NEW YORK REVIEW BOOKS
CLASSICS

WARLOCK

OAKLEY HALL (1920–2008) was born in San Diego and grew up there and in Honolulu, where his mother moved after his parents' divorce. After graduating from the University of California, Berkeley, Hall joined the Marine Corps and was stationed in the Pacific during the Second World War. Following the war, and with the aid of the GI Bill, he continued his studies in France, Switzerland, and England, returning to the United States to earn an MFA in creative writing from the Iowa Writers' Workshop. Hall published his first book, *Murder City*, in 1949 and his last, *Love and War in California*, in 2007. In between he wrote more than twenty works of fiction and non-fiction, including the novels *The Downhill Racers*, *Separations*, and *Warlock*, which was a finalist for the Pulitzer Prize in 1958; a libretto for the opera based on Wallace Stegner's *Angle of Repose*; and two guides to writing fiction. Hall was the director of the writing program at the University of California, Irvine, for twenty years and, in 1969, co-founded the Community of Writers at Squaw Valley, an annual writers' conference. Among his many honors are lifetime achievement awards from the PEN Center USA and the Cowboy Hall of Fame.

ROBERT STONE was born in Brooklyn in 1937. He is the author of seven novels: *A Hall of Mirrors*, the National Book Award–winning *Dog Soldiers*, *A Flag for Sunrise*, *Children of Light*, *Outerbridge Reach*, *Damascus Gate*, and *Bay of Souls*. He has also written essays, and screenplays, and published a short story-collection, *Bear and His Daughter*, which was nominated for the Pulitzer Prize. He lives in New York City and Key West, Florida.

WARLOCK

by OAKLEY HALL

**INTRODUCTION BY
ROBERT STONE**

NEW YORK REVIEW BOOKS

New York

This is a New York Review Book
Published by The New York Review of Books
435 Hudson Street, New York, NY 10014
www.nyrb.com

Copyright © 1958 by Oakley Hall
Introduction copyright © 2006 by Robert Stone
All rights reserved.

Library of Congress Cataloging-in-Publication Data
Hall, Oakley M.
   Warlock / Oakley Hall ; introduction by Robert Stone.
     p. cm. — (New York Review Books classics)
   ISBN 1-59017-161-6 (alk. paper)
   1. Shooters of firearms—Fiction. 2. Social conflict—Fiction.
3. Social control—Fiction. 4. Violence—Fiction.   I. Title. II. Series.
  PS3558.A373W3 2005
   813'.54—dc22

                                                       2005023653

ISBN 978-1-59017-161-5

Printed in the United States of America on acid-free paper.
10 9 8 7 6

CONTENTS

INTRODUCTION

ONE YEAR in the early Sixties, shortly after I met my literary agent Candida Donadio for the first time, she gave me a novel to read. To my surprise it was a western, by Oakley Hall, a writer of whom I had heard good things. The last western I had read was a book of Zane Grey's about hunting mountain lion somewhere around the Grand Canyon. I had no idea what I would think.

I remember thinking how wonderfully clear the book was. Not only clear, as I remember, but full of light. The sensation of reading back into time was very strong because the style made itself invisible as good style will when it is accomplishing its purpose.

Rereading *Warlock* I found again the light I remembered, an afternoon brightness, a clarity that is, I think now, the essence of good realism. In an almost literal way it illuminated the characters. When it focused on individual lives it seemed to vary its distance from each character as though there existed a different extension of sympathy or a withholding of it for different individuals in the narrative. The light I guess I had recognized the first time as western light. Big Sky light. *Realism*, I had thought at that time. This is good *realism*. And I became aware of the skill, the strategy of placing one line upon the other.

Now I know—I think I know—that modalities like realism, magic, hyper, or otherwise, have only the vaguest application. Nothing is *real*; life is life and language is language. Really excellent prose like Oakley Hall's is the creation of sound, of songs, unheard, which, as they say, can be very sweet. Overall I felt the artistry at work, or maybe I should say at play. But at the core of *Warlock* was something stronger and more mysterious.

Years ago Richard Slotkin wrote the third, concluding volume of his work on the mythology of the American frontier. Published in 1973, the final section bore a title intensely evoking the era of the trilogy's composition—the Vietnam War and its inglorious concluding years. The title is *Gunfighter Nation*.

Slotkin's books on the frontier are very wise and insightful. They are particularly relevant to the work of Oakley Hall and, of course, to *Warlock*. If I had read the title presenting America as a "gunfighter nation" a few years ago I would have believed that it bore the ugly mark of the domestic conflict over the Vietnam War. Perhaps too deeply. The country in its cowboy suit—a double disguise behind which lurks a posture of innocence and of menace, infantile self-deception enhanced by cheap theatrics. The contemptuousness is very nearly savage.

In fact, though, the professor's arraignment by nomenclature is far less facile, trivial, or even sarcastic than it seems. Slotkin's work is scholarly, and it sets out to untangle the strands of myth and mythopoetics in America's perception of itself. Much of the energy of the study goes into examining American mythmaking and defining different kinds of myth. At one point Slotkin quotes the great master and observer of myth D. H. Lawrence, a stranger in a strange land:

> But you have there the myth of the essential white American. All the other stuff, the love, the democracy, the floundering into lust are a sort of by play. The essential American soul is hard, isolate, stoic and a killer. It has never yet melted.

Slotkin uses this citation to distinguish between the kinds of created mythologies America characteristically requires to "do what it has to do." The good sheriff, a strong peaceful man; this is pop myth. The killer-stoic who lurks just below the surface of an essential collective consciousness is the real thing. No one realizes this better than Oakley Hall.

Warlock recounts a series of violent events in and around a town of the same name set in a southwestern territory during the 1880s. The account, placed partly in a fictional character's journal, is an examination of the deeper portending of these events. Goodpasture, the diarist, reflects on the balance of justice in the light of which the first series of killings might be viewed. A deputy has "buffaloed" a local cowboy on a drunken spree, beaten him and inadvertently caused his death. Eventually avengers come and succeed in settling the score. Things like this happen, Goodpasture writes, "in this rough-and-tumble corner of creation . . . happen . . . and are usually considered no more than too bad."

The "rough-and-tumble corner of creation" referred to is the American frontier in the last decade of its formal delineation, for the frontier will be officially terminated by the Department of the Interior in 1890. In fact, as the diarist knows but denies, nothing in this last resort of misfits, opportunists, professional killers, and impossibly long odds gamblers is ever accepted in fact as "no more than too bad." An overriding and thoroughly hopeless necessity to come out ahead, to come out ahead "of the next strong man" or of precarious things themselves, drives everyone as they put one more day of frontier existence on top of the last.

The stories of the Old West that Americans have grown up on render aspects of the frontier experience mythical, while reflecting the central American myth that Slotkin calls "regeneration through violence." These stories are not myths themselves, though; they are the substance of America's mythopoesis. For *Warlock* Oakley Hall uses bits of the gunfight at the OK Corral, the Lincoln County War, the Johnson, Wyoming, cattle fight, and a few others. As Slotkin writes and Oakley Hall subtly demonstrates:

> In American mythogenesis the founding fathers were not those eighteenth-century gentlemen who composed a nation at Philadelphia. Rather, they were those who (to paraphrase Faulkner's *Absalom, Absalom!*) tore violently a nation from implacable and opulent wilderness—the rogues, adventurers, and land-boomers; the Indian fighters, traders, missionaries, explorers, and hunters who killed and were killed until they had mastered the wilderness . . .

In the evocatively named town of Warlock (shades of Young Goodman Brown) the Apaches kill and die and are followed by the Mexicans who slaughter the gringo cowboys and are killed by them. The US Cavalry having helped decimate the Indians and Mexicans are now used against white labor by mine owners. The murderous cattle barons who made their own law in the Rattlesnake Valley are driven down and out. America, aspiring toward her self-generated pseudo-myths, remains a prisoner of her deepest true ones.

—ROBERT STONE

WARLOCK

This book is for my son Tad

PREFATORY NOTE

This book is a novel. The town of Warlock and the territory in which it is located are fabrications. But any relation of the characters to real persons, living or dead, is not always coincidental, for many are composites of figures who live still on a frontier between history and legend.

The fabric of the story, too, is made up of actual events interwoven with invented ones; by combining what did happen with what might have happened, I have tried to show what should have happened. Devotees of Western legend may consequently complain that I have used familiar elements to construct a fanciful design, and that I have rearranged or ignored the accepted facts. So I will reiterate that this work is a novel. The pursuit of truth, not of facts, is the business of fiction.

—Oakley Hall

BOOK ONE

 The Fight in the Acme Corral

I. Journals of Henry Holmes Goodpasture

August 25, 1880

DEPUTY CANNING had been Warlock's hope. During his regime we had come to think, in man's eternal optimism, that progress was being made toward at least some mild form of Law & Order in Warlock. Certainly he was by far the best of the motley flow of deputies who have manned our jail.

Canning was a good man, a decent man, an understandably prudent man, an honorable one. He coped with our daily and nightly problems, with brawling, drunken miners, and with Cowboys who have an especial craving to ride a horse into a saloon, a Cyprian's cubicle, or the billiard parlor, and shoot the chimneys out of the chandeliers.

Writing of Canning now, I wonder again how we manage to obtain deputies at all, who must occupy a dangerous and frequently fatal position for miserly pay. We do not manage to keep them long. They collect their pittance for a month or two, and die, or depart, or do not remain long enough even to collect it at all. One, indeed, fled upon the first day of his employment, leaving his star of office awaiting his successor on the table in the jail. We have had bad ones, too; Brown, the man before Canning, was an insolent, drunken bully, and Billy-the-kid Gannon gained a measure of fame and gratitude by ventilating him in a saloon brawl down valley in San Pablo.

Canning, too, must have known that some day he would be thrown up against one of that San Pablo crew, incur, prudent as he was, the

3

enmity, or merely displeasure, of Curley Burne or Billy Gannon, of Jack Cade or Calhoun or Pony Benner, of one of the Haggin brothers, or even of Abe McQuown himself. I wonder if, in his worst dreams, it ever occurred to him that the whole down valley gang of badmen would come in against him at once.

There is no unanimity of opinion even now amongst those of us who believe them at least to be a regrettable element in Warlock. There are those who will say that of the lot only Cade is truly "bad," and possibly Calhoun when in his cups; who will say that Luke Friendly may be something of a bully, and Pony Benner scratchy at times, but that Billy Gannon is, if you know him, a fine boy, Curley Burne a happy-go-lucky, loyal friend, and McQuown not actually an out-law, since his forays after stock into Mexico are not really rustling.

However many good men die at their hands, or are driven out for fear of them, there will, it seems, always be their defenders to say they are only high-spirited, mischievous, fun-loving, perhaps a little careless—and even I will admit that there are likeable young fellows among them. Yet however many Saturday evenings are turned into wild carnivals of violence and bloodshed, however many cattle are rustled and stages held up, there will always be their champions to claim that they steal very little from their neighbors (I must admit, too, that Matt Burbage, whose range adjoins McQuown's, does not blame McQuown for depredations upon his stock); that they confine their rustling raids to below the border; that the stages are robbed not by them, but by lonesomers hiding out here from true-bills further east; that, indeed, matters would be much worse if it were not for Abe McQuown to keep the San Pablo hardcases in hand, and so forth and so forth. And it may be so, in part.

McQuown is an enigmatic figure, certainly. He and his father possess a range as large and fertile as that of Matt Burbage, and, it would seem, could be ranchers as eminent and respected. Certainly they seem no more prosperous, in their lawlessness. Abe McQuown is a red-bearded, lean, brooding fellow, who has about him an explosive aura of power and directionless determination. He has protruding green eyes, which, it is said, can spit fire, or freeze a man at fifty feet; is of medium height, almost slight, with long arms, and walks with a curious, backward-leaning gait, like a young cadet, with hands resting upon his concho belt, his beard tipped down against his chest, and his green eyes darting glances right and left. Yet there is about him a certain paradoxical shyness, and a certain charm, and in con-versation with the man it is difficult not to think him a fine fellow.

His father, old Ike, was shot through the hips six months or so ago on a rustling expedition, is paralyzed from the hips down, and is, reportedly, a dying man. Good riddance it will be; he is unequivocably a mean and ugly old brute.

I say, Deputy Canning must have known the clash would come. In retrospect I suffer for him, and at the same time I wonder what went on in McQuown's cunning and ruthless mind. What kind of challenge to himself did he see in Canning? Merely that of one strong man as a threat to the supremacy of another? The two were, to all appearances, friendly. Certainly Canning never interfered with McQuown, or with McQuown's. He was too prudent for that. Canning was widely liked and respected, and a man as intelligent as McQuown must have had to take that into consideration, for is there a man of stature anywhere who does not wish to be the more admired? And will any such man commit a despicable act without attempting to color it in his own favor?

I will put down, then, what I think: that McQuown carefully chose the time, the place, the occasion; that this was deeply premeditated; that McQuown is not merely high-spirited, mischievous, careless, that he is not simply a spoiled and willful youth; that, further and specifically, McQuown was jealous of what his henchman Billy Gannon had won for himself by dispatching an obnoxious bully of a deputy, and sought to repeat a winning trick.

About a month ago, Canning buffaloed a young Cowboy named Harms. It was a Saturday night and Harms was in town with a month's pay, which he promptly lost over Taliaferro's faro layout. With whisky under his belt and no more money in his pocket, and so nothing to do for excitement, Harms vented his feelings by proceeding to the center of Main Street and firing off his six-shooter at the moon—for which he is not much to be blamed. Canning, however, accosted him, for which the deputy was not to be blamed either, and, at some danger to his person, grappled with Harms in order to relieve him of the offending Colt's. In the end he had to clout the boy over the ear with the weapon to quiet him, which is acceptable practice. Canning then bore Harms off to see Judge Holloway, who presented him with a night's accommodation in the jail. Released the next morning, Harms started back down valley, but was thrown from his horse en route, was dragged, and died. No doubt his death was in good part brought about by the buffaloing he had received.

It was too bad. We felt badly, those who thought of it at all, and I am sure Canning was as sorrowful as anyone. Still, in this rough-and-tumble corner of creation, such things will happen, and are usually considered no more than too bad.

I think there is some East Indian doctrine to the effect that our fate is shaped in the most inconsequential of our acts, and so it was with poor Canning. Enter, then, a further minister of providence, a week or ten days later, in the person of Lige Harrington, a braggart, blowhard fellow more ridiculous than dangerous, but a minor hanger-on of McQuown's. Harrington announced himself a bosom friend of Harms, and his avenger. Harrington was patently seeking to make himself a reputation at Canning's expense, and to give himself prestige among the San Pabloites. Well primed with liquid courage, Harrington sought Canning's demise, but was dispatched in short order, crated, and immured upon Boot Hill.

Again, I think, no one was much concerned. This sort of asinine bravado must be the bane of any peace officer's existence. Yet I wonder if Canning did not have a fearful vision of how Right carries the seeds of Wrong within it, and Wrong its particular precariousness for a man in his position. For what are Right & Wrong in the end, but opinion held to? Certainly there were men who said that Canning had murdered the unfortunate Harms, and so had murdered Harrington his avenger, bad rubbish or not. Is not the semblance of guilt, however slight the tinge, already a corruption?

And I wonder if Canning did not feel the web beginning to encase him and the red spider gently shaking the strands. For soon rumors started. Canning had better get out of town. The threat was nameless at first, but after a time it was joined with McQuown's name. What other name would do?

I had heard rumors of impending trouble between Canning and McQuown, and dismissed them as idle gossip. At some point, I cannot say when, I realized they were not; I realized it as Warlock itself did, with a jerk to deadly anxiety as of a rope pulled suddenly tight and singing with strain. I have said that Canning was a prudent man. Had he been prudent enough he would have left town as soon as these rumors started, while still he could have done so without too great a loss of face. Yet he had come too far along the course. He had his own reputation as man and gunman now. He was caught in his own web as well as in McQuown's. He did not get out in time, and McQuown came in from San Pablo day before yesterday with all his men.

They hurrahed the town that night. Not so wildly, though, as to be much out of the ordinary, and I see that, too, as cunning upon Mc-

Quown's part: there was cause, but perhaps not urgent or completely justifiable cause (by our standards!), for Deputy Canning to step in. But Canning made no trouble; we did not see him abroad that night.

By then, however, the handwriting was etched upon the wall for all to see, and early yesterday men were loitering in the street, and Canning was early at the jail. I watched from my window as avidly as the rest of Warlock, in that crackling deadly tension, waiting for the trouble to start.

It was noon before McQuown came down the center of Main Street in his shining sugar-loaf hat and his buckskin shirt, stepping with disdain through the powdery dust. He fired into the air and shouted his taunts, such as, "Come out into the street, for you have murdered too many good men!" etc. Canning came out of the jail and I retreated—no more cowardly, I say in defense of myself, than any other citizen of Warlock—from my store to my rooms upstairs where I could watch from a more protected coign of vantage. There I watched Canning advance unfalteringly down the street toward McQuown. Once he looked back, and I saw behind him, almost hidden in the shadows under the arcade—two men. One from his short stature I knew to be Pony Benner, the other I have heard since was Jack Cade, both henchmen of McQuown's.

Canning came on still, but a few yards more and his steps slowed. They quickened again, but not with courage. He ran down Southend Street and got his horse from the Skinner Bros. Acme Corral, and fled Warlock.

My eyes smarted with rage and shame that there was not a man in Warlock to get out in the street with a Winchester and face down those devils behind him, and to see McQuown tip his white hat back on his head and laugh, as though he had won a trick at cards. My eyes smart still.

Last night honest men barricaded their doors, and no lights were left burning for fear they would be shot at. The Cowboys roamed the street and quarreled, and loudly joked, and shot at the moon to their hearts' content. They only quieted, like stallions, when they trooped off to the French Palace and the cribs along Peach Street. After a brief respite their unholy din began again, and lasted until morning, when the wagons that transport the miners out to the mines were held up, and the mules set loose and chased out of town. The doctor's buggy was commandeered and put to a wild race down Main Street against the water wagon, and many other pranks were played. Before noon they had departed for San Pablo with much hilarity, leaving our poor barber dying at the General Peach with a bullet through his lungs. Pony Benner shot him, evidently because he cut Pony's cheek while shaving him.

So the wild boys have had their fun, and played their mischievous games, driving a good man from this town, and murdering a poor, harmless fellow whose razor slipped because he was deadly afraid.

I think we would have done nothing about Canning, for his shame was ours. McQuown must know our cowardice well, and count on it, and despise us for it. So he should, and so should we despise ourselves. Yet, as with Canning, an inconsequential act may have set in train forces of adversity against McQuown. Our little barber's death has caused a congealing of feeling and determination here such as I have never seen before. If we cannot give voice to our indignation over Canning's shame, since it is too much our own, we can cry out in righteous wrath against the murder of the barber.

The Citizens' Committee meets tonight, called upon to defend Warlock's Peace & Safety, not righteously, only sensibly, for as this town is affected adversely by anarchy, violence, and murder, so are we, its merchants. Furthermore, Warlock has no other possible protector. It is to be hoped that the Citizens' Committee can, on this occasion, pull itself together and gain for itself, at last, the name of action.

The original organization, from which the Citizens' Committee sprang, was perhaps more fittingly titled the Merchants of Warlock Committee, including Dr. Wagner in his capacity as proprietor of the Assay Office, Miss Jessie in hers as boardinghouse mistress, and the judge as the operator of a commercial enterprise in his judgeship.* Some time ago, however, when it became obvious that the granting of a town patent, and so of some measure of government, to Warlock, was not imminent, it was resolved that the original committee be expanded into something more. Since we were the only organiza-

---

* The Citizens' Committee at this time consisted of the following members: Dr. Wagner, Miss Jessie Marlow, Judge Holloway, Goodpasture (the General Store), Petrix (Warlock and Western Bank), Slavin (the Warlock Stage Co.), Pike Skinner (the Acme Corral), Hart, Winters (Hart and Winters Gunshop), MacDonald, Godbold (superintendents, respectively, of the Medusa and Sister Fan mines), Egan (the Feed and Grain Barn), Brown (the Billiard Parlor), Pugh (Western Star Hotel), Kennon (Kennon's Livery Stable), Rolfe (Frontier Fast Freight), Swartze (the Boston Café), Robinson (lumber yard, carpenter shop, and Bowen's Sawmill), Hake (the Glass Slipper), and Taliaferro (owner of the Lucky Dollar and the French Palace).

tion that existed, except for the Mine Superintendents Assn., we, the merchants, seemed the ones to initiate some sort of pro-tem governing assembly.

The old town-meeting style of government was immediately proposed. The suggestion was met with high democratic enthusiasm, which, however, waned rapidly. I, who made this proposal myself, immediately came to regard it as patently unworkable here, in a place where passions in all things run high, and men go armed as they wear hats against the sun, and where such a large proportion of the inhabitants is of the ignorant and unwashed class, if not actual renegades from the law elsewhere.

There are, for instance, the miners, the bulk of the town's population. Are they intelligent and responsible enough to be entrusted with the vote? They are not, we feel, perhaps a little guiltily. Then there are the brothel, gambling, and saloon interests; it is true that Taliaferro and Hake belonged to the Merchants Committee, but could we afford to give them and their disreputable employees proportionate power over the more decent citizenry? The question also arose as to how extensive the city-state should be. If it were to include ranchers from the San Pablo valley, what of such as Abe McQuown, not to speak of the Haggins, Cade, and Earnshaw, all of them landholders at least in a small way, and at the same time Warlock's scourges?

Our projected state was thus gradually whittled down, to become a kind of club restricted to the decent people, the right-thinking people, the better class of citizens; became, ultimately, restricted to the merchants of Warlock—ourselves; with a few additions, for Warlock had grown meanwhile; and a new name: The Citizens' Committee of Warlock. Now we must act, or abandon all claim to that name.

The situation is indeed fantastic. Keller * never appears here. We are none of his concern, he says firmly. When given argument by various volunteers passing through Bright's City, or by any of the numerous subcommittees that have been assigned to plead with him and General Peach † himself on the subject of law enforcement here, Keller gives it as his opinion that the country beyond the Bucksaws is not properly Bright's County at all, and that General Peach and his aides are presently working on boundaries of the new county, which will soon be established. Warlock will then be given a town patent, and will, of course, be the county seat. This will be any day, he says;

* Sheriff Keller of Bright's County.
† General G. O. Peach, the military governor in Bright's City.

any day, he repeats, and again repeats—but it has not been yet. Keller
points out, when badgered further, that he did not campaign for our
votes when running for his office, and promised us nothing, which is
true; and that he has given us deputies, when they could be hired,
which also is true enough.

Despairing, consequently, of aid from above, savaged beyond patience by McQuown and his San Pablo crew, some of us of the
Citizens' Committee have decided that we must put it strongly in meeting tonight that our only solution is to hire a Peace Officer on a commercial basis. This is common enough practice, and there are a number
of renowned gunmen available for such positions if the pay is high
enough. They are hired by groups such as we are, or by town coun-
cils in luckier and more legitimate localities, and paid either a monthly
fee or on a bounty system.

Something must be done, and there is no one to do it but the
Citizens' Committee. It will be seen tonight whether the determined
among us outnumber the timid. I think not a man of us has not been
badly frightened by Canning's flight, and fear can engender its own
determination.

August 26, 1880

At last, it seems, Something Has Been Done. The meeting last night
was quiet and brief; we were of one mind, except for Judge Holloway.
We have sent for a man, a Marshal, and have obliged ourselves to
open our pocketbooks in order to offer him a very large sum of money
monthly. He is Clay Blaisedell, at present Marshal in Fort James. I
know little of his deeds, except that it was he who shot the Texas badman, Big Ben Nicholson, and that his name at present is renowned—
names such as his flash up meteor-like from time to time, attaching
to themselves all manner of wild tales of courage and prowess.

We have made him a peerless offer, for what we hope will be a
peerless man. Such, at least, is our prospective Marshal's reputation,
that he was one of the five famous law officers to whom Caleb Bane,
the writer, recently presented braces of gold-handled Colt's Frontier
Models, as being most eminent in their field, and so, no doubt, most
lucrative to Bane as a chronicler of deeds of derring-do. A fine act
of gratitude on Bane's part, certainly, although it is cynically rumored
that he asked for their own many-notched pacifiers in return, and
from the sale of these to collectors of such grim mementoes realized
a very tidy profit on the transaction.

So Clay Blaisedell has been sent for—not to be Marshal of Warlock, for there is no such place, and no such position, legally; but to be Marshal acting for the Citizens' Committee of an official limbo.* This is our third, and most presumptuous, action as the government-by-default of this place—the local government "on acceptance," a term Judge Holloway often uses to refer to himself as a judge, who has no legal status either. Our first act was to build Warlock's little jail by subscription among ourselves, in the hope that the presence of such a structure might have a steadying influence upon the populace. It has had no such effect, although it has proved useful on at least two occasions as a fortress in which deputies were able to seek refuge from murderously-inclined miscreants. Our second was to purchase a pumping wagon, and to guarantee a part of the salary of Peter Bacon as jointly the driver of Kennon's water wagon and as Fireman in Chief. Taxes are no less painful under another guise.

I write with levity of what have been serious decisions for small men to make, but I am elated and hopeful, and the members of the Citizens' Committee, if I am representative, feel a great pride in having overcome our fears of offending the Cowboys, and our natural reluctance to part with any of the profits we extract from them, from the miners, and from each other, and at last having made an attempt to hire ourselves a Man. It will be the luck of the camp to have its savior ventilated by road agents en route, and arrive here boots before hardware.

He is to be hired, as we said last night, to enforce Law & Order in Warlock. He is actually to be hired, as no one said aloud, against the San Pabloites. What one man is to do against the legion of wild Cowboys of McQuown's kin or persuasion, we have, of course, asked ourselves. The question being unanswerable, like sensible men we have stopped asking it. We do not demand Law & Order so much as Peace & Safety, and a town in which men can go about their affairs without the fear of being shot down by an errant bullet from a gun battle no concern of theirs, or of incurring in a trifling manner

* Warlock's situation was much as Goodpasture has described it. General Peach was a notoriously inept administrator, sulking because he felt his fame and services to the nation justified a more exalted position than military governor of the territory. Despite repeated pleas and demands, no town patent had been issued Warlock, which had a population almost as large as that of Bright's City, both the county seat and territorial capitol; and the rumor was so strong that the western half of Bright's County was to be formed into a new county, that Sheriff Keller was able to ignore almost completely, and evidently thankfully, the Warlock and San Pablo Valley area. There was, however, provision for a deputy sheriff in Warlock.

the murderous dislike of some drunken Cowboy. Warlock's Marshal will have to be a Warlock indeed.*

It is not known when Blaisedell will arrive here, if he accepts our offer, which we are certain he will. At any rate we pray he will. He is our hope now. I think we must have, in him, not so much a man of pure, daredevil courage, but a man who can impart courage to this town, which is, in the end, no more than the sum of every one of us.

September 1, 1880

Evidently Canning managed to pass on some of *his* limited portion. Carl Schroeder, who was, I understand, Canning's closest friend, has given up his position as shotgun messenger for Buck Slavin's stage line, to undertake the post of deputy here at one-third the pay. He is a fool. God protect such fools, for we will not.

September 8, 1880

Blaisedell has accepted our offer! He will be here in about six weeks. This delay is unfortunate, but presumably Fort James must be possessed of a suitable substitute before he departs. On the other hand, McQuown and his gang are reported in Mexico on a rustling expedition, so Warlock may still be inhabited when our new Marshal arrives.

September 21, 1880

A gambler named Morgan has arrived, and purchased the Glass Slipper from Bill Hake, who has departed for California. The new

---

* The town took its name from the Warlock mine, which was inoperative by this time. One story of the naming of the Warlock mine is as follows: Richelin, who made the silver strike, had been prospecting in the Bucksaws under exceedingly dangerous conditions. The inhabitants of Bright's City, to which he returned from time to time for supplies and with specimens for assay, viewed him as mad, and his continued existence, in close proximity to Espirato's band of marauding Apaches, as miraculous. On the occasion of his actual strike, he had, on his journey into Bright's City, an encounter with some Apaches in which his burro was killed. He managed to reach town, however, and, when news of his escape was heard, someone remarked to him that he must have flown back, riding the handle of his shovel like a witch. Richelin is supposed to have made an obscene gesture in reply to this, and cried, "Warlock, damn you!" Be that as it may, he named his first mine the Warlock, his second the Medusa. The Warlock, after producing over a million dollars' worth of ore, played out, and was closed down in 1878, shortly after the Porphyrion & Western Mining Company had purchased Richelin's holdings.

proprietor of Warlock's oldest gambling and drinking establishment has brought with him two attendants; a huge, wall-eyed fellow who serves as lookout and general factotum; and a tiny, bright, birdlike man of whose function I was uncertain until it developed that Morgan had imported for his shabby and run-down establishment (besides a fine chandelier, which much enhances the interior of the Glass Slipper), a piano, and the Little Man is its "professor." It is Warlock's first such instrument, and the music issuing from the saloon is a wonder and joy to Warlock, and a despair to Taliaferro and the Lucky Dollar. It is rumored that Taliaferro will now bring in a piano himself, either for the Lucky Dollar or the French Palace on the Row, to meet the competition.

Morgan is a handsome, prematurely gray fellow, of a sardonic aspect and reserved nature. His deportment, as a newcomer, has been subject to much comment, and his manner with his customers seems bad business practice, in a place where men are apt to be friends or enemies. But his "professor's" music remains much admired.

October 11, 1880

McQuown and several of his comrades have been back in town twice now—not including Benner, the barber-killer. They have been very much on their good behavior, as though ashamed of their last excesses here, and aware of the hostile attitude toward them that now generally obtains. Or else McQuown may be aware that we have hired a Nemesis.

2. Gannon Comes Back

WARLOCK lay on a flat, white alkali step, half encircled by the Bucksaw Mountains to the east, beneath a metallic sky. With the afternoon sun slanting down on it from over the distant peaks of the Dinosaurs, the adobe and weathered plank-and-batten, false-fronted buildings were smoothly glazed with yellow light, and sharp-cut black shadows lay like pits in the angles out of the sun.

The heat of the sun was like a blanket; it had dimension and weight.

The town was dust- and heat-hazed, blurred out of focus. A water wagon with a round, rust-red tank moved slowly along Main Street, spraying water in a narrow, shining strip behind it. But Warlock's dust was laid only briefly. Soon again it was churned as light as air by iron-bound wheels, by hoofs and bootheels. The dust rose and hung in the air and drifted down in a continuous fall, onto the jail and Good-pasture's General Store, onto the Lucky Dollar and the Glass Slipper and the smaller saloons, onto the Billiard Parlor, the Western Star Hotel, the Boston Café and the Warlock and Western Bank, onto the houses in the Row, the cribs along Peach Street, Kennon's Livery Stable and the freight yard, onto Buck Slavin's stage yard and the Skinner Brothers Acme Corral in Southend Street, onto the Feed and Grain Barn and the General Peach boardinghouse in Grant Street, onto the tarpaper shacks of the miners and the wagons and the riders pass-ing through and the men in the street. It got into men's eyes and irritated their dry throats, it dusted them all over with a whitish sheen, and turned to mud in the sweat of their faces.

Trails, and stage and wagon roads, led into the town like twisted spokes to a dusty hub—from the silver mines in the nearer Bucksaws: the Medusa, Sister Fan, Thetis, Pig's Eye, and Redgold: from the hamlet of Redgold and the stamp mill there; from the more distant hamlet of San Pablo in the valley and on the river of that name; from Welltown to the northwest, where the railroad was; from Bright's City, the territorial capitol.

Dust rose, too, where there were travelers along the roads: a pros-pector with his burro; a group of riders coming in from San Pablo; great, high-wheeled, heavy-laden ore wagons descending from the mines; loads of lagging timbers for the stopes being hauled from the forests in the northern Bucksaws; a stage inbound from Bright's City; and, close in on the Welltown road, a single horseman slowly making his way up through the huge, strewn boulders toward War-lock's rim.

John Gannon rode bent tiredly forward against the slope, his hand on the dusty, sweated shoulder of the gray he had bought in Welltown, urging her up this last hill out of the malpais and over the rim, where she increased her gait at the sight of town. He glanced down the rutted trail to his right that led out to the cemetery called Boot Hill, and to the dump, where he could see the sun glint-ing on whisky bottles and a skirl of papers blown up by a wind gust. The mare plodded heavy-footed past the miners' shacks on the edge of town. Beyond, and looming above them, was the tall, narrow-windowed rear of the French Palace. A woman waved a hand at him from one of the windows and called something lost in the wind. He looked quickly straight ahead of him, and laid his hand on the mare's shoulder once more. At Main Street he swung to the left and the mare's hoofs sucked and plopped in thicker dust.

The sign over the jail swung and creaked in a gust of wind as he passed it. The sign was barely legible; weathered, thick with dust, dotted with clusters of perforations, it humbly located the law in Warlock:

DEP. SHERIFF

JAIL

Gannon reined left into Southend Street and turned at last into the Acme Corral. Nate Bush, the Skinner brothers' hostler, came out to meet him. Bush took the reins as he dismounted, spat sideways, wiped his mustache, and, without looking at Gannon directly, said, "Back, huh?"

"Back," he said.

"McQuown pulling them back in from all around, I guess," Bush said, in a flat, hostile voice, and immediately turned away and led the mare clop-hoofing toward the water trough.

Gannon stood looking after him. He felt heavy and tired after a day in the murderous sun, heavy and tired with coming back to the valley as he watched Nate Bush's back carefully held toward him. He had tried to hope he was not coming back to trouble, but he had heard in Rincon that Warlock had hired Clay Blaisedell as town marshal, had known without hearing it that the Fort James man had been hired against Abe McQuown; and he knew Abe McQuown. He had ridden for McQuown—even in Rincon they had known it—and in Warlock they would never forget it. Billy, his brother, rode for McQuown still.

He spat into his bandanna and closed his eyes as he tried to scrub some of the dust from his face. Then he walked slowly up to Main Street, stopping on the corner before Goodpasture's store as a wagon rolled by in the street, dust rising beneath the mules' hoofs in clouds and streaming from the wheels like liquid. He turned his face away and blew his breath out against Warlock's dust, remembering its smell and prickly taste; as it settled behind the wagon he saw a thin figure appear and lean against the arcade post before the jail. It was Carl Schroeder; in his depression at the hostler's greeting he had forgotten that there were a few men in Warlock he would be glad to see. He started catercornered across the street as Carl stared, and then raised a hand.

"Well, Johnny Gee!" Carl said, as Gannon came down toward him along the boardwalk. Carl's lean, hard-calloused hand wrung his. "How's the trains running over in Rincon, Johnny?"

"Coming and going. What's that on your vest there, Carl?"

Carl Schroeder glanced down and thumbed the star out where he could see it. He did not smile. His plain, sad-mustached face was older than Gannon had remembered it, tired and strained. He said, "Bill Canning got run out and I kind of fell into the hole he left. You knew Bill, didn't you?"

"I didn't know him."

"I guess you have been gone a good while at that." Carl's eyes flickered at him, not quite casually, and then away. "Canning come in after Jim Brown got shot."

He nodded. His brother Billy had shot Jim Brown. The only letter he had had from Billy during the six months he had been in Rincon had been a strange mixture of brag and apology for having shot a deputy. "Dirty-mouth, bull-ragging son of a bitch," Billy had written. "He had it coming bad. Everybody says he had it coming. Abe says he'd choose him himself if I didn't choose him out first, Bud."

"Come on in and sit," Carl said, turning and moving into the jail. As he followed Carl inside he read the legend neatly lettered on the square of paper fastened to the adobe beside the door:

2ND DEPUTY WANTED
SEE SCHROEDER

The sign above his head creaked in another gust of wind. Judge Holloway was staring up at him from the shadow inside the jail, his sick face darker, thinner, more closely hatched with red veins than ever, on one cheek the wart or mole like a peg driven into the flesh, his bloated body hunched over the battered pine table that was his bench. The crutch that substituted for the leg he had lost at Shiloh leaned against the wall behind him with his hard-hat hung from its armrest. Peter Bacon, the water-wagon driver, sat at the back, beside the alley door, with a knife and a bit of gray wood in his hands.

"Well, Bud Gannon," Peter said, raising an eyebrow.

"Peter," he said. "Judge."

The judge didn't reply. Peter said, "How's the telegraphing going, Bud?"

No one had called him "Bud" for a long time now, but the name was as familiar and disagreeable as Warlock's dust. He felt a silly, apologetic grin cramp his face. "Well, I gave it up," he said.

"Come back for good, then?" Carl asked, turning toward him. He hitched at his shell belt. "Here or San Pablo, Johnny?" he asked quietly.

Gannon rubbed his hands on the dusty thighs of his store pants. "Why—" he said, and paused as he saw something very hard, very sharp, show for an instant in Carl's eyes. "Why, San Pablo, I guess. The only thing I know besides telegraphing's running a branding iron."

Peter bent to his whittling. The judge stared, darkly brooding, at the line of late sunlight that came a little way into the jail. Carl propped a boot up on the chair beside the cell door. "How come you to give it up, Johnny?" he asked. "Looked like you was going to make something of yourself."

"Laid off," he said. He could feel their unspoken questions. Although there was no call to answer them, he said, "Fellow I was apprentice to went and died, and they brought in another had his own apprentice." And he was pretty sure they had brought in another because it was known he had once run with McQuown, which was what Carl and Peter were surmising. But he had said enough, and he watched them both nod, almost in unison, apparently without interest.

Carl turned away from him to gaze at the wall where former deputies of Warlock had scratched their names brown in the whitewash. Carl's name had been added at the bottom. Above it was WM. CANNING, above that, in big, crooked letters, JAMES BROWN, above that, B. EGSTROM. Higher on the list was ED. SMITHERS, whom Jack Cade had shot in a cruel fuss at the Lucky Dollar. Gannon had seen that.

"Matt Burbage might be needing some hands," Peter Bacon said, without looking up from his whittling. "Usually comes in town Saturday nights, too."

"Thanks," he said gratefully. "Well, I guess I'll go have myself a drink of whisky." No one volunteered to accompany him. The judge's fingers drummed on the table top.

"Got ourself a marshal now," Peter said.

"I heard. Did Peach come around to giving Warlock a town patent?"

Carl shook his head. "No, the Citizens' Committee hired him."

"Gunman from Fort James," Peter said. "Name of Clay Blaisedell."

Gannon nodded. A gunman from Fort James hired against Abe McQuown, against McQuown's people, against Billy, who was one of them. The town had turned against McQuown. The taste and smell of Warlock was not merely that of its dust, but the taste of apprehension, the smell of fear and anger like a dangerous animal snarling and stinking in its cage. He had come back to it, that had changed only for the worse since he had run from it. And now the town was waiting. He said quietly to Carl, "Trouble?"

"Not yet," Carl said, quietly too, his hand rising to pick at the dull five-pointed star limply hanging from his vest, his face, in profile as he still stared at the names on the wall, showing clearly anger and fear, determination and dread.

As Gannon started out the judge's hot, bloodshot eyes with their yellow whites slanted up to meet his own. No one spoke behind him. Outside, in the sun that came in under the arcade, his bootheels resounded on the planks as he started down toward the central block.

He would look up Matt Burbage tonight, he thought, doggedly. He knew it was useless. He had been one of McQuown's, and he would have to go back to McQuown, in San Pablo. Once he had thought he was quit of them.

3. The Jail

THE sun, misshapen and red, was resting on the jagged spine of the Dinosaurs when Pike Skinner turned into the jail. Halting in the thick arch of the doorway, he cleared his throat and said, "I guess McQuown's coming in tonight."

Inside were Judge Holloway and Peter Bacon, Carl Schroeder, leaning back in the chair beside the cell door, with a hand grasping one of the bars to balance himself, and old Owen Parsons, the wheelwright at Kennon's Livery Stable, squatting against the wall at the back.

Schroeder nodded once, gently let his chair down, and stretched one leg out with a slow, careful motion. "Heard about it," he said. Then he said, "Bound to come in some time."

Peter Bacon said, "We was just saying it was none of Carl's worry." He bent down to sweep his whittlings into a neat pile between his boots.

"It's sure none of your put-in, Carl," Skinner said quickly.

No one looked at Schroeder. At a sound of hoofs and wheels in the street Parsons spat. The spittoon rang deeply. Bacon glanced up at the door, and Skinner turned to watch a buggy roll by in the street, its yellow and red striped wheels bright with motion in the last of the sun.

Skinner hooked his thumbs into the sweat-stained shell belt that hung over his broad hips, and teetered on his bootheels. He was a tall, heavy, slope-shouldered man and he filled the doorway. The others watched him remove his hat and slap it once against his leg. He scowled sideways at the square of paper tacked to the wall before he turned back inside. He had a clean-shaven, red, ugly face, and great protruding ears.

"Blaisedell buggy-riding Miss Jessie again," he said.

Peter Bacon nodded. "Fine-looking man."

"Him and Morgan is friendly," Old Owen Parsons said disapprovingly. "Heard they are partners in the Glass Slipper, and was before in a place in Fort James."

"Signifies what, if they are?" said Skinner, who was a member of the Citizens' Committee, scowling.

He stood aside as Arnold Mosbie, the freight-line mule skinner, came in. Mosbie's handsome, blackly-sunburnt face was marred by a great scar running down his right cheek.

"Heard Dechine was in town saying McQuown and them was maybe coming in tonight," he said, to no one in particular.

Schroeder said nothing. The judge raised his eyes to the round, dented bowl of the lamp suspended above his head. Peter Bacon sighed and said, "What Owen here was saying."

"Abe's been a while making up his mind to come," Mosbie said.

Skinner said to Parsons, "What's it to you if Blaisedell is friendly with Morgan, old man?"

Parsons spat, rang the spittoon, and jerked his fingers through his tobacco-stained beard. "Morgan is a damned high-rolling son of a bitch."

"It don't make Blaisedell one."

"Maybe it don't."

"A man has got a right to a friend," Bacon said.

"Why, what if it does make Blaisedell one?" Mosbie said, in his heavy, rasping voice. "What he is here for is against sons of bitches, and maybe a man has got to be one himself to make it. A real son of a bitch that shot Ben Nicholson loose from his boots and chased those wild Texas men out of Fort James till they are running yet, I hear— that's the kind we need here bad."

The judge folded his hands over his belly and turned his muddy-looking eyes to watch Schroeder plucking at the star on his vest. Milky dust drifted into the jail as riders passed in the street.

"Five hundred dollars a month, I hear the Citizens' Committee is paying him," Parsons said. "Five *hundred*, and what's Carl here—"

"Four hundred, God damn it!" Skinner broke in. "By God, how the talk in this town makes everything something it isn't. Old man, you'd set yourself where he sets for four hundred a month?"

Tim French, who worked at the Feed and Grain Barn, squeezed inside past Skinner. He had a round, cheerful, bright-eyed face, like a boy's. "Heard the news, Carl?"

Schroeder nodded tightly, and, with the same slow, careful movement, tipped his chair back again. "Heard it. Some fellow named McQuown's coming in."

There was a silence. Then French said, "Saw Bud Gannon down the street. I thought he was over at Rincon."

"Come back," Schroeder said. "Just came in an hour ago."

"Expect McQuown figures he needs all the help he can get," Mosbie said. "Pleasant to see Abe with the nerves."

"If Bud Gannon's any shakes of a gunhand I never heard anything about it," Skinner said scornfully.

"Johnny's all right," Schroeder said. "I don't care he's Billy's brother or whose. He quit them down there."

"Come back, though," Parsons said, grinning sourly.

"He got laid off over at Rincon," Bacon said.

"I wait and see," Parsons said. "Looks like he come back at the right time for McQuown." He grunted and said, "I wait and see on Blaisedell, too. Maybe he's no son of a bitch, but all I've seen so far is him hanging over a faro layout or whisky-drinking with Morgan. Or buggy-riding Miss Jessie Marlow. He—"

He broke off, for the judge was speaking. "Any man," the judge said, and paused for their attention. "Any man," he went on, "who has got himself set over others and don't have any responsibility to something bigger than him, is a son of a bitch." He stared from face to face, his cheek twisting around the great wart, his mouth drawn out flat and contemptuous. "Bigger than all men," he said, "which is the law."

Then he looked at Schroeder again. "And those the same that take the law for a fraud. For the law is for all, not just against some you hate their livers."

Schroeder had flushed, but he said without heat, "Can't see every-body's livers from where I sit, Judge."

"See just toward San Pablo from where you sit," the Judge said. "So where is the law?"

"In a book, Judge," Tim French said gravely.

"Never been a man yet to know what it was he swore when he put on that badge," the judge said. "Maybe you thought you swore blood on Abe McQuown and his people, Deputy. But that wasn't what you swore."

The front legs of Schroeder's chair tapped to the floor; his hand, where it still clutched a bar of the cell door beside him, was white with strain. In the easy voice he said, "Judge, I went up to Sheriff Keller and told him I'd come in here because Bill Canning got run and not a man to stand up for him. I come in here against Abe McQuown and people getting run or else burnt down by sons of bitches like him and Cade and Benner and Billy Gannon and Curley Burne. That's what I swore to, and your law for Warlock's in a book still, the way Tim said, if you don't like it." Then he laughed a little and said, "Though I have kind of got this ice water in my bowels right now."

The others silently avoided his eyes, except for Peter Bacon, who was watching his friend steadily. Bacon said, "I guess you could leave things up to Blaisedell, Horse."

"None of your put-in, Carl," Tim French said.

"Never said it was," Schroeder said. "Only—" He was silent for a time, and the others stirred nervously. He drew a long breath and said, "Only if they run him. If they run him and think they are going to whoop this town like they did before." He paused again and his face stiffened. "I guess that'd be my put-in. I guess you'd say I was looking the right way if I took that for my put-in, wouldn't you, Judge?"

The judge moved his head in what might have been a nod, but he didn't speak. Skinner said, in an embarrassed, too-loud voice, "Well, now, I expect you can count on Clay Blaisedell not running, Carl."

"There was Texas men tried to run him out of Fort James," French said. "I expect maybe Abe is going to bust a few teeth on Blaisedell, and choke on them too."

"I just wait and see," Parsons said.

"Every man is waiting to see, Owen," Bacon said.

"Well, Blaisedell looks a decent one to me," Mosbie said. "Don't look to be holding himself above a man, being what he is and all. I expect he will make out tonight. I expect he will make a fine marshal here, and Carl an easy job out of it."

Schroeder's lips twitched beneath his colorless mustache as he glanced up at the names of predecessors scratched in the whitewash. The judge was shaking his head.

"No," the judge said. "Not an easy job for Carl if he does his job. No, and not enough for Blaisedell to look decent either. For he has set himself to kill men and judge men to kill. And the Citizens' Committee has." He glared up at Skinner as Skinner started to interrupt. "No, not enough!" he said.

"Blow!" Skinner said. "By God, you are on the Citizens' Committee the same as me. It seems like you could go along with what the rest of us decided had to be done or shut up about it. Blaisedell isn't costing you nothing."

"He costs me," the judge said hoarsely.

"You damned drunken old fraud!" Skinner cried. "Nobody ever got any money out of you for anything yet but whisky. I am sick of your damned blowing! You are no more judge than I am, anyhow!"

"On acceptance," the judge said. He looked flustered. Clumsily he opened the table drawer against his belly, took out a bottle of whisky and started to pry the cork out with his thumbnail. Then, as he saw the others all watching him, he changed his mind and only set the bottle down before him. "On acceptance only, in this law-forsaken place," he said.

Tim French said suddenly, "Well, I will sure say this, Carl. How you ought to let Blaisedell take on what he is paid good money for. It is his showdown tonight and none of yours."

"Surely," Schroeder said.

Mosbie, his dark face flushing more darkly, said, "There is others but you have come hard against McQuown now, Carl."

"Not a man here that isn't with you," Pike Skinner said heavily. "Me included. And not a man here that won't back off when it comes time to scratch, I guess. That has been proved on us hard."

No one spoke. The judge sat staring at the whisky bottle before him.

"But with you all the same," Skinner said. He slapped his hat against his leg and turned to leave, but stopped.

"Got a help-wanted sign outside there," Schroeder said, with an edge to his voice. "Keller says I can have another deputy in here, can I hire one."

Skinner grunted explosively and flung on outside. His heels hammered away on the boardwalk. Owen Parsons rose and stretched, and

Peter Bacon bent forward to sweep up his shavings. His face hidden, he said, "People have been shamed, Horse. I expect next time a man needs help, there'll be help."

"Uh-huh," Schroeder said. His mustache twitched again, but his voice still held the bitter edge. "There'll maybe be help, but I haven't heard much about anybody offering it to Blaisedell tonight. That might need it bad." He rubbed his hand over his mouth. "Me included," he said.

4. Morgan and Friend

IN HIS office at the rear of the Glass Slipper, Tom Morgan changed into a clean linen shirt and tied his tie by the dim last dregs of daylight. From the mirror the image of his pale face with the silver-white sleek hair and the black slash of mustache gazed back at him, expressionless and shadowy. He put on a bed-of-flowers vest, his shoulder harness, and short holster that carried his Banker's Special flat against his side, and his fine black broadcloth coat.

Then he poured a quarter of an inch of whisky into a glass from the decanter on his desk, and rinsed it through his mouth, gazing up now at the dull painting of the nude woman sprawled lushly on a maroon coverlet that hung, slanting sharply, on the wall over the door into the Glass Slipper. He raised his empty glass to her in a formal salute, and swallowed the whisky in his mouth. As though it had been a signal, the piano began to fret and tinkle beyond the door, the notes muted sourly in the increasing busy hum of evening.

He went out into the Glass Slipper. The big chandelier was still unlighted. To his right the long bar was lined with men's backs, the mirror behind it lined with their faces, but the miners had not started coming in yet and only one faro layout was going. Two barkeeps were hustling whisky and beer. The professor sat erect and narrow-shouldered at the piano, his hands prancing along the keys, a glass of whisky before him. He turned and smiled nervously at Morgan, the little tuft of whiskers on his chin popping up. Murch, brooding over the faro layout, his shotgun lying across the slots in the arms of his highchair, nodded down at him. Morgan nodded back, and, as he passed on, nodded to Basine, and to the case keeper, and to the dealer, shadowy-eyed in his green eyeshade; to Matt Burbage and Doctor Wagner. He sat down at an empty table in the corner to the left of the louvre doors, and raised two fingers to one of the barkeepers.

There was a deck of cards on the table, and he began to sort the cards by suit and number, his pale, long hands moving rapidly. When he had finished the sorting he quickly cut, recut, and shuffled. He frowned as he examined the result. The barkeeper arrived with a bottle and two glasses, but he did not look up, sorting, cutting and shuffling as before. This time the cards had reformed in proper order. He regarded them more with boredom than with pleasure. He was thirty-five, he thought suddenly, for no reason; half done. He poured a little whisky in his glass and touched it to his lips, but only to taste it, and his eyes glanced around the Glass Slipper. It was the same, here as in Fort James, here as anywhere. He had been pleased to sell out there and come ahead when Clay had told him he was going to take the place as marshal in Warlock; he had been eager to move on, eager for a change, but there was no change. It was the same, and he was only half done.

The batwing doors swung inward and Curley Burne and one of the Haggins came in. They did not see him, and he watched them go down along the bar, Curley Burne with his sombrero hanging against his back from the cord around his neck. They shouldered their way up to the bar, McQuown's first lieutenant and McQuown's cousin. And McQuown himself was coming in tonight, Dechine had said. He felt an anticipatory pleasure, and, almost, excitement.

He sat regarding the slight nervousness within himself as though it were some organic peculiarity, watching the heads turning covertly toward the newcomers and listening to the heavy conglomerate noise of men drinking, quarreling, whispering, gossiping, and to the little silences from the nearby layout when a card was turned and then the sudden click of chips and counters. The piano notes flickered through the noise like shards of bright glass. The sounds of money, he thought, and raised his glass again.

"Here's to money," he said, not quite aloud. After a time you discovered that it was all that was important, because with it you could buy liquor and food, clothes and women, and make more money. Then, after a further time, you went on to discover that liquor was unnecessary and food unimportant, that you had all the clothes you could use and had had all the women you wanted, and there was only money left. After which there was still another discovery to be made. He had made that by now, too.

Still, though, he thought, putting his glass down untouched and turning again to gaze at the two at the bar, there was a thing or two worth watching yet. The eyes that chanced to meet his in the mirrors behind the bar glanced away; they all disliked him already, as always, and he could enjoy that, and enjoy, too, their displeasure and surprise that Clay should associate with him, that Clay was his friend. There were a few things yet.

Basine had lowered the chandelier and was lighting the wicks with the long-handled spill. As each flame climbed and spread, the room lightened perceptibly. He noticed that the piano notes no longer filtered through the sounds around him; the professor was coming toward him, in his shiny black suit.

"Well, sir!" the professor said, sitting down opposite him. "Place should be filling up pretty soon now, shouldn't it?" His eyes were like bright beads.

"Why, yes, sir, Professor. I believe it should."

"Well, now, this place has done fine here, Mr. Morgan. I wouldn't have believed it, coming in here cold like we did. Nice town too, but noisy." He leaned forward, conspiratorially. "However, I see that a couple of McQuown's people are in tonight. Expecting trouble, sir?"

"Always expect trouble, Professor," he said, conspiratorially too. "That's my practice."

The professor cackled, but he seemed distressed. The professor leaned toward him again as he shuffled the cards once more and dealt them out for patience.

"I've been thinking, Mr. Morgan."

"Now, why is that, Professor?"

"You know me, Mr. Morgan. I have worked for you for two years now, here and Fort James, and I'm an honest man. You know, I have to speak my mind when I see a thing that's wrong. Well, sir, money is being wasted here. By you, Mr. Morgan, on me!"

The professor had spoken dramatically, but Morgan did not look up from his cards. "How is that, Professor?"

"Mr. Morgan, I am an honest, outspoken man, and I have to say it. No one can hear that piano going, with the runkus in here. It is a waste of money, sir, and I made up my mind I was just going to say it to you."

"Play louder," he said; now he saw, and was bored. Taliaferro, who owned the Lucky Dollar and the French Palace, had been after the professor again. He flipped the cards rapidly, red onto black, black onto red, the aces coming out one by one; cheating yourself, he thought, as the kings appeared, queen to king, and jack to queen, and ten to jack—what use to play it out? But he continued to turn and place the cards, cheat himself, and laugh at himself for it. The last day, he thought, would be the day when he could laugh at himself no longer.

The professor was staring at him with his face askew as though he were about to cry. "Why, I play as loud as I can, sir!" the professor said, in an aggrieved and trembling voice.

Morgan said, "Taliaferro?"

The professor licked his lips. "Well, sir, it is that fellow Wax that works for Mr. Taliaferro. You know that Mr. Taliaferro went and got a piano for the French Palace, but there is no one around can play one but me. Well, they have been after me, Mr. Morgan, and you know I wouldn't leave working for you for double pay, but— Well, I was thinking, like I said, since it is a waste of your good money me playing here with nobody can hear it, so much runkus going on—I thought I might go up there to the French Palace and waste Mr. Taliaferro's money."

"You are too good to play a piano in a whorehouse, Professor," he said, and sat staring steadily at the other until the professor left him and went slowly back over to the piano.

Morgan watched a man he had never seen before enter and move over to the faro layout to stand behind Matt Burbage. The newcomer wore dusty store pants and a dust- and sweat-stained shirt. He was not heeled, was thin, not quite tall, with a narrow, clean-shaven face and a prominent bent nose. He bent over to speak to Burbage, and straightened suddenly, his lips bent into a strained grin. As he turned away and moved toward the bar, somebody cried, "Hey, Bud!"

Haggin flung himself upon the newcomer, and Curley Burne came up to slap him on the back. "Why, Bud Gannon!" Burne said. One on either side of him, they dragged him to the bar.

Morgan watched the three of them in the mirror. He had heard that Billy Gannon had a brother off somewhere. A group of miners came in, in their wool hats and faded blue clothes and heavy boots, two of them sporting red sashes—heavy, pale, bearded men. It was difficult to tell one from the other among them, but they were trade. Clay appeared behind them in his black frock coat.

Clay held the batwing doors apart as he halted for a fraction of a second, and in that fraction glanced, without even appearing to turn his head, right and left with that blue, intense and comprehensive gaze. Then, removing his black hat, he came over and sat down on the far side of the table and placed his hat on the chair beside him. "Evening," he said.

Morgan grinned. "Is, isn't it? And a couple or three San Pablo boys over there at the bar, too."

"Is that so?" Clay said, with interest. "McQuown?"

"He's supposed to show tonight."

"Is that so?" Clay said again. He stuck out his lower lip a little, raised his eyebrows a little. "Hadn't heard. I guess I ought to be tending to business instead of buggy-riding around."

Now the professor's piano playing carried well enough. Morgan could see the eyes watching Clay in the mirror. Murch had shifted the shotgun slightly, so that the muzzle was directed toward the three at the bar.

"Been a hot day," Clay said. He propped a boot up on the chair where he had laid his hat. Beneath the black broadcloth of his coat his shirt was wilted.

"Hot," Morgan said, nodding. As he poured whisky into the second glass he watched Clay's pursed, half-smiling mouth beneath the thick, blond crescent of mustache. "And it looks like a hot night," he said.

Clay grinned crookedly at him and they raised their glasses together. "How?" Clay said.

"How," he replied, and drank. "Look at them," he said, and indicated the people in the Glass Slipper with a nod of his head. "They are all in a twitch. If they stay around they might see a man shot dead—you or one of McQuown's. Only there might be stray lead slung and bad for their hides. But the money's been paid and time for the show to begin. You like this town, Clay?"

"Why, it's just a town," Clay said, and shrugged.

"Just a town," Morgan said, grinning again as Jack Cade came in. "Smaller than most and about as dull. Hotter than most, and dustier, but it has got a fine pack of bad men. Not just tourists like those *Tejanos* in Fort James, either."

"Who's that one?" Clay said thoughtfully, as Cade swung on down the bar, dark-faced with a stubble of beard, his round-crowned hat exactly centered on his head, his holstered Colt swung low.

"Jack Cade," Morgan said; he had made it his business to know who McQuown's people were. Cade joined the others at the bar, elbowing a miner out of the way. "Next to him is Curley Burne—number two to McQuown. That'll be Billy Gannon's brother in the store pants, and the other is one of the Haggin twins, cousins of McQuown's. One's right-handed and one left. This's the left-handed one, but I forget his name."

Clay nodded, watching them with a slight shine now in his blue eyes, a little more color showing in his cheeks. The room had quieted again, and there was traffic moving toward the door. The doctor and Burbage left the faro layout. As they went out they encountered another bunch of miners entering. "Doc," each miner said, as he passed the doctor. "Doc." "Evening, Doc." "You'll be needed later, I hear, Doc."

Clay grinned again. Luke Friendly came in. With him was a cocky, mean-faced little man who swaggered like a sailor walking the deck in rough weather. They joined the others, where the little man turned to glance at Clay, and spat on the floor.

"I expect that might be Pony Benner, that shot the barber a while back," Morgan said. "I haven't seen him in before. The big one is Friendly. By name, not nature. But watch out for Cade. He is a bad one."

"So I hear."

"McQuown is sitting off to let you chew your fingernails up a while. He won't play it your way, Clay. He will play it with a back-shooter, which is his style. Watch out for Cade."

"Why, I will play it my own way, Morg. And see if they don't have to, too."

Morgan shrugged and raised his glass. "How?"

"How," Clay said, nodding, and they drank.

"I hope you have got on your gold-handled pair. There will be a lot disappointed here if they don't get to see them flash."

He laughed, and Clay laughed too, easily. Clay said, "Why, they are for Sunday-go-to-meeting. This is a work day."

Carl Schroeder was approaching, and Clay got politely to his feet. "Evening, Deputy," he said, and put out his hand. Schroeder shook it, said, "Evening, Marshal," nodded tightly to Morgan, and sat down, pushing his hat back on his head. Above the brown of his face his forehead was a moist, pasty white. Little muscles stood out along his jaw, like the heads of upholstery tacks.

"I will stick by tonight, Marshal," Schroeder said, in a strained voice that was almost a stutter. "I am no shakes of a gunhand, but it'll maybe help to have me by."

"Why, I kind of thought I could count on you, Deputy," Clay said. He paused a moment, frowning. "But when it comes right down to it, this is no trouble of yours. You are not paid for it and I am—no offense meant."

"Pay is not the only reason for a thing, Marshal," Schroeder said. He looked down, scrubbing his hands together as though they itched.

Clay said, "Morg, would you call for another glass, and—"

"No, not for me. No, thanks," the deputy said. He looked sick with dread. His back was to the bar and he tried awkwardly to glance around, and then he said, "Is Johnny Gannon with them over there, can you see, Morgan?"

"He's there," Morgan said, and picked up the cards again. Schroeder bared his teeth in some kind of grimace. Clay got to his feet. His Colt was out of sight beneath the skirt of his black frock coat.

"Might take a little *pasear* around town, Deputy," he said. "There is no reason to sit in here and give ourselves the nerves." Schroeder scrambled up quickly, and Clay took up his hat.

"I'll probably clean them out myself," Morgan said, "if they get noisy." Schroeder stared, and Clay grinned at him. Morgan watched them leave, taking a cigar from his breast pocket and clamping his teeth down on it. Schroeder kept close as a shadow to Clay's heels.

As soon as they had gone, Murch signaled to Basine to replace him as lookout. Murch clambered ponderously down and came over toward Morgan. He looked like a carp, with his wall eye and his great slit of a mouth.

"Something going to come off in here?" Murch said, in his gravelly voice.

"Yes."

"How you want to handle it?"

"Tell Basine I want him behind the bar. You on the stand. They'll play one behind him. It'll probably be Cade. You hold on whoever it is with the shotgun and let go if he moves."

"Holy Jumping H. Jupiter!" Murch muttered. "I can't let that thing off, it's crowded in here! It'll mash half the place full. I'll—"

"You'll let it off if one of them makes a move at Clay's back," he said, through his teeth. He stared into Murch's straight-on eye. "I don't care who you mash."

Murch said, "All right," unemotionally. The piano began to play again. Murch poured whisky into the glass Clay had left; his throat worked as he drank.

"What's chewing the professor?" he asked.

"Taliaferro wants him to play that new piano at the French Palace. That Wax's been scaring him."

"That's poor of Wax," Murch said.

"He just works for Taliaferro, and Taliaferro's got a new piano and nobody to run it."

Murch nodded stolidly. "What'll we do about it, Tom?"

"I'll see," Morgan said. "Get back up on that stand. I meant what I said about backshooters, Al."

Murch nodded again. Sweat showed on his forehead in a delicate fringe beneath his receding hair. He went back over to the faro layout.

Morgan poured himself another quarter-inch of whisky, leaned back, and waited.

It was dark outside when McQuown came in, wearing a pale buckskin shirt, smiling pleasantly, his face slanted down and his red beard against his chest, the lamplight catching glints off the big silver conchos on his belt. With him were Billy Gannon and Calhoun. Billy looked like his brother, Morgan thought, except that he was six or eight years younger and had a sparse young mustache sprouting on his lip, and his nose was straight, his eyes narrower and warier. His walk was a copy of Curley Burne's slow-gaited, cocky stride.

Morgan nodded to McQuown as the three of them went on down the bar. Billy yelled with surprise and jumped forward to embrace his brother, while McQuown glanced casually around the room. Now there was a steadier exodus. When McQuown's eyes met his for a moment, Morgan grinned back. "All right, McQuown," he whispered, hardly aloud. "Clay Blaisedell won't play your game, but I can, and better than you."

5. Gannon Sees a Showdown

STANDING beside his brother at the bar of the Glass Slipper, John Gannon looked from one to another around him—at Pony Benner's mean, twisted little face; at Luke Friendly, who could, at least, be dismissed as a blowhard and braggart; at the sour, cruel, dark features of Jack Cade, whom he had always feared; at Calhoun, with whom he had learned to be merely careful, as with a rattlesnake out of striking distance; at Curley Burne, who, with Wash Haggin, had been his friend, whose droll, easy manner of speech he had once tried to copy, and whose easy gait he had seen that Billy was copying now. He looked at Abe McQuown's keen, cold, red-bearded face. Once, when he had been Billy's age, he had admired Abe more than he ever had any other man.

Now he was back among them, and he tried to smile at Billy, his brother. Billy looked thinner and taller in his double-breasted flannel shirt and his narrow-legged jeans pants. It was like seeing a photograph of himself taken five years ago—same height, same weight, the same quick, not quite sure movements that he recognized as having been his own, but surer than his own had been; the same narrow, intent, deep-eyed face, with the only differences the mustache Billy was trying to grow, and Billy's nose straight still, whereas his own slanted off to one side, broken-bridged and ugly. Billy was watching Abe McQuown.

"Blaisedell'll be about halfway to Bright's by now," Pony said, in his shrill voice, and Luke Friendly laughed and glanced toward the batwing doors.

"Don't you wish it, Shorty," Wash Haggin said, and winked at Gannon. He had a big mustache, whereas his twin was—or had been—clean-shaven, silent, and reserved. Chet was home, Wash had said, disgustedly, when Gannon had asked.

"Blaisedell'll be around," Wash went on, to Pony. "This one is a different breed of horse."

Abe smiled and bent his head forward as he lit a cheroot. In the brightness of the match flame, his skin looked clear and fine as oiled parchment. Long, harshly cut wrinkles ran down his cheeks into his beard. He shook the match out, blew smoke, glanced up to meet Gannon's gaze, and smiled again.

"It is surely nice to see you back, Bud," he said. His eyes were bright as wet green stones. Casually he turned his buckskin back, and Cade leaned forward to whisper to him. Abe nodded in reply.

Gannon saw the big, flat-faced lookout staring down at them. "What's going on?" he said to Billy.

"New marshal," Billy said. "Clay Blaisedell, that's a gunman from Fort James. Citizens' Committee hired him to run us out of town. We'll see who's going to run tonight."

"Well, I expect he won't run," Wash said cheerfully. "He's the one that shot Big Ben Nicholson," he told Gannon. "And got a pair of gold-handled Colts from some Wild West writer for it."

Gannon nodded, watching Billy's stony young profile. "Pretty bad odds against him, isn't it?" he said, more drily than he intended.

Billy's face turned sullen. "Why, we'll make a play in here," he said.

"Not so bad odds in here," Wash explained. He jerked a thumb and whispered, "Morgan over there is kin to him, I heard; anyway they are partners here. And a charge of buckshot up there," he went on, indicating the lookout. "Only I hope to God it is birdshot. And count up Morgan's dealers and barkeeps and who knows what the hell else besides. Morgan is supposed to've cut plenty score himself. It is a fair enough shake."

Cade finished his conversation with Abe and turned to the bar with his back to the others. Calhoun was watching the door, scraping a thumbnail along his boneless nose.

"Billy," Abe said. "Maybe you and me and Curley and Wash could have a hand of cards over there."

Billy nodded tautly, and, with Wash and Curley, moved off after Abe. As they sat down in the rear, beyond the piano, a group of miners hurriedly vacated a nearby table. The piano player banged his hands down in a sour chord, and got up too, bumping, in his departure, against Calhoun and Friendly as they moved down to the end of the bar, and apologizing profusely. Pony Benner swaggered over toward the lookout's stand. Men were crowding out the door.

Gannon felt leaden as he stood alone against the bar, watching, in the mirror, McQuown's disposition of his men. At the table Billy sat facing the bar, with Abe and Wash on either side of him, Curley across from him, back to the room. So it would be Billy. He remembered that his father, dying, had charged him with watching out for Billy until Billy was grown. But Billy had grown too fast for him, and already Deputy Jim Brown was dead by Billy's six-shooter. His responsibility had been long ago dissolved in incapacity, and now the dread he felt as he stared into the mirror was more disgust and hopelessness than fear. He had fled this hard and aimless callousness where a human life was only a part of a game, and never, so far as he had seen, a fair game. He had thought he could escape it by fleeing it. But he could not escape having been one of McQuown's, nor the nightmare-crowded memory of what they had done, himself as much as any of them, one day six months ago, in Rattlesnake Canyon just over the border; and he could not escape himself.

The Glass Slipper continued to empty, men abandoning the bar and the gambling layouts without apparent haste, but steadily, clotting together as they thrust their way out the doors. The gambler, Morgan, came down along the bar against the traffic, his hair gleaming smoothly silver under the light of the chandelier, his face dead pale with the black bar of the mustache across it. Icy eyes touched his briefly. Morgan disappeared through the door at the back, beyond where Calhoun and Friendly stood.

Then Gannon was aware of the congealing silence. He saw the men crowded at the louvre doors pushing back out of someone's way. Among them appeared a man in black broadcloth, wearing a black hat. A step behind him was Carl Schroeder.

Carl halted there, among the others, but the man who must be Blaisedell came on, a tall, broad man with long arms, and a way of carrying himself that was halfway between proud and arrogant. His faintly smiling mouth was framed between a thick, fair curve of mustache and a prominent, rounded chin. For an instant the most intensely blue eyes Gannon had ever seen glanced directly into his. The marshal halted at a vacant stretch of bar between him and Jack Cade, who was bent forward over his glass.

"Whisky," the marshal said. A reluctant barkeep brought it. The sound as he set the bottle down on the bar was very loud, as was the slap of a coin on wood. The bartender, his hands in his apron, glided rapidly backward. Then there was no sound at all.

In the mirror Gannon saw that Curley Burne had risen and turned, and was standing to the right of McQuown, facing the room now. So it was not to be Billy; but he felt no relief.

Curley was grinning. Glints of light flickered in his black curls. Billy and Wash were sitting with their hands on the table before them. McQuown shuffled the deck of cards with a sound like tearing cloth.

"Oh, Mister Marshal!" Curley said.

Out of the corners of his eyes Gannon watched the marshal raise his glass to his lips and toss down the whisky. Then he set the glass down, and turned.

Curley's face wore a mock sheepish expression. "Marshal," Curley said. "I wonder could I make a little complaint?"

Blaisedell inclined his head once, politely.

"I guess it is up to me, Marshal," Curley went on. "There is a lot of complaint around about it—but folks have just kind of gone and left it up to me. Those gold-handles of yours, Marshal. They are awful hard on a fellow's eyes."

Someone laughed shrilly.

The door through which Morgan had disappeared stood open now, and Morgan leaned there casually.

"I mean, speaking for myself now, Marshal," Curley said. "I would surely hate to get a case of eyestrain from those gold-handles. They are so bright in the sun and all. A fellow is not much use without his good eyes. I hear they have been strained bad in Warlock lately."

"You could close your eyes," Blaisedell said, in his deep voice, but pleasantly still.

With a deprecating gesture Curley said, "Aw, Marshal. I'd just be bumping and wumping all over the place, trying to get around with my eyes closed. And look foolish! Marshal, *por favor*, couldn't you just not polish them handles so bright, hand-rubbing on them like they say you do?"

"Why, I guess I could do that. If things fell right in town here."

Curley nodded seriously, but long dimples cut his cheeks. Blaisedell stood with his boots set apart, his arms hanging loosely. Beyond him Gannon saw Jack Cade's head half turned, his lips drawn tight and bloodless over his teeth. Carl Schroeder stood alone just inside the batwing doors; he looked as though he were in pain.

"Marshal," Curley said loudly. "What if somebody painted them handles black for you?"

"It might do," Blaisedell said. He walked forward, not directly toward Curley, but at a slant to the right, and Gannon knew the marshal had not moved until he had worked out the geometry involved. Gannon found himself sidling doorward along the bar. He stepped past Jack Cade, but Cade's hand caught his arm and held him there, between Jack and the lookout on the stand. He stared up into the lookout's sweating face and the round huge muzzle of the shotgun.

"But who is to do it?" Blaisedell said. He moved another step toward Curley.

Gannon felt the movement of Cade's arm behind him. Instinctively he jerked his elbow back, and slammed his hand down on Cade's Colt, gasping as the sharp point of the hammer tore into the web of flesh between his thumb and forefinger, and staring up at the shotgun barrel. He fought the Colt down, looking wildly toward the table now, and saw, past Blaisedell's broad back, Curley's hand snatch for his sixshooter; and saw the swifter flick of the bottom of Blaisedell's coat. Curley's hand halted, the gleaming barrel of his Colt not quite level, and his left hand held spread-fingered and protective before his belly. His face was twisted into a grimace that was half grin still, half shock and horror as he stared at Blaisedell's hand, which was hidden from Gannon. In that same frozen instant McQuown flinched forward away from Curley, Wash straightened stiffly, and Billy sat perfectly still with his hands held six inches above the table top. Gannon saw him glance to his right, where Morgan had produced a short-barreled shotgun, which he held trained on Calhoun and Friendly. Then, as Gannon turned back to face the lookout again, he had a glimpse, behind and below the stand, of Pony Benner's baffled, furious face gaping at Blaisedell.

"Whooooo-eee!" he heard Curley whisper. Jack Cade's breath was scalding on the back of his neck. The upward pressure on the gun beneath his hand was released, the hammer drew loose from his flesh. He saw Blaisedell make a peremptory motion with his head at Curley.

Curley gave his hand a little shake and his Colt fell with a thump shockingly loud. Blaisedell returned his own piece to the holster hidden by the skirt of his coat. It was not gold-handled, Gannon saw.

He felt blood sticky and warm in the palm of his hand; he pressed it hard against his pants leg, his back to Cade still. Sweat stung in his eyes, and above him he saw sweat dripping from the lookout's chin. The muzzle of the shotgun was drawn back a little. Glancing toward the door he saw that Carl Schroeder had disappeared.

"McQuown," Blaisedell said. McQuown sat in profile, his head bent forward, deep shadows caught in the lines in his cheeks. He acted as though he had not heard. "McQuown," Blaisedell said, again.

Billy's hot eyes swung toward his chief, and Abe McQuown slowly pushed his chair back and rose. He slowly turned, one hand braced on the back of his chair, his eyes moving jerkily from side to side, his nostrils flaring and slackening with his breathing. His beard twitched as though he were trying to smile. Morgan was leaning casually in the doorway again, the short-barreled shotgun under his arm.

"McQuown," Blaisedell said, for the third time. Then he said, his deep voice without expression, "My name is Blaisedell and I am marshal here. I am hired to keep the peace here," he said, and stopped, and waited, just long enough for McQuown to speak if he wished, but not so long that he had to.

Then Blaisedell glanced around as though he were talking to all now, in the breathless silence. "Since there is no law for this town I will have to keep the peace as best I can. And as fair as I can. But there is two things I am going to lay down right now and back up all the way. The first one is this." His voice took on an edge. "Any man that starts a shooting scrape in a place where there is others around to get hurt by it, I will kill him unless he kills me first."

Gannon saw the furious tears in Billy's eyes. Billy got to his feet, and McQuown glanced nervously at him. Morgan shifted his shotgun around. McQuown's face was deep red.

Blaisedell continued. "Number two is what the Citizens' Committee has agreed to. I will say it again in case it hasn't got around yet. If a man makes trouble, or looks to make it and go on making it, he is going to see himself posted out of town. That is what they call some places a white affidavit. It is backed by me. Any man that comes in here when he has got himself posted comes in against me."

Again he paused, and again McQuown did not speak.

"That's all I've got to say, McQuown," Blaisedell said. "Except that you and your people are welcome here so long as you can keep them in order."

"Hear, hear!" someone yelled from the doorway. It was the only utterance. McQuown suddenly started forward. He came at a slow, steady walk along the bar. As he passed Friendly and Calhoun he nodded to them; they fell in behind him. Blaisedell half turned to watch, and Gannon could see the line of his face, calm and sure; and proud.

"Blaisedell!" Billy yelled. His voice broke. "Go for your iron, Blaisedell!" He leaned forward in a crouch, his hands hovering at his waist.

Billy, Gannon whispered, not even aloud; he tried to shake his head. He saw Morgan raise the shotgun.

Blaisedell didn't move. "Go along, son," he said gently.

Billy stood there with his upper lip working over his teeth; he twisted away as Wash put out a hand toward him. Then McQuown said, over his shoulder, "Let's go, Billy," and Billy let his hands fall to his sides.

The men who had crowded back in through the batwing doors now squeezed apart to let McQuown through, and Friendly, Calhoun, and Pony Benner behind him. Wash and Billy came down past Gannon, and Curley stooped to retrieve his gun, holstering it with a flourish. Billy stared at Blaisedell as he passed, and Wash, walking heavy-footed behind him, rolled his eyes exaggeratedly at Gannon. Curley came last, and made a little saluting gesture to Blaisedell. He looked pale, but unconcerned now.

Then Blaisedell turned squarely to face him, John Gannon. The lookout gazed down at him still from the stand, and Morgan watched him from the doorway at the end of the bar. Everyone was looking at him; he felt it like a blow in the stomach, and slowly he too started out after the rest. Behind him there was the sudden whispering of the Glass Slipper coming back to life.

They stood on the boardwalk in the near-darkness. As he came outside, slipping his still-bleeding hand into his pocket, he saw Curley standing close to Abe. He heard Curley laugh nervously. "Whooooo-eee, Abe! Fast, I *mean!*"

Gannon let the batwing doors swing closed behind him. They struck against his back on their outswing, without force. Jack Cade was sitting on the rail, his head in his round-crowned hat bent down. He rose and came forward, his face featureless in the darkness.

"You God damned yellow-livered son of a bitch!" Cade whispered. "By God, I will cut your damned throw-down interfering hand right—"

Gannon backed up a step. Billy sprang forward toward Cade. "Shut your face!" he cried, almost hysterically. "You was supposed to hold on that lookout! I saw you making for Blaisedell, you backshooting son—"

"Here!" Curley said, and Wash stepped between Cade and Billy. "Abe's going, boys," Curley said. "Let's go along now, and not stand around squawling at each other." He started after McQuown, his sombrero swinging across his back from the cord around his neck. Abe was already a half-block away, heading toward the Acme Corral.

The group before Gannon dissolved as Billy and Wash moved aside. Gannon stared into Jack Cade's face—without judgment, for he had known what Cade was for a long time; and now he knew, too, that McQuown had put Cade to the backshooting which had just failed. With a slow, upward movement of his hand, Cade hooked his thumb behind his front teeth and snapped it out viciously.

"I'll shoot that thumb off, one day, Jack," Billy said, in a quieter voice. "Come on, Bud," he said to Gannon.

Gannon stepped past Cade, and ducked under the tie rail to join the others in the street. Billy laid an arm over his shoulders; it felt like wire rope.

"Back to old San Pablo with our tails between our legs," Wash said.

"Did you see that damned Morgan?" Luke Friendly said, in an aggrieved voice. "Brought that God damned short-barreled out of somewhere and had it on us before you could say spit."

Cade caught up and fell into step with Benner. "Who is going to get hisself posted first?" he said, and there were curses.

"He had it his way this time!" Pony said shrilly. "But there'll be another time!"

"We should've known better than to make a play in that damned place," Friendly said. "Too bad odds."

Gannon trudged through the dust between his brother and Wash Haggin, Billy's arm heavy on his shoulders. He had never felt so tired, and his dread of Cade was lost in his revulsion against them all. Ahead, alone, Abe McQuown disappeared in the shadows on the corner before Goodpasture's store. He heard muffled laughter behind them, and Billy cursed under his breath. Someone called, "Say, did you see those gold-handles good enough, Curley Burne?"

"Ah, sons of bitches!" Calhoun muttered. Curley, strolling ahead of the rest, began to hum a mournful tune on his mouth organ. Gannon remembered that mouth organ, and Curley playing it on quiet evenings in the bunkhouse—that had been one of the pleasant things. There had not been many.

And suddenly he knew he was not going with them back to San Pablo. He slowed his steps; he felt the strain of stubbornness in him that was as strong as the same strain in Billy, tighten and halt him like a snubbed rope caught around his waist. Billy's arm slipped off his shoulders.

Gannon turned to face his brother. "I guess I will be staying in town, Billy," he said.

6. The Doctor and Miss Jessie

DOCTOR WAGNER, bag in hand, watched the riders appear against the whitish dust of the street and the night sky. They turned west toward the rim, one of them riding well ahead, the others bunched behind. The suspirant music of Curley Burne's mouth organ was mingled with the confused pad of hoofs as they disappeared into the darkness.

Clearly they were leaving town. There had been no shooting, no need for his bag of medicines and his small skill. He heard a man near him sigh with relief.

He turned and pushed his way through the crowd of men along the boardwalk. "Doc," one said, in greeting. Others took it up: "Doc!" "Evening, Doc." Behind him the piano in the Glass Slipper began tinkling brightly. A man caught his arm. "What happened, Doc?" Buck Slavin cried excitedly.

"The marshal got the drop on Curley Burne in the Glass Slipper. The cowboys have all gone out of town."

Slavin let out an amazed and pleased ejaculation. The doctor disengaged his arm and hurried on, for he must go and tell Jessie, who would be waiting.

He crossed Broadway. Several men were standing on the veranda of the Western Star Hotel, outlined against the yellow windows there.

"What happened, Wagner?" MacDonald called, in his harsh voice.

A burst of whooping from the men back in the central block gave the doctor an excuse not to hear the superintendent of the Medusa mine. He hurried away across Main Street. There was no reason not to be civil, he thought, and he was irritated with himself. When the miners came to him with their complaints and wrongs, he could patiently explain that MacDonald's ways were only company policy, common practice—yet it was hypocrisy, for he shared their hatred of MacDonald.

He turned down Grant Street toward the high, narrow bulk of the General Peach. A lamp was burning in the window of Jessie's room, on the ground floor to the right of the doorway. All the other windows were dark, the boarders in town to watch trouble, to see one of the gun fights that were at the same time Warlock's chief source of entertainment and Warlock's curse. They had been disappointed this time, he thought.

Panting a little, he mounted the plank steps to the porch, opened the door, and set his bag down inside the dense block of darkness of the entryway.

"Jessie!" he called, but before her name was spoken the darkness paled and she was standing in the doorway of her room.

"I haven't heard anything," she said quietly.

"There was no shooting."

She smiled a flickering, tentative smile. He followed her into her room and sat down in the red plush chair just inside the door. Jessie stood facing him, slight and straight in her best black dress with its lace collar and cuffs. Her hands were clasped at her waist. Her hair, parted neatly in the middle, fell almost to her shoulders in cylindrical brown ringlets that slid forward along her cheeks when she inclined her head toward him. Her triangular face was strained with anxiety. It was a face that some thought plain; they did not see the light behind it.

"Tell me," she said pleadingly.

"I didn't see it, Jessie. I had gone to get my bag. But from what I heard, the marshal got the drop on Curley Burne, and took the occasion to announce to McQuown his intentions here. There was no trouble, and McQuown and his people have gone."

The tip of her tongue appeared, to touch her upper lip. When she smiled, tiny muscles pulled at the corners of her mouth. "Oh, that's good," she said, in a curiously flat voice. She turned half away from him, and laid a hand on the edge of the table. "Was he—" She paused, and then she said, "Did he look very fine, David?"

"I'm sure he did," he said. "Although I didn't see him, as I have said."

"Oh, that's good," she said again.

He glanced away from her, at the bookcase with the set of Scott gleaming with gold titling; at the lithographs and mezzotints upon the walls—Bonnie Prince Charlie in heroic pose, Cuchulain battling the waves, The Grave at St. Helena; at the curved-fronted bureau next to the bed, on top of which were two daguerreotypes, one of Jessie as a girl, with the same ringleted hair and her eyes cast demurely down at a little book held lovingly in her hands. The other was of her father, sad-faced with his neat triangle of mustache and beard, seated against a manufactured backdrop that spread away behind him to dreamy distance.

"Are you angry, David?" Jessie asked.

"Why would I be angry?"

She sat down on the black horsehair sofa, her hands still clasped at her lap. He was, he thought, only angry that she should have seen so easily that he was jealous. "Don't be angry with me, David," she said, and he was moved despite himself, by the girlishness that was her manner whenever she was alone with him; by her sympathy and her sweet guilelessness that were her stock in trade, and, at the same time, her armor against rough men. She smiled at him, with the incisive understanding that always surprised him. Then her eyes wandered from his face, and, though she smiled still, he knew that she was thinking about Clay Blaisedell, who had come riding to her one day out of the half-calf and gilt-titled set of Waverley Novels.

She cocked her head a little, to something he could not hear. "Cassady is coughing again," she said.

"There is nothing more I can do for him, Jessie. There never was anything. I don't know how he is still alive."

Her face saddened. He knew that sympathy was as real as anything about her, and the tears when Cassady died would be real, and yet he wondered if any of it really touched her. He had always the feeling that death could not touch her, as rough men could not. He himself had always hated disease and death, and all the other outrages of nature upon man. But he himself became always less removed; hating them, he had, slowly, come intensely to hate Warlock, where death was so commonplace as to be a sort of rude joke, and especially to hate the mines that were the real destroyers of men. Most of all he hated the Medusa, the worst destroyer; and so he had come to hate its superintendent, MacDonald.

Yet Jessie, too, had seen much of death. She had spent her girlhood nursing her father to his slow demise, and now she had nursed more dying men in Warlock than he could count any more, holding their hands as they departed quietly and bravely—as they usually did if she was with them, for they knew it was what she wanted, though others wept, or fought and cursed death, as though they could drive death off or shout it down. And now in the last week or so he had come to see that she was in love with Clay Blaisedell, had fallen in love with him immediately, was in love as obviously and unaffectedly as she was Angel of Warlock. He wondered if *that* could touch her, either.

Maybe it depended upon Clay Blaisedell, he thought, and felt a stricture knot his throat.

She was listening again. This time he heard it too, the heavy, helpless, muffled coughing. Footsteps came hurrying down the hall, and Jessie lifted the brass lamp from the bright-colored yarn lamp mat on the table.

"Miss Jessie!" Ben Tittle cried, from the doorway. "He has gone and started it again!"

"Yes, I'm coming, Ben. And Doctor Wagner's here now." She hurried out with the lamp, and he retrieved his bag and followed her down the hall, reluctantly; Cassady only made him feel his helplessness the more. Shadows swung and tilted in the hallway as Jessie hurried along it with the lamp, toward the room at the back that she had converted into a hospital. Tittle hobbled after her on the crippled, twisted foot. They had not taken him back on at the Medusa because of that foot, and now he worked for Jessie as an errand boy and orderly.

When he entered the hospital, Jessie was already bending over Cassady's cot. Tittle was holding the lamp for her. Rows of cots extended into the shadows, and men were sitting up watching as Jessie poured water from an olla into a glass, and tipped the glass to Cassady's lips. The coughing continued, fleshy-sounding and murderous in the man's crushed chest.

"He sounds like a goner, Doc," Buell said softly from his cot nearest the door. "We sure thought he was going about three times tonight, and a blessed relief it would be, God help me for saying it."

The doctor nodded, watching Jessie lay her hand on Cassady's chest; he had never known another woman who would have done that, except a hardened professional nurse. "Drink it!" Jessie said. "Drink it, please, Tom. Drink as much as you can!" She spoke urgently, she sounded almost angry; and Cassady drank, and choked. Beneath a fringe of curly beard his face was drawn tight over the bone, and freckles stood out on the clean, gray flesh like bee stings on an apple. Water streamed down his beard.

"You can stop, Tom," Jessie said. "Try now. *David!*" she called, as Cassady began to gasp, horribly. The water might choke and kill him as easily as the coughing fit, the doctor thought, but he did not move. Cassady would not die simply because Jessie commanded him not to.

The gasping ceased, and the coughing. Jessie straightened. "There, Tom!" she said, as though she had merely talked a child out of a willful pet. "Now, that's better, isn't it?"

The doctor picked up Cassady's limp wrist. The pulse was almost imperceptible. Cassady was staring up at Jessie with worship in his eyes. The man could not possibly live for more than a day or two, and, heaven knew, there would be another along soon to need his cot. The cots were always needed, for the men were continually being broken and crushed in rock falls, in the collapse of a stope or the failure of a lift, or were poisoned at the stamp mill, or knife-slashed or shot, or got broken jaws or heads in saloon fights.

It would be merciful to let Cassady die, but Jessie adhered to a sterner philosophy than his. It was not that she considered death a sin, as he had once; she considered it a failure, and could not believe that there were wills less strong than her own. He knew her persuasion to duty, too, and he wondered if she did not also refuse to let Cassady die because her duty as the Miners' Angel, the Angel of Warlock, was to be just that, to the limit of her powers, and of her will. Perhaps, he thought, almost guiltily, in this singlemindedness she was incapable of any interest in Cassady, or any other, as a person at all, but saw them only as objects for her ministrations and as proofs of her office.

He shook his head at her, as Cassady tried to speak.

"Hush now, Tom," Jessie whispered, smiling down at the dying man. "You mustn't try to talk, the doctor says. It is time you tried to sleep."

Cassady's pale tongue appeared, to swipe at pale, dry lips. He closed his eyes. In the lamplight spilled water shone like jewels in his beard.

Jessie handed the olla to Ben Tittle and took back the lamp. She raised it so that its light spread farther, and smiled around the hospital room at the others. "Now you boys try to be quiet, won't you? We must let Tom get some sleep."

"Surely, Miss Jessie," young Fitzsimmons said, cradling his thickly bandaged hands to his chest. "Yes, Miss Jessie," the others said, in hushed voices. "We sure will, Miss Jessie."

"Good night, Miss Jessie. Doc."

"Good night, boys." She started toward the door. Her skirts rustled as she walked. They all stared after her.

"Doc," MacGinty whispered, as Jessie went out. MacGinty's thin, pocked face was raised to him; it did not look so feverish tonight, and he pressed the back of his hand to the dry forehead and nodded with satisfaction.

MacGinty said, "I guess you heard how Frank tried to get a contrib from MacDonald for—" He rolled his eyes toward Cassady. "But MacDonald said how if he gave anything we'd think the Medusa owed us something when we hurt ourself."

"Frank was stupid to ask."

"Lumber's too high to run in enough laggings," Dill said. "But it don't cost them nothing when we get busted up."

The doctor only nodded, curtly. It was difficult to meet their eyes. Sometimes that was even harder than trying to excuse MacDonald and the mine owners. "I'll come in in the morning," he said. "Good night."

"Good night, Doc."

He took up his bag, went out, and closed the door behind him. Halfway along the hall, Jessie was standing in conversation with Frank Brunk, a miner whom MacDonald had fired a month ago.

"He won't last long," Brunk was saying, in his heavy voice. "Not busted up the way he is. He can't."

"He can if he will," Jessie said. She raised the lamp, and Brunk drew back a little, as though to avoid the light. He was a huge, almost square man, with a square, red, clean-shaven face. He wore a bowie knife slung from his broad belt.

"Hello, Doc," he said. "Well, I went to MacDonald and I asked him straight out to—"

"You knew there was no use asking."

"Maybe I did," Brunk said. "Maybe I just wanted it clear what a son— Pardon me, Miss Jessie."

"Asked him what, Frank?" Jessie said.

"Well, told him. How the Medusa ought to pay part of Tom Cassady's keep."

"Tom doesn't have to worry about his keep, Frank."

Brunk nodded a little; his eyes were pits of shadow. "No, I guess it won't run to much, either," he said. "But *I* worry about it, Miss Jessie. And it was the Medusa smashed him."

"You are beginning to talk like Lathrop," Jessie said.

"And maybe MacDonald will put Jack Cade to run me out of town, too?" Brunk said. "Well, I am just saying there is going to be trouble when Tom dies, is all."

The doctor said, "Do you need him to die? So you can have your trouble?"

Brunk looked at him reproachfully. "That kind of hurts, Doc." He leaned against the wall. "Do you think I want that? I only know what all of us want, and that's help."

"I have tried to talk to Charlie MacDonald about the laggings," Jessie said. She put a hand on Brunk's arm. "But he is no easier for me to talk to. He—"

"I think maybe he is, if you'll pardon me, Miss Jessie," Brunk said. "Doc, it is a fact. I am a miserable no-account miner. We all are. We are dirty, ignorant bullprod drillers and muckers, as everybody knows. No one will listen when the animals try to talk. We will have to have a union."

"Have it, then," the doctor said, with an irritation he did not understand. "If you break your heads fighting for a union or in the stope it is the same broken head."

"It is not the same," Brunk said.

Jessie said in her quiet voice, "Frank, my father used to say that men could do anything they wanted if they wanted it enough. Just to look at history to see what they have done, because they wanted it with all their hearts. He was going to write a book about it and he had collected pieces for the book—the impossible things that men have accomplished because it is in them to do anything if—"

"It's not so," Brunk broke in, roughly.

The doctor saw Jessie's eyes widen. "You can be civil, Brunk," he said.

Brunk rubbed a hand over his mouth. "Sorry. But it is not so, Miss Jessie. We can't have a union because we are not strong enough to make it and never will be, and what we want's nothing to do with it. That's all," he said bitterly. "Jim Lathrop was a good man and he did his best, and all he got was run out by a hired hardcase for his pains. Wanted enough!" he said, with scorn.

"Jim Lathrop did not have courage enough," Jessie said.

"Jesus Christ!" Brunk cried. "I will not hear that from anybody, Miss Jessie!"

Jessie's face was stiff as she gazed back at Brunk, the lamp steady in her hand, her breast rising and falling, and all the power of her will in her eyes.

And Brunk sighed and said in a humble voice, "I am sorry, Miss Jessie. I guess I have got the nerves tonight."

"All right, Frank," Jessie said. "I know Tom Cassady is your friend. And I know Jim Lathrop was." Footsteps sounded in the entryway, and she excused herself and hurried away down the hall, carrying the light with her.

The doctor said to Brunk, "Don't you know how to be civil? Don't you ever consider what she has done for you?"

"Christ knows she helps us enough," Brunk said, in his heavy, tired voice. "And Christ knows you do, Doc. But—" Brunk stopped.

"But what?" He put his bag down and stepped closer to the miner. He could not see Brunk's features now in the darkness.

"But Christ knows we shouldn't ought to be dirty charity cases," Brunk groaned. "We are people like anybody else. When we are charity cases it just makes it worse what everybody thinks of us. We—"

"Just a moment," the doctor said. "Let me tell you something. Who will you blame for the fact that you are charity cases? Jessie? Is it MacDonald's fault that Cassady has saved no money and must become a charity case? You make more money by far than any other laboring men in Warlock. Have any of you ever thought of saving any of it? I will grant you that the saloons, gambling halls, and the Row are snares constructed to relieve you of your earnings. But must all of you fall into those snares payday after payday? Saving is good for the moral fiber—a quality extremely rare among you. Saving your pay might also keep you from becoming charity cases, since you resent that status so much."

Brunk said, "If we had a union we could—"

"There is not moral fiber enough among you to make a union."

Brunk was silent for a time. Then he said, "Doc, I'm not saying what you just said isn't so. But it isn't all there is to it. We have got to have help to have a union, Doc. And the help we have to have is from respectable people. Like you."

He had told Brunk many times he would not engage himself in trying to form a miners' union; he had told himself, as many times, that there was no reason why he should. He said with finality, "I am a doctor, Frank. That's all I am."

"That's a funny way to be. For I am a miner, but I am a man too."

He didn't answer; he picked up his bag.

Brunk said bitterly, "Well, don't worry—they won't fight when a man dies, not having any of that moral fiber you said. But maybe they will try to cut wages one of these days. I have never seen a man yet that wouldn't fight for money."

Brunk moved away from him, down toward the hospital room. Carrying his bag, the doctor walked rapidly to the entryway, and the stairs that led to the rooms on the second story of the General Peach. Outside the open front door a group of boarders on the porch were talking together in the darkness.

As he started up the stairs he could see through Jessie's door, which she always left open, when she had company, for the sake of propriety. She was sitting stiffly on the horsehair sofa, with her hands clasped in her lap and her face alight. Just past the edge of the door a black strip of Blaisedell's coat sleeve was visible, on the arm of the red plush chair.

"They were reasonable enough," Blaisedell was saying. "Most men are, when you can talk to them straight. I don't know as McQuown is one I'd trust far, but then I don't know him."

Blaisedell's voice ceased for a moment, and Jessie glanced toward the door. The doctor went on up the stairs. Below him they began talking again, but now he couldn't hear the words. In his room, as he poured a glass of water, and, into the water, the carefully measured drops of laudanum, he could not hear them at all.

7. Curley Burne Plays His Mouth Organ

IN THE night Curley let Spot pick his own way, only pushing on him when he began to fritter. By day it was a six-hour ride from Warlock to San Pablo, but by night it was slow. The stars were out and a burnt quarter-moon hung in the west, but the darkness was thick, and shapes came suddenly out of it to make his heart start and pound. From time to time he brought out the mouth organ that hung on a cord inside his shirt, and blew a tune through it.

He had dropped the others behind, but Abe had dropped him, too. Still, it was pleasant riding alone in the night, hearing now the wind whispering through trees he couldn't even see. He reined up a moment to locate himself by the sound; he must be on the slope where, below, the river made a bend around a thick stand of cottonwoods. He turned downhill toward the river, Spot picking his way along with care. He heard the river itself and immediately, as he always did when he first heard it, he reined up again and dismounted to make water.

He rode on alongside the river, with its trembling rapid sheen under the moon and the trees soaring against the black sky, light-streaked where the wind turned the leaves. He listened for the thick rush of the rapids, and saw before him the outline of a horseman. He raised his mouth organ and blew into it, tunelessly. Spot scrambled down a rocky ledge, striking hoof-sparks.

"Curley?" Abe said.

"Ho," he replied, and Spot whinnied at Abe's black. They were on the northwest corner of the spread now, and Abe always stopped and watered here.

"Pretty night for a ride," Curley said, dismounting and giving Spot a slap on the flank. "But I sure don't own night eyes like you do. It is lucky Spot knows the route."

"Where's the others?" Abe asked.

"Back somewhere, bickering and whickering."

Abe said nothing, and Curley waited to see if he would start off or wait. If he started off he would let him go in alone. But Abe waited until he remounted, and together they rode on down along the river beneath the cottonwoods.

After a time Curley said, "Quite a one, the marshal!"

"Yes," Abe said. "He is quite a one." Abe didn't pick it up any more than that, nor, although his voice had seemed short, quite cut him off either.

Curley was silent for a time, thinking that it was still all right between the two of them, but thinking painfully now, too, that if he, Curley Burne, left San Pablo and moved west, or north, or down to Sonora somewhere, the way he had been considering lately, Abe would turn into pure son of a bitch. Like Jack Cade, only a bigger one; and that would be too bad. Abe had been knocking at it close for a good while now—he knew well enough that Abe had put Jack there to backshoot Blaisedell if it came to it—and it seemed to him more and more that but for him, and some kind of decency Abe owed him, Abe would go all the way over.

And the old man, he thought, shaking his head. The old man was a trial and a terror, and born unholy mean.

"Let's go on along the river instead of cutting in," Abe said.

"Sounds nice tonight, don't it?" He reined right as Abe cut back down under the deep shadow of the cottonwoods. He spat, scraped his hand over his face, and braced himself to try again. Once he and Abe had been able to talk things out.

"Well," he said loudly. "Looks like I am some beholden to him. He could've burned me down there as well as not."

"No," Abe said.

"Surely," he insisted. "I was looking right down it, six feet long and six deep. And lonely!"

"No," Abe said again. "It looks better for him like this."

He grimaced to think of having to try to figure everything that way. "Well, he is greased lightning, sure enough," he went on. "I never saw a man get unhooked that fast and have himself in hand enough so he didn't have the trigger on the pull. I am some pleased to be with us here, tonight."

Abe didn't turn, didn't speak.

"Well, it was coming anyhow," Curley said. "Warlock was about due to get fed up with folks. There's been things done that would make *me* mad, I know. Pony, now; Pony is an aggravating kind of man. Sometimes I think he don't have good sense. Looks like Warlock was due for somebody like this Blaisedell."

"I was here before he was," Abe said, in a stifled voice. "But now he is set up to say who comes and goes in Warlock."

"Aw, Abe," he said. He didn't know how to go on, but he was filled with it now and he had to try to say it out. "What's got into you, Abe?" he asked.

"Meaning what?" Abe said.

He couldn't bring himself to reproach Abe for setting Jack Cade to backshoot Blaisedell. He said, "Well, it used to be you'd come out and shoot tomato cans off fence posts with the rest of us. And mostly you'd win, but sometimes you'd lose out—that will happen to any man. And Indian wrestle and hand wrestle with us when we got to fooling, and that the same. But you have stopped it."

The black cantered ahead, but when Curley caught up again he kept at it.

"Like you had got to be too big a man to lose any more." His voice felt thick in his throat. "Like if you lost even one time at anything now you lost face, or some damned foolish thing. Like—" He cleared his throat. "Like I kind of think you couldn't stand to lose tonight."

This time Abe glanced back at him, and Curley turned in his spurs in order to draw up even.

"Abe," he said. "Anything where you stand to win, you have got to be able to stand to lose, too. For that's the way things go. Abe," he said. "Maybe I know how you feel some. But say you kept on being the biggest man in the San Pablo valley and Warlock too. You still wouldn't be the biggest man in the territory by a damn sight. And say you called out old Peach and the cavalry, and massacreed them and took Peach's scalp—where'd you go then? What'd you have to be the biggest of then?"

It sounded as though Abe laughed, and his spirits rose.

"Why, Curley," Abe said. "The last time I saw that scalp of Peach's there wasn't a hell of a lot of hair to take. Come to think of it, maybe that's why Espirato took his Paches out of here—when he saw old Time had beat him to Peach's hair."

He laughed too. It sounded like the old Abe.

"Bud Gannon coming along with the others?" Abe asked.

"He stayed in town."

"He did?" Abe said. When he spoke again his voice had turned somber. "I know there is some that's turned against me."

"That's not so, Abe!" he protested.

"It's so. Like Bud. And Chet—you see how he has been staying clear. And I felt it hard in Warlock tonight. But you can't back off."

"Nothing ever stopped me from it." Curley tried to say it lightly. "I surely backed tonight, and glad to."

"I couldn't have done that," Abe said. "I guess you know that's why I let you take it."

He nodded sickly. He thought again of Cade, and he thought of how it had been worked when they had run Canning; he had tried to shut that from his mind, but it had been as clear as this tonight. He felt sick for Abe. "Surely I knew it," he said. "But what the hell? Abe—I am damned if I think poor of myself for backing off tonight. Or why you—"

"There gets a time when it don't matter what you think of yourself," Abe broke in. "That's it, you see. Maybe it is what everybody else thinks instead." The black cantered on ahead again. "Let's get on in," Abe called back to him.

Curley spurred Spot to a half-trot, but he stayed behind Abe all the way.

As they walked up from the horse corral, the dogs barked and jumped around their legs. Curley sighed as he looked up at the squat ranch house, where a little light showed in a window. Behind it soared the monolith of the chimney of the old house, which had burned down. The lonely chimney seemed incredibly high and narrow against the night sky, pointing its stone and crumbling mortar height at the stars. He wondered if that chimney would not fall some day, despite the poles that propped it up, and mash them all to smithereens.

He said to Abe, "Well, I'll be going over to the bunkhouse."

"Come inside and take a glass of whisky," Abe said. His voice was bleak. One of the dogs sprawled away in front of him, yelping. They mounted the slanting steps to the porch, and Abe jerked on the latch-string and shouldered the door open. "What the hell are you doing out here, Daddy?" he said.

Following him in, Curley saw the old man on his pallet on the floor. He was raised on one elbow, his skinny neck corded with strain. There was a Winchester across his legs, a jug and lamp on the floor beside him. His beard was thick, pure-white wool in the lamplight, and his mouth was round and pink as a kitten's button.

"Didn't stay long, did you?" Dad McQuown said. "Think I'm going to stay in that bedroom and burn?"

"Burn?" Abe said. He picked up the lamp and set it atop the pot-belly stove. With the lamplight on it the stovepipe looked red. "You're not dead yet. Burn?"

"Burn is what I said," the old man said. "Don Ignacio is going to hear some time you have left me all alone. You think he won't send some of his dirty, murdering greasers up here to burn me in my bed?"

It was strange, Curley thought, that those Mexicans, killed six months ago in Rattlesnake Canyon, had turned almost every man of them into a greaser-hater—afterward. It was a strange thing.

"There's three men out in the bunkhouse," Abe said. He picked up the jug, hooked it to his mouth, and took a long draught. He handed it to Curley and went to sit on the old buggy-seat sofa against the wall.

"Burn them too," the old man said. "Sneakier than Paches. Those sons of bitches out in the bunkhouse'd sleep through a stampede coming over them anyhow." His eyes glittered at Curley. "What happened up there?"

From the buggy seat Curley heard a clack and metallic singing. He turned to see Abe bend to pull his bowie knife loose, where it was stuck in the floor. Abe spun it down again, the blade shining fiery in the light.

"Let me tell you," Curley said to the old man. "Bold as brass I went in there against him. In the Glass Slipper, that was packed with guns to back the bastard up. 'Let's see the color of your belly, Marshal!' I said to him."

The old man said, "Son, how come you let Curley—"

"Hush now, Dad McQuown. I am telling this. How come he let me? Why, he knows I am the coolest head in San Pablo, and that saloon stacked hard against us." Feeling a fool, he bent his knees into a crouch and heard Abe spin the knife into the floor again. The old man stared as Curley jerked out his Colt and took a bead on the potbelly stove. "I don't mind saying that was the fastest draw human eye ever did see," he said. "Fast, and—" He stopped, straightened, sighed, and holstered his Colt.

"Kill him clean off?" the old man demanded.

"He was way ahead of me," he said, and glanced toward the buggy seat. He had hoped for a laugh from Abe, to clear things a little; he knew what Abe was going to have to take from the old man. But Abe only flung the knife down again. This time the point didn't stick and it clattered across the floor and rang against a leg of the stove. Abe made no move to retrieve it.

"Run you out of town," the old man breathed.

"He surely did."

The old man lay back on his pallet, and sucked noisily at his teeth. "Son of mine running," he said.

"Yep," Abe said, tightly.

"That all you can say?" the old man yelled.

"Yep," Abe said.

"Go in myself," the old man said. "See anybody run me out."

"Walk in," Abe said.

"I will drag in, by God!" Dad McQuown said, straining his head up again. "See anybody run me out. I have been through Warlock when it wasn't but a place in the road where me and Blaikie and old man Gannon used to meet and go into Bright's together. Went together because of Paches in the Bucksaws, thick as fleas. Many's the time we fought them off, too, before Peach was ever heard of. Took my son with me sometimes that I thought was going to amount to something, and not get run out of—"

"Say, now, speaking of Gannons," Curley broke in. "Bud's come back from Rincon. We saw him in town."

"Bud Gannon," the old man said, lying back again, "never was worth nothing at all. Billy, now; there is a boy any man'd be glad for a son. Proud."

"Well, Dad McQuown, he run with the rest of us. Maybe not so fast as me, but he run all right."

"How fast did my boy run?" the old man whispered, and Abe cursed him.

Curley took a long pull on the jug, watching the old man's fingers plucking at the Winchester while Abe cursed him, harshly and at length.

"You will answer to the Lord for that cussing some day, boy," Dad McQuown said, at last. "Cussing your daddy when he is crippled so he can't beat your teeth down your throat for it. Well, it is sire and dam in a man like a horse, and no way to get yourself a boy without there is half woman in him."

"One way," Abe said, in a dead, strained voice. "Breed one mule on another like did for you."

"Cuss your father, and his ma and pa before him, do you? You will answer for that, too."

"Not to you," Abe said.

"You will answer to another Father than me."

"I'll answer maybe for killing a pack of greasers for what they did to you. I won't answer for calling you what every man knows you are, and the Lord too."

Standing there listening to them, trying to grin as though they were just joking each other, it came on Curley strongly that he had to move on. He had been here too long now; he had seen the beginning, which he had not even known was the beginning, and he did not want to see the end. Abe was a man he had respected and loved as he had no other man, and did still, but lately he could not bear to see where Abe was heading. Or maybe he had to stay, and watch, he thought, and felt a kind of panic.

The dogs set up another clamor outside, and hoofbeats came in through the yard. The old man said, "They didn't run so fast as you."

"That is some greasers of Don Ignacio's come up to burn you in your bed," Abe said savagely. "By God, how you would burn and stink!"

The hoofbeats and the barking and yelping diminished, going down toward the horse corral. "Well, I will be getting over to the bunkhouse," Curley said, pretending to yawn. "Good night, Dad McQuown. Abe."

"We'll be going down tomorrow after supper," Abe said.

"Down where?" the old man demanded. "What you going to do now?"

Abe ignored him. "That will put us through Rattlesnake Canyon after dark," he said. "Tell the boys."

Curley tipped his hat back and scratched his fingers through his hair, grimacing. "Hacienda Puerto?" he said. "I thought you figured we ought to lay off that awhile, Abe. They followed us a good way last time and we didn't make off with hardly enough head to count. It is getting tight."

"We will take more people this time."

"Well, there is talk Don Ignacio's got himself an army down there now, Abe. They are going to be waiting for us, one of these times. If they catch us—"

Abe swung toward him. "God damn it, there will be nothing happen because I will be along! You only get caught when I am not there. One shot through and another one dead, and then run home to me to back them off you!"

Curley had brought the old man back that time, leaving Hank Miller dead; and he had refused to go back with Abe and the rest to the ambush in Rattlesnake Canyon. Abe had not forgiven him that, and had not forgiven Bud Gannon, who had left San Pablo afterward. And Abe had not, he thought, forgiven himself either. Rattlesnake Canyon still ate at them all.

"All right, I'll tell them, Abe," he said, and went outside and closed the door behind him. He stood on the porch looking up at the stars past the old chimney. He should go, he thought; he should get out now. As he walked tiredly down the steps and over toward the bunkhouse, he took out his mouth organ and began to blow into it. The music he made was sad in the night.

8. Journals of Henry Holmes Goodpasture

November 16, 1880

Venit, Vidit, Vicit. The recent dramatics at the Glass Slipper were eminently satisfactory to all, except, no doubt, McQuown and his men, and Clay Blaisedell has succeeded almost past our wildest hopes in subduing the Cowboys. We have been most marvelously impressed with his demeanor here so far.

A man in his position is, of course, handicapped, but he is evidently experienced with makeshift arrangements. A tiny, one-cell jail, no court, no proper judge this side of Bright's City—except for a J.P. who is only that on his own mandate and general tolerance, have not fazed our Marshal at all. Thus he has for weapons only his reputation and his own six-shooters, with which to threaten, to buffalo, to maim, or to kill. The first, the inherent threat of his reputation, we hope will serve our purposes.

Blaisedell had various suggestions to make. One was that we set up a deadline; no firearms to be carried past a certain part of town. We were uneasy about this, and Blaisedell readily agreed that the edict might cause more trouble than it prevented. Another suggestion of his was met with more enthusiasm: this is what is known as a "white affidavit." If it is felt that the peace of this town or the safety of its inhabitants are threatened by any man, or if a criminal is transported to Bright's City for trial for a major crime, and the Bright's City jurymen fail to render a true judgment (as is often the case), a white affidavit is to be issued. This is no more than an order on the part of the Citizens' Committee that an offender is to be forbidden entry to the town by the Marshal. If such a one disregards this posting, he then enters under pain of death—which is to say, he must face Blaisedell's six-shooter prowess, which, we are hopeful, will strike fear into the bravest hearts.

We are most pleased with ourselves, and with our Marshal, so far. As Buck Slavin points out, Warlock's bad reputation has long stood in the paths of Commerce and Population. If Blaisedell can effect order here we may expect both to increase, for the peaceable and the timid must certainly shy away from the violence well known to have ruled here. Thus, with an influx of citizens of finer stamp, in time the better element of the population will come to overbalance by far that of the violent and irresponsible, peace will come to enforce itself, and Commerce will flourish. To the good fortune of the members of the Citizens' Committee of Warlock.

Still, there are doubts. I have been troubled in wondering whether we of the Citizens' Committee have fully realized the responsibility we have assumed. We have hired a gunman whose only recommendation is a certain notoriety. We are responsible for this man of whom we know, actually, nothing. I suppose our troubled consciences are assuaged by the thought that we have assumed a makeshift authority for a makeshift situation, and a temporary one.

The question of our status remains frozen in suspension. Are we in Bright's County, or in a new, yet-to-be-surveyed county? What keeps us from being granted a town patent before this matter is settled? Is there more to it than merely General Peach's carelessness and senility? Is there, as Buck Slavin hints in his darker moods, some official feeling that Warlock is not worth troubling with, since it will soon fade away with its subterranean wealth exhausted, or its mines gradually closing down as the market price of silver continues to fall, or becoming flooded and unworkable? *

Poor and makeshift our efforts may be, yet there would seem proof in them that a society of sorts is possible in an anarchistic state. We feel we are ultimately in the Republic, separated from her only by an incredibly inept and laggard territorial government, and so obedience to the forms is necessary. Or are those forms themselves so ineradicably imbedded in men's minds that we cannot think but in terms of them? The general passive acceptance of Judge Holloway's fines (which everyone knows he pockets), and his imposition of sentences to our little jail or to unpaid community tasks, would seem to indicate this.

Be that as it may, I think the Citizens' Committee has been most lucky in their employment of Blaisedell. He might have begun his action here in Warlock against the lesser fry. Instead he waited (and incurred some initial criticism for his inaction), and made his play against McQuown himself. I understand that his handling of Mc-Quown, Burne, et al. in the Glass Slipper was masterful. He could have shed blood, but correctly chose not to do so. It is said that Curley Burne actually saluted Blaisedell in tribute to his gentlemanliness and forbearance, as he departed.

We have not seen McQuown since, nor any of his men. There has been no bloodshed since Blaisedell's arrival. Blaisedell has had to buffalo a few recalcitrants, and has escorted some Cowboys and drunken miners to the jail, but violent death has removed itself from our midst temporarily.

Blaisedell is an imposing figure of a man, with a leonine fair head, an erect and powerful carriage, and eyes of an astonishing concentration. He seems guileless and straightforward, very dignified, yet I have seen him laughing and joking like a boy with his friend Morgan in the Glass Slipper. It is rumored that Blaisedell has an interest in that

---

* The Sister Fan and Pig's Eye were already at this time having difficulty disposing of the water encountered at the lower levels.

gambling hall. He spends much time there in company with Morgan, and on several occasions has engaged himself in dealing faro there. From what we have seen of Blaisedell thus far, he seems to have no excesses; he is not given to whoring, drunkenness, or profanity. I think he must needs be a blessedly simple man, in his position, for does not the capacity to deal in violence without excesses, to deal actually in men's lives as he must do, denote an almost appalling simplicity?

Or is he, in the end, only a merchant like myself, with his goods for sale as I have mine, knowing, as I know, that the better the goods the better price they will command, and the price variable as well with the Need? I see my mind must seek to bring this man to my terms, or perhaps it is to my level.

November 27, 1880

Pranksters have poured cement into the new piano at the French Palace. The piano, which Taliaferro had brought here at what I am sure must have been enormous expense, is ruined, the culprits unknown. It was a mean and thoughtless trick, in that coarse vein of frontier humor of which I have seen far too much. I have offered my sympathy to Taliaferro, who merely glowered. I suppose he suspects that since I mentioned it, I may be the guilty one.

There has also been another rash of rumors about the presence of Apaches in the Dinosaurs, that Espirato has returned from Mexico and is gathering his band again, preparatory to going on the warpath. This is not given much credence, since it has been several years since Espirato was last heard from. He is widely believed dead, and the bulk of his warriors secretly returned to the reservation at Granite.

In consequence of these rumors, however, we have had the pleasure of again seeing General Peach, who is always sensitive to news of his old adversary. He came through Warlock last Sunday with one troop of horse, another having swept up the far side of the valley. It was a shock to see him, for he has grown incredibly gross, and, viewing him, it is easy to believe that his mind is eaten away with paresis. Still, there is something inherently heroic about him; it is like watching an equestrian statue of the Cid or George Washington wrapped in a cloak of heroic deeds, to the accompaniment of stirring martial music. The man has had the capacity throughout his career for giving miserable and inexcusable fiasco the semblance of a thrilling victory. He rode down Main Street at the head of his troop as in a Fourth of July Parade, wearing his huge hat, his white beard blowing back, his strange, pale eyes fixed straight ahead while he saluted right and left with the leather-covered shaft which is supposed to be that of an arrow that almost ended his days at the battle of Bloody Fork. We watched him fresh from a fool's errand to the border, and reminded ourselves that he has a harem of Apache and Mexican women out of which he has produced (supposedly) a get of half-breed bastards numerous enough to increase by a good percentage the population of this territory; that, in his senility, he wets his trousers like a child, and must have his hand guided by Colonel Whiteside when he writes his name; and still we could not forbear to applaud his passage—badly as he has treated us here.

There have been rumors that silver will drop again on the market, and there is unrest among the miners, who fear a cut in their wages. Especially those of the Medusa. Some weeks ago, in the collapse of a stope at that unlucky mine, two miners were killed outright, and a third horribly crushed—the doctor says the man, Cassady by name, did not die the same night only because he seemed to feel it would put Miss Jessie out, and so clung to his life until early this week, when he finally gave up the ghost. The Medusa miners are incensed about these deaths, and I understand that talk of the Miners' Union has begun again. They claim that insufficient lagging-timbers are furnished to support their burrowings. This MacDonald denies heatedly, and calls them overpaid and pampered as it is. The price of lumber is certainly fantastic. There are trees of any size only in the northernmost Bucksaws, Bowen's Sawmill is small, the water power to run it often insufficient, and breakdowns frequent.

There is this time more sympathy than usual with the miners, of whom a large number have been killed and maimed in mine accidents this year. The doctor is quite beside himself about it, a man rarely given to shows of anger. Still, as I said to him, the fellows do make wages of $4.50 a day, and are free to take themselves elsewhere and to other work, if they choose.

December 14, 1880

A death of note has been that of the little professor, whose piano playing at the Glass Slipper all of Warlock had enjoyed. Poor fellow, apparently, while in his cups, he fell insensible into the street at night, where his skull was crushed by a hoof or wagon wheel; not found until morning. God rest his soul, his passing so tragically has saddened us all.

December 28, 1880

Christmas has come and gone and a New Year is almost upon us. The cold spell has broken, and in this the peaceful season there is peace, but perhaps no more than the usual amount of good will. I have a crèche in my store window, Mary and Joseph bending over the Infant in the manger, attended by kings and shepherds. It is surprising how men stop and stare. I think they are not enraptured at the old story; the star of Bethlehem interests them not, nor do the shepherds and the kings. The baby fascinates them, a hideous little piece, out of scale to the rest of the figures, pink plaster with daubs of deeper pink upon the cheeks. It is not that there are no babies here, for the miners beget them upon their Mexican "wives" in some quantity. But they are not proper babies, being illegitimate; and not pink, being half-breed tan to begin with, which soon becomes a deeper hue due to the lack of frequent applications of soap and water. Most important, I think, is that the Babe is surrounded by His family. For there are no proper families here, and pitifully few proper women. There are Cyprians in quantity (more attentive to my crèche even than the men), there are a few ranch women whom we see from time to time, shapeless and bonneted against the sun and rude eyes. There are, in town, besides Miss Jessie, Mrs. Maple and Mrs. Sturges, the one, as is said, twice the man Dick Maples is and as tough as bootsole leather, the other ancient, huge, and a reformed harlot from the look of her.

The reigning queen is Myra Burbage, to court whom, of a Sunday, a great procession of Warlock's most affluent young bachelors rides down valley to irritate Matt Burbage. Men are made slaves to women by a cunning nature, who designed lust as the means to the continuation of our kind; we are made slaves as well by a trap of our own devising, whereby we desire to stand, as it were, for one of those stiff and smug photographer's portraits, as man and wife amid our offspring in that proud and self-contained protective society, a family.

A Christmas party at the General Peach, and all were invited to sip a cup of Christmas cheer—paying two dollars to the miners' fund for the privilege. Myra Burbage distributing her favors among her admirers, and, wonder of wonders, Miss Jessie apparently much interested and amused in conversation with the Marshal! She looked very pretty with her face flushed by the warmth of her labors—or was it something else that had caused her color to rise? There will be much surmise about this, I have no doubt. The Marshal and Miss Jessie have been observed, before this, buggy-riding together, and now, I am sure, more notice will be taken of their activities.

January 2, 1881

I suppose we should have realized that if the infection were only thrust down here, it would crop up elsewhere. There have been a great number of rustling raids in the lower valley, and stage hold-ups on the San Pablo and Welltown roads—so many, in fact, that Buck Slavin has instructed his stage drivers not to resist road agents, and is refusing to transport any shipments of value, as well as warning his passengers to carry none. The Welltown stage was robbed day before yesterday. This is laid at McQuown's door by some, while others claim that worthy has merely relaxed his control over the San Pablo hardcases, who are consequently running wild.

Road agents are none of Blaisedell's affair, unless a coach were to be assaulted within the limits of Warlock. Schroeder, however, is showing signs of life. There is another deputy with him now: I understand that one of his conditions to Sheriff Keller for taking up the post was that he be allowed an assistant. The other is John Gannon, elder brother to Billy Gannon and at one time a rider for McQuown himself. He seems an odd choice for an assistant on the part of Schroeder (an honest man, although heretofore exceedingly timid), but there has been a sign attached to the wall of the jail for some time now, advertising the need of another deputy, and no doubt Gannon has been the only one to apply. There has been some talk about this, and some suspect darkly that Gannon has come at McQuown's bidding to corrupt the Warlock branch of the law in some kind of plot against Blaisedell.

Gannon and Schroeder did collaborate to capture a road agent when an attempt was made on the Bright's City stage a week or ten days ago. The stage, although under fire, ran for it and gained the town quickly, where Schroeder immediately organized a posse including Gannon and a number of Schroeder's friends, who happened to be passing the time of day at the jail. The posse lost one of the bandits, but captured the other, one Nat Earnshaw. Schroeder then took Earnshaw to Bright's City for trial, where he now resides, awaiting court session. Great praise has been heaped upon Schroeder for his quick action, and his courage—for Earnshaw, although not actually a member of McQuown's band, is a San Pabloite, a rustler, and a badman of some repute.

Possibly Schroeder's triumph has been made the more of because Blaisedell has had a failure of sorts. Wax, one of Taliaferro's dealers, was shot in the alley behind the Lucky Dollar, and his murderer has not been apprehended. It could have been almost anyone, since the victim was a gunman himself, quarrelsome and overbearing. Wax is not widely mourned. There has been some hint, however, that Morgan was the murderer, in some unnoticed and growing feud between the Lucky Dollar and the Glass Slipper, whose rear doors both open upon the same fatal alley. Morgan has made a great number of enemies here. He can be most unpleasant, brusque and rude, and has a way of looking at a person that expresses all too explicitly an almost unbounded contempt for his fellow man.

January 10, 1881

There has been a Social Event, a Wedding, and we are stuffed with punch and wedding cake, and, perhaps, with envy. Ralph Egan * has married Myra Burbage, and the happy couple is by now entrained from Welltown to a honeymoon in San Francisco at Matt's expense, the bride's fondest wish having been to see the ocean before she settled down in Warlock.

I wonder how many of us have realized the change inherent in this event, the first such a one that we have had. Civilization is stalking Warlock.

The bride was very attractive indeed, particularly, I am sure, to the unsuccessful swains, Jos. Kennon, Pike Skinner, and Ben Hutchinson. There have been a horde of others along the way, including Chet Haggin, but these were the ones who galloped cheek by jowl down to the finish line, with Ralph, in the opinion of the pretty judge, the winner.

Curley Burne was on hand, as pleasant, humorous, and eminently likable as always; with him the Haggin twins, the bantering Wash and the silent Chet—alike as two peas, they are commonly identified by the side upon which they wear their six-shooters, Wash being left-handed, his brother right. All three were very much upon their good behavior, and Curley in particular went out of his way to ingratiate himself to one and all. It is difficult to think badly of the fellow. As

* Proprietor of the Feed and Grain Barn.

Blaikie puts it, who is something of a philosopher, McQuown is like a coin, with Curley Burne imprinted upon one side, and the evil physiognomy of Jack Cade upon the other. A man's attitude toward McQuown depends upon which side of the coin he has seen.

Matt Burbage fixed me with his glittering eye; I was the wedding guest in fact. He tells me not only of the dangers he has passed, but of those that beset him on every hand. He has lost much stock, he says, but is not inclined to hold McQuown responsible. He says he has never known McQuown to steal from his neighbors, and that he has heard that McQuown recently brought back from Mexico nearly a thousand head, which he will fatten and drive up to sell to the reservation at Granite. He has seen McQuown very little of late. He thinks —this in a most discreet whisper—that Benner, Calhoun, and possibly Friendly have been responsible for a good part of the road-agentry.

Matt is worried about squatters coming in, a good proportion of downright outlaws among them. San Pablo, he says, has grown, and has become even more tough-town, calky, and dangerous than ever. He intends to do all his purchasing in Warlock now, a much longer trip for him, but good news for me. I think Matt longs for the peaceful past (he was one of the first to settle along the San Pablo River) when he had only Apaches to worry about. He has heard that Bright's City is about to unleash hordes of tax collectors upon us; on the other hand he bewails the lack of law officers to pursue his lost stock. Some of us love Freedom not so much as Safety, but are given pause by Safety's Cost.

Miss Jessie attended as bridesmaid, and afterward played on the melodeon, which tended to wheeze and rattle under her ministrations but still produced most pleasant harmonies. She has a high, sweet soprano, and it was wonderful to hear her render such favorites as: "She Wore A Wreath of Roses"; "Days of Absence"; and "Long, Long Ago." All joined in with a will on "Tenting Tonight" and "A Life on the Ocean Wave," etc.

It is rare to see her without Blaisedell these days. (I should imagine that Matt did not wish to offend his neighbor McQuown by inviting the Marshal.) The occasion of Myra Burbage's wedding was a romantic one to a populace of bachelors, for Ralph is a well-liked young fellow, and his spouse has long been the belle of the valley. Still, they are as nothing compared to Miss Jessie and the Marshal, who are as romantic a match as Tristram and Isolde.

The Angel of Warlock is a fascinating woman, not beautiful certainly, although she has a wealth of ringleted brown hair and fine eyes. She arrived in Warlock during the first boom, perhaps six months after I did. She was preceded by a lawyer, who purchased the old Quimby boardinghouse from the crippled prospector who was the proprietor of that riotous and unsavory place. The lawyer remained to have it refurbished into a decent boardinghouse, repainted, and rechristened in honor of the governor, upon which Miss Jessie herself arrived, in a clamor of speculation. She quickly won our hearts, as much by her gentle demeanor and apparent defenselessness, as by her actions during the typhoid epidemic of that summer, when she converted a part of her establishment to a hospital, which she has maintained as such ever since on what must be some regular and not inconsiderable income which she receives from elsewhere, for surely the money paid by her boarders cannot support the General Peach.

The doctor, who knows her best, says she comes from St. Louis, and that her father was a wealthy sickly man, whom she nursed until he died, which was shortly before she came to Warlock. This is all the information the doctor will give, and is perhaps all he possesses. Beyond this I have only my own speculations.

I would deduce, for instance, that she began nursing her father on an intensive basis, so that she was completely occupied with him, before she reached her twentieth year. Her girlish mannerisms and dress, which at first I thought affected, now seem to me to indicate that before this age she was removed from the normal social contacts of feminine society, to become so preoccupied with her duties to her parent that many of her habits of dress, speech, etc., remain those of a young girl.

Beneath her gentleness is a great strength of character. We have had occasion to see this in Citizens' Committee meeting, where she often locks horns with MacDonald, a bullheaded and rude man, over matters pertaining to the miners. Indeed, upon occasion she can don an almost repellent schoolmarmish attitude. To continue with my deductions about her, however: she has a strong will, she is a romantic, she is also quite plain. I think she came to Warlock in order to be Someone. Possibly she came, too, because this is the Frontier, which term I understand is a romantic one to those not there residing. I imagine she had been a nonentity in her own locality and society. If this is true, she has achieved entirely her object in coming here. She is certainly unique, a Personality, and her stature here is immense.

Her reputation is spotless, which is, in itself, astonishing in this place where foul rumor is a favorite pastime, and gossip vicious and pervasive. Indeed, I think one of the quickest ways to commit suicide in Warlock would be to cast aspersion against her good name. She lives with one fat Mexican maid in a house full of the roughest kind of ignorant, crude, dishonorable fellows, with only the doctor in one of her rooms as, I suppose, a sort of duenna. She walks streets which rock with catcalls when such an old harridan as Mrs. Sturges passes by, and where women from the Row are all but physically assaulted if they dare to promenade, and is greeted always in the most polite and gentlemanly manner. She can nurse miners mouthing dreadful obscenities in their pain, and yet find men completely tongue-tied before her for fear they will utter some slight impropriety of speech that might offend her ears. She is a miracle without being in the least miraculous.

She is also, now that I find myself thinking of her, a lonely and slightly pitiful figure, and I am pleased by Blaisedell's attentions to her, and by her reception of them.

The Marshal has, very recently, taken up residence at the General Peach, takes tea with Miss Jessie in the afternoon, and, the doctor says, submits amiably to having poetry read him. All in all, Blaisedell's courtship of her is fitting, and I think there will be few to resent it. This romance is an ennobling thing for this foul-minded, whore-ridden town, a showing-forth to limited minds that there can be more to the conjunction of men and women than a befouled and sweating purchased trick in bed.

January 15, 1881

Blaisedell has posted a man from town. We knew it must come eventually, and I have dreaded it. For if he posts a man out, and that man comes in, he comes under threat of death. If it is carried out are not we of the Citizens' Committee, who have hired Blaisedell and directed the posting, executioners? So I have waited in dread for this to happen, and waited in more dread still to see if the edict would be honored. Earnshaw, however, has reportedly left the territory.

Earnshaw had been acquitted by a jury of supposedly good men and true in Bright's City. I suppose there is no reason to damn the jurors, who were bound to abide by the evidence; and ten witnesses had ridden in from San Pablo to swear that Nat Earnshaw was seen by all of them in San Pablo on the day that the prosecution claimed he had tried to rob the Bright's City stage, and that he had been mistakenly apprehended by the posse while innocently riding into Warlock. It was not stated why he sought to flee the posse with his accomplice, who was not named.

Unfortunately, no one on the stage could identify Earnshaw as one of the bandits, for both had been masked, and the only witnesses for the prosecution were Schroeder and the possemen, whose evidence that they had followed the tracks of Earnshaw's horse from the scene of the assault upon the stage to the point of capture, was not given as much credence as that of the San Pablo hardcases, whose threatening demeanor was no doubt more effective than their verbal testimony.

The Citizens' Committee met upon the subject of Earnshaw, and discussed posting him with a considerable lack of resolution. Blaisedell spoke to the effect that if we ever intended to post anyone, Earnshaw was a good place to begin. Upon which we entrusted our consciences to the Marshal's capable hands. There was no dissent, although Miss Jessie was not present, nor Judge Holloway, who, I am sure, would have loudly damned the illegality of our action. Luckily the judge had drunk himself into insensibility that day, and was not heard from for several days thereafter.

We would have heard from him had Blaisedell been forced to ventilate Earnshaw, I am sure. He can be as nettlesome as various of the wild-eyed Jewish prophets must have been to their rulers. But thank God the fatal day when we must look at each other and try to shrug off some stubborn fellow's death as being only his own doing, is put off a little longer.

9. Gannon Calls the Turn

IT HAD turned chilly with the sun gone down and some quality in the atmosphere did not hold the dust, so that the air was clear and sweet now as Gannon walked back from supper at the Boston Café. The stars were already showing in the soft, violet darkness that shaded off to a pale yellow above the peaks of the Dinosaurs, where the sun had disappeared. Men lounged in groups along the boardwalk in the central block, leaning against the saloon fronts or seated on the tie rail, where a number of horses were tied. They talked in quiet voices and here and there among them was the orange glow of a cheroot or a match flame—wool-hatted miners, and cowboys in flannel shirts and shell belts, striped pants or jeans, and star boots, with the shadows cast by their sombreros making of their faces only pale ovals. They fell silent as Gannon passed. No one spoke to him, or spoke at all; there was only the stamp and snort of a horse at the rail, the hollow clumping of his bootheels.

He walked through the thin stripes of light thrown out by the louvre doors of the Glass Slipper. Other groups of men fell silent before him. Unwillingly he felt his steps hasten a little, his wrist brushed against the butt of his Colt, and his stomach twisted with its own cold colic. He glanced down to see a little light glitter on the star pinned to his vest.

It was quiet tonight, he told himself calmly, quiet for a Saturday night; the concentrated jumble of sound from the Lucky Dollar faded behind him.

When he descended into Southend Street dust prickled in his nostrils. To his right were the brightly lit houses of the Row; to his left, across Main Street, the second-story window above Goodpasture's darkened store was a dim yellow rectangle. Light from the jail spread out across the planks of the boardwalk, beneath the hanging sign.

Carl sat alone at the table, one hand on the shotgun. "Seen the marshal?" he asked.

"I expect he's in at the Glass Slipper."

"Pony and Calhoun and Friendly's in town," Carl said. He leaned back in his chair, stiffly. "See them?"

"No."

"And your brother," Carl said.

Gannon went over and sat down in the chair beside the cell door. The key was in the lock and he withdrew it, and hung the ring on the peg above his head.

"They are in the Lucky Dollar, I heard," Carl said. He chewed on the end of his mustache; he stretched. "Well," he said, in a shaky voice. "He handled the whole bunch at once, I don't know why he can't four of them."

"I expect he can," Gannon said. At least Cade was not in, he thought, and despised himself.

"I don't know," Carl said, rubbing a hand over his face. "Seems like I face up to it every night as soon as I close my eyes. But damn if I can—" He shook his head, and said, "When you see a real man it surely shames you for what you are, don't it?"

"Meaning Blaisedell?"

"Meaning Blaisedell. You know, I had got to thinking that if I didn't go up against McQuown sometime I would know I was dirt. But maybe that's wrong. Maybe *he* is the one—I don't know, maybe I mean big enough or clean enough or something—to do it. My God *damn* how I have chewed myself to ribbons over that bunch. But maybe McQuown is Blaisedell's by rights."

Gannon said nothing. It seemed to him that hate was a disease, and that he did not know a man who didn't have it, turned inward or outward. He had felt the hate when he had walked along Main Street tonight, hate for him because he was suspected of being friendly with McQuown; he wondered if McQuown, in San Pablo, could not feel the hate all the more. Maybe McQuown had gotten used to it long ago. Carl hated both McQuown and his own self, and that was the worst kind, the pitiful kind.

"Dirt," Carl said. "Me"—he laughed breathlessly—"that thought I was the finest thing to walk the earth when I put this star on here. Not because of Bill Canning exactly, either," he said. "But because I was ashamed of every damned man in Warlock. And hating that red-bearded son of a bitch so much. And Curley."

Gannon looked down to examine the little scar in the fold of flesh stretched between his thumb and forefinger. It had healed quickly. "Why, Carl, I believe you have the Saturday night jim-jams!"

"Something awful," Carl said, laughing and stretching again. "Well, I have never seen one yet that didn't pass on by come Sunday morning. And a damned comfort when they do."

After a long time Carl spoke again. "Had a delegation from the Citizens' Committee come to call this afternoon. Buck and Will Hart."

"What did they want?"

"Wanted some action about all this road-agenting. I told them there'd been some starch took out of us running any more posses, since Keller hadn't got pay sent down yet for those boys that run the last one for me. It turned out they had a proposition, which was the Citizens' Committee guaranteeing posse pay."

"That will make things easier," Gannon said. "It is good to know we can jump if we get another clear shot."

"It is," Carl said. He leaned back in his chair again. "I told them it was fine and public-spirited and all, but Buck is hard to get along with sometimes. We got along better when I rode shotgun for him; he was always afraid I was going to quit. We had some words."

Gannon saw that Carl had flushed; Carl avoided his eyes, and he thought that Carl and Buck Slavin might have had words over him.

"Well, I told him if he didn't like the way I did my job he could hang this star on himself and welcome," Carl went on. "I told him and Will to look at those names over there," he said, nodding toward the scratchings in the whitewash. He glanced toward Gannon now, and his deep-set eyes looked very hot. "Like I have to every time I turn around in here. See if they could count a man on there didn't turn in his star and run, or get shot out from behind it. And I told them they wouldn't see me run. I might not maybe go out on the prod for Curley Burne or any of them, but I won't ever run. Made a damned fool of myself," he said, flushing more darkly.

"Curley?" Gannon said carefully.

"Well, there is a lot that thinks high of Curley. Will Hart is one. Said he didn't think Curley ever robbed a coach in his life. We had some words on that, too." Carl scrubbed his hands up over his face. "I don't know—I am pretty down on Curley, Johnny," he said, in a washed-out voice. "I guess it is a laughing backshooter makes me madder than any other kind. I don't know. Or maybe it is McQuown is Blaisedell's size, but maybe Curley is mine."

Speaking very carefully again, Gannon said, "Like you said, there are a lot that don't think bad of Curley."

Carl nodded jerkily. "Part of it, too. For he is what the rest is and can fool folks to think he is not. And so he is worse." He glanced at Gannon again with his hot eyes, and Gannon knew enough had been said.

He nodded noncommittally.

Carl sighed and said, careful-voiced now in his turn, "Well, it was sure a surprise to me when it was you come in here with me, Johnny. I guess you know there is some that won't take to you kindly, right off."

"Surely," he said, and he felt the questions Carl wanted to ask, but hadn't yet.

"Well, you come in and that's the main thing," Carl said. "But I guess you don't really hate San Pablo the way I do, do you?"

"I guess not, Carl."

"Don't mean anything by mentioning it," Carl said apologetically. "But I remember there was some talk at the time—I guess it was Burbage. How what happened to that bunch of greasers down in Rattlesnake Canyon that time wasn't Apaches' doing."

Gannon didn't reply as footsteps came along the planks outside.

Carl stiffened in his chair, slapped his hands on the shotgun, started to rise. Pony Benner came in, with the marshal a step behind him.

"This one is getting a little bit quarrelsome," Blaisedell said, putting Pony's Colt down on the table before Carl. "Maybe he'd better cool off overnight, Deputy."

Carl got to his feet. The Colt rattled as he slid it into the table drawer and closed the drawer with a slap. Pony looked past Carl to meet Gannon's eyes. He spat on the floor.

Blaisedell said, "If the judge comes in tell him this one was picking away at Chick Hasty in the Lucky Dollar. It looked like trouble so I took him out of circulation."

"Surely, Marshal," Carl said. Blaisedell nodded to Gannon, turned, and went out, tall in the doorway before he disappeared.

"Well, Mister run-chicken, pee-on-your-own, Deputy Bud Gannon," Pony said, his small, mean face contorted with fury and contempt. "Why didn't you get down and kiss his boots for him?" he cried, swinging toward Carl. "Gimme that damned hogleg back, Carl!"

Carl straightened his shoulders, hitched at his shell belt, and, with a swift motion, picked up the shotgun and slammed the muzzle against Pony's belly. Pony yelped and jumped back. Carl said, "G-get in there before I blow you in!"

Pony retreated into the cell before the shotgun, and Carl slammed the door. His face, when he turned to take the key Gannon handed him, was blotched with color.

In the cell Pony was cursing.

"Hear anything?" Carl said, winking at Gannon. "I believe it is those rats moaning in there again. One of these days we are going to have to clean them out, I expect."

"All right!" Pony cried. "All right, Carl, you have chose the way you are going to choke yourself. All right, Bud Gannon, God damn you to hell—we'll see, God damn you all!"

"Damned if that one rat don't squeak just like old Pony Benner," Carl said.

"You will chew dust, you stringy, washed-up old bastard!" Pony yelled. His face disappeared. Immediately it returned. "And that gold-handled, muckering, God-damned long-haired son too!" Pony shouted. "He has threw his weight around for the last time, the last God-damned rotten time. We give him his chance and now he'll eat dust, too. You hear I said it, you kiss-boot sons of bitches!"

He retreated into the cell, and the cot creaked.

"Quieted down," Carl commented. "Sounds like somebody set a cat after those rats." There was a triumphant flush to his face, but Gannon saw the flicker of fear in it, and was embarrassed to see it there. He went to lean in the doorway and stare out into the street.

"No reason to bother the judge, I guess," Carl said, behind him. "Judge was taking on freight heavy this afternoon, and he would need a lot of sobering up by now. We'll just leave this one wait the night, and sweep him out with the cockroaches in the morning."

Gannon watched Billy coming down the boardwalk. "Billy," he said.

"Bud," Billy said, casually. Gannon stepped back inside and Billy followed him in. Pony's face reappeared between the bars.

"Some day you will get just too feisty," Billy said to Pony. He would not look at Gannon. He said to Carl, "What's the fine, Schroeder? I guess I can make it up."

"Judge hasn't been in," Carl said. "I'm holding him for disturbing the peace till he comes, or morning, one."

"He wasn't disturbing it that much," Billy said. "Let him out and we'll settle when the judge shows."

"I guess not, son."

"Kiss-boot bastards!" Pony cried, and kicked the door. Gannon stood watching his brother's face. It was sullen and hard, with only the shadowy mustache to show the youth in it.

"Let him out," Billy said to Carl. He dropped his hands to his shell belt, as though to hitch at it; in an instant his Colt was in his hand, and trained on Carl behind the table.

Gannon heard Carl's sudden ragged breathing, and Pony's laugh, but he stared still at Billy's face. Those cut-steel eyes might have been Jack Cade's, and they were eyes that had looked at Deputy Jim Brown with the same expression in the San Pablo saloon, just before Billy had shot him dead for making too much fun of his youth and his claim to being the best marksman in San Pablo.

But it was a copy of Abe McQuown's shy grin that twisted the corners of Billy's mouth, and a copy of Curley Burne's bantering tone in which he said, "*Por favor,* Carl. *Por favor.*"

"Go to hell," Carl whispered.

"Listen to the rats squeaking now!" Pony crowed. "Squeaking awful quiet, seems like."

Billy said, "Get the keys, Bud."

Gannon stepped between Billy and Carl, as though he were going for the key. He stopped there, blocking Billy's Colt. Billy started to jump sideways and Pony yelled, "*Watch the shotgun!*"

Gannon stepped out of the way. Pony was cursing again.

"Buckshot," Carl said.

"Birdshot," Billy said, and again there was a reflection of Curley Burne in his tone. He grinned slightly. "I know what you carry in that piece."

"Buckshot," Carl said. "On Saturday nights." His voice was stronger. "Son," he said. "Buckshot beats a Colt's just like a full house does a pair."

Billy slipped his Colt back into its scabbard. He gave Gannon a blank look, not so much of anger as appraisal.

"You threw me, Bud," he said. "And took kind of a chance too."

"You wasn't going to go to shooting. Whoever it was."

"Maybe I wasn't, but it wasn't a bluff you had to call. I had you and Carl covered fair enough."

"Get out of here," Carl said. "Before I decide to chuck you in there with Mister Squeaky."

Billy said, "The marshal doesn't run this town."

"Looks like he does tonight," Carl said.

"Nah, he doesn't. Just some cowardy-cats in it." Billy inclined his head almost imperceptibly at Gannon, and went out.

Pony yelled, "You, Mister throw-your-brother! I guess maybe next time he won't be so quick to take big Jack off you!"

Carl slammed the barrel of the shotgun against the wooden bars, just as Pony leaped back away from the door.

Gannon cleared his throat. "Well, I guess I will take a walk around town, Carl."

"Feel easy," Carl said, grinning at him hugely. "It is a quiet night after all."

Gannon went out along the boardwalk. Billy was a lean shadow slanted against the wall just around the corner on Southend Street. "We had better talk some, Bud," Billy said.

He stepped down off the boardwalk into the dust. Up the street behind Billy were the lighted windows of the French Palace, and there were men passing on the far side of the street, laughing and talking. He heard Pony's name, and Blaisedell's.

Billy had turned to face the adobe wall beside him; he kicked a boot against it. "What's gone and got into you, Bud? Went off to Rincon to be a telegrapher and then come back, only not going back to Pablo, you said. Warlock is no kind of place to come back to. And deputying. What's got into you, Bud?"

Gannon shrugged.

Billy kicked the wall again. "Well, maybe I know why you lit out. But what the hell, Bud! What would you have done else, let them shoot us down and run that stock back?"

"I guess if you steal stock you have got to shoot to keep it sometimes. But not the way it was done, Billy."

"You've stole before that."

"I never saw it run all the way through like that before, though."

"So you come back and went to deputying to stop it, huh?" Billy sneered. "Well, you have changed, Bud. Got religion or something."

"I guess you have changed, too, Billy, since you made your score. People change."

"Ah, Christ, Bud!" Billy said, and now for the first time in the darkness it sounded like his brother again, and not some awkward and snarling boy-man out of San Pablo. "Well, I wanted to say I didn't blame you for what you did just now, which was slick, and— Hell, I knew it was what you had to do in there! But this is the bad thing, this God-damned marshal that thinks he is Lord God of Creation here. Where does he think he gets off, posting Nat out like that and running Pony into jail?"

"I don't know what Pony was doing, Billy," he said. "I didn't see what happened. But I know Pony—so do you."

"Christ, you have sure gone over, haven't you?" Billy said. He leaned back against the wall. "Like Blaisedell pretty good now, do you? Think he is pretty fine?"

"I don't know him, except to say hello to."

"Well, sometime when you get real good sucked up to him, ask him something for me! Ask him who the hell he thinks he is. Lording it over everybody. Running everybody around and telling them when they can come and go and all. This is a free country, isn't it? God damn it!"

"Billy," he said. "It's been free the way you mean, maybe, but it is going to have to be free the other way. So people are free to live peaceable, and free of being hurrahed and their property busted up, and their stock run off, and stages robbed. And killed for no more—"

"Who's the killer?" Billy broke in. "It is him! He got those gold-handled guns for the grand turkey-shoot prize for killing, didn't he?"

"I guess he is what we have to have here, then. For people like I am afraid you have got to be."

He had meant to say the people Billy has got to be like, but he didn't try to correct himself, and Billy whispered, "Jesus!" A group of horsemen turned into Southend Street and rode up toward the Row. They were laughing, and without even listening to what they were saying he knew they were laughing about Pony Benner.

"I don't mean to take up preaching," he said. "But I guess if I have changed it's because I've seen there has got to be law. It seems like you were always quicker and smarter to see a thing than I was. Can't you see it, Billy?"

"I can see this much," Billy said, in a contemptuous voice. "Who your law is for. Petrix at the bank and Goodpasture's store, and Buck's God-damned stages and Kennon's livery stable and all."

"Not just them. It is decent people running things, not rustlers and road agents and hardcase killers."

"Blaisedell isn't a hardcase killer? I heard he killed ten men in Fort James. Ten!"

"You can hear anything you want to hear. But there is something I saw, and got a hammer pin through my hand to prove it. Jack would have shot him in the back if I hadn't stopped it."

"Oh, I know Jack is a son of a bitch," Billy said. "Everybody knows that."

"Do you think Abe didn't put him to it?"

"Abe didn't have anything to do with it! God damn it, Bud, there is not another man but my own brother I'd let say a thing like that about Abe! Damn, you are wrong! Damn, I don't know how you turned so fast. You have got so damned holier-than-anybody because of us rustling a few old mossy-horns they never get around to rounding up even, they have got so many down at Hacienda Puerto. And a few sons-of-bitching greasers killed." Billy's voice ceased abruptly.

"Did they get to be sons-of-bitching greasers when they came after their stock, Billy? And got shot down by a bunch dressed like Apaches—and worse than Apaches. Is that when they got to be sons of bitches?"

Billy didn't answer, and Gannon leaned against the wall too, and looked up at the cold stars, shivering in the wind that had come up. A newspaper rolled slow and ghostly across the street and flattened itself against the wall beyond Billy.

Billy said in a low voice, "Listen, Bud, you don't want to get Abe thinking you have gone over to Blaisedell's side against him."

"Why not?" he said quickly.

"Well, you couldn't blame Abe for being down on somebody that's trying to throw him!"

Billy would not see, he knew. There had never been any use arguing with Billy. He laughed a little and said, "I was thinking how Daddy told me once I was to watch out for you. But I guess it got so you had to watch out for me—with Jack anyhow. That wasn't the only time I thought he'd drink my blood, but for you."

He reached over and slapped Billy's shoulder, awkwardly, and Billy punched him in the ribs. "*That* son of a bitch. I hate that dirty, cold-hearted, mean son of a bitch. I'd drink his blood, but it would probably poison a toad." He went on in a rush. "Christ, Bud, Christ, how things get muckered up! Why, here we are— I mean, there is never going to be any real trouble between you and me, is there, Bud? It seems like we had trouble enough when I was a pup."

"I guess we didn't have enough," he said, and tried to laugh again. Billy's fist punched into his ribs again; then Billy stepped away from him, to stand flat and faceless against the lights up the street.

"Well, see you, damn it all, Bud."

"See you, Billy," he said wearily.

Billy backed up another step. He seemed about to speak again, but he did not, and turned and walked up Southend toward the Row.

Gannon did not watch him go, but moved slowly over toward the boardwalk that ran along before the saloons and gambling houses. It was time he took a turn around Warlock. Carl did not leave the jail much on Saturday nights.

10. Morgan Doubles His Bets

I

STRIPPED to the waist, Morgan was leaning over the basin with his face close to the mirror and the razor sliding smoothly over his cheek, when there was a knock on the alley door.

"Who is that?"

"It's Phin Jiggs, Morgan. Ed sent me down from Bright's."

He dropped the razor into the soapy water, went around the desk to the alley door, and slid the bolt back. Jiggs, who did odd jobs for Ed Hamilton who had been Morgan's partner for a time in Texas and now had a place in Bright's City, slipped inside, caked with dust from head to foot except for the part of his face his bandanna had covered.

His eyes were muddy around inflamed whites, and there were sweat-tracks on his forehead and cheeks. He swiped at his face with his neckerchief.

"Ed said you might be pleased to know there is a woman named Kate Dollar coming down here."

He stared at Jiggs. At least he was pleased to *know* she was coming.

"She put her name down as Mrs. Cletus at the Jim Bright Hotel there," Jiggs said. "But Ed said to tell you it was Kate Dollar, all right."

"Mrs. Cletus?" he said, and felt stupid as he watched Jiggs nod. He turned uncertainly and went back to the basin, where he fished the razor out of the water. Mrs. Cletus. "Did you see her?" he asked, and stared at his face in the mirror.

"I saw her. Tall woman. Black hair and eyes and a fair-sized nose. About as tall as you, I'd say."

He nodded and raised the razor to his cheek again. Mrs. Cletus. Pleased. "She is on the stage now," Jiggs said. The stage would come in a little after four; Jiggs had ridden through the Bucksaws, instead of going around them as the stage had to do.

"Anybody with her?" he asked casually.

"I guess it is this Cletus she was down as Missus of."

He contemplated the razor with which he might have removed an ear to hear that, while Jiggs continued. "He is a big feller. Heavy-set with a kind of chewed-up looking face. They was down as Mr. and Mrs. Pat Cletus at the hotel there, Ed said to tell you."

Morgan sighed, and his mind began to function again. It was no ghost; she had found kin of some kind, a brother maybe. God damn you, Kate, he thought, without anger. He should have known she would not let it alone. In the mirror he saw Jiggs staring up at the painting over the door.

"Handsome woman," Jiggs said. It was not clear whether he was talking about the nude in the painting, or Kate.

"How many on the stage?"

"There's four of them. Her and him and a drummer, and the little sawed-off from the bank down here."

Money in the box then, he thought. He finished shaving, rinsed the lather from his face, and toweled it dry. He slipped his money belt up where he could get to it and drew out a hundred dollars in green-backs, which he gave to Jiggs.

"Oh, my!" Jiggs said, in awe.

"Forget about the whole thing and tell Ed thanks. Going right back?"

"Well, I—"

"Surely, I guess you might as well. You know Basine's place, out on the north end of town? Tell him to give you a fresh horse. He'll be there still if you hurry."

Jiggs stuffed the money down into his jeans pocket. "Well, thanks, Morgan! Ed said you'd be pleased to hear it."

"Pleased," he said. When Jiggs had gone he put on his shirt, whistling softly to himself. He opened the door; the Glass Slipper was empty still, and a barkeep was dispiritedly sweeping Saturday night's clutter along in front of the bar.

"Go find Murch," he called, and went back to his desk and poured himself a larger portion of whisky than usual. He raised it before him, squinting up at the painting of the woman over the tilted flat plane of the liquor. "Here's to you, Kate," he whispered. "Did you find one after all that had the guts to come after him? You damned bitch," he said, and drained the glass. Then he remembered that Calhoun and Benner, Friendly and Billy Gannon had been in town last night, and he laughed out loud at this continuing evidence of his luck.

II

Two hours later he was five miles out of Warlock on the Bright's City road, riding slowly, not hurrying. He was hot and uncomfortable with jeans on beneath his trousers, and a canvas jacket was tied in an inconspicuous bundle behind the saddle. A few torn bits of cloud floated in the sky, and their shadows moved swiftly across the yellowish-red earth and the sparse, bristling patches of brush. His horse flung her head back and danced sideways as a tarantula scurried across the stage tracks, heavy-bodied and tan-furred in the dust.

Now he kept off the stage road on the hard-packed earth, and, fifty yards from the rim, dismounted, ground-tied his horse, and went the rest of the way on foot. He grinned as he watched the column of dust moving east along the valley bottom. He could see the riders, two of them, very small in the distance below him. Crouching on his heels beside a staghorn cactus he watched them threading their way through one of the mesquite thickets that grew in patches over the valley bottom, until they were out of sight. The dust they had been raising also ceased. They had stopped at Road Agent Rock, a stony ridge through which the stage road threaded its way before starting up the long grade from the valley floor.

Presently he saw another plume of dust; horse and rider appeared, gradually enlarging, coming up the slope toward him. It was Murch, whom he'd sent up the valley. He stood up and waved his hat. Murch's horse was blowing and heaving as he spurred up the last steep piece. Murch dismounted, sweating and dusty in shotgun chaps and a flannel shirt.

"It is Benner and Calhoun," he said, mouthing the words over a cheekful of tobacco. His left eye studied Morgan's face, his right roving toward the flanks of the Bucksaws. "Them and the other two went on down toward Pablo a couple of miles in the malapai. Then they split, and Billy and Luke went on down valley, and these two come around up here."

"Now what do you suppose they are up to?"

"Couldn't guess," Murch said.

"Well, if I were you I would get on back to town quick where everybody could see me. In case the Bright's City stage runs into trouble. You wouldn't want to get taken for a road agent."

"No," Murch said, and spat.

"Let me have the Winchester."

Murch drew it from the saddle boot and handed it to him, mounted, and started back along the stage road at a fast trot. He looked like a gallon jug in the saddle.

Morgan walked back to his horse, remounted, and, leaving the stage road, headed east to meet the lower slopes of the Bucksaws. He crossed the first ridge and swung downhill in the barren canyon behind it. To his right now was the upper end of the rock outcrop that slanted like the edge of a long, curved knife to the valley floor.

He tied his horse in a mesquite thicket, removed his suit, and in jeans and the canvas jacket, a bandanna tied around his neck and Winchester in hand, scrambled up the ridge. Just on the other side of it, hidden by the crest, he began to work his way down.

Once he stopped to rest, breathing deeply of the clear air, and looked about him. He could see the valley for many miles east from here, with the cloud shadows moving across it. He could make out the cut of the stage road through the low brush for a long distance too. He felt a growing excitement. He accepted it with reluctance at first, cynically, but more and more fully as he made his way on down the ridge. He chuckled to himself from time to time, and paused more often to breath great sucks of the sweet air and gaze out on the colors of the valley. His senses felt alive, as they had not for a long time; he felt unburdened, young, and larking, but still the dark cynicism in himself kept careful watch, nagging and sneering at him. Once, as he edged his way around a steep rock, he whispered, "Well, Clay, I have never crawled on my belly for any other man."

Finally he heard the sound of voices, and he crawled to the crest of the ridge, where, hidden between two rocks, he could look down to the west side. The stage road cut in close to the ridge below him, swung to the right through a narrow defile, and angled to the left again. He could see the two of them not fifty yards away.

They were sitting on a low ledge just beyond the defile, which was called Road Agent Rock—it was said that so many stages had been stopped there that Buck Slavin had had to send out a crew to fill the rut made by the dropping strongboxes. They were in the full sun and Pony had his hat off and was mopping his face with a blue bandanna. Their horses weren't in sight.

"Just like the bitching coach to run late today," one of them said. The words came to him clearly. He edged the Winchester up beside him, and rested his cheek against the warm stock.

From time to time Calhoun would move into the defile to gaze east along the stage road. Then Benner, a head shorter, would go. They muttered back and forth. Once they both went out together. They sat and quarreled in the sun. Then Calhoun went out to look for the stage.

"Here it comes!" he cried, and ran back. They both tied neckerchiefs over their faces and jammed their hats down to their ears. They arranged themselves on either side of the stage road just beyond the cleft in the rock, facing each other tense and motionless like firedogs of unequal size.

Morgan glanced back to see the dust the stage was raising; it would be ten minutes yet. He watched an ant edging its way along the perpendicular side of one of the rocks that concealed him. It was carrying something white many times its own size. He watched the ant struggling; often it almost fell, but it never let go of its burden.

He whispered to it, "When you get home you'll find it wasn't worth the trouble, you damned fool!"

At last he heard the stage, the squeal of wheels, the whip crack and shout from the driver. It occurred to him suddenly that Kate was there, not a hundred yards away. He heard a steel rim scrape on rock. The lead team came into his field of vision, then the coach itself, Foss holding the reins with a boot up on the brake, Hutchinson, the messenger, with one hand braced behind him for balance and the shotgun ready in the other, leaning forward to try to see around the bend.

"Pull up and reach!" Calhoun bellowed, and fired into the air. Pony leaped out before the leaders, who bucked and plunged sideways. Hutchinson half rose as Pony ran around toward him, a six-shooter in either hand; Calhoun laid the Winchester on Foss.

"Throw it down, God damn you!" Pony shrilled, and Hutchinson pitched the shotgun away from him.

"Box down!" Calhoun said.

Foss had his hands raised shoulder-high, his foot on the brake, his eyes squinted against the sun. Hutchinson dragged the strongbox out. Morgan heard him grunt as he lifted and dropped it at Calhoun's feet.

"Let's see what the passengers got," Calhoun said. He flung the door open, and jumped back with his rifle leveled. Pony dragged the box away from the coach.

Morgan eased his own Winchester forward a little and grimaced as the sun caught fire along the barrel. He framed the door of the coach in the cleft of the rear sight, and gently raised the front sight blade beneath it. The blade danced, suddenly, as he saw Kate's face sharply outlined in the window. A man in a black hat squeezed out the door and dropped lightly to the ground, raising his hands.

Morgan stared at the man's face down his sights. It was a Cletus clearly enough, a tougher, meaner, harder version of Bob Cletus; he felt a weakening run through him and tensed his body against it as though he were clenching a fist. He lowered the sights to the man's shirt front. Kate appeared, a white hand on the door frame, her head bent down so that her hat hid her face.

He stroked the trigger. The rifle jarred in his hands; the coach was obscured in smoke. Ragged and shrill through the crash of the Winchester came the scream, and through the smoke he saw Cletus pitch forward with his broad-brimmed hat rolling free like a cartwheel. A Colt fell from his outstretched hand. Kate jerked back inside the coach. One of the leaders bucked up, hoofs boxing the air, and there was a chorus of yells. Then suddenly the coach was moving, and Foss was thrown back hard upon the seat. Hutchinson ducked down and turned, and, a Colt appearing in his hand, fired at Pony—smoke drifting from the muzzle an instant before the sound of the report. Calhoun raised his rifle and fired, levered and fired again, and Hutchinson slumped. Now Foss was standing and his long whip cracked out alongside the leaders. The stage fled, the door slamming open and shut and Kate's face showing once again in the window as the coach ran out of Morgan's view, with a loose tarpaulin flapping over the boot.

Calhoun fired again, and then he and Benner stood gazing after the coach. Presently Pony went over to where Cletus lay, and, thrusting at his shoulder with a boot, turned him on his back. Neither of them glanced up to where Morgan lay hidden. They bickered over Cletus's body for a while, went through his pockets, and then Pony went out of sight at a run. He reappeared, leading the horses. In a flurry of activity they raised and lashed the strongbox to the saddle of one, mounted, and started down the valley at speed.

Morgan sighed. The sun felt very warm on his back; his face was wet. He rose, stretched, untied the bandanna and wiped his face with it, staring down at the body sprawled on the ground below him, boots twisted together, arms outstretched and the glisten of red on the white shirt front. He felt the excitement slipping away.

He leaned on one of the rocks that had concealed him, and watched the high, tan plume run down the valley. Now he could also see the coach rolling slowly up the long grade toward the rim—the driver still standing and his whip arm working mechanically. Then he looked down at the dead man again. He wondered where Kate had had to go to find him.

"Damn you, Kate," he said aloud. "Why can't you leave a thing alone? It is done." He said it as though he were pleading with her, but half-humorously; it caught in his throat. "It is done," he said again, as though saying it could make it so.

Finally he turned away from the man he had killed. He made his way without haste back along the ridge and down the canyon where he had tied his horse. He buried the Winchester and the canvas jacket, and, in his black broadcloth, rode back along the stage road to Warlock. Before he reached town he cut over to the north side, where he left the horse in Basine's little corral, and walked to the Glass Slipper.

As he entered through the alley he saw Lew Taliaferro's dark, mole-spotted face watching him from the alley door of the Lucky Dollar. He tipped his hat and grinned, and would have spoken, but Taliaferro's face disappeared and the door closed. He was still grinning when he went in through the back door of the Glass Slipper, and stripped off his dusty clothes and began to wash. But he should, he thought, have been more careful, especially since Taliaferro was down one faro dealer named Wax to him. Still, he knew, his luck was good. His luck would stand as long as he believed in it.

II. Main Street

THE Bright's City coach turned into Main Street with its body swinging far over on the thoroughbraces, the team running scared, and the coach sucking a whirlwind of dust behind it. It came fast down the street with the driver yelling, the popper of the whip snapping out alongside the lead team, and the shotgun messenger swaying on his seat with a hand clasped to his shoulder.

Schroeder, walking along before the Glass Slipper, stopped and stared. Then he spat his chew of tobacco into the street and vaulted the rail, coming down hard in the dust with his knees buckling. He cupped his hands to his mouth and shouted at Chick Hasty, who was standing in his dirty canvas apron before Goodpasture's store, "Chick! Get the posse together! Get Pike!"

Hasty went around the corner toward the Acme Corral at a run. "*The Doc!*" Foss, the driver, yelled, standing now as he set the brake. The coach skidded and slowed, and came to a stop before the Assay Office, the lathered, muddy horses crowding and shifting together. Foss leaped down, and, with Schroeder's assistance, helped down Hutchinson, whose sleeve was soaked with blood. They sat him on the rail; holding him, Foss said, "Threw down on us at Road Agent Rock. Shot a passenger, and the team took out, so we run for it."

A crowd began to collect, men running up from all directions. Old Man Parsons halted his team of mules at the corner of Southend Street and Carl yelled at him, "Old Man, you are deputized. We are going out instanter!"

"One of them was Pony Benner, I hope to spit!" Hutchinson said, leaning limply against a post. The doctor came up, panting, his valise slapping against his leg as he ran; he and Sam Brown helped Hutchinson into the Assay Office.

The door of the coach opened and the pale face of a drummer appeared, his sidewhiskers standing out like the fur of a scared cat. He descended, followed by Pusey, the bank clerk, and they both turned to hand a woman down. She looked like a sporting woman, in her fancy clothes, but she did not carry herself like one, and the men on the boardwalk greeted her politely. Her face was chalk white beneath a hat covered with black cherries. Her eyes were black, her nose long and straight, her mouth reddened with rouge. There was a crescent-shaped court-plaster beauty mark at the corner of her mouth.

"The little one was Pony, all right," Foss said to Schroeder.

"Two of them," little Pusey broke in. "They got the strongbox."

"More than two," Foss said. "Couple up on top the ridge. It was one of them killed that big feller."

"I only saw two," the drummer said.

"There were three," the woman said. She looked at Schroeder's star, and up into his face with her hard black eyes. Her face was stiff with shock. "There was one on top of the ridge."

"Shot what big feller?" Schroeder said to Foss.

"Passenger that was with this lady here," Foss said. "We had to leave him lay, for the team took out wild when he got shot. He was dead, miss," he said, apologetically. "You going after them, Carl?"

"Surely am," Schroeder said.

"Went down valley. We could see them raising dust coming up the grade to town."

John Gannon forced his way in through the crowd. There was a lull in the excited talk around them.

"Stage got run, Johnny," Schroeder said. "Hutch shot and a passenger killed and still out there at Road Agent Rock."

"Pony and Calhoun and Friendly and Billy Gannon," someone in the crowd said. "Headed out of here like they was going back to Pablo, and went up valley to agent the coach instead."

"By God if it wasn't!"

Gannon licked his lips. He looked from Foss to Schroeder with his deep-set eyes in his bone-thin face. "Are we going after them, Carl?"

"Well, I thought maybe I'd ask you to ride out after that passenger." Gannon flushed, and Schroeder went on quickly, his voice loud in the hush. "What was his name? Anybody know?"

Everyone looked at the woman, who said, "I think it was Cletus."

"Thought I heard you calling him Pat, ma'am," the drummer said politely. The woman did not reply.

"What'd they kill him for?" someone asked.

"He drawed, looked like," Foss said.

"Fool thing to do," Schroeder said.

The woman said, "He didn't draw till he'd been shot."

Tim French and Chick Hasty, mounted, came into Main Street. Then Peter Bacon appeared, leading an extra horse, and, a moment later, Pike Skinner, Buchanan, and Phlater. Each of them had a rifle in his saddle boot, and Pike Skinner had belts of rifle and shotgun cartridges slung over his saddlehorn, and a shotgun hanging from a saddle strap. Old Owen Parsons came after them in a hurry, on a rat-tailed bay, his hat brim blown back flat against the crown.

"Come on, Carl!" Skinner shouted.

"You go bring the dead one in, Johnny," Schroeder said. "And watch things here." He clapped Gannon on the shoulder. Buck Slavin came through the crowd crying, "Foss! God damn it, Foss!"

"Out of my way fellows," Schroeder said. The crowd parted before him as he hurried out into the street to mount the extra horse.

"Looks like one we're after's Billy," Tim French said.

"Maybe," Schroeder said. "Chick, you ride out with Johnny and track back down valley after them. So we'll have that squarer in court this time. Watch for them shedding the strongbox, too."

Hasty nodded, and Schroeder surveyed the others. He grinned suddenly. "Well, boys," he said. "We will ride to hit the river low down, and try to head them."

They all nodded. Schroeder set his spurs and his horse leaped forward. The posse fell in behind him and went out of Warlock at a fast trot. There were cheers from the crowd standing around the dusty coach in Main Street.

12. Gannon Meets Kate Dollar

IT WAS after dark when Gannon brought back the body of the big man whose name seemed to be Pat Cletus, and left it, covered with a tarpaulin, at the *carpintería*, where old Eladio would make a coffin for it in the morning.

He went home to Birch's roominghouse to wash, and stopped at the jail to sit at the table in the dark for a while; then he went up to the Western Star for dinner, carefully oblivious under the silent stares of the men he passed upon the way.

But his eyes felt hot and gritty as he listened to them whispering behind him. They were sure that Billy had been one of the road agents, and probably they were right.

In the lobby of the hotel Ben Gough, Pugh's clerk, nodded distantly to him from behind the counter. It was late and the dining room was deserted except for the woman who had come in on the Bright's City stage. She sat at a table near the window, and he moved uncertainly over toward her.

He took off his hat. "Mind if I sit here, ma'am?"

She looked up at him through long lashes that were very black against her white skin. She glanced around at the empty tables, then at the star pinned to his shirt. She said nothing, and he sat down opposite her. Obsidian eyes watched him over her cup as she drank coffee.

"Catch them?" she said finally, setting her cup down in its saucer with a small clatter.

"No, ma'am. At least the posse's not back yet."

"Do they catch them here?"

"I expect they might this time. They got off fast."

She nodded, uninterested. She was a handsome woman, except that her nose was too big. The black cherries on her hat shone overripe with red tints in them in the lamplight.

The waiter wandered over, switching a cloth at the flies and crumbs on the tables he passed.

"Supper," Gannon said. When the waiter had gone switching away again, he said, "Maybe you wouldn't mind answering a few questions?"

"All right."

"Well, I'll ask your name to start off with."

"It's Kate Dollar."

Her eyes regarded him hostilely, and he hesitated. He had hardly talked to a woman before he had gone to Rincon, and very few there except in the course of his duties. He didn't know whether to call her Mrs. Dollar or Miss. You said Mrs. to a sporting woman, if you wanted to be polite, but he was uncertain whether this one was or not. It was not that she was better dressed than a whore, for some of them wore finery to put your eye out, but her dress was expensive looking without being flashy and eye-catching, and there was a certain dignity about her. She was young, but her face was wary and there were bitter lines at the corners of her eyes.

"And yours?" she said.

"Gannon," he said, and added, "John Gannon."

"Oh," she said. "One of them was supposed to be your brother."

He felt his face burn painfully. He looked down quickly and nodded.

"What was it you wanted to ask, besides my name?"

"Why, there seems to be some mix-up, miss. About how many road agents there was. The driver—"

"I saw three of them," she said. "But there might've been four."

"There was one up on top of the ridge there, you mean? You are sure? I mean—" He stopped.

"I saw a rifle barrel up there clear enough," she said. "And gun-smoke." She raised a finger and pressed it to the beauty mark at the corner of her mouth. "When I heard the shot I didn't know who had fired, because I could see the other two road agents, and it wasn't either of them. Then I happened to look up at the top of the ridge and saw the smoke. And I saw the rifle barrel pull back out of sight."

"You didn't see the man?"

"No."

The waiter brought a plate of steak, fried potatoes, and beans. He pushed at the potatoes with his fork. His eyes were burning again. Kate Dollar patted at the corners of her mouth with her handkerchief.

"The driver said you got on with this Cletus at Bright's City."

"So did that little bank clerk, and the drummer."

"I heard the drummer say you called him Pat."

"Maybe I did."

"You wouldn't want to say, then?"

"Say what?"

"Whether you'd been coming out here with this Pat Cletus, or what for. Or who he was."

"What difference does it make?"

"I don't know," he said, hopelessly. He forked a mouthful of po-tatoes, chewed, and tried to swallow; they were at the same time greasy and dry as dust.

"What do you want me to say?" Kate Dollar asked, in a different voice. "That there were only two of them? Because then one might not have been your brother?"

"I don't know," he said. "The driver and the shotgun seem pretty sure it was Pony Benner and Calhoun. But the third one could've been Friendly. Or— I don't know," he said again. "I just thought you might've got mixed up—with everything happening so sudden and all. I guess you didn't."

"What were you trying to blackguard me into, asking about the man that was killed?"

"I don't know," he said dully. "Just—deputies're supposed to ask questions about a thing. I was just trying to find out what happened," he said. He put his fork down.

"Aren't you going to eat?"

"I guess not," he said, and pushed the plate away from him.

Kate Dollar said, "From what I've heard, it sounds like nobody gets convicted of anything at the Bright's City court. Why are you so worried? Because of being deputy?"

"It's not that. I guess they would probably get off in Bright's, all right. If they get caught."

Kate Dollar was frowning a little; she looked at him questioningly.

"Well," he said, "that's it, you see, miss. I expect they will get off all right. But then they'll get posted out of town."

There was a slow tightening around her mouth. Suddenly her face seemed filled with hate, but the expression was gone so quickly that he could not be sure what he had seen. She said, in a curiously flat voice, "I knew Clay Blaisedell in Fort James."

"Did you?" he said.

"So you are worried about him posting your brother out of town," she said. "He is just a boy, I heard somebody say." He saw that she looked very tired.

"He is eighteen. No, he's not a boy." He was embarrassed that he had let the subject of Billy come up. But it was big in him and there was, it seemed, no one else he could speak to like this. He said, "Have you ever seen a gambler in a game of cards and you can tell he knows just where every card is?"

She nodded, as though immediately she had caught his thought; and he went on. "Well, I guess I am like that right now. Cards have been dealt out and they are face down yet, but I know what they are."

Kate Dollar continued to regard him with her black eyes, her expression one of expectant interest. But now he was confused and jarred by the thought that she was estimating him, and was not interested in Billy at all. He thrust his chair back and got to his feet.

"Well, I didn't mean to bother you with all that, Miss Dollar. I just came to ask you some things, and I thank you."

"You are welcome, Deputy."

Halfway to the lobby he realized he had forgotten his hat, and he had to return for it, apologizing to her again. She did not speak this time, although she smiled a little; he noticed that her eyes looked pink and swollen in her tired face, and he thought, as he started back to the jail to begin the long night's wait, that the man Cletus must have been more to her than she wanted to admit.

13. Morgan Has Callers

I

MORGAN had been waiting for her to come all evening, but still he started at the knock on the alley door, which he knew was her knock. He rose and smoothed his hands back along the sides of his head, pulled down the tabs of his vest, buttoned his coat. He slid back the bar and opened the door; at first he could see nothing, and he didn't speak, waiting for his eyes to accustom themselves to the dark.

She was standing back and a little to one side, where the light did not touch her.

"I've told you tommies to quit bothering me," he said, and made as though to slam the door.

"Tom," she said, and moved closer. "It's Kate."

He was supposed to blow to pieces at the sight of her. "Well, I'll be damned," he said. "Now they are following me out from all over."

"Yes," Kate said. She sounded disappointed, which pleased him. He moved aside and she entered, tall, all in black; black hat with black cherries on it, black skirt draped in thick folds over her hips, black sacque jacket—with only the white ruffled front of her shirtwaist to relieve it.

She clutched her hands, in black mesh mitts, to her waist, watching him close the door. Her dead white face was controlled, and stiff, but filled with hate.

"Couldn't you get along without me, Kate?" he asked, and managed to meet her black eyes and grin. But, when she did not answer, against his will he retreated to his desk and took a cheroot from the silver box there, and lit it. "You should have let me know you were coming."

"Didn't you know?"

"I'd've had a brass band out."

"Didn't you?" she said.

He frowned, as though he'd been struck by a thought. Then he burst out laughing. "I guess you came in on the stage this afternoon," he said. "Well, you had a little excitement at that, didn't you?"

"You don't know who it was that was killed?" Kate said. She was staring at him not quite so intently, and he thought he had got past her. If not, in the end he had only to tell her the truth and she would not believe it, either, from him. She looked very tired, he thought; she looked older than he had remembered, who was not even two years older.

"Somebody said he looked like a high-roller." He paused, frowned again, grinned again. "Why, was he with you? I thought you had had enough of high-rollers, Kate."

"It was Bob Cletus's brother."

He stared at her as if incredulous. He began to laugh again. He put down his cheroot and laughed and watched her upper lip twitching, with hate of him, or as though she were going to cry. "My God, how you run through those Cletuses!" he said.

She made a humming sound in her throat. She said, in a shaky voice, "You knew I would come, Tom. I told you—I would!"

He turned the laughter off like a tap. He stared back into her black eyes that were glazed with tears now, and said, "If I'd known you were coming out here with some cheap gunman you spaded up somewhere, you'd have never got here either. You damned vulture."

"Oh, I don't think *you* shot him," Kate said. "I think you hired Clay to do it. The way you did with Bob."

That was supposed to pin him to the wall. But she could not keep her voice from shaking, and he almost felt sorry for her.

He said, "Or I might've just done nothing and let him choose Clay out and commit suicide. The way it was before."

She turned half away from him, dropping her hands tiredly to her sides. He saw her glance up at the painting over the door. He felt an almost savage relief that she had not got to Fort James with Pat Cletus during the time when he, Morgan, had come on ahead to Warlock, and Clay had remained in Fort James.

"So you went out and hunted up his brother to do Clay down for you. It took you a good while."

"I couldn't find him," Kate said, in a dead voice. "So I gave up. But then I ran onto him." She stopped, as though there were nothing more to say.

"And all for nothing, too. Well, bad luck, Kate. But maybe there is another brother, or cousins. In Australia or somewhere."

She shook her head a little. She reminded him of a clock-work figure running down.

"Haven't you got the fare? Why, there is money I owe you, at that." He put his hands to his money belt, and saw her face come back to life.

"Would you pay me to go? I hope you would pay a lot, for I won't go!"

"Come back to me after all?"

He shouldn't have said it. He saw the revulsion show clearly in her face, and the strain of maintaining the grin that painfully stretched his lips became immense. But he continued. "I have got a nice place out front, and a nice apartment back here. I could set you up in style. You might have to work your trade from time to time if I ran short of cash, but . . ."

She only stared at him.

"Leaving then?" he asked. He had better not underestimate her, he knew, tired as she was now, and shocked. He felt enormously tired himself. He had thought hate did not affect him. He had thought he was used to it.

"No," she said. "No, I will stay and watch Clay Blaisedell shot down like he shot Bob down."

"Do it yourself?"

"Are you afraid I would? No, I won't do that."

He sat down in his chair, inhaled on his cheroot, blew smoke. "Maybe you can get somebody to go after him here. Like the one you just lost." His voice rasped in his throat. "There are some that might be hard up enough to try it for a chance to sleep free with a hydrophoby skunk bitch."

He felt a lift of pleasure to see her face dissolve. But she quickly regained control of it. She only shook her head.

"Why, you have gone soft, Kate."

"No," she said, and again he saw how exhausted she was. "No, not soft. I went all over looking for Pat Cletus," she said, in the dead voice. "I went more than five thousand miles looking for him—different places I had heard he might be. I couldn't find him so I thought I would give it up. Then a month ago I met him in Denver, and we came out here and he was killed. I don't know whether you did it or not—except—except I should've known he would be killed. Like I should've known Bob would be killed if he went to tell you he was going to marry me."

"I told you once before he didn't ever come to see me."

She didn't seem to hear him. "So that was my fault too. I should have seen you dead before I thought of wanting to marry Bob Cletus. Or we should have run—to Australia. But I killed him when I let him go to you. And killed Pat when I made him come out here. I have had enough of killing."

He nodded sympathetically, and saw the despair crumple her face again.

"But I will see Clay Blaisedell shot down!" she said. "I will see that, I'll follow him wherever he goes to see it." She took a deep breath, and her lips tightened as though she were trying to smile. "I saw him tonight," she went on. "He looked at me as though he'd seen a ghost, and I thought how fine it would be to be a ghost and haunt and torture somebody who—who"—her voice began to shake again— "who took away the only chance I ever had!" she cried. "Who killed the only decent man I ever knew! And you had Clay shoot him down!" Tears shone suddenly on her cheeks.

"Why, then you should look for somebody to shoot me down."

"No! Because you don't care about yourself—I know you that well. But I know you care about Clay. I think I might've let it alone if I thought you didn't care what happened to him. But I will follow him and haunt him. And you."

"And yourself too, isn't it?"

"Maybe so," she said, with a tired lift of her shoulders. "Haunt myself too for not knowing you would always do the foulest thing you could do. To me or anyone." Her voice rose shrilly, "But I'll stay here and wait it out, and watch! Whenever you see me you will know I am waiting to see him die like Bob died. Or wherever he is when somebody finally shoots him down, I will be there too. And then I'll come and laugh at you!"

"We will have a good laugh together, Kate."

She sobbed. She raised a hand to her eyes and then dropped it, as though she were too proud to hide that she was crying. She was ugly when she cried; he remembered that.

"Come in any time and we will have a good laugh," he added, pleasantly. She did not answer, moving toward the door. He watched the swing of the thick pleats of her skirt, her hair, blue-black in the light, where it showed beneath her hat. Her white, lined face turned toward him once, and then she was gone and the door slapped shut behind her.

Her scent of lavender water was strong in his nostrils. He was shivering a little, and he stretched, hugely. He had done well enough tonight, he thought; he had given her nothing. He had never given her anything. He saw, indelible in his mind's eye, her tired, hate-filled face. Once there had been good times.

II

Kate had not been gone ten minutes when Clay came in from the Glass Slipper. Clay took off his hat, brushed his fingers back through his thick, fair hair, and sat down on the other side of the desk. He placed his hat on the desk before him and then moved it a little to one side, as though it were of great importance where it was placed.

"Posse back?" Morgan asked.

Clay shook his head. His eyes were deeply shadowed, his mouth a thin shadow beneath the sweep of his mustache. He had been doing some drinking, from the look of him.

"Whisky, Clay?" Morgan asked, and his hand caught the neck of the decanter as though to strangle it. But Clay shook his head again.

"I've just found out something to shake a man," Clay said.

"What's that?"

"The passenger those road agents shot. I heard his name and I didn't believe it. But I went over to the carpenter shop for a look."

"Somebody you knew?" Morgan said, and put the decanter down.

"Knew of. I'd heard Bob Cletus had a brother up in the Dakotas somewhere."

Denver, he commented to himself. "Cletus?" he said aloud.

"Pat Cletus," Clay said, looking down at his hat. "This one's name was Pat Cletus. You would know it was his brother, looking at him."

Morgan whistled.

"Come after me, I guess," Clay said.

"I don't know. Looks like he might just have happened out this way."

Clay shook his head again, and Morgan leaned back in his chair and hooked his thumbs in his vest pockets. He said easily, "What would you have done?"

"Run."

"If he'd come after you like you think, I expect he'd've followed if you'd run."

After a time Clay nodded. "Why, yes," he said. "That's so, isn't it?"

"Then it seems like those San Pablo boys that shot him down did you a favor," Morgan said. He tried to grin, and felt his lips slide dry over his teeth.

"Yes," Clay said. His elbows on the desk, he made a steeple of his hands and gazed through, as though he were shading his eyes to sight at something a long way off.

"Foolishness!" Morgan said suddenly, savagely. "I don't know how you managed to settle it in your mind that Bob Cletus wasn't on the prod for you. You heard he was. It looks to me like you just chose he wasn't so you could chew yourself forever. Foolishness. God damn it, Clay!"

"What is foolish to one man maybe isn't to another, every time," Clay said. "It is different with you. If you lose a stack at your trade you can push out another and win it back. If I lose a stack like that one I can't."

"If you lose at your trade they leave your boots on," Morgan said. He tried to grin, and saw Clay try to grin back. But Clay only shook his head; that wasn't what he had meant.

Morgan said, "Let one Cletus shoot you down because you shot down another—what kind of trade is that?"

"Fair trade," Clay said, and his lips twisted again, more weakly still.

Damned fool, Morgan thought, not even angrily any more; oh, you damned fool! "Why, then it is a funny kind of trade and a funny kind of fair," he said carefully. "It is a trade where you will have to kill a man sometimes. But any time their kin come after you, there is nothing for it but throw down your hardware and go to praying."

"Only Cletus's kin," Clay said. "You know what I mean. Don't try to make a fool of me, Morg." Clay carefully moved his hat two inches to the right. "There's more to it than Pat Cletus," he said.

"I know."

"You've seen her?"

"I heard there was a women came in on the stage with him. So if it was a Cletus—"

"I guess she went looking for him when she left Fort James."

"There are people I'd rather see in Warlock than Kate."

"You didn't use to feel that way."

"There was a time when I could eat hot chiles too. That was when I was younger."

"I can't look her in the face," Clay said, in an expressionless voice. "I think I could look any Cletus in the face, but I can't her."

Morgan reached for the decanter again. Clay did not take on this way very much, and when he did Morgan was angry, first at Clay, and then at himself; and part of the time it would seem a foolish joke, and part of the time it would sit his back heavy as pig lead because it sat Clay's so. He had not yet discovered how he must act with Clay when Clay was like this. "A little whisky, Clay?" he said.

"*Por favor.*"

He poured whisky into the two glasses, and wondered if Clay had any idea that the man drinking with him had done it to him. "How?" he said.

"How," Clay said. He drank the whisky off at a swallow and got to his feet, putting his hat on. Standing, his face remote and calm, Clay said, "There was a time when I used to pray it wasn't so, what I'd done. It is hard to blame a person for what he does when he is scared, but you can blame yourself. Trigger-nervous and edgy like I was, and seeing a *Tejano* coming at me around every corner. But maybe a man has to have something like that on him." Abruptly he stopped, and turned away from the desk.

"Why, Clay?" Morgan said.

"Why, just so he'll know, I guess," Clay said distantly. He went out. The sounds of gambling and drinking and monotonous talking were loud for a moment before Clay shut the door behind him.

Morgan took a cheroot from the box. He lit it with steady fingers, and inhaled deeply until he felt the smoke gripe his lungs. "How?" he said, raising his glass to the fuzzy, fat nude on her red couch. She smirked back at him, flat-faced, and he said, "Don't smile at me, for I would hire you out in a minute if I needed a stake."

He brought the cheroot up close before his slitted eyes, until all he could see in the world was the hoared cherry ember. Inverting the cigar, he mashed it out against the back of his hand, curling his lips back against the fierce, searing pain, and breathing deep of the stink of burning hair and flesh.

Then he sat grinning idiotically at the red spot on the back of his hand, thinking of Clay saying that he had prayed.

14. Gannon Watches a Man among Men

I

GANNON waited alone at the jail. About ten o'clock the judge appeared, coming in the doorway with his hard hat cocked over his eye, a bottle under one arm and his crutch under the other, his left trouser leg neatly turned up and sewed like a sack across the bottom. Heavy and awkward on the crutch he moved around to the chair behind the table, which Gannon vacated, and sank into it, grunting. He put the bottle down before him, and leaned the crutch against the table.

"Left you behind, did they?" he said, swinging around with difficulty to confront Gannon, who had seated himself in the chair beside the cell door. The judge's face was the color of unfresh liver.

Gannon nodded.

"You see any reason why they should have?" the judge demanded, continuing to regard him with his muddy eyes.

"Yes."

"What reason?"

"I expect you know, Judge."

"I asked you," the judge snapped.

"Well, one they are after is maybe my brother."

"By God, if you are the law you arrest your own brother if he breaks it, don't you?"

"Yes."

"But maybe you lean a little toward McQuown's people," the judge said, squinting at him. "Or Carl is afraid you do. Do you?"

"No."

"Lean toward Blaisedell then, like most here? Seeing he is against McQuown?"

"I don't guess I lean either way. I don't take it as my place to lean any way."

Footsteps came along the boardwalk and Blaisedell turned into the doorway. "Judge," he said, nodding in greeting. "Deputy."

"Marshal," Gannon said. The judge turned slowly toward Blaisedell.

"Any word from the posse?" Blaisedell asked. He leaned in the doorway, the brim of his black hat slanting down to hide his eyes.

"Not yet," he said. He felt Blaisedell's stare. Then Blaisedell inclined his head to glance down at the judge, who had muttered something.

"Pardon, Judge?" Blaisedell said.

"I said, who are you?" the judge said, in a muffled voice.

"Why, we have met, Judge, I believe."

"Who are you?" the judge said again. "Just tell me, so I will know. I don't think it's come out yet, who you are."

Gannon stirred nervously in his chair. Blaisedell stood a little straighter, frowning.

"Something a man's got a right to know," the judge went on. His voice had grown stronger. "Who are you? Are you Clay Blaisedell or are you the marshal of this town?"

"Why, both, Judge," Blaisedell said.

"A man is bound by what he is," the judge said. "An honest man, I mean. I am asking whether you are bound by being marshal, or being Clay Blaisedell."

"Both, I expect. Judge, I don't just know for sure what you are—"

"Which first?" the judge snapped.

This time Blaisedell didn't answer.

"Oh, I know what you are thinking. You think I am a drunk, one-legged old galoot pestering you, and you are too polite to say so. Well, I know what I am, Mister Marshal Blaisedell, or Mister Clay Blaisedell that is incidentally marshal of Warlock. But I want to know *which* you are."

"Why?" Blaisedell said.

"Why? Well, I got to thinking and it seems to me the trouble in a thing like law and order is, there is people working every which way at it, or against it. Like it or not, there has got to be *people* in it. But the trouble is, you never know what a man *is*, so how can you know what he is going to *do?* So I thought, why not ask straight out? I asked Johnny Gannon here just now what he was and where he stood, and he told me. Are you any better than another that you shouldn't?"

Blaisedell still did not speak. He looked as though he had dismissed the judge's words as idle, and was thinking of something else.

The judge went on. "Let me tell you another thing then. Schroeder has gone after those that robbed the stage and killed a passenger. I expect him and that posse would just as soon shoot them down *ley fuga* as bring them back. But say he will catch them, and say he gets them back whole. Well, there will be a lynch mob on hand, like as not, from what I've heard around tonight. But say the lynch mob doesn't pan out, or Schroeder sort of remembers what he is here for and stops them. Then those road agents will go up to Bright's City to trial, and likely get off just the way Earnshaw did.

"Then it is your turn, Mister Marshal, or whatever you are. Which is why I am asking you now beforehand if you know what you are, and what you stand for. If a man don't know that himself, why, nobody does except God almighty, and He is a long way off just now."

"Judge," Blaisedell said. "I guess you don't much like what you think I stand for."

"I don't *know* what you stand for, and it don't look like you are going to tell me, either!" Gannon heard the judge draw a ragged breath. "Well, maybe you can tell me this, then. Why shouldn't the

Citizens' Committee have gone out and made itself a vigilante committee like some damned fools wanted to do, instead of bringing you here?"

Blaisedell spread his legs, folded his arms on his chest, and frowned. "Might have done," he said, in his deep voice. "I don't always hold with vigilantes, but sometimes it is the only thing."

"Don't hold with them why?"

"Well, now, Judge, I expect for the same reason you don't. Most times they start out fine, but most times, too, they go bad. Mostly they end up just a mob of stranglers because they don't know when to break up."

"Wait!" the judge said. "You are right, but do you know why they go bad? Because there is nothing they are responsible to. Now! Any man that is set over other men somehow has to be responsible to something. Has to be *accountable*. You—"

Blaisedell said, "If you are talking about me, I am responsible to the Citizens' Committee here."

"Ah!" the judge said. He sat up very straight; he pointed a finger at the marshal. "Well, most ways it is a bad thing, and it is not even much of a thing, but it is an important thing and I warrant you to hang onto it!"

"All right," Blaisedell said, and looked amused.

"I am telling you something for your own good and everybody's good," the judge whispered. "I am telling you a man like you has to be always right, and no poor human can ever be that. So you have got to be accountable somehow. To someone or everybody or—"

"To you, you mean, Judge?" Blaisedell said.

Gannon looked away. His eyes caught the names scratched on the wall opposite him, that were illegible now in the dim light. He wondered to whom those men, each in their turn, had thought they were responsible. Not to Sheriff Keller certainly, nor to General Peach.

The judge had not spoken, and after a moment Blaisedell went on. "Judge, a man will say too often that he is responsible to something because he is afraid to face up alone. That is just putting off on another man or on the law or whatever. A man who has to always think like that is a crippled man."

"No," the judge said; his voice was muffled again. "No, just a man among men." He drank again, the brown bottle slanting up toward the base of the hanging lamp above him.

Blaisedell stood with his long legs still spread and his hands upon his shell belt beneath his black frock coat. Standing there in the doorway he seemed as big a man as Gannon had ever seen. When he examined Blaisedell closely, height and girth, he was not so tall nor yet so broad-chested as some he knew, yet the impression remained. Blaisedell's blue gaze encased him for a moment; then he turned back to the judge again.

"Maybe where you've been the law was enough of a thing there so people went the way the law said," he said. "You ought to know there's places where it is different than that. It is different here, and maybe the best that can be done is a man that is handy with a Colt's—to keep the peace until the law can do it. That is what I am, Judge. Don't mix me with your law, for I don't claim to be it."

"You are a prideful man, Marshal," Judge Holloway said. He sat with his head bent down, staring at his clasped hands.

"I am," Blaisedell said. "And so are you. So is any decent man."

"You set yourself as always right. Only the law is that and it is above all men. Always right is too much pride for a man."

"I didn't say I am always right," Blaisedell said. His voice sounded deeper. "I have been wrong, and dead wrong. And may be wrong again. But—"

"But then you stand naked before the rest in your wrong, Marshal," the judge said. "It is what I am trying to say. And what then?"

"When I have worn out my use, you mean? Why, then I will move along, Judge."

"You won't know when it is time. In your pridefulness."

"I'll know. It is something I'll know." Gannon thought the marshal smiled, but he could not be sure. "There'll be ones to tell me."

"Maybe they will be afraid to tell you," the judge said.

Blaisedell's face grew paler, colder; he looked suddenly furious. But he said in a polite voice, "I expect I'll know when the time comes, Judge," and abruptly turned and disappeared. His bootheels cracked away to silence outside.

The judge raised his bottle to drain the last of the whisky in it. With a limp arm he reached down to set it beside his chair, and knocked it over with a drunken hand. It rolled noisily until it brought up against the cell door, while the judge leaned forward with his face in his hands and his fingers working and scraping in his hair.

After a long time he rose and clapped his hat on his head, staggering as he fitted the crutch under his arm. Gannon had a glimpse of his face as he swung out the door. Hectically flushed, it was filled with a sagging mixture of pride and shame, dread and grief.

II

It was well after midnight when the posse returned. Gannon stared at the doorway with aching eyes as he heard the tramp of hoofs and shouting. Men began running in the street past the jail, and he felt his heart swell in his chest as though it would smother him. He thrust down hard on the table with his hand, forcing himself to his feet, and went outside.

The street seemed filled solid with horsemen and men on foot milling around the horses. Someone was swinging a lantern to illuminate the faces of the riders—he saw Carl's face, Peter Bacon's, Chick Hasty's; the lantern showed Pony Benner's scowling, frightened face, and the men in the street howled his name. The pale light revealed Calhoun, and another shout went up. Then Gannon saw Billy sitting straight and hatless in the saddle, with his hands tied behind him.

The lantern swung again to show a riderless horse; but not riderless, he saw, for there was a body tied over the saddle.

"Ted Phlater!" someone said, in a sudden silence.

Immediately a roar went up. "Hang them!" a drunken voice screamed. "Oh, hang the sons of bitches! Hang them, boys!"

"Shut that up!" Carl shouted. Gannon swung off the boardwalk and made his way through the crowd as Carl dismounted. Carl looked into his face and gripped his arm for a moment.

"Got Ted Phlater shot and lost Friendly, damn all," he said.

Another drunken voice was raised. "Where's Big Luke, Carl?"

"Where is McQuown? You went and forgot Abe and Curley, boys!"

"They got the barber-killer!"

There was laughter, more shouting. "Hang them, boys! Hang them!" the first voice continued, shrill and mechanical, like a parrot.

"Horse!" Carl called to Peter Bacon. "You and Pike bring them inside." He started for the jail, and Gannon made his way toward Phlater's horse, to help Owen Parsons with the body. Men surged and shouted, mocked and joked and threatened as Pony, Calhoun, and Billy were dismounted. The crowd pressed toward the jail now, as the prisoners came up on the boardwalk, where a man held a lantern high as they moved past him.

"Hang them! Hang them!"

Gannon and Parsons lifted Phlater down and tried to make their way to the jail. "Get the God-damned jumping hell out of the way!" Parsons cried hoarsely. "Got any respect for the dead?"

Inside they put Ted Phlater's stiffening body on the floor at the rear of the jail, and Peter appeared unfolding a blanket, with which he covered it. Pike Skinner was untying Calhoun's arms; he thrust him roughly into the cell with Billy and Pony, and Carl slammed and locked the door.

Chick Hasty and Tim French came inside with the strongbox from the stage, which they shoved under the table. The hanging lamp swung like a pendulum when one of them brushed against it, and shadows swung more wildly still. The dusty window was crowded with bloated, featureless faces pressed against the glass, and men were pushing in at the door.

"Out of here!" Carl shouted. His face was lined with fatigue and gray with dust. "Isn't any damned assembly hall. Out of here before I get mad! You!" Pike Skinner swung around and with his arms outstretched forced the men back.

"Hang the murdering sons of bitches!" someone yelled from outside. Pony's scared face appeared at the cell door, and Calhoun's lantern-jawed, cadaverous one; Gannon could see Billy's hand on Calhoun's shoulder.

"Expect they mean to try something, from the sound of them," Peter Bacon said calmly.

"No they won't," Carl said. He stretched and rubbed his back, and grinned suddenly. "Well, three out of four," he said. "That is better than one out of two like we made last time, anyhow."

"You going to want some of us here tonight, Carl?" Parsons said, and Gannon saw that he tilted his grizzled head in his direction. He looked quickly away, to meet Calhoun's eyes. Calhoun pursed his slack mouth, hawked, and spat.

"Go home and get some sleep," Carl said, and slumped down in the chair at the table. "We are all right here."

"I'm staying," Pike Skinner said.

"Stay then. Chick, you and Pete go get some sleep. We'll be taking them into Bright's in the morning."

There was muttering among the men bunched in the doorway. A muffled shout went up outside. The possemen pushed out the door, spurs clinking and scraping.

When they had gone, Pike Skinner swung the door closed and slid the bar through the iron keepers. The goblin faces still pressed against the window glass. There was another burst of shouting and hurrahing outside. Pike Skinner walked heavily to the rear, let himself fall into the chair there, and stared hostilely at Gannon. At the table Carl sighed and rubbed his knuckles into his eyes.

"Didn't take you long," Gannon said.

Carl laughed. "We ran onto them just before they hit the river. Pony and Calhoun, that is. They separated but we rode them down easy. Ted and Pike here kind of flushed Billy out of some trees down there and—"

Pike said abruptly, "It was Billy shot Ted."

"He was shooting at me," Billy said, in a harsh voice, from the cell. "What was I supposed to do, sit and let him do it?"

"Carl," Pony said. "You are not going to let those bastards take us out of here, are you, Carl?"

"Shut your face," Pike said. "You chicken-livered ugly little son of a bitch."

"Thought you wanted me to let you go," Carl said. "Thought you told me I might as well, for a jury up at Bright's would do it anyhow. Save me trouble, you said."

"I got something to tell you, Bud Gannon," Calhoun said. "Come over here so's I can whisper it."

"Never mind," Billy said. "Never mind, Bud."

Gannon didn't look toward the cell, leaning against the wall where the names were scratched, and watching within himself the slow turn of the cards, knowing each one as it turned. He stared at the goblin faces at the window and listened to the shouting and muttering outside. It was the only card he had not foreseen.

"You are so God-damn sure you caught your road agents!" Pony yelled.

"Hush!" Carl said.

"Be damned if I do! You got the wrong people! You—"

Carl got up, swung swiftly and hit Pony in the face through the bars. Pony fell backward, cursing.

"Wrong people!" Carl said, rubbing his knuckles. "You just happened to pick up that strongbox where somebody else dropped it, I guess."

"One wrong, though," Calhoun said quietly, and laughed; he moved back as Carl raised his fist again. Gannon stared in the cell at Billy and he felt his heart swell and choke him again; he had almost missed another card. Billy just looked back at him, scornfully.

"Listen to those boys yell out there," Pike said.

Gannon started and Carl reached for the shotgun as there was a knock. Carl motioned to Gannon to unbolt the door. It was the Mexican cook from the Boston Café; he slipped in, carrying a tray covered with a cloth. The men outside set up a steady whooping, and the Mexican looked very frightened as he put the tray down and departed. As Gannon swung the door closed behind him he had a glimpse of the vast, dark mass in the street, and groups of pale, whiskered faces showing here and there by lanternlight. Someone was haranguing them from the tie rail at the corner. He bolted the door again.

Carl passed bowls of meat and potatoes into Calhoun. Pony threw his to the floor. "Go hungry then," Carl said.

Pike took a steak in his hand and wolfed it down, and Carl attacked his hungrily too. Gannon set his plate on the floor beside him. There was another round of shouting outside, with one voice rising above the rest. The words were lost in the uproar. The faces at the window had vanished.

"Bud," Billy said. Pony and Calhoun had retreated into the darkness. Gannon felt Pike Skinner watching him. "What the hell would you do, Bud?" Billy said. "People after you and throwing lead all over the landscape. What the hell would you've done?"

"I don't know," he said. Carl was pretending not to listen.

Pike said, "You might've thought how come there was a posse after you in the first place."

Gannon saw Billy's face twist, and something in him twisted with it. Another yell went up outside, and Pony appeared at the cell door again.

"Sit there and lap your supper!" he shrilled at Carl. "They are coming! Can't you hear them coming?"

"We'll stop them," Carl said, "if they come. You can quit wetting your pants."

"Bud," Billy said again.

"Never mind it now, Billy," Gannon said tightly. Pike glowered at him from the chair beside the alley door. Carl sat hump-backed at the table, forking food into his mouth.

"Long ride to Bright's," Carl said, over a mouthful. "You boys in there better get some sleep."

"We'll never get to Bright's!" Pony cried.

"Oh, hush that!" Calhoun said.

Bud—Gannon could hear it, repeated and repeated, although Billy hadn't spoken again. Reluctantly he turned his head to look at Billy again, and he saw Billy's lips tilt beneath the pitiful young mustache.

"Go ahead and say you told me what I was heading for," Billy whispered. "Go ahead, Bud."

"What good would that do?"

"No good," Billy said, and disappeared. The cot springs creaked. Gannon could hear them whispering in the cell. "Why don't you tell him?" he heard Calhoun say; then the tumult outside grew suddenly louder, and faces were pressed against the window again.

Someone beat on the door with the flat of his hand. "*Carl!*"

Carl grunted and rose. He wiped his mustache, hitched at his shell belt, and glanced significantly at Gannon and Skinner. He took up the shotgun and nodded at Gannon to unbar the door.

Gannon did so, and leaped back, jerking his Colt free as the door burst inward. Two men hurtled in, to stop suddenly as they saw Carl's shotgun. There was a knot of others jammed in the doorway, and behind them Gannon could feel the whole huge and violent thrust of the mob. Pike leaped forward with his Winchester in his hands. Outside they were whooping steadily again.

"You are going to have to give them up, Carl," Red Slator said loudly, as he and Fat Vint backed up to join the others in the doorway. Close behind these two, Gannon could see Jed Smith, a foreman at the Thetis, Nate Bush, Hap Peters, Charlie Grace, who was one of Dick Maples' bakers, Kinkaid, a cowboy from up the valley, several miners, and Simpson and Parks, who were both macs for some of the crib girls. Their faces were grim. Fat Vint looked drunker than usual.

"Get out of here, you miserable sons of bitches!" Carl said.

"You can't stop us!" Charlie Grace shouted, and cheers went up from the dark, featureless mass behind them.

"See if I don't," Carl said. "If you think a bunch of pimps and drunk bullprods is going to bust this jail, you are mistaken. Get out of here!"

"We will tramp you down!" Vint yelled blusteringly. "You hear, Pike?" He looked at Gannon with his bloodshot pig-eyes, and sneered, "And you'll keep out of it if you know what's good for you, Johnny Gannon."

"Get out of here!" Carl said, in a level voice.

"We'll get out of here taking them with us!" Slator said. "We are going to hang the murdering bastards and bust over you if we have to, Carl Schroeder. You know what'll happen at Bright's; by God, everybody knows. They'll get off sure as hell, with McQuown to send up lying hardcases by the dozen and scare the jury green too. You know that, Carl!" The men in the doorway began all to shout at once, and the shouting gathered power outside until the whole world seemed to be shouting.

Carl waited until the noise had subsided a little; then he said, "Red, I'd like to see them hang as much as you. I caught them and lost Ted Phlater doing it." His voice rose. "And we went out and caught them while you and this bunch was sitting on your slat-asses drinking whisky. So I will be damned if you will take them off us now the hard work is done! Now get!"

He jammed the shotgun against Slator's chest and Slator backed up. Vint grabbed at the shotgun and Gannon slammed the barrel down on the fat hand. Vint yelped. Pike started forward, and, feinting blows with the butt of the Winchester, drove them all back through the doorway.

"Tromp them down! Tromp them down, fellows!"

"Christ, give us something to help stand them off with, Bud!" Calhoun cried.

They pushed the mob leaders before them out the door, and the crowd in the street gave way. Then it surged forward again with a wild yelling. Hands caught Carl's shotgun and pulled him forward. He stumbled to his knees, then fought and scrambled back away from the men crowding in on him. Gannon fired twice into the air. Someone yelled in terror and the mob fell back again.

The three of them stood close together before the jail door. Carl was panting.

"They won't shoot!" a hoarse voice yelled from the rear of the mob. "They know better than to shoot!"

"Give us a God-damned iron, Carl!" Calhoun shouted.

"Good Christ, Carl, for Christ's sake, give us a gun to hold them off with! Bud!"

"Don't be a damned fool, Carl!" Slator said.

"Get the hell out of the way, Johnny Gannon! You two-way son of a bitch!"

"What the hell are you doing, Pike? Leave us take them!"

Slator, Vint, and Simpson started forward again; Vint was grinning. "You dassn't shoot, Carl!"

"One step more," Carl panted.

"Give us a chance, Carl!" Pony screamed.

"One step more, you bastards!" Pike said, and Gannon started to swing his Colt at Simpson's head.

There were three shots in rapid succession from Southend Street, and then silence, sudden and profound. Craning his neck, Gannon saw men hurrying to get off the boardwalk, and Blaisedell appeared, walking rapidly, the Colt in his hand glittering by lanternlight. A whisper ran through the crowd. "The marshal!" "Blaisedell!" "Here comes the marshal!" "It is Blaisedell!"

Blaisedell joined them before the jail. "Need another man?" he said.

"Surely do," Carl said, and let out his breath in a long, shaking, whispering laugh. "We surely do, Marshal."

"We are taking those road agents out to hang, Marshal!" someone cried from across the street.

"You are not going to stop us, Marshal!" Fat Vint blustered. "We will tromp you with the rest. We are—"

"Come here and tromp me," Blaisedell said.

Vint stepped back. Those around him retreated further.

"Come here," Blaisedell said. "Come here!" Vint came a step forward. His face looked like gray dough.

"This is none of your put-in, Marshal!" someone yelled, but the rest of the mob was silent.

"Come here!" Blaisedell said once more, dangerously. Vint sobbed with fear, but he came on another step. Blaisedell's hand shot up suddenly, the Colt's barrel gleaming as he clubbed it down. The fat man cried out as he fell. There was silence again.

"Damn you, Marshal!" Slator cried. "This is none of your—"

"Come here!" Blaisedell said. When Slator didn't move he fired into the planks at his feet. Slator jumped and yelled. "Come here!" Slator moved forward, trying to cover his head with his hands. Blaisedell slashed the gun barrel down and he staggered back. Hands caught him and he disappeared into the crowd.

"Take that one off, too," Blaisedell said, and the same men hurriedly dragged Vint off the boardwalk.

"You have done McQuown's work tonight, Blaisedell!" a man yelled.

"If you have got something to say, step up here and say it," Blaisedell said, not loudly. "Otherwise skedaddle." No one spoke. There was a movement away down Main Street. "Then all of you skedaddle," Blaisedell said, raising his voice. "And while you are doing it think how being in a lynch mob is as low a thing as a man can be."

There was bitter muttering in the street, but the mob began to disperse. Blaisedell holstered his Colt. Gannon could see his face in profile, stern and contemptuous, and thought how they must hate him for this. But he had saved shooting; he had probably saved lives.

Carl was mopping his face with his bandanna. "Well, thank you kindly, Marshal," he said. "I expect there isn't a one in there worth any man's trouble. But damned if you don't hate to be run by a bunch of whisky-primed, braying fools like that."

Blaisedell nodded. Pike Skinner, Gannon saw, was looking at the marshal with a reluctant awe on his face.

"Prisoners get a scare?" Blaisedell asked.

"Caterwauling like a bunch of tomcats in there," Carl said, and chuckled breathlessly.

Blaisedell nodded again. Suddenly he said, with anger in his voice, "A person surely dislikes a mob like that. They are men pretending they are brave and hard, but every one so scared of the man beside him he can't do anything but the same." He glanced from Pike to Gannon. "Well, I didn't go to butt in so," he said, as though apologizing. "I expect you boys could've handled it. It is just I surely dislike a mob of men like that."

"I guess we couldn't've handled it, Marshal," Pike said. "Things had got tight."

Gannon said, "I guess we would've had to go to shooting," and Blaisedell smiled with a brief, white show of teeth below his mustache. He made a curt gesture of salute, as though acknowledging that as the proper compliment.

The four of them stood in awkward silence, watching the men drifting away before them in the darkness. Then Carl turned and went inside, and Pike followed him. When the others had gone, Blaisedell said to Gannon, "Your brother was with them, I heard."

"Yes," he said.

"Too bad," Blaisedell said. "Young fellow like that." Blaisedell stood with him a moment longer, as though waiting for him to speak, but he could think of nothing to say and after a time the marshal said, "Well, I'll be going." With long strides he faded off into the darkness.

Gannon slowly turned back inside the jail. His clothes were soaked with sweat. Billy stood alone at the cell door. "Well," Carl was saying to Pike, leaning against a corner of the table with his arms folded over his chest, "good lesson on how to run off a mob. Haul them out and knock their heads loose one at a time."

"More lesson than that," Pike said ruefully. "For it takes a man to do it." He nodded toward the door.

Gannon looked down at the blanket-wrapped body that was Phlater, whom Billy had shot. So the cards he had missed had not mattered. The lynch mob was gone. He knew that Billy had not been at the stage, but with Phlater dead and Billy's stubborn pride, that would not matter either. So the rest of the cards would continue to play themselves out.

Pony said savagely, "Shut up about that gold-hanneled son of a bitch and leave us get some sleep in here."

Carl's face stiffened. Pike said hoarsely, "Gold-handled son of a bitch that just saved your rotten lives for you!"

"Sleep good on that," Carl said.

Billy's voice was bitter as gall. "Bring his boots and we'll kiss them for him. Like he wants. Like you all do. Bring us his damned boots."

Pike took a step toward the cell door and Billy retreated. Now none of them were visible in the deep shadow of the cell, but it was as though Gannon could see through it, and beyond it, and beyond Bright's City even, see all the massive irrevocable shadows with only the details not clear.

He went out to the Boston Café, after a while, for a pot of coffee to take back to the jail, and sat the night, sleepless himself, watching Carl and Pike fighting sleep. In the morning Buck Slavin furnished a special coach, and Carl, Peter Bacon, Chick Hasty, and Tim French took the prisoners into Bright's City for trial.

15. Boot Hill

WARLOCK'S Boot Hill was not a hill at all, but a knoll protruding from the plateau next to the town dump, where flies hovered in great black swarms. From Boot Hill itself the valley all the way to the Dinosaurs was visible: near at hand the jumble of great rocks of the malpais, farther down the cottonwoods lining the river in irregular stretches, the greasy-green mesquite thickets, and the drier green of the grama grass along the bottoms. To the south were the barren, tan sides of the Bucksaws, marked here and there with winding mine roads, the neat ugly smears of tailings below the gallows of the shafthead frames. Farther to the west were the chimneys of the stamp mill at Redgold, with the smoke blowing southwest in gray chunks.

Today there were two open graves, two pine coffins resting on the stony ground beside them. It was windy among the mounded graves. Men stood hatless and their hair blew askew and their trouser bottoms flapped—groups of townsmen, a few cowboys, two women in deep bonnets, and a number of curious Mexicans standing close by. A little apart stood Miss Jessie Marlow, with her hand on Marshal Clay Blaisedell's arm, and, on the other side of her, Dr. Wagner in his old black suit. Further along, all in black and standing alone, was the new woman, who, it was rumored, had paid for the coffins. Beyond her were six women from the Row, bunched close together as though for protection, from time to time one painted, powdered face or another glancing curiously sideways at the strange woman. Morgan was also alone, his hat in his hands like the rest of the men, his sleek hair shining in the sun and undisturbed by the wind, standing with one foot on a rock and brooding down at the first coffin.

The four gravediggers, who had been assigned a month's duty as such by Judge Holloway in penance for being drunk and disorderly on various occasions, leaned on their shovels while Bill Wolters, one of Taliaferro's barkeepers, recited the service from memory in a loud, sing-song, former-Baptist-preacher's voice, that was broken into snatches of sound by the wind. The coffin was let down into the first grave with new yellow ropes, and Wolters moved to the second grave and recited again. The second coffin was lowered, and the gravediggers began shoveling dirt and rocks into the holes. The Mexicans, the strange woman, and one of the women from the Row crossed themselves. Morgan brought a cheroot from his pocket and chewed on it. Some of the other men took turns with the shovels. Dick Maples produced the two crosses he had fashioned and painted —it was his hobby. On the first was:

PATRICK CLETUS
Murdered by Bandits
January 23, 1881
"How long, oh Lord?"

On the second:

THEODORE PHLATER
Shot by Billy Gannon
January 23, 1881
"A time of war—"

A group of Citizens' Committee members began moving away from the graves together. "Who is the tall woman?" asked Joseph Kennon.

"Came in on the stage yesterday," Buck Slavin said. He nodded back at the first grave. "With that one. Somebody said they were going to put up a dance hall here."

"Married?" Fred Winters inquired.

"I don't know."

"Her name is Kate Dollar," said Paul Skinner, Pike Skinner's brother, as he limped up to join them. "That's how she's got it down at the hotel, anyhow."

The doctor joined them and Winters said, "That is a good arm Miss Jessie is walking on, Doc. Did you see him in action last night?"

The doctor shook his head.

"I saw him," Henry Goodpasture said. "He made fifty or sixty men run with their tails between their legs."

"Who were they?" the doctor asked.

"The usual no-accounts. Slator and Grace among them. A bunch of drunken miners."

"I see you will blame the miners for everything, too," the doctor said.

Goodpasture rolled his eyes heavenward, and Kennon and Winters laughed. The new woman had moved away from Morgan to join Deputy Gannon. Slavin informed the others of this in a whisper, and each found occasion to glance back and confirm the fact.

"It seems Gannon has a friend after all," Winters said.

Morgan passed and one or two of them nodded to him, but no one spoke. Morgan glanced from face to face with his contemptuous eyes, and nodded back with a kind of insulting deference.

"Damned hound," Will Hart said, when Morgan was out of ear-shot. "There's a man I wouldn't trust my back to."

"There's talk Taliaferro's man Wax trusted his to him," Slavin said. "Damned if I don't believe it, too."

"Blaisedell seems to trust him well enough," Goodpasture said.

"It does not say much for Blaisedell, I'm afraid," Winters said. "Which is too bad."

They all fell silent as the deputy and Kate Dollar caught up with them. The deputy's eyes flickered at them as he passed. The woman walked with him, but separately too. Her face was pale and set.

No one spoke until these had gone on past, and they all stopped when they reached the doctor's buggy. The fat bay mare swung her head from side to side, cropping stubble. Goodpasture and the doctor climbed into the buggy. "Is there a Citizens' Committee meeting, Buck?" the doctor asked.

"Why, I hadn't heard," Slavin said. "Is there, Joe?"

"I don't know," Kennon said, glancing quickly away.

The doctor took up his whip, shook it, and clucked to the mare. They waited while the buggy rolled off. Hart looked at Kennon,

who flushed. Hart said to Slavin, "You know damned well there is
a meeting, Buck! MacDonald called it."

"You know why he called it?" Kennon said. "He wants to vote
Blaisedell to post some troublemaker at the Medusa out of town."

"I don't like that!" Hart said swiftly.

"Cheap," Winters said. "Cheaper than hiring Jack Cade to do it,
the way he did with that man Lathrop. This way we all foot the bill."

"Well, I will go along with him," Slavin said. "It's that one called
Brunk, Will. You have one man like that and he stirs everybody up.
I think Doc is pretty friendly with him, is why I didn't want to
say anything."

"Isn't that pretty?" Paul Skinner said, pointing. Ahead of them,
cutting across toward the Row, the whores with their pastel clothing
fluttering in the wind looked like bright-colored birds.

"I wish Doc would leave those damned jacks alone," Kennon said.
"My God, he has got touchy about them."

"Well," Winters said, "in my opinion the troublemaker at the
Medusa is Charlie MacDonald himself. Maybe he is the one that should
be posted, and I don't know that I wouldn't vote for it."

"I don't like anything about this," Hart said.

"I expect we'll want the marshal to post those three of McQuown's,
won't we?" Kennon said. "If they get off at Bright's, I mean."

"They will. They will."

"Four of them," Slavin said. "Friendly was with them, that's for
sure. Maybe it'd be better to post that Brunk then, come to think of
it. I'll tell Charlie."

Hart was shaking his head worriedly. Winters slapped him on
the shoulder. "Do you know what Warlock's second industry is,
Will? Coffin manufacture," he said, and laughed. But no one else
joined him in his joke, and now they all walked in silence back
along the dusty track to Warlock, returning from the burial of
yesterday's dead.

16. Curley Burne Tries to Mediate

CURLEY BURNE rode beside Abe up into Warlock from the rim. As
they entered Main Street he could feel Abe's tenseness ten feet

away, see him sitting up straighter, his left hand stiff with the reins and his right braced upon his thigh, his green eyes flickering right and left at the almost empty street. Up in the central block there were a few horses tied before the saloons, and, beyond, two teams and wagons stood before Egan's Feed and Grain Barn. Peter Bacon drove the water wagon across on Broadway, water slopping from the top of the tank.

"Got quiet in Warlock," Abe said, in a flat voice.

"Surely has," Curley said, nodding. He pulled his mouth organ from inside his shirt and started to blow on it—and saw Abe frown. He let it drop back. "Chunk of them gone to Bright's for trial tomorrow, I expect," he said. "I hear there's a lot of feeling."

Abe's lips tightened in his red beard. He glanced toward the jail as they passed. The morning sun brightened the east face of the bullet-perforated, weather-beaten sign.

"Bud in there?" Abe asked.

"Didn't see."

"Probably gone up to witness against Billy," Abe said bitterly. He swung his black into Southend Street, so evidently he meant to stop in Warlock instead of just riding through. Curley supposed he felt he had had to come through, and had to stop, just to show himself.

Goodpasture's *mozo* was sweeping the boardwalk in front of the store; when he saw them he began to swing his broom in a burst of animation. A high, battered old Concord stood in the stageyard and a hostler was backing a wheeler into harness. He stared at them as they turned into the Acme Corral. Lame Paul Skinner came out to meet them, silent and hostile. Nate Bush spat on his hands and rammed the tines of his hayfork into the hay as though he were killing snakes.

Abe stood watching Paul Skinner lead Prince and the black off to water with his eyes cold and color burning in his cheeks. "Now, easy, Abe," Curley whispered.

They moved out of the corral, Abe very straight in his buckskin shirt, his shell belt riding his hips low beneath his concho belt. "Easy, now, Abe," Curley said sadly, again, and said it still again but not aloud.

"Sons of bitches!" Abe hissed, as they went along past the buckled, leaning plank fence toward Goodpasture's corner. "They will turn on a man as soon as spit. They will lick up to a new dog and turn on the old every time."

At the corner he started cater-cornered across Main Street toward the jail, and Curley followed a step behind him.

Inside the jail Bud Gannon sat behind the table. His stiff, dark brown hair was neatly combed and his hat lay on the table between his hands. Beside the alley door was a rusty, dented bucket with a mop handle leaning out of it, and the floor was still damp in spots.

Bud nodded to them. He looked tired, and thinner than ever. His star was pinned to the breast of his blue flannel shirt. Abe stopped just inside the door, and, standing at ease, glanced around the jail with careful attention. The cell was unoccupied, the door standing open.

"Well, how's the apprentice deputy?" Curley said, squeezing in past Abe. He had liked Bud Gannon as well as anyone at San Pablo, quiet and sober as he had always been. He had been a top hand with the stock, and he was missed. The killing in Rattlesnake Canyon had hit Bud the worst, he knew; immediately after it he had left for Rincon. He knew Abe hated Bud for that, and for not coming back to San Pablo now.

"All right," Bud said, nodding. "How are you, Curley?"

"Fine as paint."

"We are going up to Bright's," Abe said.

Bud nodded again.

"Where's your big-chief deputy?"

"Bright's City."

"Looks like half Warlock's gone up." Curley flipped his hat off, so that it hung down his back by its cord. Whistling through his teeth, he stepped over to the cell door and batted it back and forth between his hands.

"Lot of yours going up, Abe?" Bud asked.

"Some," Abe said gravely. "Some people down there are interested pretty good."

"Be jam-packed up there," Curley said, pushing the door in faster, shorter arcs. "People all squunched together in court there and everybody calling everybody else a liar." He laughed to think of it, and to think of the fat, sweaty-faced townsmen in the jury box.

Abe leaned back against the wall and crossed his legs. "You look worried, Bud," he said. "Don't worry about Billy. It'll come right."

"Will it?" Bud said, and he sounded hoarse. "I'm glad to hear that." His thin face had paled. "How will it?" he said.

"Because I will see it does," Abe said. "Because they are friends of mine and I intend to see they are not blackguarded and false-sworn into hanging for something they didn't do—by people that's after me. I will stand up for my own, Bud."

Curley looked down as Bud's eyes turned toward him; he knew Abe had meant what he said, not just about Billy, but about Pony and Calhoun as well. But Luke had told them that Pony and Calhoun had planned to stop the stage. It was all right to stand up for your own, it was the first principle; but there was no need to throw up a dust cloud about what they had or had not done. It was as though Abe were trying to fool himself as well as the rest.

"You wouldn't see what you are doing to your own," Bud said, in the hoarse voice.

"Doing!" Abe said. With a lithe movement he leaned his hands on the table and stared into Bud's face. "What would you do, let them hang? Let your own brother hang? By God, I think you would do it, just so Blaisedell would pat you on the head and call you a good boy."

"I'd let them have a fair trial," Bud said.

"Fair trial!" Abe said, and straightened and grinned. "I hear Buck is running passengers up free so everybody in Warlock can go swear against them. Fair trial?"

Bud said nothing, and it came over Curley with a sickening shock that Bud would *not* do anything, that he would let Billy hang and not make a move. "Holy smoke, Bud!" he said. "I believe you— What the hell has happened to you?"

Bud swung toward him. "Do you think I want—"

"I know what's happened to him," Abe broke in. "Clay Blaisedell is what's happened to him."

He went on, but Curley didn't listen, staring at Bud who was, in turn, watching Abe. It came on him strongly, all at once, that Bud did not hate Abe, that maybe Bud felt something of the way he did toward Abe. Yet there was some cold lack in him, where friends didn't matter, or even his brother.

"Whose town is it?" Abe was saying. "I mean, who was here to begin with? You know who, when Warlock was nothing but Cousins' store and Bill Hake's saloon. But then Richelin got his silver strike and everybody comes crowding in, and now it's beginning to look like there is no more room for the ones that was here first."

"There is room, Abe," Bud said.

"Just if I make room, it looks like. Bud, I was friendly with people and took care of my own and got along, and people looked up to me some. But not any more. Because there is someone come in that is trying to run me off like you would a dirty, stinking dog. Turning people against me—" His voice began to shake, and he stopped.

Bud said, "So now you are going up to Bright's City and have your own lied free, or the jury scared off, one. Or both. You will trick and mess the law around like you want it until—" He hesitated. "Until you get Clay Blaisedell brought in against you, and then you can't understand it."

"I understand it," Abe said. "I understand he has got people thinking he is Jesus Christ, so that makes me a black devil from hell. I understand it, and you too, Bud. I put you and Billy on when your Daddy died, Bud, but I guess you have surely forgot that."

"No," Bud said. "I haven't forgot it. But there is other things I can't forget either."

Curley said quickly, "There is some things better forgot."

"You son of a bitch!" Abe whispered. Curley saw that he had his hand on the haft of his knife. His lips were pulled back white against his teeth, and the long wrinkles in his cheeks were etched deep. "You son of a bitch!"

Bud licked his lips. When he spoke his voice was dead and dry. "I've come against things like that, is all," he said. "A thing happened there at Rattlesnake Canyon that I guess had to happen because of what'd gone before. So what went before was wrong, and I will try to see— Do you think it is easy?" he said loudly. "Because you think I am for Blaisedell against you, when I am not. And people here think the other way around, when I am not. But I am come against what we did in Rattlesnake Canyon, Abe. And against what was tried that night in the Glass Slipper when Jack would have shot a man in the back like you'd kill a fly. One fly, or seventeen flies."

Abe sucked his breath in; he cried, "If you say I fixed it to back-shoot Blaisedell you are a liar!"

Curley tried to say jokingly, "Why, Bud, that kind of hits at me, don't it? I thought that was my fight. My back-off, anyhow." But he felt sick all the way down. He sighed and said, "Where you've gone wrong, Bud. You know where you went wrong? There's been bad things done, surely, but you went wrong lining up against your own instead of trying to change them. Against your friends, Bud; against your brother! That's no good! They are the most important people there is to a man; why, nobody else counts. Your friends and kin—Billy. You know that's wrong!"

"He doesn't think so," Abe said, easily now. "You can see that."

Curley said, "Do you think Billy run that stage and killed that passenger, Bud?" He watched Bud look down at his hat, and crease the top with the edge of his hand.

"Happen to know he didn't," Abe said.

"Luke says he didn't, Bud."

"But you'd have him hang," Abe said.

"He killed a posseman," Bud said tiredly.

"Oh, that's right," Abe said, mockingly. "Banging away at him and he was supposed to just let himself get shot up. Hang for just trying to defend himself."

"Let him plead it then," Bud said. "He wouldn't hang if he got a fair trial. But he will be lied off for what he didn't do in the first place, and stuck with it. No, he won't hang and he won't even go to the territorial, for you will get him off. And I don't guess you will ever see how you killed him by it."

Curley stared at him, uncomprehending, and Abe laughed and said, "My, you are a real worrier, aren't you?" His voice tightened as he went on. "Well, I know what you want—you want us all to hang for that in Rattlesnake Canyon. Don't you? You are like a hellfire-and-damnation preacher gone loco on bad whisky. All for a bunch of stinking, murdering greasers that wasn't worth the lead it cost to burn them down!" He stopped and rubbed a hand across his mouth, and Curley thought of Dad McQuown in one of his fits as he saw the shine of spit in Abe's beard. "But you were there!" Abe cried. "Shooting and hollering with the rest!"

Then Abe said softly, "Well, I am warning you, Bud."

Bud got to his feet and stood, stoop-shouldered, facing Abe. All at once he looked angry. "Warning me what?"

"Why, how Cade knows you have been making talk he was out to backshoot Blaisedell." Abe swiped at his mouth again, and Curley saw his eyes waver from Bud's; they would not meet his, either. Then Abe grinned and said, "But maybe Billy will keep him off you, if he doesn't get hung."

"Cade must be scared I'll tell Blaisedell," Bud said slowly. "Are you, Abe?"

Abe grunted as though he'd been hit in the belly, and snatched for his knife. Curley leaped toward him and caught his wrist. It took all his strength to thrust that steel wrist down, and the knife down, while Abe glared past him at Bud, panting, his teeth bared and beads of sweat on his forehead. "You are to quit this, Abe!" Curley whispered. "I mean right now directly! You are making a damned fool of yourself!" And Abe's hand relaxed against his. Abe resheathed the knife.

"Because I won't," Bud said. "And haven't. That's done. You can get out of here now. We have said all we have to say, I guess."

Abe's eyes glittered as Curley stepped back away from him. "Why, Bud," Abe said. "I'll take almost anything off you, and have today—because we've been friends. But I won't take you telling me to get out."

"Let's go get some whisky and get along to Bright's, Abe," Curley said. "I mean! I'm not going to hang around here if I'm not wanted."

"Go, if you want," Abe said. Footsteps came along the planks outside, a shadow fell in the door. Abe swung around with his hand jerking back.

Pike Skinner came in, and Curley almost laughed with relief. Pike looked uncomfortable in a tight-fitting suit; he wore a new black, broad-brimmed hat and his shell belt under his sack coat. He halted as he saw them, and scowled. His flap ears turned red.

"Well, howdy, Pike," Curley said. "That is a mighty fine-looking suit of clothes you have got on there."

"Friends come in to see you, did they?" Pike said to Bud, in a rasping voice.

"Anything wrong with it?" Abe said.

"Yes!" Pike said, his face going as red as his ears. He squinted suddenly as though he had a tic. "Looks like something going on to me. There is two sides clear now, Gannon. You've got your pick!"

"You've picked, have you?" Abe said. "It was clear enough brother Paul already did."

"I surely have," Pike said. He stood with his hands held waist-high, as though he didn't really want to make a move, but thought he'd better have them handy in case his mouth got away from him.

"Boo!" Curley said, and laughed to see him start.

Pike flushed redder still. He said to Gannon, "If you are with these people, say so. And get out of here. You have got your pick now, and I will—"

"What if I don't pick?" Bud said.

Pike's eyes kept moving, watching Abe's hands, and Curley's. Curley heard Abe laugh softly. "Nobody sits the rail any more!" Pike said.

Grinning, Curley rested his hands on his shell belt and stretched his shoulders. "Why, give me a good rail to sit for comfort. I will do it every time."

Bud said nothing, and Curley realized that Bud could have made to please Pike, who was on the Citizens' Committee, and decent enough for a townsman, by repeating the order to get out. Bud didn't, and he respected him for it. Bud looked as though he didn't give a good God damn about anything right now.

"Let's move along, Abe. I can't stand this being picked against. Hurts my feelings."

"Going to Bright's City, Pike?" Abe asked.

"God-damned right I am!"

"See you there." Abe moved sideways toward the door. "See you, Bud," he said. "See you when we all hang together."

Abe went on out. Curley tipped his hat back onto his head, saluted Pike, and followed Abe out. He didn't look at Bud. Silently he walked back along the boardwalk beside Abe.

"Let's get riding to Bright's," Abe said in a stifled voice. "I hate this rotten town."

"Sure is down on you," he said. He felt for Abe. It was hard when everybody turned against you. It would be hard on any man, but it was a terrible thing on Abe.

"Sons of dirty whore bitches," Abe said. "Damn them to burning hell and Bud Gannon the first of them!"

Reluctantly Curley said, "Abe, you shouldn't have gone at him so. He is a cold one and no mistake, and I couldn't see it the way he does and ever look at myself shaving again, but—" He broke off as Abe halted and swung toward him. Abe's face was fierce again, his eyes like green ice. "—but you have got to hand it to a man that's doing what he thinks is right," he went on, staring straight back. "Whatever."

"I'll hand him what he handed me," Abe said. "Which is shit."

"Abe—" he started again, but Abe moved off across the street toward Goodpasture's store. Following him, he felt a dull anguish, for Abe, for Bud, for everyone. He wondered how everything had got so messed up; worse, it seemed, all the time. Maybe it was Blaisedell after all.

He glanced down toward where Mosbie stood. He and Mosbie had drunk together many a time; now he felt the anguish sharpen to see the carefully blank expression on Mosbie's face, and the same expressions on the faces of the other men watching. Why, they all hated Abe, he thought; and they hated him, too.

As he followed Abe through the dust to Goodpasture's corner, and then down the boardwalk toward the Acme Corral, he felt anger begin to stir in him, and a retaliation of hate. What had done it to them all, he wondered? It must, he thought again, have been Blaisedell, after all.

17. Journals of Henry Holmes Goodpasture

February 1, 1881

THE latest bag of road agents has been acquitted by a Bright's City jury. There is high feeling here, and those who journeyed to Bright's City to give evidence or as spectators are exceedingly violent in their anger against judge, jury, lawyers, Bright's City in general, and Abraham McQuown in particular. Since Benner was the only bandit positively identified by his victims, the defense mounted the outrageous presumption that the other two were consequently innocent, and, that since both of these swore that Benner had been with them all day and that they had engaged in no crimes whatsoever, then Benner was also innocent. The witnesses who identified Benner were tricked into admitting that the main factor in their identification was his small stature, which was made to seem ridiculous. The posse itself, it was claimed, was responsible for Phlater's death, since it had begun firing wildly at the "innocent cowboys" as soon as they were within range, and the Cowboys plainly could not be blamed for defending themselves from such a vicious assault. It was implied even further that the whole affair was staged by "certain parties," and the strongbox carefully disposed where it would implicate the poor Cowboys most foully.

It is said that the prosecution was pursued with less than diligence. It is also said that judge and jury were bribed, and that the courtroom was crowded with McQuown's men brandishing six-shooters and muttering threats. Along the way my credulity begins to fail, amongst all this evidence of perfidy, but the fact remains that the three men have been freed. They rode through here yesterday on their way back to San Pablo. They encountered a sullen and most unfriendly Warlock, and had sense enough not to linger here in their triumph.

I think next time it may be very difficult to discourage a lynching party from its objective.

Still, certain good has come out of the affair. Public opinion, as it did when our poor barber was killed and Deputy Canning driven out of town, has again congealed, so that the Citizens' Committee feels itself in not so exposed and arbitrary a position in trying to administer some kind of law in Warlock.

The Citizens' Committee has not met yet. We are not in a hurry to face the situation, and feel it best to move slowly. The question foremost in everyone's mind is, of course, whether or not Blaisedell should be called upon to post the "innocent Cowboys" out of town, and, insofar as I can see, the great majority of the Citizens' Committee, and of Warlock itself, is for this. There is much talk of a Vigilante Army convened to ride upon San Pablo and "clean the rascals out." There is also talk of posting McQuown and *all* his men, and backing up Blaisedell in whatever action might ensue with a vigilante troop, which would be only operative within Warlock and for this one purpose.

As to the wholesale posting, you may hear it being argued on every hand, but with qualifications almost as numerous as the arguers. I think some of us are obsessed with the pleasure and presumption of dictating Life & Death.

There are also some who seem to be having grave second thoughts about the whole system of posting. Will Hart, I notice, is beginning to sound remarkably like the judge in his arguments. True, these say, posting worked in the case of Earnshaw, who is definitely reported to have left the territory—but is it not asking for trouble? Does not posting actually make it a point of honor that a man come in to fight our Marshal? What if a number come in against him at once and he is killed—are we not then still more at the mercy of the outlaws? What, if this be carried too far, is to prevent the enemies of each among us from seeing that he himself is posted?

I must face the fact, of course, that Public Opinion is not so unanimous as I would like to think. There are issues at stake, but as too often happens, we are apt to look to men as symbols rather than to the issues themselves. There are two sides here; one is Blaisedell, the other McQuown. So, alas, have the people chosen to see it. Blaisedell is, at the moment, the favored one by far; the *profanum vulgus* is solidly for him, and, as evinced by the lynch mob (which, curiously, Blaisedell had a large hand in putting down), against McQuown and the "innocents." The Citizens' Committee, of course, is behind Blaisedell too, but, as is usual when some are more violently partisan than we are, we edge away a little and restrain our own enthusiasms.

Still, McQuown retains some of his adherents. Grain, the beef butcher, who, I am sure, buys stolen beef from McQuown, remains loyal to him. Ranchers, such as Blaikie, Quaintance, and Burbage, view the outlaw as a necessary evil, point out that their problems would be greatly increased without the presence of a controlling hand, and in any case are apt to view Blaisedell, possibly because he is a townsman and an agent of townsmen, with suspicion.

I do not think the Citizens' Committee intends to do more than post the three road agents (or more probably four, including Friendly) out of town, but that remains to be seen. There is some talk of posting at the same time a chronic malcontent and agitator among the miners, but I feel this would confuse the present issue. I presume a meeting will be called by this week's end, at the latest.

February 2, 1881

I am sorry for Deputy Gannon. He must know that his brother's fate is being decided, all around him, by the jury this town has become, and he looks gaunt and haunted, and as though he has not slept in days. He, Schroeder, and the Marshal have not had much to occupy their time of late. Warlock is in a fit of righteousness, and men are exceedingly careful in their actions. The presence of Death does not make us feel pity for the dead or the condemned, but only a keen awareness of our own ultimate end and a determination to circumvent it for as long as possible.

February 3, 1881

A despicable rumor is being circulated, to the effect that the Cowboys are truly innocent, and that the bandits actually were Morgan and one or more of his employees from the Glass Slipper; that Morgan was seen riding furtively back to town not long after the stage arrived here, etc. This is an obvious tactic of McQuown's adherents here to backhandedly attack Blaisedell, as well as of Morgan's enemies, of whom there are a great number. Why Morgan should have taken up road-agentry, when he has a most lucrative business in his gambling establishment, has not been stated.

Morgan is certainly roundly hated here, with good reason and bad. I might venture to say that unanimity of opinion comes closest to obtaining in Warlock as regards dislike of him. Personally, I think I would choose him over his competitor, Taliaferro, and I am sure that Taliaferro relieves his customers of their earnings no less rapidly or crookedly than Morgan. Yet Morgan does it with a completely unconcealed disdain of his victims and their manner of play. His contempt of his fellows is always visible, and his habitual expression is that of one who has seen all the world and found none of it worth while, least of all its inhabitants. He has evidently acted viciously enough upon occasion too. There was the instance of a Cowboy who worked for Quaintance, a handsome and well-liked young fellow named Newman, who, unfortunately, had larcenous tendencies. He stole three hundred dollars from his employer, which he promptly lost over Morgan's faro layout. Quaintance learned of this and applied to Morgan for the return of the money. Morgan did return it, possibly under pressure from Blaisedell, but dispatched one of his hirelings, a fellow named Murch, after young Newman. Murch caught him in Bright's City and, following Morgan's instructions, beat the boy half to death.

Like others of prominence here Morgan has been the object of many foul, and, I am sure, untrue tales. Unlike others, he seems pleased and flattered by this attention (I suppose this furnishes further evidence to him in support of his opinions of his fellow man), and has even sometimes hinted that the most incredible accusations of him may be true.

Because of all this, however, Blaisedell, in his fast friendship with Morgan, is rendered most vulnerable. I hope Morgan does not become the Marshal's Achilles' heel.

18. The Doctor Arranges Matters

THE doctor hurried panting up the steps of the General Peach and into the thicker darkness of the entryway. He rapped on Jessie's door; his knuckles stung. "Jessie!"

He heard her steps. Her face appeared, pale with the light on it, framed in curls. "What's the matter, David?" she said as she opened the door wider for him. He moved in past her. A book lay open on the table, a blue ribbon across the page for a bookmark. "What's the matter?" she said again.

"They have instructed him to post five men out," he said, and sat down abruptly in the chair beside the door. He held up his hand, spread-fingered, and watched it shake with the sickening rage in him. "Benner, Billy Gannon, Calhoun, and Friendly. *And* he is to post Frank Brunk."

She cried out, "Oh, they have not done that!"

"They have indeed."

She looked frightened. He watched her close the book over the blue ribbon. She stood beside the table with her head bent forward and her ringleted hair sliding forward along her cheeks. Then she sank down onto the sofa opposite him.

"I have talked myself dry to the bone," he said. "It did no good. It was not even a close vote. Henry and Will Hart and myself—and Taliaferro, of course, who would not want to offend the miners' trade. The judge had already left in a rage."

"But it is a mistake, David!"

"They did it very well," he went on. "I will admit myself that Brunk is a troublemaker. His activities could easily lead to bloodshed. Lathrop's did. Brunk has been posted to protect the miners from themselves—that is the way Godbold put it. And to protect Warlock from another mob of crazed muckers running wild and smashing everything—that is the way Slavin put it. What if they fired the Medusa stope? Or all the stopes, for that matter? I think the only thing Charlie MacDonald had to say in the matter was what would happen to Warlock if the miners, led by Brunk, succeeded in closing all the mines out of spite? Evidently they are thought entirely capable of it."

He beat his fist down on the arm of the chair. And so we fell into the trap we had set for ourselves when we brought Blaisedell here, he thought. "It was so well done!" he cried. "But Jessie, if you had been at the meeting, they could not have done it."

"Posting men from Warlock is nothing I can—"

"You should have gone!"

"I will go to see every one of them now."

"It will do no good. Each one will lay it on the rest." He slumped back in the chair; he told himself firmly that he would not hate Godbold, Buck Slavin, Jared Robinson, Kennon, or any of the others; he would only try to understand their fears. What angered him most was the knowledge that they were, in part, right about Frank Brunk. But he knew, too, that he himself was now inescapably on the side of the miners. Heaven knew that a blundering, stupid leader such as Brunk was no good to them; but Brunk was all, at present, that they had. It was as though he had, at last, come face to face with himself, and, at the same moment, saw that the man who was his own mortal enemy was Charles MacDonald of the Medusa mine.

"Poor Clay," he heard Jessie whisper.

"Poor *Clay!* Not poor Frank? Not those poor fellows—" He stopped. She had said it was a mistake, and he saw now what she meant. The miners' angel had become the guardian of Blaisedell's reputation. All at once he could regard her more coldly than he had ever done before.

"Yes," he said. "It is a terrible mistake. Do you think you can persuade Blaisedell that he must do no such a thing?"

"I must try," she said, nodding as though Clay Blaisedell were the object of both their concerns.

"Yes," he said. "For if he does this to Brunk, how is he any better than Jack Cade, who was hired to do it to Lathrop? And you know what Frank is like as well as I do. I think he would not go if ordered to, and how would Clay deal with him then? Frank is no gunman."

He glanced at her from under his brows. She was sitting very stiffly, with her hands clasped white in her lap. Her great eyes seemed to fill the frail triangle of her face. "Oh, no," she said, with a start, as though she had not been listening but knew some reply was called for. "No, he can't be allowed to do it. Of course he can't. It would be terribly wrong."

"I'm glad we agree, Jessie."

She frowned severely. "But if I can't persuade him to—to disobey the Citizens' Committee, then Frank will have to go. That's all there is to it. He will go if I ask him to, won't he, David?"

He did not know, and said so. She announced decisively that she wished to speak with Brunk first, and he left her to find him. In the entryway, with her door closed behind him, he stood with a hand to his chest and his eyes blind in the solid dark. He had thought she was in love with a man, but now he saw, with almost a pity for Blaisedell, that she was in love merely with a name, like a silly schoolgirl.

The doctor moved slowly along the tunnel of darkness toward the lighted hospital room. The faces in the cots turned toward him as he entered. Four men were playing cards on Buell's cot—Buell,

Dill, MacGinty, and Ben Tittle. The boy Fitzsimmons stood watching them, with the thick wads of his bandaged hands crossed over his chest.

There was a chorus of greetings. "What about the road agents, Doc?" someone called to him.

"Did Blaisedell post those cowboys yet?"

He nodded curtly, and asked if anyone had seen Brunk.

"Him and Frenchy's up in old man Heck's room, I think," Mac-Ginty said.

"You want him, Doc?" Fitzsimmons said. "I'll go tell him." He went out, his bandaged hands held protectively before him.

"Hey, Doc, how many got posted?" a man called.

"Four," he said. Someone laughed; there was a swell of excited speculation. He said. "Ben, could I see you for a minute?"

He stepped back out into the dark hall. When Tittle came out, he told him to go find Blaisedell in half an hour. Then he went back down to Jessie's room; she glanced up at him and apprehensively smiled when he entered, and he went over and put out a hand to touch her shoulder. But he did not quite touch it, and, as he stared down at the curve of her cheek and the warm brown glow of the lamplight in her hair, his throat swelled with pain, for her. He turned away and his eye caught the dark mezzotint of Bonnie Prince Charlie, kilted, beribboned, gripping his sword in noble and silly bravado.

He heard heavy footsteps descending the stairs. "Come in, Frank," he said, as Brunk appeared in the doorway.

Brunk came inside. "Miss Jessie," he said. "Doc. What was it, Doc?"

"The Citizens' Committee has voted to have you posted out as a troublemaker," he said, and saw Brunk's eyes narrow, his scar of a mouth tighten whitely.

"Did they now?" Brunk said, in a hoarse voice. All at once he grinned. "Is the marshal going to kill me, Miss Jessie?"

"Don't be silly, Frank."

Brunk held out his hands and looked down at them. Then, with a ponderous, triumphant lift of his head Brunk looked up at the doctor and said, "Why, I expect he is going to have to, Doc. Do you know? The boys wouldn't move for Tom Cassady, but maybe they will if—"

"Don't be a fool!" he said.

"Now, Frank, you are to listen to me," Jessie said, in a crisp, sure voice, and she rose and approached Brunk. "I am going to ask him not to do this thing, whatever the Citizens' Committee has decided. But if I—"

"Ah!" Brunk broke in. "The miners' angel!"

"You will be civil, Brunk!"

A flush darkened Brunk's face. He took hold of his forelock and pulled his head down, as though in obeisance. "Bless you, Miss Jessie," he said. "I am beholden to you again."

"I have promised to try," Jessie went on. "But as I was saying when you interrupted me—if I cannot, then you must promise to leave."

"Run for it?" Brunk said. "Run?"

"Do you have to go out of your way to be offensive, Brunk?"

"Doc, I am trying to go out of my way to be a man! But she won't let me, will she? She will nurse me off this. She is too heavy an angel! She wouldn't let Tom Cassady die when he was begging to. She won't let me—" He stopped, and his mouth drew sharply down at the corners. "If I had courage enough," he said. "But maybe I don't."

"I don't know what you are talking about, Frank."

"I don't know what I am talking about either. Because they would not move even for me, and I would be a fool. But what would *you* do, Doc?"

"I think I would do as she asks," he said, and could not meet Brunk's eyes.

"Why, I have to, don't I?" Brunk said. "She has kept me since I was fired at the Medusa. Put up with me, and fed me. But, Miss Jessie—you said Jim Lathrop didn't have courage enough. Why won't you let me have it? Maybe I have got enough."

"I'm sure I don't know what you are talking about," Jessie said. "But if you will not do this for your own sake—and I understand that men must have their pride, Frank—then you must do it for mine. I hope it will not be necessary."

Brunk stared at her. "Why, I would be a fool, wouldn't I?" he said in his heavy, infinitely bitter voice. "And ungrateful too, since it is for your sake, Miss Jessie. But don't you see, Doc?"

The doctor could say nothing, and Jessie put a sympathetic hand on Brunk's arm. But Brunk drew away from her touch and backed out the door. His heavy tread slowly remounted the stairs.

"I don't understand," Jessie said, in a shaky voice.

"Don't you?" he said. "Brunk was just wishing he might be a hero, and knows he cannot be. It is difficult for a man to bring himself to be a martyr when he is afraid he might look a fool instead. Do you think you can persuade Blaisedell?"

She did not answer. She was staring at him strangely, tugging at the little locket that hung around her throat.

"It is very important that you do," he went on. "Because of what the miners would think of you if Blaisedell went through with this. Whether Brunk fled, or not. And because of what everyone would think of Blaisedell."

He felt a blackguard; he turned so as to confront himself in her glass, and saw there a short, gray man with bowed shoulders in a shabby black suit, undistinguished looking, not handsome, not heroic in any way, almost old. The eyes that gazed back at him from the glass looked like those of a man with a dangerous fever.

"There is Clay," Jessie whispered, as footsteps came along the boardwalk outside her window.

"I wish you luck with him, Jessie," he said. He went out into the entryway just as Blaisedell entered; a little light from Jessie's open door gleamed in the marshal's hair as he took off his hat.

"Evening, Doc," he said gravely.

"Pardon me," the doctor said, and Blaisedell stepped aside so that he could pass.

Outside he stood on the porch for a moment, breathing deeply of the fresh, cool air, and gazing up at the stars bright and cold over Warlock. Behind him he heard Blaisedell say, "Did you want to see me, Jessie?" Quickly the doctor descended the steps to get out of earshot. He went up the boardwalk, across Main Street, and on up toward Peach Street and the Row.

19. A Warning

IN THE jail Carl Schroeder, Peter Bacon, Chick Hasty, and Pike Skinner were talking about the posting, while at the cell door Al Bates, from up valley, watched them with his whiskered chin resting on one of the crossbars.

"You suppose the news got down to Pablo yet?" Hasty asked.

"Dechine was in," Bacon said, from his chair at the rear. "And went back down valley yesterday. I expect he'd take it as neighborly to stop in and tell McQuown the news on his way home."

"They won't come," Schroeder said, hunched over the table, scowling, gouging the point of a pencil into the table top.

Hasty said, "I guess Johnny's plenty worried Billy'll show."

"Worried of getting in bad with McQuown, mostly," Skinner said. "He—"

"You!" Schroeder said. "I am sick of hearing you picking at Johnny Gannon!" He flung the pencil down. "He come in here and put on that star, *you* didn't! You quit fretting at him, Mister Citizens' Committee Skinner!"

Peering up at Skinner from under his hat brim, Hasty said, "Is MacDonald going to see the Committee fires Blaisedell for saying them no on that jack, Pike?"

"He did right," Skinner said, with a sour face. "Nobody's thought of firing him. MacDonald fired that son of a bitch Brunk how long ago, but he still hangs around trying to drum up a fuss. It's the Committee's business to post out troublemakers, but Blaisedell can't go against a dumb jack that doesn't know one end of a Colt from the other."

"Old Owen was saying he heard some muckers talking that if the Committee fired Blaisedell over it, the miners would get together and hire him themself," Schroeder said. "And put him to post MacDonald first thing."

The others laughed.

"There is talk Miss Jessie had a hand in the marshal changing his mind about Brunk," Hasty said.

"Lot of talk up our way them two is going to come to matrimony right quick," Bates said from the cell. "Make a fine-looking couple."

Nobody spoke for a time, and finally Bacon sighed and said, "You suppose the four of them is going to come against him? Or not?"

"They won't come," Schroeder said again, grimly. He began to jab his pencil at the table top once more.

Standing in the doorway Skinner worriedly shook his head. He turned as there was an approaching cracking sound on the boardwalk.

"Here comes old Judge," Bates said. "Charging along on that crutch of his to give everybody pure hell again."

The judge entered past Skinner. With his shoulders hunched up by the crutch and his claw-hammer coat hanging loose, the judge looked like a big, awkward, black bird. He halted and his bloodshot eyes glared fiercely around the jail. "Where's the deputy?"

"Here!" Schroeder said. He raised himself reluctantly from the judge's chair, and leaned against the cell door.

"Not you. The other one."

"Sleeping, I guess. He was on late last night."

"There's no sleep any more," the judge said. He shifted his weight from the crutch to a hand braced on the table, and sat down with a grunt. His crutch clattered to the floor.

"Aw, please, Judge," Hasty said. "Leave us sleep sometimes. We got little enough else."

The judge scraped his chair around to face the others. "You would sleep through the roof of the world caving in and not even know it," he said. He removed his hat, using both hands, and set it before him. He glared around the room.

"By God, you stink, Judge," Skinner said. "Why don't you come down to the Acme and me and Paul and Nate'll scrape you down in the horse trough?"

"I don't stink like you all stink." The judge rubbed at his eyes, muttering to himself. "Where is Blaisedell?" he said suddenly. "He is running from me!"

Everyone laughed. "Laugh!" the judge cried. "Why, you poor, ignorant pus-and-corruption sons of bitches, he is afraid of me!"

"He's went for his gold-handles, Judge," Schroeder said. "Then he'll show."

They laughed again, but the laughter broke off abruptly as a shadow fell in the door. Blaisedell came in, bowing his head a little as he stepped through the doorway. He was coatless, wearing a clean linen shirt and a broad, scrolled-leather shell belt, with a single cedar-handled Colt holstered on his right thigh.

"Judge," he said. He nodded to each of them. "Deputy. Boys. Looking for me, Judge?"

"I was," the judge said, and Bates snickered. The judge said, "I am warning you, Marshal. You are now standing naked and all alone. The Citizens' Committee has gone and disqualified itself plain to everyone from pretending to run any kind of law in this town. Ordering you to something that wasn't only illegal and bad but was pure damned outrage besides. And you have gone and disqualified yourself from them by refusing to do it. Now!" he said, triumphantly.

Blaisedell took off his hat and idly slapped it against his knee. He looked at once amused and arrogant. "You are speaking for who, Judge?" he asked politely.

"I am speaking—" the judge said. His voice turned shrill. "I'm speaking for— I'm just warning you, Marshal!"

"Listen to him go at it!" Bates whispered. "By God, he is a real Turk, that old Judge."

Blaisedell glanced at him and he looked abashed.

"For what you have done," the judge went on, more calmly, "you have run up a ukase on those four boys all by yourself now."

"Pardon?" Blaisedell said.

"Now, hold on, Judge—" Schroeder began.

"Ukase!" the judge said. "That is a kind of imperial king I-want. What the king does when he makes the rules as he goes along. You have run one up the flagstaff and yourself with it. For what was behind you has blown itself out to nothing, and you have walked off away from it anyhow. I told you it was the only thing you had! And a poor thing, but even it gone now."

"Don't listen to the old cowpat, Marshal," Skinner said placatingly. "He has got a load on and raving. He is not talking for anybody. He is surely not talking for the Citizens' Committee."

"I am talking for his conscience," the judge said. "If he can hear it talking in his pride!"

"Why, I can hear you, Judge," Blaisedell said. He stood looking down at the judge with his eyebrows hooked up, and his mouth, beneath the fair mustache, flat and grave. "But saying what?"

"Saying there is nothing you are accountable to any more," the judge said. "You have got no status, you have chucked it away. No blame to you for that, Marshal, but it is gone. What I am saying is you can't post those four fellers out. You are no law-making body. You can't make laws against four men. Neither could the Citizens' Committee, but they had a better claim than you. Mister Blaisedell, you are running up a banishment-or-death ukase and it is illegal and outlaw and pure murder. There is no law behind you!"

"Fry your head in your God-damned law!" Skinner said. "We saw enough of it, up in Bright's City."

The judge massaged his eyes with his hands again. Then he squinted cunningly up at Skinner. "You saw lynch law here in town just before that," he said. "You didn't like that either, did you? Liked that some less, didn't you?" he cried. Pressing down on the table top, he half-raised his thick body, and cords stood out on the sides of his neck. "Did you like that mob? I tell you he is a one-man lynch mob if he goes on like he is headed!"

"By God!" Bates whispered, admiringly. "I bet he could beller a brick wall down."

The judge sank back into his seat. Blaisedell's intense blue stare inspected, one by one, the men in the room. They fastened last upon the judge again, and he said, coldly, "One man is a different thing from a mob. If a man runs with a pack like that he is only a part of the pack and the whole thing hasn't got a brain or anything. I say what you said just now is foolishness, and I think you know it. I am not scared of myself so I have to look around every second to make sure the Citizens' Committee is standing right behind, nodding to me. Or the town either," he said, glancing at Hasty. "Because in a thing like this I know best and can do best by myself."

"You have said it out loud!" the judge whispered. "You have said it. You have set yourself above the rest in your pride!"

Blaisedell's face tightened. "If I am hired to keep the peace in this town," he said, slowly and distinctly, "why, I will do it and the best I can. Judge, I would keep those four birds out of town whether anyone told me to or not."

"You are not going to keep them out! You are going to kill them! You are going to shoot them down dog-dead in the street, or them you. Keep the peace! Why, if that don't make somebody a murderer and somebody dead that didn't need to be then I can't see across my nose! Keep the peace! Why, you will bust it wide open with your hail-to-the-king ukase!"

"Maybe," Blaisedell said. "But most likely they won't come in."

"They will come!" the judge said. "I'll tell you why they will come. Because now they are guilty-as-sin road agents to every man, and they know it. They are that if they stay out, and yellow-bellies besides. If they come in they will think they are honest-to-genuine, gilt-edged heroes proving they are innocent to all, and striking a blow for freedom too. Men have died for that many's the time, and God bless them for it!"

"They know better than to come," Skinner said.

"They will have to come. And you, Mister Marshall of Warlock Blaisedell, have made it so. There is no way out of it. So you will have to kill them. And that will put you wrong. You will fall by it, son."

"Don't call me son, Judge," Blaisedell said, very quietly. A vein began to beat in his temple.

The judge said in a blurred voice, "Marshal, if you understand me and go your way anyhow, God help you. You will be killing men out of pride. You will be doing foul murder before the law, and you will stand trial in Bright's City for it or these deputies here ought to throw their badges in the river. For you will be an illegal black criminal and outlaw and murderer with the blood fresh on you as bad as any of McQuown's and worse, and every man's hand should be against you. Murder for pride, Marshal; it is an ancient and awful crime to go to book for."

Blaisedell backed up a step, to stand in the patch of sunlight just inside the door. He put his hat back on and tapped it once, and glanced around the jail again. This time no one met his eyes.

Blaisedell said gravely, "Maybe somebody will get killed, Judge. But that is between them and me, for who else is hurt by it?"

"Every man is," the judge whispered.

Blaisedell flushed, and the arrogant, masklike expression came over his face again. But his voice remained pleasant. "You have been going on about pride like it was a bad thing, and I disagree with you. A man's pride is about the only thing he has that's worth having, and is what sets him apart from the pack. We have argued this before, Judge, and I guess I will say this time that a man that doesn't have it is a pretty poor specimen and apt to take to whisky for the lack. For all whisky is, is pride you can pour in your belly."

The judge flushed too, as Bates snickered and Schroeder grinned. "That was a mean thing you said, Marshal," the judge said. "But I won't say it isn't so, so maybe I am honester than you. And I don't have to be scared of you, either, Marshal."

Skinner said disgustedly, "You a poor, one-legged, loud-mouthed old—"

The judge raised a finger toward Blaisedell's face. "Being decent like you are—and I didn't say you wasn't!—I think you can brace no man that has got right on you; I think you know that. It is what I am warning you. What you are working toward in your pride is some day meeting a man that has got to kill you or you him, only he is righter and you know it. Because you have gone wrong. And what are you going to do then?" His voice sank until it was almost inaudible. "That is the box, Clay Blaisedell. What are you going to do then?"

There was a taut silence. Blaisedell's face had paled, except for the spots of color on his cheeks. "Judge Holloway," he said, in his deep voice. "I think you haven't only been drinking." He paused ominously. "I think you have been drinking out in the hot sun."

Everyone laughed explosively in the sudden release of tension, and Blaisedell himself grinned. "Well, I guess I will go have a glass of whisky for my bruised-up pride," he said, and turned to go out.

"Marshal," Pike Skinner said. "I just want to say—" His angular, ugly face reddened furiously. "I just wanted to say the judge wasn't speaking for me just now, and I know he wasn't speaking for Carl Schroeder. I expect he wasn't speaking for anybody but Taliaferro's bad whisky."

"That's right, Marshal," Schroeder said.

"That goes for me, Marshal," Hasty said, and got to his feet.

Peter Bacon said nothing. His brown, lined face was sad. The marshal glanced at him. Then he nodded silently to the others and went on outside.

The judge rubbed his hands over his face. Then he turned to Schroeder; his dark face was drawn and puckered around the wart on his cheek. "You mark what I have said, Carl Schroeder. He is going to kill men and it will be on you to arrest him for it. Hear?"

"I don't hear," Schroeder said. "You are acting like a damned virgin, Judge. Like you have never known a man to be shot down before. It'll be a day when I try to arrest Blaisedell."

The judge bent, grunting, to recover his crutch, and then, red-faced with effort, thrust himself upright and hooked the crutch under his armpit. He set his hat, which was too small for him, on his head. He said contemptuously, "Maybe you will see, some day, how if you are bound to arrest some of McQuown's people for a thing, you are bound to arrest another man the same. So if Blaisedell goes out and murders—"

"Great God, Judge!" Schroeder cried. "You are getting it all switched around who is murderers here!"

The judge hobbled toward the door, his crutch tip racketing. Pike Skinner glared at him. At the door the judge turned again, the hat slipping forward over one eye. "We all are, boys," he said. He swung on outside on his crutch and his one good leg.

20. Gannon Has a Nightmare

IT IS a dream, he told himself; it is only a dream. Sweating, naked, daubed with mud, he crouched behind a crag upon the canyon wall and watched against the curtain of his memory the sandy river bottom of Rattlesnake Canyon, listening in the waiting silence to the pad of hoof irons in the sand and the sharper, urgent sound as a hoof struck stone, and, nearer, the musical clink of harness, and nearer still, voices soft-mouthed with Spanish; his heart turning over on itself as the first one came around the far bend upon a narrow-faced white horse, looking very tall at first in his high, peaked sombrero, but small, compact, brown, watchful-eyed, with pointed mustachios, behind him another and another, some with striped serapes hung over their shoulders and all with rifles carried underarm; seven, eight, and more and more, until there were seventeen in all, and Abe's Colt crashed the signal. The echo was instantaneous and continuous. Smoke drifted up from all around the canyon where the other mud-daubed figures were concealed, and it was as though an invisible flash flood had in that instant swept down the canyon: horses reared and screamed, swept backward in the flood, and died; men were thrown tumbling, a rifle flung up in a wide arc turning end over end with weird slowness, and there were gobbling Apache cries mixed with the screams of dying men. There was the white horse lying on the reddening sand, there was the leader in his high, silver-chased hat crawling in the stream; then the hat gone, then a part of his head gone, and he lay still in the channel with his jacket shiny and bloated in the water that ran red over him. And now the half-naked, muddy Apache figures stood all around the canyon, yelling as they fired into the mass of dying men and horses below them, the faces magnified and slowly revolving before his eyes —Abe, and Pony and Calhoun and Wash and Chet, and on the far side Billy and Jack Cade, Whitby and Friendly, Mitchell, Harrison, and Hennessey.

And at the end there came the Mexican running and scrambling up the steep bank toward him, hatless, screaming hoarsely, brown eyes huge and rimmed with white like those of a terrified stallion, and the long gleam of the six-shooter in his hand, slipping and sliding but coming with unbelievable rapidity up the canyonside toward him, John Gannon. He changed as he came. Now he came more slowly; now it was a tall, black-hatted figure walking toward him through the dust, slow-striding with the massive and ponderous dignity not of retribution but of justice, with great eyes fixed on him, John Gannon, like ropes securing him, as he cried out and snatched in helpless weakness at his sides, and died screaming mercy, screaming acceptance, screaming protest in the clamorous and horrible silence.

It is only a dream, he told himself, calmly; it is only the dream. But there was another reverberating clap of a shot still. He died again, in peace, and waked with a jolt, as though he had fallen. There was another knock in the darkness of his room.

"Who is it?" he called.

"It's me, Bud," came a whisper. He swung off his cot in his underwear and went to open the door. Billy came in, stealthily. A little moonlight entered through the window, and Billy was visible as he moved past it, wearing a jacket and jeans, his hatbrim pulled low over his face.

"What are you doing in town?"

"Come to see you, Bud." Billy laughed shakily. "Sneaked in. Tomorrow I don't sneak in."

Billy took off his hat and flung it down on the table. He swung the chair around and sat down facing Gannon over its back. The moonlight was white as mother-of-pearl on Billy's face.

Gannon slumped down on the edge of the bed, shivering. "Just you?" he said.

"Pony and Luke and me. Calhoun weaseled."

"Why Pony?"

"What do you mean, why Pony?"

"He hasn't any right to come—he was at the stage. Was Luke in on it, or not?"

"Not," Billy said shortly. Then he said, "It doesn't matter who was at the stage or not."

"No, it doesn't matter now. They were lied off and you with them, so it is too late to tell the truth."

"I don't know what you mean," Billy said. Gannon could see that he was shivering too. "But I have got to do it, Bud."

"Got to get yourself killed?" He had not meant to speak so harshly.

"Don't be so damned sure about that!"

"Got to kill Blaisedell then?"

"Well, somebody's got to, for Christ's sake!"

Gannon closed his eyes. It might be the last time he saw Billy; probably it was; he knew it was. And they would wrangle meaninglessly over who was the son of a bitch, Blaisedell or Abe McQuown. It seemed to him that if he was any kind of man at all he could let Billy have his way tonight.

"Listen, Bud!" Billy said. "I know what you think of Abe."

"Let's not talk about it, Billy. It's no good."

"No, listen. I mean, what is different about him? He goes along the way he always did that used to be all right with everybody, but everybody's got down on him. He gets blamed for everything! He—"

"Like the Apaches used to," he said, and despised himself for saying it.

Billy said in a husky voice, "I know that was a piss-poor thing. Do you think I liked that? But you make too much of it."

"I know I do."

"Well, like the Paches; surely," Billy went on. "But you know what it's like all around here. Every son with a true-bill out against him ends up here, and he has got to eat so he swings a wide loop or tries to agent a coach or something. And Abe gets blamed for it all! But you know damned well—"

"Billy, you are not coming in tomorrow because of Abe."

"Coming in because a man has to stand up and be a man!" Billy said. "That suit you? Because it is a free country and sons of bitches like Blaisedell is trying to make it not."

He looked at Billy's taut, proud young face with the glaze of moonlight on it, and slowly lowered his head and massaged his own face with his hands. Billy's voice had been filled with righteousness and it tore him to hear it, and to hear Abe McQuown behind it furnishing the words that were true enough when Billy spoke them and yet were lies because they came from Abe McQuown.

"But I guess you don't think that way," Billy said.

Gannon shook his head.

"He is after Abe," Billy went on. "He is after all of us! A person can't stand it when there is somebody on the prod for him all the time. Trying to run him out or kill him. A man has got to stand up and—"

"Billy, Blaisedell saved your life when he backed off that lynch party. And Pony's, and Cal's, and maybe mine. And he could have killed Curley that night in the Glass Slipper, if that was what he was after. And you too. And Abe."

"He just wanted to look good, was all. And us to look bad. I know how it would've been if he'd had us alone and nobody to see."

"What if he kills you tomorrow?" he whispered.

"I've got to die some day, Christ's sake!" Billy said, with pitiful bravado. "Anyway he won't. I figure Pony and Luke can stand off Morgan and Carl, or that Murch or whoever he's got to back him. I figure I can outpull him and outshoot him too. I'm not scared of him!"

"What if he kills you?" he said again.

"You keep saying that! You're trying to scare me. You want me to run from him?"

"Yes," he said, and Billy snorted. "Billy—" he said, but he knew it was useless even before he said it. "You weren't at the stage and you shot Ted Phlater in self-defense, but not the way it looked in court. Billy, I can't see you die a damned fool. I—"

"Don't you ever say a thing to anybody about any of that," Billy said coldly. "I am with them, whatever way it happened. That is gone past now. You hear? That's all I ask of you, Bud."

That hurt him, as part of the long hurt that Billy had never been able to think much of him. He sat shivering on the edge of the bed, and now, when he didn't look at his brother, Billy seemed to him already to have become just another name on Blaisedell's score, and just another mound on Boot Hill marked with one of Dick Maples' crosses. With horror he looked back to Billy's moonlit face.

"Billy, I don't mean it any way and you don't have to say if you don't want to, but—do you want to die?"

Billy was silent for a long time. He leaned back and his face was lost in shadow. Then he laughed scornfully, and one of his bootheels thumped on the floor. But his voice was not scornful: "No, I am afraid of dying as any man, I guess, Bud." He rose abruptly. "Well, I'll be going. Pony and Luke are camped out in the malapai a way." He started toward the door, pushing his hat down hard on his head.

"Sleep here if you want. I'm not going to try to argue with you any more. I know you are going to do what you are set on doing."

"Surely am," Billy said. He sounded childishly pleased. "No, I'll go on out there, I guess. Thanks." At the door he said, "Going to wish me luck?"

Gannon didn't answer.

"Or Blaisedell?" Billy said.

"Not him because you are my brother. Not you because you are wrong."

"Thanks." Billy pulled the door open.

"Wait," he said, getting to his feet. "Billy—I know if somebody shot me down you would take after them. I guess I had better tell you I won't do it. Because you are wrong."

"I don't expect anything of you," Billy said, and was gone. He left the door open behind him.

Gannon crossed to the door. He couldn't see Billy in the darkness of the hallway, but after a moment he heard the slow, stealthy descent of bootheels in the stairwell. He waited in the darkness until the sounds had ceased, and then he closed the door and returned to his cot, where he flung himself down with his face buried in the pillow and grief tearing at his mind like a dagger.

21. The Acme Corral

I

(From the sworn testimony of Nathan Bush, hostler in the Acme Corral, as reprinted in the Bright's City Star-Democrat.)

NATE BUSH was alone in the Acme Corral when Billy Gannon, Luke Friendly, and Pony Benner rode in. Calhoun wasn't with them. They had come in up Southend from Medusa Street. It was about nine o'clock in the morning, maybe a little later.

"Go tell Blaisedell we have come in," Billy Gannon said to him. Billy Gannon was wearing two guns. Pony Benner did some fancy swearing about what they were going to do to Blaisedell and Morgan. Friendly didn't have anything to say.

When Bush left the corral they were dismounting. He went to find Blaisedell, and met Carl Schroeder and Paul Skinner coming out of the Boston Café. Schroeder told him to go on and tell Blaisedell. Blaisedell was shaving in his room at the General Peach. Bush told him, and the marshal only asked where they were and said he would be along directly, and went on shaving.

Bush went back then, and told some others he met that the cowboys had come in. There was already a good-sized crowd of people collected at the corner of Southend and Main, by Goodpasture's store.

II

(From the testimony of Deputy Carl Schroeder)

It was a little after nine o'clock when Deputy Schroeder saw the marshal come around the corner from the General Peach. Blaisedell wasn't wearing a coat and he had on his pair of gold-handled Colts. It was the first time, so far as Schroeder knew, that anybody had seen them in Warlock.

He told Blaisedell that there were three of them, and said he stood ready to help any way he could, but Blaisedell said, "Why, thank you, Deputy, but I guess it is my fight."

Schroeder wanted to help, but it did not seem strange to him that the marshal did not accept him. He was no gunman, he knew that.

Blaisedell went on up the center of Main Street toward Southend. There were four or five horses tied to the rail along by the Lucky Dollar, and some men there. A few of them called out to Blaisedell as he passed, warning him to watch out and wishing him well. A wind had come up and dust was blowing, which was worrisome. Schroeder didn't see Morgan till Morgan was out in the street and buckling on his shell belt as he ran after the marshal.

III

(From the testimony of S. W. Brown, proprietor of the Billiard Parlor.)

Sam Brown was standing before the Lucky Dollar with some others when he saw Morgan run out of the Glass Slipper, vault the rail, and, with his vest flapping and buckling his shell belt on, run after Marshal Blaisedell.

The marshal was walking straight up the street toward the corner, and men were calling out to him such things as, "Don't give those cowboys any break this time, Marshal" and "Watch out for some trick of McQuown's, now," "We are holding for you, Blaisedell," and "Good luck, Marshal!"

The marshal didn't act like he heard any of it. He didn't look worried, though. He had on his gold-handled pair everybody had heard about, and they looked fine in the sunshine. His shirt sleeves were gartered up like a bank clerk's. He was a sight to see, plowing toward the corner of Southend Street. Morgan caught up with him before he got there.

Brown heard Morgan say, "Hey, wait for a man!" Morgan fell into step beside the marshal. He had his shell belt hooked on now, and he was coatless like Blaisedell. Usually Morgan wore a shoulder gun, but it seemed more proper to see him this way, and he and the marshal looked pair enough to go against any three cowboys.

He heard Morgan say, "I am always one for a shooting match." Blaisedell said, "It is none of your fight, Morg," and Morgan said, as though he was hurt, "That is a hell of a thing to say to me, Clay!"

They went on up the street to the corner and Morgan was still talking, but by then they were out of Brown's hearing.

IV

(From the testimony of Oliver Foss, driver for the Warlock Stage Co.)

Oliver Foss was on the corner by Goodpasture's store, along with Buck Slavin, Pike and Paul Skinner, Goodpasture, Wolters, and some others, when the marshal and Morgan walked up Main Street. There was a wagon coming up Southend, Hap Peters driving a team of mules. Dust was blowing from the team and wagon and there was a dog running and yelping at an offside wheel. Foss called to Hap to hurry it along because the dust was bad and it had better have time to clear before the marshal went down to the Skinner Brothers' corral.

Foss couldn't see into the Acme, where Billy Gannon, Pony Benner, and Luke Friendly were supposed to be. He heard Morgan say to the marshal, "Maybe there are only three, or maybe there is a nigger in the woodpile." Morgan was grinning in that way of his, like he didn't think much of anybody but Tom Morgan and didn't mind rubbing it in either. They both stopped when Deputy John Gannon came at a run across from the jail, calling to the marshal.

John Gannon said to the marshal, "Can you give me five minutes to try and get them out?" He didn't say it like he expected anything to come of it, and a man had to feel sorry for him.

Blaisedell said he had warned the road agents they weren't to come into Warlock any more, but he didn't move on right away and it sounded to Foss as though he were willing to listen to reason. Gannon said, "Marshal, give me five minutes and I will go down there and—" He didn't finish saying what he would do; he talked in fits and starts, and he looked like he was chewing on something that had got gummed in his mouth. A man had to feel sorry for him. Finally he said to the marshal how he might disarm them, but by then his voice had got so low you could hardly hear it.

Blaisedell asked him if he thought he could disarm them but John Gannon didn't answer, and Morgan nudged the marshal with his elbow. Then Gannon looked about to say something more, but he never did, and the marshal and Morgan went on down Southend Street, past the old, bowed-out corral fence there. Morgan walked spread out from the marshal a little, so when they came up even with the corral gate he and the marshal were about ten feet apart; and Morgan went on a few steps after the marshal had turned toward the corral gate, so he was a little behind and maybe ten or fifteen feet beyond the marshal when the two of them stood facing into the Acme.

It was a little while yet before the shooting started.

V

(From the testimony of Clay Blaisedell and of Thomas Morgan.)

When Clay Blaisedell and Thomas Morgan faced the gate of the Acme Corral, halfway across the street from it, they both saw Luke Friendly first. He stood on the south side of the corral about twenty feet inside. There were three horses tied behind him, and the one nearest him had a rifle in the boot on the near side. Friendly was bent forward so he looked smaller than he really was, and had his hands held out at his waist for a fast draw. Crouched like that, with his hands like that, he looked to be backing away, though he didn't move. He looked to both Blaisedell and Morgan as though he didn't much want a fight, now that he had stopped to think about it.

Billy Gannon stood in the center and Pony Benner on the north side, close by the gate. Billy Gannon was wearing two guns, Benner one. They were both outlined against the wall of the Billiard Parlor at the back of the corral. Dust was blowing straight out of the corral in gusts of wind, but both Blaisedell and Morgan noticed that a door to the Billiard Parlor there stood a little way open.

Blaisedell considered Billy Gannon to be the leader, though Benner might be the more dangerous one. Friendly was not much to worry about unless he went for the rifle in the saddle boot. Blaisedell called to Billy Gannon by name and said, "You don't have to fight me, Billy."

Billy didn't answer. They could hear Benner cursing to himself. Morgan saw Friendly look toward the door to the Billiard Parlor and he said to Blaisedell behind his hand, "I will hold on that door. Don't you worry about it."

Blaisedell tried to talk to Billy Gannon again. "You don't have to fight me, Billy. You and your partners just mount up and ride out."

Billy said, "Go for your guns, you son of a b—!"

Blaisedell started moving forward then. He still thought the road agents might be backed out. This time he spoke to Benner. "Don't make us kill you, boys. Clear on out of here."

Billy Gannon yelled at them again to go for their guns, but did not start to draw his own yet, and Blaisedell kept moving forward. He thought he might get close enough to buffalo the boy, and then the others might fold. He had seen they had no stomach for it.

Morgan saw the door of the Billiard Parlor flung open, and yelled to Blaisedell. Blaisedell had seen it too, and he stepped sideways as a man with a Winchester showed there. He didn't know that it was Calhoun till later. The man let fly with the rifle and Morgan fired back, three times. Those were the only times that Morgan fired. The man yelled and fell sprawled out into the corral. Morgan swung around to cover Friendly, in case Friendly thought of going for the rifle in the boot, but he could see that Friendly had lost interest in the whole business.

When Calhoun had fired from the back, Benner had started for his Colt, and Blaisedell drew and fired. Pony went back hard with his hat rolling off, and didn't move again. Billy Gannon had looked back over his shoulder and seemed to be trying to dodge when the rifle went off. It sounded to Blaisedell as though he yelled, "No! No!" and when Billy turned back to face him he thought that Billy was going to put his hands up. But then Billy changed his mind, or else it had been a trick, and made his move. Blaisedell called his name again, but Billy was too close to count on his missing, and Blaisedell fired just as Billy got his six-gun clear of the holster. Billy spun around and dropped his Colt. His right arm was hanging broken, but he grabbed for his left-hand Colt and got a shot off.

Morgan saw Blaisedell stumble back, and jumped forward to try to get out from behind Blaisedell for a shot at Billy. But then Blaisedell fired again and Billy went down.

Friendly came running and yelling toward them with his hands held up. He caught hold of Blaisedell, crying out that he hadn't had anything to do with Calhoun being there and hadn't wanted anything to do with any of it. He was crying like a baby. They had made him come, he said, and he hadn't had anything to do with robbing the stage.

Blaisedell shook him off and said, "Get to shooting or get out of town!"

Friendly went running back toward the horses, still holding his hands up. Morgan thought he looked like he was going to dive into the horse trough. He could see that Blaisedell had been shot in the shoulder, but it looked no more than a crease. He saw Billy trying to get his six-shooter out, where he had fallen on top of it.

Blaisedell walked over to Billy and took the Colt away just as he pulled it free. Billy said to him, "I could have killed you if they hadn't done that." And he said, "I didn't know they was going to do that. Oh, the dirty sons of b----es!"

Morgan went over to the man who had fallen out the door of the Billiard Parlor and turned him over. He called to Blaisedell that it was Calhoun. Calhoun was already dead, and so was Benner. Friendly took out on his horse and went down Southend Street at a run.

Men were starting to come into the corral now, and Blaisedell
called to them to get the doctor.

VI

(From the testimony of Deputy Carl Schroeder.)

Deputy Schroeder was one of the first into the Acme Corral after
the shooting stopped. He saw Luke Friendly light out on his horse as
though the fiends were after him. Pony Benner was dead just inside
the corral gate and Blaisedell was standing by Billy Gannon, who was
still alive. Blaisedell handed Schroeder Billy's Colt, and pointed out
another where Billy had dropped it. Blaisedell had been creased on
the right shoulder and it was bleeding some.

Billy Gannon was gasping and choking, and Johnny Gannon ran in
and knelt beside him. Blaisedell moved off then. Morgan was over
toward the back of the corral, where Calhoun was lying dead on a
little adobe walkway outside the open side door of Sam Brown's Billiard Parlor. There was a rifle beside Calhoun. He was shot three
times, once through the throat and the other two not a finger apart
on the left side of his chest.

Schroeder asked Morgan if Calhoun had tried to ambush them from
there, and Morgan said he had, and pushed Calhoun back over on his
face with his foot.

Some others came over to look at Calhoun and congratulate Morgan, who moved off. A good lot of others were standing around Blaisedell. Dr. Wagner had shown up and was bending down over Billy
Gannon, but anybody could see there wasn't anything to do.

After a while the doctor went to bind up Blaisedell's shoulder, and
Johnny Gannon laid Billy flat on the ground. Then Gannon went up
to Blaisedell, and some seemed to think there was going to be trouble,
for they backed away. But Gannon only said to Blaisedell that Billy
hadn't known about Calhoun, and Blaisedell answered that he was
sure of it.

Schroeder busied himself asking if anybody had seen Calhoun come
in, or hiding in the Billiard Parlor or anything. The Billiard Parlor
didn't open till eleven o'clock, except Sundays, but Sam Brown told
him the corral door was open sometimes in the mornings. Nobody had
seen Calhoun at all, which didn't particularly mean anything as far as
he, Schroeder, was concerned; because the fact was that Calhoun had
been in the Billiard Parlor to try to dry-gulch Blaisedell, and it didn't
have to be proved how he had got in there.

Maybe Billy Gannon and the rest of them hadn't known about Calhoun being there in the Billiard Parlor; he didn't see that it made any difference. For it was all McQuown's doing, any man could tell that.

VII

(From the testimony of Lucas Friendly, cowboy.)

Lucas Friendly had come into town with William Gannon, Thaddeus Benner, and Edward Calhoun, to protest to Marshal Clay Blaisedell that they had been unfairly and illegally posted from Warlock.

They had not come in to make trouble. They had only wanted to reason with the marshal. There had been no cause for posting them out of Warlock, which everybody knew was illegal anyway, except that some people had got down on them and their friends. They had heard that the marshal was a reasonable man, and had felt they could convince him that they had had no part in the stage robbery of which they had been so foully accused, and justly acquitted by a Bright's City jury. There had been some talk among them on the way up that their entrance into Warlock might be dangerous, but they had felt they had to talk it over with the marshal man to man.

Calhoun's horse had gone lame just before they reached Warlock, so the rest of them had got into town ahead of him. They told Nate Bush to go for the marshal and ask him to come to the Acme Corral so they could talk. They had not wanted to go abroad in Warlock, fearing trouble with certain townsmen who were unjustly set against them, and edgy toward them.

Calhoun had arrived while Bush was gone. They waited a long time, but the marshal did not appear, so, fearing that Bush had gone astray, Calhoun had gone into the Billiard Parlor to try to find someone there to send for the marshal.

But just then the marshal came down Southend Street. When they saw Morgan with him they knew it looked bad, and he, Lucas Friendly, was sick to see the marshal with that high-roller and both clearly coming after trouble.

Both he and Billy Gannon tried to reason with Blaisedell, but the marshal only shouted at them to go for their guns, and called them foul names.

Billy was a hot-headed boy, and Friendly was afraid that he and Benner would not stand for being called names like that. He had cautioned them to hold steady, while he tried to argue with the marshal some more. But he could see it was no use, and that the marshal and

Morgan had murder in their hearts. Morgan began to curse them for being yellow—trying to get them to draw so it would be on them for starting the trouble.

Unluckily it was just then that Calhoun came back out of the Billiard Parlor, and right away Morgan started shooting, and Blaisedell drew and shot at Billy and Pony Benner. Billy and Pony started shooting back, but Blaisedell and Morgan had got first draw and shot them down as they had already shot Calhoun.

He, Friendly, kept yelling at Blaisedell that they had not come to make trouble, and trying to stop the shooting. But it was too late. They had killed the others by then, and he could not draw himself for both Blaisedell and Morgan had their six-shooters aimed at him. So he ran for his horse because he could see they were going to shoot him down whatever he did. He heard them arguing behind him which one was going to shoot him. Luckily for him, a lot of people came down Southend Street toward the corral just then, thinking the shooting was over, and the marshal could not backshoot him for all these others to see it.

There had been nothing for him to do but jump his horse and ride for his life. They would have found some way to kill him if he hadn't.

He thought they would find some way to kill him yet. He had heard that both of them had sworn to do it. He knew they would try to shoot him down in cold blood as they had three fine young fellows with nothing in the world against them except that they had somehow got the marshal of Warlock down on them.

22. Morgan Sees It Pass

MORGAN sat at the table in the front corner of the Glass Slipper that was always reserved for Clay and himself. What the Professor had called a "runkus" was in full bloom. The barkeepers were hustling whisky and beer and the conversation along the bar was shrill and reverberating; men called to each other over the heads of those around them, contended for attention, showed hands shaped into six-shooters in illustration, gesticulated with vehemence; in the mirrors behind the bar their eyes were bright and their faces excited. They were hashing over the fight in the Acme Corral. He could hear his own name coupled with Clay's, and the names of the cowboys, repeated and repeated.

Three men came in together. "Morgan," each said, in turn, and nodded to him, friendly and respectful. "That was a good piece of shooting, Morgan," one said. He nodded in reply, and grinned at himself that he should enjoy this. Others came in, and each one had a greeting for him.

"Put two in Calhoun about a finger apart and from clean across the street, I heard," someone said at the bar. Laughter wrenched at him that he should be a hero to them now. They were jackasses and school-boys; either they saw that the men who had been killed might have been themselves, which made their own miserable lives more precious and engendered gratitude for the increase of value, or else they imagined themselves doing the shooting—and killing made a fellow quite a man, it made his whisky taste better and gave him a brag with the tommies at the French Palace.

Buck Slavin entered and approached him, with a hand out and his jaw shot out grimly; he was one of the second kind. "Morgan," Slavin said. "This town ought to thank you and the marshal. I thank you."

He shook the proffered hand, without rising. "I thank you for thanking me, Buck. But it was nothing."

"That was fine shooting."

"I was lucky, Buck," he said, solemnly, and shot his jaw out too.

Slavin clapped him on the shoulder and swaggered over to the bar. Morgan laughed to himself, as much at himself as at Slavin and the rest. Oh, I am lucky by trade, he thought. More men came in and congratulated him, and he folded his arms on his chest and looked stern, or grinned boyishly, and tried to keep his contempt from showing, the better to enjoy it. Someone sent over a bottle of whisky, which he raised in thanks.

"It will pass," he said to himself, as he poured a little whisky into his glass. He listened to his name coupled with Clay's, proud with the old pride of being counted with Clay. But it would pass. All things would pass, even the passing itself. But for once the pleasure and excitement drowned the sourness in him, and he was very pleased that it had worked so well for Clay. They would produce a brass band for Clay if they would send him a bottle of whisky.

"*Billy was the wrong man, though.*" He heard it, sharp-edged, from the bar. He did not even look to see who had said it, for immediately frozen in his mind's eye was the deeply etched track that led from Bob Cletus to Pat Cletus, from Pat Cletus to Billy Gannon. But it was all right, he reassured himself, so long as Clay did not see the track, see the wrong man again, see him, Tom Morgan— Yet abruptly his mood was broken. All things passed, he thought, except for that one thing.

There was a sudden hush in the Glass Slipper as Clay came in through the batwing doors. Then there was a chorus of greetings and congratulations, and men crowded around Clay to shake his hand, ask about his shoulder, praise him, curse McQuown for him, offer him drinks. Morgan poured whisky into the other glass and looked at nothing until finally Clay made his way over to him, dropped his hat on the table, and sat down with a long leg propped up on an empty chair. He had put on his coat, which would be a disappointment to those watching in the mirrors. Seeing his blood was something they could have told their grandchildren about.

"How?" he said to Clay.

"How," Clay said. His face was drawn and tired-looking. He drank his whisky and set his glass down. "Thanks for coming along, Morg."

"I'd like to have seen you try to stop me."

His heart pumped sickeningly when Clay said, "I was wrong about that boy." Then he sighed with relief as Clay continued. "I thought I could back him down."

"A wild-eyed gunboy trying to be a man."

"Man enough," Clay said. He raised a hand toward his shoulder but didn't touch it.

"McQuown ought to get a better sniper. That one wasn't much good."

Clay frowned, and said, in his deep voice, "Looks like it might've been McQuown behind it, sure enough. I guess I am going to have to have it out with him after all."

"You won't," Morgan said, and Clay glanced at him questioningly. "You won't have it out with him. He is not going to play your game when all he has got to do is use his own rules."

Clay shook his head.

"McQuown is right, too," Morgan went on. "If you are out to kill a man, kill him. It is war, not a silly game with rules."

"There are rules, Morg," Clay said.

"Why?"

"Because of the others—I mean the people not in it."

"Oh, you have started worrying about the people watching, have you?"

"No," Clay said. "But it is just so."

"You are in damned poor shape then against someone that doesn't think it is so. Or care a damn if it is or not. I say you can't beat McQuown for he won't play your rules."

"Why, Morg, I will beat him either way. I will beat him *by* playing the rules, if he won't. Because he will have to pretend there are rules whether he thinks there are or not, just like he had to today. And if he has to pretend, it means he is worrying about the others pretty hard." The corners of Clay's lips tilted up. "See if I'm not right," he said.

Morgan pushed at his glass with a forefinger. He did not know anyone like Clay who would observe the rules to the end, live or die by them. There were some who would observe them insofar as they were a benefit, and, beyond that, would not, and there were those like McQuown who would make a fraud of the rules. That was the danger, but he did not see that Clay could do anything but ignore it. Clay had to, to be what he was, and Clay was the only man he had ever known, except for himself, who knew exactly what he was. It was the basis of his admiration for Clay. He had never understood their friendship on Clay's side. He only knew that Clay liked and trusted him, and it was the only thing that had become more precious to him than money, which, at the same time, he had come to realize was worth nothing, for it bought nothing. And so, somewhere along the line, his friendship for Clay had become all there was.

Clay's chin jerked up as the batwing doors swung in, and the number two deputy came in. There was a deeper hush than before, and a longer one, as Gannon came over toward them. Gannon's face was gray, his bent nose too big for his thin face; his hair was rumpled when he took off his hat. "Have a seat, Deputy," Clay said gently.

Gannon sat down and put his hat on the floor beside him, folded his hands on the table before him.

"Whisky?" Morgan asked.

"Yes," Gannon said, without looking at him. "Thanks."

Morgan beckoned for a glass. Gannon did not speak until it had been brought, and Clay was silent too. The faces still stared in the mirrors, but the noise began again.

Gannon said suddenly, "I guess I had better tell you, Marshal. Before it comes out another way. Billy wasn't with them when they stopped the stage. I don't know whether Luke was or not, but Billy wasn't."

Carefully Morgan did not look at Clay; he felt the sickening rapid pump of his heart again.

"What good does this do, Deputy?" Clay said harshly.

Gannon shook his head, as though that were not the point. "He wasn't there," he said. "He held with them because he was caught with them and I guess it was all—he thought he could do. And came in because of being posted out, I guess, Marshal."

"There was three of them at the stage at least," Clay said.

"Not him," Gannon said stubbornly. He cleared his throat. "Marshal, I know. Billy said so, and—"

"You could have told me," Clay said.

"What good would that have done?" Gannon said. He sounded almost angry now, and he brushed his fingers back nervously through his hair. "What could you have done different than you did?" he said. "He would have come in against you whatever. He was that kind."

"What difference does it make?" Morgan said, staring at the deputy. "He shot that posseman, didn't he?"

Gannon looked back at him with his deep-set, hot eyes. "That is nothing to do with it." He said to Clay, "Marshal, I am just saying there is probably others than me that know. So I thought you better had."

Clay sat with his head bent down and his mouth drawn tight. He nodded his head once, as though in thanks, and in dismissal. Gannon pushed his chair back and rose. He hesitated a moment, and then, since Clay did not speak again, plucked up his hat and went outside.

Morgan leaned forward toward Clay and said, "What the hell difference does it make? He killed that posseman and was out to kill you. Everybody knows that!"

Clay nodded a little, but when he raised his head the flesh of his face looked eroded, and his eyes were shuttered. He said in a quiet voice, "One time wrong and then every time wrong after it."

To himself Morgan cursed Clay and his rules, his scruples and his conscience. He cursed the Cletus brothers, the Gannon brothers, and himself. He said through his teeth, "You did everything but beg him to get the hell out of town!"

Clay did not reply; Morgan refilled Clay's glass, and filled his own. "How?" he said.

"I guess I had better do it," Clay said, and got to his feet.

"Where are you going?"

"Bright's City," Clay said. He put on his hat and patted the crown. "What for?"

"Stand trial," Clay said, and went outside. The batwing doors swung through their arcs and came to rest behind him.

Morgan rinsed whisky through his mouth, and finally swallowed it. He smoothed his hands back over his hair, and halted them midway to press his head hard between them. "Damn you, Clay!" he whispered. Yet he should have foreseen, as soon as Gannon had spoken his piece, that Clay would feel he had to do this. One time wrong and every time wrong after it; Bob Cletus to Pat Cletus, and Pat Cletus to Billy Gannon; and not a one of them worth a minute's bother.

He rose and started down along the bar. Men were standing there two-deep now, and thick around Basine's layout. He caught Murch's eye and nodded to the other layout. Men greeted him cordially as he passed; he ignored them, listening to the names dropping out of the loud whine of talk—Billy Gannon, Pony, Calhoun, Curley Burne, Cade, McQuown, Johnny Gannon, Schroeder, and his own name and Clay's. Eyes watched him in the mirror and the talk died a little. He heard his name again, and halted.

A short, heavy-set miner with an arm in a dirty muslin sling was talking to McKittrick and another up-valley cowboy. "Why, this fellow I knew was up there at the trial and he said there wasn't anything but smoke blown against those poor boys there. They wasn't within fifty miles of that stage! So I say it is clear enough who stopped that stage if they didn't, and they didn't. Oh, there is plenty knows how come the marshal and Morgan had to shoot those poor boys down dead crack-out-of-the-box like they did, and you can bet they are sick Friendly got away. For what's dead is dead and don't talk back, and what's dead's forgotten about too. If the marshal and Morgan didn't throw down on that stage, I'll eat—"

His voice faltered as one of the cowboys nudged him, and he broke off. Slowly he raised his eyes to meet Morgan's in the mirror. The cowboys edged away.

"Eat what?" Morgan said.

The miner turned toward him. His mouth was pursed as though he had been sucking on a lemon. With his left hand he shifted the sling around before him. McKittrick moved farther away from him, with disclaiming gestures.

"Eat what?" Morgan said again. "I want to know what you are thinking of eating."

"Sneak around listening you will hear a lot of things," the miner said. He glanced around to see if he was getting any support. Then he said, "I just don't aim on ruckusing with anybody, Mr. Morgan, with this smash elbow I got."

"I want you to get started eating whatever it was you were fixing to eat," Morgan said. He stared into the miner's frightened eyes until the miner shifted the slinged arm again, with a fraud of a grimace of pain as he did it. "Because," Morgan said, "you are a dirty-mouth, stinking, lying, buggering, pissant, yellow-belly, mule-diddling, coyote-bred son of a nigger whore. Which is to say a mucker."

The miner's Adam's apple bounced once. He wiped his free hand across his mouth. "Why, I guess you wouldn't talk like that and still be standing if I had the use of my right arm here," he said. "I said what I said, Mr. Morgan."

"You said it in the wrong place."

The miner said stubbornly, "I guess a man can still talk—"

"Eat this, then," Morgan said, and hit the miner in the mouth. He kicked him in the crotch and the miner screamed and doubled up, clutching himself, and fell. Morgan kicked him in the face as he fell.

The miner lay face down by the rail at the base of the bar, his slinged arm beneath his body, one leg stretching and pulling up rhythmically. He groaned in a hoarse monotone. Murch came stumping up with the toothpick sticking out of the corner of his mouth.

"Get him out of here."

Murch picked the miner up by his belt and carried him like a suitcase toward the louvre doors.

Morgan swung around and went over to the second faro layout, and seated himself in the dealer's chair. He held his hands out over the box. His right knuckle was torn whitely and a trickle of blood showed, but his hands were as steady and motionless as though they were a part of the painted layout beneath them.

When he looked up to meet the eyes that watched him from the glass behind the bar, no longer friendly, he saw that what had been bound to pass had already quickly passed.

23. Gannon Witnesses an Assault

GANNON stood in the doorway of the *carpintería* staring at the greasy tarpaulin furred with sawdust and fine curls of wood. It was so stiff that the separate shapes beneath it were not discernible. He could not even tell which of the three pairs of boots that protruded beyond its edge was Billy's.

Old Eladio, with a maul and chisel, was cutting dovetails in a yellow pine board, and beyond him the other carpenter pushed his long plane along the edge of another board, freeing crisp curls of wood, which he shook from the plane from time to time. One of the coffins was already finished, and Gannon seated himself upon it. He tried to keep his eyes from those three pairs of narrow-toed boots. Eladio fitted an end and a side together, and meshed the dovetails with sharp raps of his maul.

"*Va bien?*" Gannon said, just to be saying something.

"*Sí, bien,*" Eladio said. He bowed his bald, wrinkled brown head for a moment. "*Que lástima, joven.*"

Gannon nodded and closed his eyes, listening to the clean scuff of the plane and the tapping of the maul. Then abruptly he went out into the hot sunlight, and started up Broadway toward the jail. His Colt felt very heavy upon his thigh, his star heavy where it was pinned to his vest; his boots scuffed and tapped along the boardwalk. The men he passed watched him with carefully indifferent side glances.

In the thick shadow of the arcade on Main Street a knot of them, standing before the Billiard Parlor, moved aside to let him by, and he saw a horseman swing out of Southend Street, turning east. It was the marshal, riding a big-barreled black with white face and stockings. Blaisedell rode stiff-backed and heavy in his black broadcloth, trouser legs tucked into his boots, black hat tipped forward against the sun. The black's hoofs danced in the dust. Blaisedell glanced toward Gannon briefly, and he felt the intense blue stare like a physical push. The horse broke into a trot. He heard the men before the Billiard Parlor whispering as the black danced on down Main Street, horse and horseman gradually smaller and more and more dimly seen in the dust, until they disappeared on the Bright's City stage road.

As he went on again, toward the jail, he felt relieved; he had not been sure that Blaisedell had believed him.

The judge sat at the table, his crutch leaning beside him, before him his hard hat, his pen, bottle of ink, Bible, rusty derringer, and a half-empty pint of whisky—all the accoutrements of his office, which he brought out when he sat to fine or jail an evening's transgressors. He frowned when he saw Gannon; he had not shaved, and there was a thick gray stubble on his cheeks and chin. Carl sat on his heels against the wall, teasing a scorpion with a broomstraw. His jaw was shot out and he looked sullen and stubborn.

"Deputy Schroeder has resigned," the judge said.

"I haven't either, you old fool!" Carl got up and smashed the scorpion with his heel. "Damn, how you badger a man!"

"Badger you to do your duty like you are sworn to," the judge said. "You won't, so you have resigned." He looked up at Gannon and said, "Will you do your duty, Deputy?"

"Damned old bastard!" Carl cried. "Murderer, hell!" Then he said apologetically, "Johnny, I am sorry talking this way now, but he has drove me to it. What kind of judge are you?" he said to the judge. "Four hardcases trying to burn down a peace officer and it isn't self-defense? I never heard—"

"Not for you to judge what it is," the judge said.

"Or you!"

Gannon sat down beside the cell door and leaned back. Watching the two angry faces, his eyes felt as though they were bleeding.

"Warned him!" the judge said. "Warned him what he was doing. Making a murderer out of himself, issuing ukases and banishments like a duke. Now he has to stand trial like any ordinary mortal man and poor sinner, and I will witness against him if I have to crutch it into Bright's City."

"You couldn't," Carl said. "There is no place to buy whisky on the way."

"I'll witness against you for malfeasance of duty while I am at it. Will you arrest Blaisedell, Deputy Gannon?"

"He's gone," Gannon said.

The judge stared at him.

"Gone where?" Carl said.

"He rode out toward Bright's City. I expect he's gone up to court."

"What the hell would he do that for?"

"To be shriven," the judge said. He smiled and stretched, smugly. "Ah, he listened after all, did he? Yes, to get it off himself."

"Nothing on him, Christ's sake." Carl swung toward Gannon. "He only did what he had to do. Johnny, you heard him trying to talk Billy out of it!"

Gannon nodded with an incomplete and qualified assent. Carl was right to the boundaries of what he had said; Blaisedell had done what he had to do, given the circumstances. Yet the judge was right when he said that Blaisedell must be accountable. Billy would not have died had the Citizens' Committee not decided to post him, and had Blaisedell not decided to honor their decision, as he had not in the case of the miner Brunk. But on the other hand Billy would not have been posted had McQuown not loaded the court in Bright's City with perjured witnesses, tricked it with a clever lawyer, menaced it with gunmen and the threat inherent in his name. And, in the end, Billy would not have died had he not set himself to kill Blaisedell.

Carl furiously scraped his bootheel over the shredded stain that had been the scorpion. "By God!" he said thickly. He sounded as though he were in pain. "Johnny, what the hell did he think he had to go for?"

"The law is the law, Mister Malfeasor of Duty," the judge said smugly. "And no good getting hysterical—"

Carl took a long stride toward him, swung an arm, and slapped him on the side of the head. The judge screamed and toppled; Carl caught him by the shirt front and set him upright, slapped him again, forehand and backhand. The judge snatched for his derringer and Carl knocked it aside. The judge screamed and tried to cover his face. Gannon leaped out of his chair, caught Carl around the waist, and pulled him away.

"Witness!" the judge cried. "Assault and battery and—"

"Shut up!" Carl shouted. He stopped struggling in Gannon's grip, but when Gannon released him Carl darted for the judge again.

This time he only bent down close to the judge's blotched face. "The law is the law!" he panted. "But there isn't enough of it to go around out here. So when we get a good man protecting this town from hell with its door open I am not going to see him choused and badgered and false-sworn and yawped at fit to puke by a one-legged old son of a bitch like you!

"Until he gets fed up and rides the hell somewheres else and this town left pie on the table again for those San Pablo cowboys to pick it clean and kill anybody fool or awkward enough to get in their way. A good man, God damn you! That gives some of us here some pride and gets our peckers up for a change. God damn you, if by God because of you he has went up there to court and gets frazzled out of patience by it and sets his back against us here I will tear your other leg off and bust it around your God-damned neck for a God-damned necktie and run your God-damned crutch through it for a God-damned stickpin!" He stopped, panting.

"Witness!" the judge said hoarsely, covering his face with his hands.

"Shut up!" Carl yelled. "You don't know what assault and battery is yet, and by God I want witness to what I am saying! Because that's the word with the bark on it—if you have got him turned against us here with your law's-the-law bellywash, I swear to God people will walk ten miles out of their way around what happened to you, so as not to see the mess!"

Carl stepped back from the table. The judge snatched up his whisky bottle and tilted it to his mouth; whisky trickled over his chin.

Carl leaned back against the wall, chewing furiously on a mustache end. "By God, Johnny, it is a shameful thing," he said, in a shaky voice. "Here I am making a damned yelling fool of myself, and you with your brother killed. I am sorry."

"That Blaisedell killed," the judge whispered.

"It wasn't Blaisedell killed him," Gannon said, and Carl gave him a confused look.

Bootheels racketed on the planks outside and Pike Skinner came in. "Where the hell's Blaisedell gone to?"

"Bright's, it looks like," Carl said.

The judge said, in a loud, trumpeting voice, "He knew he had to go, because no man can set himself above the law!" He turned toward Gannon suddenly. Red marks showed on his pale, stubbled cheeks. "That's why, isn't it, Deputy?"

"I guess so," Gannon said.

"You two have been drinking out of the same bottle," Carl said, disgustedly.

"It is the only bottle there is," the judge said.

Pike stared at Gannon with wide eyes in his red face. Pike came forward around the table. "I don't know," he said, with difficulty. "I don't know what's happened or what's going to happen. But Johnny Gannon, I know if you throw Blaisedell down some way because of Billy I will—"

Carl caught Pike by the shoulder and jerked him around. "Shut your face!" Carl drew and jammed his Colt into Pike's side. His face was contorted with fury. "You have shot your mouth one too many times!"

Pike backed up a step and Carl moved after him. "Johnny, I will hold on him and you can beat the holy piss out of him for that if you want."

"Never mind it, Carl," Gannon said.

"Take it back then!" Carl said, through his teeth. "I say back down, you bat-eared ignoramus! You don't know what you are talking about even!"

"I'll not!" Pike said stiffly.

"It doesn't matter, Carl," Gannon said, and Carl cursed and holstered his Colt.

"Pus and corruption," the judge said, in the smug voice. "Small men bickering and quarreling and killing at each other, a whole world full and not one worth the trouble it is to law them. But there is one did a right thing one time in his life."

"Shut up!" Carl cried. He hit his fist back against the wall. "Just shut that up. I'm warning you! Just shut up about it!"

24. Journals of Henry Holmes Goodpasture

February 10, 1881

THE pipers play "The World Turned Upside Down." Clay Blaisedell is in Bright's City awaiting trial. He took himself there upon his own warrant, evidently preferring not to present himself to the deputies here for arrest, as is fitting his Dignity & Station.

The rumors fly. His action has astounded everyone. We cry that there is no need for him to seek justification in court, and further that he puts himself in grave danger by thus surrendering himself to the mercies of a judge and jury too often proved weak creatures of McQuown's will. Yet perhaps I do see a need. Blaisedell must have come to suspect immediately after the fight what is being more and more widely bruited about here—that Billy Gannon was not one of the road agents. And he must have felt that the fact that Billy Gannon had killed a posseman and had joined with those who were actually and clearly the road agents in order to ambush him (Blaisedell), does not alter this original case. If this is true, I must feel that he has acted correctly and honorably.

I wonder if Blaisedell realizes that he will stand trial for us of the Citizens' Committee as well as for himself.

February 15, 1881

It is too bad that Blaisedell left so soon for Bright's City and was not here to enjoy the luster of his feat in the Acme Corral while that luster remained intact. For within a week his triumph has become somewhat tarnished. Ah, the pure shine of a few moments of heroism, high courage, and derring-do! In its light we genuflect before the Hero, we bask in the warmth of his Deeds, we tout him, shout his praises, deify him, and, in short, make of him what no mortal man could ever be. We are a race of tradition-lovers in a new land, of king-reverers in a Republic, of hero-worshipers in a society of mundane get-and-spend. It is a Country and a Time where any bank clerk or common laborer can become a famous outlaw, where an outlaw can in a very short time be sainted in song and story into a Robin Hood, where a Frontier Model Excalibur can be drawn from the block at any gunshop for twenty dollars.

Yet it is only one side of us, and we are cynical and envious too. As one half of our nature seeks to create heroes to worship, the other must ceaselessly attempt to cast them down and discover evidence of feet of clay, in order to label them as mere lucky fellows, or as villains-were-the-facts-but-known, and the eminent and great are ground between the millstones of envy, and reduced again to common size.

So, quickly, as I have said, Blaisedell's luster has been dimmed. As if ashamed of our original exuberance, we begin to qualify our praises, and smile a little at the extravagant recountings of the affair. For would we not look fools, were facts to arise that showed Blaisedell's part in the Acme Corral shooting to have been despicable? What cowards we are!

Still, it is a reaction against his having at first been made too much over. The pendulum inevitably swings, and, I hope, may come to rest dead center. But at the moment some scoffing has replaced the adulation, as I will now recount:

Blaisedell had, after all, Morgan with him—a gunman of no small accomplishments.

Blaisedell's antagonists are reconsidered. We realize that there were only four of them, and one did not even participate in the shooting. Pity is felt for their ineffectuality.

I feel some pity for them myself, but I am infuriated when I hear attitudes expounded that go beyond mere pity. For instance, I have heard Pony Benner remembered as a kindly albeit rough-cut spirit, who had unfortunately incurred general displeasure when he killed our poor barber in *self-defense!* Now it seems that the barber insulted a nice woman in Pony's presence, Pony called him down for it, whereupon the barber flew at him brandishing a razor! Who this nice woman could possibly have been, I have no idea.

Even Calhoun's good lives after him, while the evil has been interred with his bones. The fact that he was indisputably trying to shoot down Blaisedell from ambush is glossed over by the claim that he was trying to protect his friend Billy Gannon.

Poor Billy, too, becomes no longer "Billy-the-kid," who shot down Deputy Brown in the San Pablo saloon for trying to force a glass of whisky upon him, but has changed into a lad forced into a fight he did not want. He has grown younger after death, and I have heard him spoken of as a mere sixteen, instead of eighteen or nineteen as formerly.

How the tide of sentiment can swing, and how it has changed in many since the night when a good portion of this town attempted to lynch these same three "innocents," and only the presence of Blaisedell saved them. Men are wild, not wicked, said Rousseau, who knew not Warlock.

There is one wicked rumor that sets me in a rage. It has obviously sprung from another that was current here before the Acme Corral fight. This was that it was not the "innocents" who robbed the stage at all, but Morgan in company with unnamed accomplices. Now the accomplices have been named. They were Morgan's lookout, Murch, and Blaisedell! It seems that the Cowboys became, somehow, advised of this, had definite proof, and came into Warlock to establish their innocence by broadcasting it. Consequently they had to be shot down immediately by Blaisedell and Morgan, so that the truth would not be known.

Oh, foul! I have not, as a matter of fact, heard it uttered, I have only heard men say they disbelieve it completely. It is said that the original rumor came from Taliaferro, Morgan's competitor, and a vile blotch of a man. The new one can only come from someone who hates Blaisedell completely and ruthlessly. I suspect McQuown, who must hate Blaisedell thus—as one must hate a man he has tried foully to wrong, and failed.

February 18, 1881

Blaisedell will go on trial to determine whether the deaths of Billy Gannon and Pony Benner were acts of murder or of self-defense.*

* It should be noted that the question seems never to have arisen as to whether or not Morgan should have been tried for the death of Calhoun.

If guilty, we of the Citizens' Committee cannot be punished for our Crime, while Blaisedell can.

My thoughts are much occupied with Blaisedell now, as, of course, are those of everyone in Warlock. I find myself thinking of him with sadness, because of the canards visited upon him *in absentia*, that surely will in some degree and over the years stick to his name in the minds of men. Sadness, too, because he is, I am convinced, a good man, a fair, temperate, and reasonable man, a decent man and an honorable one; and, in the end, of course, he must die. Probably he will die by just the sort of foul trickery that was attempted upon his person in the Acme Corral. If not here, elsewhere. He is, after all, a killer; living by the six-shooter, he will no doubt perish by it. Other killers or would-be killers will be moved from time to time to try his mettle or to usurp his fame, and one day, even if he is not removed by treachery, his hand will lack the necessary swiftness.

It is curious that a man like Blaisedell, no less than outlaws such as Calhoun, Benner, Curley Burne, and McQuown, is referred to as a "Badman." This describes more a man who is dangerous to meddle with than one murderously inclined, and yet the term has unhappy connotations, and I am more and more displeased to hear it applied to our Marshal.

Obviously Blaisedell must enjoy his role as angel with a sword or he would not undertake so dangerous a role, but can he endure to be called devil? Surely he will be acquitted and his name cleared in court. There are many men here who would walk to Bright's City to testify in his behalf, were it necessary.

February 22, 1881

The trial is to begin tomorrow. Buck has gone in with the doctor, Morgan, the Skinner brothers, Sam Brown, and a number of others. I did not choose to make the onerous journey into Bright's City myself since there is nothing except my high opinion of Blaisedell that I could offer the court. Nor do I wish to see our Marshal being questioned before a jury box full of Bright's City fools. Those of the Citizens' Committee who went in to attend the trial are to carry another appeal to General Peach that he legalize our situation in Warlock. I wish I had counted how many of these appeals have already been made. Doubtless this will meet the same fate as the others, although some hope is felt that General Peach will be forced to see, because of the trial, the extremes we have been brought to by his neglect.

Those who are witnesses have been cautioned to mention this in court whenever possible.

A prospector has been reported murdered in the Dinosaurs, and in consequence there has been another rash of Apache rumors. It is embittering to think that Peach will no doubt get wind of this and bring the cavalry down to investigate, but will not hear our appeals for law. Not all Apaches are dark-skinned.

There are also reports of Mexican troops along the border again, probably on watch against rustlers crossing. One of Blaikie's hands was wounded in an encounter with rustlers, and Deputy Gannon, I hear, has gone down to investigate. I wonder why he did not go up for trial. He roams the streets by night, while Schroeder has kept the jail by day; more morose than ever, cadaverously thin, his eyes like holes burnt in his skull. Poor fellow, he is condemned by some for having attempted to shield a villain of a brother, by others for not having attempted to avenge an heroic one.

February 25, 1881

The trial has been put off another week, and the witnesses have returned, grumbling. It appears that Friendly, who was thought to have fled the territory, is in Bright's City where he will give evidence against Blaisedell. He is a fellow whom anyone but a fool would know on sight as a born liar. Blaisedell is not in jail, but resides at the Jim Bright Hotel and spends his days gambling. There is some talk about his not returning here to await the trial, but I can understand his not wishing to do so.

25. Gannon Goes to a Housewarming

I

From the doorway of the jail, Gannon saw her coming across the street from Goodpasture's corner, her hands lifting her skirts as she waded through the dust, the cord of her reticule twisted around her wrist. Buck Slavin, walking up from the stageyard, tipped his hat and she stopped briefly to talk to him. But then she came on, and it was clear that she was coming to the jail.

He stepped back inside and sat down on a corner of the table. He had seen her many times in the last few weeks; always she would smile at him and more and more often stop to pass a few moments with him, which moments were always difficult ones, because he could think of nothing to say to her and always he had the feeling, after she had gone on, that he had disappointed her in some way.

He heard her steps. Then she was framed in the doorway, smiling at him, with the little court-plaster beauty mark very black against her pale face. "Good morning, Deputy."

"Good morning, Miss Dollar," he said, standing quickly upright. She glanced at the empty cell and took a handkerchief from her reticule and daubed at her temples. The bottom of her skirt was white with dust. Still, perspiring and dusty as she was, she was a handsome woman, and, standing before her, incapable of easy conversation, he felt intensely his own awkwardness, his own inadequacy and ugliness.

"It's cool in here," she said, and came a little farther inside.

"Yes, ma'am. And hot out."

"I've rented a house."

"You are lucky to find a house. Are you—I mean, I guess you are going to stay in Warlock awhile, then."

"I've been here a month. I guess I am staying." She was looking at the names scratched in the whitewashed wall. "It's a pretty fair house," she went on. "I rented it from a miner. Some boys from the livery stable are bringing my trunks around this afternoon." She smiled at him with a mechanical tilt of her reddened lips. "I wondered if you would help me move in."

"Why—" he said. "Why, I would surely appreciate to help, Miss Dollar. What time would you—"

"Toward five. I will try a hand at cooking some supper for us." Then she smiled again, not so mechanically. "You don't have to look worried. I can cook, Deputy."

"I am sure!" he protested. "I will surely be pleased to come."

Her eyes examined him in that way she had that was both careless and intense, as though she could see right through him, but at the same time as though she were searching for something. He had felt it most intensely when, after Billy's death, he had met her on the street and she had stopped to say she was sorry about his brother.

She remained and chatted a little longer, but he became more and more tongue-tied and stupid, as he always did, and finally she left. From the doorway he watched her cross Southend and walk past the loungers in front of the saloons. They did not bother her, he noticed.

He saw the lead mules of a freighter swinging wide into Main Street from the Welltown road, and he moved back inside the jail to get out of the dust. The mules plodded past, almost invisible in the dust they raised, with Earl Posten trotting alongside the swing team, and Mosbie standing and cracking his long whip from the lead wagon. Carl came in and sailed his hat toward the peg on which the key ring hung.

"Damn!" Carl said, and went to pick up his hat, where it had fallen. He sat down at the table and said, in a gloomy voice, "I've been up at the stable talking to Joe Kennon. You don't suppose they are going to find against Blaisedell, do you?"

Gannon shook his head, while Carl guardedly watched his face. "I don't see how they can, Carl."

"Well, I don't like them putting it off a week like this. Like they think if they keep putting it off there'll nobody go in to witness for him. By God, if that's what they think they're trying to do, I'll set up camp on the courthouse steps!"

"Do you think I ought to go in?"

Carl sat scowling down at his hands. He sighed and said, "No, I guess I don't know what good it'd do. I don't know—I have just got the nerves, I guess."

Gannon watched a bluefly circle past Carl's head, to strike and buzz angrily against the window glass. Hoofs clopped by in the street —two of Blaikie's riders. One waved in to him, and he raised a hand in reply.

Carl said, "Saw that Kate Dollar woman coming out of here. What did she want?"

He found himself grinning foolishly. "Well, she wants me to come and help her move her things for her. She has rented herself a house."

"You!" Carl said, in an awed voice.

"Me, sure enough."

"You!" Carl said. "By God, a lady-killer underneath all. I never thought it of you."

"Well, she said she had picked the handsomest man in town here to help her."

"Thought I was," Carl said. He squinted at Gannon. "Well, I'll just pass on what my Daddy said to me. 'Look out for women!' he said, and I have done it all my life. But not a one went and looked back." He laughed a little. "Well, now, that's fine," he said. "She is a handsome-looking woman. What is she doing out here, did she ever say to you, Johnny?"

"Looking for me," he said, and felt himself flush. He grinned at Carl, who snorted.

"A lady-killer underneath," Carl said. "Well, if that don't beat all."

II

At four o'clock Gannon went to the Mexican barber on Medusa Street for a haircut and shave, and, reeking of toilet water, hurried back to his room at Birch's roominghouse and washed off the stink and put on his best shirt and his store suit. Surveying himself in the shard of mirror over the washstand he thought there had never been a face so ugly, and the suit did not look like anything but what it was, a cheap store-bought, with the jacket pinch-waisted and short and the store creases still in the trousers.

He took off the suit and put on clean moleskin pants; anyway he was going to help her move her things, not to a soiree. He dusted and oiled his shell belt, put on his new star boots that were too small for him, and spent some time brushing his hat and adjusting it upon his head. Then he limped out. He looked in at the jail, where Carl was poring over a Wild West magazine.

"In a pure sweat, aren't you?" Carl said. "I was betting on that store suit of yours, though."

"It's that red-trim house over on Grant Street. If you need me for anything."

"I'm too soft-hearted a man to pull you out of there short of McQuown coming in to burn the town down," Carl said. "Then I guess you'd hear the shooting anyway."

Gannon grinned and went on east along Main Street, walking pigeon-toed and wincing in his star boots. He turned into the Lucky Dollar for a glass of whisky, taking a place at the bar where he could watch the thin hands of the Seth Thomas clock.

He had finished his whisky and was marveling at the incredibly slow movement of the minute hand, when there was a sudden silence in the Lucky Dollar, and then a scuff of bootheels and clink of spurs. In the mirror he saw Abe and Curley entering. They walked past him, unnoticing, and he watched them find a table and seat themselves.

A barkeeper took them a bottle and two glasses; the hum of conversation was resumed, in a lower, sibilant key. In the mirror Gannon watched Curley whispering to Abe behind his hand, and Abe glancing around him continually with little nervous movements of his head, the lines in his cheeks deeply cut, his face bitter, watchful, and—Gannon thought with a shock—almost fearful.

When the minute hand stood two minutes away from straight up, Gannon turned to go. He nodded to Abe, who stared back without recognition; he nodded to Curley, who wrinkled his nose a little, as though he had smelled something bad. Gannon went on outside. He did not think there was going to be any trouble. Probably they were on their way into Bright's City and Abe had felt he had to show himself in Warlock on the way. The red-bearded face with the clawed-looking lines in the cheeks remained in his mind's eye as he went on east toward Grant Street. He had never thought that he would see Abe McQuown frightened.

The house Kate Dollar had rented was of tarpaper and wooden battens, with red trim around the door and a single narrow window at the front. The door stood open and he knocked on the red frame and waited, hat in hands. Inside he could see two scuffed leather trunks with curved lids, one with a valise on top of it, the other standing open. In the room were three rawhide straight chairs, a love seat with one corner propped up on some bricks, an oilcloth-covered table beneath the pulley lamp, and, on the wall opposite him, a painting in a chipped gilt frame of a shepherd tending some sheep. The glass over it was cracked.

Kate Dollar came out of the doorway beyond the trunks. She had on a soiled apron and a white frilled shirt with a high collar. Her black hair was tied up in a scarf, and her face, clean and scrubbed-looking, seemed strangely different until he noticed that the beauty mark was missing. She did not look so tall, either, as she came across the creaking plank floor toward him. "Come in, Deputy," she said.

He entered, and she stepped past him to close the door with a slap. "How do you like my house?"

"It's a fine house."

She looked at him in the almost rude way she had. "I see you didn't know whether to come dressed for work or supper. There'll be no supper till there's some work done. I want you to slide those trunks into the bedroom for me, and then I want these walls washed down. Can you bring yourself to do that kind of work?"

"If nobody catches me at it."

She raised an eyebrow at him, and raised a finger to touch the place where the beauty mark usually was. She smiled a different kind of smile. "I will have something on you, won't I?"

She stood aside as he lifted the valise to the table, and slid the larger trunk into the bedroom. In the bedroom was a brass bed and an unpainted crate with dirty muslin curtains covering the front. On the crate, on a purple scarf, was a glass-covered picture of the Virgin. There was a wire stretched across one corner of the room, on which hung the clothes she had been wearing when she had come to the jail.

When he returned to the living room he could hear her in the kitchen, and a bucket of water and some cactus-fiber wads were on the table. He went to work on the tarpaper walls.

While he scrubbed the walls Kate Dollar worked in the kitchen and the bedroom, occasionally talking to him from whatever room she happened to be in, and once or twice, as she passed him, pointing out places he had missed. He thought it was as pleasant a time as he had ever spent.

Finished with the front room, he took his bucket into the bedroom. Now the wire in the corner was sagging with clothes. One of the trunks was empty and stood open; there was a mirror in the lid with red roses and blue stars painted around it. The top of the crate had been heaped with her things—a little black book, a silver cross on a beaded chain, a silver-chased box, a derringer, a tinted photograph in a gold frame. The picture of the Virgin stood apart from the clutter. She had a sad, sweet face, full of pity.

He moved closer to the crate. His hand hesitated, as his eyes had hesitated, to pry into her personal things there. But he picked up the tinted photograph. It showed a man with a reddish walrus mustache —a smiling, well-dressed, plump, handsome, touchy-looking man; at first the face seemed familiar and he thought it must be that of the dead man, Cletus, who had come to Warlock with her. Yet he decided it was not. He heard the slap of Kate Dollar's slippers in the front room, and guiltily he put the photograph down and moved quickly away from the crate. Through the door he saw her pull down the lamp and light the wick with a paper spill. The room brightened around her, and she turned and smiled at him, but some essential part of the pleasantness had vanished, and he felt uncomfortable in the bedroom with the brass scrolled bed, and her private things.

He was nearly done when he began to smell the damp, sweet smell of cornbread, and cooking meat. She called to him that it was time to wash up, and he finished quickly. The oilcloth table was set with dented metal plates and thick white mugs. Kate Dollar had put out a crockery bowl of water and a cake of Pears soap for him, and he washed his hands carefully and wiped them dry on his trouser legs. He could see Kate Dollar in the little kitchen, before a charcoal fire set into a brick counter; her face was pink and prettily beaded with perspiration.

"You can sit down, Deputy," she called. He did so, and continued to watch her working. She seemed very slim, and it occurred to him that she must not be wearing certain of her usual undergarments. She brought in a dish of cornbread, with a cloth over it, and he rose hurriedly, and seated himself again when she had returned to the kitchen—to rise again when she brought in the meat and greens. Finally she sat down opposite him.

"We'll have to eat the cornbread dry," she said. "I haven't got anything to put on it."

"Everything certainly smells fine," he said. He watched her hands to see how she would use her knife and fork, and followed her example. He remembered that his mother had switched her fork to her right hand after she had cut her meat, and he was glad to see that Kate did it that way. In the lamplight he watched the dark down on her bare arms. Her knife scraped painfully on the metal plate.

"Eat your greens, Deputy."

He grinned and said, "I remember my mother saying that."

"It is a thing women say." She had taken off her head scarf and her hair gleamed blue-black. Her teeth were very straight and white, and there was a fine down also on her upper lip. "Where is she?" she asked.

"Well, she's dead, Miss Dollar."

"Kate," she said. "Just Kate."

"Kate," he said. "Well, she died, I don't know—twelve years ago. That was back in Nebraska. She and the baby died of the influenza."

"And your father?"

"Apaches shot him. That was in the early days here."

"And Blaisedell killed your brother," Kate said.

He looked down at his plate. Kate didn't speak again, and the silence was heavy. He finished his meat and greens and took a piece of cornbread from under the cloth. It was warm still, but it was dry in his mouth. He knew he was not being very good company. With an effort he laughed and said, "Well, there's not many men in Warlock tonight, I guess, eating home-cooked food. And good, too. I mean with white women," he added, thinking of the miners' Mexican women.

"I'm not all white," Kate said. "I'm a quarter Cherokee."

"That's good blood to have."

"Why, I've thought so," she said. "My grandmother was Cherokee. She was the finest woman I ever knew." She looked at him intently, and then she said, "When my father was killed in the war she was going to go after the Yankee that did it, except she didn't have any way of knowing what Yankee. I was five or six then and the first thing I remember was Grandma getting ready to go with her scalping knife. The only thing that held her back was not knowing how to find out who the Yankee was. Then when I was ten she just died. It always made me think the Yankee'd died too, and she knew it some way, and had gone off to get him where she knew she could find him."

She smiled a little, but the way she had told it made him uncomfortable. It seemed to him they had talked only of death since they had sat down. He said, "I guess I would have known you for part Cherokee. With those black eyes."

"My nose. I think I might've given up a little Cherokee blood for a decent-sized nose."

He protested, and put his hand to his own nose, laughing; it was the first time he had ever been pleased with it.

"How did you break it?" Kate asked.

"Fight," he said. "Well, Billy did it," he said reluctantly. "We got in a fight and he hit me with a piece of kindling. He had a temper."

Silently she rose and went into the kitchen. She brought back the coffee pot and poured steaming coffee into the two cups. When she had seated herself again, she said, "The first time you talked to me you knew he was going to kill your brother. Didn't you?"

"I guess I did."

When she seemed to change the subject he was grateful: "Where were you from before Nebraska?"

"From Pennsylvania to begin with. I don't remember it much."

"Yankee," she said.

"I guess I am. Where are you from, Kate?"

"Texas." She sat very stiffly, not looking at him now but attentive, as though she were listening to something within herself. She said, "I don't know about Yankees. In Texas if a man killed your brother you went after him."

He picked up his cup. The coffee burned his tongue but he drank it anyway, and when he put the cup down he spilled coffee in a thin brown stain on the oilcloth.

"But you're not going after Blaisedell," Kate said, in a flat voice.
He shook his head. "No."

"Afraid of him?"

"I have got no reason to be afraid of him."

She shrugged her shoulders. All at once she seemed very cold, and bored.

"Men brace people they are afraid of," he said. "That's nothing to do with it. I just don't expect I have to set out to kill a man because some people think I ought to."

"Who?" Kate said.

"Some people here. But I am not going to go against Blaisedell just because I don't want people to think I am yellow. I don't care that much what they think of me." He felt himself flushing, as though he had been caught in a brag. Kate was looking at the star on his shirt, her mouth tucked in at the corners.

"Meaning what I think?" she said.

"Why, no. Anyhow all that is nothing to do with it. It's that I don't see how any blame is due Blaisedell. Or not—not much."

"You have called him not guilty before the jury in Bright's City got around to it, have you?"

"Well, it was self-defense clear enough, when you come down to it. They'd come in to kill him. Billy told me that."

Kate drank her coffee. Her eyelashes made delicate shadows upon her white cheeks. He finished his own coffee, disappointed and ill at ease in this silence. Finally he said, "Well, I had better be going now, Miss Dollar."

"Kate," she said. "No, don't go yet. There might be somebody coming by and I think I had better have a man here."

"Who?"

"The jack I rented this house from. I thought he might be planning on paying a call."

He nodded, and he felt better. She poured another cup of coffee, and he said, "You said you knew Blaisedell in Fort James?"

"I knew Tom Morgan. If you knew him you knew Blaisedell."

"What did they think of Blaisedell in Fort James, Kate?"

She didn't answer right away, and he saw the tightening in her face. She said, "About the same as they do here. The way they feel about a badman anywhere. Some like him because they think if they show they like him he'll like them. Others don't like him and stay out of his way. People are the same most places."

Her black eyes met his expressionlessly as she went on. "He dealt faro for Morgan and people knew he was a gunman from the start. Though nobody knew anything about him. Then one day a man named Ben Nicholson came in. A real bad rattlesnake of a man. He was shooting things up. Drunk and cursing everybody and trying to get a fight. He was trying to get the marshal to fight. So Blaisedell went to the marshal and said he'd brace Nicholson, and the mayor heard him and fired the marshal and made Blaisedell marshal. So Blaisedell went out in the street and told Nicholson to get out of town. Nicholson drew on him so Blaisedell killed him."

She stopped, but it didn't sound as though she was finished, and he waited for her to go on.

"So he was marshal but he still worked for Morgan," she said. "Morgan had given him a quarter interest in the place he had there."

"A lot of marshals do that."

"I didn't say there was anything wrong with it."

"I'm sorry. I didn't mean to bust in."

"That's all I was going to say. He killed four or five others—badmen mostly. That writer came and gave him those gold-handled guns. I guess you've seen them. I was gone by then. I left pretty soon after he killed—Nicholson. Fort James was dying off by then and everybody was beginning to move on."

"What did you mean," he said slowly, "that the four or five others was badmen *mostly?*"

She said, in a voice so thick he could hardly understand her, "I am sick and tired of talking about Clay Blaisedell and who he killed."

"I'm sorry. I guess it's not a thing women are interested in much." He tried desperately to think of something to say that would interest her, but it seemed to him that he didn't know anything that would interest anybody. He wondered why she had gotten so angry.

"I've heard people saying you'd come out here to start up a dance hall," he said, tentatively. "Seems like it would be a good thing."

She shrugged. Then she sighed and said, "I don't know. Maybe I am waiting to see if this town is dying off too." Something in the way she said it made him think it was a kind of apology for her anger, and after that it was almost all right again. They discussed the rumors that wages were going to be dropped at the mines, and she told him of the strike she had seen at Silver Mountain. She regarded him brightly now when he spoke, and so he found himself not so tongue-tied, although he marveled at how much more she knew, and had seen, than he. It was almost like talking to a man, and almost he could forget he was having supper with Kate Dollar in her house and alone, and that they were man and woman. But he would be brought back to it sharply from time to time, by something she said, or by some movement, and it was a very intense thing to him, except that it always made him begin to wonder again what had brought her to Warlock, who she was and what she was; but now he did not want to know. And he marveled too at how fine-looking she was in the lamplight, and at how soft her sharp black eyes could be sometimes, and the crooked way her mouth twisted when she smiled the smile he liked. He could not keep his eyes from the soft shadows her lashes made upon her cheeks.

Then she asked about McQuown. "What sort is he? I've heard a lot about him since I've been here, but I don't think I've ever seen him in town."

"He and Curley are in tonight. I guess on their way up to Bright's for the trial." He paused, to see if she was really interested; she was watching him intently. "Well, he is a rustler, mostly," he went on. "I know him pretty well. He took Billy and me on to work for him after our father died—the Apaches'd run off all our stock."

"How bad is he?"

He laughed shakily and said, "Why, Kate, I guess I don't like to talk about him sort of the way you don't about Blaisedell."

She touched a finger to the corner of her mouth. She looked wary, suddenly. "I see," she said. "You are against McQuown. So you are for Blaisedell."

"No, that's not so. Not like Carl is; not—" He stopped and looked down at his hands. "Maybe I am in a way," he said. "For Abe is bad. Worse than he ought to be, and worse all the time, it seems like. I used to think pretty high of him."

"But you left," she said. "You left and your brother stayed on there."

He stared down at his hands. He was going to tell her; it surprised him that he was. It seemed to him that Kate was gathering information not because she was interested in him, but for some purpose of her own that he had no way of deciphering. Yet, he thought, he would tell her, and only waited to get it calm and in proportion in his mind, so that he could tell it correctly.

"It was eight or ten months ago," he said. "Maybe you've heard about it. Some Mexicans that was supposed to have been shot by Apaches in Rattlesnake Canyon. Peach came down with the cavalry. I guess everybody thought it was Apaches."

"I've heard about it. Somebody said it was McQuown's men dressed like Apaches."

He nodded, and wet his lips. "We'd rustled more than a thousand head down at Hacienda Puerto," he said. "But Abe wasn't along. Abe always ran things like that pretty well, but he wasn't along that time. He was sick, I guess it was, and Curley and Dad McQuown was running it, but there was nobody so clever as Abe. Anyway, they just about caught us, and Hank Miller was shot dead, and Dad McQuown shot and crippled. We lost all the stock, and they trailed us pretty close all the way.

"We got across the border all right, but then we found out they were coming right on after us. Abe was there by then, for Curley had rode the old man back to San Pablo. So a bunch of us stripped down and smeared ourselves with mud and boxed those Mexicans of Don Ignacio's in Rattlesnake Canyon. We killed them all. I guess maybe one or two got away down the south end, but all the others. Seventeen of them."

He picked up his coffee cup; his hand was steady. The coffee was cold, and he set the cup down again.

"That's when you left?" Kate said; she didn't sound shocked.

"I had some money and I went up to Rincon and paid a telegrapher to apprentice me. I thought it would be a good trade. But he died and I got laid off. So I came back here."

It struck him that he had been able to tell her all there was to know about him in a few minutes. He shifted his position in his chair and his scabbarded Colt thumped noisily against the wood. He went on. "I can't say I didn't know what Abe aimed to do there in Rattlesnake Canyon. I knew, and I was against it, but everybody else was for it and I was afraid to go against them. I guess because I was afraid they'd think I was yellow. Curley wouldn't go, though; he wouldn't do it. There was some others that didn't like it. I know Chet Haggin didn't. And Billy was sick—to his stomach, afterwards. But he stuck down there. I guess he figured it out some way inside himself so it was all right, afterwards. But I couldn't."

"If you don't like to see men shot down you are in the wrong business, Deputy," Kate said.

"No, I'm in the right business. I was wrong when I went up to Rincon—that was just running away. There is only one way to stop men from killing each other like that."

He looked up to see her black eyes glittering at him. She smiled and it was the smile he did not like. She started to speak, but then she stopped, and her eyes turned toward the door. He heard quiet footsteps on the porch.

He rose as a key rattled in the lock and the door swung inward. A short, fat, clean-shaven miner stood in the doorway, in clean blue shirt and trousers. His hair gleamed with grease.

"Oh, hello, Mr. Benson," Kate said. "Meet Mr. Gannon, the deputy. Did you want something, Mr. Benson?"

The miner shuffled his feet. He backed up a step, out of the light. "I just come by, miss."

"I guess you came by to give me the other key," Kate said. "Just give it to Johnny, will you? He's been asking for it, but I'd thought there was only one."

"That's it," the miner said. "Remembered I had this other key here and I thought I'd just better bring it by before I went and forgot, the way a man does."

Gannon stepped toward him, and the miner dropped the heavy key into his hand. The miner watched it all the way as Gannon put it in his pocket.

Kate laughed as he fled, and Gannon closed the door again. He couldn't look at Kate as he returned to the table.

"He's sorry he rented it so cheap," Kate said.

"I guess I'd better talk to him tomorrow."

"Don't bother."

He stood leaning on the back of his chair. "Anytime anybody fusses you, Kate. I mean, there's some wild ones here and not much on manners. You could let me know."

"Why, thank you," she said. She got to her feet. "Are you going now?" she said. Dismissing him, he thought; she had just asked him for supper because of the miner.

"Why, yes, I guess I had better go. It was certainly an enjoyable supper. I surely thank you."

"I surely thank you," she said, as though she were mocking him.

He started to put the key down on the table.

"Keep it," she said, and his hand pulled it back, quickly. It was clear enough, he thought. He tried to grin, but he felt a disappointment that worked deeper and deeper until it was a kind of pain.

He started around the table toward her. But something in her stiff face halted him, a kind of shame that touched the shame he felt and yet was a different thing. And there was something cruel, too, in her face, that repelled him. Uncertainly he turned away.

"Well, good night, Miss Dollar," he said thickly.

"Good night, Deputy."

"Good night," he said again, and took his hat from the hook and opened the door. The blue-black sky was full of stars. There was a wind that seemed cold after the warmth inside.

"Good night," Kate said again, and he tipped his hat, without looking back, and closed the door behind him.

Walking back toward Main Street he could feel the weight of the key in his pocket. He wondered what she had meant by it, and thought he had been right about it at first. He wondered what had happened inside her that had showed so in her face at the end; he wondered what she was and what she wanted until his mind ached with it.

26. Journals of Henry Holmes Goodpasture

March 2, 1881

JED ROLFE in on the stage this afternoon, and everyone gathered around him to hear about the first day of the trial. Evidently the delay came about because at the last moment General Peach decided he would hear the case himself, as Military Governor, from which illegal and senile idiocy he was finally dissuaded. General Peach, however, did sit in at the trial and interrupted frequently to the harrassment of everyone and the baffled rage of Judge Alcock. Peach is evidently inimical to Blaisedell, for what reason I cannot imagine. My God, surely Blaisedell cannot be found guilty of anything! Yet I must remind myself that anything is possible in the Bright's City court.

If Blaisedell were to be found guilty I think this town would rise almost to a man and ride into Bright's City in armed rebellion to free him. Opinion has swung violently back to his behalf in light of this newest report, and his critics are silent. Miss Jessie Marlow in my store this afternoon ostensibly to purchase some ribbon, actually to learn if I had heard anything beyond the news Rolfe had brought. I had not, and could only try to reassure her that Blaisedell would be speedily acquitted. She was sadly pale, ill-looking, and far from her usual cheerful self, but she thanked me for my pitiful offering as though it were of value.

McQuown's absence from Bright's City's courthouse has been remarked upon. He and Burne passed through Warlock on Sunday, and it was presumed they were en route to the trial. But only Burne was there; indeed, he seems to have been the only other San Pabloite other than Luke Friendly to appear. Rolfe said he heard that Burne and Deputy Schroeder exchanged hot words upon the courthouse steps, and would have exchanged more than words had not Sheriff Keller intervened. McQuown is no doubt more frightened that Blaisedell will be acquitted and return, than we are that he will not.

March 4, 1881

Buck Slavin, the doctor, Schroeder, et al. back. The jury is deliberating. They had waited over a day after the jury had left the box, but it was still out. They seem certain Blaisedell will be acquitted, and that the jury's delay is only to enjoy as many meals upon the county as possible. Still, I notice that they seem worried that Luke Friendly's outrageous lies may have told heavily against Blaisedell. Buck is bitter about the prosecuting attorney, Pierce, and that Judge Alcock did not cut him short more often than he did.

Evidently Pierce sought to inflame the jury with Billy Gannon's youth, with the fact that less than a month ago the three Cowboys had been declared innocent in the same court, and with Blaisedell's "murderous presumption" in setting aside the court's decision and declaring himself "Judge and Executioner." Buck says that the same rumor we have had here—that Morgan and Blaisedell were actually the road agents themselves, and murdered the "innocents" in an effort both to silence and permanently affix the blame on them—has been sown in Bright's City, and, although not much believed there (Bright's City has not seen as much of McQuown as we have, but they have seen enough) had evidently been heard by Pierce, and it was Pierce's hints and implications along these lines that Buck felt Judge Alcock should have dealt with more firmly. As all agree that Friendly was a poor witness against Blaisedell, so do they agree that Morgan was the best witness in Blaisedell's behalf; that he was cool and convincing, and gave as good as he got from Pierce, several times calling forth peals of laughter from the courtroom at the prosecutor's expense.

From all I have heard I am glad I did not attend the trial. Poor Blaisedell; I pity him what he has gone through. Yet it was at his own instigation, and I am certain no charges would have been brought against him had he not wished it. Buck says, however, that he has been most calm throughout, and apparently took no umbrage at Pierce's blackguardly accusations.

> "What stronger breastplate than a heart untainted?
> Thrice is he armed that hath his quarrel just;
> And he but naked, though locked up in steel,
> Whose conscience with injustice is corrupted."

March 5, 1881

Blaisedell was acquitted yesterday. Peter Bacon arrived this morning with the news, having ridden all night. I sent a note around immediately to Miss Jessie, expressing my pleasure at hearing it, but there was no reply other than her verbal thanks to my *mozo*.

Now that Blaisedell is free and absolved, I am neither pleased nor relieved. The blackguardly statements with which Pierce harangued the jury, the jury's inexcusable delay, Friendly's damnable lies about what happened in the Acme Corral, and General Peach's actions throughout *—how must these have affected him? He must have gone to court wishing absolution, and received only a poor, grudging, and besmudged verdict in his behalf. The official verdict, however, will not affect the verdict here, and I think in days to come there will be bad blood between Warlock men and Bright's City men. Although I will say that the Bright's City paper has treated Blaisedell with great respect in its columns and especially in its editorials, and I will congratulate Editor Jim Askew on these when next I see him.

I find myself deeply emotionally subscribed to all this. It seems to me that I, and all of us here, have a stake and an investment in the Marshal. He has produced, and, looking back, I see that he did from the beginning produce, an intense division for or against him. But Clay Blaisedell is not the rock upon which we are divided, he is only a symptom. We do not break so simply as some think into the two camps of townsmen and Cowboys. We break into the camps of those wildly inclined, and those soberly, those irresponsible and those responsible, those peace-loving and those outlaw and riotous by nature; further, into the camps of respect, and of fear—I mean for oneself,

---

* General Peach evidently, upon one occasion, shouted down the judge to say that Blaisedell should properly have been tried by a military tribunal, and that he, General Peach, would have had him shot. Why the military governor was not declared in contempt of court for his interference is perhaps understandable, and references to his peculiar actions, most delicately handled, are contained in the *Bright's City Star-Democrat's* reports of the trial.

and for all decent things besides. These are the poles between which we vibrate, and Blaisedell has only emphasized the distance between them. It is too simple perhaps to say that those who fear themselves and fear their fellow men, fear and hate Blaisedell, while those who respect themselves, and Man, respect him. Yet I hold that this is true in a broad sense.

For the arguments continue, what happened in the Acme Corral compounded by the Bright's City court and those who spoke there. I feel strongly that not merely I, but everyone here, sees himself affected personally by all this, and that, somehow, the truth or falsity of the whole affair reflects through and upon each of us. Fine points are argued as heatedly as the whole—how many shots, how many paces, who was stationed in exactly what position, and so on *ad infinitum*. So must the schoolmen have argued in their day, in their own saloons, the number of angels who could dance on the head of a pin.

27. Curley Burne and the Dog Killer

CURLEY rode in from the river on his way back to San Pablo from Bright's City, blowing on his mouth organ. The music was pleasant to his ears in the silence around him, and the sun was pleasant upon his back as the gelding Dick plodded over the bare brown ridges and down the grassy draws. The Dinosaurs towered to the southwest with the sun on their slopes like honey, and from the elevation of the ridges he could see the irregular line of cottonwoods marking the river's course toward Rattlesnake Canyon.

His cheerful mood vanished as he saw the chimney of the long-gone old house, and the windmill on the pump house. He was not bringing good news from Bright's City.

Finally he came in sight of the ranch house, low to the ground and weathered gray as a horned toad; and now he could see the bunkhouse, cook shack, horse corral—the porch of the ranch house. There were two figures seated there.

Going down the last slope Dick quickened his pace expectantly. Curley dropped the mouth organ back inside his shirt, flicked Dick with his spurs, and went down toward the house at a run, bending low in the saddle with his hat flying off and its cord cutting against his throat. He drew up with a yell before the porch, dismounted in a whirl of dust and barking dogs, and went up the steps. The other man he had seen was Dechine, Abe's neighbor to the south, dropped in to pay a call. Dad McQuown was lying on a cot in the sun.

Abe sat staring at the mountains with his hat tipped forward to shade his face, scratching a thumb through his beard. He was leaning back with his boots crossed up on the porch rail.

Curley said, "Well, howdy, Dechine. How's it?"

"Fine-a-lee," Dechine said, fanning dust away with his hat. He was a short, pot-bellied fellow with little reddened eyes and a nose like half a red pear stuck to his face.

The old man propped himself up on one elbow. "Well, what happened, Curley? They set him loose?"

"They did," he said. Abe sat there silently, staring off at the Dinosaurs with the long creases in his cheeks like scars. All the starch had gone out of him since the boys had got killed in the Acme Corral; sometimes he acted as though there were nothing left in him at all.

The old man spat tobacco juice in a puddle beside his pallet, swiped at his little red mouth, and said, "Buggers."

"I was just telling Abe, here," Dechine said, "how people has got down on Blaisedell in Warlock there, over murdering those poor boys."

"One of them's not Carl," Curley said. "I don't know what's got into Carl. Used to be a man could get along with him."

"You have trouble with Schroeder?" the old man said eagerly.

"We went and scratched some. He is taking lawing pretty hard."

"He is one of those thinks Blaisedell is probably Jesus Christ there," Dechine said. "I've been telling Abe they are not all like that, though."

Still Abe didn't move, didn't speak. Curley took out his mouth organ, then put it back. He didn't know what had happened to everybody but it had begun to seem to him more and more that it was time to move on. Everything was nasty now, except when he was off by himself. Dad McQuown scraped his nerves like a rasp, and it was poor to see a man scared loose from himself, which was the case with Abe, who was the best friend he had ever had. He had got Abe to come as far as Warlock with him on his way up to Bright's City, and Abe hadn't said as much as two words the whole time and had acted as though he were madder at him, Curley, than at anybody else. He had stayed in the Lucky Dollar about an hour and then headed on back without an aye, yes, or no, except to say Warlock turned his stomach now. Everything had turned bad because of Blaisedell sitting in Warlock like a poison spider in its dirty web.

"Where's Luke?" Abe asked.

"Well, he decided he'd go over toward Rincon and see what the country's like there. Said he was tired of the territory."

Abe made a sound that was a fair try at a laugh. The old man yelled, "Hollow pure yellow son of a bitch!" He began fretting and cursing to himself, and scratching viciously at his legs. They itched all the time now, he said.

"Well, now," Dechine said. "I didn't get up to the trial there, but I heard Blaisedell had himself an awful hard time up there." His little red eyes sought Curley's. "Isn't that right, Curley?"

"Joy to see it. I wished you'd been there, Abe."

Abe said nothing.

"Well, I mean," Dechine said. "What I come by to tell you, Abe. I was talking to Tom Morgan, kind of talking around it to him there, and he sounded like Blaisedell wasn't going to stand for being pissed on up there at Bright's like he was. Sounded like he thought Blaisedell might move on."

"He won't move on," Abe said. "He's got work to do still." Curley watched him stretch, and knew it was a fraud. "Killing to do yet," Abe said.

Curley averted his eyes to see Dechine scowling down at his knees, and the old man grimacing horribly.

Dechine said, "There is this new woman up in Warlock. Kate Dollar her name is, and high-toned as that madam they used to have at the French Palace there. Won't have anything to do with anybody, but I see her passing the time there with Johnny Gannon the other day. Never thought of him much as being a long-boy, before."

"Hope she gives him the dirty con," the old man said. "Any son of a bitch that would stand by and see his brother burnt down by that hog butcher."

"Dog killer," Abe said, in that way he had, as though he were talking to no one. "He will come back because he didn't get all the dogs killed yet."

"I swear!" Dad McQuown cried. "It makes a man want to puke to hear a son of mine talk like you do!"

Abe didn't even appear to hear. Dechine was studying his knees some more.

"Son, what's got into you?" the old man said. "I never heard such fool talk."

Curley heard snarling beneath the porch. One of the dogs dashed off around the corner; it was the big black bitch, with the little feisty brown one after her. Abe stirred a little, and moved his shoulders in his grease-stained buckskin shirt.

"Why, they make you out a dog," Abe said. "Run everything onto you. Then they put the dog killer after you and it crosses out everything. I see how it works," he said, nodding like that, to himself.

Curley said, "Maybe they will take it far enough back so they can make out it was you all the time, instead of Apaches out here."

Abe looked at him with his green marbles of eyes. "Do you think you are joking, Curley? They could do it if they tried. Because time was when every foul thing any man did it was Paches did it. And so old Peach came dog-killing down and cleaned them out. And so start all over clean. It is like a woman every month. Now it's Abe McQuown is the dog and Blaisedell dog killer so they can start clean again. I see how it works."

"*Jesus!*" the old man said.

"Watch I'm not right, Daddy," Abe said. "They have piled all the foul on me now. Then they will bleed it out and start clean. A man'd been educated he could follow it all the way back through history, I expect. How it's worked just like that. You can't blame them. Can't blame Blaisedell even."

"*Jesus Christ!*" Dad McQuown said. Curley looked at Dechine and shook his head a little, and Dechine found a place on the back of his hand that needed studying more than his knees.

Curley said, "Abe, I guess I never knew a man with as many friends as you. And talking this crazy stuff."

Abe blinked and stared off at the mountains. After a long time he said, "You think I have gone yellow. But I'm not scared. I just feel like one of those calves in the Bible that's going to get its throat cut by a bunch of wild Jews set on it. Only those calves never knew what was happening to them."

"Holy Jesus Christ, son!" the old man yelled. "You have been chewing on the wrong weed. Son—"

But Abe continued, not even raising his voice. "Can't blame Blaisedell even. He is just doing what all the rest want. He is just the one with the knife to do the cutting."

Dechine said, "I never heard about Blaisedell being any shakes with a knife."

Abe's eyes glittered with anger as he glared at Dechine. But he did not speak, and Curley sighed to see him.

"Son," the old man said. "Now listen here, son. Why, God-damned right it looks like Blaisedell is itching to kill you. But the thing you have to do is kill him first."

"He'll kill me if he gets a chance," Abe said. "I'd be a fool to give him the chance."

Curley said slowly, "Blaikie would surely like to buy this spread, Abe." He met Abe's eyes that blazed at him, sorrier for Abe than he had ever been for anyone else; Abe's eyes wavered away from his, and he was sorry for that, too.

"Do you think I would run out like Luke?" Abe said hoarsely.

"What're you going to do, Abe?" Dechine asked.

"Only one thing for a man to do," Dad McQuown said, "that's being chased out of his own country."

"Wait it out," Abe said.

"Why, son, there's them that fought your fight for you moldering on Boot Hill in Warlock! Why, if I was anything but half a man myself I'd—"

"You're not," Abe snapped.

Curley said, "I've been thinking of moving on myself, Abe."

"Run then."

"I wouldn't look at it I was running. Things have gone bad here, is all. I wouldn't look at it that you was running either."

"I don't run," Abe said. He shook his head, his face in shadow beneath his hatbrim, the sun red-gold in his beard.

"Or fight," the old man said contemptuously. "Or anything."

"Wait it out, that's the best thing, Abe," Dechine said. Curley saw Abe's face twist again, as though with pain, and Curley stood up a little straighter, where he leaned against the rail. He could feel the strangled violence in Abe and he was afraid that if Dechine said one more stupid thing Abe would jump him.

But Abe only shrugged and said, "Can't go against what everybody thinks of you." Then, after a time, he said, "Can't run and I can't go against him. He is fast. He is faster than anybody in the country. He's— He'd—"

He stopped, staring, and Curley turned to see the brown dog trotting around the corner of the house, his dark-spotted tongue lolling from his mouth. Abe leaned back stiffly. His hand flicked down, and up; his Colt crashed with a spit of fire and smoke and the dog was knocked rolling in the dirt with about a half a yelp. The Colt crashed and spat again and again, and with each shot the brown, bloody, dusty body was pushed farther away as though it were being jerked along on the end of a rope.

"Like that!" Abe whispered, as the gunsmoke blew away around him. He holstered his Colt. "Like that," he said again.

28. Journals of Henry Holmes Goodpasture

March 12, 1881

I HAD thought this affair of only local importance. It did not occur to me that it had spread beyond the territory. I was surprised to read a long account of it in a San Antonio paper which someone brought here, and now I have come into possession of a magazine called the *Western Gazette*. This so-called journal combines cheapjack writing with smudged print upon coarse paper, and is devoted almost entirely to an affair vaguely resembling, and called, "The Battle in the Acme Corral." It is a strange experience to read an account such as this, where an occurrence one is closely acquainted with is transformed into something wild, woolly, and improbable, with only the names true, and not all of *them* by any means. There is a crude illustration upon the cover, depicting a huge St. George of a man whose six-shooter is almost as long as a sword, confronting a host of sombreroed dragons. The execrably written text might be the more infuriating if Blaisedell were held to be the villain of the piece, but possibly nothing could be more intolerable than the fulsome praise, the impossible prowess and nobility, and the heroic speeches that make the gorge rise. The author listed nine dead, of whom Morgan was credited with three. It is fantastic to think of people reading, and believing, this vile fiction, which is solemnly presented as Truth. Buck says there were a number of newspapermen at the trial, however, some of whom had come from great distances to attend it. Presumably Warlock will now go down in History as the site of "The Battle in the Acme Corral," as well as of the Medusa Mine. Blood is as stirring to the human imagination as silver.

I was struck by the artist's depiction of Blaisedell as a huge man.

Since the corral shown has nothing to do with the original, other than its name, and the representation of Blaisedell the same, I find myself wondering why the artist chose to draw a great brute of a fellow. A rough-and-tumble Hero for a rough-and-tumble people? Feats of strength being more appealing than feats of finesse? No doubt the artist knows better than I the correct heroic image to present to a republican mentality.

This magazine has affected me more deeply than merely with the contempt and anger I felt upon first examining it. For are we not, perhaps, here in Warlock, sitting in upon the childbed of a Legend? Are we watching such a momentous birth all unknowingly, and, unknowing too, this one or that one of us helping it along, acting as midwife, boiling the water, holding the swaddling clothes, etc? As time goes on and if the infant does not die (literally!), and continues to grow, will not this cheap and fabulous account in this poor excuse for a magazine become, on its terms, a version much more acceptable than ours, the true one? It is a curious thought; how much do these legends, as they outstrip and supersede their originals, rest upon Truth, and how much upon some dark and impenetrable design within Man himself?

March 18, 1881

A most pleasant evening last night, spent with Buck, Joe Kennon, Jed Rolfe, Will Hart, Fred Winters, and the doctor. I held forth mightily, I talked my mouth dry, and my listeners' ears to tatters; but I must hold that Blaisedell is a virtuous man (against no opposition in that company), and that the Acme Corral was a tragedy for him since it was not a clear-cut victory. For he deserves no other kind.

We speculated on the fact that Blaisedell has not yet returned to Warlock, although it has been two weeks since his acquittal. Morgan has been to Bright's City, undoubtedly to see him, but has made no comment or explanation that I have heard. My fear is that Blaisedell will not return at all. This would be a blow to us, for I fear our uneasy peace is coming to an end. A miner was killed by one of his fellows in a quarrel at the French Palace last Thursday night. The survivor was arrested and has been sent to Bright's City for trial, but it is felt that this would not have happened had Blaisedell been here. Will Hart has heard he is riding a tiger in a Bright's City gambling hall and does not wish to quit while he is winning. Buck is irritated with him; after all, there were no provisions made for long vacations in the terms of his employment. We all, of course, fear that Warlock will revert to her former state of violence and lawlessness in his absence, temporary or permanent.

Will, I think, feels that Blaisedell would do better not to return. That, for instance, he might take offense at talk and be forced into petty quarrels. This has occurred to me too. Yet I myself want Blaisedell to return, not merely for the sake of peace here, but in order that he may in some way redeem himself in a further and completely unambiguous action. Joe Kennon, a straightforward man, wishes Blaisedell to return and kill McQuown. Buck Slavin, not so straightforward, fears that McQuown may be feeling vengeful toward him because he has sided with Blaisedell, and wishes devoutly for the same consummation. Buck proclaims that all disorder and lawlessness would die with the San Pabloite, peace would reign, and commerce flourish forever after.

McQuown's death by gunplay, I am afraid, is the climax I also desire. Blaisedell's reputation is important to me. It is as though, through him, I can see a bit of myself immortalized, and the others of this town, and even the whole of this western country. For how can this be done but through those men who, because of their stature among us, we raise still further in tall tales and legends that denote our respect, and which are taken by the world and the generations, from us, as standing for us?

March 20, 1881

It is said that Blaisedell's decision to go to Bright's City and endure trial was to a large degree brought about by Judge Holloway's righteous rantings at him. I have heard the judge cursed for this often of late. Pike Skinner is especially bitter toward him, and there is a rumor that when Schroeder heard that Blaisedell had departed for Bright's City, he physically assaulted the judge as being the cause. The old story, that arises whenever the judge is in an unpopular phase, is also current again: that he was run out of Dade County, Texas, where he was a J.P., for drunkenness and other more sinister vices. But I must defend him, and counter with the story which seems to me at least complementary to the other: that he was run out of Dade County because he tried to expose a criminally inclined sheriff who was, unfortunately, much better liked by the Texans than Judge Holloway and Rectitude.

I have also heard that he was at one time judge on a bench of some importance in Kansas, where people became so inflamed against him because of a series of unpopular decisions—I have no doubt that these were righteous ones, righteously delivered—that they tarred, feathered, and rode him out of town on a rail.

Certainly he is a bitter man, and one impossible to know, but if there are kernels of truth in these two tales of him, the outlines of his bitterness begin to show; nor will I condemn a man for trying to drown an abysmal bitterness in alcohol. He is a lonely man, too; he has no friends, nor even any regular drinking companions. He is uncomfortable company.

He can be awesome enough on occasion, in his wrath, although he usually ends by making a fool of himself, when he is pitiable. Yet he is, to me at least, more often than not an admirable man, and Warlock owes a debt of gratitude to him. As judge "on acceptance" he has long dealt successfully with our minor disputes and misdemeanors, and he has, almost singlehandedly, as the deputies have come and gone and Sheriff Keller has done neither, maintained at least an awareness of the law here, where there has been no law.

March 28, 1881

Blaisedell has returned. He has resigned his position as Marshal and is dealing faro at the Glass Slipper. Disappointed and heartsick as I am at this turn of events, I cannot find it in my heart to blame him.

BOOK TWO

 **The Regulators**

29. Gannon Looks for Trouble

GANNON was alone in the jail when he heard the pound of bootheels on the boardwalk, and Carl hurried in. Carl sailed his hat toward the peg and grunted with satisfaction when it caught and swung there. But he said, "Trouble," as he sat down at the table.

"What?"

"They are dropping wages at the Medusa and the Sister Fan," Carl said. One end of his mustache was wet where he had been chewing on it. "They are going to do it," he said. "And the others'll follow what the Porphyrion and Western Mining Company does, sure as shooting. MacDonald just told me. He is worried about it; he by God ought to be!"

"They knew it was coming."

"Not by a dollar a day, they didn't!"

Gannon whistled.

"Cutting them a dollar a day. MacDonald says it's got to be that much because the price of silver's went down, partly, and partly because they are getting all that water down on the thousand-foot level. Unprofitable labor, getting rid of water, he says. There is going to be hell broke loose when they hear about it."

"They don't know about it yet?"

"He'll tell them payday." Carl took a dirty, irregularly bitten piece of plug out of his pocket, and wrenched a corner off with his teeth.

"That's almost twenty-five per cent."

"It is, and there is going to be hell. MacDonald's not likely to step out of his way to miss any trouble, either. Well, and easy enough to wreck a mine, to give him his due. Charge of giant powder somewhere, or a fire in the stope. There was that one on the Comstock burned for three years and then had to be all retimbered before they could work it again. So MacDonald is getting ready to bust them before they bust him."

"Bust them how? Did he say?"

"He has got his mind set on running out that Brunk he fired a while back, the one he tried to get Blaisedell to post. And Frenchy Martin and old Heck, and some others he says're agitators too. Wants us to run them out for him." Carl looked up at him and grinned a little.

"No," Gannon said.

"What I told him," Carl said. The lump of tobacco moved in his cheek like a mouse. "So Mister Mac is down on me; he is a man that doesn't take kindly to anybody saying him no. I told him we would come out to the Medusa Saturday when they announced it—try to stop trouble. But he'd got other ideas by then."

Carl sighed and said, "And I think what he's got in mind now is rounding up a crew of hardcases to do his dirty work for him. Regulators was what he said, and I thought he meant some Citizens' Committee people he'd get together. But now I wonder if he wasn't thinking San Pablo."

"It's what he did before."

"Cade," Carl said. "By God, I forgot about that. Damn it to hell!" he burst out. "I wish we could count on Blaisedell if MacDonald intends on pulling something like that. By God if I want to see Warlock run by MacDonald and a bunch of San Pablo hardcases any more than McQuown and Curley and the same. What the hell's got into Blaisedell, you suppose, anyhow?"

Gannon went over to sit down beside the alley door, and Carl scraped his chair around to face him. "Maybe he is just waiting for McQuown to come in," Carl went on. "Maybe that's what he is doing. Except why'd he quit marshaling?"

"Maybe he is sick of killing."

Carl stared at him; he licked his lips. "Johnny, you haven't gone and turned against him because of Billy? I thought you hadn't."

Gannon shook his head, patiently. He had prayed that he could remain patient. Always he could feel the accusations, from both sides, picking at him like knives whenever he walked the streets. He had ignored them so far, but he was afraid he was not always going to be able to.

"Well, somebody's got to be peace officers," Carl said. "And killing is part of it. I don't see—" He stopped, and shook his head and said, "I wonder if it wasn't that Miss Jessie went and turned against him. That'd sour a man. He is not rooming there any more, and they say he don't see her any more. That would turn a man sour."

He rose and paced the floor, his hands gripping his shell belt, his face puzzled and angry. "There is Blaisedell banking faro for Morgan and a glass of whisky right near all the time—and why? And there is McQuown keeping down to San Pablo. Scared to death, some say, but I think he is just waiting like a damned coyote. Everything is too quiet. It is so quiet it sets my nerves to banging like a dinner bell. Everybody just sitting around waiting for something to happen. What to happen?"

"I've felt it too."

"Well, there's going to be fireworks and the band playing with this pay drop, anyhow."

Carl went over and kicked the cell door; it swung slowly shut. Carl stood facing the cell, his head bent down dejectedly. "Well, I never said I wasn't a scaredy-cat," he said. "But it sure comes on me hard sometimes. If we just had Blaisedell to yell for if MacDonald starts up anything, or those jacks either. Like that night they tried to lynch Billy and the other two, out of here. That was a night! A man knew what he had to do that night, and it was surely a comfort to have Blaisedell by."

Gannon kept silent while Carl brooded—over Blaisedell, he knew, more than that there might be trouble at the mines. Gannon found himself almost looking forward to trouble. It had been too quiet. More than once, faced with the fact that some thought him one kind of coward, and some another, one kind of traitor, or another, it had all seemed hopeless and he had thought of quitting. Now, he thought, he might be of some use.

30. The Doctor Considers the Ends of Men

THE doctor sat opposite Jessie with the checkerboard between them. He watched her take his king; he was used to letting her win because he loved to hear her laugh and clap her hands in triumph. But these days she did not laugh, nor even smile much. She had been this way since Blaisedell had come back from Bright's City, and had not come back to the General Peach. Blaisedell had not even been to see her, so far as he knew. But still she kept his room for him, and still she turned expectantly toward the door whenever anyone entered.

Her white, nervous hand moved her checkers out, and his own square, short, hairy hand retreated. She took his last king. "Oh, I have beaten you again, David!" she said.

"You can't do it three times in a row," he said, and began spreading the checkers out on the squares for another game. Footsteps sounded; her eyes swung toward the door. He turned too, and saw that it was only a miner, who leaned heavily upon the rail as he mounted the stairs.

"There are many of them drunk tonight," Jessie said. "Almost every one."

"They know a wage cut is coming tomorrow. I'm afraid they will do more than get drunk when they find it is to be a dollar a day."

"Yes," she said listlessly. She leaned forward to study his move.

"We may be very busy," he said. "It is always sad when we are busy, isn't it?" But he thought it would be angry this time.

"I hear them talking about the Miners' Union again," Jessie said. She jumped his checker and snatched it up, and looked up at him with her pale mouth bent into a smile and her eyes alight for an instant. But only for an instant.

"In the end they are going to have to have their union, Jessie," he said. "They will have to have their union to get out from under the manipulations of a bunch of conniving speculators in San Francisco and New York. And maybe to get out from under—our charity just as much as that."

"They hate charity, don't they?" Jessie said, matter-of-factly.

He stared at her. She let the checker in her hand drop to the board. "I am tired of living like this," she said, with infinite weariness. "What is there here for me?" He saw the sheen of dampness in her eyes. The little muscles at the corners of her lips flexed to form an ashamed smile. Then she whispered, "Do you ever feel you were made for something, David? Made to do something—oh, something fine! But not know—" She stopped and shook her head, and the ringlets danced.

"I think everyone feels that sometimes, Jessie."

"Oh, no! Oh, I don't think everyone does. Most of them just live along. But there are a few who can do—I suppose I mean *be* something. Something that can go on even after them. And shouldn't those people be trying every moment to *be* that? I mean, God gave it to them to do or be, and if they didn't try I should think they would be very afraid of God."

"It is your move, Jessie," he said.

She was leaning forward with her hand on the locket that hung at her throat, a vertical frown line creasing her forehead, and her eyes were far removed from him. She said, "How terrible for a person to know what he could have been. How he could have gone on. But instead having to live along being nothing, and know he is just going to die and that's the end of it."

She was talking about Blaisedell, and he did not know what to say to her. He removed the checker she had dropped upon the board. Her eyes turned toward the door again; Brunk appeared there, with his cap pulled low upon his forehead and one big hand grasping the door frame. He was grinning, and his face was flushed with liquor.

"Miss Jessie," he said thickly. "And the good doctor Wagner. Good night." He said it with a peculiar inflection.

"Oh, good night, Frank!" Jessie said.

"Good night, Brunk."

"No," Brunk said, with a solemn shake of his head. "I mean, it *is* a good night. Mostly, just before payday, it's not. But this payday—" Brunk grinned again.

"Looking forward to it, are you?" the doctor said grimly.

"Am," Brunk said. He glanced around with exaggerated caution. "Because you know what?" he whispered. "It is going to go down to *three*-fifty a day and they are not going to stand for it." He raised a thick finger to his lips. "Oh, but I won't tell them! Let them hear it from Mister Mac. Then they will bust!"

"And then we can try to patch the bloody heads they bring here."

"Bloody heads to you, but men to me!" Brunk said proudly. "For some'll have to get bloody heads so the others can hold theirs up. It's what I've been waiting for." He turned to Jessie. "Well, Miss Jessie, maybe Lathrop hadn't courage enough. But *I* have. *I* have!" he said, and hit his fist upon his chest.

"That's fine, Frank," Jessie said, in a colorless voice. "But I wish you wouldn't shout so."

Brunk stared at Jessie and his face was at once shocked, hurt, and furious. "You don't think I am good enough, do you, Miss Jessie?"

"Of course I do, Frank!"

"No, you don't," Brunk said. He glanced at the mezzotint of Bonnie Prince Charlie on the wall behind Jessie's head, and his face twisted. "Because I am no *gentleman*," he said. "Because I am no—no long-haired, white-handed gunman. Oh, I know I am not good enough and it is only a bunch of dirty miners anyhow."

The doctor thrust his chair back and rose. "You are drunk," he said. "Get out of here, you drunken fool!"

"Not so drunken as her fair-haired boy-killer!" Brunk cried. "That is so drunk his high-rolling friend's got to half carry him away from the French Pal—"

The doctor darted forward and slapped Brunk's face. Brunk staggered a step back. The doctor slapped him again. "Get out of here!" he cried, in a voice that tore in his throat.

Brunk put his hand to his cheek. He turned slowly away. He moved toward the foot of the stairs, where he leaned against the newel post, a thick, dejected figure in the darkness of the entryway.

Jessie was sitting up very straight, her mouth tightly pursed in her stiff face, her eyes glancing sideways at the checkerboard as though she were considering her next move. Her hand plucked nervously at the locket at her throat.

There was a scuffling sound outside on the stoop, a low cursing. More drunken miners, the doctor thought; he was tired of drunken miners beyond patience. He stepped out toward them just as they came in through the door—two men who were not miners. Clay Blaisedell had come back to the General Peach.

Morgan edged his way inside with an arm around Blaisedell, who was hatless, sagging, stumbling—not wounded in brave battle, merely drunk to helplessness. Brunk had turned and was watching them.

"Come on, Clay boy," Morgan was saying. "Sort those feet out. Almost home now—where you were bound to go." He was panting, his white planter's hat pushed back on his head. "Evening, Doc," he said. Then Morgan said, "Evening, Miss Marlow," and the doctor felt Jessie's fingers grip his arm.

Blaisedell pulled away from Morgan and stood swaying, his boots set apart and his great, fair head hanging as he faced Jessie. Jessie moved a step forward to confront her drunken hero. He had thought she would be shocked and disgusted but she was smiling and looked, he thought, with a painful wrench at his heart, triumphant.

But she did not speak, and after a moment Blaisedell started for the stairs, holding himself very straight. He stopped at the foot, as though realizing his incapacity to mount them, and leaned upon the newel post as Brunk backed away.

Morgan said to Brunk, "You look like you have a strong back, Jack. How about a hand upstairs?"

"Let him lay in the gutter for all of me!" Brunk said. "One that would shoot down a sixteen-year-old boy in—"

"Don't say that, bullprod!" Morgan said; his voice was like metal scratching metal. Blaisedell clumsily tried to turn, and Morgan caught his arm as he staggered.

"Help you either!" Brunk said. "That would kick a broken-arm fellow's teeth in!" His voice rose hysterically. "High-rollers and road agents and murdering pimps and worse! Well, I am not afraid to talk out, and there's things—"

"Stop it!" Morgan snapped, just as the doctor heard Jessie utter the same words, her fingers tightening on his arm again. Brunk stopped and looked from Morgan to Jessie with his tortured red face.

"I have been looking for coyotes howling that tune," Morgan said, in the metallic voice. His eyes, glinting in the light from Jessie's room, looked as cold as murder.

"You will have a lot of teeth to kick in then!" Brunk cried.

"I'll know where to start!"

"Never mind it, Morg," Blaisedell said. He started up the stairs, and Morgan grasped his arm again and helped him upward, grunting with the effort and glancing back over his shoulder once at Brunk. The two men disappeared into the darkness of the stairwell, laboring and bumping against the railing.

"Frank," Jessie said. Slowly Brunk turned, his scar of a mouth strained wide, his fists clenched at his sides. "You are to get out of my house."

"Miss Jessie, can't you see—"

"Get out of my house!" Jessie said. Her fingers left the doctor's arm; he heard her go back into her room. Brunk stood gazing after her with dumb pain on his face.

"You had better leave, Frank," the doctor said, with difficulty. He knew now that he was not the only man who had been jealous of Clay Blaisedell. He followed Jessie into her room, and heard, behind him, Brunk's slow departing footsteps; above him, shuffling ones.

Jessie was staring up at the ceiling with round eyes. "Are they saying things like that about him?" she whispered.

"I suppose there are a few that—"

"Frank said it," she broke in. "Oh, the fools! Oh—" She put her hands to her face. "Oh, they are!" she whispered through her hands. "It is Morgan's fault! It is because of Morgan! Isn't it, David?"

"I suppose in a way it is," he said, nodding. He could not say more, and he was sorry now for Brunk, who had tried to.

"It is!" Jessie said, and he heard Morgan coming back down the stairs.

Morgan stopped and looked in the doorway, taking off his hat. His figure was slim and youthful, and his face, too, seemed young, except for his prematurely gray hair, which looked like polished pewter in the light. Slanting hoods of flesh at the corners of his eyes gave his face a half-humorous, half-contemptuous expression.

"I am sorry to bring him home in a state like this, Miss Marlow," he said, with a mock humility. "But he would come. And sorry for the fuss with the jack."

The doctor said, "You will have to excuse Brunk, Morgan. Stacey is a friend of his."

"Stacey?" Morgan said, with a lift of his eyebrows.

"Whose teeth you kicked in, at your place. That was a cruel thing."

"Was it?" Morgan said, politely.

"Mr. Morgan," Jessie said in a stiff voice. "Possibly you could tell me what's the matter with him. I mean, what has happened to him since he came back to Warlock."

"What's happened to him is for the best," Morgan said. "Though I don't expect you will agree with me."

"What do you mean?" Jessie said.

Morgan smiled thinly, and said, with the polite and infuriating contempt, "Well, Miss Marlow, he is a man with some good in him. I don't much like to see him broken down under things. He is better off out of marshaling."

"Dealing faro in a saloon!" Jessie cried. The doctor was shocked at the venom in her voice, but Morgan only grinned again.

"Or anything. But that's handy and pays well. Good night, Miss Marlow. Good night, Doc."

"Just a moment, please!" Jessie said. "You didn't want him to come back here, did you, Mr. Morgan?"

"It is hard to argue with him sometimes."

"You don't like me, do you?"

Morgan put his tongue in his cheek and cocked his head a little. "Why, ma'am, I am very respectful of you, like everybody else here in town." He made as though to leave again, but seemed to change his mind. "Well, let me put it this way, Miss Marlow. I am suspicious by nature. I know what sporting women are after, which is money. But I am never quite sure what nice women are after. No offense meant, Miss Marlow."

Again he started to leave, and again Jessie said, "Just a moment, please!" The doctor could hear her ragged breathing. She said to Morgan, "You said you didn't like seeing him broken down under things."

Morgan inclined his head, warily.

"So how you must *hate* yourself, Mr. Morgan!"

Morgan's face looked for an instant as it had when he had confronted Brunk; then it was composed again, like a door being shut, and he bowed once again, silently, and took his leave.

Jessie put her hand down on the checkerboard and with a quick motion swept the checkers off onto the floor. "I hate him!" she whispered. "No one can blame me for hating him!" She raised her face toward the ceiling. He saw it soften and she whispered something inaudible—that must, he thought, have been addressed to Blaisedell, who had come back to her.

She seemed to become aware of him again; she smiled, and it lit her whole face. "Oh, good night, David," she said. "Thank you for playing checkers with me."

It was a dismissal, he knew, not merely for this evening, but of a companion with whom she had passed the time while she waited for Blaisedell to return. He nodded and said, "Good night, Jessie," and backed out the door. She came after him, to close it, the opening narrowing into a thin slice of lamplight that framed her face. The door shut with a gentle sound.

He went up the steps to his room, and sat down on his bed. He felt as though he were smothering in the thick darkness. He felt old, and drained of all emotion except loneliness. Through the window he could see the bright stars and a narrow shaving of moon, and from here he could hear the sounds of laughter and drinking from the saloons on Main Street. He rose and fumbled on the table for the bowl of spills and matches. He lit the lamp, the darkness paled around him; he stood with his hands on the edge of the table, staring into the bright mystery of the flame. He had taken the bottle of laudanum from his bag when there was a soft knock.

"Who is it?"

"It's Jimmy, Doc. Can I come in a minute?"

"All right," he said.

"You'll have to open the door for me, I guess."

He put down the bottle and went to open the door. Young Fitzsimmons came in, carrying his bandaged hands before him as though they were parcels. He had dark wavy hair and thick eyebrows that met over the bridge of his nose. His long, young face was grave.

"Some things bothering, Doc."

"Worried about those hands, Jimmy? Here, let me cut the bandages off and have a look." The boy's hands had been burned so terribly he had told him he might lose them. But miraculously they were healing, although it would be a long time yet.

"No, it's not that," Fitzsimmons said. He held out his hands and grinned at them. "They are coming fine—they don't stink like they used to, do they?" He sat down on the end of the bed and his face turned grave again. "No, it's I am kind of worried about Frank, Doc."

"Are you?" he said, without interest.

"My daddy was a miner," Fitzsimmons said. "And his before him and on back. I know about mines, and I know what you can do and can't do when there is trouble with the company. They had troubles back in the old country my grandaddy used to tell about. I know one thing you don't do is fire a stope."

"Are they talking about that?"

"Plenty. They won't listen to me because I am only twenty, but I know rock-drilling better than most of them, and union and company too. I know you don't wreck a mine; because there may be trouble, but there is always a time when trouble is over for a while."

"I know, Jimmy," he said. He watched the boy's brows knit up; they looked like black caterpillars. The boy shook his head and sighed, then held up his bandaged hands again.

"It's been kind of good for me to be this way awhile, Doc," he said. "It is fine to be quick with your hands, and hell not to be able to even button your fly or open a door the way I can't. But it makes you understand, too, how you can be too quick with them. Now I have got to think every time before I reach out for anything. That's a caution these others would be better off with."

"But they won't listen to you," he said, and smiled.

Fitzsimmons grimaced. "There's not three of them could beat me single-jacking before I got burnt—Brunk couldn't. But there's not three of them will listen to me, either. All they'll listen to is Frank and Frenchy and old Heck. But they'll listen to me some day!

"Frank's all right in a way," he went on. "He didn't want nothing for himself, and I expect he would jump down a shaft if it would help get a union. Except he would just as soon jump everybody else down-shaft too, and then look back and find there wasn't anybody to make a union with."

"I have noticed that in Brunk," the doctor said.

"He is that way, all right. They are all too wrapped up in how they hate MacDonald's guts. Well, I do too, but it doesn't do anybody much good—hating Mister Mac. He is not the only super there'll ever be. The way they are thinking, union now is only something against MacDonald. If the company was smart enough to fire MacDonald the whole union idea'd blow up in Brunk's face."

"Yes, I suppose that's true, Jimmy," he said. Fitzsimmons looked pleased.

"I've tried to tell them MacDonald is nothing but company policy, and policy will change a good deal faster if the company sees it is good sense to change. Burning the stope or the rest of it'll just bring in a harder man than MacDonald. But they won't listen."

He sat there frowning. This was the most serious the doctor had ever seen Jimmy Fitzsimmons; even when he had warned him about his hands he had been cheerful. He was a strange boy, though not a boy. He wondered if there was not more iron in him than there was in Brunk. There was certainly better sense.

"Well, Jimmy," he said. "I would vote for you for president of the union rather than Brunk, I'll say that."

He had meant it jokingly; he saw that Fitzsimmons had not taken it so. "No," the boy said, very seriously. "I'm too young yet." He looked up from under his thick eyebrows and grinned again. "But I would vote for you, Doc."

"Don't be silly," he said; his heart began to labor, as though he had been running.

"No, I'd vote for you," Fitzsimmons said. "There's others that would too. There's a lot that's sensible but just get carried along by the wild ones like Brunk because they're loudest. Doc, what we need is somebody that can talk straight with MacDonald and Godbold and the rest of them and not be made a fool of. Somebody that is quick and smart, but somebody that is respectable too. It's true what Frank says. But because we are not respectable don't mean a man doesn't have pride in being a miner. My grandaddy and my dad had pride in it, and me too. Brunk doesn't much, underneath all. That is his trouble trying to deal with MacDonald—so that all he can think to do is things like stope-burning. But there is talking and dealing has to be done too, and that is where you would do for us, Doc. Some of us have talked of it already."

"I'm no miner, Jimmy."

"You are *for* us, Doc. Everybody knows that. That's the main thing."

He wondered if he really was; he knew he was against the things that destroyed and maimed them.

Fitzsimmons said quickly, "Well, I guess there is no use talking about it just yet. I guess they are going to have to bust loose this time again, and maybe they will learn from it." Then he said, "I thought of even going to tell Schroeder they was thinking of firing the Medusa, but I couldn't do that. That would bust me with them if they ever found out."

The doctor was surprised at the calculation in Fitzsimmons' voice; it was a side he hadn't seen before.

Fitzsimmons gazed back at him boldly, as though aware of what he was thinking. He grinned again, not quite so boyishly. "What's wrong with that?" he said. "Sometimes if you know better than a bunch what has to be done you have to undercut them a little. You have to be careful, though, for they are hard when they think a man is against them. They will listen to me some day," he said, and rose. Then he laughed. "And don't think you are out of it, Doc. I have got plans for you."

The doctor rose to open the door for Fitzsimmons, who now thanked him for his time and said good night very formally. He went back to the table and took up the bottle of laudanum and held it until his hand warmed the glass. But finally he put it back into his bag, and undressed and went to bed.

In bed he could not sleep, not merely because he had not taken his evening potion, but because always, in the darkness, Jessie's face hung in his eyes. He saw Blaisedell drunken and sagging, and yet, try as he would, he could not look upon him with contempt. He saw Brunk's face, with the jealousy as pitiful and hopeless as his own behind the hate. He saw Morgan's face, full of murder, and yet it was the face of a man much more than the mere unscrupulous and violent gambler he had seemed. He remembered Jessie and Morgan crying at the same instant to Brunk to stop, in their different voices that were as one voice, and remembered them only minutes later facing each other as deadly enemies.

It seemed to him that in this night he had seen many symptoms of the obsession which he had already known in Jessie. He had seen that both Jessie and Morgan accepted the importance of Blaisedell's name and all that it implied even in their antipathy for one another. He had seen the same obsession, though not for Blaisedell, in possession of Brunk, and even stronger in Jimmy Fitzsimmons. It seemed to him, as he considered it, more than an obsession, a disease of the spirit; and yet he wondered if this disease, this obsession, this struggle to preeminence, was not the reason for mankind's triumph on the earth—the complex brain developed to plot for it, the opposing thumb to grasp at it—if it was not what set mankind apart from the animals. No animal cared what was its name.

He stared out at the bright stars over Warlock, regarding, now, himself, and what Fitzsimmons had said about his leading the miners. He felt no call within himself. He felt no urge to strive to be anything more than what, long ago, he had been content to be. He considered his freedom and his bondage, his own soul's sickness and his own particular health, and wondered at the will he did not possess.

31. Morgan Uses His Knife

Across from Morgan at the desk in the office of the Glass Slipper, Clay sat with his fair head canted forward, his lips pouting a little. He looked white and ill, Morgan thought; Clay had had a bellyful of whisky last night, but he looked sicker than that.

"What do you hear from Porphyry City, Morg?" he said. "I hear it is booming some."

"It is booming right here."

"Not for me," Clay said.

"Why, Porphyry City sounds fine, from what I hear. You thinking of going there?"

"I don't know," Clay said. "I suppose it wouldn't be much different."

Morgan laughed and said, "You were surely bound and determined to go back to the General Peach last night. See the lady today?"

Clay glanced up at him and nodded tersely. Then he leaned back in his chair and said, "I shouldn't have gone back there."

He nodded too.

"It is not her, Morg," Clay said, as though to answer what he, Morgan, had not wanted to ask. "It is everybody. I can feel it walking down the street or anywhere. Even if there is nobody around I can feel it. I can't do what they want. They don't even know what they want, and I can't do anything, for anything I do is either all the way wrong or not right enough."

"Eat your guts out!" Morgan said, and all at once he was angrier at Clay than he had ever been before. "You are either a peace officer eating your guts up, or you are a faro banker. God damn it, Clay, wherever you go you are going to have to not give a damn what people want of you. You can quit marshaling and make it stick here as well as anywhere."

"I should have quit before I started."

"Chew on yourself!"

Clay said, "Abe McQuown is sitting bad on their stomachs and I am supposed to give them a purge. I want no part of it. For it is me that is poisoned every time. Every time now. Who am I to do their killing for them? I just want shut of it, but I can feel them at me all the time. And Jessie—" He did not go on.

"Well, you have quit," Morgan said. "You did the right thing, Clay."

Clay's mustache lifted, as though he were grinning, and his eyes crinkled a little. He said, "There was a time when I thought I could do the right thing."

Morgan poured himself a quarter of an inch of whisky, and, turning it in his hand, frowned carefully at the flat tilt of the liquor. "You were going to say something about Miss Jessie."

"What she says," Clay said heavily. "She says there is a thing a man needs to be—" Morgan saw something uncertain and almost frightened cloud his eyes. "It is hard to say, Morg," Clay said, and sighed and shook his head.

So it was Miss Jessie pushing Clay; his mind closed down on it like a trap. It was as though in a card game with strangers he had picked on sight the one he must play against as most dangerous, and had seen himself proved right on the first hand.

"But she is wrong," Clay said. "For it has gone past and the rest is poison."

"And you have quit."

Clay nodded; Clay's clouded eyes met his for a moment. "But it is not so easy here, Morg. With Kate to see every time I turn around. I see she has taken up with Billy Gannon's brother. Came out with Cletus's brother, and now she has taken up with Gannon. It is a thing to scare me screaming, isn't it?"

"Scare you?" Morgan said, and didn't know if he should laugh at that or not.

"Why, yes. If every man I shot down wrong had a brother, and every one came after me, I would have to die that many times."

"Hard to do," he said, and still he did not know. Anxiously he watched Clay's face. He felt a quickening lift as he saw the rueful smile starting.

"Surely," Clay said. "But I could do it the way I feel now. Like a cat."

"Listen to me now," he said to Clay. "For a change. First thing where you have gone wrong is worrying over what everybody wants of you, or thinks. To hell with them! That is the nugget of it, Clay. And look at it like this—like a hand of cards. It is like throwing in your hand because you made one bad play."

"No, not one," Clay said. "Take your card game another way. The stakes are too high now, it has got too big for me. It was jacks to open once, now it is kings."

Queens, he thought; he felt as though Clay were arguing with Jessie Marlow, through him. "Clay, I don't know what we are quarreling over," he said. "You have quit it."

"That's so," Clay said, and sighed again.

A racket was starting up in the Glass Slipper. It was time for the miners to be coming in, but it sounded to Morgan as though every one of them in Warlock were crowding into the Glass Slipper at once. He heard their raised voices and the confused tramp and scuffle of boots on the floor. Clay turned to glance at the door. "What the hell is going on?" Morgan said, and rose just as the door opened.

Al Murch looked inside; behind him the racket was louder. "There is some jacks here to see you, Blaisedell," Murch said. He stood barring the door with his broad frame, but behind him Morgan could see the big miner, Brunk, and another one with a red welt along the side of his head.

"What about?" he said, as Clay rose.

"Proposition to put to Blaisedell, Morgan!" someone called.

"Let us in, Morgan," Brunk said, and Morgan nodded to Murch, who let four of them in.

"That's enough, Al," he said, and Murch fought the door closed against the rest.

Brunk looked as though he would rather be somewhere else. With him was an old miner with a goat beard, another heavy-set one with a black waxed and pointed mustache, and a fourth, the one with the bruise on his head, who was bald and had an Adam's apple like a billiard ball.

"You do the talking, Frank," Goat-beard said. He said to Clay, "We have went out at the Medusa, Marshal."

"He is not marshal any more," Morgan said, and Goat-beard looked at him with dislike.

Brunk, who had a rough-cut, square face and hands the size of shovels, pointed to Bald-head's bruise. "Wash Haggin did that," he said. "They have dropped wages at the Medusa a dollar a day, and MacDonald's hired himself about fifteen hardcases in case there was any complaint about it. Wash Haggin did that to Bobby Patch."

"Don't do to complain," Bald-head said, and grinned toothily. But he looked scared.

"Winchesters and shotguns around to fit out an army," Waxed-mustache said. "Both Haggins was there, and Jack Cade and that one Quint Whitby."

Morgan said, "McQuown?"

Brunk shook his head. "Not him or Curley Burne."

"Put it to him, Frank," Goat-beard said, and nudged Brunk.

"Well, MacDonald's got these people up there to try to scare everybody to going back to work," Brunk said. "We kind of think they will do more, too. We think MacDonald is going to send them in here to run some of us out of town. Like he did with Lathrop last year."

"Run *you* out, you mean?" Morgan said, and Brunk's big, red face twisted angrily.

"What did you want to see me for?" Clay asked. "It sounds like you had better see the deputies."

Waxed-mustache said, "They are no good for us, Marshal." He spread his hands out. "You are the man for us."

"We've got to keep those hardcases off us some way," Brunk said stolidly. "They've got too much artillery. We need a gunman." He stopped and swallowed; it looked, Morgan thought, as though it swallowed hard.

"You are the one that could do it," Brunk went on. "Schroeder is not much friendly with us, and him and Gannon couldn't do anything against that bunch even if they wanted to. We are having a meeting tonight as soon as we see what's happened at the Sister Fan and the rest." He licked his lips. "And we'll get organized and the union will collect dues. We can pay you for kind of marshaling for us," he said. "That's our proposition, Marshal."

"I guess not, boys," Clay said. "Sorry."

"Told you," Bald-head said. "Told you he wouldn't."

"I guess MacDonald got to him first," Goat-beard said. "Mac-Donald is a step ahead of us all the way, looks like."

Morgan watched Clay shake his head, apparently without anger. "Nobody's got to me, old man. I am not against you or for you either. I'm just not in it."

Morgan nodded to Murch, who caught hold of Brunk's arm. "Let's skin out, fellows," Murch said, in his rasping voice. "Mr. Morgan and Mr. Blaisedell's busy."

"Told you he wouldn't," Bald-head said, starting for the door.

"Why should he?" Brunk said, and jerked his arm away from Murch.

"What do you mean by that?" Clay said.

"Well, why should you?" Brunk said loudly. "We can't pay you like any rich-man's Citizens' Committee, with MacDonald sitting on it. We don't want killing done to hire you for. Only killers kept off us. So why would you be interested?"

"Al!" Morgan said, and Murch caught hold of Brunk's arm again. Waxed-mustache was grimacing violently.

"Let him be," Clay said. More color showed in his pale face. "Let him have his say out."

Brunk glanced down at Clay's shell belt, which showed beneath his coat; he glanced quickly at Morgan. He said in a stifled voice, "I'm not saying anything but that we need help, Blaisedell."

"Let me tell you," Clay said. "So there is no misunderstanding here. I was hired marshal here, and I have quit it. I'm not hiring out again to the Citizens' Committee, or MacDonald, or you, or anybody. What more is there to say than that?"

"Nothing, by damn!" Goat-beard said. "Let's get out of here, Frank!"

"No, wait a minute," Clay said to Brunk. "There is something you are choking on yet, and was last night. Go ahead and spit it out."

"Do you think I am scared to?" Brunk said.

"Who asked you to be?" Clay said.

"Get him out of here, Al," Morgan said, but Clay looked at him angrily.

"I want to hear what he has to say, Morg."

"Never mind it, Frank!" Waxed-mustache said. "Let be, can't you?"

Clay stared steadily at Brunk, and Brunk took a step back away from him. His face working, he said, "I was just saying—I mean, rich men can have themselves a marshal, but no dirty, ignorant muckers can. Surely; that's all. It's clear enough."

"That wasn't what you was going to say," Clay said. It was as though he were calling Brunk a liar. "That wasn't what you was saying last night, either. Say it out. Say it clear out, Brunk. I would rather a man said a thing to my face than behind my back."

Brunk just stood there facing him with his hands at his sides and his thick shoulders hunched a little. Murch moved toward him and Brunk snatched a hand to the haft of his bowie knife. Suddenly he said, "All right, I will say it to your face! I say you would have shot me down like your Citizens' Committee told you to, only Miss Jessie begged me off." Brunk stopped and his head swung sideways, as Morgan moved to lean forward with his hands on the desk top.

Then Brunk's voice rose. "But even your respectable friends threw you down when you and your high-roller partner went to robbing stages!"

"Holy Christ, Frank!" Bald-head whispered.

Brunk sucked his breath in, and then cried explosively, "And when you and him went to killing cowboys to make like it was them had done it! And Morgan kicks out a broken-arm fellow's teeth for saying it! Well, I say if your high-toned Citizens' Committee don't want you any more, then the damned miners don't either!"

Morgan slowly turned toward Clay. Nothing showed in Clay's face. He reached for his hat, and Brunk drew back at the movement. Brunk shifted his feet to keep facing Clay as Clay slowly came out around the desk. Bald-head and Waxed-mustache backed out of his way. Clay put on his hat, and, without a word, went out the alley door and pulled it closed behind him.

In the silence the noise of the crowd of miners in the Glass Slipper was very loud. Murch started to slide the bar back and open the door.

"Keep it shut," Morgan said, in a voice he could hardly recognize as his own.

"Here, now!" Bald-head said fearfully.

Morgan stripped off his coat, unbuckled his shoulder holster, and dropped Colt and harness on the desk with a thump. He opened the drawer and brought his knife out. Brunk's scarlet face swam in his eyes. "Do you know how to use that sticker of yours, mucker?" he said.

"Now hold on, now!" Waxed-mustache said. "Now, listen, Morgan; Frank here said things he had no cause to say and didn't mean. Now let's not—"

"Get it out, if you know how to use it," he said to Brunk. He pricked the palm of his hand with the knife's point. "You had better know," he said. He came out from behind his desk, and the others moved away from Brunk.

"He is big, Tom," Murch said. "You had better leave me—"

"This is mine. Get it out!" he said. Brunk was hesitating with his hand on the haft of his bowie. "Why, I am giving you a fair shake, aren't I?" Morgan said, grinning. "Prove you are right by sticking me. Or I'll prove you are an over-grown, yellow-livered lying hog that's not fit to lick his boots you just pissed all over. Get it out and talk like that to me!"

Brunk pulled his bowie loose. He held it waist-high, his left hand out and spread-fingered, his thick forearm blocking.

"Fair fight now, boys!" Goat-beard shrilled. "We are here to see it is fair, Frank!"

"Come on, then, Mister high-roller," Brunk said hoarsely, moving sideways to get his back away from Murch and toward his partners. He swung the bowie blade in a circle before him.

Morgan did not move now, watching Brunk's guard and holding his own knife low in his right hand, with his left close to it. He met Brunk's eyes, and saw, in their black pupils, his own image. He heard the quickened breathing of the men watching as he thrust his right hand up, the knife cutting out. Brunk leaped back, and then immediately pressed forward, feinting with the bowie. Morgan exposed his neck, hoping that Brunk would make a high stroke.

The bowie swept toward his throat, and he dodged to the left and shifted his knife to his left hand. He thrust it up and felt it catch home, and tear away; Brunk's arm was too long.

He heard the gasp, not from Brunk but from the others. He had drawn blood that darkened the breast of Brunk's dirty blue shirt, but he had wasted his best stroke. For the first time it occurred to him that he might die.

The knife in his right hand again, he raised the blade to touch his forehead, dropped it low once more, feinted left, feinted right. The blood spread on Brunk's chest. Brunk lunged toward him.

Brunk's wrist crashed against his, the bowie blade passing over it. His own knife snubbed into the bone of Brunk's forearm, and immediately Brunk's big hand caught his wrist. With a wrench he freed it and dodged aside, but he had felt the power in those hands and arms, and their quickness. Brunk's arm was bleeding now too, but he saw a light of confidence in the miner's eyes.

Morgan swung in to the right to get under Brunk's guard, and the elbow crashed down against his hand. He feinted right again and drove straight in, but had to leap back again as the long arm swept around. He felt the slight tug at his shoulder, and heard the gasp again. He didn't look.

His breath began to tear at his lungs. There had been too many cigars, too many women, too much whisky; he laughed out loud and saw Brunk disconcerted by it. He drove in once more and this time slashed Brunk's upper arm; he jumped back as the bowie flashed past, and immediately thrust up and in and this time his knife ripped into flesh and caught, and Brunk gasped a harsh cough. But his knife did not pull free as he retreated, and Brunk's left hand clutched down on his. In turn he caught Brunk's wrist as the bowie swung down. Brunk's weight forced him back, and Brunk's height bore him over. He tried to wrench back away, and tripped; he fell and Brunk fell with him. Brunk's grip loosened on his knife hand and he rammed the knife farther into Brunk's belly as he crashed to the floor with Brunk sprawled on top of him. Brunk cried out once.

Brunk's hand caught his wrist again between their bodies, but still he could move his hand a little, to twist and turn the knife blade in Brunk's flesh. He felt the warm wet flow of blood on his own belly, as, grunting and straining, his elbow set and bruised against the floor, he fought to keep Brunk's bowie from his throat.

Brunk's hand bore down impossibly hard. What was the use? he thought suddenly; he did not love life enough to bother to fight this to its end. What was the use? He grinned into Brunk's crazed face and replied to himself: because he would not let a clumsy, stupid mucker beat him; or any man. He twisted the knife in Brunk's body, to kill Brunk before the bowie pierced him, and knew he could not as the huge weight of Brunk's arm came down against his own. Brunk's sweat fell into his face and the muscles in Brunk's neck were spread out like batwings; there was no sound in the world but Brunk's grunting and his own.

He strained his own blade from side to side and Brunk gasped. But he felt his wrist begin to tilt. He had to bend his arm to retain his grip, and so the post he had made of his forearm was gone and there remained only the inadequate strap of his muscles, and his will—not to be beaten. He could feel his arm bending as the blood flowed from Brunk's belly.

He laughed and panted up into Brunk's contorted face, and smelled the stink of him, and watched the bowie that was not a foot from his throat. He worked his own blade up toward Brunk's vitals, up toward Brunk's heart; for Brunk must die too. Why? he thought. What did it matter? There seemed no reason, but his hand needed none. He grinned up at the bowie's point, not six inches from his throat now. Now three, as his arm gave like a rusty ratchet, pure pain now, and caught somehow again; now two inches, as it gave again.

Then out of the corners of his eyes he saw Murch move suddenly, and saw the little double-barreled derringer in Murch's hand. "*No, Al!*" he grunted, and his words were lost in the crash. Brunk's head fell on him, and Brunk did not move again. "No!" he panted.

Weakly he struggled to slide the heavy body off himself, and to his feet. His vest was soaked with blood. He stood there swaying. Murch had the derringer trained on the three miners. Someone was hammering on the door and shouting, "Frank! Hey, Frenchy!"

"Shut up!" Murch whispered to Bald-head. He turned white-rimmed eyes to Morgan. "Christ, what the hell was I supposed to do, Tom?"

"Fair shake!" old Goat-beard cried. "Son-of-a-bitching gambling man, never gave anybody a fair shake in your life!"

Bald-head was leaning back against the wall with a hand in front of him as though to keep the derringer off. The door creaked as the miners in the Glass Slipper tried to force it.

Morgan took up his shoulder holster and Colt, and could not think for a moment. He glanced at his bleeding shoulder.

"Christ, what'll we do, Tom?" Murch said desperately. "Christ, Tom!"

"Sons of bitches!" Waxed-mustache said. "Play fair so long as you win. He had you by the—"

"Shut up!" Murch cried. "Christ, Tom!"

Morgan looked down at Brunk on the floor, with one arm under him and the other flung out, the blood beneath his head and much more blood spreading on the floor beneath his body. He sighed and said, "You had better make tracks, Al."

Murch started for the alley door. The inner door creaked and strained again, and there was another volley of shouting and cursing. Murch turned and the straight-on eye regarded him worriedly. "What about you, Tom?"

Morgan didn't answer, and Murch went out. Morgan stood facing the three miners, trying to get his breath back. As they would not think of blaming the derringer that had put the bullet through Brunk's head, so they would not think either of blaming merely Murch. The bar on the door began to squeal as a more concerted weight crashed against it. He drew the Colt from its holster as Waxed-mustache took a step toward him.

"Bust that door in, boys!" Goat-beard yelled. "For there is rats in here need cleaning out!"

One of the iron keepers sprang loose from the door and flew like an arrow to smack against Waxed-mustache's shoulder. Morgan grinned suddenly to watch Waxed-mustache rubbing his arm, and unhurriedly went to the door and stepped out into the alley. Murch was nowhere in sight. He started to the left. When he heard the crash as the door burst open, he broke into a run. He had reached the end of the alley before he saw, over his shoulder, a flock of them come out of the Glass Slipper and start after him. He laughed as he ran down Southend Street toward Main. It would be quite a run, he thought, if neither Schroeder nor Gannon were at the jail.

32. Gannon Takes a Trick

GANNON was in the jail with Carl when Tom Morgan ran in, panting, covered with blood, hatless, a holstered Colt in his hand. "Lock me up, boys!" he panted. "Or there's a lynching coming off!" He ran into the cell and slammed the door on himself.

Carl sprang up, knocking his chair over backward. There was a roar outside; it came down Main Street like a flood, and Gannon snatched the shotgun down from its pegs. "What the hell?" Carl cried.

"Lock the damned door!" Morgan said, and Carl leaped to do it, and flung the key inside the cell. Gannon ran to the door. Behind him he heard Morgan laughing like an idiot.

Miners were streaming around the corner out of Southend Street, more were coming out of the Glass Slipper to join them, and all of them were yelling.

Gannon held the shotgun out before him with his finger tight on the trigger and felt the sweat starting from his face. "Hold off!" he shouted, "Hold off!" the words lost in the tumult. Beside him Carl was shouting too. Then the leaders halted.

Gradually the whole mass came to a halt, forming a broad semicircle on the boardwalk and in the street around the front of the jail, all of them yelling still, until Carl raised his Colt and fired into the air.

"Now, what the hell?" Carl said, in the silence.

There was a disturbance in the front rank and Frenchy Martin stepped forward through the settling dust; then old man Heck came out.

"Now you turn over that son of a bitch in there, Deputy!" Frenchy Martin cried.

"He is our meat and no business of yours at all!" old man Heck shouted. "Dirty dog killed Frank Brunk and we are—"

The clamor began again and the miners crowded forward. Gannon thrust the muzzle of the shotgun against the belly of the one nearest him. Slowly the shouting died.

"—fair fight," Frenchy Martin was saying. "And then Frank got him down and that lookout of his shot Frank through the head!"

"Where's Murch?" someone yelled. "Somebody'd better get that wall-eyed son too!"

"He lit out on a horse!" another replied. "He was moving!"

"You turn over that bloody-bellied gambler, hear!" old Heck said. "I mean, we will tromp you down, Schroeder!"

Gannon swung the shotgun toward Heck. Another miner made a grab for it and he slammed the barrel against the man's elbow. "Get back!" he said.

Somebody was singing, "We'll hang Tom Morgan to a sour apple tree!"

Frenchy Martin jumped up on the tie rail, and, clinging to a post, motioned for silence. "Boys, are we going to let them stop us? Are we going to take out that murdering bastard or not? Good old Frank was a friend to us all, and MacDonald set Morgan to kill him, most likely." The miners roared.

Gannon looked toward Carl, for this had better be stopped, and Carl leaped forward and clubbed the barrel of his Colt down behind Martin's ear. Martin fell forward into the street, where the miners caught him; the yelling increased in volume and violence. Old man Heck was shaking his fist. Carl fired into the air again. Gannon began edging toward old Heck again, to buffalo him next. He was only worried that it would get dark before they could run the mob off. Already the light was fading with the sun gone.

"Listen!" Carl shouted. "There's been men took out of here and hung but not while I was here and by God there won't be, either! Because I can play hell with a good lot of you and Johnny will just make pure mincemeat with that shotgun. Now; if you want Morgan that bad maybe you can get him, but it's going to cost you dear. You hear now!"

The solid roar went up again, the shoving back and forth. Old man Heck turned and cupped his hands to his mouth to yell, and Gannon slammed the shotgun barrel against the side of his head. He fell to his knees.

"Watch that bull moose over there!" Carl cried, and Gannon swung the shotgun toward a big bearded miner who was moving toward him.

"Back off!"

The miner retreated a step, grinning. Past him, over the heads of the men in the street, Gannon saw riders coming down Main Street from the direction of the rim. They were riding abreast, two ranks of them, and they filled the street. Heads began turning toward them. Abruptly the miners fell silent.

"It's MacDonald!" Carl said.

MacDonald was in the lead, on a white-faced horse, wearing a checked suit and his hard-hat. In the gathering dust Gannon began to recognize the other riders: Chet and Wash Haggin, and Jack Cade, Walt Harrison, Quint Whitby, Jock Hennessey, Pecos Mitchell, and more, and still more in the second rank. Some of them had Winchesters over their arms, and belts of cartridges hung from their saddle-horns.

Abe McQuown was not with them, Gannon saw, straining his eyes; nor Curley. The big miner near him was now flattened against the wall as though he wished he could push back on through it.

"He has brought his Regulators in to do us all down!" Gannon heard someone say. The miners in the street began to retreat, some, on the fringes of the crowd, fading back into Southend Street. Now there was no sound but the pad of oncoming hoofs in the dust.

"MacDonald's come to run his agitators out himself," Carl said. "Damned if he isn't, and damned if it is pleasant to be bailed out by such a bunch."

Someone yelled, "Morgan already did your dirty work for you, Mister Mac!"

"Hold together, fellows!"

"Damned if we will run before a pack of rustlers, MacDonald!"

Carl said mournfully, "What the hell are we going to do, Johnny?" and Gannon took a deep breath and then ducked under the tie rail and jumped down into the street. He moved through the miners as rapidly as he could, pushing right and left with the shotgun butt as though it were an oar. Sweating, dusty faces turned to stare at him. There was muttering behind him. A hand reached out to grasp his shotgun.

"Let me by," he said, and the hand fell away.

"Let the deputy through, boys," a voice said, and the miners began to move more rapidly aside before him. He came out of the mob not fifty feet from the riders, and he walked on through the dust straight toward MacDonald.

"Pull up!" he said, bringing the shotgun muzzle up to bear on the white-faced horse. MacDonald reined in and the horse stood steady, swinging his head around to feign a bite at MacDonald's leg. The others reined up also. Wash Haggin gazed contemptuously down at him, Chet Haggin grinned a little, Jack Cade lifted his round-crowned hat and ran his fingers through his hair, his dark, whiskered face sullen. Gannon looked from face to face. Those in the rear rank were the kind of San Pablo scum that even Abe McQuown was too proud to ride with. Except for the Haggins they were all bad ones, but after the first glance around he looked only at MacDonald. He felt calm enough.

"What's going on here, Mr. MacDonald?" he said.

"This has nothing to do with you, Deputy," MacDonald said coldly. "We have constituted ourselves a regulation committee and we know our objectives. It is none of your business. Stand aside."

"It is my business. You are not coming in here with these people."

"You caught this posting people out from the marshal, Bud?" Chet Haggin asked.

Gannon saw Cade casually draw his Colt and rest it on his thigh. He kept the shotgun trained on MacDonald. "Take them out, Mr. MacDonald."

"You fool!" MacDonald said. His mouth looked like a trap in his ascetic, coldly handsome face. "We intend to round up some agitators who are bent on making trouble at the Medusa. You won't stop us. You—"

"Take them out," he said again. His ribs ached where the butt of the shotgun was clamped against his side, his hand sweated on the barrel. "Out," he said.

"We'll come through shooting if we have to, Bud," Wash said.

Gannon heard the iron snap as Cade cocked his Colt; he tried not to flinch, not to look. He stared straight at MacDonald over the muzzle of the shotgun, and MacDonald licked his lips.

"Morgan already killed Frank for you, Mister Mac!" a miner yelled, and MacDonald scowled.

"Take your people out of town, Mr. MacDonald," Gannon said once more. "There will be no rounding up done in Warlock."

"Schroeder!" MacDonald cried. "Tell this idiot to get out of the way."

"Do like he says, Mister Mac!" Carl called back. His voice was shrill. "And Jack Cade, you had better hang up that hog leg, for I am laid in on your belt buckle."

Gannon stood watching MacDonald and he thought he had won.

"What do you say, Mister Mac?" Cade said, in his flat, harsh voice. "Shoot in or crawl out?"

Wash said, "You had better back off and let us handle it, MacDonald."

"He doesn't go unless you all go," Gannon said.

"Very well!" MacDonald said. "Your piece there speaks with more authority than you do. I'm forced to honor it, since I want no bloodshed. You will hear more about this from Sheriff Keller." He stood in his stirrups and called to Carl, "This is not the end of this, Schroeder!" He sawed viciously with the reins, and the white-faced horse bucked, scaring Chet's mare sideways. Gannon swung the shotgun toward Wash and Jack Cade. Cade nodded once, thumbed his teeth, nodded again. The Regulators became, for a moment, a milling mass of horsemen, cursing and muttering among themselves as they turned away. Then they sorted themselves out into the same two ranks, and, with MacDonald again at the head, faded into hazy shapes in the twilight as they retreated. A roar went up from the miners; taunts were shouted after them. Gannon made his way back to the boardwalk and mounted it once more. Pike Skinner was standing with Carl; Pike watched him come up with his mouth pursed, and his hat brim shadowing his eyes. Carl was laughing.

"They'll be back, deputy!" someone yelled from among the miners in the street. "Don't think they won't be back!"

Gannon leaned against the adobe wall. The sign above his head creaked a little. He let the shotgun barrel droop.

"Why, I guess you had better clear out of the street then," Carl said. "So they won't ride you down."

"We want Morgan!" someone shouted. A few took it up, but soon the cry died away. Gannon leaned against the wall and watched the miners drift off. A tension had gone out of the air. "Meeting!" somebody was yelling. "Meeting!" The crowd began to break up into small clots of men. A wagon came across on Southend, breaking it up still further.

"You had better go scratch your name on the wall in there, Johnny," Carl said. "You have done smart work tonight. I thought we was due for two falls at once, but damned if you didn't take them both instead. What's that you say, Pike?" he said, turning toward Pike Skinner, who had said nothing.

"It isn't done with yet," Pike said grouchily.

"Well, I expect you are right," Carl said. "And you are deputized, you and Pete and Chick and Tim. Hunt them up for me, will you? There's a good fellow."

Pike went off along the boardwalk. Carl slapped Gannon on the back as he followed him into the jail. Morgan was leaning against the cell door, almost invisible in the darkness.

"Hanging off?" he said.

"For a spell anyway," Carl said. He pulled down the pulley lamp and lit it. Now Gannon could see Morgan's face; it looked as gray and tired as he himself felt. "I wouldn't say clear off, no," Carl went on. "Well, you surely went and roused things up. What'd you want to kill this Brunk for?"

"Bled his dirty blood all over me," Morgan said, distantly. Gannon sat on the table edge with the shotgun leaning against his leg and his arms folded, watching the gambler's face. For all the expression that was there Morgan might have meant what he said.

"I suppose you might call that a reason," Carl said. "You taken up fighting jacks as a steady thing now, Morgan. Knife fight, was it? What was all that yelling how it was supposed to be a fair fight?"

Morgan said in a disgusted voice, "Brunk had me in a little trouble so Murch shot him."

"Heard them saying Murch's lit out, but damned if I think I had better take after him the way things stand. You put Murch to shooting him?"

"He thought of it before I did."

"Get me to believe you didn't put him to it."

"Believe it or don't!"

"Now don't go scratchy, Morgan," Carl said mournfully. "If a hardcase that works for you kills a man that's got you in trouble, maybe it is on your back some."

"Nothing's on my back," Morgan said, and withdrew into the shadows.

Gannon said to Carl, "Maybe somebody'd better get the judge."

"Time enough. You're not in any hurry, are you, Morgan?"

"I'm patient by nature," Morgan said.

Peter Bacon appeared in the doorway; he nodded at Gannon, and raised an eyebrow.

"Witnesses?" Carl said to Morgan.

"All muckers," Morgan replied. "Old Goat-beard and that one with the waxed mustaches, and another one called Patch."

"Old Heck and Frenchy," Carl said. "They seemed kind of maddest, all right. You sure you didn't tell Murch to blow him loose from you?"

There was a crash and splatter of glass and a rock rebounded from the far wall, and came to rest among the shards of glass beneath the broken window. Peter Bacon disappeared out the door, and Gannon ran to look. He could see no one in the darkness, and after a moment Peter returned along the boardwalk, shaking his head. Gannon went back inside, where Carl was cursing and trying to push the broken glass into a pile with the side of his boot.

"Oh, hello, miss," Peter said from the doorway, and Kate Dollar came in.

"Good evening, Deputy," Kate said to Carl. "Deputy," she said to Gannon. She wore a tight jacket, a long, thickly pleated black skirt, and her black hat with the cherries on it. She smiled her harsh, unpleasant smile as Morgan appeared at the cell door again.

"Is that Tom Morgan?" Kate said, and her voice was as unpleasant as the smile. "I heard the miners had him on the run."

Gannon backed up uncertainly to lean against the wall, and Carl said, "It sure is him, Miss Dollar. And he sure was running. Not much of a lead on the pack, either."

"You running, Tom?" she said, and laughed.

"Oh, I can run with the best of them," Morgan said. His voice was as harsh as Kate's, his face, framed in the thick, hand-smoothed bars, was blank. "I have run before this. There was a place called Grand Fork I ran and got caught."

"Did they hang you?" Kate asked, and Gannon felt that he was witnessing something he did not want to see, or know.

"Maybe they did," Morgan said. He frowned with thought. "No, come to remember, a friend I had there set fire to the hotel where those vigilantes had me, and during the whoop-de-do I got out some way. No, I didn't hang that time."

"But no friends here?" Kate said.

"Well, now, miss, we made out all right," Carl said uncomfortably. "Johnny and me didn't need any help."

Gannon saw Peter Bacon grimacing painfully as Kate spoke to Morgan again. "But I understand you didn't kill him yourself, Tom. Was he a good man, Tom? That you had your gunman kill for you?"

"Just a big, stupid mucker, Kate," Morgan said. "But you probably would have liked him, at that."

"But what was the matter with Clay?" Kate cried. Now she sounded hysterical, and now, Gannon thought, he must stop this.

He put a hand out toward her and said, "Kate!" just as Morgan said loudly, "What kind of jail is this, where anybody can drift in off the street and bedevil the prisoners?"

"Bedevil!" Kate cried.

Gannon touched her arm. "Now, Miss Dollar," he said.

"Well, now, yes, miss," Carl said. "I don't expect you ought to be in here with a bunch of wild jacks around throwing rocks through the window and all. I guess you had better—"

"I just came down to tell you they are throwing rocks through the windows of the Glass Slipper, too," Kate said, calmly now. "There are some people trying to stop them, but I don't know if they will."

"Durn!" Carl said. "I should've thought of that. I'd better go, Johnny." He took up the shotgun and hurried out. "Come on, Pete!"

Morgan disappeared again and Kate stood facing the cell for a moment longer. Then she bowed her head and turned away. Without looking at Gannon, she said, "Will they try again?"

"I don't know."

"Don't try to save him," she said in the ugly voice. "Don't try to do anything for him. He doesn't want you to, and anybody that ever did has been sorry for it the rest of their lives." She stopped and he saw that she looked almost ashamed; then her face tightened again, and she swept on out of the jail.

In the cell Morgan was laughing softly.

Gannon went outside to stand beneath the gently creaking sign in the cool night breeze. He could hear shouts and see the dark shapes of men against the whitish dust of the street up before the Glass Slipper.

He heard the sad, suspirant music of a mouth organ. A thin figure was coming toward him.

"Well, howdy, Deputy Bud Gannon."

"Hello, Curley," he said. "Did you come in with MacDonald?"

"No, just rode in to watch the fun," Curley said. "Should have; Mister Mac is giving six dollars a day and expenses. There is going to be a lot of expenses, too, up at the French Palace and around."

"No, there's not. They're not coming in here."

Curley looked at him with his eyebrows crawling up. He ran his fingers back through his black curls, and took a step back, raising his hands in mock terror. "By God, posted out of town by Bud Gannon! Not me too, Bud? Say it isn't so!"

Gannon shook his head and tried to grin.

"Whuff!" Curley said. "I was ready to fork it and crawl. Well, I guess I'll have the French Palace to myself then." He looked at Gannon sharply, and his clownish expression vanished. "What're you going to do if some of them come back anyway, Bud?" he said quietly. "Brace a man?"

"They haven't come back in."

"Might, though," Curley said. He pried at a crack in the boardwalk with the toe of his boot. "You know, people don't take to posting so good. Billy didn't."

"I'm not posting anybody," he said tightly. "We are just not going to have MacDonald and that crew in here chasing miners around."

"Strikers," Curley said. "Agitators, what MacDonald said. Bunch of damned, over-paid—"

"Why didn't you hire out with the rest, then?"

Curley laughed cheerfully. "Well, I just don't like Mister Mac much, Bud. One of a few I don't."

"Including me. Are you down on me too, Curley?"

"Yep," Curley said.

"All right," he said, and felt his eyes burning.

Curley sighed and said, "Well, I kind of am and kind of not. I see you think you did right and maybe I see how you could think it honest. But I can't think that way. How a man is brought up, I guess, and you are a cold one, Johnny Gee."

"Maybe I am."

"That was your brother, Bud. The only kin you had."

Gannon said in a shaky voice, "Most people here think Blaisedell only did what he had to."

"You think that way, don't you?" Curley said. His boot toe scuffed at the planks again. "No, I am not all the way down on you, Bud. But I am about the only one. You sure ought to think about putting distance between you and here—when you get a chance."

"Thanks."

"*Por nada*," Curley said.

A group of men was coming across Southend Street and onto the boardwalk. Gannon heard the crack of the judge's crutch; with him were Carl, Pike, Peter Bacon, and some others. Carl stopped while the rest went on into the jail.

"You ride in with the Haggins, Curley?" Carl said, in a rasping voice.

"Oh, no!" Curley said. "No, sir, I am separate. I just swore it in blood to your partner here. I'm just having a little chin with Bud about this posting fellows out of town. You boys have come pretty hard against us cowboys, haven't you?"

"Yeh," Carl said, in a kind of grunt. "Hard."

"The Acme Corral for you boys, huh? Big medicine. Run up a score, maybe they'll make you marshal, Carl, now Blaisedell has quit. Money in it, I hear. Scalp money for—"

"D-don't you say anything against Blaisedell to me!" Carl said.

Gannon could feel the hate. "Carl," he said. But Carl didn't look at him.

"Don't even say his name to me," Carl said hoarsely. "You God-damned picayune rustler."

"You have rewrote the laws, have you?" Curley whispered, dangerously. "A man can still talk, I guess."

"Not to me," Carl said. "Not here or Bright's City either. You or any other rustler."

Gannon took out his Colt and held it pointed down before him. Curley glanced toward him, only his eyes moving in his rigid face. "Better move along, Curley," Gannon said.

Curley shrugged and sauntered off into the darkness. The sound of the mouth organ drifted back. Carl stood staring after him, rubbing his right hand on his pants leg.

"Schroeder!" the judge shouted from the jail, and Pike Skinner appeared in the doorway: "Come on, Carl!"

"Let's go in, Carl," Gannon said.

"Kind of pleasant not to be scared of a man for a change," Carl said in the hoarse voice. "Sure, let's go in and get the hearing started."

33. A Buggy Ride

THE strikers from the Medusa and the sympathetic miners from the other mines held their meeting on the vacant ground next to Robinson's wood yard on Peach Street. Torches made an orange glow there and smoke from the torches overlay the meeting like a milky sheet illuminated from below. There was a steady roar of shouting and clapping as they listened to various of their number harangue them, or broke up into smaller groups to attend half a dozen different speakers at once.

The town had fortified itself against riot. Shopkeepers sat inside their stores with shotguns close to hand. Horses were kept off Main Street. The Glass Slipper was dark, its front windows broken and a frame of timbers nailed up before the batwing doors. Men stood along the arcades listening to the sounds of the miners' meeting. Inside the Lucky Dollar the gambling layouts were packed and townsmen stood three deep along the bar. Among them were Arnold Mosbie, the freight-line mule skinner, Fred Wheeler, who worked at the Feed and Grain Barn, Nick Grain, the beef butcher, and Oscar Thompson, Kennon's blacksmith. These four were sharing a bottle of whisky, Mosbie and Wheeler squeezed against a narrow strip of bar, while the others stood behind them.

"Listen to those sons of bitches yell up there!" Mosbie said.

"Think they're going after Morgan again?" Thompson said, glancing worriedly toward the doors.

"Working themselves up to it?" Wheeler commented. "I'll bet Carl and Gannon's wetting their pants."

"Looks like they might've done better not to let out the judge wasn't holding Morgan for Murch killing that jack," Thompson said. "Just keeping him in jail for his own good."

"I heard old Owen wouldn't go stand by the jail with the rest," Grain said, reaching past Wheeler for the bottle. "I sure agree with him about Morgan. I don't hold with miners much, but I'll whistle when they set out to hang Morgan." He glanced at the others from beneath his colorless lashes. "Blaisedell is going to let him hang, too. See I'm not right."

"Sure been scarce today," Wheeler said, shaking his head.

"What's wrong with Morgan?" Mosbie asked.

"Well, you heard about him and that little Professor of his, didn't you?" Grain said. "Morgan wasn't paying him enough so he was going to go to work for Lew Taliaferro, playing that new piano Lew got for the French Palace. So Morgan had that Murch of his fill Lew's piano with lime mortar, and the Professor knew about it and was going to tell—you know what happened to him. Looked like he got tramped by a horse out here, but it wasn't any horse."

Wheeler snorted. "I heard it," he said. "I didn't have to believe it, though."

Mosbie had turned to face Grain. "That is Lew's story, Nick," he said. "And bull piss just like his whisky."

"Well, it is just hard for a man to like Morgan, Moss," Thompson said.

Someone near them said, "Whooo, listen to them crazy muckers!"

Mosbie turned to face Thompson. "Listen," he said. "I have said it, and you have said it too—hooray for Blaisedell for going against those sons of bitches of McQuown's. He has made McQuown eat it till it comes out of Abe's ears, and hooray for him, I say. So I say hooray for Morgan too, that is the only man in Warlock that ever helped another out against those backshooting bastards." He looked back at Grain again, "And I say piss on those that piss on Morgan, for he is a better man than them, whatever he's supposed to've done."

Grain flushed. "Now, listen, Moss—"

"I'm not through," Mosbie said. "Now it is funny how all of a sudden McQuown and Curley and them is smelling sweeter and sweeter to people again, I don't say who, the mealy-mouthed sons of bitches. And all of a sudden it is clear somehow that it is Morgan that's done everything mean and rotten that ever happened around Warlock, killing piano players and such. And in the whole valley besides, it looks like—riding around dropping off strongboxes to make it look bad for poor, innocent murdering rustlers. It surely is nice for Abe McQuown."

"Now, see here, Moss," Grain said. "I don't hold with McQuown, but—"

"That's good," Mosbie said, turning back to the bar again. "I am glad to hear you don't."

"They're coming!" somebody cried. The Lucky Dollar fell abruptly silent. The yelling of the miners was louder.

"Jesus, here they come," Thompson said, and he and Grain were borne along by the men crowding toward the batwing doors. There was a tramping and a rhythmical shouting now in the street, a burst of singing. The bankers at the layouts were swiftly cashing in the chips. Wheeler tossed his whisky down and looked at Mosbie.

"Want to go watch the hanging, Moss?"

"Hanging, hell," Mosbie said. "Let's go watch Blaisedell." They shouldered their way into the press of men moving toward the doors.

The miners came along Main Street, marching in what must have been ranks when they started, and with a semblance of the martial in their blue shirts and trousers and red sashes. Many of them carried torches or lanterns, and their bearded faces shone sweaty and orange-red in the torchlight. They sang in ponderous unison:

"Oh, my sweetheart's a burro named Jine!
We work at the old Great Hope mine!
On the dashboard I sit,
And tobacco I spit
All over my sweetheart's behind!

Good-by, good-by, good-by, Tom Morgan, good-by . . ."

The singing broke off in a ragged yell. Some tried to continue the tune, while others merely shouted as they went on down Main Street toward the jail, with the dust rising beneath their marching feet and hanging like fog in the darkness. There was a crash of glass as a rock was thrown through Goodpasture's store window, followed by an outcry of argument and laughter. There were other crashes. Torches were swung from side to side, shedding sparks like Catherine wheels.

"Christ, they will burn the town down!" someone exclaimed, as the men streamed out of the Lucky Dollar in their wake. The street began to fill behind the miners as townsmen came out of the saloons and the Billiard Parlor, and, with the sidewalk loungers, drifted along after the marchers. Outlined against the front of the jail, in the light of the torches, stood a small group of men.

Mosbie and Wheeler crossed Main Street and made their way down to Goodpasture's corner, where their bootheels grated on broken glass. Goodpasture stood within the darkened store with a shotgun in his hands. "*Morgan!*" the miners were shouting, all together. "*Morgan! Morgan!*" They approached the boardwalk before the jail in a broad semicircle, the near end of which moved slowly, the far more rapidly. Carl Schroeder shouted something that was lost in the yelling.

"My God!" Wheeler said. "Look at them go! They're going right on in!"

The miners advanced steadily toward the six who opposed them: the two deputies, Pike Skinner, Peter Bacon, Tim French, and Chick Hasty. Three of them had shotguns, Bacon a rifle, Gannon and Hasty only handguns. The miners in the front rank began swinging their torches and sending up great arcs of sparks.

Finally they halted and Schroeder's voice was heard: "First one across this rail gets shot!"

"Tromp them down!" the miners cried. "Morgan! We want Morgan!"

"Give him up, Schroeder! We'll tramp you down!"

Mosbie said to Wheeler, "By Christ, it looks to be two hundred of them there!"

"Where the hell's Blaisedell?" a man near them said. "He had better damn well hurry!"

"He'll be along and back them off," said another.

"Hell he will," a third said, with a snicker. "He is soaking it over at Miss Jessie's. She'll keep him there, being for those stinking jacks—" He cried out as someone hit him in the mouth.

Mosbie struggled to free himself from those who pressed around him, and flung himself at the man who had spoken; they went down in a cursing pile. Others tried to separate them. "Foul-mouthed son of a bitch!" Mosbie yelled.

On the far corner a miner was haranguing Schroeder. He tried to climb over the rail and Schroeder swung the shotgun barrel down on him. Instantly a wave of miners poured forward over the tie rail. "Moss!" Wheeler shouted. "There they go!"

The boardwalk before the jail was a mass of fighting men. A shotgun was discharged; there was a scream, and the blue-clad figures fled back into the street, leaving one crumpled and shrieking on the boardwalk, with Carl Schroeder standing over him.

"Shot one, by God!" Wheeler said, as Mosbie rejoined him, panting. "Best thing for it, too."

"Who did it?"

"Carl, looked like."

"Hey, Carl shot one!"

The miners began to roar with one voice, and the tightly packed mass of them in the street weaved and swayed, the torches waving wildly above them. *"Kill them! Kill them! Hang them with Morgan!"*

"Boys, they have killed Benny Connors!"

Mosbie leaned against one of the posts that held up the arcade, with Wheeler pressed tightly against him by the men around them. "Oh, Jesus!" a man near them said, over and over, like a prayer. The weaving, uncertain movement of the mob changed, section by section, into a single forward thrust forcing the men in the front rank against the railing. One of the deputies raised his six-shooter and discharged it with a flat shock of sound; still the miners pressed forward, almost in silence now.

"Here he comes!"

"It's Blaisedell, all right. Here he comes!"

"Thank the good Lord!" Wheeler said.

"Look at the buggy!" someone said, but no one paid any attention to him.

Mosbie clambered up on the tie rail and clung to the post. "You ought to see him!" he called down to Wheeler.

Blaisedell came down the center of Main Street, with the townsmen moving quickly aside before him. He came at a swift, certain, long-legged stride, with his black hat showing above the heads of the men he passed. He did not pause as he came to the edge of the mob of miners, forging straight ahead through them like a knife splitting its way through a pine board. Torchlight gleamed on the barrel of his Colt as he knocked a miner aside with it.

"Kill him too!" someone among the miners cried suddenly. "Don't let him get up there, boys!"

But Blaisedell went on, unhindered, and finally he stood before the jail among the deputies, taller than any of them. His voice was sudden and loud. "Back off, boys. There'll be no hanging tonight."

"I believe he could stand off the U. S. Cavalry," Wheeler said. The miners in the street remained silent.

"You had better get this one to Doc Wagner," Blaisedell said, motioning to the miner still groaning on the boardwalk.

Still there was silence. The torches flared and smoked. The front rank had drawn back from the rail.

Then someone shouted, *"He won't shoot!"*

Others took it up. "He won't shoot to save that murdering high-roller! He's bluffing! Run him down!"

The yelling mass began swaying forward once more, compressing those who tried to hold back away from the rail. Then the railing

went down and miners leaped and crowded onto the boardwalk. Blaisedell and the deputies were swamped by the blue-clad bodies in a
melee of flailing arms and gun barrels. There were two shots, two furry
spurts of flame reaching upward. Again the miners retreated. Gannon
and Schroeder appeared, and Blaisedell with his hat gone. One of the
deputies was down; Pike Skinner and Tim French helped him inside
the jail.

"Who was that, Moss?" Wheeler cried.

"Chick Hasty."

"*He won't shoot!*" the same voice shouted again, and again the
miners took up the cry.

"They are going to run him," Mosbie said hoarsely.

Blaisedell stood before the jail door with a lock of hair fallen over
one eye, his chest heaving, and both his Colts out. Schroeder, shouting unheard, stood on one side of him, Gannon on the other. Skinner
and French came out of the jail again and took up their posts. Once
more the torches began to swing, and sparks flew upward in the
wind.

"They are going to bust over him," Mosbie said.

"There they go again!"

The miners flung themselves forward and Blaisedell and the deputies
were thrown back before them. Blaisedell went down; there was a
yell as the watchers saw it, and a groan; the other deputies went
down. One retreated inside the jail, dragging another with him, and
slammed the door. The miners crashed against it, drew back, and
crashed against it again.

"Look at that! Look!" cried the man beside Mosbie on the railing.

But no one noticed him as the jail door broke and the miners streamed
inside, yelling in triumph. Almost immediately they began thrusting
themselves back out again, while others still fought to enter. The
deputies began to appear among them.

"What the hell happened?" Wheeler demanded.

"Look! It's Miss Jessie!"

A buggy was coming out of Southend Street. Miss Jessie Marlow
was in it, and there was a man on the seat beside her. She was trying
to turn the bay horse that drew the buggy east into Main Street and
the horse was scaring in the crowd. Miss Jessie sat very straight with
a bonnet on, and a white frilled blouse with a black necktie. The man
lounging on the seat beside her was Morgan.

"It's Morgan with her!"

"It is Morgan, for Christ's sake!"

Miss Jessie flicked the buggy whip down once, and the bay pranced ahead. Men moved out of the way. The lighted tip of a cigar glowed in Morgan's hand. The two of them looked as though they had been out for a pleasant ride.

"She took him out of the back!" a man cried. "I saw that buggy turning in the alley there a while ago. Look at that, will you?"

"She won't get away with it," Mosbie said, in the hoarse voice.

"Hurry up!" Wheeler whispered, hitting his fist against the tie rail. "Hurry up, ma'am! Bust that bay again!"

The buggy continued its slow progress through the men in the street. The miners had fallen silent, and now the main traffic was away from the jail. Some of them appeared out of the alley in Southend. "He's gone!" a miner shouted. "Got out the back!"

"There he is! In the buggy!"

Miners surged around the buggy, the whole mass of them changing direction now, and pressing back up Main Street. But the miners who surrounded the buggy began to drop away from it. Others ran after it, looked in, and dropped back too. Mosbie began to laugh.

"Did it!" he said. "They are going to make it, by God! Came right through them, and the best thing she could've done, too."

The buggy began moving more swiftly now, out of the press; it disappeared into the darkness up Main Street.

"Taking him to the General Peach," someone commented calmly. "Well, they'll never bust over her."

"Where's Blaisedell?"

"He just went inside the jail. He's all right, looked like."

"He held them long enough for her to get Morgan out. Slick!"

"I'd a lot rather seen him cut a few of them down."

Miners stood in uncertain groups in the street. The deputies were shooing them off the boardwalk. Two of them carried off the miner who had been shot. Schroeder had a long, bloody cut over one eye. Gannon retrieved Blaisedell's black hat from a miner who had picked it up.

Mosbie climbed down from the tie rail. "What the hell did Blaisedell let those sons of bitches run over him for?" he said to Wheeler. "That's what I don't see. God damn it to hell."

Nick Grain appeared beside Wheeler. "Did you see him get run over, Fred?" he cried, in an excited voice. "They sure called his bluff."

"Shut up!" Mosbie said. He caught Grain by his shirt collar. "Shut up! You push-face cow-turd of a butcher! Shut up!" He flung Grain away from him, and Grain disappeared hurriedly into the crowd.

"I hate that stupid asinine flap-mouth son of a bitch," Mosbie said. He and Wheeler started back along the boardwalk with the others. The men around them were talking in low tones; one of them laughed and Mosbie glared at him.

Groups of men stood in the street, looking toward the jail, or up toward the General Peach where the buggy had gone. The miners were heading into the saloons, or congregating along the boardwalks.

Wheeler and Mosbie walked on east in the deep shadow under the arcade, crossed Broadway, and continued up to Grant Street, where they joined a group standing by the side of the Feed and Grain Barn. All the windows were lighted in the General Peach. The buggy stood in front, the fat bay scratching her neck against the hitching post. Eight or ten miners stood near the buggy, and the crippled miner, Tittle, was watching them from the porch with a rifle in his hands.

"The Doc's buggy," someone commented.

"Not a one to try and stop her!" Paul Skinner said. "Not a one!"

"There's a woman with more guts than any man I know."

"Shame to see them bust over Blaisedell," said another.

"Should've shot one for himself like Carl did."

"I heard Carl didn't go to. The stupid muck got hold of his shotgun and yanked on it, and Carl's finger on the trigger."

"Looks like maybe Blaisedell's a human being like the rest of us though," another man said. Mosbie started toward him, but Wheeler grasped his arm.

"There comes Curley Burne," someone whispered.

Curley Burne came across Grant Street toward them with the light from the General Peach gleaming on his black curls.

"Curley," someone said, and several others also greeted him.

"Big night, boys," Curley said. "You boys fun it like this every night in Warlock?"

There was some laughter. "Where's those Regulators of Mac-Donald's, Curley?" a man drawled from the shadow of the adobe wall. "Just when we needed those Regulators bad they didn't show for beans."

"Warlock's too calky for them," Curley said. "Curl a man's hair just to walk down the street here." He indicated his own head with a sweep of his hand, and there was more laughter.

"There's Blaisedell."

They all fell silent. Blaisedell rounded the corner; he limped a little as he walked down toward the General Peach. As he mounted the porch past Tittle he held to the hand rail, and, in the light there, he did not look so tall. The front door closed behind him with a hollow whack.

"The marshal got himself some chewed up tonight," Curley Burne said.

Wheeler gripped Mosbie's arm, but Mosbie pulled away with a curse. "Go tell it to Abe McQuown, Curley!" he said thickly. "Maybe it will bring him out of his hole."

"Who said that?" Curley said.

Mosbie crouched a little. "I said it!"

"Hold off now!" Paul Skinner said. "Hold off! Curley, you leave be! Moss!" Wheeler stepped between Curley and Mosbie.

"You shouldn't have said it, Moss," Curley said, and his voice was as thick as Mosbie's.

"I'll say it again!"

"Take it and forget it, Curley," a voice said from the darkness. "He has got friends here and you haven't."

"We are pretty sick of cowboys up here," another man said.

Curley glanced toward the two who had spoken, looked past Wheeler at Mosbie, shrugged, and turned away. His hat swung across his back as he disappeared into the darkness.

"Soooooo-boy!" Wheeler said. "He is no man to mess with, Moss!"

"I am no man to mess with tonight either," Mosbie said.

Behind him someone laughed a little, relievedly.

"God damn it to hell!" Mosbie said, and kicked in fury and frustration at the dust.

34. Gannon Puts Down His Name

I

GANNON leaned limply against the cell door, pressing a hand to his ribs. Pike Skinner and Peter Bacon were hunkered down with their backs to the wall opposite him, Pike with a bloody ear over which he kept cupping the palm of his hand, Peter supporting himself on the shotgun. Tim French had helped Hasty, who had been badly shaken up, home to bed.

"Nothing to do now," Carl said. He sat at the table brushing his hand back over his graying, thinning, sweat-tangled hair. "It is off our back anyhow. Blaisedell is probably right, there is less chance of trouble if we stay away from the General Peach." He sat looking down at the crooked trigger finger of his right hand.

Gannon slowly seated himself in the chair beside the cell door, holding his breath at the sudden ache in his ribs.

"Damn them," Carl said, without heat. "Looked like they might've saved that one I shot. But they had to let him bleed it out and then tramp what was left of him. Course, any man that's fool enough to give a jerk on a gun barrel when it's pointed right at him and cocked, and your finger—"

"Sure, Horse," Peter said. "None of your doing."

"Well, he held them off long enough for Miss Jessie to get Morgan out the back," Carl said. "What we was after, after all—save a lynching."

"Yes," Gannon said, and Peter Bacon glanced up at him and nodded.

"I guess he did pure right not shooting," Peter said. "But that didn't make it a better thing to see."

"I admire to see a woman cool as Miss Jessie was," Carl said. He straightened and stretched. "You boys go home and get some sleep. This deputy's office is just about to close up for the night."

Pike said, "I'm going out and drink some of the meanness out of me."

"You stay out of scrapes with jacks, now!" Carl said. "I don't want anything more to mess with tonight. If I don't get some rest for my old bones I am going to have to lay right down and die."

" 'Night," Peter said, rising; he nodded to Carl and Gannon, and he and Pike went outside into the darkness.

Carl went over and kicked at the broken glass on the floor, and inspected the broken latch of the door. "You suppose the Citizens' Committee'll pay for fixing these? Place could fall down for all of Keller. All I asked him for here was a new sign, but I guess I am not going to get it unless I pay for it myself." Blood had scabbed over the long scratch above his right eye, and run and crusted on his cheek. "Bad night," he said, in a sad voice. "Let's close up, Johnny."

Gannon pulled down the lamp and blew out the flame, and followed Carl out. Outside, in the thick dark, the town seemed very still.

"Quiet," Carl said, and sighed. "I guess I'll have a whisky before I go home. You, Johnny?"

"I guess not; thanks." He watched Carl go off along the boardwalk, frail-looking and limping a little, his bootheels cracking unevenly on the planks.

II

Gannon went along past the wood yard to Grant Street and turned down toward Kate's house. He could see a light burning at the back.

He mounted the two steps, knocked, and waited. He felt for the key in his jeans pocket, and his face prickled; he knocked again. He heard her footsteps inside, and the door was opened a crack.

"It's me," he said.

The crack widened and he was aware of her close to him, although he could not see her yet in the darkness. "Oh, it's my gentleman caller," she said.

"I just came by to tell you Morgan is all right now."

"Come in, Deputy," Kate said. He went inside; Kate was outlined for a moment against the lighted bedroom doorway, but she moved aside to become invisible again. Something thumped on the oilcloth-covered table and he realized that she had had the derringer in her hand.

"Blaisedell?" she said.

"He showed up, but he couldn't stop them either. It was Miss Jessie got him out. She came in the doctor's buggy and took him out through the alley. He's at the General Peach now."

"Is he?" Kate said, as though she were not interested. She was silent for a long time, and he felt like a prying fool. He turned to go.

"Well, I'll be going. I just—"

"The angel of Warlock," Kate said. He couldn't make out her tone. "Is she Blaisedell's sweetheart?"

He nodded, and realized that she could not see him nod. But before he could speak, she said, "I'd heard of her before I came here. She is what you hear of when you hear of Warlock. And I've seen her on the street. What's she like?"

"Why, she is a fine woman, Kate. It took some doing what she did tonight."

"She is a nice woman," Kate said, in the tone he could not make out.

"She is. She—"

"I hate nice women," Kate said. It shocked him to hear her. Again he turned to go; he felt strangely angry.

"Anxious to go, Deputy?"

"It's not that. But I just came by to tell you about Morgan."

"Did you think I cared what happened to Morgan?"

He licked his lips. He could see her now, standing across the table from him. There was some kind of shawl draped over her shoulders. "Well, I couldn't help hearing what you was saying to him earlier tonight," he said. "When you came in the jail. And I thought—"

"Is it any of your business?"

He nodded, and the anger ached in him like the savage ache in his ribs where the miner had kicked him.

"Is it?" Kate said.

"Yes."

"All right. I saved him like that once."

"In Grand Fork."

"He'd killed a man that called him for cheating. That was when he still let himself get caught cheating once in a while. The vigilantes took him to the hotel to hold him till they could hang him. I started a fire and—"

"I understood what he was saying."

"Did you?" Kate said, in a flat voice. "And you want it your business? If you don't want it, say so now." She sounded as though she were warning him. "Maybe you don't," she said.

"I want to know." He leaned on the back of a chair.

"I was Tom Morgan's girl for four years," she said. His fingers tightened on the chair back, not to hear her telling him what he had already sensed, but to hear her say it as though it were no different than telling him where she was born, or how old she was, or who her parents were.

"Most of the time he was flush," she continued. "There were scrapes and sometimes we'd have to run, and sometimes he would bust; but mostly he was flush. He is a real high-roller. He has owned places here and there, the way he does now, but he would always sell out sooner or later and go back to playing against the bank. He did that best. He liked that best. He will get tired of running the Glass Slipper here and sell out and go somewhere else to buck the tiger. That's all he really wants to do. But he has to have a stake to start.

"After we'd run from Grand Fork we went to Fort James. He didn't have a dollar—except me." She laughed a little. Then her voice went flat again as she said, "So he wanted me to make a stake for him. Going back to what I'd been doing when he took me up. Back," she said, as though he might not have understood.

"I did, and I made him his stake. But I told him I was through with him. I didn't even see him for a long time—but I should have known I wasn't through with him. Anyway, Bob Cletus was going to marry me. He had a ranch near Fort James." Her voice began to shake. "Maybe I did know, for I told Bob he had better tell Morgan. And see if it was—all right." She stopped then.

"Cletus?" he said. "The one you came out here with?"

"That was his brother. Blaisedell killed Bob in Fort James that day."

"Oh," he said.

"So you see," she said, her voice so low he could hardly hear her. "Did you want to know?"

"Why, yes," he lied.

He could smell the perfume she wore; she had moved closer to him. She said, "I looked for his brother for a while—Blaisedell shot Bob in Seventy-nine. Then I just happened to run onto Pat in Denver, and I—he came out here with me. And they killed Pat, too."

He was aware again of the shape of the key in his pocket, and of its weight. He cleared his throat. "You got his brother to come out here with you to try to—"

"Yes," she broke in, curtly, as though he had been stupid even to ask. Then she said, "I want to see Blaisedell shot down like that. It is all I want."

He heard the scrape of her slippers and the creak of the floor as she moved again. She halted so close to him that he could have touched her, and he could see the shape of her face and the rounded pits of her eyes. But all at once she said, "No," and drew back a little. Her voice began to shake once more as she said, "I don't know. Maybe I only want to see it happen and not—do anything. Maybe it is enough. Maybe I have done too much already. But I would like to know the man who was to do it. Beforehand. I thought it might be you."

"No," he said hoarsely.

"After he killed your brother I was almost glad. For I thought there would be reason enough. . . ."

"It won't be me. I couldn't anyway."

"I think you could. But I won't ask you, Deputy. Are you afraid I am going to ask you?"

"Why *him?*" he cried. "I should think it would be Morgan you are after!"

He saw her turn away. When she spoke her voice was clear and small, and she sounded as though she were reasoning with herself as much as with him. "Because I should have known what Tom would do. So maybe it was part my fault. Because it was just the sort of rotten, dog-in-the-manger thing Tom would do. But Blaisedell—"

Her voice ceased, but he saw, and was sick with jealousy and pain at what he saw. How much those four years must have been to her, and Morgan; she must have loved Morgan very much.

He raised a sour, damp hand to rub it over his face. He tried to speak calmly. "Kate, maybe Blaisedell did that. But I don't believe he is bad. He has done good here, killed my brother or not. Kate, do you think it will be someone decent who will kill him? It will not be!"

"Decent to me."

"Do you know who will kill him? Someone like Abe McQuown, or some kid after score like Billy. No, not even that. It will be some backshooter, like Calhoun. Or Cade. It will be somebody like Jack Cade, somebody worse than you think *he* is even. Somebody all bad. Don't you see?"

"It doesn't matter."

"It matters! Don't you see he is a man for men to look up to? There are not many good ones like that, and it will be an all bad one that will kill him, and then the bad one looked up to for it. Don't you see that?"

"Maybe not a bad one," Kate said. She sounded almost indifferent. "Maybe a better one. Someone like you, I mean."

"Don't say that."

"I think it is so."

"That's foolishness, Kate!"

"Why, then it is none of your business after all," she said. There was an edge of anger to her voice, and as she went on it was more and more angry, and filled with hate. "You look up to him, don't you?" she said. "You should know how men look up to him, since you do yourself. Because he is so *fine*. He is quick on the draw—does that make him fine? He has killed I don't even know any more how many men—does that make him fine? He is a hired killer! Morgan hired him to kill a man and Fort James hired him to kill men, and Warlock has. It must be fine and brave and *manly* to be a hired killer, but you can't expect a woman to understand why men will worship him like a saint because he—"

"Stop it!"

"All right, I will stop it. And you get out of here. You are not a *man*. Not the man I want."

"More man than you are woman, I guess, Miss Dollar." He spoke in anger; instantly he was sorry. "I am sorry," he said quickly. "I didn't go to say a thing like that. I'll ask you to forgive me, Kate."

But she didn't speak, and he could feel the hate. It was as though he were in a cage with an animal. He turned and moved toward the door.

He heard a shot. It came from the direction of Main Street, and there was a yell, and a chorus of yells. But still he did not leave. "Kate—" he said.

"Maybe they have killed him for me," Kate said, viciously, and he went outside. He ran down toward the corner of Main Street with his ribs aching and the scabbarded Colt slapping against his leg.

It was some time before he could find out what had happened; no one seemed to know. Someone said that Blaisedell had shot Curley Burne, who had been taken dying to the General Peach; another thought that some of the Regulators had come in and scared up a Medusa miner. He crossed the street finally, to another group of men before the Billiard Parlor. Hutchinson, Foss, and Kennon were there.

"Carl got shot," Foss told him. "It was Curley."

"Dirty hound!" Kennon said, in a cracked voice.

"Where is he?"

"Forked a horse and lit out running," someone said. "There is a bunch going to take out after him. They're down at—"

"No—*Carl!*" he said.

"They took him over to the General Peach," Hutchinson said. "He was bleeding bad."

As Gannon ran back down Main Street, Kennon shouted after him, "You had better start getting a posse together, Gannon!"

There was another bunch before the General Peach, and a number of horses. "It's Gannon," someone said. "Here comes Johnny Gannon." He made his way through them and up the steps, where Miss Jessie's man Tittle barred his way with a Winchester.

"Listen, nobody else comes—"

He shouldered past, and Tittle stumbled back clumsily, banging his rifle butt against the door. "Where is he?" Gannon panted, starting back toward the hospital room. Then he saw Pike Skinner and Mosbie through Miss Jessie's open door. Buck Slavin was there, and Sam Brown and Fred Wheeler. Morgan leaned on the foot of the bed, with the doctor beside him, and Blaisedell stood apart. Miss Jessie was sitting beside the bed, where Carl was.

"Well, hello, Johnny," Carl said, in a breathless voice. He looked like a scared, white-faced boy with a pasted-on, graying mustache. Gannon hadn't realized how gray Carl was. He moved over to kneel

beside the bed, next to Miss Jessie's chair. Carl wet his lips and carefully turned his head toward him.

"You will have to deputy alone awhile, Johnny."

"Sure," he panted. "Surely, Carl. We'll make out."

Behind him Pike Skinner said roughly, "We will help him till you
are up and around again, Carl."

Carl grinned thinly; he turned his head a little farther toward
Gannon, and winked. "Sure," he whispered. "There is some good
boys to help. They have been rallying round. You'll be all right,
Johnny."

"Hush, now, Carl," Miss Jessie said, and patted his hand. She wore
the high-necked, frilled blouse with the black necktie she had worn
when she had come to the jail, and she smelled cleanly of sachet and
starched linen. "You mustn't talk so much, Carl," she said.

"It's all right," the doctor said, in his clipped, curt voice.

"I have always been a talker, ma'am," Carl said. "It is hard to quit
being one now."

Leaning on the brass foot of the bed in a clean shirt and trousers,
his cigar bobbing in the corner of his mouth as he spoke, Morgan
said gently, "A man needs a little rest after fighting those wild-eyed
jacks off my neck half the night."

Carl grinned again. Behind Morgan, Blaisedell stood with his arms
folded over his chest, and only his blue eyes alive in his cold, bruised
and scraped face. There was a tramp of hoofs outside the window,
and Gannon could hear the men talking there. "Let's get moving," one
said. "Where's Gannon. He going to weasel on this?"

"What happened?" Gannon said quickly, to Carl.

"Just stupid," Carl said, in an embarrassed voice. "Curley and me
had some more words. That was there by the Billiard Parlor and I
kind of surprised myself and him too getting drawed before he did."
He laughed shakily. "Durned if I didn't! Well, I kind of cooled off,
seeing I'd got the drop; so I thought I'd camp him in jail for the night.
So I called for his piece—" His voice trailed off.

"Curley went to let him take it and then spun it on him," Mosbie
said. "I saw him do it, and a good lot of others standing there saw it.
Run the road-agent spin on him, by God—pardon me, Miss Jessie.
I should have chose him myself, I just about did earlier."

"We'll see he is caught, Carl," Buck Slavin said solemnly.

Gannon saw a little cluster of bluish veins at Carl's temple, and the
slow beat of blood in them. He had never seen those veins there before.
The flesh of Carl's face looked as though it had been waxed.

"Better get a posse riding, Johnny," Pike said. "There is a good lot gathered outside already."

"Not much use till morning," Carl said. "If I was doing it I'd wait. Nobody could follow sign till light."

Miss Jessie patted Carl's hand. Her hand was white and small beneath the long cuff of her sleeve, the nails cut shorter than Kate's. Carl's brows knit together beneath the long, crusted scratch on his forehead, and Carl's eyes took on an inward expression.

"Feels like something's broke loose again, Doc," Carl said easily. "I don't want to bleed up Miss Jessie's nice bed."

"It will stop," the doctor said.

"Let's go on outside," Pike whispered, and he left the room, followed by Buck, Wheeler, Mosbie, and Sam Brown.

Gannon could hear more horses in the street now. He saw Carl's eyes close and he quickly looked up at the doctor, who had on his nightshirt beneath his rusty black suit. The doctor shook his head.

Gannon saw that Blaisedell was watching him expressionlessly. Above Blaisedell's head was a mezzotint of a man thrashing at some ocean waves with a long sword.

Carl opened his eyes again. "You know?" he said. "It makes a person sort of mad—I mean I was just watching it go by in my head here. Say you catch him, Johnny, and the judge binds him over to trial in Bright's. He will just get off." He laughed a little and said, "Are you going to post him out of town for me, Marshal?"

Gannon heard Miss Jessie draw in her breath; he saw Morgan's face harden. Blaisedell didn't give any sign that he had heard.

Miss Jessie said, "David, I think he ought to rest a little now. I think everybody ought to leave and let him rest." She said it as though she were talking to the doctor, but it sounded like a command. Gannon started to get to his feet.

"Except Johnny," Carl said. "Leave Johnny stay."

Miss Jessie rose with a quick movement, brushing her hands together in her skirt. Her eyes looked tired, but very bright; her brown ringlets swung as she turned toward Blaisedell. She went over to take Blaisedell's arm, as though she must lead him out, and Morgan's cold eyes followed her all the way. They all left the room.

Gannon knelt uncomfortably beside the bed, watching Carl's face, in profile to him, and the steady throb of the little cluster of veins. Carl whispered, "I'm going, old horse."

Gannon shook his head.

"It is like big gray curtains coming down. You can kind of see them trailing down—like the bottom of a tornado cloud coming down. Getting black like that too, but slow."

"I'm sorry, Carl," he said.

"Surely," Carl said, as though to comfort him. "We have been friends and got along, haven't we? I was a good enough deputy, wasn't I? Whatever old Judge had to say about it."

Gannon tried to speak and choked on it.

Carl laughed soundlessly. "Well, I don't know what I am crying about now. I knew one of those cowboys was going to score me, and I guess I'd just as soon it was Curley.

"Ah, I came in all big medicine brave on account of Bill Canning," he went on. "And saw what I was into, and caved in for a while. Pure fright. But I come up again, I'll say that for myself. I picked up there toward the last. Why, I was right proud of myself standing up to Curley like I did. I just wish I didn't have to go out on killing that poor, stupid jack, though; that was no kind of thing. And sorry to leave you right in the middle of all hell, Johnny. With Curley to get, and I suppose somebody ought to get word in to Bright's City on Murch, in case he went that way. And muckers and Regulators." He began to chuckle again, his shirt trembling over his chest with it. "Maybe I picked the best time after all," he said. "But damn Curley Burne anyhow."

Carl looked exhausted now, and his eyes seemed suddenly sunken. After a moment he said, "Me and Curley scrapped over Blaisedell mostly. I guess you figured that."

"I thought it'd been that, Carl."

Carl's eyes flared in their sockets, like candles guttering. "Once in a while—once in a long while there's a man— Blaisedell made a man of me, Johnny. But now—"

"I know," he said quickly.

"Things getting him down," Carl whispered. "Bringing him low. Like those jacks tonight, and nothing for a man to do to help him back. Then somebody comes along and you can speak up for him. And maybe because it is the only thing you can do—you push it too hard. Maybe I pushed Curley too hard."

"Never mind it now, Carl." Gannon could hear now, in the street outside, the pad of hoofs and the jingle of spurs and harness, and voices, diminishing as the men rode away.

"I always was a talker," Carl said. His eyes drooped closed. His hands moved slowly to fold themselves upon his chest. He looked as though he were aging at tremendous speed.

Gannon rose from his knees and sank into the chair. He saw Miss Jessie standing in the doorway behind him, one hand to her throat and her round eyes fixed on him steadily.

Carl whispered something and he had to bend forward to hear it.

"—post him out," Carl was saying, smiling a little, his eyes still closed. "And right down the middle of the street with no two ways about it, like that in the Acme was." His voice came more strongly. "Why, that'd be epitaph enough for a man! Carl Schroeder that was deputy in Warlock, shot by Curley Burne. And right next to me: Curley Burne, killed for it by Clay Blaisedell, Marshal. Cut that in stone! That'd be—" His words became a kind of soft rustling Gannon could no longer understand.

Gannon sat watching with fascination the slow movement in the little veins, knowing he should be both with the posse, which was not a posse without him, and here with Carl.

"That stupid jack!" Carl said suddenly. His eyes opened and all at once fright was written with cruel marks upon his face. He reached for Gannon's hand and gripped it tightly. "Johnny! Bring out your Colt's and hand it here!"

"Carl, you—"

"Quick! There is not much time!"

Gannon drew his six-shooter and held it out where Carl could see it, which seemed to be what Carl wanted.

"Hold it right," Carl said. "Finger on the trigger." Carl caught hold of the barrel and gave it a jerk. Then he groaned. "Yes!" he whispered, as Gannon withdrew the Colt. "I pulled on it the same as that damned, stupid jack did to me with the shotgun. *No*, not the *same!* But by God it was!"

Carl turned his head from side to side with a tortured movement. "Oh, God Almighty, there is no way to know! But maybe he didn't go to do it, Johnny."

"But he ran—" he started.

"Because there was half a dozen there would've cut him down! Johnny—" Carl stopped, his throat working as though he could not swallow. Finally he got his breath; he lay there panting. "Forgive as you would be forgiven," he whispered. "And I will be going to that judgment seat directly. Oh, God!" he whispered, dully.

Tears squeezed from beneath his eyelids. His throat worked again.

He whispered, "Johnny—I guess you had better tell them that Curley didn't go to do it."

That was all. Still a faint flicker of life showed in the blue veins. Gannon stared at them, slowly thrusting the muzzle of his Colt toward its scabbard, until the barrel finally slid in; he sat hunched and aching, watching the little veins, and at no given instant could he have said that the movement in them ceased. There was only, after a time, the realization that Carl's life was gone, and he rose and disengaged the counterpane from beneath Carl's arms, folded the hands together on the thin chest, and drew the counterpane up over all.

He backed away, upsetting the chair in his clumsiness, and catching it as it fell. Jessie Marlow still stood in the doorway. She nodded, just as he said, "He's gone," and raised her finger to her lips in a curious, straitened, intense gesture he did not understand.

He moved out past her into the dark entryway. Blaisedell stood across from him, his legs apart, hands behind his back, his head bent down—as still as a statue. Morgan sat on the bottom step, smoking.

"He's gone," he said again. Still Blaisedell didn't move. The doctor came out of the shadows near the front door and followed Miss Jessie into her room. Gannon knew these out here had not heard Carl's last words; he wondered if even Miss Jessie had.

"They went on down toward San Pablo," Morgan told him. "Skinner said he thought you would just as soon not go anyway."

He nodded dumbly, and went on outside. There was no one now in the street before the General Peach. He walked to the jail and in the darkness there sank down in the chair at the table, with his head in his hands. He did not know if he could face telling them what Carl had said. They would say he lied, with utter condemnation and contempt, and the lie thrown in his face until he would have to fight back. But how would he be able to blame them for thinking that he lied? He could only pray that the posse would not catch Curley. Surely they would not catch Curley Burne.

He groaned. Finally he rose, with broken glass scraping beneath his boots, and lit the lamp, staring, in the gathering light, at the names scratched on the wall. He slid open the table drawer and took out Carl's pencil. With his ribs aching, he squatted before the list of the deputies of Warlock, and, carefully, in small, neat lettering, he added, beneath Carl's name, the name of John Gannon.

35. Curley Burne Loses His Mouth Organ

CURLEY was half asleep in the saddle when the sun came up, sudden and painfully bright just above the peaks of the Bucksaws. As he cut in from the river his eyes felt sandy and his spine jarred into the shape of a buttonhook. The gelding he had taken plodded along, stiff-legged, and he was grimacing now at every jolt.

"That is some gait you got, horse," he complained, leaning both hands on the pommel to ease his seat. "I never heard of a horse without knee joints before." He reached for his mouth organ inside his shirt; somehow the cord had got broken, and he had to dig for the mouth organ inside his shell belt. He blew into it to wake himself up, and now he began to feel a growing elation. For now he could go, now he must move on, and there was good news for Abe about Blaisedell's comedown for him to leave on.

The elation faded when he thought of Carl Schroeder. Carl had been an aggravating man, and more and more aggravating and scratchy lately, but he had not wanted to see Carl dead. He wondered if there was a posse out yet, and he looked back for dust; he could see none.

"Poor old Carl," he said aloud. "Damned scratchy old son of a bitch." In his mind's eye he saw Carl go down with the front of his pants afire, and he winced at the sight. He knew that Carl was dead by now.

The gelding went grunting pole-legged down a draw, and labored up the rise beyond it. He had a glimpse of the windmill on the pump house with the blades wheeling slowly in the sun, and the tall chimney of the old house. He pricked the gelding's flanks with his spurs. "Let's run in there with our peckers up, you!" The gelding maintained the same pace. "Gait like banging an ax handle on a fence post," he said.

By dint of jabbing in his spurs, yelling, and flapping his hat right and left, he got the gelding into a shambling, wheezing run down the last slope. He fired his Colt into the air and whooped. The gelding fell back into a trot. Joe Lacey and the breed came out of the bunkhouse and waved to him. Abe appeared on the porch of the ranch house in an old hat and a flannel shirt, and no pants on. The legs of his long-handled underwear were dirty and baggy at the knees.

Curley gave one last half-hearted whoop and jumped off the gelding; his knees gave beneath his weight and he almost fell. Abe leaned on the porch rail, sleepy and cross-looking, as Curley mounted the steps.

"Where'd you get that bottlehead?"

"Stole him, and a bad deal too." He leaned against the porch rail beside Abe. "I'm leaving, Abe," he said. "Things look like they'll be getting hot for me here."

Abe said incuriously, "Blaisedell?"

"Carl and me come to it."

A shadow came down over Abe's red-bearded face, and he blew out his breath in a whisper like a snake hissing.

"Abe!" the old man called from inside. "Abe, who is that rode in? Is that you, Curley?"

"It surely is," he called back. "Coming and going, Dad McQuown. I'm on the run."

"Killed him?" Abe said sharply.

"Looked like it. I didn't stay to see." When he flipped his hat off, the jerk of the cord against his throat made his heart pump sickly.

"Killed who?" Dad McQuown cried. "Son, bring me out so's I can see Curley, will you? Killed who, Curley?"

"Carl," Curley said. He tried to grin at Abe. He said loudly, for the old man's benefit, "Run the road-agent spin on him. Neat!"

The old man's laughter grated on him insupportably, and Abe cried, "Shut up, Daddy!" One of Abe's eyes was slitted now, while the other was wide; he looked as though he were sighting down a Winchester. Curley saw Joe Lacey coming toward the porch.

"You are not needed here!" Abe snapped, and Joe quickly retreated. "What happened?" Abe said.

"Why, it seems like they get a new set of laws up there every time a man comes in. Now you can't even talk any more. And scratchy! Well, I was there by Sam Brown's billiard place, minding my own business and talking to some boys, and Carl comes butting in and didn't like what I was saying. We cussed back and forth some, and—"

"God damn you!" Abe whispered.

Curley stiffened, his hands clenching on the rail on either side of him as he stared back at Abe.

"You did it now," Abe said. He didn't sound angry any more, only washed-up and bitter.

"What's the matter, Abe?"

Abe shrugged and scratched at his leg in the dirty longjohns. "Where you going?" he asked.

"I guess up toward Welltown, and then—*quién sabe?*"

"In a hurry?"

"I don't expect they got a posse off till sun-up. But it's not something I better count on. Why'd you get so mad, Abe?"

"People liked Carl," Abe said. He hit his fist, without force, down on the porch rail, and shook his head as though there were nothing that was any use. "They'll hang this on me too," he went on. "That I put you to killing Carl. But you'll be gone. It's nothing to you."

"Ah, for Christ's sake, Abe!"

"They have got me again," Abe said.

"Sonny, you shut that crazy talk!" the old man shrilled. "Now, you bring me out there with you boys. Abe!"

"I'll get him," Curley said. He went inside to where the old man lay, on his pallet on the floor by the stove, and picked him up pallet and all. The old man clung to his neck, breathing hard. He didn't weigh over a hundred pounds any more, and the smell of him was the hardest part of carrying him.

"Got the deputy, did you, Curley?" the old man said, blinking and scowling in the sun as Curley put the pallet down on the porch. "Well, now; I always thought high of you, Curley Burne!" His mouth was red and wet through his white beard. "Well now," he went on, glancing sideways at Abe. "That's all there is to it. Man's pushing on you, all you do is ride in there—"

"By God, you talk," Abe said, in a strained voice. "Daddy, I've told you I don't mind dying, if that's what you want of me. I just mind dying a damned fool!"

"Abe," Curley said. "I guess I had better be moving."

Abe didn't even hear him. "I mind dying a damned fool, and I mind dying one for every man to spit on," he went on. He began to laugh, shrilly. "Pile everything on me! By God, they will have a torchlight parade and fireworks when I am dead! They will carry him around Warlock on their shoulders and make speeches and set off giant powder, for him; that never did a sin in his life. And tramp me in the dust for the dogs to chew on—that never did anything else but!"

The old man gazed at his son in horror, at Curley in shame. There was an iron clamor from Cookie's triangle, and the dogs began to bark out by the cook shack.

"Well, there is breakfast now," the old man said in a soothing voice. "You boys'll feel better after some chuck."

"Blaisedell don't stand so high now, Abe," Curley said. "I heard a thing or two about Blaisedell, and saw a pack of miners tramp over him too." He told about the miners storming over Blaisedell to try to lynch Morgan. Abe looked barely interested.

"And maybe things're getting stacked against him some, for a change," Curley went on. "There is plenty talk it was Morgan stopped that stage, and maybe Blaisedell with him."

"That's stupid," Abe said, but he stood a little straighter.

"And that those boys was killed in the Acme Corral to cover it over."

"That's a stupid lie," Abe said. He grinned a little.

"No, there is something there. Pony and Cal stopped that stage, surely. But you remember Cal and Pony being kind of suspicious back and forth about who it was shot that passenger, and then they finally decided it must've been Hutchinson trying to sneak a shot at Cal and the passenger jumped out and got hit instead. But maybe it wasn't Hutchinson, either."

Abe was nervously running his fingers through his beard.

"There is something there," Curley said again. "Taliaferro had some news might interest you, and it is spreading around Warlock pretty good, I hear. There is some whore named Violet at the French Palace that was in Fort James when Morgan and Blaisedell was. And this Kate Dollar woman that Bud Gannon is chasing after now. Lew says this Violet says the Dollar woman was Morgan's sweetie in Fort James, and she took up with another fellow and Morgan paid Blaisedell money to burn him dead. How a lot of people knew about it in Fort James— Wait a minute, now!" he said, as Abe started to interrupt. "And then this Dollar woman was married to the passenger that got shot on that stage. Now if Pony or Cal didn't shoot him, who did? Lew likes it it was Morgan—he is down on Morgan something fierce— but there is talk that if Blaisedell hired out to Morgan for that kind of job once, why not twice? There is all kind of things being said around Warlock, Abe."

"Boys, what is this hen-scratch low gossip you are talking here?" the old man said indignantly.

"Shut up," Abe said, but he began to grin again.

He had better go, Curley thought. There was more than he had told Abe, but he did not like to hear himself saying all this. Lew Taliaferro was a man he could stand only if the wind was right; and what Taliaferro had told him, part of which he had just repeated to Abe, had made as poor hearing as telling, medicine though it was to Abe.

"So I expect you will be going into Warlock one of these days your-self," he said, and tried to grin back at Abe's grin. "There is a time coming. I wish I could go in with you when you go, but you won't need me, Abe."

"By God!" the old man whispered.

"I'd sure like to stay to see it," Curley went on. "But it has come time for me to make tracks. Like you said, people liked old Carl." He took a deep breath. "I'm telling you things are running the other way, Abe. You have done right, staying down here till they started chang-ing. And it was the smartest thing you ever did, too, telling MacDonald you wouldn't have nothing to do with his Regulators. Just wait it out. It won't be long. Abe, Blaisedell is starting to come down like a pile of bricks."

He felt exhausted watching the life and sharpness coming back into Abe's face. He had given Abe what he had to give, and he would do it again, but he had lied when he had said he wished he could see the end. He could stomach no more of it.

"Thanks, Curley," Abe said, softly. "You've been a friend." With a lithe swing of his body he turned to gaze off at the mountains. His face, in profile, looked younger. He said, "Well, you will hear one way or other when the time comes."

"I'll drink a bottle of whisky to you, Abe."

"Do that for me. One way or the other."

"One way," Curley said, grinning falsely.

"You have sure bucked him like a dose of kerosene," the old man said, in a breathless voice. The clanging of the iron triangle sounded again.

"Better eat before you go," Abe said.

"I'll grab something and say so long to the boys."

"What do you want to move on for, Curley?" the old man com-plained. "How'll we make out? Have to break in a new hand on that mouth organ of yours."

"You'll never get one as good as me."

"Wait a minute till I get my pants on," Abe said, and disappeared inside.

Curley took the mouth organ out of his shirt and began to play the old man a tune. "Curley," Dad McQuown said, scrounging up on one elbow. "Tell me how it was you popped that deputy before you go. Ran him the road-agent spin, did you?"

It was sour music he was making. He wiped the spit from the mouth organ, and put it down on the rail beside him. "No, it wasn't that," he said.

"You said—"

"It wasn't so," he said. "The whole thing was poor all around. He had the drop on me and I went to give him my Colt's like a good boy. But he grabbed hold of the barrel—" He stopped, for Abe was standing in the doorway with his hands frozen where he'd been buckling his shell belt on. Abe's eyes were blazing.

"You always was a God-damned liar, Curley Burne," the old man said disgustedly, and lay back again.

"You didn't mean to do it?" Abe whispered, and his face was crafty and cruel as Curley had not seen it since Abe had heard the Hacienda Puerto vaqueros were coming after them through Rattlesnake Canyon.

He shook his head.

"Carl went and did it himself? Pulling on the barrel with your finger on the trigger. Like that?"

"That was it." The expression on Abe's face frightened him a little, but then it was gone and Abe bent to attend to buckling his belt on. "It was poor," Curley said. "It don't set so good either, but it is done. I kind of thought I'd better not stick around and try and explain it to folks, what with five or six of them getting ready to pop away at me. Well, I guess I'll go get some breakfast."

Abe nodded. "I'll go down and saddle up for you," he said, in a strange voice. "You send the breed around and I'll put him on that you rode out here on, and send him on down Rattlesnake Canyon in case they have got somebody following sign. You head for Welltown and I'll get a herd run over your track." Abe nodded again, to himself.

"Well, that's fine of you, Abe."

"So long, Curley," the old man said. "You take care of yourself, hear?"

Curley hurried down the steps. "So long, Dad McQuown!" he called back over his shoulder. At the cook shack he shook hands around with the boys who hadn't gone with MacDonald, and told them to say so long for him to the rest when they got back from Warlock. He sent the breed to Abe, and got some bread and bacon and a canteen of water from Cookie. Hurrying, he went on out to the horse corral, where Abe had saddled a long-legged, big-barreled, steady-standing gray he had not seen before. "He'll take you in a hurry," Abe said, and slapped the gray on the shoulder. Curley swung into the saddle, and Abe reached up to wring his hand.

"Curley," he said.

"So long, boy, *Suerte*."

"*Suerte*," Abe said, grinning, but not quite meeting his eyes. Something had gone wrong again, but now Curley was only in a hurry to get out. He swung the big gray out of the corral on the hard-packed red earth. He could see the dust the breed was making, heading south. The big gray moved powerfully; he drew up as Abe yelled something after him, and cupped a hand to his ear.

"I say!" Abe yelled. "They catch you all you do is see you get to Bright's City for trial all in one piece. No worry then!"

Curley waved and spurred on again. When he had crossed the river that was the border of the ranch, he had never felt so free. He reached for his mouth organ. But he had left it on the porch rail.

His mood was not affected; he began to sing to himself. The gray loped steadily along. The land stretched board-flat away to Welltown, the gray-brown desert marbled with brush. The sun burned higher in the sky. He glanced back from time to time—at first he thought it was only a dust-devil.

Then he whistled. "We had better stop loafing, boy," he said. "Look at them come!" But he was not worried, for the big gray was strong and fresh, and the posse must have been riding hard from Warlock. The gray broke into a long, swinging stride that ate up the ground, and he laughed to see the dust cloud fading behind him.

Then the gray grunted and went lame.

He dismounted to examine the hoof; carefully he looked over the leg for something wrong, but he could see nothing. The gray stood with the lame leg held off the ground, looking at him with unconcerned brown eyes. "Boy, why would you do such a thing?" he complained, and remounted and dug his spurs in. The gray limped along, grunting, more and more slowly; he bucked half-heartedly at the spurs.

Curley looked back at the oncoming dust. It was a big posse. The gray stopped and would go no more, and he sighed and dismounted, shot the horse through the head, and sat down on the slack, warm haunch to wait in the sun. "Boy," he said again, "why would you do such a thing?" His hand fumbled once more after his mouth organ which he had left behind him.

36. Journals of Henry Holmes Goodpasture

April 10, 1881

It is impossible to watch these things happening and feel nothing. Each of us is involved to some degree, inwardly or outwardly. Nerves are scraped raw by courses of events, passions are aroused and rearoused in partisanships that, even in myself, transcend rationality.

It must be a wracking experience to stand before a mob as Schroeder and Gannon did last night; to do it not once, but twice, and to be trampled at the last by men no more than crazed beasts. I write this trying to understand Carl Schroeder, as well as in memoriam to him. I see now that his office had served to ennoble him, as it had done with Canning before him. We gave him not enough credit while he lived, and I think we did not because he was too much one of us. God bless his soul; he deserves some small and humble bit of heaven, which is all he would have asked for himself.

He was an equable and friendly man. Perhaps he was inadequate to his position here. Yet who would have been wholly adequate except, perhaps, Blaisedell himself? I think a part of Schroeder's increasing strength (has it not been a part of all our increasing strength?) was Blaisedell's presence and example here. I think he must have been badly shaken by Blaisedell's decline from Grace. As he drew his strength from Blaisedell, so must he have been all too rawly aware of the cruel vicissitudes of error, or rumored error, or of mere foul lies, to which such dispensers of rough-and-ready law as Blaisedell, and himself, were prey.

Poor Schroeder, to die not only in an undignified street scrape, but in one of the multitudinous arguments over Blaisedell and McQuown. Buck Slavin heard the quarrel, and saw it at the end; he says it seems to him that Carl was as much at fault in it as Curley Burne. He says there was a deeper grudge there than the mere quarrel, but I think of my own feelings of that time last night, and know it would have taken little to rouse me to a deadly rage.

Buck was present at the General Peach almost until Schroeder's death, and says that Schroeder chided himself bitterly for being tricked with what is called the "road agent's spin." This is a device whereby the pistol is proffered butt foremost, and then spun rapidly upon the trigger finger and discharged when the muzzle is level. It is a foul trick. Curley Burne has had more friends in this town by far than any other creature of McQuown's. He has only sworn enemies now.

Gannon did not accompany the posse that went out after Burne, perhaps, as Buck suggests, because Curley has been an especial friend of his, or perhaps, as the doctor says, because Carl expressed a wish that Gannon remain with him in his final hour. The miners set fire to the Glass Slipper shortly after Schroeder's death and Gannon has been much occupied in putting out the fire. The feeling is that he was too much occupied with it, and that his proper business lay with the posse. It is to be hoped that his office will be as ennobling to Gannon as it has been to his last two predecessors.

I think that Carl Schroeder would have been pleased to know that his death has taken men's minds away from Blaisedell's failure before the jail, and concentrated hate upon one man. I fervently hope that the posse will catch Curley Burne and hang him to the nearest tree.

I burn the midnight oil, I bleed myself upon this page in inky blots and scratchings. How can I know men's hearts without knowing my own? I peel back the layers one by one, like an onion, and find only more layers, smaller and meaner each than the last. What dissemblers we are, how we seek to conceal from our innermost beings our motives, to call the meanest of them virtue, to label that which in another we can plainly see as devilish, in ourselves angelic, what in another is greed, in ourselves righteousness, etc. Observe. The Glass Slipper is burned, gutted to char and stink, and the pharmacy beside it saved by a miracle. The fire was set by the miners; they have got back at Morgan. They are devils, I say, to so endanger a town as tinder-dry as this. But is that it? No, they have endangered my property. I will forgive being shamed, discountenanced, and insulted; threaten my property and I will never forgive. Take everything from me but my money. With money I can buy back what I need, the rest is worthless.

Poor devils, I suppose they had to destroy something. Men rise to the heights of courage and ingenuity when they avenge their slights or frustrations. It has always been so. It is comforting to some to see men work together with a good will against catastrophe. Humanity at its best, they say. Yet *against*, as I have written. When will humanity work with all its strength, its courage and ingenuity, and all its heart, *for?*

Morgan is burnt out. Will he rebuild, or accept this as earnest of the widespread sentiment against him here and depart our valley of Concord and Happiness? And in that case what of Blaisedell, who has been banking faro for him? Will he go too, or will he undertake the position of Marshal here again? I am sure the Citizens' Committee intends to ask, or beg, him to reassume his office, next time it meets.

Blaisedell and Morgan: it is said that Blaisedell did not shoot his assailants before the jail because he would not kill for the sake of Morgan, who had wrongfully murdered Brunk (if not a number of others!). Yet Blaisedell's prestige would have been even more grievously damaged had Morgan actually been taken out and hanged, and so I see Miss Jessie's part in this. Blaisedell is obviously very much her concern, and, with the friendship of Blaisedell and Morgan an established fact, did she not realize that Morgan had to be saved at all costs, distasteful as the object of her salvage must have been to her?

There has been some talk to the effect that Blaisedell began his career as a gunman in a position similiar to that of the now-departed Murch, as pistolero-in-chief for Morgan's gambling hall in Fort James, and that he killed at Morgan's behest various and sundry whom Morgan found bothersome in his affairs of the heart, as well as in his business. Morgan once saved Blaisedell's life, it is further said, so Blaisedell is sworn to protect Morgan forever and serve whatever purpose Morgan assigns him. Morgan becomes possessed of horns, trident, a spiky tail, and Blaisedell's soul locked up in a pillbox.

Morgan is replacing McQuown as general scapegoat and what might be called whipping-devil. McQuown has remained in San Pablo and out of our ken for so long that he is becoming only a name, like Espirato, and someone readier to hand is needed. So are the witches burned, like coal, to warm us.

April 11, 1881

The posse has returned with Curley Burne, and Deputy Gannon has shown his true colors.

Burne has gone free on Gannon's oath that Schroeder's death-bed words were that his shooting was accidental, caused by his pulling on the barrel of Burne's six-shooter and thus forcing Burne's finger against the trigger. Judge Holloway, whatever his feelings in the matter, could not under these circumstances remand Burne to Bright's City for proper trial; there would be no point in it with Gannon prepared to swear such a thing. Joe Kennon, who was at the hearing, says he thought Pike Skinner would shoot Gannon then and there, and called him a liar to his face.

It is fortunate for Gannon that this town has had a bellyful of lynch gangs lately, or he and Burne would hang together tonight. Oh, damnable! Gannon must have been eager indeed to please McQuown, for in all probability Burne would have been discharged by the Bright's City court, as is their pleasure. Certainly Gannon is in danger here now, and, if he is here to serve McQuown in any way he can, has destroyed any further usefulness he might have had to the San Pabloite by this infuriating, and, it would seem, foolish, action. It is presumed that he will sneak out of town at the first opportunity, and that will be the last Warlock will see of him. Good riddance!

The posse was evidently divided to begin with as to whether they should capture Curley Burne at all, a number of them feeling he should be shot down on sight. His horse had gone lame, however, and, luckily for him, he offered no resistance. Opportunities were evidently made for him to try to escape, so *ley fuga* could be practiced, but Burne craftily did not attempt to take advantage of them. No doubt he was already counting on Gannon's aid.

It must have taken a strange, perverted sort of courage for Gannon to stand up with such a brazen lie before so partisan a group as there was at Burne's hearing. Evidently he tried to claim that Miss Jessie had also heard Schroeder's last words. Several men promptly ran to ask her if this was so, but she only increased Gannon's shame by replying, in her gentle way, that she had been unable to hear what Schroeder was saying at the end, since his voice had become inaudible to her. Buck says now that he knew all the time that Gannon was trying to play both ends, and was just biding his time to pull one coup for McQuown such as this. I must say I cannot myself view Gannon as a villain, but only as a contemptible fool.

Burne has promptly and sensibly made himself scarce. Some say he has joined the Regulators, who are encamped at the Medusa mine. If Blaisedell will resume his duties as Marshall here, and this town has its say, Curley Burne will become his most urgent project.

Toward this end the Citizens' Committee is meeting tomorrow morning, at the bank.

April 12, 1881

Blaisedell has resumed his position, and Curley Burne has been posted from Warlock. I have never felt the temper of this place in such a unanimously cruel mood. It is fervently hoped that Curley Burne, wherever he is, will take the posting process as what we have never before considered it to be—a summons, instead of a dismissal.

April 13, 1881

Word seems to have come, I'm sure I don't know how—perhaps it is some kind of emanation in the air—that Burne will come in. It seems to me that at one moment there was not a man in Warlock who believed he could be fool enough to come, and at the next it was somehow fixed and certain that he would. He is expected at sun-up tomorrow, but I still cannot believe that he will come.

April 14, 1881

I saw it, not an hour ago, and I will put down exactly what I saw. I will then have this record so that, in time to come, if what others perceived is changed by their passions or the years, I may look back at this and remind myself.

Before sun-up I was on the roof of my store, sitting behind the parapet. Others came up a ladder placed against the Southend Street wall, made apologetic gestures to me for invading my premises, and squatted silently near me in the first gray light. There were men to be seen in the street, too, occupying doorways and windows, and a number of them established within the burnt-out shell of the Glass Slipper. From time to time whispering could be heard, and there were frequent coughs and a continual rustle of movement, as in a theater when the curtain is about to rise.

Some of our eyes were trained east, for the sun, or for Blaisedell, who would presumably appear from the direction of the General Peach; some west, as the proper direction for Curley Burne's entry upon the stage.

There came the rhythmic creaking of wheels; it was the wagons taking the miners out to the Thetis, the Pig's Eye, and the farther mines, ten or twelve of them, with the miners seated in them knee to knee. Their bearded faces glanced from side to side as the wagons passed down Main Street, with, from time to time, a hand raised in greeting to a fellow, but none of the cheerful, disgruntled, or profane calling back and forth we are so used to hearing of a work-day morning. The water wagon, driven by Peter Bacon, crossed Main Street on its morning journey to the river. It was seen that the harness of the mules glittered, and all eyes turned to see the sun.

It climbed visibly over the Bucksaws, a huge sun, not that which Bonaparte saw through the mists of Austerlitz, but the sun of Warlock. I felt its warmth half gratefully, half reluctantly. There was an increasing stirring and rustling in the street. I saw Tom Morgan come out of the hotel, and, cigar between his teeth, seat himself upon the veranda. He leaned back in his rocking chair and stretched, for all the world as though it were a bore but he would make the best of what poor entertainment Warlock had to offer. I saw Buck Slavin with Taliaferro in the upstairs window of the Lucky Dollar, Will Hart in the doorway of the gunshop, Gannon leaning in the doorway of the jail, a part of the shadow there, appearing as tiredly and patiently permanent as though he had spent the night in that position, in that place.

"Blaisedell." Someone said it quite loudly, or else many whispered it in chorus. Blaisedell debouched from Grant Street into Main. He waited there a moment, almost uncertainly, with his shadow lying long and narrow before him. He wore black broadcloth with white linen, a string tie; beneath his open coat the broad buckle of his belt was visible, his weapons were not. With almost a twinge of fear I watched him start forward. He carried his arms most casually at his sides, walked slowly but with long, steady strides. Dust plumed about his feet and whitened his boots and his trouser bottoms. Morgan nodded to him as he passed, but I saw no answering nod.

"He'll just have a little walk and then we'll go home," someone near me whispered.

Blaisedell crossed the intersection of Broadway, and from all around I heard a concerted sigh of relief. Perhaps I sighed myself, with the surety that Curley Burne was not going to appear after all. Hate can burn itself out in the first light of day as readily as love can. I could see Blaisedell's face now very clearly, his broad mouth framed in the curve of his mustache, one of his eyebrows cocked up almost humorously, as though he, too, felt he would only have a little walk and then go home.

The sun had separated itself from the peaks of the Bucksaws by now; it glinted brilliantly upon the brass kick-plate on the hotel door. I saw Morgan, slouched in his rocking chair, raise his hand to take the cheroot from his mouth, then hold cigar and hand arrested. He leaned forward intently, and I heard a swift intake of breath from all around me, and knew that Curley Burne had appeared. I was reluctant to turn and see that this was so.

He was a hundred yards or so down Main Street. I saw Gannon, without changing his position, turn with that same slow reluctance I had felt in myself, to watch him. I found in myself, too, a grudging admiration for Burne, that he managed even now to accomplish that saunter of his we in Warlock knew so well. His shoulders were thrown back at a jaunty angle, his sombrero hung, familiarly, down his back, his flannel shirt was unbuttoned halfway to his cartridge belt as though in contempt of the morning chill, his striped pants were thrust into his boot tops. He looked very much a Cowboy. He was grinning, but even from where I was I could see his struggle to maintain that grin; it was exhausting to see it. I had to remind myself that he had murdered Carl Schroeder by a filthy trick, that he was a rustler, road agent, henchman of McQuown's. "Dirty son of a b - - - -!" growled one of my companions, and summed up what I had to feel, then, for Curley Burne.

He and Blaisedell were not a block apart when there was another gasp around me, as Burne broke stride. He halted, and cried out, "I have got as much right to walk this street as you, Blaisedell!" I felt ashamed for him, and, all at once, pity. Blaisedell did not stop. I saw Burne raise a hand to his shirt and wrench it open further, so that his chest and belly were exposed.

"What color?" he cried out. "What color is it?" He glanced up and around at us, the watchers, with quick, proud movements of his head. The skull-like grin never left his face. Then he started forward toward Blaisedell again. He sauntered no longer, and his hand was poised above the butt of his six-shooter. My eyes were held in awful fascination to that hand, knowing that Blaisedell would give him first draw.

It flashed down, incredibly swift; his six-shooter spat flame and smoke and my ears were shocked by the blast despite my anticipation of it—three shots in such rapid succession they were almost one report, and Burne and his weapon were obscured in smoke. Blaisedell's own hand seemed very slow, in its turn. He fired only once.

Burne was flung back into the dust and did not move again. He had a depthless look as he lay there, as though he were now only a facsimile of himself laid like a painted cloth upon the uneven surface of the street. Blood stained his bare chest, his right arm was flung out, his smoking Colt still in his hand.

Blaisedell turned away, and as he retraced his steps I watched that marble face for—what? Some sign, I do not even know what. I saw his cheek twitch convulsively, I noticed that he had to thrust twice for his holster before he was able to reseat his Colt there. I could not see whether it was gold-handled or not.

The doctor appeared in the street, to walk through the dust to where Burne lay, carrying his black bag. A short, stocky, bowed figure in his black suit, he looked sad and weary. Gannon did not move from his position in the jail doorway. His eyes, from where I watched, looked like burnt holes in his head. Other men were coming out along the far boardwalk, and there was no longer silence.

"Center-shotted the b------ as neat as you please," a man near me said, as he got to his feet and spat tobacco juice over the parapet.

"Give him three shots," said another. "Couldn't give a man any more than that. I call that fair."

"Give him all the time in the world," agreed a third.

But I could feel in their voices what I myself felt, and feel more strongly now. For all that Blaisedell had given Burne three shots, for all he had given him all the time in the world, we knew we had not witnessed a gunfight but an execution. I leaned upon the parapet and looked down upon the men who had surrounded the mortal remains of Curley Burne, and I saw, when one of them moved aside, a little patch of bloody flesh. I thought of that gesture he had made, opening his shirt and confronting us with the color of his belly; showing us, more than Blaisedell.

It had been an execution, and at our order. Perhaps we had changed our mind at the last moment, but there was no reprieve, no way, before the end, to turn our thumbs up instead of down, and save the gladiator. And I think we felt cheated. There should have been some catharsis, for Carl Schroeder had been avenged, and an evil man had received his just deserts. There was no catharsis, there was only revulsion and each man afraid, suddenly, to look into the face of the one next to him. And there was the realization that Curley Burne had not been an evil man, the remembrance that we had once, all of us, liked and enjoyed him to some degree; and there was the cancerous suspicion spreading among us that Gannon might not, after all, have been lying.

I feel drained by an over-violent purge to my emotions, that has taken from me part of my manhood, or my humanity. I feel scraped raw in some inner and most precious part. The earth is an ugly place, senseless, brutal, cruel, and ruthlessly bent only upon the destruction of men's souls. The God of the Old Testament rules a world not worth His trouble, and He is more violent, more jealous, more terrible with the years. We are only those poor, bare, forked animals Lear saw upon his dismal heath, in pursuit of death, pursued by death.

I am ashamed not only of this execution I myself have in part ordered, but of being a man. I think the climax to my shame for all of us came when Blaisedell was walking back up the street, dragging his arrow-thin, arrow-long shadow behind him, and Morgan came down from the veranda of the Western Star to put a hand on his shoulder, no doubt to congratulate his friend. At that moment I heard someone near me on my rooftop whisper—I did not see who, but if I believed in devils I would have been sure it was the voice of one come to yet more hideously corrupt our souls than we have ourselves corrupted them this day—whisper, "There is the dirty dog he ought to kill."

37. Gannon Answers a Question

"COME IN, Deputy," Kate said. She was tall in her white shirt with a velvet band around the collar, and her thickly pleated black skirt. Her hair hung loose around her head, softening the angular lines of her face. She looked neither pleased nor displeased to see him. "Haven't left town yet?" she said.

"No," he said, and sat down at the table, as she indicated he was to do. The oilcloth was cool and cleanly greasy to his touch. He felt something in him relax suddenly, here, for the first time since the posse had returned with Curley. He had become used to men falling silent as he passed them, and whispering behind his back, but now all his strength and will were spent staying out of quarrels, or worse. They no longer whispered behind his back.

"Well, they haven't got a lynch party after you yet," Kate said.

He tried to smile. "I'm not so worried about lynch parties as I am a shooting scrape."

Kate seated herself opposite him, and, regarding him steadily, said, "What did you expect when you swore him out of it?"

"What I said was so." His voice took on an edge he had not meant to have, here.

"Was it?" Kate said. The corners of her mouth pulled in deeply; with contempt, he thought. "Not because he was a friend of yours?"

"No."

"That doesn't signify? No, I thought what you swore was probably so, Deputy. The rest of this town hates you because they think you lied, but I don't think much better of you because I know you didn't. Because you would have sworn it the other way just as well if it had been the other way, friend or not—just what is true out of your cold head. But nothing out of hate or love or anything."

He said roughly, "I don't have any friends."

"No, you wouldn't have. Nor anything." She put out her hand and laid it cool against his for a moment, and then withdrew it. "Why, it's warm!" she said.

Even here, he thought, and he felt as though he had gone blind. He had tried to tell himself it did not matter what everyone thought of him; but it mattered, and he did not know how much longer he could stand under it.

But Kate continued, mercilessly. "You had a brother. Didn't you love your brother?"

"I knew what he was."

"God!" Kate said. "Isn't there anything—haven't there been any people you loved? That you'd do things for because you loved them even if you saw in your cold head it was wrong, or bad?" Her chair scraped back as she rose suddenly; she stood staring down at him with her hands held spread-fingered to her breast. "What do you see here?" she said hoarsely. "Just a bitch, and you know all I want is Blaisedell dead and that's wrong? Well, it may be wrong, but it comes out of *here!*"

"Stop it, Kate!"

"I want to know what you see! Have you got eyes to see just exactly what is there and no more—no blur or warmth in them ever? Then what do you come here for?"

He couldn't answer, for he did not know. Today, he thought, he had only wanted a respite. He shook his head mutely.

"Just to talk?" Kate said, more quietly. "To unload a little. And you have picked me to unload on?"

He nodded again, for maybe that was it.

"You need me?" she said, as though it were a condition she insisted upon.

"Yes; I guess."

"Holy Mary!" Kate said. "There is something to shake the world—that you need anything but your cast-iron conscience." She sat down again, and he heard the drowsy buzzing of flies against her window, and found himself listening for the distant crack of Eladio's maul in the *carpintería*. He could not hear it from here.

"Are you afraid of Blaisedell now?" Kate said.

He shook his head.

"Every other man here is. Or ought to be."

"No, Kate."

"Don't you know why he went back to marshaling and posted Burne out of town?"

"He didn't post him, Kate. The Citizens' Committee did."

"Wait!" she said. "Deputy, there are some people who might kill a man because they hated him. And there are some that might because they thought it was right; cold, like you. And then there is Blaisedell. Do you know why he killed Burne?"

"Because the Cit—"

"He killed him because his reputation was slipping. Do you know why he took the job as marshal again?"

He didn't answer.

"Because he knew the Citizens' Committee would tell him to post Burne out of town. Because he knew that was what everybody wanted, and so he could be the Great Man again. It is like a gambler starting to double his bets because he is losing. Recouping like that. Not hating Curley Burne, or not even thinking of the right or wrong of it. Just his reputation to keep. And where is your brassbound conscience now, when Schroeder told you Burne hadn't done it on purpose?"

"Blaisedell thinks I was lying. Everybody does. They knew I'd been friends with Curley and Abe, and they think I lied because—"

Kate said, "Do you know that the Citizens' Committee almost asked him to post *you* out with Burne? Buck Slavin told me. And Blaisedell would have done it. And killed you, too."

"I don't believe he would have done it. He wouldn't with Brunk."

"He would have posted you and killed you just to feed the kitty. Because people hated you and it would make him a bigger man."

"Stop it!" he said, as anger rose sudden and sickening in him. "Don't do it any more. Trying to pimp a man into going against Blaisedell."

Kate's mouth fell half open; then she closed it tightly, but not, it seemed to him, in the fury he had expected. He watched the rims of her nostrils whiten and slacken with the rhythm of her breathing. Her black eyes stared back into his. Then, at last, she shook her head. "No. No, I don't mean that, Deputy. Not any more."

She was silent for a long time, and all at once it came to him what he must do. Ride to Bright's City to see Keller, to see Peach himself if he could. He could go now, for the Regulators were disbanded and gone, and maybe if he himself were absent for a few days it would not be so bad when he returned. He would go and see Keller and even Peach himself and seek the means of warding off more tragedy, even knowing that those means would be whimsically or ruthlessly withheld, as they had always been.

"What kind of man was Curley Burne?" Kate asked.

"Why, I guess about everybody liked him, even though he rode for McQuown. He was pleasant to talk to, and friendly, and there was no scratch to him. Though he could be hard enough if he wanted to be, and he was man enough to go as he pleased. I told you he wouldn't go along on that in Rattlesnake Canyon." He scraped his fingernails along the oilcloth in little wrinkled tracks.

"He was strong on kin and friends and that," he went on. "We argued that after Billy got killed. He was always Abe's best friend." He looked up at Kate. "I guess you would have liked him."

"Why did he do it?"

"Come in against Blaisedell? Why, you heard about what he said. Just to show the color of his belly. Just to show he had as much right to walk the street as Blaisedell."

It was not enough, he knew. He sighed and said, "I don't know, Kate. I have been thinking maybe it was for McQuown."

"I guess I would have liked him," Kate said. Then she frowned and said, "Why for McQuown?"

"Well, he said something funny when he was let go and he knew he'd better get out in a hurry. He said he guessed he had been chosen to clear the air. But that he guessed he just couldn't oblige. I didn't know what he meant exactly, but—"

"Blaisedell," Kate said scornfully.

"No, I thought he meant McQuown some way. But then he came in after all. I don't know—probably it was just what he said; how he wanted to show he wasn't yellow."

"Or just being a man," Kate said, in her most contemptuous voice. "I have seen men bucking cards they knew were stacked against them and losing their stake and borrowing more and losing that. All the time knowing they couldn't win."

"I don't know," he said. He tried to formulate what was disturbing him more and more. "I've tried to think it through. Why Billy came in, and why Curley did, when it looked at first as though he wasn't going to. I'm afraid—what I'm afraid is that there is something about Blaisedell so they—"

He stopped as Kate cried, as though she had won something from him, "So they have to! Yes, so they have to; like flies that can't stay out of a spider web."

"Maybe it is something like that," he said. "Well, part that and part different things. For instance, I was thinking about Billy, and how my father used to whip him. He had to whip Billy a lot, for Billy was always wild. And he'd never cover up a thing he'd done." He touched his nose, remembering that time. "He would always tell right off, like he was proud of it. And it seemed like he got whipped for things he hadn't done when he could have got off by speaking up.

"So I've got to wondering if he wasn't just taking the whippings to clear off things he'd done, inside himself. I mean things he felt guilty about. So that if he got whipped it paid him up for a while. I wonder— I wonder if—" He could not quite say it.

"Killed?" Kate said.

"Maybe it would pay for everything."

"*Killed?*" Kate whispered.

"Why, yes." He tried painfully to grin. "Maybe you haven't ever felt that way, being a religious woman. If a person hasn't got any religion there's some things he can't get forgiven for because he can't forgive himself. I wondered if it wasn't partly that with Billy."

"*Killed* for it?" Kate said, and he was pleased to see there were things about men she did not know, after all her bragging that she knew them so well.

"Even that. Though I think it was more than that with Curley. He and Abe was close, and I think he was maybe trying to prove something to everybody about Abe. Or else he couldn't admit he was wrong about Abe and was trying to prove to himself he wasn't. It is hard to see in a man's heart."

"It's not for you to do, Deputy," Kate said. She was staring at him with a curious concern.

He nodded. "But what I was thinking was all the reasons there might be for going against Blaisedell. To prove yourself some way, or cancel something out. Or he is somebody and you are nobody and even if he kills you, you get to be somebody because of it; I have known men to think backwards like that. Or see him a devil, so you are good and fine if you go against him. Or—or just what it would make of you if by luck you managed to kill him. I think of all the reasons and—"

"You had better stop this," Kate said.

"—and I think it is pretty terrible. I hope it isn't so, but I can see how it might be to some, and it is a terrible thing. I think Blaisedell couldn't stand it if he knew."

He gazed back into her eyes and was sorry for what he saw there. He got quickly to his feet. "Oh, I was just talking foolishness," he said. "Just unloading foolishness. I thank you for listening to me. Now I have got to ride up to—"

He heard a sound of heels outside; they thumped on the steps. There was a knock. Kate came around the table and opened the door. Past her, Gannon saw Blaisedell standing on the porch, his black hat in his hands. His fair hair was matted where the hat had compressed it, in a circle around his head.

"Hello, Kate," Blaisedell said, in his deep voice. "I thought the deputy might be here. I wanted to talk to him."

Kate's hand tightened into a claw, gripping the edge of the door. She moved aside; she looked as though she had grown faint. "Talk?" she whispered.

"I wanted to ask him something," Blaisedell said. He stepped inside past Kate, who still clung to the door, her head turning slowly as Blaisedell passed her, until she was staring into Gannon's eyes, and he could feel the fear and hate in her so strongly that it seemed to fill the room.

"What is it, Marshal?" he asked, resting a hand on the back of his chair.

Blaisedell said almost casually, "What Schroeder told you."

"He has already sworn what Schroeder told him!" Kate cried.

"I asked *him*, Kate," Blaisedell said, and did not look at her.

"I told the truth, Marshal," Gannon said.

"Now kill him for saying it!"

"You think badly of me, don't you, Kate?" Blaisedell said. Still Blaisedell's eyes remained fixed on him, and he had the sensation of being examined completely. "Jessie has decided she might have been wrong," Blaisedell went on, after a time. "So I thought I would ask you face to face."

Then Blaisedell nodded as though he was satisfied. "Why, I guess it has been hard, then, Deputy," he said, "with every man down on you for it. You will understand it would be hard for her to come out now and say she has changed her mind, though. Because of what's happened," he said.

"Surely," Gannon said, stiffly. It occurred to him that Miss Jessie might not have admitted willingly even to Blaisedell that she had changed her mind, or that she had lied. "That doesn't matter, Marshal," he said, and Blaisedell started to turn away.

"Marshal," Gannon said. "Carl didn't know for sure. You know he killed that miner that way, when the jack pulled on his shotgun. That was on his mind at the end. And he said—that a man ought to forgive if he wanted to be forgiven, and that he was going to judgment directly. He—" He stopped, and Blaisedell nodded to him again.

Blaisedell turned to face Kate, who drew back away from him. "I have killed another one, being too quick on the draw, Kate," he said. "I had swore I would never do that again."

Then he moved on outside and down the steps in the sunlight, replacing his hat. He walked with his head tipped back a little, as though he were watching something above him. Kate leaned on the door staring after him.

When she flung the door shut the tarpaper walls shivered with the shock. She swung around to face Gannon and there was a kind of wonder in her face. "I thought you had never *felt* anything in your life," she said, in a stifled voice. "But you pity him."

"I guess I do, Kate," he said, and bent to pick up his hat.

"Him!" Kate said, as though she could not believe it. She made a sound that was halfway between a laugh and a sob. "Pity *him!* Why, you were suffering because you had to tell the truth. You would have backed down except that it would have been a lie, and a lie is wrong." She said it not angrily, as he had expected, but as though she was trying to understand.

He strained his ears for the crack of Eladio's maul knocking Curley Burne's coffin together. He could hear it in his mind, and hear the scrape of shovels on the rocky ground of Boot Hill, and the rustle of the wind blowing through the brush and rocky mounds and the grave-markers there. The retreating slow crack of Blaisedell's boot-heels had been a sound as lonely, and as fatal.

"What did he mean, too quick?" Kate said, in a breathless whisper, but he did not know what Blaisedell had meant, nor did Kate seem to be speaking to him or even aware of his presence any more. She did not appear to hear when he said good-by and told her he would be going up to Bright's City. He walked slowly back to the jail the long way around, by Peach Street, so he would not have to pass so many men on his way.

38. The Doctor Attends a Meeting

AFTER the Citizens' Committee meeting the doctor walked with Jessie and some of the others to the stage yard to see Goodpasture, Slavin, and Will Hart depart for Bright's City. Buck waved from the window as the coach swung out of the yard, carrying another frantic delegation to General Peach, with another series of demands and pleas. And with threats this time.

With Jessie's hand on his arm, he moved on to Goodpasture's corner. The coach was already almost lost to sight in the dust that followed its rapid progress east along Main Street. Jessie, beside him, was silent; it had been a difficult meeting for her, he knew. She had hardly spoken a word throughout, and she seemed listless and tired. There were unhealthy-looking smudges beneath her eyes.

"And how is the miners' angel today?" MacDonald said, coming up behind them. His hands were thrust down into the pockets of his jacket; his derby hat was cocked over one eye. His pale, petulant, handsome face was coldly hateful. He inclined his head to the doctor. "And the miners' sawbones?"

Jessie did not speak, peering at MacDonald past the edge of her bonnet. Her hand tightened on the doctor's arm, and he said, "Idle. There have not been many broken men to try to put back together now that the Medusa is shut down."

MacDonald's upper lip drew up tautly as he sneered. "I'd heard you had taken up *other* work."

"Have you put me on the list of men your Regulators are to deal with?"

"Please stop this!" Jessie said.

Pike Skinner had come up beside MacDonald. "He hasn't got any Regulators any more," Skinner said. "Why'd they quit on you, Charlie? Did you drop their pay?"

MacDonald said hoarsely, "I see you have all turned against me. I know that lies are being told about me. I know who is telling them, and who is plotting against me, and in what boardinghouse." He pointed a finger suddenly, his upper lip twitching up again. "And I know who is the chief troublemaker now!"

The doctor looked from the finger, pointed at him, into MacDonald's face. It was plain enough that the man was half mad with fear of losing his position. MacDonald was in a pitiable condition, but he felt no pity. He would be pleased to see him completely broken. Biting his words off sharply to keep his voice from shaking, he said, "Charlie, I am very proud that you count me among your enemies."

"Oh, please stop it!" Jessie cried. "Aren't there more important things than this silly bickering over the Medusa mine? I wish there were no Medusa mine!"

"I'm sure that everything will be done to see that you get your wish, Jessie!" MacDonald retorted. "I'm sure—" He stopped as Pike Skinner caught his shoulder and wrenched him around.

"Watch who you are talking to! She asked you to stop it; you stop it!"

MacDonald's face reddened in hectic blotches; he pulled away from Skinner's grasp, readjusted the hang of his coat, and silently marched away around the corner.

Watching him go, the doctor saw Taliaferro crossing Main Street, followed closely by the half-breed pistolero, who, it seemed, accompanied him everywhere of late. He saw the deputy coming down Southend Street toward the jail. "Poor Charlie is unhinged," he said, and patted Jessie's hand.

"Gannon keeps off Main Street, I notice," Skinner was saying bitterly to Fred Winters. The doctor felt Jessie's fingers bite into his arm as Skinner continued his denunciation of Gannon.

"I have an errand, David," she said, and left abruptly. Her errand, he saw, involved Gannon, whose dismissal from his position had been one of the objectives of the delegation that had just left for Bright's City. He himself had not voted for it, and he knew the majority had hoped that firing Gannon would somehow be proof that he had lied.

He waited until he saw Jessie enter the jail, and then he started alone for the General Peach, where there was to be a meeting of the miners. Strikers from the Medusa greeted him as he walked along under the arcade, and Morgan was watching him from his rocking chair on the veranda of the Western Star. Morgan inclined his head to him, but he ignored the greeting.

There were a few miners loitering on the porch of the General

Peach, but the dining room, where the meeting was to be held, was empty yet, and he went on down the hall to the hospital. As he had said to MacDonald, with the Medusa closed down there had been almost a moratorium on mine accidents, and, in addition, a number of sick men had moved out in what they must have thought was a protest against Jessie's saving Morgan from the mob. There were not many beds occupied now.

The curtains were drawn back on the tall, narrow window, and a long block of sunlight streamed in over the empty cots. Barnes, Dill, and Buell sat on Barnes' cot, engaged in their endless game of red dog, and Ben Tittle and Fitzsimmons stood watching them. Nearby, Stacey, with his bandaged head and jaw, lay on his side reading a tattered newspaper.

Dill flung a card down. "What's happened?" he said, in a flat voice. "Who's shot now?"

"What's the news, Doc?" Barnes asked.

"Is it so the Regulators have gone home?"

"They've gone," he said.

"Who's murdered now?" Dill said, to no one, staring sullenly down at the cards on the bedclothes before him.

"Where is Miss Jessie these days, Doc?" Buell said, and would not meet his eyes. "She has kind of went and forgot us in here, hasn't she?"

"You can shut your face!" Ben Tittle said.

"Good lot of quarreling going on in here today," Fitzsimmons said. Then he said, "I don't know what to make of the Regulators going, do you, Doc?"

The doctor shook his head, and knew that Fitzsimmons was worried that now there would be more definite talk of burning the Medusa stope, since it was unguarded; it was what had terrified MacDonald. Fitzsimmons brushed his hands together worriedly. The fingers of the right one looked like bent sausages where they rested on the left, which was still bandaged.

"Got tired is all," Dill said. "Nobody to shoot. Well, I say it is plain dull myself, no shooting for about twenty minutes, I guess it is now—nobody new killed?" He threw down another card. "Well, it's come fine, I guess," he said, "though not quite even yet. Schroeder kills Benny Connors and Curley Burne kills him, and Blaisedell him. But when Morgan kills Brunk there is Miss Jessie to—"

"I say shut your face!" Tittle cried. He swung his arm and the flat of his hand cracked against Dill's cheek. Dill sprawled on top of Barnes, cursing, and awkwardly got to his feet to face Tittle. The long scar on his forehead was red and shiny. Watching them brawl, the doctor wondered if they were worth anyone's trouble; he was ashamed to realize that he cared nothing for any one of them, except, perhaps, Fitzsimmons. He only hated what oppressed them, and sometimes he was afraid it was not enough.

"You shut that talk, Ira!" Tittle said. "Damn you, Ira! I'll not hear it!"

Dill cursed him, and Fitzsimmons propped a foot on the rail of the cot between them.

"We've been talking, Doc," Buell said apologetically. "And worked up a little heat before you came in. Ira and me was holding that Frank Brunk was right, and it bears hard on a man to be a poor-house case. You can see that, Doc."

"Pay for your keep then!" Tittle said. "I say if you can pay, pay. Or shut up about it. Damned if I see why she'd keep such ungrateful, dirty-mouth bastards anyhow."

"And what have you and Ira decided, Buell?" the doctor said.

"Well, this is a boardinghouse and she has got to make a living of it," Buell said. "And on the other side it is poor to be on somebody's charity. So we was just saying that those that can pay her ought to do it."

"All right, do it."

"Not a one of them's got anything saved to do it," Fitzsimmons said disgustedly. "They are talking gas. Mostly what they are worrying on is some way to make her feel bad because she did for Morgan."

"You talk too much for a young squit," Dill said, and Fitzsimmons grinned at the doctor.

"Yes, it is all right for her to save their lives. But not that of anyone they don't like."

"That's all right, Doc," Dill said. "We know who she likes. I guess her long-hair gunman smells sweeter than we do."

"I'll kill you, Ira!" Tittle cried, starting forward.

"Stop it, Ben!" the doctor said; he was struck by the fury in Tittle's face. He nodded his head toward the door, and Tittle obediently turned away. He hobbled toward the door, his clothing hanging loosely on his stick of a body.

The doctor turned to Dill, whose eyes reluctantly met his. "I take it you are the one who can't pay, Dill," he said. "What do you want her to do, dun you so you can insult her?"

Dill said nothing.

"Others who seem to have felt the way you do have had the decency to leave here," he went on, still staring into Dill's ugly face. "I suggest that you do so. You are not worth her care, nor my trouble. You are not worth anyone's trouble."

"Oh, I'll be moving out," Dill said. "I know when I'm not wanted."

"I suggest that you buy a stock of pencils from Mr. Goodpasture and sell them on the street. That way you will not be a charity case."

"I'd rather. Don't think I wouldn't."

The doctor took a step toward Dill, who backed away. He saw Jimmy Fitzsimmons watching him worriedly and he fought to keep his voice level. "Let me tell you something, Dill. I don't know what you have been saying here, but if you manage to cause her any pain in your stupid spite, I will do my best to break that head I mended for you."

"Easy, Doc," Fitzsimmons whispered.

"I mean exactly what I say!" he said, and Dill retreated before him. "Did you hear me, Dill?"

"Like Morgan busting Stacey, huh, Doc?" Dill said.

"Exactly."

Dill shrugged cockily, and moved over to his own cot; he stood there glancing back out of the corners of his eyes.

"Go on!" the doctor said. "Get out, Dill!"

He heard Ben Tittle call him from the doorway, and he swung around. "Miss Jessie wants to see you, Doc."

Abruptly his rage died. Almost he could feel sorry for Dill and the others, each of whom fought his own lonely battle to maintain a semblance of pride. He walked out past Tittle and went down the hall. There were a number of miners standing inside the entryway now, worried-looking, stern-faced men in clean blue clothing, several with six-shooters stuck inside their belts. All greeted him gravely. There were some, he knew, who were responsible men, men with dignity who could act for themselves if they were shown the way. He wondered why he must always be so short with them.

He knocked on Jessie's door, and entered when she called to him. She stood facing him with her fists clenched at her sides, and tears showing in her round eyes. He had never seen her look so angry.

"What is it, Jessie?" he asked, closing the door behind him.

"That hateful little man! Oh, that hateful, jealous little man!"

"Who?"

"The deputy!" she said, as though he had been stupid not to know. "I don't see why he couldn't do it! It is just that he is so jealous. So *little!* He—"

"I don't know what you are talking about, Jessie. Gannon wouldn't do what?"

She made an effort to compose herself. The little muscles tugged at the corners of her mouth, and it was, he thought, as if those same muscles were connected to his heart. "What is it, Jessie?" he said, more gently.

"I went to tell him that Henry, Buck, and Will had gone to Bright's City to see that he was removed," she said. "I told him I—that I didn't know whether they would succeed or not. And I— Well, I thought he would leave if I asked him, David."

"Did you?" he said, and wondered how she could presume such a thing, and what she hoped to gain by it.

"I thought if *I* asked him," she said. The tears shone in her eyes again; she daubed at them with her handkerchief. "I thought if I made him understand—" Then she said furiously, "Do you know what he said? He said that Clay could not do it!"

"You asked him to quit so that Blaisedell could be deputy," he said, and, although he nodded, he knew that Gannon was right. There were many reasons why Blaisedell could not do it, but he would rather have slapped her face than try to reason with her.

"Hateful, jealous, *smug* little man!" Jessie said. She put her handkerchief to her mouth in what seemed an unwarranted degree of grief.

"What is it, Jessie?" he said again, and put an arm around her straining shoulders.

"Oh, it is Clay," she whispered. "Clay told him I had lied, and he was so *smug*. Oh, I hate him so!" She drew away from him, and threw herself down on her bed. She sobbed into the pillow. He thought he heard her say, "If he would leave no one would know!"

He went to sit beside her, and after a time she took hold of his hand with her tight hand, and held it against her damp cheek. "Oh, David," she whispered. "You are so kind to me, and I have been such a terrible person."

"You are not terrible, Jessie."

"I lied to him. And he found it out."

"Blaisedell?" he asked, for it was not clear.

She nodded; he felt her tears warm and wet on his hand. "I lied to him about what Carl Schroeder said."

He said nothing, staring down at her tumbled ringlets; gently, awkwardly, he stroked his left hand over them. She sobbed again.

"I told him I had even *lied* for him. That's how he knew. But I did it for *him!* I thought if I could just ask the deputy to—"

"Hush!" he said. "Not so loudly, Jessie. It will be all right."

"Clay hates me, he must hate me!"

"No one could hate you, Jessie."

There was a knock at the door. "Doc, it's time for the meeting." It was Fitzsimmons' voice.

"Just a moment," he called. He stroked his hand over Jessie's hair, and said, "It will be all right, Jessie," without even thinking what he was saying. He looked down at the brown head beneath his hand. She had done something that had been unworthy of her—for Clay Blaisedell. She had dedicated herself to him. He prayed with a sudden fury for a return of the days when there had been no Clay Blaisedell in Warlock.

"But what am I going to do now?" Jessie said. "David, if Gannon would only leave no one would believe him!"

He did not answer, for Fitzsimmons was knocking again. "Doc, they are starting! You had better come."

Jessie was sobbing quietly when he left her, and Fitzsimmons looked relieved to see him. "Come on! Daley is saving us a place!"

There were about thirty men in the dining room. The plank tables and benches had been pushed back against the walls, and men sat on them and on two ranks of chairs at the far end of the room beyond which were Frenchy Martin and old man Heck, at Jessie's table. There were a number of miners standing. The doctor noticed that although most of the men were from the Medusa, there was also a contingent from the Sister Fan, and, it seemed, at least one from each of the other mines. This was the skeleton of the Miners' Union that had been set up under Lathrop's leadership, had lapsed since, but had not been forgotten.

Daley had saved two chairs for them in the front row. Fitzsimmons sat down stiffly, adjusting his hands before him, and the doctor was aware that Fitzsimmons' habit of holding them so, was, in part, to call attention to them—like a soldier's wounds, as some kind of proof of adulthood and initiation before the rest.

Old man Heck waved at the rear of the dining room, and the door there was shut and latched. Heck was scowling beneath his wiry gray eyebrows as he slapped his hand on the table for order. There was a nasty bruise along the side of his head, and a scraped place on his forehead that gave him a fierce expression. Martin, beside him, had a bruised eye, and, with his long, waxed mustaches, looked equally fierce.

Old man Heck said, "The Regulators have gone for sure. We have been up to see for ourself. There is a pack of foremen there and a barricade they put up on the road, but that's all. Now; everybody knows what's the question here."

"I'm for it," someone said quietly, and the doctor swung around to see that it was Bigge who had spoken. He had thought better of Bill Bigge, who flushed to meet his gaze.

"I am for it," Frenchy Martin said. "They have pushed it down our throat long enough. Now we bite it off, eh?"

Fitzsimmons got to his feet.

"Who let *him* in?" someone growled.

Fitzsimmons stood holding his burnt hands before him. He said, "I'd like to ask Doc what he thinks, if everybody is agreeable."

There was a burst of clapping. They called his name, apparently with good grace, although they must know what he would say to them. He rose and glanced around at Daley, Patch, and Andrews, who had asked him to come.

"Very well," he said. "I will say what you all know I will say. Shall I?"

"Go ahead, Doc," Daley said.

"Give them hell!" Fitzsimmons whispered.

"I will say that you had better think before you act, which you already should know. I will say that you have a much greater chance of achieving what you want by sensible means rather than by violent ones. Unless what you want is merely senseless violence, in which case you have proceeded correctly at every turn, and I congratulate you."

There was laughter, and catcalls mixed with it. As the noise ceased he went on more grimly. "I know the reason for this meeting, and I refuse even to discuss the subject. There has been too much lynch-mobbing and burning already, all of it stupid. I hope that whoever it was among you that took it upon himself to fire the Glass Slipper realizes by now how he has hurt you all. For what you need is friends in Warlock, who will help you with your cause. If you feel you do not need friends, you do not need me. I should like to know if this is the prevailing attitude, for if it is there is no reason for me to waste my breath further."

"We sure do need you, Doc!" Fitzsimmons said loudly.

"Hear! Hear!" Patch called, from the back of the room. Martin was chewing on a thumb knuckle, and Heck wore a look of sour disapproval.

"Very well," the doctor said. "I will say again that you need all the friends you can get. MacDonald has made you friends by stupidly trying to bring his Regulators into Warlock. You will just as stupidly lose them by your disgraceful behavior. If I were you I would see to it that there is no more playing with fire, or hurling of rocks through store windows, and the like. In particular, you will throw away every advantage you now possess in the instant it takes to light another match—do you understand me?"

"By God, Doc—" old man Heck cried, but a voice from the rear drowned him out: "We have to do something, Doc! We can't just sit and wait till MacDonald starves us back."

"You can't eat fire!" another broke in, and the dining room resounded with cries and argument. Old man Heck pounded for silence, and the doctor waited patiently with his arms crossed on his chest.

Finally he said, "You will remember a thing that Brunk had to say— that people look down on you miners. I think Brunk never saw why this should be; he only resented the fact. I will tell you why. I know, for it is the reason I am out of patience with you a good part of the time myself. They look down on you because of the wild and irresponsible vandalism you have indulged in all too often. Some idiot among you might have burned this town down. Do you wonder that such things might make you unappealing to the decent citizens?

"As I have said before, MacDonald is a stupid man. Because of his stupidity there is a certain sympathy for you now, despite your own actions. It is your business to see that in the future you are not more stupid than MacDonald, so that this sympathy for your plight may continue to grow. There is a force in public opinion that even Mac-Donald will have to feel. He—"

"MacDonald wouldn't feel a shafthead frame if it fell on him!" Bull Johnson said, and there was laughter.

"MacDonald has already felt it. The deputies may have stopped the Regulators the first time they tried to come in, but have none of you wondered why he didn't bring them in again? He did not because he knew this town was solidly against such a thing. The marshal—"

There was another outcry at the word, and suddenly he was furious. He sat down. "Now, Doc!" Fitzsimmons said. "You don't want to get mad!" Daley leaned toward him to try to get his attention. The shouting slowly died.

"All right, Doc," Frenchy Martin said. Old man Heck only scowled. "No offense, Doc!" a voice called. They began to chant his name in unison, and he felt a surprised exultation that he could speak to them as he had and make them accept it.

But when he rose again he looked from face to face with contempt. "Why should I take no offense? You yourselves are quick enough to take it, it seems. Anything done in this town that is not exactly what you wish, you feel is traitorous. If you are going to turn on Miss Jessie like sulky boys, or on the marshal or poor Schroeder who defended you as well as Morgan in defending the law—"

There was a louder outcry; the names were shouted—Blaisedell, Morgan, Brunk, Benny Connors, Schroeder, Curley Burne. This time he shouted back at them until he made himself heard. "You contemptible fools! What is the use of trying to help you? Who cares for your piddling dollar a day? I do not. I hoped there might be some decency and common sense somewhere among you, but I see there is none. Have your damned violence and arson and see where it will get you. You will burn that stope and cut off all your noses to spite one face you hate!"

He sat down again, and again they pleaded with him to go on, but he did not rise. He thought that he could sway them in the end, he was not even particularly angry, but he thought it best to let them whistle for his advice for a while. They would covet it the more if he withheld it.

Fitzsimmons rose, to be met with catcalls. He cried in return, cheerfully, "Cut away, boys! Cut those noses!" He held his burned hands out before him and waited for silence.

"You can laugh at me because I am younger than you," Fitzsimmons went on. "But I am more a miner than three-quarters of the ragtag and bobtail around here. I've been underground since I was twelve, and I know some things about a strike it looks like you don't know. I know when there is a strike the mine don't produce and the miners don't eat. But a mine can go a long time without producing."

Fitzsimmons seemed a little surprised that he had not been shouted down yet, and, watching the boy, the doctor was aware again of the iron in him, and more and more, too, he was aware that Fitzsimmons was as patient, calculating, and ruthless as any gambler.

"And I know another thing it looks like you don't," Fitzsimmons went on. "I know if a stope gets burnt it stays burnt a long time, and you don't eat during that time either. Or after."

"There are other mines, boy," old man Heck said. "There is other camps besides Warlock."

"Not for those that burnt a stope, there isn't!"

"The kid is right on that, old man!"

Again everyone began to talk at once. Fitzsimmons tried to make himself heard, but the others quieted only when Bull Johnson got to his feet, grinning and waving his arms.

"I say we can bust Mister Mac," Johnson said, in his great, deep voice. "Him and the Haggins and Morgan and Blaisedell and the Citizens' Committee and any other sons of bitches in league with him. I say we have got stronger arms than they got, and all we have to do is get guns and—"

"Dig silver ourself then?" Patch broke in. "Do you think Peach wouldn't be down here with the cavalry?"

"Ah, you couldn't get Peach out of Bright's City with a pry-bar."

"Better Peach than a bunch of hardcase Regulators!"

Old man Heck pounded on the table. Fitzsimmons shook his head despairingly and dropped into his chair.

"Doc!" They began chanting his name again. As soon as he got to his feet again they fell respectfully silent.

"I understand your fear." He spoke quietly now, so they would have to be silent in order to hear him. "Now that you have begun this strike, you must get something for your efforts or look like fools. I would hate to see MacDonald's satisfaction, if you were able to gain nothing, as much as any of you. But what do you want in the end? Your wages raised, or the Miners' Union established?"

He looked from face to worried face, and no one answered him. "I think you will get neither of those things," he said. "Lathrop made the Miners' Union too much of a bugbear here for MacDonald even to tolerate the notion, and MacDonald has put himself into a position where to save his face he cannot put wages back to where they were. They were due to come down in any case, and I am sure he was ordered by the company to lower them, though possibly not so much as he did.

"My advice to you is to accept these two facts. Make no issue of the Miners' Union as yet, and let MacDonald have his way about the wages. Then what can you hope for? I know you must save your own faces, and I think you must try to save your lives as well—by which I mean the timbering in the stopes.

"I think you should prepare a series of demands to present to MacDonald. He will refuse them, and then you should submit slightly different ones. If he goes on refusing them, he will come to look more and more unreasonable to everyone—including the Porphyrion and Western Mining Company. I think that is the way you can beat him."

He saw that he had most of them with him. He took a deep breath.

"Some of your demands should be these: Demand above all proper timbering, especially in that number two shaft. And demand that the number two lift be made safe. Demand ventilation at the lower levels. There are a great many more items that concern your personal safety which you know much more about than I. People are going to sympathize with demands of this nature, as they will not sympathize with the drop in your wages, or with the Miners' Union as yet.

"You have every right to demand these things, but I would demand much more at first so that you can bargain downward. I would—" He paused a moment; what he was going to say seemed, in a way, a betrayal of Jessie, but he could see that they must, one day, have it. And, he though bitterly, Jessie had Blaisedell now. He said, "I would demand some kind of hospital for the injured, the cost to be shared between you and the mine owners." He held up a hand for silence, and raised his voice above the muttering. "And there is to be a committee of miners established to supervise that, and to advise on what is to be done about safety in the Medusa. This is the most important thing. A committee," he said, and paused again so as to catch their full attention, "that will be the basis for your Miners' Union!"

They cheered in one voice, and he could not help smiling. He sat down quickly, amid the prolonged yelling and clapping. Fitzsimmons sprang to his feet.

"Listen!" he cried. "The Doc has told us the right way, I guess we all know; but there is something else to bring up. What we are waiting for is the day Peach gives this town a patent. Stop and think how the vote'll run when *we* have got a vote. We—"

"Sit down! Young one—sit!"

"Listen! Why won't you listen to me? I am telling you we can elect the mayor and council and all—and sheriff! We—"

"Sit down, boy!" Bull Johnson growled.

"Peach's forgot us here. He thinks we are in Mexico."

"Brunk was after MacDonald about that retimbering too, Doc. He never got anywhere but fired."

"I say burn the Medusa for Frank's sake!" Bull Johnson shouted. "Then they'll *have* to retimber."

"Hear! Hear!"

Old man Heck pounded on the table. Fitzsimmons sank into his chair again, and turned to grin bitterly at the doctor. "They won't listen. Damn them, they just won't."

"Well, I guess Bull has got us back to what we come here to vote on," old man Heck said. "All this other is interesting and maybe edifying, Doc, but we are here to vote on the first thing. All right, all for it!" Old man Heck got to his feet to count the hands.

The doctor did not turn to see how many had gone up, watching old Man Heck's face. Fitzsimmons, who had looked around, grinned and winked at him.

"Seven for," old man Heck said sourly. "Well, all right; against."

"No fire tonight," Frenchy Martin said.

"Yellow-belly bastards!" Bull Johnson said. All around the room men began to stir and rise. There would be no fire tonight.

The doctor sighed and got to his feet; he had better get back to Jessie. He excused himself and hurried from the dining room, waving a hand and nodding to the men who tried to talk to him.

He crossed the hall and entered Jessie's room without knocking.

Blaisedell was there, sitting where he had sat, and Jessie's head was against his chest. It did not appear that Blaisedell hated her, as she had feared. They both stared at him, Blaisedell with the color flushing to his cheeks, Jessie with her eyes round and bright. She smiled at him, and Blaisedell started to his feet.

"You had better keep your door locked, Jessie," the doctor said, and backed out and pulled the door quickly closed behind him. The entryway was full of miners, but he thought no one had seen.

Someone called to him, and he went to join Fitzsimmons, Daley, and Patch, and the two or three others who seemed to make up Fitzsimmons' clique. Fitzsimmons asked if he would like to come to the Billiard Parlor for a game with them, and they all seemed surprised and pleased when he said that he would.

"You can hold my cue for me, Doc," Fitzsimmons said, as they left the General Peach together. "But maybe you could let me call the shots."

39. Morgan Looks at the Deadwood

Tom Morgan sat in the sun on the porch of the Western Star Hotel in his only suit of clothes, his only boots, his only hat. He rocked, smoked a good Havana cheroot, and watched the activity of Warlock in the afternoon—the bustle down the street of horsemen and wagons and men afoot, the loungers along the arcades, the groups of Medusa strikers standing along the far side of Main Street. There was a racket of whistling and catcalls as three whores in their finery promenaded down Southend Street and stopped to look into Goodpasture's store window.

As he leaned forward in his chair to try to see down to the ruin of the Glass Slipper, his money belt pressed into his flesh. Quickly he leaned back. In it was his stake; his place was burned, and he had long been sick to death of Warlock. His mind began to poke pleasureably at place names, at things he had heard of this town or that one.

He spun his cigar out into the dust of the street, where it disappeared as into water. He rocked back and stared up at the sun past his hat-brim, and grinned—a painful stretch of flesh over his teeth. He could not go. Clay would not because of Miss Jessie Marlow, and he could not because Clay would not, and because of McQuown, and because he did not know what Kate was up to with the deputy

At that moment the deputy came into sight, mounted, from Southend Street. He came jogging down Main Street on a shabby buckskin horse, his hat pulled low on his forehead, his face turned aside against the wind. He nodded gravely as he passed, and Morgan turned to see that he took the Bright's City road.

As he watched the deputy ride out of town he saw Kate coming toward him with her skirt blowing and one hand holding her feathered hat on her head. He rose as she came up the steps to the veranda.

"I want to talk to you," she said.

"Fine. Sit and talk."

"Not here."

"Your deputy rides out of town and first thing you are out hunting a tomcat," he said, as he took her arm. They started back toward Grant Street to her house. "You will get yourself a bad name walking with me," he went on. "I am a devil, as everybody knows. What's this about you and Buck Slavin going to build a dance hall?"

"We've talked about it," Kate said shortly. "He'll put up the money if I'll run it."

"Just Buck?" He grinned at her.

"No, I think there is somebody else in it, Tom," she said, in an uninterested voice. He noticed that she was very pale. "I don't know who."

"It is Lew Taliaferro, and if you think I am going to let what's left of the Glass Slipper go to *him* for nothing you can have another think."

But she shook her head; that was not what she wanted to talk about. She unlocked the door of her house and let him in, watching him with her black eyes as he entered. Then she moved to stand across the table from him, as though it were necessary to have something between them.

"What's bothering, Kate?"

"Clay was here. He said he had killed another one being too quick on the draw. I want to know what—"

"He said *what?*"

She repeated it. He stared back at her and slowly he took off his hat and dropped it on the table, and brushed a hand back over his head. "Why did he come here?" he asked.

"He came to ask the deputy if he had lied about what Schroeder told him—there was something about Miss Jessie Marlow being mistaken. But I want to know what he meant about Bob Cletus! Tom, what did he *mean*, he'd been too quick on the draw?"

He hardly listened; he felt a rage at Jessie Marlow that filled him until he thought he would burst with it, then pity and rage for Clay, who had killed Curley Burne wrongfully now by his lights—one time wrong, and every time wrong after it, Clay had said. More and more, it seemed, everyone looked upon Clay as only a name, a thing, a machine to which they fed their pennies and out of him came the same trick which they could then class good or bad for their amusement. Even Miss Jessie Marlow; he knew she had done it to Clay without even wondering how she had. Talked him into going back to marshaling, for one thing. God damn her to hell! There was no one but Tom Morgan to see the man inside the machine any more.

But Kate was not interested in Curley Burne or Miss Jessie Marlow; she was interested in Bob Cletus.

"I don't know what he meant, Kate," he said. "Why didn't you ask him?"

"What did he mean, Tom?" She hit her fist on the table, and then she leaned on it heavily and the feather swayed on her hat. She looked suddenly as though she were going to break apart. "Now I don't *know!* Don't you see? Now I—" She got control of herself with an effort. "Tom," she said. "Tell me the truth about what happened!"

"Told you and told you, but you won't believe me. Cletus called out Clay over Nicholson."

"Bob didn't care anything for Nicholson! I *know* that!"

He shrugged. "You are going to believe Clay shot him down because I asked him to, whatever I say."

He watched her face crumple. He could smile as he told the truth; "I didn't tell Clay to shoot him down. I wouldn't have if I'd *wanted* him shot down, for Clay wouldn't have done it." And he leaned toward her and said, "Kate, I wish you had gone and married Bob Cletus and that I'd given you away to the happy bridegroom. And that you were fat as a pig and worn out right now cooking chuck for him and all his hands on that spread he had, and a couple of dozen children. Don't you believe I wish it?"

He heard her make a high sound in her throat. "What did Clay mean by that, Tom?" she whispered hopelessly.

"Ask him. But let me ask *you* something. What are you up to with the deputy, Kate? A person would think you had a thing on about somebody whose brother Clay shot. Are you trying to make something out of it?"

She shook her head a little; her eyes were swollen. "No. Nothing. I can't make anything with anybody, for you would just have him killed. Wouldn't you?"

"I don't know which way you mean that. One way I might." He sat down and leaned his chair back and crossed his boots up on the table. She was staring at him with her red lips half open.

"Let me tell you something straight and for all, Kate," he said, and he spoke as seriously as he had ever spoken in his life. He pointed a finger at her. "There have been damned few people I have ever thought anything of. Maybe only two, when it comes down to it. And those I have never thrown down and never will."

"Two!" she cried. "Do you mean *me?* You crucified me!"

"Why, Kate, you'd been a whore and it was your own doing. No mac brought you to it. I thought you figured the way I did, and whoring is a way to make a stake like any other. I didn't know you were going to be so damned delicate about it. A person is what they are and what's there to be ashamed of?"

"I didn't mean that!"

"Oh, you meant Cletus. Well, there is no point talking if you are going to hold I put Clay to that."

"You can't even look at me and say you didn't!"

He looked at her and said he hadn't. He wondered suddenly if he would have done it any differently if he had known he was never going to have Kate back, whatever. "I was saying," he said, "that there have been a couple I held high like that. One was you, the other is Clay. I suppose you wouldn't understand that, being a quarter-breed bitch, but it is so."

He paused and gazed back into her wide eyes and saw her mouth open again, as though she would speak again. But she did not, and he went on. "And I am talking about Clay now, for you have gone your way and it's not mine. I call Clay friend and I don't know that I've ever had another. Do you know what a friend means? I don't expect you do, for all you've known is a bunch of other whores you thought poorly of, and said so. I call Clay friend, and I don't give a damn that some go around holding him up as God's salvation to this country, and others call him a dirty dog of a killer. And I don't expect it makes much of a damn to him either what everybody thinks of me."

He pointed his finger at her again. "Now, that is a thing that is just so, whether you understand it or not, which I expect you don't. But that holds strong with me. Now let me tell you some more. There are people who are trying to throw him down. I am speaking in particular of you, and maybe your deputy. And McQuown. And there are others, like Miss Jessie Marlow, though I don't expect she thinks she is. Now: I think I will see Clay Blaisedell die, like I told you once. For that is the trade he is in. But I intend to see that he dies decently, and his name held good, and honor to him. Though not the same way some others want it. Listen to me: I will stick with him and try to do in every backshooter there is, and I mean you among them, and Gannon, if you two are up to something. And McQuown; and *all*. You want to see him die, in your woman-meanness, but I will fight you down the line. Maybe you will think you have won when he is dead, but I will win too, for I will see he goes down in the end like he wants to."

Again she started to speak, again he leveled the finger at her. "There is nothing I have ever set myself to do yet I haven't done. Hear me and think if it isn't so. And this is what I have set myself to. I will see it through in spite of every son of a bitch in the world against it. I will kill anybody I think is dangerous to him that way. Or get killed for it either without giving one good God damn, if it would do any good. Do you understand me, Kate?"

"Tom," she said shakily. "I don't want to hear anything more about it. I don't—"

"Just one more thing," he said. His throat felt very dry. "Listen. There is going to come a day when I cash in. When I get up to the Gate they will look at the records, like they do. They will scream to see mine. But I will say to them that I was made the way I was, but I did a decent thing in my life. And I don't know that there are so many decent things done that they can sniff at it. I can say I did this, and by God I did my best, and it was a good thing. I can say I had a reason to *be,* and I don't see many around me that have. I can say I had a reason for being alive that was mine, and that was worth something, and—"

"I have got my reason to be!" Kate cried, but he felt a vast triumph as her voice broke.

"Why, it isn't worth anything and you know it. Two bits' worth of forgiveness would cancel it out. To see a man that never *meant* to do you or yours any harm brought low! You a Catholic, with your Virgin to pray to and your candles and all—do you think you can go up there and when they ask you what reason you had for being alive, say it was to see a man dishonored and killed? It won't pass, Kate." He began to laugh. "They will send you to a lower part of hell than me. Wouldn't that gripe your everlasting soul!"

He shouted with laughter and beat his hand upon his leg. He tried to suck the laughter back at the sight of her face, but he could not. "Oh, that *would* be hell!"

"Stop it!"

He stopped. He put his feet down and leaned toward her, and said, seriously again, "Kate, do you think I would give a rap for Clay if I could tell him to go out and shoot down a randy son of a bitch that was after my girl?"

He watched her fighting uncertainty. She shook her head and the feather on her hat swooped and swung; he could make her believe the truth a lie, he knew, but not a lie the truth.

"Wait!" he said, as she started to speak. "Let's try to work it out. Maybe I see how it went, come to think of it. You had a few rolls in bed with Clay, didn't you?"

"I did not!"

"Are you sure, now?" he said, grinning, feeling hate of himself like black bile rising in his veins. "Because *I* thought you did, Kate. Wait now! I was just wondering if Cletus might've got wind of it too. Was he a jealous kind? Maybe that was why."

She clutched her hands to her face and he thought he had won; he wondered what he thought he had won. He said softly, "Maybe that was why Cletus called out Clay, Kate. Do you think that might've been why? You knew him better than I did."

"It's not so!" she said, through her hands. "That I— Tom, I knew he was your friend. I—"

"Well, lots of things that aren't so get fought over all the same."

She leaned forward, her hands on the table, her swollen eyes fastened to his. "You—" she whispered. "You—"

"I'm just saying that somebody could have told him that," he said easily. "And if he was a jealous fellow. I've heard—"

"I don't believe you!" she cried. "You didn't. You are just trying to— I can't believe you, I can't ever believe you! Get out of here, Tom!"

All at once he was very shaken by the sight of her face, and he picked up his hat and started for the door. He had only meant to try to take her off Clay's back a little and let her sit his own. He thought of the times he had seen her in anger, the times in grief; it occurred to him, now, that he had never felt sorry for her before. He turned and said, "Kate—"

"Oh, *please* get out!"

He went on outside, where his eyes recoiled from the brightness of the sun. He could hear her sobbing behind him. Why couldn't he tell her the truth? Why wouldn't it be easy? He almost turned to go back to her, but, after a moment's reflection, he did not. He could not, he thought, ever go back.

40 Bright's City

BRIGHT's City lay just to the east of the Bucksaws, along Bright's Creek. There was a heavy traffic of wagons across the rumbling wooden bridge over the creek, where, straight ahead, on Main Street, lay the Plaza. To the right, half a mile down Fort Street, was Fort Jacob Collins, with its flag rippling and colorful in the wind, and, to the left, the three-storied red-brick courthouse, its tall windows shuttered against the sun, its copper-sheathed cupola raised like a helmeted dragoon's head.

Soldiers from the fort paced the streets or stood upon corners. There were many women in Bright's City, and many men in store suits among the more roughly dressed ranchers and cowboys. Townsmen and housewives kept to the north side of Bright's City's Main Street, while sporting women in their finery passed in promenade on the south side, accompanied by the whistling of cowboys and soldiers.

The delegation from the Warlock Citizens' Committee exited from the Jim Bright Hotel. A Bright's City deputy, chewing on a toothpick, greeted them pleasantly as he sauntered on his rounds.

"How enviable it is," Will Hart said, "to see the same deputies on hand every time you come in here."

"I wish we'd see a different sheriff," Buck Slavin said irritably.

"Well, let's go see what sheriff there is," Goodpasture said, and they proceeded to the sheriff's office, which adjoined the courthouse. Sheriff Keller was visible through the dusty glass of the window. He sat at ease with his scrolled boots propped up on his pigeon-holed desk, his fine, white, sugar-loaf hat tipped over his eyes.

Keller rose ponderously as they entered, a bull-necked, heavy man with the face of a jolly bloodhound, a tobacco-stained mustache, and a gold watch chain with links like barbed wire strung across his massive midsection. Behind him the cell doors stood open, and in one of them a number of prisoners were playing cards.

"Why, it's some gentlemen from Warlock," Keller said, removing his hat and smiling in greeting. Then his face turned sad as he said, "I certainly was distressed to hear about old Carl Schroeder. A good man." He shook his head sadly, and clucked.

The prisoners dropped their cards and crowded into the door of the cell. "What's happened?" one cried.

"Blaisedell throw down on McQuown yet?"

"You boys hush, now!" the sheriff roared. "You! Get back in there!" The prisoners moved back inside, and Keller went over to slam the door on them. "I'll have a little peace and quiet in here!" he said severely, and turned back to the delegation again. Another deputy came in.

"Branch, you run for Jim Askew," the sheriff said. "Here is some more news from Warlock and he'll apoplexy sure if he gets gone to press before he hears it. Now; what's up now, gentlemen?"

"We want some law in Warlock, Sheriff!" Slavin said. "The Citizens' Committee has sent us up here to insist—"

"Well, now, hold on," Keller said. "You people are all right. That young Gannon come up here ahead of you people, and told me he was going to *re*sign, but I have talked him out of it. Anyway, you have got Blaisedell still, haven't you?"

"Damn," Slavin said.

"Well, we wanted to get rid of Gannon, Sheriff," Will Hart said. "I must say we are a little sorry to hear you talked him out of resigning."

The sheriff sat down, frowning heavily. "Well, now, gentlemen; he said people was kind of down on him, thinking he had swore false over Curley Burne. Maybe he did too, but it come right in the end, now, didn't it?" He eyed them each in turn. "You people down there have got to realize it is hard to get a decent man to deputy in Warlock. You don't just chuck one out when he does something you don't like once or twice; no, sir." He scowled at the deputy, who had not left yet. "Run along now, Branch. Get Jim Askew here, boy." The prisoners were whispering together excitedly.

"Like I say," Keller went on. "It came right anyway what with Blaisedell cutting down Curley Burne, so I can't see what you people are so excited about."

"We insist that you fire Gannon!" Slavin said. "The Citizens' Committee has sent us up here to tell you—"

"Huh!" Keller said. "Now, I mean! Who is the Warlock Citizens' Committee to tell me who I am to fire? I mean, I like to get along with you folks, but it is hard to hire a man for that place down there."

"What did he want here, Sheriff?" Goodpasture asked.

The sheriff leaned back in his chair, his face crinkling with amusement. "Why, he didn't really want to resign. He was just trying to blackguard me with it. He wanted four more deputies down there. Four!" He held up four fat fingers. Well, he's young, but he is all right. I promised him if he'd wait over a day or so, I'd get him a new sign made for that jail down there, though."

"That will be an improvement," Goodpasture said.

"Now, see here, Sheriff!" Slavin said heatedly, and then he stopped and sighed.

Keller sat rubbing his red-veined nose and glancing from face to face again. "You gentlemen ought to try to get on with your deputies down there. Down on him, are you? Well, let me tell you. Either he went and lied to get Curley Burne off, or else he didn't lie. You gentlemen know for sure he went and lied?"

"Everybody knows he lied," Slavin said.

"Well, now, I meant proof, Mr. Slavin. No, now, you don't know for sure. You have got to look at it this way, anyhow. I mean, say he did lie; what're you going to do if a man lies for an old partner of his? You'd do it; maybe I'd do it, though I won't admit it straight out. I mean, that is a poor place to be down there, terrible bad pay, and a man doesn't live long enough to take much of it home, either. Look at poor old Carl. And he lasted a coon's age compared with most. I mean, you have got to give a man with a job like that a little leeway."

"There's another way of looking at it, too," Hart said. "Burne probably would have gone free anyway if he'd come up here to trial."

The prisoners broke out laughing. Keller scowled and scratched his nose. "Well, now!" he said. "You know what the man said when he saw the black-headed Swede, don't you? That's a Norse of a different color!" He roared with laughter, amid a further chorus from the cell. The delegation from Warlock looked at each other despairingly.

Then Keller's face assumed a serious expression, and he said, "Well, now, about McQuown's boys getting off up here. I might doubt it some. Things've gone and changed in people's eyes up here a little. I don't expect no jury here is going to let those Pablo 'cases run quite so pecker-up any more. What I mean—it looks like Abe's just about run his string. People used to take a fright you just creep up behind them and whisper '*McQuown!*' It's not so any more, not with Clay Blaisedell salting his tail for him and lopping his gun hands off like he is doing. It is like when the old general got after Espirato and made him run for cover."

Hart said, "You make it sound almost safe enough for you to come down and be a proper sheriff, Sheriff."

"Now it is not going to do any good for you to get insulting, Mr. Hart. I swear, you people come up here and play me the same tune every time, and all I can tell you is just any day now there is going to be a separate county set up down there. Peach County, I expect it'll be called. You will have your own sheriff to pick at then. I was talking to Whiteside just last week, and he was saying any day now that—"

"I do hate to remind you, Sheriff," Goodpasture said. "But it has been any day now for over a year."

"Two years," Hart said.

"Well, it is any day *now* for sure. I'd put money on it—not more than a month, for sure."

"Bellywash!" Slavin cried. "I'll tell you this, Keller. If we don't get some satisfaction from you this time, we will see Peach himself!"

"See him!" Keller said, smiling, nodding. "Do that."

"And if we don't get any satisfaction from him we will by God go to Washington, if we have to!"

"Go," Keller said. "You will probably have to. I'd sure like to go back there myself. I hear it is pleasant this time of year, back there."

"We are asking for your help, Sheriff," Goodpasture said. "The situation in Warlock is much more difficult than you realize."

Keller's eyes flickered a little. He hunkered forward in his chair, and spread his hands. "But what would you want me to do, Mr. Goodpasture? I mean! I'd be all my time riding back and forth between here and Warlock, and I am too old for that foolishness. And don't mind saying I am scared. Mr. Goodpasture, I just don't claim to be anything I'm not. I run for sheriff here, surely, but to my mind this county stops at the Bucksaws there and that is all I run for. That is so, now; you know I didn't come down there beforehand, either. Now, I like this big belly here as it is and not all shot full of holes. Like Carl, and that feller Brown and how many others before that? I am not sheriff down there, that's all. If it was put to me hard I had to be, why, I'd quit. What's the matter with Blaisedell all of a sudden you are so dissatisfied again? Sounds from here like everything is going nice as pie."

Will Hart said, "It has not worked out, Sheriff. He has had to kill too many men."

"Why, my stars! You fellows aren't shedding tears for those rustlers he is popping off, are you?"

"Sheriff," Goodpasture said. "He has no authority. And we had none when we hired him. He and the Citizens' Committee have had to take too much upon themselves."

"It looks from here like it is going nicely. He has got McQuown tramped down and Pablo thinned out some. Those cowboys will stop getting their fingers burnt pretty quick, and settle down. I will give you gentlemen the same advice I gave Gannon. Let Blaisedell work it out. There is no better man nowhere, from what I have heard. I told Gannon to quit worrying, and you too. The time to worry's when things is in bad shape, not—"

"They are in bad shape," Hart said.

"You are an officer of the court!" Slavin cried.

"Not down there."

Hart said, "Well, maybe if we had three or four more deputies, as Gannon suggested—"

Keller shook his head. "You would have to collect taxes down there to have your three or four, and that would take a dozen. And fighting men! Now, maybe you gentlemen wouldn't mind paying taxes, and maybe Mr. Slavin wouldn't even mind having it run into his franchise about transporting prisoners up here, but you gentlemen ought to know those ranchers down that way never even heard of taxes. They'd think a tax collector was a road agent! Why, it'd take Peach and the whole shooting match from the fort to collect taxes down there. All that for some deputies? Why, Blaisedell is serving you better than ten deputies could in a month of Sundays. Now, isn't that so, Mr. Goodpasture?"

"Blaisedell is a very fine man," Goodpasture said. "We have had no cause to be anything but highly satisfied with him. It is a matter of authority. We are in a position of ordering him to kill men. We are in a position of trying to administer severe laws that do not exist, when the responsibility is yours."

"No, sir! It is not mine either. No, sir, you just take all the authority you need."

Goodpasture sighed and said, "And the kind of thing that Blaisedell can deal with is necessarily limited. You should be able to understand that."

"You mean those Cousin Jacks running wild and tearing things up? MacDonald was up here complaining about that just lately, but I thought you people had worked up some sort of regulation committee to deal with those wild men."

"MacDonald has," Hart said. "Please don't connect us with that pack of mongrels."

"I thought it was a Citizens' Committee thing," Keller said. "So did everybody. Well, it goes to show you."

"Say!" one of the prisoners called. "Does it look like McQuown is going to make a play against Blaisedell? There is betting here he won't."

The sheriff regarded them questioningly too, but, sunk in gloom, no one of the delegation answered. The sheriff chuckled and said, "I'd ride down to see that."

"Let's get out of here and see Peach," Slavin said. "I knew there was no damned use in our coming here."

"See him," Keller said, approvingly.

"We are going to! Right now!"

"Let me tell you something first," Keller said, in a confidential tone. "Just like I told Gannon, that's bound and determined he is going to see him too. Don't mention about Blaisedell if you see him. Old Peach doesn't like anything to do with Blaisedell for beans." He winked hugely. "Jealous! Jealous as a lap dog. For you know what used to be the biggest thing in this territory? Peach cleaning out the Apaches. Now it's been so long people's forgotten there ever was Apaches, and new people coming in all the time that's never even seen one. Why, now the biggest thing out here is Blaisedell. By a mile! Jim Askew is coining money from newspapers all over the country.

"He sends out stories by telegraph, for heaven's sake! And those papers back east of here pay for it and beg for more, he says. Nothing new on Blaisedell, he writes about some fool gossip or other, anything. Back East Peach is only some has-been of a general, maybe he is dead by now, it's been so long since anybody heard anything about him. But Blaisedell! Why, Jim got rich on that Acme Corral shoot-up alone, and never stopped a minute since. Jump, when he heard about Curley Burne! You should have seen him!

"Oh, Blaisedell has got to be the biggest thing that ever happened out here, and you remember what I say and keep kind of quiet if you have to mention him to the general. Or talk him down. Here comes Jim right now," he said, nodding toward the window.

Jim Askew, editor and publisher of the *Bright's City Star-Democrat*, came hurrying in. He was a little, wrinkled, side-whiskered man with a green vizor over his eyes, ink-smeared paper cuffs, and a canvas apron. The deputy was a step behind him, and the other deputy, whom the delegation had seen before the hotel, appeared also.

"What's happened now? What's happened now?" Askew demanded, taking a newsprint pad from beneath his apron, a pencil from behind his ear. He stared from one to the other of them with his eyes enlarged and rolling behind his steel-rimmed spectacles. "What's happened in Warlock, fellows?"

"Warlock is gone, Jim," Hart said. "It was a terrible thing. The old Warlock mine opened right up and the whole town fell in. Nobody left but the few miserable survivors you see before you."

"Now, now, fellows," the editor said reprovingly. "Now, seriously, what's been going on lately? What's Blaisedell been up to now?"

41. Journals of Henry Holmes Goodpasture

April 15, 1881

IT HAS been said, with the exaggeration by which truth is memorialized in a kernel, that the reason people remain in Warlock is that death is preferable to a journey to Bright's City, and damnation better than the stage to Welltown. It is not quite so bad as that, although the trip is a long day's horror, and upon arrival at Bright's City the spine feels like a rock drill that has lost its temper.

This morning, then, to see Sheriff Keller. He is a shameful excuse for a sheriff, venal, cynical, and cowardly, and yet it is difficult to dislike him. Gannon, we found, had preceded us to Bright's City—having ridden through the Bucksaws, a shorter route by half than the stage road—and Keller out-argued our demands for his dismissal, I think more from force of habit than from loyalty to his deputy. His reasoning was: 1) deputies for Warlock are hard to come by, good or bad; 2) Gannon is willing to be deputy in Warlock; ergo, 3) Gannon remains deputy in Warlock.

We are so used to being defeated and thwarted by Sheriff Keller that we no longer feel animus against him. Still, we were depressed by our encounter with him, and when we were kept from seeing General Peach by Whiteside at his most obstructionistic. We will try again tomorrow with renewed determination, revived by a night's rest at the Jim Bright Hotel.

It is curious to talk to the inhabitants here about recent events in Warlock. Bright's Citizens are defenders of Blaisedell to a man, and they are, indeed, surprised and insulted that we should feel there are two sides to the matter. They will not accept the fact that there are things in heaven, earth, and Warlock undreamt of in their philosophy. To them, Blaisedell is an uncompromised and untainted Hero, battling a Villain named McQuown. There are none of the shadows and underbrush that have so haunted us in Warlock. Morgan is Blaisedell's right bower, and is somewhat revered himself. The miners and their quarrel with MacDonald are of no interest, although it is disturbing to hear the Regulators described as a band of eminent Warlockians convened in aid of Blaisedell.

April 16, 1881

Colonel Whiteside guards his lord like a lion. He is a colorless little man, thin, worried-looking, and nervous to infect the most placid. He is uneasy with civilians, and his manner alternates between chill command and an inept cajolery. He routed us again this morning. This afternoon we won through to the Presence.

I had not seen the General since November, when he passed through Warlock en route back from the border after one of his idiotic dashes after a rumor of Espirato. Since then, I think, he has not been out of Bright's City. That he is insane, I have now no doubt.

Whiteside was fending us off again, although with increasing desperation, when the General himself stormed down the corridor of the courthouse where we were seeking to obtain an audience, shouting incoherently in his great blown voice. He was followed by a company of aides, orderlies, and sergeants, all in dress uniform, and was in dress uniform himself, although his blouse hung open and some kind of liquid had been spilled upon his shirt front. He waved his gauntleted hands and shouted something at Whiteside which seemed to have to do with the presence of dogs upon the post, and how they were to be dealt with. With him chaos came, as he roared meaningless sounds, and all his company sought to speak at once, while Colonel Whiteside, with pad and pencil in hand, called simultaneously for silence, sought to make sense of what his chief was saying, and watched us nervously for evidences of a flank attack.

Then, out of the uproar he himself had brought into the corridor, or out of the decay of his brain slipping into senilty or worse, or because of our unaccustomed presence, General Peach fell silent and confusion spread over his face. It was pitiful to see it. The little blue eyes, fierce and determined a moment past, wandered distraitly around, all but lost in the fat, red folds of his face. He stripped his gauntlets off hands as fat as sofa cushions, and, as soon as he had them off, struggled to put them on again, while all the time his eyes worried from face to face as though he did not know where he was, nodding from time to time as poor Whiteside tried to prompt and question him into repeating what the order, so urgent a minute before, was about— with a desperation that called forth pity not only for his master but for Whiteside himself, who must be the one to govern this territory under a madman while trying to conceal that madness from the world.

At last Peach's eyes fixed themselves upon me with an enraged and defiant glare, and he cried, "Has headquarters sent out some more damned politicians to try to run my brigade for me, sir?"

I stammered that we were a deputation from Warlock with urgent business for his attention, to which he retorted even more forcibly that I was to tell them that the damned devil had hidden himself in the Sierra Madre and he could do nothing unless he was given permission to cross the border in pursuit. "Nothing, damn his red eyes!" he cried, while Will, Buck, and I tried to explain where we were from and something of our mission. Finally either some sense broke through or we were mistaken for still other emissaries, for all of a sudden we were swept into the inner temple beyond Whiteside's desk.

It is a great room with westward-looking windows, crowded with the mementos of his career: an umbrella stand in which are tattered banners, bullet-torn regimental colors, a pair of confederate standards; on the wall a large painting of the Battle of the Snake River Crossing, with Peach leading his men through Lame Deer's painted ranks and the teepees beyond them; on the wall also a varnished plaque on which was the scalp of some vanquished foe, with long, dusty braids; and there were quivers of arrows, moth-eaten war bonnets, Apache shields, war clubs, peace pipes, and framed photographs of Peach shaking hands with various chieftains. Upon his desk was the leather-wrapped stick he often carries, which is supposed to be the shaft of an arrow that almost killed him. The whole room seems a dusty and unkempt museum, or perhaps it is only a facsimile of his mind—a vacant space, inhabited by heroic memories.

Peach seated himself behind his desk, swept off his hat and flung it over the inkstand, stripped off his gauntlets again, transfixed us with his glittering, pale eyes, and said that he sympathized with our position, but that he could only fight a defensive campaign until those damned, do-nothing politicians in Washington decided to put it up to the Mexican government, and that there was no way, at present, he could go after the "murdering red rascal."

I was, I remember, terrified lest Buck or Will blurt out that Espirato is presumably dead, and any threat from his renegades extremely improbable. They did not, however, and stood as stupefied as I, while Peach arose and paced the floor in an agitated manner. His actions are a series of mechanical and fustian gestures, each one anticipated by a slight pause, as though, inside him, gears and levers prepare the proper muscles for their roles—almost you can hear the whirr of the aged and imperfect clockwork. Then he will toss his head as though flinging back from his eyes the mane of white hair he no longer possesses (he is quite bald except for a matted ruff that gives his head the broad, flattened look of a badger's), fold his arms with massive dignity, and stare down his nose; or fling himself into his chair with a crash that seems sure to smash it, or rise out of it with labored gruntings. He paces the floor with his hands locked behind his back like a man in a prison cell, or stands glaring at nothing with his great boots spread splay-footed apart and a hand held Bonaparte-like within his blouse, or strokes his beard with the expression of one giving birth to an infinitely cunning stratagem. Now, I find, I am able to sort out these various poses and attitudes one by one; yet, at the time, accompanied by the steely glare of his small, bright, mad eyes, there was a kind of majesty about them.

But it is a variety of dumb-show. The words that accompany these postures and gestures have no relation to them. The mildest words may be set to the most violent gesticulation, and conversely. His speech, gushing from the rusted pipes within him, is of the most monumental and dreadful nonsense.

From time to time poor Whiteside appeared at the door, to be waved away with irritable condescension. At least, when I was able to get a word in edgewise, I sought to tell the General of the plight of Warlock. He let me speak, flinging himself down in his chair again and studying me the while with his bearded chin propped upon his fist, and on his face an expression of terrible dismay, as though I were relaying to him news of some dreadful defeat and rout. But presently his attention wavered, and his eyes began to flicker confusedly around the room—and I to falter in my speech as the impression grew stronger that not a word of what I said was understood, and, moreover, if it had been, would be of no more import to him than reports of injustices among the sparrows to a Zeus brooding over Troy. Buck was of no assistance, paralyzed into dumbness, and Will has confessed that all his energies were taken with stifling a fit of giggles which had smitten him as though he were a schoolboy in church.

I was reduced, in the end, to stammering like a schoolboy myself. Peach made interjection only once. He reared back in his chair, frowning at something I said, took up his hat from the inkwell and cast it to the floor, snatched up a pen and scribbled furiously upon a piece of paper, and stared down at what he had written with an awesome concentration. Then he threw down the pen also, and muttered, "By God, if they come around that way, Miller and half a company could—"

It finished me. Buck gave me a wild, desperate glance. Will had already turned to go, and I retreated also, uttering apologies, statements that perhaps we should return another time, etc., that must have sounded as eccentric and irrational as what we had heard from him. But he spoke calmly behind us, saying, "Warlock," as though my explanations had won through at last.

He was standing behind his desk now, glowering at us from under the white bushes of his eyebrows with eyes that looked sane at last. "Tell him he is getting too big for his boots," he said. "Tell the scoundrel I am governor here. Tell—" he said, and once again confusion showed in his eyes and he was lost. But still he made an effort to recover his train of thought. He slapped a hand down on his desk and said we were to tell Whiteside we were to have fresh mounts and the best Indian Scouts he could furnish us!

We left the room. Before Whiteside's desk there was still the clutter of aides and orderlies. Whiteside, writing busily, took no notice whatever of our exit, and we had nothing to say to him, nor to John Gannon, whom we met outside the courthouse and who seemed anxious to ingratiate himself with us. We ignored his overtures and walked back to the hotel more in awe than in black depression. "Mad as a hatter," was all Buck could say, and it has seemed to me an understatement of shattering proportions.

We determined to send our telegrams to Washington, as we had been directed to do, all else failing. The wording had been set down, and we engaged ourselves in copying them out, and, further, in making up a statement in the form of a letter which Askew had offered to print for us, to be sent by mail to follow our telegrams, expanding upon our grievances. Whereupon Whiteside burst in on us (for we had made our threats to him before we had seen the General), seized a copy of the telegram, read it, and burst out with the most astonishing threats against us should we send them. He said he would hale us into military court and prosecute us to the full extent of his power, which he hinted was substantial; he said further that he would have us arrested immediately, that he would have the telegraph office closed down, etc. We were in no mood to be frightened, however, and said we knew perfectly well he could not arrest us, and that, if the telegraph office was closed to us, we would travel on to Rincon to send our telegrams.

Threats failing, he turned to pleading; his motivation was plain, and, indeed, he stated it. Obviously he is insanely loyal to his insane chief. The General is old, he said; a famous man, a great man, but failing now, obviously dying. Could we not see that he was a dying man? Could we not wait a little while? Will said that it looked to him as though Peach might live forever, and that we would not, Warlock remaining in its present state. Whiteside is not much impressed with the importance of Warlock or its inhabitants, but sought our sympathy and strove desperately not to offend us. He turned to procrastination. Give him a little time; a month or six weeks. General Peach was failing rapidly, he could see it day by day. The General had certain prejudices against Warlock, but if we gave him, Whiteside, six weeks, he would see that the necessary orders were given for the issuance of a town patent, and, indeed, the establishment of another county with Warlock, of course, the county seat (here I saw Buck's eyes light up). He would do his utmost to bring the General to these dispositions, but, that failing, would forge the General's name as he has evidently already done on various minor administrative documents.

I think we were all moved with pity for Whiteside. At any rate we promised to wait six weeks, after which, if he failed us, we would bombard Washington with letters and telegrams detailing All. Whiteside thanked us most gratefully, and retired, and we drank a bottle of whisky together, most grim and depressed, wondering how many men we might have condemned to death in this delay and subjection of the public good to one man's already engorged reputation. And I found myself wondering what we might be doing to Blaisedell's reputation, which is precious to us, by making this concession to Peach's, which is not.

We could comfort ourselves only in the hope, and I pray it is a legitimate one, that we had more to gain by enlisting Whiteside's aid than by offending him, and that, though our telegrams could easily become lost among bureaucratic desks and wastebaskets, unsent they became a spur to hasten Whiteside to action.

Will and Buck have gone off to their own rooms, to their own dreams or nightmares. Bright's City is gay tonight outside my window. I can feel strongly a difference in the atmosphere here, the presence of order and of the knowledge of, and trust in, order. Is it too much to hope that Warlock will be like this one day? Or will our mines play out and our town dissolve to an abandoned ruin before it has even come to peace?

We will return to Warlock, I am afraid, despite Whiteside's promises, with heavy hearts and guilty ones, and with little appetite for the explanations we will have to give our fellows.

42. Morgan Is Dealt Out

SITTING on the bed in his room in the hotel, Morgan unfolded the piece of stiff paper with steady fingers. He glanced up once at the frightened face of Dechine, in from San Pablo, and then held the paper under the lamp. The words were printed in large, carefully shaped letters:

3–7–77

CLAY BLAISEDELL

FOR THE FOUL MURDER

OF WILLIAM GANNON

AND CHARLES BURNE

3–7–77

BY THE HAND OF

ABRAHAM MCQUOWN

CHIEF OF REGULATORS

"What am I going to do, Tom?" Dechine whined. "Jesus, what am I going to do?"

Morgan refolded the paper carefully. Then, holding it with his thumb and forefinger at one end, snapped it open again with a loud pop. Dechine flinched.

"How many have you got?"

"Ten of them," Dechine said. He rubbed his red nose. "Jesus! Three or four of them I'm supposed to post up somewheres—by the stage depot there, and by the Lucky Dollar and Goodpasture's store. The rest's for him, and you, and Buck, and some others—I got a list here." He made motions toward a vest pocket. "I am supposed to see *he* gets one, for sure. Jesus, what am I going to do, Tom?"

Morgan studied the paper again. It was neatly done. He felt a kind of admiration for McQuown, that he had listed only Billy Gannon and Curley Burne. McQuown had known the cards that were high in Warlock; they were higher still with Clay, though McQuown could not have known that. McQuown had been smart enough not to overload a thing. Well, Clay, what do we do now? he said to himself.

Dechine's voice rattled in his ears. "I was going to chuck them off somewheres and just make tracks. Give *him* one! Then I thought I'd bring them up here for you to see, Tom. I—"

"Who spelled them out like this for McQuown?"

"Joe Lacey. He can write good. Jesus, Tom! What am I going to do?"

"Like you were told. If you don't, Joe Lacey will just have to run up another batch."

"Oh, no! I am getting right on out of the territory. I know God-*damn* well I'm not going to give one of these to Blaisedell." Dechine's shoulders were hunched as though he were afraid someone was standing behind him; gingerly he placed the stack of papers on top of Morgan's bureau. "I told Abe straight out that I wasn't going to do it, but there's no talking to him. He has got a look on him like he's been chewing peyote berry. So I thought I'd just make like I was going to, and get scarce fast and far. I know I—"

"When are they coming in?"

"Not right away, I don't expect. There was everybody there drinking and jawing when I left, but they was laughing there how they would let Warlock stew awhile. I guess not right off. They are all coming, though; that bunch the Haggins rounded up for MacDonald, and all Abe's people this time. The old man even—they are going to bring him in the wagon to see the sport. You should have heard the old son of a bitch! But not me, no sir! Tom, I am not going to post up those damned things!"

"Put them out. If you don't they'll just have to send somebody else to do it." He folded the paper again. His hands remained steady, but there was a taste of copper in his mouth as he wondered what Clay would do. But there was no way of stopping these, or others like them, from showing up.

"I don't know whether I am scareder of Blaisedell or Abe, which," Dechine went on. "Abe is on the prod for a caution!" He hesitated and licked his lips, his eyes flickering. "Well, I guess I ought to tell you, Tom. They almost put you down there too. But Abe said not. They was thinking of putting you and Blaisedell down for killing that Cletus—"

"Who?" Morgan said, raising an eyebrow.

"Well, he was that passenger that got killed that time Pony and Cal shot up the Bright's City stage there. Abe was trying to figure on some way to make like you and Blaisedell did it, or just him. But finally Abe decided this was all he'd put there. I tell you he has gone crazy wild down there, and it's not just over Curley either. Jesus, Tom, I will be glad to get out of this country. This country has went to hell. I'll say this straight out, Tom, even knowing Blaisedell is a friend to you. And even if I have known Abe and liked him too. There's times I've hoped to God they would come to it and burn each other dead so a man could get his breath out here again!"

Dechine jammed his hat on his head, and said, "I wonder if you couldn't give me a little stake, Tom?"

"Why, surely. How much do you owe me—five or six hundred? Take that."

"Tom, I—" Dechine swung around to face the door as footsteps sounded, on the stairs, in the corridor. There was a knock.

"Tom?" Clay said.

"Come on in," Morgan said, and grinned at Dechine.

Dechine backed into the corner and took off his hat and began wrenching it between his hands. Clay glanced toward him as he entered.

Morgan handed Clay the piece of paper.

"I was nothing to do with it, Marshal!" Dechine cried. "They would have cold-cocked me there if I didn't bring these in! But I brought them straight to Tom here!"

"I thought you were in a hurry to get moving, Dechine."

Dechine made a sound like a leaky pump. He edged toward the door, nodding ingratiatingly; he went down the stairs at a heavy-footed run.

Clay stood reading the paper for what seemed a very long time. Finally he said, "The old vigilante sign. Three feet wide by seven long, by seventy-seven inches deep." And then he said, "Chief of Regulators." He folded the paper carefully.

"They are all coming in," Morgan said. "Those that were Regulators for MacDonald and more besides."

"Fair enough," Clay said.

"What are you going to do?" Morgan said evenly. "Run for it?"

"Not for McQuown."

"What are you going to do?" he repeated, not so evenly. "Lie down and die?"

"Not for McQuown," Clay said. Suddenly he grinned. He looked like a boy when he grinned like that, and he said, "Have you got any whisky, Morg?"

"Have," Morgan said. He got it and poured two glasses. "How?" he said, and chuckled with excitement.

"How," Clay said, nodding, and they drank together.

"Remember that time in Fort James when Hynes and that bunch got the drop on you?"

"Well enough," Clay said. He sat down, taking off his hat and dropping it on the floor beside him. His fair hair looked gold in the lamplight. "I swear, Morg, you were a sight coming out through those batwing doors. It looked like you had about six arms going like a windmill and a gun in every hand. I thought they would tramp each other to pieces getting out of there, and you and me yelling and shooting up the air behind them."

Clay sounded excited, and reenforced his own excitement; he had never felt so pleased, or proud. But then Clay looked down at his lap, and frowned as he said, in a different voice, "There was some good times in Fort James."

"Well, it looks like you will need some help again this time."

He saw Clay's hand tighten around the glass of whisky he had not finished. "No," Clay said. "I won't need help, Morg."

Morgan swung away to face the window. The full moon hung in it like a jack-o'-lantern. All the pocks showed on the round, gold, blind face. He felt as though he could not get his breath as he stood there, following through Clay's thoughts, trying to understand Clay's judgment. It seemed a judgment on him, and it was something he had never known Clay to do before.

His voice sounded very flat when he spoke. "Clay, do you think it is just McQuown coming in? It is all San Pablo."

"It is between McQuown and me."

"Surely. The rest will faint at the sight of those gold-handles."

He heard the paper rustle behind him. "I won't need help this time, Morg," Clay said.

Damned fool, he thought, not even angrily; damned fool. But there was no use in calling Clay a damned fool, no use arguing. He saw what he must do. He had told Kate he would not throw Clay down, but he must throw him down this time.

"Are you moving on, Morg?" Clay asked, in an expressionless voice.

Thank you, but no thanks, and why don't you move on while you are at it? It must be Miss Jessie Marlow speaking. You used to be yourself, Clay Blaisedell, he thought bitterly, staring out at the moonlight pale as milk in Warlock. Now they have talked you into being Clay Blaisedell instead. "You don't mind if I stay and watch, do you?" he said. "Buy you a drink of whisky after, to settle your nerves. Or pall-bear."

"You understand about it, don't you, Morg?"

"Surely. I can't hurt you if I'm not in it, and I have hurt you enough here."

Clay made a disgusted sound. "That's foolishness. Don't pretend you don't understand about this. This is on me alone."

Morgan did not turn from the window. The stars were lost in the moonlight; he could make out only a few dull specks of them. "Well, you won't mind if I don't move on right away, will you?" he said. "I have got business here still."

"What's that, Morg?"

He did not know why he should feel so ugly now. He turned to face Clay, and grinned and said, "It wasn't jacks that burnt the Lucky Dollar, you know."

"It wasn't?"

"Haven't you noticed Taliaferro lately? He has got that pistolero from the French Palace tied on his heels like a shadow."

Clay nodded almost imperceptibly. "Did you shoot that dealer of his, Morg?"

"You mean Wax? That beat my Professor's head in for him?"

Clay picked up his hat and held it in his lap while he dented the crown with blows from the heel of his hand, crosswise and then back to front, continuing it with a kind of abstracted attention as though there were nothing else in the world to do. But at last he said, without looking up, "I have never asked you a thing like this before."

"Like what?"

"Leave it alone about Taliaferro."

"All right."

"For a favor," Clay said. He got to his feet and put his hat on. He held the paper in his hand, and glanced toward the others on the bureau. "That's a silly thing," he said. "For me to be putting those up against myself. Do you know anybody you can get to do it?"

"I'll get Basine."

"Might as well get it over with," Clay said. He moved toward the door.

"For a favor?"

Clay stopped. "Don't go sour, Morg. This is nothing between you and me. I thought you would understand that."

"Why, I suppose I do," he said. He went to the bureau and took up the whisky bottle again. Standing with his back to Clay he poured whisky into his glass in a slow trickle until he heard the door close and Clay's footsteps departing.

He stepped to the window then, and, in the darkness, watched the tall figure appear below him. He raised his glass and whispered, "How?" and drank deeply. "Why, Clay, I understand well enough," he said. "But I won't let you do it. Or McQuown."

Abruptly he sat down on the edge of the bed. "Why, you damned sanctimonious school marm virgin bitch!" he said, to Miss Jessie Marlow. It was time he had a talk with her, and he addressed himself to her and to the whisky in his glass.

You, he said; *you* put Curley Burne on that list to crucify him, and I suppose you would let him stand alone against that pack of cowboys because he would look so fine? Don't you know that McQuown has been sitting down there as patient and tricky as a hostile waiting for the right time to move? You handed him Curley Burne to move on.

"How you must *hate* yourself, Miss Jessie Marlow," he mimicked, aloud. "Do you think they will curl up and die at the sight of him because he is so fine? *He* would curl up and die, they would blast him loose from his boots, backshot, sideshot, and frontshot too.

"Well, you saved my life, and with damned bad grace. And you wish I was gone, don't you, and you have told him so, haven't you? Are you satisfied with what are making of him? You have got him so he doesn't know himself any more. And I am the ugly toad whose life you saved because there wasn't any way you could get out of it, and I will save his from McQuown. I suppose it would turn you to screaming to think of me doing it, and how, wouldn't it? But what do you say, Miss Jessie Marlow?"

He laughed at her horrified face in his mind's eye.

But damn you to hell, can you let him be, afterward? Can you ever let him be? You will have him alive. "Can you let him deal faro in a saloon?" he said aloud, mimicking her scorn again. Let be, Miss Jessie Marlow, before you have killed him dead trying to make him into a damned marble statue!

43. Journals of Henry Holmes Goodpasture

April 17, 1881

WE HAVE returned this night to a Warlock seething with surmise. Posters appeared mysteriously this morning in several places about the town—one of them upon my wall!—to the effect that Blaisedell is condemned to death for foul murder, his victims listed as Curley Burne and Billy Gannon, and the posters signed by Abraham Mc-Quown as Chief of Regulators!

I did not see any of these, for they have been torn down, but there are tack holes in the adobe to the right of my door, and Kennon says he saw the one upon the Feed and Grain Barn. Dechine, a small rancher and neighbor of McQuown's, was seen in town last night, and it is presumed that he was the one who affixed the posters. It is not known who tore them down, possibly they were merely wanted for keepsakes; it is variously rumored, though, that either Morgan is responsible for their disappearance, or the lamed miner who works for Miss Jessie, or Blaisedell himself.

The name of McQuown, springing to everyone's lips again, is like the reappearance of a ghost long thought laid. Many think it is all only a practical joke, perpetrated by some townsmen, but for most of us the phrase "Chief of Regulators" rings most ominously. If it is a joke, it is a cruel one; it strikes too close to our fears, the names of Billy Gannon and Curley Burne are too aptly chosen.

There has been talk of nothing else since we returned early this evening. The town is crowded; somehow news of this nature is disseminated instantaneously throughout the valley. We, the delegation, returned full of defense and explanation of our defeat in Bright's City; what happened to us there is of no interest to anyone.

The feeling among the more intelligent here is that these posters are probably more than a joke, but less than an open declaration of war—that it may be a gambit, a bluff, a theatrical gesture of righteousness. They have certainly done their work in arousing and confirming suspicions over the Curley Burne tragedy. The seeds they may have been intended to broadcast have fallen on rich soil. On the other hand can McQuown afford to make such a bluff if it is to be an empty one? Or is this an attempt to rouse Warlock against Blaisedell so that we ourselves will run him out, thus saving McQuown the trouble and the danger? If so, McQuown has woefully misjudged our tempers.

The miners, I understand, feel this is some trick of MacDonald's, since MacDonald was the proprietor of the original Regulators. They feel that McQuown may have been won over by MacDonald, but that they, the Medusa strikers, are the actual quarry, and Blaisedell only a ruse.

The town seethes with argument, speculation, and fearful expectation. Yet many in Warlock are eager for a showdown, and, in their minds, this can only satisfactorily be a street duel between Blaisedell and McQuown. McQuown would surely not be such a fool (ah, but I said this of Curley Burne!), and yet McQuown may feel he has some moral advantage now.

There will be a Citizens' Committee meeting in the morning.

44. The New Sign

PIKE SKINNER swung into the jail doorway and stopped there, with his red face set into a scowl. Inside, Peter Bacon sat at the table spooning juice from a can of peaches into his mouth, and Tim French sat beside the cell door, just outside the circle of light cast by the lamp. A flat, square, newspaper-wrapped package leaned against the wall.

"Gannon back yet?" Skinner demanded.

"Come and gone," French said.

"I am deputying tonight," Bacon said, wiping his mouth with his shirt sleeve. "But I don't want to hear about any trouble. I am just what you might say sitting here so nobody can look in and see nobody's sitting here."

"Where the hell'd he go now?"

"Pablo," French said.

"Threw us again, did he?" Skinner cried. "Gone down there so's he can come in with those Regulators—"

"Hold on!" French said.

"You get down on a man he can't do nothing right, can he?" Bacon said. "He went down there to stop them from coming in here."

"He told you that, did he?"

"Did," Bacon said.

"You believed it, huh?"

"Did."

"There was a time before I didn't believe him," French said. "But it looks like I was wrong about it."

"I still say he was lying in his damned teeth!" Skinner said.

Bacon shrugged. "Well, anyway, I told him I'd sit it out till he got back. Or till somebody brought his poor, shot-up, hacked-on, chewed-to-pieces corpse back to bury."

"How's he think he's going to stop them?" Skinner sneered.

"Didn't say. He come in blown from riding it down from Bright's, and when he heard the news he just said he'd better go stop them, and borrowed Tim's mare and went." Bacon began spooning peach juice into his mouth again.

Skinner kicked the door jamb. "Buck and them just got back from Bright's," he said. "Buck said Johnny got Keller to half-believing what Carl was supposed to've told him."

"Some do," Bacon said.

"God damn it, Pete; I thought Carl was a friend of yours! God damn it, it played right to McQuown, didn't it?"

"That don't make it not so, Pike," French said.

Skinner shook his head and said, "You mean to say Gannon went down there all by *himself* to tell them not to come in here?"

"Bound to go he was bound to go by himself, I guess," Bacon said. He looked at Skinner with his pale eyes.

"Catch *me* going down there," Skinner said. He glanced almost furtively down the wall to where the names were scratched in the whitewash. "What's that wrapped up there?"

"New sign Keller gave him," Bacon said. He stared down into the empty can. "Would've pleased Carl."

Skinner went over to where the package leaned, picked it up, and stripped off the string and newspaper. The sign was square, with black letters on a white ground within a black border:

WARLOCK JAIL
DEPUTY SHERIFF

Skinner turned it over; it was the same on the reverse. "Nice piece of work," he said. "The old one's got so you can't hardly make it out any more."

"Looks like we might hang it for Johnny tomorrow," French said. "While we're waiting."

Skinner set the sign back where it had been. "I see Gannon got his name scratched on the wall there," he said, straightening and turning away.

"He's deputy," French said. "Deputies get to set their names down there. Why shouldn't he?"

"I just noticed he had it down there, was all."

"You had better quit looking at them names there, Pike," Bacon said, not quite humorously. "Or they will reach out and grab you one of these times."

45. Gannon Visits San Pablo

GANNON counted the horses as he reined up before the ranch house—
ten, eleven, twelve of them. Light shone out on the glossy sweep of
manes and rolling eyewhites. The dogs began to bark down by the
horse corral.

In the lamplit windows he could see the shadows of the men. He
heard the sour, thin chording of a guitar. A voice was raised in
drunken song, and was lost in laughter.

He dismounted slowly, leaden with fatigue. He tethered Tim's mare
to the rail with the others, sighed, hitched on his shell belt, and started
up the steps. On the porch he paused to wipe the palms of his hands
on his jeans; then with anxious haste he knocked on the door. It swung
inward under the pressure of his knuckles, and the voices died. The
guitar chorded on for a moment longer; then it too ceased, in a strum
of strings.

The faces were all turned toward him, pale and oily-looking in the
lamplight. Abe was leaning on the pot-belly stove with his hand gripped
around the neck of the whisky jug. Old man McQuown lay on his
pallet on the floor. Chet Haggin was slumped, spread-legged, on the
buggy-seat sofa beside Joe Lacey, and Wash sat on the floor before
them with a crockery cup in his hand. Beyond Abe were Pecos Mitchell, hunched over the guitar, Quint Whitby, with his fat face and
cavalry mustaches, the breed Marko cleaning his nails with a knife,
Walt Harrison, Ed Greer, Jock Hennessey, and five or six others
he did not know—all staring at him. Standing behind Chet was Jack
Cade, his round-crowned, leather-banded hat pulled low upon his
forehead, his prune of a mouth bent into a disagreeable smile.

"Why, it's Bud Gannon come back to San Pablo," Abe said, and
put the whisky jug down.

"Bud," Joe Lacey said. No one else spoke. Mitchell began to strum
the guitar again, humming to himself and watching Gannon with an
eyebrow cocked in his smallpox-pitted face. The old man hunched
himself up on his pallet.

"Well, come on in, Bud," Abe said. "Don't stand there acting like you mightn't be welcome." He wore a buckskin shirt that reached below his hips and was belted with a concho belt from which hung his knife, in a silver-chased scabbard. He looked drunk, but bright-eyed, keen, young—Abe looked as he had when he had first known him.

"Blaisedell run him out!" the old man said suddenly.

Gannon shook his head. He met Jack Cade's eyes and nodded. He nodded to the others. "Joe," he said. "Chet. Wash. Pecos. Quint. Dad McQuown." He knew them better than he knew anyone in Warlock, he thought; he had known them to get drunk with, work with, rustle with, play cards with. He had fought and whipped Walt Harrison, fought and been whipped by Whitby, had had for his special friends Chet and Wash Haggin, for his enemy Jack Cade; with his brother Billy, and perhaps with all of them, he had hero-worshiped Curley Burne and held Abe McQuown in awe. With all of these except the new ones he did not know, he had killed Mexicans in Rattlesnake Canyon.

Now, he knew, every one of them was contemptuous of him, and more than Jack Cade hated him.

"Where is that big old shotgun, Bud?" Wash said, and laughed.

"Where's Billy, Bud?" someone said, behind him.

Dad McQuown said, "It is kind of bad manners coming in here with that star hanging on you, Bud Gannon."

"Whisky, Bud?" Abe said.

"Thanks," he said, and shook his head.

"Didn't come to drink? Nor talk either? Just come to stand there tongue-tied?"

Mitchell strummed on the guitar, and Joe Lacey glanced at it and then significantly back at Gannon. "Always favored a mouth organ myself," he said. Jack Cade folded his arms and grinned, and Abe grinned too, his teeth showing in his red beard.

"Nothing to say, Bud?"

"Are these your Regulators?"

Abe nodded curtly. "Regulators."

"You are all coming into Warlock?"

"Planned to," Abe said. He raised an eyebrow. "Why? Any objection, Deputy?"

Gannon nodded, and watched the color rise in Abe's cheeks.

"Why, you pissant son of a bitch!" Cade cried.

"Rip that star off him, boys!" the old man said.

"Are we posted out already, Bud?" Wash said, in a mock whining voice. Cade continued to curse.

"If there's names to be called I'll call them," Abe said, and Cade stopped. "Objection, Bud?" he said, grinning again. "Are we posted?"

"Nobody's posted. But no wild bunch calling themselves Regulators is coming in to make trouble, Abe. Not so long as I've got power to deputize every man in Warlock against them."

"That's the way it is?" Abe said, in a level voice. "That way, Bud?"

Gannon nodded, and there was a rising muttering around him.

"But I can come alone, you mean?" Abe said. "Surely, that would be fine, with Blaisedell and Morgan and half a dozen other gun-slinging pimps to burn me down. No; not likely. I am coming in with some friends to back my play, is all. Like he has got them to back his." Abe rubbed a hand over his bearded chin. "I am going to kill him for murdering your brother, Bud," he said, more quietly. "And kill him for murdering Curley down." His voice began to shake. "What the hell do you mean?" he cried. "Coming down on my place and telling me I'm not to go in there?"

Gannon stood very stiffly facing Abe McQuown, and said, "I say you are not to come, Abe."

"You damned snot pup!" the old man yelled.

"Run and hide, Abe," Whitby said. "Look out! Bud is getting mad!"

"You know the trouble with you, Bud?" Abe said easily. "You are so yellow of him you can't bear it for everybody not to be yellow of him too. It makes you look too bad if they aren't. Shot down Billy and all you did was lick his boots for him. Shot down Curley," he said, his voice rising. "After you had swore Curley didn't go to kill Carl. And what'd you do, that'd sworn to it? Licked his boots some more. You are a fine deputy."

Abe took a step toward him. "A whole town-full of them like you. Your hats shy off in the wind when he blows a breath. You can't call yourself men so you can't let anybody else be one either. But there won't be a *man* left anywhere unless somebody kills that black foul devil out of hell! You damned—"

"You are not bringing a bunch of Regulators into Warlock, Abe," he said, raising his voice over Abe's. "I came down to warn you I will have to deputize every man jack in Warlock against you."

"You have sure turned hard against us, Bud," Chet Haggin said.

"I'm deputy, Chet. There's things I'm bound to do."

"For Blaisedell," Chet said.

He shook his head.

"Yeah, for Blaisedell!" Wash Haggin cried, and everyone began to talk at once until Abe shouted angrily for quiet.

But Chet went on. "Just one more thing I want to ask him, Abe. Bud, you think Blaisedell isn't going to choose us out and cut us down one by one unless we go in there against him all together?"

"He's got nothing against you. That'd be a thing I'd be bound to stop too, I expect."

Chet grinned contemptuously and Wash shouted with laughter. They all laughed.

Abe leaned his hands on his concho belt and tilted back on his heels. "Like you stopped him from cutting Curley down, Deputy?"

Gannon felt himself flush painfully. "It was a fair fight, Abe. But you don't mean to fight him fair. You are going in to—"

"Why, you are a liar," Abe broke in. "Fair fight."

"There will be no fight. You are not to bring these people in."

"Be damned to you!" Walt Harrison said.

"Stop us, Bud!" Whitby said.

"I will stop you."

"Let me talk to him a minute, Abe," Jack Cade said, in his grating voice. Cade came forward toward Gannon, his thumbs in his shell belt. Gannon stared back into his hard eyes.

"*You*," Cade said, and paused for a long time. His dirty teeth scraped on his lower lip. "You are," he said, "a yellow-belly suck-up." He grinned and hitched at his belt. "You are a *pure* yellow, pissant, chicken-livered, coyote-bred, no-*cojones* son of a bitch. I say that's what you are. I say—"

Gannon stood listening to the level, grating voice taunting him, mouthing increasing foulness. He was not especially frightened of being forced into a fight, for he did not think it was Abe's wish. He hardly heard the words, for they did not matter to him, but he realized that they would have to be stopped because where the law was merely a man there had to be some respect for that man or the law did not exist and so his journey down here had been worse than useless. He glanced from face to face around him and his heart sank to see them not merely contemptuous, but pleased and crudely eager. Only Wash Haggin looked a little ashamed, and Joe Lacey embarrassed. Chet had turned his face away. Abe was grinning faintly, watching out of the corners of his eyes.

The vile words droned on, without meaning. He unhooked the star from his jacket, and reached over to hand it to Chet Haggin. "Hold it," he said. "I don't want him to be able to say he killed another deputy."

"I'll say it!" Cade said, triumphantly. "Outside, Deputy!"

"Here," Gannon said. "So it will be a fair fight." He untied the bandanna from around his neck, and rapidly fixed a knot in either end. "You count for us," he said to Chet. "We will draw on three." He bit down on one knotted end of the bandanna, and held the other out; he saw immediately that Cade would not do it.

"I'm no God-damned fool for a handkerchief fight!" Cade said hoarsely.

It was enough, Gannon thought, and quickly he stuffed the bandanna into his pocket and took his star back. No one spoke.

It had meant nothing, and yet he hoped he had recovered something in their eyes. But he knew that Abe saw his bluff and the necessity for it, and with dread he realized that in backing Cade down he had challenged Abe himself. Now he wondered if Abe was sure enough of his own authority to let his recovery stand."

"Man doesn't have to be a damned fool!" Cade said. "Come on outside and fight decent!"

"Pure iron," Abe said. "Why, a man with iron in him like that deserves a medal." He swung toward the breed. "Where's the medal, Marko?" The breed looked confused. Abe made a gesture toward his mouth and Marko produced something from his pocket. Abe took it, and, with a swift movement, plucked off Gannon's hat and dropped a cord around his neck. From it was suspended a mouth organ. "Curley won't be needing this any more," Abe said loudly. "How is that for a medal for Bud, boys?"

He recognized the release of tension in their laughter; what had passed between him and Jack Cade was set at nothing and he was a fool to them again as well as a traitor. He stripped the cord from around his neck and handed the mouth organ back to Abe, and took his hat back. "I think you'd better have it," he said, and saw Abe's eyes narrow dangerously.

"I'll be going," he said. "Abe, you have heard me about the Regulators. That's the word with the bark on it." It gave him a start to hear Carl's phrase on his own lips.

"Abe!" the old man cried. "Are you going to let the son of a bitch walk out like that?"

"Just a minute," Abe said. The others leaned forward, attentive and expectant. They were all afraid, Gannon thought suddenly. Maybe they felt, as Chet had said, that Blaisedell would destroy them one by one if they did not destroy him.

"What right have you to stop us?" Abe said quietly. "When you didn't stop Blaisedell from killing Curley? Tell me that, Bud. How are you going to tell me I can't post Blaisedell and kill him if he don't run, when you didn't stop him with Curley? That was my friend," he said, more quietly still.

"Mine too, by God!" Wash said.

"He ought to be shot down on Billy's grave, what he ought," Dad McQuown said. "Billy was a fine boy, and him nothing."

"I am talking about Curley," Abe said. He waited, his face a bearded, furrowed mask, his eyes hooded. Then he said, "You ought to be riding in with us, Bud."

He shook his head.

"But you swore to it, didn't you?" Abe went on. "You swore Carl told you he'd done it himself, didn't you? Or did you crawfish on that?"

"Not yet," he said, and instantly he knew that what he had meant as only a passing threat was too much more than that. He heard the whistling suck of Abe's breath, and saw Abe's right eye widen while his left remained a slit.

"What do you think you mean by that?" Abe whispered.

He didn't answer right away. But he had not, he thought, come here merely so he could get away without trouble. He had come to tell them they must not come into Warlock as Regulators. He said tiredly, "There is going to be peace and law in Warlock, Abe. Or there is going to be Blaisedell. If you will let be, he will go. He knows he has to go now, for he has been wrong."

"Let him go, then."

"You will have to let be for him to go. And I will see that you let him be, and Warlock will. I have more ways than deputizing people for stopping you."

"I am sure scared of that pack of fat-butt bank clerks he is going to round up in there," Whitby said. "Whoooo! I—"

"Shut up!" Abe snapped. He stared at Gannon with his head tipped forward so that his beard brushed his chest, and his green eyes were wild. "What other ways, Bud?"

"I would crawfish to stop you."

"What the hell are you talking about?" the old man said. "I can't make out what—"

"Shut up!" Abe put a hand on top of the stove and leaned on it heavily. "Damn your dirty soul to hell!" he cried. "God damn you, coming down here mealy-mouthing what you are bound to do. I will tell you what you are bound to do! You damned lick-spittle, you will swear here and now to what Carl said to you and what is true!" Abe took a step toward him. "Swear it, damn you!"

"I guess I'll not—" he started, and tried to dodge as Abe's hand swung up against his cheek. He staggered sideways with the blow; his cheek burned maddeningly, and his eyes watered. He heard a murmur of approval from the others, whom, for a moment, he could not see.

"Swear it! You will swear to the truth or I'll kill you!"

He shook his head; he saw the buckskin arm swing again. He did not dodge this time, but only jerked his head back to try to soften the blow. There was pain and the taste of blood in his mouth.

"Hit him all night," the old man said.

"Cut him, Abe!"

"Say it!" Abe said.

He shook his head, and swallowed salt blood.

"*Say it!*"

The fist he hadn't even seen coming this time exploded in his face once more, and he stumbled back in a wild shouting with the room spinning around him. Abruptly the shouting stopped as he caught his balance, and felt in his hand, with horror, the hard rounded shape of the Colt he had drawn. In his clearing eyes he saw Abe McQuown twisted slightly with his right fist down in the uncompleted recovery of the blow. Abe straightened slowly, his chest heaving in the buckskin shirt as he panted, his left hand massaging the knuckles of the right, his eyes glancing from the Colt to Gannon's face. A grin made sharp indentations in his beard.

Gannon spat blood. The Colt felt unsupportably heavy in his hand. Abe grinned more widely. "Uh-uh, Bud," he said, and came a step forward. He came another; his moccasins lisped upon the floor. "Uh-uh, Bud."

Abe's hand snapped down over his hand as sharp and tight as a talon, and wrenched the Colt away. Abe flung it to the floor behind him, and laughed. Abe swung his arm again.

He hunched his shoulder up to catch the blow. He brought his right hand up to catch the next on his forearm. With a sudden wild elation he swung back, and his fist met hair and bone. Abe staggered back and he jumped in pursuit.

A foot tripped him. He fell heavily past Abe, who dodged aside. A fist slammed against his back as he caught himself on his hands and tried to scramble up. He cried out in pain as a boot smashed into his ribs, and fell back again. Beneath him he felt the hard shape of his Colt where Abe had dropped it.

He fumbled it free with his left hand, still trying to rise with his right hand braced on the table beside the buggy seat, dodging aside as Whitby aimed another kick at him, and the men on the buggy seat leaped out of the way. Then he had the Colt free and he swung it desperately to cover Cade, who had drawn. He saw only the long flash of the knife blade in the lamplight.

He screamed, frozen half up, with his right hand pinned to the table top by a white-hot shaft.

Whitby kicked the Colt from his left hand.

"Get up!" Abe panted.

He struggled to stand, with his shoulder cocked down so that his hand lay flat upon the table. He could hardly see for the sweat pouring into his eyes. Abe was leaning on the shaft of the knife with both hands, not forcing it down but merely holding it there. "Move and I'll cut it off, Bud," he said.

He didn't move.

"Geld him, son," the old man said calmly.

Now his hand merely felt numb and the faintness began to leave him. Leaning on the knife still, Abe disengaged his right hand, and, with a careful, measured movement, slapped him, not hard.

"Don't move, Bud," Abe said, grinning. The hand slapped his cheek harder. It came again and again, each time harder. The faintness bore down on him again as the knife edge tore his flesh. He felt only the sensation of tearing, rather than the pain. "Don't move, Bud," Abe warned, and slapped him. The faintness began to crush him.

"Swear it for us, Bud!"

He shook his head. He could feel the blood beneath his hand now, so that it seemed glued to the table as well as nailed there. "Swear it, damn you to hell!" Abe cried, and there was hysteria in his voice.

"Lever that handle a little, son. Let's hear him squeak."

"This isn't doing any good, for Christ's sake, Abe!" Chet Haggin said.

"Let me take that knife to him!" Cade said.

Abe pressed downward on the handle, and Gannon closed his eyes. The pressure ceased and he opened them. He could see the shine of spittle at the corners of the mouth in the red beard. He gazed around at the others, dimly pleased that he could stare each one of them down.

"Hold off, Abe!" Chet said.

"Swear it, Bud!" Abe whispered. "Or I swear to God I will cut your hand off! I'll kill you!"

"You had better kill me if you want to take your Regulators into Warlock," he said. "For I will stop you otherwise."

It was a way out if Abe wanted to take it, and he knew Abe did. Abe turned his face in profile, his long jaw set wolfishly and sweat showing on his cheeks. He looked pale. Wash said quickly, "I would surely like to see him trying to stop us!"

"I'd like to see that," Walt Harrison said.

Abe jerked the knife free, and he gasped as the air got into the wound like another knife. He left his hand on the table to support himself now, as he watched Abe wipe the knife blade on his trouser leg. The old man was muttering.

"Get that neckerchief out and bind that hand up," Chet said roughly. "There may be some that like the stink of blood, but damned if I do."

"Kind of surprised to see he's got any in him," Whitby said.

Gannon fumbled the cloth from his pocket and tried to bind it around his bleeding hand. Joe Lacey came forward to help him, pulling the bandage tight and tying the ends together.

"Stop us then," Abe said, in a cold voice. "We'll be in tomorrow."

"He'll just ride back and warn Blaisedell out of town, God damn it, son!" Dad McQuown cried. "I say kill him or hold him down here!"

"Let me settle my account with him, Abe," Cade said.

McQuown grinned mockingly. "Well, move along, Bud. Before my mind gets changed."

Gannon looked around for his Colt. "Give it to him," Abe said. "He can't do anything with it."

Walt Harrison handed him the Colt. He took it with his wounded hand. It slipped through his fingers and he caught it by slapping it against his leg. Awkwardly he slid it into his holster. Whitby thrust his hat on his head. He walked slowly through them toward the door. There he turned. Abe was still standing at the table, jabbing the point of his knife into the wood with a kind of listless viciousness.

"I've warned you," Gannon said. "You are not to come into Warlock like you are set to do." This time no one laughed.

He went outside into the buzzing darkness. Carefully he descended the steps. A dog began to bark, and the others joined in a chorus. They would be locked up, he remembered; they always were when men were coming and going at night.

In the saddle he sat motionless for a time, his eyes closed, his left hand clutching the pommel. One by one, gingerly, he sought to move the fingers of his right hand; his little finger, ring finger, middle finger, trigger finger. He sighed with relief when he realized that nothing had been severed, and swung the reins. Gripping the pommel, sitting stiff, heavy, and unsteady in the saddle, he touched in his spurs and whispered, "Let's go home, girl."

The mare mounted the first ridge in the pale moonlight, went down the draw, up the second ridge—he didn't look back. A falling star crossed the far flank of the sky, fading, as it fell, to nothing. There was a cold wind. He shivered in it, but drew himself up straighter, released his grip on the pommel, and raised a hand to set his hat on straight. Lowering his hand, he brushed his thumb past the star pinned to his jacket, as though to reassure himself he had not lost it.

He felt a fury that was pain like a tooth beginning to ache. He said aloud, "I am the law!" The fury mounted in him. They had insulted him, cursed him, threatened him. They had beaten and stabbed him, and deliberated his death. They had presumed to judge him, and, finally, to release him in contempt of his warning. The fury filled him cleanly, at their presumption and their ignorance.

But how would they know differently? They had never known differently. He had tried to show them courage to make them see. Once, at least, they had known courage and had respected it. Maybe they would simply not respect it in him, or maybe they knew it no longer, knew now only fear and hate and violence. The clean fury drained from him; he had been able to show them nothing. And now he could almost pity Abe McQuown, remembering the desperation he had seen in Abe's eyes as he leaned upon the knife, Abe fighting and torturing for the Right as though it were something that could be taken by force. For Right had been embodied in Curley's death, and perhaps Blaisedell was as desperate in his way for Right as McQuown was. But he knew that Blaisedell would not cold-bloodedly kill for it, would not plot to take it by trick or treachery—not yet.

He had been riding for an hour or so in the heavier darkness under the cottonwoods along the river when he heard the shot. It was a faint, flat, far-off sound, but unmistakable. There was a silence then in which even the liquid rattle of the river seemed stilled, and then a ragged volley of shots. After another pause there were two more, and, after them, silence again.

He rode looking back over his shoulder. He could see nothing, hear nothing but the riffling of the river and the wind in the trees, the steady pad of the mare's hoofs with the occasional crack of shoes against a rock outcrop. Finally he settled himself in the saddle again and into the weary rhythm of the ride back to Warlock, dozing, snapping awake, and dozing again.

Much later he thought he heard, off to the east, the clatter of fast-moving hoofs, but, coming awake with that unpleasant, harsh grasping at consciousness, he could not be sure. Awake, he did not hear it, and he thought the sound must have been only something he had dreamed.

46. Journals of Henry Holmes Goodpasture

April 18, 1881

In view of the importance of this morning's Citizens' Committee meeting, I will set down what happened there in some detail.

One of Blaikie's hands arrived last night with the information that a great number of San Pabloites were gathered at the McQuown ranch, and, with this proof of McQuown's intentions, all the members of the Citizens' Committee with whom I spoke prior to the meeting were resigned to the conclusion that we were forced to undertake the formation of a Vigilance Committee at last. Obviously Blaisedell could not be expected to face alone this force of Regulators patently assembled to bring about his destruction, or his flight. The parallel with poor Canning's fate was all too clear, and we would not be shamed again. Some were eager for war, and some were frightened, but almost all seemed firm in their resolve to back Blaisedell to the hilt.

The meeting was at the bank. All but Taliaferro attended: Dr. Wagner, Slavin, Skinner, Judge Holloway, Hart, Winters, MacDonald, Godbold, Pugh, Rolfe, Petrix, Kennon, Brown, Robinson, Egan, Swartze, Miss Jessie Marlow, and myself. And Clay Blaisedell, not a member, but our instrument.

The Marshal has not been looking well lately. Yet he seemed himself again in Petrix's bank, as though he had recovered from an illness, and he had an air of ease and confidence about him that reassured us all. He did not, however, join us at the table—usually he sits to the right of Miss Jessie when she attends—but remained standing outside the counter while Petrix brought the meeting to order.

Jed Rolfe stated the premise: that we had, many times in the past, rejected the idea of a Vigilance Committee, but now, in his opinion, it was unavoidable.

Pike Skinner moved that a Vigilance Committee be established, he was seconded by Kennon, and the meeting was thrown open to discussion.

The doctor rose to state that it was obvious that the true mission of the Regulators was to punish, murder, or drive from Warlock the leaders of the Medusa strike; this had been their original purpose and was still their purpose, although now they saw that the Marshal would have to be disposed of before they could accomplish it, since he would most certainly stand in their way. MacDonald replied that the Regulators had been originally engaged to defend mine property, but that they were no longer in his employ, that he had no understanding with them whatsoever, nor did he hold patent to the title of Regulators. MacDonald then claimed, in his turn, that the doctor was responsible for a miners' conspiracy against him, MacDonald, and was responsible for an outrageous and threatening set of terms upon which, a delegation of strikers had informed him, they would end the strike.

The doctor responded to this violently, and it was with some difficulty that Petrix restored order. Blaisedell was asked if he wished to speak, but he replied that he would rather hear us out before he expressed his own sentiments.

Will Hart obtained the floor and said with great seriousness that he knew what he was about to say would be unpopular, but that he must, in all honesty, speak out. He felt, he said, that it was the duty of the Citizens' Committee to prevent bloodshed and not to form Vigilante Committees. The whole system of posting had, in his opinion, proved a failure, and had only led to the bloodshed it had been intended to prevent. He felt strongly that a battle with the Regulators should be avoided if it was humanly possible. This could be accomplished, although he was sorry to be the one to suggest such a thing, by Blaisedell quitting Warlock. The Regulators could then be sent word of this, and they would be deprived of their purpose, which now they could endow with a certain degree of righteousness.

He was afraid, he went on rather nervously, that this might be interpreted as cowardice on Blaisedell's part. He, of course, knew that Blaisedell had no fear of McQuown—quite the opposite. As for himself, he would regard it as a much greater, and nobler, courage upon Blaisedell's part were he to go and leave us in peace.

There was an instantaneous and outraged protest to this on every side. Miss Jessie cried out that Will wanted to drive Blaisedell out, and berated him with a violence that embarrassed us all. "After what he has done for Warlock!" she cried. "For everyone here! When all of us used to be afraid of being murdered on the street by a drunken Cowboy, and you speak of his leaving us in peace!" and so forth. She was out of order, but Petrix, usually the strictest of parliamentarians, was too dumbfounded to call her to order. She desisted only when Blaisedell called her name, and the doctor spoke quietly to her.

Jared Robinson stated loudly that he considered Will Hart's idea a bad one and in bad taste, and that the rest of us apologized to Blaisedell for it. If Blaisedell departed, he said, Warlock would be thrown into chaos again, McQuown would be in the saddle, and any here who had been friendly with Blaisedell—and especially we of the Citizens' Committee—would be in deadly danger. Succeeding speakers agreed with, and expanded upon, this, until MacDonald reiterated his former statement within this context: that chaos had already descended upon us, and had done so as soon as Blaisedell had permitted the miners to overrun him at the jail, in the attempt to lynch Morgan.

Miss Jessie promptly called him a liar, to which rebuke MacDonald knew better than to retort, although he was plainly infuriated by it. The doctor then said, with what was obviously a stern attempt to control his temper, that it took considerably more of a man to let himself be overrun by momentarily crazed (and with good reason, he added) creatures, than to fire among them as MacDonald no doubt would have preferred. But, he pointed out, Blaisedell, at the time of the attempt on Morgan's life, had not been in our employ with the status of Marshal, and in any case, his object, which had been to save Morgan from a lynching rather than to preserve his own dignity, had been accomplished.

Judge Holloway, who had been sitting in a gloomy and alcoholic trance, now seemed to have accumulated enough strength to deliver one of his harangues. He rose, was recognized, and beat his crutch upon the floor for silence. He clung to the edge of the table, as fierce of mien (and as noisome of breath) as a vulture, and glared about him. He can be awesome enough, even when falling down drunk. He called us fools and said there was a man to deal with the present situation and it was not Blaisedell. There was a sheriff's deputy in Warlock to uphold the law. There were, he said, always bloodthirsty fools to cry for a Vigilance Committee or a hired Vigilante, but Deputy Gannon was the one to deal with the Regulators.

His voice was drowned in a sudden burst of speculation as to Gannon's whereabouts, and condemnation of him. Some thought him fled, some still in Bright's City (as I did), others claimed he had gone to join McQuown's forces. Pike Skinner informed us that Gannon had indeed gone to San Pablo, but with the announced intention of warning McQuown that he was not to come into Warlock; at which there were hoots of disbelief.

When order was restored, the Judge reiterated that the situation was the Deputy's responsibility. Then, as is his custom, he began to rack us for our sins and presumptions. He accused us of inciting Blaisedell to the murder of an innocent man—to our considerable discomfiture, with Blaisedell present; he called us fools and mortal fools, idiots and monstrous idiots. He shouted down, in his wrath, all interruptions, and was, in short, magnificent in his fashion. I think I might have applauded him had not what he was saying been so painful.

He said to us, more temperately, that if we had not been blind we might have seen that we had almost had a man in Carl Schroeder, and that we unmistakably had one now, in Gannon. He expounded with painful sarcasm the complete illegality of Blaisedell's position as Marshal, a point all too sore with the Citizens' Committee. Not one of us had the temerity even to glance Blaisedell's way while this diatribe continued, but at last Miss Jessie jumped to her feet and cried that he was no more a real Judge than Blaisedell was a real Marshal, and that he was a hypocrite to speak as he had.

The Judge replied that he was well aware of the fact that he was a hypocrite, and that he considered himself something worse than that for even belonging to the Citizens' Committee. He added, "But I do not presume to send men to hang, Miss Jessie Marlow."

Then, as Miss Jessie started to speak again, he gave her an awkward but courtly bow and said he refused to listen to her, for she was a special pleader, as everyone knew; and, finally, with the look of a man who has collected his courage to approach a rattlesnake, he turned to Blaisedell himself.

The Judge addressed Blaisedell deferentially at first, saying he had intended nothing personal by his remarks, and that his criticism was not so much of Blaisedell as of all of us. Soon, however, he recovered his hectoring style, and he raised his voice, lifted his crutch and shook it, and cried that Blaisedell was a crutch like the one he held, had been useful, and we should be grateful to him. But it was only an idiot who continued to use a crutch when the limb had grown whole. Including us all in his glare, he informed us that we no longer needed the crutch of an illegal gunman, that we had better begin properly using the law or it would wither away, and now we had a man to uphold the law, who was the deputy.

Petrix asked Blaisedell, who had been showing signs of wishing to speak, if he desired the floor. Blaisedell replied that he would like to answer some of the things the Judge had had to say. As he spoke I saw Miss Jessie watching him with her great eyes, tugging a little handkerchief between her hands, and if ever I saw a woman's heart in her eyes I saw it then.

Blaisedell's face was very stern as he proceeded upon a track that surprised us. He said that he thought it would be a shame to put too much on the Deputy too soon. He said a new horse should not be racked too hard. "You will bust him to running, or kill him, putting too much on him," he said, to the Judge. And he said, "He has stood up to every man here calling him a liar when he was not, but I don't think he is able yet to stand off a wild bunch from San Pablo."

He went on in this vein. But after we had grasped the fact that he believed that Gannon had not lied, and seemed to favor him—even though he did not feel he was qualified to stop McQuown yet—our comprehension of what he was saying ceased and we stared at him in confusion. I saw Buck Slavin's jaw hanging open like that of a dull-witted boy, and Pike Skinner's face grow fiery red. Miss Jessie had put her handkerchief to her mouth, and her eyes were round as dollars.

"Gentlemen," Blaisedell said. "I have done some service here and I think you know it. But I think a good many of you are beginning to wish I would move along, and not just Mr. Hart." He smiled a little then. "I had better, before you all start thinking of me like the Judge here does."

Skinner and Sam Brown protested emotionally, as did Buck, but Blaisedell only smiled and went on to thank the Citizens' Committee for having paid him well, and backed him as well as he could have wished. "But," he said, "there is value in knowing when to move on. For the Judge is right in more ways than one, though I have argued with him and got as mad at him as the rest of you do."

Blaisedell said, however, that he had one thing which he would ask of us. "I will ask you to let me handle McQuown and his Regulators my own way." He said this in such a way that it was clearly a command for us to stay out of his affair. "It is my job," he went on. "And he is coming after me, so it is my job two ways. If there are going to be Vigilantes I'll ask that they stay out of it unless *I* go down." He looked straight at MacDonald and said, "For I have been known to go down."

There was a general gasp as it was realized that Blaisedell meant to stand alone, or perhaps only with Morgan, against the San Pabloites. A storm of exclamations and protests broke out, to which Blaisedell did not even attempt to reply, while Petrix exercised his gavel violently.

It was at this moment that Gannon made his entrance. He was freshly shaven, his hair neatly combed, but his upper lip was bruised and swollen and his face was drawn with exhaustion. I noticed that his right hand was bound up in a white cloth. He said, in a truculent tone, that there would be no Vigilantes in Warlock.

We were all as shocked at the arrogance of his first words as we had been at the implication of Blaisedell's last ones. I had the impression, however, that Gannon had been steeling and rehearsing himself to his statement for some time, and was prepared, too, for a violent response to it. When there was none he seemed suddenly timid in our august presence.

In a more reasonable voice he said that he was sorry to butt in upon us, but that he had heard the Citizens' Committee intended to form a Vigilante Troop, and he had come to inform us that there would be none of that in Warlock.

Jed Rolfe asked him if those had been his orders from McQuown.

Gannon replied without heat that he did not take orders from Mc-Quown. Neither did he take them from the Citizens' Committee. He had just come back from San Pablo, he said, whence he had ridden to tell McQuown there would be no Regulators. He was now telling us there would be no Vigilantes either. I felt a certain respect for the fellow then, thinking that he must not have pleased McQuown any more than he was pleasing us.

Skinner sneered that he would bet Gannon had scared McQuown out of his foolishness, and it was certainly nice that Warlock, and Blaisedell, had nothing to worry about. At this Gannon looked childishly angered and hurt. He said, however, that if McQuown did come in he would deputize whoever was needed to meet him, and reiterated his statement that there were to be no Vigilantes. I noticed that he studiously avoided Blaisedell's eye.

Joe Kennon cried out that no one trusted Gannon enough to be deputized by him, to which Gannon replied that whoever he deputized would be deputized or go to Bright's City to explain why not to the court. This exchange was followed by other angry statements, until Blaisedell interceded to say that it was his part to make a play against McQuown and whoever came in with him. "It is against me," he said. "So it is me against them, Deputy."

He spoke in a firm voice, and Gannon blanched noticeably. He stood still not facing Blaisedell, with his bandaged hand upon the counter and his forehead creased with what must have been painful thought. To our surprise he shook his head with determination.

"If it was just you against McQuown, I would keep out, Marshal," he said. "I can't when it is the whole bunch coming in and calling themselves Regulators."

"Yes, you can," Blaisedell said. It did not seem to me he said it particularly threateningly, but he drew himself up to his full height as he looked down at the Deputy.

Gannon, however, stood his ground. He said in an emotional voice, "I have told McQuown he is not to come in here with those people. I told him I will stop him if he does. I mean to stop them."

With that he swung around to depart, and, although we waited breathlessly for Blaisedell's reply, he made none. It was the Judge who broke the silence. "Hear! Hear!" he cried, in obnoxious triumph. His voice was drowned in the ensuing outcry, and Gannon was verbally flayed, drawn and quartered, and otherwise disposed of.

In the end, however, nothing was done about the Vigilance Committee.

April 19, 1881

I will confess that for a time I subscribed to a higher opinion of our Deputy than I had previously held. That was yesterday. Today the mercury of my esteem has sunk quite out of sight, for Gannon, in claiming he would stop McQuown from coming into Warlock, has perpetrated one of the most monstrous, grotesque, and completely senseless frauds of which I have ever heard.

Gannon is, in short, accused of murder. McQuown will not bring his Regulators into Warlock because he is dead, shot in the back, and Gannon is named by a host of witnesses as his murderer.

The Regulators have, indeed, arrived, but not in that role. They are pall-bearers, and Abraham McQuown is their charge. The story I have from Joe Lacey, who swears he was witness to it all.

As he informed the Citizens' Committee yesterday, Gannon had ridden down to San Pablo the night before. He accosted the Regulators, who were gathered at McQuown's, with the same brusquerie he showed the Citizens' Committee at the bank. Hot words passed, and shortly, Lacey claims, Gannon drew his six-shooter on McQuown. Here I become a little dubious as to whether I am hearing the whole story, since drawing upon McQuown in the bosom of his friends sounds an act of incredible asininity. Be that as it may, McQuown then closed and tussled with Gannon, and, defending himself, stabbed Gannon through the hand, which accounts for the bandage we saw yesterday. Gannon was then allowed to depart, which he did ungraciously, calling back that he and Blaisedell would "get even."

Lacey claims he thought Gannon might still be skulking about, for the dogs, which were locked up, had started barking when he first left the ranch house and were never entirely quiet thereafter, as though sensing a sinister presence. About an hour later the door was flung open and Gannon fired upon McQuown, who was standing with his back to the door, killing him instantly. He then fled, but not before he was recognized by old Ike McQuown, Whitby, and several others.

All crowded outside to fire after him in his flight, but pursuit was impossible, for he had unhitched the horses and these were stampeded by the shooting. By the time the mounts were recovered it was clearly useless to try to follow him, and some were afraid that Gannon had been accompanied by a whole party of murderers from Warlock, and that he desired to be pursued so that he could lead the Cowboys into an ambush. There is no doubt in Lacey's mind that Gannon was the assassin, for, although he did not see him himself, a number of others did.

The funeral party arrived not two hours ago. It was well known that the Regulators were coming, since they could be seen a long way off from the rim. Gannon had deputized, without the difficulty some had foreseen, more than twenty good men, whom he had stationed up and down Main Street and on the rooftops. He rode out alone to meet the Regulators and their funeral wagon as they came up the rim. I have not heard what transpired there, and am surprised they did not shoot him down on the spot, but he immediately returned to the jail and surrendered himself to Judge Holloway. He is to have a hearing shortly and will have another chance to appear and swear before the judge, this time not as a witness but as a defendant; Ike McQuown being plaintiff, a curious role for him.

This turn of events has staggered us all.

47. Dad McQuown

Judge Holloway poked right and left with his crutch to clear a path for himself through the jail doorway. "Out of my way! Out of my way, damn you, boys!"

Inside, he glanced worriedly at Gannon, who leaned against the cell door looking listless, exhausted, and profoundly dejected. The judge glared around at Skinner, Bacon, Mosbie, and the others inside the jail. "Turn that table around for me," he said.

It was done and the judge sat down with his back to the door. His crutch fell with a clatter as he moved his chair, and, grunting, opened the drawer against his belly and took out his Bible, derringer, and spectacles. There was a continual mutter of talk from the men crowded into the doorway.

"I will have some order here!" the judge said, and slammed his hand down on the table top. "Or I will clear you people out into the street. Now, I am not going to have that whole bunch from San Pablo in here cluttering, either. Anybody hear who was witnesses in particular?"

"Looks like all of them," Bacon said, in an unhappy voice.

"Send out and tell old Ike he and three others can come in."

Bacon went outside, and the judge drummed his fingers on the table top. Skinner glanced covertly at Gannon with mixed anxiety and disapproval. Mosbie chewed on a cheekful of tobacco and leaned on his shotgun. French and Hasty stood together against the rear wall. There was a silence outside, and a shuffling of feet. The top of a woman's hat appeared among the sombreros, and men moved aside to let Kate Dollar through. She entered the jail, tall and richly curved in a black jacket and pleated skirt. There was a string of jet beads around her neck.

"Here now, Miss Dollar!" the judge said. "This won't do! This is no place for a lady. Now, see here!" he said, as she came on in. Gannon looked up.

"Why not?" Kate Dollar said. "Aren't ladies allowed in a court of law?"

"Well, now—this isn't any real court of law."

"Well, I am not a real lady, Judge," Kate Dollar said, with a tight smile. There were titters behind her, and the judge pointed a finger at the men in the doorway.

"Miss Dollar, it just won't do. Dirty, stinking, foul-mouthed men—"

"I don't mind. Pretend I'm not here."

"Well, get a chair for her. You, Pike!" Skinner hurriedly set out a chair and she sat down, carefully spreading out her skirt and folding her hands in her lap. She looked once at Gannon, without interest.

There was another disturbance outside and the men in the doorway parted again, this time to let through Wash Haggin and Quint Whitby, who were carrying old man McQuown on his pallet. Chet Haggin entered behind them, his face grave; the others were angry and wary. They set the pallet down and the old man raised himself on an elbow and gazed around him with venomous, grief-filled eyes that settled finally upon Gannon.

"Well, Ike," the judge said. "Lost your son."

Old man McQuown nodded curtly. His white beard had been brushed until it looked as fine and light as silk. "Never thought I would live to see it," he said in his harsh voice. "Backshot by one he'd took in an orphan and befriended too. God damn your black Blaisedell-bought soul, Bud Gannon!"

"Johnny says he didn't shoot your boy. You prepared to swear he did?"

"I God damn am!" old McQuown cried. "And how Blaisedell sent him to—"

"We'll have no cussing in here!" the judge said. "There is a lady present and this may not be any court of justice but we will pretend it is. All right now! Hearing's in session and you are to show cause why Johnny Gannon ought to be sent up to Bright's City to proper court, Ike McQuown. Now: I am nothing here but judge on acceptance, like I have said in here about three thousand times already. Johnny, are you going to accept me here?"

"Yes," Gannon said.

"You, Ike?" the judge asked. "Being plaintiff?"

Old McQuown nodded again.

"Pike, you are appointed sergeant-at-arms. I'll have the artillery collected and put by."

Skinner, moving as stiff-legged and cautious as a dog among unfriendly dogs, took six-shooters from the Haggins and Whitby, and then from the others inside the jail. He stacked the Colts on the table before the judge and hung Mosbie's shotgun on the pegs on the wall.

The judge had donned the steel-rimmed spectacles, from which an ear-piece was missing. He held out the Bible to Skinner and nodded toward Gannon. "Swear to tell the truth and nothing but the truth, Johnny. Put your hand on the book and swear."

"I swear," Gannon said, and Skinner turned with the Bible to old McQuown.

"I swear," old McQuown said contemptuously, and Skinner moved along to the others, who also swore.

"All right," the judge said. "Did you shoot Abe McQuown, Johnny Gannon?"

"No," Gannon said.

"Who says he did?"

"I say so," old McQuown said. The judge looked at the others.

"I say so!" Whitby and Wash Haggin said, at the same moment.

"Tell me about it then, one of you," the judge said, and leaned back in his chair. Old McQuown told how it had happened, in his harsh, fierce, old voice. "You saw him, huh?" the judge said, when he had finished. "You and these boys saw Johnny clear in the door there, did you?"

"Said I saw him and swore to it," old McQuown said.

"I saw him clear, Judge," Whitby put in.

"All right. Now you tell it your way, Johnny."

Gannon told his version of what had happened, while old McQuown stirred and muttered and cursed to himself upon his pallet, Wash Haggin and Whitby scowled, and Chet Haggin bit his lip.

"You drawed on Abe McQuown twice then, like Ike said?" the judge asked. "But you claim you didn't go back there after leaving. Heard shots, though?"

Gannon nodded. Pike Skinner was watching him closely, while Mosbie scowled back at Wash Haggin.

"Did you say how you and Blaisedell was going to get even?"

"No."

"He said it!" old McQuown cried. "Didn't he, Quint?"

"He said it all right," Whitby said. There was a stirring and whispering among the spectators in the doorway. Kate Dollar stared at Whitby, and, when she caught his eye, shook her head a little. Whitby flushed.

"You?" the judge said, to Wash Haggin.

"Oh, he said it all right," Wash Haggin said, evading Kate Dollar's gaze.

The judge shifted his attention to Chet Haggin.

"I didn't hear him say it," Chet Haggin said.

"You are saying he didn't say it, then?"

"I didn't say that. I just didn't hear it. He might've said it without me hearing it."

"Uh-huh," the judge said. "Now," he said to old McQuown. "You are not claiming Blaisedell was with him, are you?"

"Might've been. I claim Blaisedell put him up to it."

"Swear it, you mean?" the judge said. "You can't—"

"Damned right I swear it!" old McQuown yelled. "And these boys'll swear it too! It stands to reason, don't it?"

"Ike, I have told you once I'm not going to have any cussing in here. There is a lady present."

"What's she doing here, anyhow?" Whitby growled.

Kate Dollar smiled, and said in a clear voice, "I am trying to see if any of you boys will look me in the eye when you lie."

The judge slapped his hand down on the table. "Ma'am, you will keep hushed or I will clear *you* out of here!"

Chet Haggin said, "Cousin Ike, I don't see how you are going to swear to a thing like that. We don't—"

His brother swung around toward him angrily. "Chet, you know well enough Blaisedell put him up to it!"

Old McQuown raised himself on his elbow again. "There is not a man in the territory that don't know Blaisedell was out to kill my boy, and was out for it ever since he came here. Abe a peaceable, law-abiding boy that—"

Someone in the doorway snickered loudly. The judge swung around and pointed a finger at the offender. "You! Get!"

Old McQuown's breathing sounded very loud in the silent room. He rubbed a hand roughly over his eyes. His voice shook as he continued. "Abe wouldn't give him cause to pick a fight, not wanting to kill a man that was marshal even if he was pure devil. So Blaisedell couldn't get at him, and he had to send a dirty, rotten, nose-picking backshooter of a—"

"Never mind that," the judge said. "That's irrelevant and a matter of opinion too. Now, you say every man knows Blaisedell put Johnny Gannon to it?"

"Said so."

"Well, now, Ike, maybe everybody knows it. But I will put it to you that everybody knows too how you and these same boys here, and your son, has gone up to Bright's City to court and swore false I don't know how many times to keep some of yours from prison or hanging for what they did and what everybody knew they did. Now what do you say to that?"

"By God!" old McQuown whispered. "By God, George Holloway, you are calling us liars!"

"I am," the judge said calmly. "Maybe not this time, but I say you have been other times. You just swore to me on the Bible to tell the whole truth, and I am asking you on your oath if you people haven't been liars in court before this time."

Old McQuown didn't speak.

"You going to answer, Ike, or not?"

"Be damned to you!" old McQuown said hoarsely.

"Judge," Chet Haggin said. "If you make us out liars it don't make Bud there not one."

"No, it don't. But the point I am making is that it don't signify that the bunch of you is swearing one way, and him another." The judge took off his glasses and tapped the earpiece against the Bible. Carefully he pushed the stack of six-shooters farther along the table. "Now, the next thing," he said, "is how you all saw Johnny firing in through the door. Kicked it open, you said? And went right to shooting? He was seen clear?"

"Swore to that already," old McQuown said, in the hoarse voice.

"You don't mind if we run through it again, though—since I wasn't there. Now there was light enough to see by, was there?"

"Three lamps burning. Ought to've been."

"It was light enough, all right," Whitby said.

"But he didn't come inside, did he? Thought you said he stayed outside and just kicked the door open."

"Said he was outside."

"Dark outside, though, wasn't it?"

Old McQuown did not reply. He looked from face to face around him, twisting his head so as to look Kate Dollar in the eye. He grunted scornfully, and lay back on his pallet, panting from the exertion.

"Now, what I am trying to get at here," the judge said, "isn't just that every man knows how a man outside can see fine into a lit-up room, but a man in a lit-up room can't see outside when it's dark anywhere near as good. That's not what I'm getting at." He scowled and held up a hand as Whitby started to speak.

"I am just trying to make certain you are sure of your man, is all," he went on. "Now I am asking you to think back hard, Ike, and you, boys—in view of the fact there's been some talk that Blaisedell rode down there himself the night Abe McQuown got murdered. I am asking you if you are absolutely dead certain sure that the man you saw shoot Abe McQuown down was Johnny Gannon here. I mean, since everybody knows Blaisedell was out to kill Abe by hook or crook, like you say. Now!"

There was a sudden excited rustle of comment in the doorway. Whitby whispered triumphantly, "Why, by God, maybe it was at that! Say! Neckerchief pulled up over his face, but—" His eyes narrowed cunningly as he swung toward the old man. "Say, what do you think, Dad McQuown? By God if it wasn't Blaisedell himself, come to think of it!"

"You was closer to the door than the rest, huh, Quint?" the judge said.

"Cousin Ike!" Wash Haggin said. "It is a trick!"

"Hold on there!" old McQuown shouted. Pike Skinner grinned suddenly, and there was laughter from the men in the doorway. Whitby's brown, fat face paled.

The judge said mildly, "It is hard to see a man clear when he is out in the dark and you in the light."

"I say it was Bud Gannon!" old McQuown cried. "By God, if you have threw us down with this fool—"

"Hush up, now," the judge said. They shouted back and forth at each other until old McQuown gave up and lay back on his pallet in exhaustion again.

"You just listen to me," the judge said. "I am going to sum things up now, and I will have quiet in here to do it. Now, here is Johnny Gannon to swear one thing, and four to swear against him—and more outside that'll do the same, I guess. But—"

"Damned right they'll swear the same!" Wash Haggin cried.

"—but as I said before, it doesn't signify. So now I'll take up things brought in against Johnny Gannon. First how he and Blaisedell planned to kill Abe McQuown in a conspiracy. Dismissed. No evidence whatsoever, except everybody's supposed to know it's so.

"Then there is that Johnny Gannon went down there and tried to pick a fight with Abe McQuown spang in front of fifteen or so of his friends and kin, drew on him, and all that. I just can't believe it. No man with a speck of sense would do such a thing. Say he killed Abe like that, it'd been pure suicide in front of all those. It doesn't stand to reason and I just don't believe it is so."

"He did it!" old McQuown shouted.

"Hush. Now the next thing, that he got stabbed through the hand somehow and went out swearing he would get even for it—that sounds reasonable, and I might believe it. And he might have said that he and Blaisedell was going to get even, knowing the people he was talking to was edgy about Blaisedell.

"But this don't get him to killing Abe McQuown, which is what is primary here. Whitby, and you, Ike, swear you saw him and it was Gannon. Only Whitby went and changed his mind a little—and I will admit I tried to fuddle him saying that about Blaisedell, who was in town that night for all to see, whatever rumors have got started about him. But now it turns out Whitby didn't see quite so clear as he first made out, and now it turns out that the killer had a neckerchief over his face, as would be natural. Only the neckerchief got forgot about, first time you told it. So now it looks to me that since Whitby thinks it might be nice if it was Blaisedell after all, it must be he didn't really see *who* it was, Gannon and Blaisedell not being two that look much alike. And so I figure that if Whitby didn't see who it was at all, then nobody did, and I think you people have accused Johnny Gannon wrong and I think you know it!"

He slapped his hand down on the table top with a report like a revolver shot. "Dismissed!" he said. "I say there is no evidence Johnny Gannon did it what-so-ever that would stand up in proper court, and I just don't believe it!"

Old McQuown spat on the floor. Whitby, red-faced still, laughed harshly, and Wash Haggin stared hard at Gannon.

"Hearing's adjourned," Judge Holloway said hastily. He took off his spectacles and put them, the derringer, and the Bible away in the drawer. "So now you can tell me what you think of me without offending the court, Ike."

Old McQuown glared around the jail with eyes full of tears and hate. "My son is killed," he said. "My son is backshot before my eyes, and not a man anywhere to do anything about it."

"There is plenty to do something, Cousin Ike," Wash Haggin said.

"I guess that is my place, Dad McQuown," Gannon said suddenly. "I will be trying to find out who did it."

Old McQuown grunted as though in pain. He didn't look at the deputy. "I reckon you won't be doing anything if there is a man anywhere," he said. He looked back at the judge. "Come here after justice, George Holloway, even knowing you was a Yankee."

"Ike," the judge said gently. "You said you'd accept what I decided. Are you going to crawfish now?"

"I am! Because I see my son shot down and the cowardly bugger that did it walk free!"

"How many walked free because your son and his people went up to Bright's City and perjured them off?" the judge said.

"I trusted you, George Holloway," the old man said, shaking his head. "And you have tricked and thrown us down today, and mocked an old man with his son dead. I come in here against my inclination, and these boys too. I thought soon or late we was going to have to face up to a change in things, but I see it is dog eat dog like always, and justice only what you make yourself."

"Bud," Wash Haggin said to Gannon. "A man could say you did Curley a disservice swearing what turned him loose for Blaisedell to kill. The judge did you a disfavor the same just now, Bud. You are a dead man."

Kate Dollar sat up very stiffly. All eyes turned on Gannon.

"Wash," Gannon said. "You have known me—what did I ever do you'd think I'd do a thing like this?"

"Know what you turned into," Wash Haggin said.

"Chet," Gannon said. "Maybe you will see that if every man is to think the worst he can think of every other man, then there is going to be no man finally better than that."

The muscles on Chet Haggin's jaw stood out, but he did not answer. Wash Haggin said in a flat voice, "You won't be around to see it get much worse, Bud."

"George Holloway," said old McQuown, "I have known you awhile and you me. I tell you it is a shame on you. You have thrown me hard and by a poor trick. You don't know what it is to lose your son and have it laughed in your face, and the bugger that did it tricked free."

"It's not laughed in your face, Ike."

"Was, and right here. I say he was a good boy and peaceable, and they laugh and scorn me for saying it. He was sitting down there how long with every man to think him yellow for it—because he didn't want to go against Blaisedell that was marshal here. Not a yellow bone in his poor dead body. Oh, I was as bad as the rest, I'll say that right out; his own daddy was as bad as the rest, that was every one of them badgering at him to go against Blaisedell. When he knew it wasn't the thing to do. Knew it better than me, God rest his soul, for I cared too much in my pride about what some coyotes thought of him. Blaisedell pushing on him and pushing on him, that only wanted to be left in peace and to do right, till finally he was pushed too far and his own best friend murdered by that murdering fiend out of hell. And he had to come then, there was nothing else for it.

"And then Blaisedell sends his lick-spittle Judas down to gulch him rather than fight it fair down the street here. But there is no justice to be had. It is bitter, George Holloway, but I will swear something else I didn't swear before because it would've only been laughed to scorn. I swear my boy will go to heaven and that foul devil to hell where he belongs and Bud Gannon along with him."

"And soon," Whitby said, in a low voice.

"That's pled to another judge than me, Ike," the judge said.

"Already been. Abe is looking down on us from heaven right now, and pitying us for poor miserable mortal men."

"He'll be happier before tonight," Wash Haggin said, looking down at his hands.

Old McQuown lay back on his pallet and gazed up at the ceiling. "What have we come to?" he said quietly. "Every man out here used to be a man and decent, and took care of himself and never had to ask for help, for always there was people to give it without it was asked. Fighting murdering Pache devils and fighting greasers, and real men around, then. Murder done there was kin to take it up and cut down the murdering dog, or friends to take it up. Those days when there was friends still. When a man was free to come in town and laugh and jollify with his friends, and friends could meet in town and enjoy towning it, and there was pleasure then. Drink whisky, and gamble some, and fight it stomp and gouge sometimes when there was differences, but afterwards friends again. No one to say a man no, in those days, and kill him if he didn't run for cover and shiver in his boots. Life was worth the living of it in those days."

"And men killed sixteen to the dozen in those days," the judge said, quietly too. "And not by murdering Apaches, either. Rustling and road-agenting all around and this town treated as though it was a shooting gallery on Saturday nights, for the cowboys' pleasure. Miners killed like there was a bounty on them, and a harmless barber shot dead because his razor slipped a little. Yes, things were free in those days."

"Better than these! Maybe men was killed, but killed fair and chance for chance, and not butchered down and backshot. And no man proud enough to raise a hand to stop it!

"But there is some left to raise a hand! There is some of us down valley not eat up with being townfolk and silver-crazy and afraid to breathe. When there is a man killed foul and unrighteous in the sight of God, there will be some to avenge his name. There is some left!"

"Every man's hand will be against you, Ike," the judge said. "It is a battle you poor, dumb, ignorant, misled, die-hard fools have fought a million times and never won in the end, and I lost this leg beating you of it once before. Because times change, and will change, and are changing, Ike. If you will let them change like they are bound to do, why, they will change easy. But fight them like you do every time and they will change hard and grind you to dust like a millstone grinding."

"We'll see who the grinder is!" old man McQuown cried.

"Blaisedell is who it is, Ike. You pull him down on you hard and harder, and on us too who maybe don't like what he stands for a whole lot better than you do. But we will have him, or you, and rather him; and *you* will have him for you will not have law and order."

"We will not have it when it is Blaisedell," Chet Haggin said.

"Blaisedell has run his string," Wash Haggin said grimly.

"Thought he had," the judge said. "But he hasn't if you are going to go on taking law and order as set pure against you every time. Ike, where I was a young fellow there was a statue out before the courthouse that was meant to represent justice. She had a sword that didn't point at nobody, and a blindfold over her eyes, and scales that balanced. Maybe it was different with you Confederates. A good many of you I've seen I've thought it must've been a different statue of her you had down south. One that her sword always poked at *you*. One with no blindfold on her eyes, so you always thought she was looking straight at *you*. And her scales tipped against *you*, every time. For I have never seen such men to take her on and try to fight her.

"And maybe with a fraud like that one you could win. But this here, now, is the United States of America, and it is *my* statue of justice that stands for here. You can cross swords with her till you die doing it, and you are always going to lose. Because back of her, standing right there behind her—or maybe pretty far back, like here in the territory—there is all the people. *All* the people, and when you set yourself against her, you are set against every one of us."

"Get me out of here, boys," old McQuown said. "It is too close in here. Let's get out and bury my son, and then tend to our business."

"Just a minute now!" Pike Skinner said. "I have heard you threatening Johnny Gannon. That is deputy sheriff in this town. I am warning you there are a deal of people watching for you damned rustlers to start trouble."

"There surely are," French said. "You count them when you go out of here."

"Get me outside, boys!" old McQuown cried. "Get me out of here where I can see some decent faces of my own kind, that's not all crooked and mean-scared and town-yellow." The Haggin brothers lifted the pallet, and the old man was borne outside through the men standing in the doorway, who respectfully made a passage for him.

48. Gannon Takes a Walk

GANNON sat with his chair tilted back against the wall and his boot-tips just touching the floor, pushing the oily rag through the barrel of his Colt with the cleaning rod. He forced it through time after time, and held the muzzle to his eye to peer up the dark mirror-shine of the barrel. He tested the action and placed the piece, awkward with his bandaged hand, in its holster, and looked up to see Pike Skinner watching him with an almost ludicrous grimace of anxiety. The judge sat at his table with his face averted and his whisky bottle cradled against his chest.

Gannon tapped the wounded hand once against his thigh, then shot it for the Colt. His hand wrapped the butt gingerly, his forefinger slipping through the trigger guard as he pulled it free, his thumb joint clamping down on the reluctant cock of the hammer spring. He did not raise it, holding it pointed toward the floor.

"Christ!" Pike said.

It had not been as slow as all that, Gannon thought. He had never been fast, but he could shoot well enough. He felt very strange; he remembered feeling like this when he had had the typhoid and had waked finally with the fever broken. Then, too, all the outer things had seemed removed and unimportant, and as though slowed somehow, so there was much time to examine all that went on around him, and especially any movement seen in its entirety, component by component. Then, as now, there had been a very close connection between the willed act, and the arm, and hand and fingers that were the objects of the will; so that, too, his life and breathing had become conscious acts, and he could almost feel the shape of his beating heart, and watch the slow expansion and collapse of his lungs.

The judge drank, spluttered, and went into a coughing fit. Pike pounded him upon the back until he stopped. "They must be about through burying by now," Pike said, scowling.

Gannon nodded.

"You just sit, son," the judge said, in a choked voice. His eyes were watering, and he drank again and wiped his mouth. "You just let them go on out if they see fit, now, you hear?" he said feebly. "There is nothing gained anywhere if you are shot dead."

"You let us handle them if they are calky," Pike said. In a placating tone he said, "No, now, not vigilantes either, Johnny. There is Blaisedell down there and no reason for him not to be, and just some of the rest of us around. Now you hear, Johnny?"

"Why, I'm not going to hide in here," Gannon said, and felt the necessity to grin, and, after it, the grin itself. He looked at the judge, whose face sagged in dark, ugly, bloated lines. "Nothing is gained if I sit it out in here, either."

"You don't have to prove anything," Pike said. "You leave it to us, now. There is some of us got to stand now like we never did for Bill Canning. You leave us that."

Gannon didn't answer, for there was no point in arguing it further. Pike said, "They ought to be about through out there. I am going down." He hitched at his shell belt, loosened his Colt in its holster, gave Gannon another of his confused and accusing glances, and disappeared.

When Pike was gone Gannon took out his own Colt again, and began to replace the heavy, vicious, pleasingly shaped cartridges in the cylinder.

"Blaisedell was right," the judge said. "He said I would put too much on you and I have done it."

"You put nothing on me, Judge. There is just a time and a place for a show. You know that."

"But what place, and what time? Who is to know that?" The judge swung a hand clumsily to try to capture a fly that planed past his head. He contemplated his empty hand with bloodshot eyes, and made a contemptuous sound. "I saw you draw just now, son. Time you got that piece out, Jack Cade or either of the Haggins or any fumble-handed plowboy would have shot you through like a collander and had a drink to celebrate and rode halfway back to San Pablo." He sighed heavily and said, "I thank you for saying I didn't put it on you. Are you scared?"

Gannon shrugged. He felt not so much fright as a curious, flat anxiety. He was only afraid that it would be Jack Cade.

"I'm scared for you," the judge said. "I don't think you have got a Chinaman's chance unless you let Pike and the marshal and those give you a chance. You too proud for that?"

"Proud's nothing to do with it," he said. It touched him that the judge felt responsible for this. "Well, maybe a little," he said. "But if a deputy is going to be worth anything he can't hole up when there is trouble."

"All men are the same in the end," the judge said. "Afraider to be thought a coward than afraid to die."

Gannon rubbed his itching palm on the thigh of his pants, grimacing at the almost pleasant pain. The judge held the bottle up before him and squinted at it.

"Some men drink to warm themselves," he said. "I drink to cool the brain. I drink to get the people out of it. You are nothing to me, boy. You are only a badge and an office, is all you are. Get yourself killed, it is nothing to me."

"All right," he said.

The judge nodded. "Just a process," he said. "That's all you are. What are men to me?" He rubbed his hand over his face as though he were trying to scrape his features off. "I told them they had put Blaisedell there, and put him there for the rest of us. I talk, and it makes me puke to hear myself talking. For Blaisedell is a man too. I wish to God I didn't feel for him, or you, or any man. But do you know what whoever it was that shot down McQuown took away from Blaisedell? Who was it, do you suppose?"

Gannon shook his head.

"What they took away from him," the judge went on. "Ah, I can't stand to see what they will make of him. They will turn him into a mad dog in the end. And I can't stand to see what they will do to you now, just when you—" He drank again. "Whisky used to take the people out of it," he said, after a long time.

Footsteps came along the planks outside. Buck Slavin appeared in the doorway, carrying a shotgun. Kate entered a step behind him. "They are coming," Kate said.

Gannon heard it now, the dry, protesting creak of a wagon wheel and the muffled pad of many hoofs in the dust. He got to his feet, and as he did, Buck raised the shotgun and pointed it at him.

"Now, you are not going out there, Deputy," Buck said patronizingly. "There are people to deal with this. You just sit."

"What the devil is this?" the judge cried.

Gannon began to shake with rage; for they had thought he would be glad of an excuse, and Kate had begged it and Buck furnished it. Kate stood there staring at him with her hands clutched together at her waist.

He started forward. "Get out of my way, Buck Slavin!"

Buck thrust the shotgun muzzle at him. "You will just camp in that cell awhile, Deputy!"

Gannon caught hold of the muzzle with both hands and shoved it back so that the butt slammed into Buck's groin. Buck yelled with pain and Gannon wrenched the shotgun away and reversed it. Buck was bent over with his hands to his crotch.

"*You* march in there!" he said hoarsely. He grasped Buck's shoulder and propelled him into the cell, locked the door, and tossed the key ring onto the peg. He leaned the shotgun against the wall. He didn't look at Kate. The hoofs and the squealing wagon wheel sounded more loudly in the street.

"Now see here, Gannon!" Buck said in an agonized voice.

"Shut up!"

"Oh, you are brave!" Kate cried. "Oh, you will show the world you are as brave as Blaisedell, won't you? I thought you had more sense than the rest behind that ugly, beak-nosed face. But go ahead and *die!*"

"That was a fool trick, Buck!" the judge said. "Interfering with an officer in the performance of his duty. And you ought to be jailed with him, ma'am, only it wouldn't be decent!"

"Shut up, you drunken old fraud!" Kate said. Her eyes caught Gannon's at last, and he saw that she had come to save him, almost as she had once saved Morgan; he felt awed and strangely ashamed for her, and for himself. He started out.

"We'll send flowers," Buck said.

"Why?" Kate whispered, as Gannon passed her. "*Why?*"

"Because if a deputy can't walk around this town when he wants, then nobody can."

Outside, the sun was warm and painfully bright in his eyes as he gazed up at the new sign hanging motionless above his head. The sound of the wagon had ceased. He remembered to compose his face into the mask of wooden fearlessness, that was the proper mask, before he turned to the east.

The wagon had stopped before the gunshop in the central block. The San Pablo men had dismounted and there was a cluster of them around the wagon, and a few were entering the Lucky Dollar. Faces turned toward him. Some of the men, who had been moving toward the saloon, stopped, others moved quickly away from the wagon; they glanced his way and then across Main Street.

Blaisedell was there, he saw, standing coatless under the shadow of the arcade before the Billiard Parlor, one booted foot braced up on the tie rail; it was where he often stood to survey Main Street. His sleeves were gartered up on his long arms, a dark leather shell belt rode his hips. He stood as motionless as one of the posts that supported the roof of the arcade. Farther down were Mosbie and Tim French, and, on the corner of Broadway, Peter Bacon, with a Winchester over his arm. Pike Skinner stood before Goodpasture's store, and in a group in Southend Street were Wheeler, Thompson, Hasty, and little Pusey, Petrix's clerk, with a shotgun. His throat tightened as he saw them watching him; Peter, who was no gunman; Mosbie, who had railed at him most violently over Curley Burne; Pike, who he had begun to think was his sworn enemy, until today; Blaisedell, who had wanted to make this his own play; and a bank clerk, after all.

He started forward down the boardwalk. He flexed his shoulders a little to relieve the tight strain there. He stretched his wounded, aching, sweating hand to try to loosen it. His skin prickled. He wondered, suddenly, that he had no plan. But he had only to walk the streets of Warlock as a deputy must do, as was his duty and his right.

He crossed Southend Street with the Warlock dust itching on his face and teasing in his nostrils. Wash Haggin was standing spreadlegged in the center of the boardwalk before the Lucky Dollar, facing him.

Old man McQuown was still in the wagon, beneath a shade rigged from a serape draped over four sticks. There was no one else in view on this side of the street.

"Dad McQuown," he said, in greeting, to the wild eyes that stared at him over the plank side of the wagon. He halted and said, "I will do my best to find out who did it, Dad McQuown."

He started on, and now Wash's face was fixed in his eyes, Wash's hat pushed back a little to show a dark sweep of hair across his forehead, Wash's face set in a wooden expression that must be a reflection of his own face. Wash instead of Jack Cade because Wash was kin to Abe, he thought. He had a glimpse of Chet Haggin's face above the batwing doors of the Lucky Dollar, and Cade, and Whitby and Hennessey shadowy behind them.

"I'll trouble you to let me by, Wash," he said.

Wash's eyes widened a little as he spoke, and he felt a thrill of triumph as Wash sidled a step closer to the tie rail. There was the scuffing of his boots, then an enormous silence that now contained a kind of ticking in it, as of a huge and distant clock. He saw Wash's face twist as he passed him and walked steadily on. Now the prickling of his skin was centered in the small of his back and the nape of his neck. Peter Bacon, across the street, was holding the Winchester higher; Morgan sat in his rocking chair on the veranda of the Western Star. He could see Blaisedell, too, now, as he came past wagon and team.

"Bud!" Wash cried, behind him.

He halted. The ticking seemed closer and louder. He turned. Wash was facing him again, crouching, his hand hovering. Wash cried shrilly, "Go for your gun, you murdering son of a bitch!"

"I won't unless you make me, Wash."

"Go for it, you murdering backshooting—"

"Kill him!" Dad McQuown screamed.

Wash's hand dove down. Someone yelled; instantly there was a chorus of warning yells. They echoed in his ears as he twisted around in profile and his wounded hand slammed down on his own Colt; much too slow, he thought, and saw Wash's gun barrel come up, and the smoke. Gannon stumbled a step forward as though someone had pushed him from behind, and his own Colt jarred in his hand. He was deafened then, but he saw Wash fall, hazed in gunsmoke. Wash fell on his back. He tried to roll over, his arm flopped helplessly across his body, and his six-shooter dropped to the planks. He shuddered once, and then lay still.

Gannon glanced at the doors of the Lucky Dollar; the faces there had disappeared. Then he had a glimpse of the long gleam of the rifle barrel leveled over the side of the wagon. He jumped back, just as a man vaulted into the wagon. It was Blaisedell, and old McQuown screamed as Blaisedell kicked out as though he were killing a snake —and kicked again and the rifle dropped over the edge of the wagon to the boardwalk.

He could see the old man's fist beating against Blaisedell's leg as Blaisedell stood in the wagon, facing the doors of the Lucky Dollar. No one appeared there for a moment, and Gannon started back to where Wash lay. But then Chet Haggin came out and knelt down beside his brother's body, and Gannon turned away. The old man had stopped screaming.

He walked on down toward the corner. After a moment he remembered the Colt in his hand, and replaced it in its holster. There was the same silence as before, but it buzzed in his shocked ears. His hand felt hot and sticky, and, looking down, he saw blood leaking dark red from beneath the bandage. At the corner he turned and crossed Main Street, and mounted the boardwalk on the far side in the shadow. Peter didn't look at him, standing stiffly with the rifle in his white-clenched hands. Tim's eyes slid sideways toward him and Tim nodded once. He heard Mosbie whistle between his teeth. Blaisedell had returned to this side of the street, and leaned against a post, watching the wagon. Now Gannon could hear the old man's pitiable cursing and sobbing, and he could see Chet still bent over Wash.

"I thank you," he said, to Blaisedell's back, and walked on. He looked neither right nor left now but kept his eyes fixed on the black and white sign over the jail doorway. Kate's face appeared there briefly. He had made his turn through Warlock, as was his right, as was his duty; but his knees felt weak and the sign over the jail seemed very distant. He could feel the blood dripping from his fingers, and his wrist brushed the butt of his Colt as his arm swung.

"Hallelujah!" Pike Skinner whispered, as he came to the corner. He did not reply, and crossed Southend Street, feeling the stares of the men—not vigilantes—who were stationed there. Again he saw Kate appear in the jail doorway, but when he approached she disappeared back inside, and, when he entered, she stood with her back to him.

The judge sat hunch-shouldered at the table, his crutch leaning beside him, his bottle and hard-hat before him, his hands clasped between them. Buck's face was framed in the bars.

"Got you in the hand, did he?" Buck said, in a matter-of-fact voice.

"I just broke it open again."

The judge didn't speak as he moved in past the table. He heard Kate gasp. "Your belt!" she cried. He reached back to feel a long gap in the leather and some cartridge loops gone. He sat down abruptly in the chair beside the cell door.

Kate stood facing him. He saw her stocking as she pulled up her skirt. She tore at the hem of her petticoat and then stooped to bite on the hem and pull loose a long strip. She took his hand and roughly bound the strip of smooth, soft cloth around it, and tore it again and tied the ends.

Then she stepped back away from him. "Well, now you are a killer," she said, with her lips flattened whitely over her teeth.

"Who was it, Johnny?" Buck said.

"Wash."

"What're they going to do now?"

"I expect they'll go out."

"He's got a brother, hasn't he?" Kate said. The judge was regarding the whisky bottle, his face a mottled, grayish red, his hands still clasped before him.

Buck cleared his throat and said, "Well, you have made some friends this day, Gannon."

"Friends!" Kate cried. "You mean men to think he is a wonder because he killed a man? Friends!" she said hoarsely. "A friend is someone who will say he did right and what he had to do, and hold to it. They will stew on this until they have figured he murdered this one like he murdered McQuown. I have seen it done too many times. Friends! They will—"

"Now, Kate," Buck said.

"I didn't murder Abe McQuown, Kate."

"What difference does that make?" she cried at him. "Friends! A friend lasts like snow on a hot griddle and enemies like—"

"You are bitter for a young woman, miss," the judge said.

Gannon hung his head suddenly, and bent down still farther. He felt faint and his stomach kept rising and swelling against his laboring heart, and he could taste bile in his throat. In his mind's eye he saw not Wash Haggin's wooden face, but the frantic dark face of the Mexican sweeping up the bank toward him still. "Bitter?" he heard Kate say, above the humming in his ears. "Why, yes, I am bitter! Because men have found some way to crucify every decent man, starting with Our Lord. No, it is not even bitter—it is just common sense. They will admire him for a wonder because he killed a man they wouldn't've had the guts to go against. But they will hate him for it, because of that. So they will say he murdered him like he murdered McQuown. Or they will say it was nothing, with Blaisedell there to back him, and those others. They will say it for they are men. Don't you know they will, Judge?"

"You are bitter," the judge said, in the same dull voice. "And scared for him too. But I know men better than you, I think, Miss Dollar. They are not so bad as that."

"Show me one that isn't! Show me one. But don't show *them*. Or they will kill him for it!"

"There are men that love their fellow men and suffer for their suffering," the judge said. "But you wouldn't see them for hatefulness, it looks like, miss."

Gannon raised his head to look at Kate's face, which was turned toward the judge—and it was hard and hateful, as he had said.

"I would show you Blaisedell for one," the judge said.

"Blaisedell," Kate whispered. "No, not Blaisedell!"

"Blaisedell. Hard as I have judged him, he is a good man. That knew better than you, miss, what had to be done just now. That let

Johnny take his play and glory just now, for he needed them, with McQuown took from him. He is a good man. And I will show you Pike Skinner that thought Johnny threw this town down with Curley Burne, but backed him now all the same. And the rest of them out there. Good men, Miss Dollar! The milk of kindness is thick in them, and thicker all the time!"

"Thick as blood!"

"Thicker than blood. And will win in the end, miss—for all your sneering at a man that says it to you. So this old world remakes itself time and time again, each time in labor and in pain and the best men crucified for it. People like you will not see it, being bitter; as I have been myself, and so I know. So they can say a town like this one has its man for breakfast every morning—" He slammed his hand down on the table top, his voice rose. "But not killed to eat for breakfast any more! Not burnt on crosses to the glory of God any more! Not butchered up—"

The judge stopped and swung around in his chair as footsteps sounded outside. Gannon rose as Chet Haggin came into the doorway. Chet wore no shell belt, and there was a smear of blood on the breast of his blue shirt. He stood in the doorway staring at Gannon with burnt, dark eyes in his carefully composed face.

"I'm sorry, Chet," Gannon said.

Chet nodded curtly. He glanced from Gannon to Kate, to Buck, to the judge, and then his burnt eyes returned. "I never thought you come back and shot Abe," he said, in a harsh, flat voice. "I have known you some, Bud. So I know just now you killed Wash because there wasn't anything else you could do, the way it was put. I come up here to tell you I knew that."

Chet made as though to hook his thumbs in his belt, and grimaced and looked down. "Thought I'd better not start up here heeled," he said, in an apologetic tone. "Things are scratchy out."

The judge sat motionless with his chin on his hands. Kate stood tall and straight with her hands clasped before her and her eyes cast down.

Chet said, "Bud, we thought pretty low of you when Billy got killed. And said low things. Now I guess I know how you felt, for when you press to kill a man and he kills you to keep you from it, who is to blame? Anyway, I guess I know how you wouldn't go against Blaisedell, and scared nothing to do with it." His eyes filled suddenly. "For I won't brace you, Bud. And I'm not scared of you!"

"I know you're not, Chet."

"They will say it. Be damned to them. I won't come against you, Bud. But they will try to kill you, Bud. Jack— They won't rest till they do it now. I won't go against you, but I can't go against what's my own kin and kind! I can't go against my own and side with Blaisedell like you have done. I can't!" he cried, and then he stumbled back outside and was gone.

"Always said he was the white one," Buck commented, and the judge gave him a disgusted look.

Gannon stood staring at the dusty sunlight streaming in the door. Presently he heard the creaking of the wagon wheels. He moved slowly past Kate to stand in the doorway. The team and wagon were coming down Main Street toward him, and the riders following in the dust it raised. Pike Skinner, who was still standing before Good-pasture's store, waved to him to get back inside.

"Going out?" the judge asked.

"Looks like it."

"You had better get out of that door, Johnny!" Buck said.

But he didn't move, watching them come down Main Street, Joe Lacey and the breed Marko on the seat of the wagon, and the serape shading the old man in the bed behind them. The horsemen fanned out to fill the street. He watched for Jack Cade.

Cade had dropped a little behind the others. He rode with his shoulders hunched. His round-crowned hat was white with dust, his leather vest hung open; his purple and black striped pants were stuffed into his high boots. A fringed rifle scabbard hung slanting forward along his bay's neck. He reined the bay toward the board-walk, and behind him on the corner Gannon saw Pike Skinner lower his hand to his Colt.

The wagon rolled past him, the men on the seat staring steadily ahead. The old man's eyes gazed at him over the side of the wagon, white-rimmed, sightless-looking, and insane. The riders had drawn their neckerchiefs up over their faces, and it was difficult to tell one from the other. They turned their faces toward him, like cavalrymen passing in review, but Jack Cade was riding toward him.

"*I'll* kill you, Bud!" Cade said in a voice that was almost a whisper and yet enormously loud in the silence. Then he nodded, and set his spurs, and the bay trotted swiftly on to catch up with the others.

They rode on down the street behind the wagon, fading shapes in the powdery drifting dust, their passage almost soundless except for the occasional eccentric creak of the dry wheel. When they had almost gained the rim, he saw one of the horses rear and a shot rang out; and at once all the horses began to rear in a confused and antic mass, and all the riders fired into the air and yipped and whooped in thin and meaningless defiance.

There was a flat loud whack above his head and the sign swung suddenly. The shooting and whooping ceased as suddenly as it had begun, and, as though team, wagon, and horsemen had fallen through a trapdoor, they disappeared over the rim on the road back to San Pablo.

He looked up at the bullet hole in the lower corner of the new, still swinging sign, and went back inside.

"Was that Cade?" Kate whispered.

He nodded and heard her sigh, and she raised a fist and, like a tired child, rubbed at her eyes. There was a new and closer whooping in the street, and suddenly Kate moved to lean on the table and stare down at the judge.

"Everything is fine now, isn't it?" she said. "Nothing to worry about now, is there? Oh, the good ones always win out in the end and it is all right if they get crucified for it, because—"

"Now, Kate," Buck said. "I don't know why you're taking on so. It's all over now, and he'll have a lot to back him from now on."

"But who is to stand in front of him?" she said, just as Pike Skinner ran in.

Pike leaped on Gannon, laughing and yelling and hugging him; then the others came until the jail was filled with them, all of them talking at once and coming up to slap his shoulder or shake his good hand, to examine and exclaim over the bullet scar on his belt, and ask what Chet had had to say. He didn't see Kate leave, he was just aware suddenly that she was gone, and the judge gone. Someone had brought a bottle of whisky and was passing it around, and others were singing, "Good-by! Good-by! Good-by, Regulators, Good-by! . . ."

He thanked Pike, and thanked the others one by one as they came up to him. "Surely, Horse, surely," Peter Bacon said. "It was a pleasure to see you and worth more than just standing there holding my boots down with a Winchester for ballast." The whisky bottle was forced upon him time and again. Someone had let Buck out of the cell. He thought, with a sinking twisting at his heart, that there had not been such jollity and merriment as this in Warlock for a long time now.

He heard someone ask where Blaisedell was and French replied that he had not come up with them. He had wanted to thank Blaisedell.

He flinched as someone slapped him on the shoulder, and in the process brushed against his hand. Hap Peters stuck a finger through the hole in his shell belt. "Drink!" Mosbie was shouting, waving the bottle at him. "Drink to the rootingest-tootingest-shootingest-beatingest deputy this side of Timbuctoo!"

Mosbie forced the bottle on him, but he gagged on the sour whisky. Suddenly he could not stand it any more, and he made his way outside, and almost ran along the boardwalk to his room in Birch's roominghouse.

BOOK THREE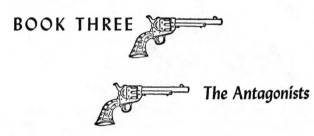

The Antagonists

49. Gannon Walks on the Right

GANNON was alone in the jail when Blaisedell appeared in the doorway, blotting out the late sun for a moment. "Evening, Deputy," he said.

"Marshal," he said, rising. He had had little occasion to speak to Blaisedell this last week. He had thanked him for his help, and Blaisedell had made acknowledgment in that uncommunicative and not quite arrogant way he had. Since then he had seen the Marshal only at a distance, usually under the arcade before the Billiard Parlor; and one night in the Lucky Dollar when there had been a quarrel between two of the Medusa strikers, which Blaisedell had already settled when he arrived.

"Mind if I sit?" Blaisedell asked.

Gannon indicated the chair beside the cell door, and pivoted his own around to face it. Blaisedell seated himself, tipped the chair back against the wall, and grasped one of the bars of the cell door to balance himself. "Quiet lately," he said.

"Been some rustling. Blaikie's lost a few head."

"I meant in town."

"Oh; yes."

Blaisedell frowned and said, "I wanted to ask you about Haggin's brother."

"Chet? Well, he came in that day to say he didn't hold it against—anyone," Gannon said, and wondered if that was what Blaisedell had meant.

"But Cade means to take it on himself?"

"He said so." Gannon licked his lips.

"A mean-looking one," Blaisedell said, and Gannon felt the full force of his blue eyes. "Backshooter," Blaisedell went on. "Worried about him?"

"I guess you can't worry about every man that's down on you."

"Some can." Blaisedell's lips bent into a stiff, almost shy grin. "Maybe you are just not the worrying kind."

"Why, I can worry with the best of them, Marshal." He forced a laugh, and Blaisedell chuckled too. It occurred to him all at once that Blaisedell was trying to make contact with him in some way, and immediately what he had hoped was going to be an easy conversation for him grew taut with strain.

"Go home and puke afterwards?" Blaisedell asked. He did not ask it humorously; it was a question of consequence.

"Not till night."

Blaisedell nodded as though satisfied. "About Cade," he said. "If he has taken it on against you I guess the Citizens' Committee would want to post him. If—" He stopped as Gannon shook his head.

"I guess not, Marshal," he said.

"No?" Blaisedell said, and now his voice had an edge to it. "Standing on your own feet now, is it?"

"It is not that so much," he said with difficulty, looking down at his bandaged hand. "It is posting I am starting to balk at. It seemed it worked for a while and it was all we had here. But something happened—I don't know what happened. I guess I don't know how to say this very well, Marshal."

"Just say it," Blaisedell said.

He felt the strain again, and he grimaced down at his hand. "I don't say it is the killing that's so bad in itself," he went on. "I mean, when people wear guns like they do, they are going to use them. But it is that after some point the killing makes people turn against what was supposed to be done for them in the first place. It is hard, and it is unfair, but it is so. I guess I mean you, Marshal. You have stood for law and order here, so if they turn against you, they—"

"I know all that," Blaisedell said. It seemed a rebuke, and it angered Gannon that this thought, so hard to put into words, should be brushed aside. He glanced up to see a bitterness in Blaisedell's face that shocked him; but instantly it was gone, so that he could not be sure he had really seen it.

"Go on, Deputy," Blaisedell said easily. "I guess there is more."

"It would be a poor thing if this town was to turn against you," he said. "Because Warlock is a safer place since you came here. And there is more to it than that, for people have got some starch into them to stand up to things. Like Carl. Why, like the other day! There was others than you that let me make that play, and come out of it. But those others wouldn't have been standing by if you hadn't done what you've done in this town.

"But there is that point, Marshal," he went on. He managed to meet the impassive blue stare. "It is like a kid with a big brother to run the bad kids off him. Some time the big brother is going to have to let the kid fight for himself. I mean even if he gets whipped—"

"That is you you are talking about," Blaisedell broke in.

"No, it is the deputy here. Which only happens to be me."

"Do you think you are ready to take it on, Deputy?"

He almost groaned, for it was the question. He shook his head tiredly and said, "I don't know."

"I don't think you are ready yet," Blaisedell said. "But then I didn't think you were before the Regulators came in, either."

He saw Blaisedell smile a little, and he supposed it had been a compliment. "I think I will stay on awhile," Blaisedell said. "It is not time yet." He said it with a certain inflection and Gannon thought he might be talking of himself now.

He remembered Blaisedell's telling the judge that he would know when it was time to go, but now he wondered what time Blaisedell had meant, Warlock's or his own. "Surely," he said quickly. "I don't think it is time yet, either. But I have got to be ready sometime. I couldn't ever have been ready at all if you hadn't been here."

Blaisedell blinked. After a long time he said, "I see you have taken up with Kate Dollar."

Gannon felt himself blushing, and Blaisedell continued, still gazing at the names on the wall. "She is a fine woman. I knew her back awhile."

"She said."

"Down on me," Blaisedell said. "I killed a friend of hers in Fort James."

She said; this time he did not say it aloud.

"It was shoot or get shot," Blaisedell said. "Or I thought it was. I had been edgy about things." He was silent for a time, and Gannon remembered what Kate had told him about it. He had thought she must be telling the truth because she had sounded so certain; but now he wondered about it just because Blaisedell sounded so uncertain.

Then Blaisedell said, "I remember when I killed a man the way you did the other day. And it was clear and had to be done, though I went home afterwards and puked my insides out. The way you did." His voice sounded removed and musing, and, after another pause he went on again. "But there was a lesson I learned. It is that a man can't ever be careful enough. Even careful as a person can be is not enough. For there will be a man you don't want to come against you, and that shouldn't, but all the same he will—"

He stopped and shook his head a little, and Gannon thought he had been speaking of Curley Burne.

Blaisedell said, "I knew a man once who said it was all foolishness— that if you want to kill a man, why, kill him. Shoot him down from behind in the dark if you want to kill him. But don't make a game with rules out of it."

This time it was Morgan; it hit Gannon like a picture slapped across his sight and then drawn back into focus so he could study it: Morgan standing masked in the doorway in the dark, and Abe McQuown with his back turned.

"But he doesn't understand," Blaisedell said. "It is not that at all, for you don't want to kill a man. It is only the rules that matter. It is holding strict to the rules that counts."

Blaisedell let his chair down suddenly, and the legs cracked upon the floor; he leaned forward with his face intent and strained, and Gannon felt the full force of his eyes. "Hold to them like you are walking on eggs," he said. "So you know yourself you have played it fair and as best you could. As right as you could. Like you did with Haggin. I admired that, Deputy, for you did just what it was put on you to do, and did it well."

Then the muscles along the edges of his jaw tightened. "So it was all clear for you," he said, with the bitter edge to his voice again. "But there are things to watch for. Watch yourself, I mean. Don't be too fast. I have been too fast two times in different ways, and it is why I asked you about Cade. For after the first time, there are people out after you, and you know it and worry it, unless you are not the worrying kind. So then, you think, if you don't get drawn first and them killed first—do you see what I mean?"

Gannon nodded. He was being instructed, he knew, and this was a very precious thing to Blaisedell. He felt embarrassed as he had been once when his father had tried to instruct him about women. And he saw that Blaisedell was embarrassed, as his father had been.

"Well, I came in to try to tell you a couple of things, Deputy," he said, in a different tone. "And a long time getting to it. A little thing I noticed watching you draw, for one."

"What was that, Marshal?"

"Well, you lose a little time and your aim, too, flapping your hand out when you pull your piece free. I would put in a little practice bringing it up straight. Down straight with your hand, up straight with your piece. I saw you flapped your hand out a little, and though you center-shot him clean, you lost time. He lost aim. He flapped out so far he didn't get the barrel back in line, was the reason he missed you."

"I'll remember. I hadn't thought of that, Marshal." He waited, tensely.

Blaisedell frowned. "The other thing," he said. "It is something you ought to know, but I don't know quite— Well, it is just something you have got to tell yourself every time. It is a kind of pride a man has to have, and it has got to be genuine. *Has* to. You will see when another man hasn't got it. I mean, when a man thinks maybe you are faster and better than him, he is already through. You can see that, and those times you don't have to hurry a shot, for he will more than likely miss. Like Curley missed," he said, in a flat voice. "I knew he would miss.

"But it is more than that," he said, frowning more deeply. "I don't—I—"

"More than just that you are faster," Gannon said.

Blaisedell looked relieved. "That's it. It is just that you *are* better. A man has to be proud, but he has to have the reason to be proud to hold him. Genuine, like I said." Blaisedell grinned fleetingly. "I guess you will understand me. It is a close thing out there, you and the other. But I mean it is like two parts of something are fighting it out inside—before there is ever a Colt's pulled. Inside you. And you have to know that you are the part that has to win. I mean *know* it."

"Yes," Gannon said, for he saw that.

"There is no play-acting with yourself," Blaisedell said. He got quickly to his feet, and stretched, and put on his hat and patted it. "Why, just some things I thought I could pass along, Deputy," he said.

"Thank you, Marshal." He rose too.

"Have you figured who killed McQuown yet?"

"There are a lot of people who could have done it."

Blaisedell nodded gravely. Then he said, "Maybe you would have a whisky with me?"

"Why, yes, Marshal—I would like to." He took up his own hat, and stood turning it in his hands. He had a feeling that Blaisedell knew exactly what he was going to say. "I've been wondering what Morgan is going to do, with the Glass Slipper burnt down."

"I guess he is thinking of moving along," Blaisedell said. "There is nothing to hold him here, with his place burned. He is one that likes a change."

"Well, maybe it is better."

Blaisedell's eyes were cold as deep ice, and his voice was cold. "Maybe it is," he said, and moved on outside.

Gannon took a deep breath and followed Blaisedell, who waited on the boardwalk. They started down toward the Lucky Dollar together, in silence. They had almost reached the corner when he realized that he was walking on Blaisedell's right, when the gunman always walked to the right in order to keep his gun hand free; and then he knew that Blaisedell had chosen to have it that way.

50. Journals of Henry Holmes Goodpasture

May 14, 1881

McQuown's death, which would have been wildly celebrated here a few months ago, has set upon us a pall that is mitigated only in part by the pride we have felt in the emergence of a home-grown hero. The means of his death, for one thing—cowardly murder—and, for another, the meaninglessness of it. There should have been some meaning, some lesson, some sense of triumph. There was none.

Moreover, in the past weeks, it has been brought home to us that perhaps his champions were in part right, and that it was McQuown, who, although himself a rustler, kept order among the outlaws down valley, and confined their depredations to certain channels. He was not called the Red Fox for nothing. Control was necessary, organization brings control; therefore McQuown.

There has been a rash of petty rustling, and both the Redgold and Welltown stages were stopped by road agents within the last week alone. Blaikie has lost over a hundred head of stock, and one of his hands was wounded, not dangerously, by a crew of thieves he encountered. Burbage is incensed; McQuown was at least a man of honor, says he, indignantly. I, however, refuse to join in the general sainting of the outlaw. The border seems to be very tightly watched now, both by elements of the Mexican Army and Don Ignacio's own vaqueros—it is said that he has declared war upon the rustlers who have harried him for so long, and will deal ruthlessly with any he can catch. Perhaps, in view of the border situation, McQuown died at the right time, or else, like those who have survived him, he might have had to turn to robbing his neighbors.

Gannon, resting on his laurels, has done nothing whatever since he dispatched Wash Haggin. Kennon does not like him, says he is a born coward and main-chancer, and only had the courage to fight Haggin because he knew Blaisedell would protect him. Buck Slavin defends him, but is losing patience. The judge, however, points out that Gannon is helpless to deal with a series of small and scattered raids in a hostile countryside, for he would have to be in constant motion with a posse increasingly difficult to assemble. The judge says that the situation will be alleviated only when backing is received from Sheriff Keller, and this will take place when outrage or notoriety have forced that worthy, or the General, to action. Perhaps Whiteside is seeing that wheels are being turned even now in our behalf; I doubt it to the bottom of my soul.

Pike Skinner, for his part, seems to have swung over to the deputy's side, and defends him wholeheartedly. He points out that Gannon, in enemy territory, puts himself in grave danger of assassination, since to all appearances the Cowboys remain convinced that it was Gannon who murdered their chief; also that the stalwarts who would have enthusiastically formed the Vigilantes to protect Warlock from the Regulators, are not enthusiastic at all about riding down valley to face the Cowboys whose deadly mien and ready weapons were so much in evidence on their last appearance here.

Gannon is looked upon with distrust by a good many members of the Citizens' Committee—or perhaps it is with jealousy. He remains, however, a hero to the unwashed elements. There is great interest on every hand in his future actions, and he is at the moment more a center of interest than is Blaisedell.

> The present eye praises the present object.
> Then marvel not, thou great and complete man,
> That all the Greeks begin to worship Ajax,
> Since things in motion sooner catch the eye
> Than what not stirs.

But Hector is dead, and what is there left for Achilles to do?

May 16, 1881

It is thought here now that McQuown must have been murdered by Mexicans in the employ of Don Ignacio, in revenge, and as assurance against further rustling of Hacienda Puerto stock.

I am sure there would be some to accuse Blaisedell of the crime, had not Blaisedell been in evidence here that night. I have heard it said, though, that Morgan was clearly seen (by whom?) riding back into Warlock the following dawn upon a winded horse, as he was also seen (by whom?) riding back from the scene of the Bright's City stage robbery, etc. No doubt Morgan is capable of such a murder, as no doubt he is capable of road-agentry, but I am unable to believe him capable of such strenuous diabolism merely for its own sake.

Yet more and more I see the conspiracy to bring Blaisedell low by gossip and canard, since it cannot be done by gunfire. They will strike at him through Morgan, against whose name is piled a higher and higher stack of guilt and sin, in the hope that this will topple over onto the Marshal. Very probably Morgan has no more moral code than a rhinoceros, and certainly he does nothing to make himself popular. He spends his time viewing and sneering at our activities from the veranda of the Western Star, and, afternoons and evenings, gambles at the Lucky Dollar, where he is having a phenomenal run of luck at the faro table, to Lew Taliaferro's great discomfiture. Morgan was attacked there the other night by two miners, but, although he is not large in stature, he is a powerful and active man, and acquitted himself well. When he had had enough of the brawl he drew his sixshooter and put his attackers to flight, and then returned to his game, Will Hart said, as calmly as though nothing had happened.

The town itself is quiet and well behaved. Our population is growing. Among others, a man named Train and his wife, a faded but indomitable-looking woman, have arrived, with the prospect of building an eating establishment, which they claim will be of high quality. They are having great difficulty obtaining lumber, but Mrs. Train says firmly that she will not have adobe, which is dirty and repellent to white people. There has also been another marriage. Slator has taken to wife a Cyprian from the French Palace. The judge performed the ceremony, the validity of which might consequently be suspect, and Taliaferro, fittingly enough, gave the bride away. The happy couple has rented a cabin from one of the Medusa strikers, who was no doubt badly in need of money. Slator, formerly an irresponsible and drunken odd-jobman, has been given steady employment by Kennon at the livery stable, and shows every sign of having become a reformed character, this being attributed to his new responsibilities. I should think it might be difficult to possess a wife whom almost every other man in town has known so intimately, but no doubt True Love Conquers All.

So peace and civilization are encroaching upon Warlock. Yet it is not a pleasant peace. There is concern as to whether the strikers will accept their defeat, or will break out in some new violence. Miss Jessie has set up a breadline at the General Peach. They stand in the street at meal times, waiting their turn to be fed by her generosity, and are silent and sullen. MacDonald must fume at her feeding them, and yet I am sure that in the end he will win, and they will silently and sullenly go back to work at the Medusa.

It is a Saturday night, and very quiet outside my window. I remember when a Saturday night was a matter of dread in Warlock— I remember the wildness, the shouts and laughter, the brawling, the shooting that would all too often punctuate and bring a bloody climax to the night. Is not this what we wanted? McQuown is dead; I have to remind myself of that. Is not that too what we wanted? Yet I am aware of the dissatisfaction on every hand. It is finished, but not finished. It is not right, but I cannot express what I feel. It is an uneasy peace in Warlock.

May 22, 1881

I have noticed that we are seeing more of Blaisedell these days. He spends much of his time on Main Street, standing at his ease beneath one or the other of the arcades. His leonine head is in continual but almost imperceptible movement—as he glances up the street, then down the street. He gives the impression of intently watching and waiting. He is a part of the furniture of Main Street, a kind of black-suited eminence—a colossus there, or is it astride the town itself?

For what does he watch and wait? The question depresses me greatly, for is not his use gone? He is like a machine primed and ready for instant service with its function no longer of value. Was not his ultimate purpose to fight, and kill, Abe McQuown? So is his use buried with McQuown? I know there is an increasing sentiment in the Citizens' Committee that he should be released. As yet this has hardly been voiced, but I know it is so. I wonder who will tell Blaisedell when, and if, it is agreed upon.

He must then go on to some other Warlock and some other Mc-Quown. There are no more McQuowns or Curley Burnes here, and he is like a heavyweight champion awaiting a challenger where there are only lightweights. I pity him that everything has gone so wrong for him. Is not all, from now on, anticlimax?

I have seen him once or twice in converse with Gannon, more often sitting upon the veranda of the Western Star with Morgan. They sit side by side, uncomfortably similar in black broadcloth suits, black hats. It strikes me that I have no impression of them speaking together. Then Blaisedell makes a round of the town, and Morgan goes to resume his bout with Taliaferro.

The quiet nights pass, and, a little after noon each day, Blaisedell reappears at one of his three or four central posts. You do not see him come and go, he is only there, or not. Once in a while you are more conscious of him. A couple of miners tumble out of the Billiard Parlor, fighting and cursing. Calmly he separates them. Upon seeing him they are at once sober and out of their fighting mood, and slink away. Or Ash Bredon rides in from up valley and thinks to do a little shooting into the air to enliven the atmosphere of Warlock. Blaisedell speaks to him from across the street, and Bredon changes his mind.

He stands and waits, and the days pass, and I wonder what will become of him. What he waits and watches for does not exist; I cannot help but feel he knows this himself. In a very brief time he has turned, almost, into a monument.

51. The Doctor Hears Threats and Gunfire

THE doctor stood in the entryway watching the miners file in through the door of the General Peach for their noon meal. As usual, they were quiet and orderly. There were more than a hundred of them now, and each one nodded to him as he came in the door, and then, carefully, did not look at him again.

The queue bent in through the dining-room doorway and past the tables where Jessie, Myra Egan, Mrs. Sturges, Mrs. Train, and Mrs. Maples served them soup, salt pork, bread, and black coffee in a rattle of plates and cutlery. Jessie looked faded and tired beside Myra Egan's pink-cheeked freshness. Those who had been served stood in the middle of the room and wolfed down their food, more, he knew, from an urge to get out than from hunger. Finished, they joined another line, where Lupe, the fat Mexican cook, watched them drop their plates into a cauldron of hot water, after which they filed outside past those who still entered.

The hot, wet smell of soup that permeated the General Peach seemed to him the stench of defeat. They were almost defeated, and he raged at it, and at his presumption in thinking he could help them, and, most of all, at MacDonald, who had beaten them so easily. They did not even send MacDonald the revised demands any more, for MacDonald only threw them away as soon as they were presented to him. More than a dozen of the strikers had left Warlock, and he knew most of the rest were only waiting for some excuse to go back to the Medusa. Leaning against the newel post, he watched their leaders, old man Heck and Frenchy Martin, filing out with the rest. Their faces were resolute still, but he knew it was only for show. Each day he stood here to watch the strikers and feel their temper, and each day he could see them weakening.

He stayed to watch the last of the miners leave before he went into Jessie's room and sat down in the chair beside the door. He rose when Jessie came in. Myra Egan stood outside in the entryway, and smiled at him as she tucked her hair up under her bonnet. Myra's face was plumper, and her breasts looked swollen in her crisp gingham dress; before many months had passed she would bear Warlock's first legitimate child.

"My goodness, I am feeling the heat these days, Doc!" she said, fanning her flushed face with her hand.

"It is natural that you should, Myra."

She flushed still more, prettily. Jessie thanked her, and thanked the other ladies, whom he could not see from where he stood. Disparate types though they were, they were beginning to form a women's organization, now dedicating their energies to the welfare of the strikers. He had heard Mrs. Maples indignantly informing Myra Egan that Kate Dollar had offered to help them; a club existed as soon as there was someone to be excluded.

Jessie closed the door and went to stand listlessly by the table. "It is very tiring," she said.

"I don't expect it will need to be done much longer."

She shrugged. He knew she did not really care, yet it was what she had chosen for her role and she would fulfill that role to the limit of her strength, and probably better than someone who cared more. She bent her head as she leafed through the pages of a little book of poems on the table. The nape of her neck under the curls was white, downed with fair hair, and heartbreakingly thin.

He heard the sound of boots mounting the porch. "Jessie!" a voice called.

She moved to the door and opened it.

"The hogs are all fed, I see." It was MacDonald's voice, and the doctor went to join her in the doorway. "How long are you going to go on feeding this herd?"

"As long as they are hungry," Jessie said. MacDonald stood facing her, his derby hat in his hand. His pale, small-featured face was savage. With him was one of his foremen, Lafe Dawson, with a shotgun over his arm.

"Well, they are going to stay hungry as long as you are going to feed them," MacDonald said. "Why should they work when they can line up at your trough for every meal? You may think you are being quite the little angel of mercy, but let me tell—"

"Maybe you had better not talk so loud, Mr. MacDonald," Dawson said, rolling his eyes toward the stairs.

"I will talk as loudly as I wish! I am talking to you, too, Wagner. You are doing them a disservice. You are going to regret this; and they are."

"There are no Regulators any more, Charlie," the doctor said. It pleased him to see how frightened MacDonald was behind his mask of anger.

"I have heard from the company," MacDonald said. "They are backing me completely—completely! There is no pressure upon me to settle this strike, whatever lying rumors have been circulated to the contrary."

"Then why are you threatening us, Charlie?" Jessie said; she said it calmly and without guile, only as though she were puzzled.

"For your own good!" MacDonald tried to smile, and failed. "I have come to tell you that I have heard from Mr. Willingham. Mr. Arthur Willingham." He folded his arms, as though in triumph. "Mr. Willingham is in Bright's City today, to confer with General Peach. You may know that Mr. Willingham, besides being president of the

Porphyrion and Western Mining Company, has very important connections in Washington. I think that General Peach will not ignore what is going on down here any longer. If these men do not go back to work immediately, or if there is any more trouble down here whatsoever, you can be sure we will have martial law down here in every sense of the word, and a Mexican crew will then be brought in to work the Medusa. That," MacDonald said, "was my communication from Mr. Willingham." He waited, as though for some attempt at rebuttal.

Tittle and Fitzsimmons had appeared at the head of the hallway, and Dawson shifted his shotgun around to point at them.

"Have you had orders to settle the strike, Charlie?" Jessie asked.

"Are you calling me a liar?" MacDonald cried. "I tell you that Mr. Willingham is backing me one hundred per cent! The mining companies cannot allow a pack of ignorant, filthy foreigners to dictate to them how stopes are to be constructed, and what wages are to be paid!" MacDonald advanced a step, pointing a finger at the doctor as though it were a weapon. "Committees interfering with the work, and all the rest of this asininity you have put into their heads, Wagner. I see well enough that your *committees* are to be the Miners' Union in fact. It was *you*—the two of you! Well, I will not be blackguarded by a pack of strong-backed louts, nor by a couple of conspiring—criminally conspiring!—busybodies! I swear to you that I will fight this until they come creeping back begging for work!"

"Charlie," the doctor said. "I swear to you that I will do my best to see that they do not!"

MacDonald bared his teeth in the facsimile of a smile again, as though he had cunningly extracted a confession. "Remember that, Dawson," he said. "When General Peach comes down here we will have things to tell him about Doctor David Wagner. And about this house. A disorderly house," he said, and Jessie gasped.

"Watch your tongue, MacDonald!" the doctor cried. Dawson was grimacing horribly; Tittle started forward and Dawson swung the shotgun toward him again.

"I said a disorderly house!" MacDonald said. "A damnable mare's nest of criminal conspiracy against the mining companies. Conspiracy to commit arson! And murder, for all I know!" He stopped, panting, his eyes flickering insanely; and then he cried, "And a disorderly house in more ways than that! This house and you are a scandal to this town, Jessie. I can ruin you!"

"Shut up!" Tittle screamed. Fitzsimmons was trying to hold him, and Dawson nervously threatened him with the shotgun. "Shut up! You lying, dirty dog!" Tittle screamed, in a mechanical voice.

"That's enough, Ben," Jessie said.

"Shoot that man if he tries to attack me!" MacDonald said to his foreman, but Tittle had quieted.

Dawson was motioning toward the stairs. "Mr. MacDonald, you had better hush!"

MacDonald sneered. "And do not think I am frightened of your adulterous scandal of a marshal, either! You may be sure he will be—"

"Charlie, I will kill you myself!" the doctor cried. He could feel his heart pounding dangerously in his chest as he started forward. Dawson turned the shotgun toward him. Tittle's eyes were glaring from his contorted face, as insane as MacDonald's; as murderous, he thought suddenly, as his own face must look. Jessie put a hand on his arm and he halted.

"Charlie—" Jessie said. She spoke in a clear, loud voice, and her tone was condescending; she might have been speaking to an obstreperous boarder. "Charlie, you must be terribly afraid of losing your position. To speak to me like this."

MacDonald made a shrill sound. "The miners' angel!" he cried. "The gunman's whore, is better; and her eunuch!"

Tittle cried out, and Dawson clutched MacDonald's arm. MacDonald glanced frantically from face to face. "You—have been warned," he said, in a voice so hoarse his words were barely understandable. He backed away, then swung around, and, with Dawson close to his heels, hurried outside.

The doctor stared at Tittle's wild eyes in his gaunt, bony face. Tittle's mouth hung half open and he did not struggle now, in Fitzsimmons' grasp. He looked as though he were in agony as he glanced at Jessie, wordlessly; abruptly he hobbled away down the hall.

Jessie turned back into her room. The doctor had thought she would be shattered, but her face was only a little pink. He wanted to cry out to her to deny it, swear to him that it was not true. He knew that she could not deny it, for, although she had lied that once to Blaisedell, she would not lie to him. The gunman's whore, and her eunuch; he stood staring at her and in his mind's eye saw his heart swelling and stretching until he thought he must faint with it. Motionless, hardly breathing, he waited for the tight pain to recede.

"He was very frightened, Jessie," he said, surprised at the calmness of his voice, "or he would not have spoken as he did."

"Yes," Jessie said, nodding, her face pink still. "Charlie was very foolish to say those things."

In the hall he heard the uneven crack of Tittle's footsteps return and break into a run. With a steady, anguished grunting Tittle hurried outside; the doctor stepped out into the entryway just as Fitzsimmons came down the hall.

Then in the street he heard the shots, and the cry, and the answering deeper blast of Dawson's shotgun. "Why didn't you stop him?" he cried, as he ran for the door.

"He got away from me, Doc," Fitzsimmons said blandly, behind him.

52. Gannon Backs Off

GANNON had just come back from lunch at the Boston Café when he heard the shots—four of them in rapid succession, and the harsh cough of what sounded like a shotgun. He went out of the jail at a run, vaulted the tie rail, and ran down the street. The hot wind plucked at his hat. Morgan sat in his rocking chair on the veranda of the hotel, and, beyond, figures milled in the haze of heat and dust.

As he approached he saw that two men were supporting a third, while a fourth with a shotgun stood in the middle of the intersection facing into Grant Street. Men were running along with him on the boardwalk. He saw Pike Skinner join the group around the wounded man, and Ralph Egan come out of the Feed and Grain Barn.

It was Lafe Dawson, one of MacDonald's foremen, pointing the shotgun toward a group of miners on the corner of Grant Street. Oscar Thompson and Fred Wheeler set the wounded man down on the hotel steps. Blood spurted from his arm as Wheeler released it, and Wheeler quickly stripped off his belt and cinched it around the arm. The man was white with dust, as though he had been rolled in flour. As Gannon ran up someone tossed a hard-hat onto the boardwalk, where it thumped and rolled erratically.

"MacDonald, for Christ's sake!" Egan said.

MacDonald wiped his left hand over his dusty forehead, and turned his head with a reluctant movement to look at his arm. "Deputy!" he cried, in a stifled voice, as he saw Gannon. His mouth hung open and his lower lip was pulled down to show pale gums; his breath was so rapid it sounded as though he were whistling. He stared at Gannon with terrified eyes.

"Somebody'd better run for the doctor," Gannon said.

"Doc took the other one back to Miss Jessie's," Wheeler said. "He'll be along."

"What other one?"

"Murder!" MacDonald shouted explosively.

"Who the hell shot him?" Sam Brown demanded.

Lafe Dawson was backing toward them, still holding the shotgun pointed at the miners. Pike Skinner said, "Who was it, Lafe?"

"It was that crippled one that works for Miss Jessie," Dawson said shakily. "He was popping away from out of range. I couldn't—"

"Oh, you hit him," Oscar Thompson said.

"Tittle?" Gannon said.

"They put him to it!" MacDonald said. His tongue appeared to mop limply at his lips. "I know they put him to it!"

"Here comes Doc now," Wheeler said, and Gannon glanced around to see the doctor hurrying toward them from Grant Street. There was a good-sized crowd now, and more miners had collected. He saw Blaisedell's back as Blaisedell walked away toward the General Peach.

Men moved aside to let the doctor through. His face was as white as MacDonald's. "This is your work, Wagner!" MacDonald cried, and his eyes rolled toward Gannon again. "He is responsible, Gannon! He put him to it!"

"Hush now," the doctor said. He put down his bag and bent to look at the wound in MacDonald's upper arm.

"Get him away from me! Lafe!"

"You had better wait until I've dressed this arm, hadn't you?" the doctor said, straightening. "Or would it serve you better if you bled to death?"

MacDonald swayed faintly, and Thompson caught his shoulder.

From the hotel porch Morgan's voice was raised tauntingly. "You muckers over there! How come you send a cripple to do a mob's work?"

"You are going to open your flap one too many times yet, Morgan!" a rough voice retorted.

"Is that you, Brunk?" Morgan called, and laughed.

"Brunk's not here. He is keeping company with McQuown and they will hang you yet!"

The doctor said, "Can a couple of you bring him over to the Assay Office?"

"Surely, Doc," Thompson said, and he and Wheeler picked up Mac-Donald in a cradle-carry. The crowd parted as they carried MacDonald off down the street, with Lafe Dawson and the doctor following them.

Gannon saw Pike Skinner looking at him worriedly. Then, in the silence, he felt all the eyes on him. With an effort he kept himself from glancing down toward the General Peach, where Tittle was, where Blaisedell had gone. He heard whispering, and heard Blaisedell's name. Peter Bacon, chewing upon a toothpick, was watching him with an expression of elaborate unconcern. Someone said, loud in the silence, "Never heard a man make such a fuss over getting shot."

Gannon took a long breath, and, as though he were preparing to dive into very deep, cold, dark waters, slowly turned toward the corner of Grant Street. He started forward and heard the sudden stir of whispering around him. He walked steadily on and the miners on the corner parted before him; there were more before the General Peach, and these also moved silently aside for him. A curtain twitched in the window of Miss Jessie's room, where Carl had died.

The door opened before he reached it, and Miss Jessie confronted him. She wore one of her white schoolgirl's blouses and a black neckerchief, a black skirt. In her face was superiority and dislike, determination and contempt. Behind her, in the dimness of the entryway, he could sense, rather than see, Blaisedell standing.

"Yes, Deputy?" Miss Jessie said.

"I've come for Tittle, Miss Jessie."

She merely shook her head at him, and the brown ringlets slid like live things along the sides of her head.

"He has shot and hurt MacDonald. I will have to take him up to jail for the judge to hear him."

"He is hurt himself. I will not let him be taken anywhere."

Gannon could see Blaisedell now, standing far back beside the newel post at the bottom of the stairs. "I guess I will have to see him, then, Miss Jessie."

"Will you force my house?" she said, very quietly, and she caught hold of the edge of the door as though to slam it in his face.

"Leave him in her custody, Deputy," Blaisedell said, in his deep voice. "He'll not be leaving here."

Gannon tapped his hat against his leg. This was not right, he thought;

it did not matter that this was Miss Jessie Marlow, and Blaisedell behind her; it did not matter that it was MacDonald who was hurt, or that it was the crippled fellow who worked for Miss Jessie that had shot him. With growing anger he gazed back into Miss Jessie's contemptuous face. But he wished it had not happened this way.

Someone called his name. The judge came hurrying through the miners on the boardwalk, his crutch flying out and his body lurching so that he looked as though he would fall at every step. The judge waved a hand at him, and, panting, made his way up onto the porch. His hat had slipped forward over one eye. "Miss Jessie Marlow!" he panted. "The prisoner is released on your recognizance. Is that all right with you, ma'am? Fine!" he said, without waiting for an answer. He turned his sweating red face to Gannon. "Fine!" he said, more loudly, as though it were a command. "Now you help me down these steps, Deputy, before I break my neck!"

The judge swung around and tottered; Gannon caught his arm. "Come on!" the judge whispered. Gannon helped him down the stairs, and immediately the judge set out back along the boardwalk with his lurching, pounding gait. The miners stared at them expressionlessly as they passed.

They turned up Main Street under the arcade. "Come on, you damned fool!" the judge said. When they were alone and out of earshot of the men in the street he slowed his pace a little, panting again. "You will leave well enough alone!" he said savagely. "Or I will take this crutch and club you senseless—which you already are. Son, any kind of a damned fool ought to know not to snatch at gnats when there's camels to be swallowed still!"

"I know what I have to snatch at. What am I supposed to do, let any wild mucker that wants to shoot at MacDonald just because nobody likes MacDonald?"

"Right now you are going to."

"You damned old fraud!"

"I am," the judge said. "I have admitted it a hundred times. It is a time for fraud and not for bullheadedness. Son, I didn't ever think it of you. Did MacDonald make a complaint against him?"

"Not yet."

"You will anyhow wait till he does. And what will you do then? Tittle has got a load of buckshot in him; will you haul him to jail regardless?"

"She wouldn't let me see him even," Gannon said. His rage was running out, but it did not change anything. He had stood in the street where MacDonald had been shot and felt the eyes upon him, and had known they thought to a man that he would not go after Tittle because of Blaisedell. He would not let it matter what they thought of him, John Gannon, but it was time that it mattered what they thought of the deputy sheriff in Warlock.

"Son," the judge said, almost gently. "Have you been watching Blaisedell these days? I thought you saw things. He will step back so you can come forward, and God bless him for it. But he is not going to step back *because* you have come forward. Don't you even think of trying to push on him."

"I was trying to arrest a man that assaulted another with a deadly weapon in this town I am deputy in."

"Son, son," the judge said, in a tired voice. "It is like hearing myself talk when I was young and thought there was nothing but two ways about a thing. Do you know what I learned in the war besides that a minie ball can take a leg off? I learned it is better to swing around a flank than charge straight up a hill."

"Judge," he said. "I am going to stand up or I'm not. If I did not go there after Tittle I backed down in every man's eyes. And it was not just me that backed down."

"There is a time when a man does best to back down," the judge said, and evaded his eyes.

Gannon started on down toward the Assay Office, where there was another knot of men watching him come. The Judge crutched along beside him, grunting with the effort. Gannon knocked on the door of the doctor's office. It opened a crack and Dawson's scared face appeared. "What do you want?"

"I want to see MacDonald." Past Dawson he could see the doctor washing his hands in a crockery bowl. The doctor shook his head.

"Not now, Deputy. He's resting now. He has lost some blood."

"I want to see him as soon as he is able," he said, and Dawson nodded and closed the door. As he started on back to the jail Pike Skinner caught up with him and caught his arm, and he heard the crack of the judge's crutch behind him.

"Johnny, for Christ's sake!" Pike whispered. "Are you trying to get Blaisedell in a brace?"

"He has caught pride like a dose," the judge said.

Gannon swung around to face them. "It is not so, Judge," he said thickly.

"Listen!" Pike whispered. "Do you know what MacDonald did, Johnny? Went in the General Peach there and called Miss Jessie a whore to her face, and it a whorehouse! Johnny, any man'd done what that crippled one did. MacDonald is lucky Blaisedell wasn't there!"

Gannon looked from Pike's face to the judge's. His mind felt as though it would burst. It did not signify, he told himself. He walked slowly away from them, past Goodpasture's store, and across Main Street to the jail. He sat down heavily in the chair behind the table and stared at the sunlight that came through the door. Nothing was ever clear, everything was incredibly difficult, complex, and suspect; there was no right way. He sat in miserable loneliness contemplating himself and his deputyship. It was a long time before he heard footsteps on the boardwalk outside, and he supposed that it was Dawson coming.

Pike Skinner came inside, grinning. "MacDonald has skedaddled," he said. "Dawson went and got his buggy and brought it around just now, and they have lit out on the Bright's City road." He grinned more widely. "The judge said you might be pleased to hear it."

He didn't answer, and Pike's face stiffened. "What are you going to do, Johnny?"

He shook his head; relief made him feel giddy. "Why, nothing I guess. I guess there is nothing to do."

53. At the General Peach

I

UPSTAIRS in the General Peach a group of miners had collected in old man Heck's room. Heck was standing; his skinny neck stuck out as he spoke. "If there is any trouble we will stand behind Blaisedell," he said. "That's what we have to do, every man jack of us. He said to me there wasn't going to be any trouble and no reason looking for any, and how the deputy'd just left Ben in Miss Jessie's custody. But I notice Miss Jessie didn't look so sure. I told him we would stand right behind him all the way. It is something we got now."

"That deputy's gone and got too big for his britches," Bull Johnson said.

"Jimmy said MacDonald called Miss Jessie a whore," Frenchy Martin said.

They all looked at Fitzsimmons, who stood before the door. He placed one disfigured hand in the other and nodded.

"Why, God damn him!" Bull Johnson said, with awe in his voice. "He did? Did you hear him, Jimmy?"

Fitszsimmons told them what he and Ben Tittle had heard MacDonald say to Miss Jessie and the doctor.

"Dirty God-damned buggering rotten son of a bitch!" Bardaman cried. Patch added his curses, and each man cursed MacDonald in turn, formally, as though it were a kind of ritual.

"We should've burnt the Medusa long since!" old man Heck said. "And run MacDonald right out of the territory."

"It's not too late," Bull Johnson said. "There's matches still."

"Is Ben hurt bad, Jimmy?" Patch asked.

They all looked to Fitzsimmons again. "He has got some shot in him. In his legs mostly." Fitzsimmons looked as though he could hardly restrain a smile.

"I'll break Lafe Dawson in half!" Bull Johnson said.

Fitzsimmons laughed, then, and said, "Do you know what is funny? MacDonald thinks he is way ahead of us now."

"How's that, Jimmy?" Daley asked.

"Why, because Ben shot him. He thinks he can hold it up to everybody now how we are a bunch of wild men."

"What's so funny about that?"

"I believe," Bull Johnson said, squinting at Fitzsimmons. "I do believe that sonny-boy here is going to lecture the grownups again, and going around the barn to do it."

Fitzsimmons flushed. "Well, MacDonald does, and he is wrong. You fellows should have seen him downstairs. Miss Jessie asked him to his face if he'd got orders to settle, and you should have heard him yell. He yelled too much," he said, and grinned. "I would just make a bet he *had* got orders to settle, and he is scared to death we can sit him out. But now he thinks he is way ahead of us, on account of getting shot. Do you know the best thing that could happen to us? If Ben got taken to the judge and heard. And better yet if he got sent up to Bright's City to court. We would be the worst kind of tom-fools to try to stop them from taking him out of here. Because then it would come out in court what MacDonald said to Miss Jessie. Threatening her like he did, and calling her what he did. You see?"

"I see we ought to cut his balls for him," Bardaman said uncertainly.

Fitzsimmons shook his head and leaned easily against the door. "No, for if we just tread soft for a while he has ruined himself for good. There'll be others to cut his balls for us when this gets out. And if it came to trial at Bright's! I expect Mister Mac might hear more from Willingham. People think high of Miss Jessie, and not just here. MacDonald is gone out in the bucket if we just play it right. If we can just last it out."

"I think maybe Jimmy is talking sense," Bardaman said.

"Good sense," Daley added quietly.

"By God, maybe we are not plowed under yet!" Patch cried.

Frenchy Martin leaned forward. "You think we might pull it off yet, eh, Jimmy?"

"I know so."

"What about the union, Jimmy?" Bardaman said. He leaned forward too. Old man Heck was scowling a little, and Bull Johnson gnawed on a knuckle, but he was watching Jimmy Fitzsimmons too. They all watched him, waiting to hear what he had to say, and he smiled triumphantly from face to face, and began to speak.

II

In the hospital room, Ben Tittle lay on his cot like a bas-relief figure beneath the bedclothes. The whisky bottle the doctor had left was on the floor beside him. When Miss Jessie and Blaisedell appeared Tittle raised his head and grinned, showing crooked yellow teeth. The flesh on his bony face was an unhealthy, tender-looking white. "They going to hang me, Miss Jessie?" he said.

"No, they are not going to hang you, Ben," Miss Jessie said. She came forward to sit on the edge of his cot, while the marshal remained in the doorway.

"Why, heck, and I was just in the mood for a hanging, too," Tittle said. "Hello, Mr. Blaisedell." The drunken grin looked pasted to his face. He said in a quieter voice, "Mister Mac cashed in yet?"

"Nobody's heard," Blaisedell said.

"You are to quiet down, Ben," Miss Jessie said. "You have been drinking too much of that whisky. The doctor left it to stop the pain."

"What did you want to take a shot at MacDonald for, fellow?" Blaisedell asked gravely. "That didn't do anybody any good."

The pasted smile disappeared. Tittle pouted. "Well, I know what is owed around here, Mr. Blaisedell. Even if no other ungrateful mutts don't. I can pay my debts as well as any man."

Blaisedell frowned. Miss Jessie, however, patted Tittle's hand, and he seemed relieved. He lay back on his pillow with the smile returning.

"Why, I don't like to make trouble for nobody, Marshal," he said. "Excepting for a man who would talk to a lady like that. Said dirty things," he said, and his voice fell with embarrassment. Then his voice grated as he said, "I hope he goes out painful, if I get lawed for it or not."

"Said what things?" Blaisedell said.

"He threatened me, Clay," Miss Jessie said quickly. "For feeding them here."

"I know that. Said what dirty things, fellow?"

Cords drew tight in Tittle's neck as he raised his head again. "Why, I guess—I guess I knew it was your place, Marshal," he said. "But it come on me so, you see. But I guess you would have got him square, and finished him." He looked pleadingly at Miss Jessie. "Did I do wrong, ma'am?"

She patted his hand. "No, Ben."

"I did it for you. The only thing I ever found to show—" He stopped, and drew a deep breath and said, angrily now, "For all of us! And if I hang for it that is fine too, and little enough."

"We won't let them hang you, Ben," Miss Jessie said. She gazed at Blaisedell with her great eyes. Blaisedell moved aside as footsteps hurried down the hall and the doctor appeared. His gray, crop-bearded face was grim.

"MacDonald?" Blaisedell asked.

"He is all right," the doctor said. He stood frowning down at Tittle. "As a matter of fact he has left for Bright's City. Ben, you have not done the Medusa strikers much good today."

Ben Tittle laughed shrilly. "I run him out!"

"Maybe you did," the doctor said, but he shook his head at Miss Jessie, and strain showed suddenly in her face. "Well, I will give you a little laudanum, Ben," the doctor said. "And start picking the lead out of your hide." He put his bag down and rummaged through it. "Jessie, you had better leave."

Miss Jessie rose quickly. She went over to join Blaisedell, and took his arm as Tittle cried happily, "Go ahead and dig, Doc. A man can stand a lot to know that he has run Mister Mac out of Warlock!"

54. Morgan Makes a Bargain

MORGAN sat in his chair in his room at the hotel, reading the magazine by the late sunlight that came in the window. From time to time he chuckled, and frequently he turned back to the cover where, on the cheap gray paper, there was a crude woodcut of a face that was meant to be his face. Beneath it was the inscription: *The Black Rattlesnake of Warlock.*

It was a narrow, dark face with Chinese-slanted eyes, a drooping mustache, and lank black hair combed like a bartender's. There was a wart high on the right cheek, close to the nose. Maybe it was only an ink smear, he thought, and brought the face closer to his eyes; it was a wart. He raised a hand to touch his own mustache, his own hair, his his own cheek where the wart was shown. "Why, you devil!" he said, with awed hilarity. "The Black Rattlesnake of Warlock!" He whooped and beat his hand on his thigh.

He skipped rapidly through the account of the Acme Corral shooting again, grinning, shaking his head. "Well, that will teach them to stand around with their backs to the Black Rattlesnake," he said. There was a knock, and he rose and stuffed the magazine under his pillow. "Who's that?"

"It's Kate, Tom."

He stretched and yawned, and went to open the door. Kate came in. She closed the door behind her and he nodded approvingly. "Dangerous," he said. "Dangerous for anybody to know you are creeping in to see Tom Morgan. That's a handsome bonnet, Kate."

"Are you going?" she asked abruptly. Her eyes were very black in her white face, her jaw seemed set crookedly.

"Why, one of these days," he said. "When I get through bleeding Taliaferro. I will have the price of the Glass Slipper back from him before long."

"Where are you going?"

"North, or east. I might go west, though, or south. Or up, or down."

She seated herself on the edge of the bed. She said, "I know you killed McQuown."

"Do you? Well, you don't miss much, do you, Kate?"

"You did it so they would blame the deputy for it."

"Here! I don't give a damn about—"

"I know you did!" she said. She bit her lip, breathing deeply. "But it went wrong. People know you did it and they are saying Blaisedell sent you. It is so wonderful when some dirty thing you do goes wrong."

He sat down again, and propped his boots up on the bed beside her. "I know I am everything bad that's ever happened in this town. I've just been reading about it. Look under the pillow there."

She felt under the pillow as though there might be a rattlesnake there, which, in fact, there was. She looked at the picture on the cover without interest. After a moment she let the magazine drop to the floor.

"I'm famous, Kate!" he went on. "I'm probably the evilest man in the West." He felt his finger touch his cheek, where the picture had showed the wart. "Women will use me to scare their babies with."

"I know you killed McQuown," Kate said. "You did it for Clay, too, didn't you?"

"I forget *why* I did it, Kate. Sometimes I just can't keep track of why I do things." He took out a cheroot and scratched a match. He blew smoke between them and regarded her through the smoke as she slowly inclined her face down away from his eyes, to stare at her clasped hands in her lap.

"Tom," she said. "I will ask you to do something for me for once."

"What do you want? The Glass Slipper for you and Buck and Taliaferro to turn into a dance hall? It is pretty poor shape."

"No, I don't want anything to do with a dance hall. I want you to do something for me. I am asking you a favor, Tom."

"Ask it."

She spoke rapidly now, and her voice sounded frail and thin. "You've heard about this afternoon. I don't know what happened exactly but— but all of a sudden everybody seems to know there is going to be trouble between the deputy and Clay."

He leaned back and blew more smoke between them.

"Not only that," Kate went on. "But there *is* talk you killed Mc-Quown. Whether you did or not, there is talk."

"You are back on that again."

"Because I think—I think he has an idea you did it. He—"

"Who?"

"The deputy! I think he thinks you did it. I think he will be after

you about it. Tom, don't you see that sets him against Clay *again?*"
He watched her eyes begin to redden, and her nose. He took the cigar
from his mouth and examined it. "I am not going to let Clay Blaisedell
kill him!" Kate continued. Now she sounded as though she had a cold
in her head.

"Another Bob Cletus," he said. "Well, I am nothing to do with it this
time, Kate."

"You can stop Clay." Her eyes glistened with tears, and the tears
made little tracks in the powder on her cheeks.

"Why, Kate, you have gone and got yourself in love with that ugly
clodhopping farmer of a deputy. Again. What do you want to do,
marry him and raise a brood?"

She didn't answer.

"Why, you pitiful old whore," he said, and it twisted within him
like a big wrench forcing a rusty bolt.

"There is no word for you!" she whispered.

"Black rattlesnake?" he suggested. "Evilest man in the West?" He
stopped; he did not know why he should suddenly feel so angry at
her.

"Tom," she begged. "You could ask Clay the way I am asking you.
How would it hurt you to do something for me? Make Clay go with
you."

"He has got Miss Jessie Marlow to hold him. And she won't go; she
is prime angel here."

"You could do something!"

"I might make a bargain with you."

"What?"

"Since your deputy is the only one that matters. If *you* went with me
I might be able to do something."

He saw her close her eyes.

"I know you would like to marry up with a famous hardcase-killer,
now that your deputy has got to be one. Like Miss Angel Marlow
with Clay. But I have got to come out of it with *something*, so you and
me is the bargain. Why, you would be a mistress to the evilest man in
the West and famous in your own right. We will go around in side-
shows and charge admission to see the worst old horrors there are, make
a fortune at it. We'd make a pair."

She did not speak, and he went on. "If I can figure some way to get
Clay out of line toward killing your deputy, this is. I might as well
set it all out for you to agree to, or not. For instance, things might
get bad from time to time so that we needed a stake. It would be up

to you to apply yourself to your line of work and make us one. Now and then."

"Yes," Kate whispered.

His voice hurt in his throat; his grin hurt his face. "Well, and you would be party to my evil schemes. Murder people together, you and me. Rob stages. Corrupt innocent people to our evil ways—all that sort of thing."

She did not speak, but she was looking up at him. He rose to stand before her, and put a hand on her shoulder. "Why, Kate," he said shakily. "You act like you don't believe what I'm saying."

She shook her head a little.

"You have gone and got yourself in terrible shape over that deputy, haven't you? Pretty decent, is he, Kate?"

"I don't want to talk about him."

He took his hand from her shoulder. He felt as though he had been poisoned. "Not to me?" he said viciously. "Pretty good in your bed, is he? That lean, hungry-looking kind."

Slowly, silently, she bent her head still farther until all he could see was the top of her hat. "Tell me what you want, Tom."

"We'll make our bargain right here and now, then. You are sitting in the right place."

Sour laughter coiled and wrenched inside him as he watched one of her hands rise to her throat. It fumbled at the top cut-steel button of her dress. The button came open and her hand dropped to the second one. Her shoulders were shaking. "Oh, stop it," he said. "I don't want you."

He stooped and picked up the magazine, where she had dropped it. He rolled it and slapped it hard against his leg as he sat down in the chair again. Kate had not moved. Her hand fumbled at the top button again; then she folded her hands in her lap.

"You have touched my black heart," he said. When he released his grip on the magazine it sprang open, but he did not want to see the picture again and he brushed it off onto the floor. He touched the place on his cheek. It occurred to him that he was making a mannerism of this, and it seemed strange that it should be like the one of Kate's he knew so well.

"So I have to give you Johnny Gannon for Bob Cletus," he said.

Her head jerked up, her wet eyes slid toward his. He said harshly, "Clay would no sooner go after him than—" He stopped.

"I am afraid Johnny will make him," Kate said. "Or—they will make him."

"They?"

She shrugged, but he nodded.

"*She,*" he said. "More likely. Miss Angel," he said, nodding matter-of-factly. That would be it, although that was a part of it that Kate didn't know enough to worry about yet.

He said, "Well, Gannon for Cletus and square," and laughed a little. "All right, Kate."

"Thanks, Tom."

"Get out of here now. People will think you are not a lady."

Obediently she rose and moved to the door. She was very tall; with her hat on she was taller than he was. She looked back at him as she started to pull the door closed, and he said, "You don't need to worry, Kate. I expect Clay would rather shoot himself than your deputy."

The door shut her face from him. He sat slumped in the chair, chewing on his cigar and listening to her retreating footsteps. He was tired of it all, he told himself. He had no interest in Kate, less in her deputy; what did he care what happened to Clay? He did not care to see how it would all come out. Nothing ever ended anyway. He sat there brooding at the sunlit window, sometimes raising a finger to his cheek with an exploratory touch. He was the evilest man in the West, he told himself, and tried to laugh. This time it would not come.

After a while he rose reluctantly. It was time to go and try himself against Lew Taliaferro again. Last night he had let Taliaferro beat him. But no one could beat him if he did not want it, and he was tired of that, too.

55. Judge Holloway

IN THE jail Judge Holloway sat at the table with his arms crossed on his chest and his whisky bottle before him, his crutch leaning against his chair. Mosbie sat with his hat tipped forward over his eyes. In the cell a Mexican snored upon the floor, and Jack Jameson, from Bowen's Sawmill, waited out his twenty-four hours looking through the bars. Peter Bacon whittled on a crooked stick in his chair beside the alley door.

Pike Skinner, standing with his hands on his hips, turned as Buck

Slavin came into the doorway. Slavin was in his shirtsleeves and wore a bed-of-flowers vest with a gold watch chain across it.

"Where is the deputy?" Slavin demanded.

"Rid out somewhere," Bacon said, without looking up from his whittling.

"Run with his tail between his legs," Jack Jameson said, from the cell. Everyone looked at him, and he winked dramatically, stooping to thrust his narrow, lantern-jawed face between the bars. "Run from the pure hypocritter of it," he said. "To see a man hoicked in the lock-up for drunk and disorderly by a judge with a whisky bottle tied on his face."

"You will have another twenty-four hours for contempt before you are through," the judge said mildly.

"Scaring all those poor girls at the French Palace with a mean old six-shooter," Mosbie said. "You ought to be ashamed, Jack."

" 'Twasn't any six-shooter that scared them," Jameson said. "It was a dommed big gatling gun. By God, what's things come to when a man hasn't seen hide nor hair of a woman for two months and comes busting into town for it, and then has to spend the night with a puking dommed greaser."

"Rode out where?" Slavin said.

"What's fretting *you*?" Skinner said. "Somebody pop another stage?"

"They've popped enough, and I'm sick of it. It's God-damn time Gannon got out of town and did something about it!"

"Tell it to him to his face!" Skinner said angrily.

"I've told him to his face! I've told him he doesn't earn his keep here. He thinks he did his job forever, shooting Wash Haggin!"

The judge sighed and said, "Buck, let me tell you the sad, sad facts of life. There will be no justice for you or for those poor ranchers weeping over their lost stock, without cash paid on the barrelhead for it. You wail and gnash your teeth for policing, but are you willing to pay for it yet? Are those ranchers I hear screaming down there willing yet? How much louder will they wail and gnash when they see the tax collector coming? Let me tell you, Buck; the deputy is doing his job exactly right. Those Philistines down there are going to be cleaned out when the sheriff is forced to do it, and that will be when the belly-aching gets so loud it hurts General Peach's ears."

"Seven stages thrown down on since McQuown got killed!" Slavin said. "When McQuown was—"

"McQuown!" Mosbie broke in, and, in a rasping voice, he cursed McQuown at length.

Jameson said, "By God if it don't look like everybody is escared of old Abe yet."

"Let him stay buried," Bacon said gloomily. "If he gets dug up he will stink to heaven."

"Morgan'll stink," Slavin said.

Skinner said uncomfortably, "I just don't see how everybody got so certain all at once it was Morgan did it."

"Johnny rode out to see Charlie Leagle," Bacon said.

"He supposed to've seen Morgan?" Slavin asked, and Bacon nodded.

"Supposed to be more than Leagle saw him," Mosbie said.

Skinner paced the floor with his hands locked behind his back. He glared at the names scratched on the wall; he swung around and glared at the judge, who had picked up the whisky bottle. "Well, tell us about it, you righteous old son of a bitch!" Skinner cried. "I remember how you used to blister Carl, and you are blistering kind of different lately. Tell us how Johnny has to go after Morgan if it looks like Morgan was the one! Tell us how Johnny has to yank Tittle out of Miss Jessie's place under Blaisedell's nose, if a warrant comes down. I saw you charging down to get him out of dutch with Blaisedell like you was trying to bust the pole-vault champeenship, you damned drunken fraud. Come on, tell us, Judge! You won't, will you? You are as sick as any man here, that used to preach at us till it came out our ears. Let's hear you preach now!"

The judge tipped his whisky bottle to his lips and drank.

"Has to pour whisky in itself before it can talk," Jameson commented.

"Shut up!" Skinner said. He leaned back against the wall with his arms folded.

But the judge did not speak, and Mosbie said, "Surely Johnny has got sense enough not to buck up against Blaisedell."

"Hasn't," Skinner said, "is the trouble." He glared at the judge. "Well, what do you say? Preach us about how he is only doing his damned duty!"

The judge nodded, and glanced up at Skinner from under his eyebrows.

"I noticed you stopping him from it the other day fast enough."

"Wheels within wheels," the judge said.

Skinner snorted. He swung around to face Slavin. "And you'd like to see him kiting off down valley so they could snipe him off from behind some rock. I suppose you can't see around a Concord far enough to see it is just what *they* want him to do."

"What they are doing," Bacon said. "They are using McQuown getting killed for an excuse for hell-roaring all over the place. So I expect Johnny figures maybe he can quiet them by sticking who did it."

"Which is Morgan," Mosbie said.

"It's a cleft stick for you," Bacon said, and shook his head.

"It is a cleft stick for Johnny Gannon," Skinner said. "Well, what do you say now?" he said to the judge. "Maybe you like all this?"

"No," the judge said thickly. "I don't like it, and don't you scorn me, you great lumbering lout! I wasn't liking it before you ever saw it."

"Say Morgan did it," Mosbie said, in his rasping voice. "Say he did and he is a dirty dog, and I won't deny it. But he is Blaisedell's friend, and I say this town owes Blaisedell one or two things, or two hundred—what he has done here. I say we can give him Morgan."

"Blaisedell has to go," Slavin said firmly. "Not just because of the friends he picks, either."

"Buck!" Mosbie said. "I want to hear you say out loud that Blaisedell has done no good here. I want to hear you say it."

"Why, I don't deny he has, fellows," Slavin said. "Nobody does. It is just time for him to move on, and mostly it is time because of Morgan."

"Tell you what you do, Buck," Skinner said. "Next meeting you make a motion he is to post Morgan out. Since you are starting to speak up so bold."

Slavin stood there biting his lip and frowning. "One thing," he said. "One thing I have got against Blaisedell that isn't Morgan. He makes people take sides hard against him or for him. He makes bad contention." He nodded to the others, turned, and departed.

"Well, I am for the marshal," Bacon said sadly. "But it certainly makes a man sick and tired—and makes him think. How Johnny is coming against him. Want it or not, looks like."

"Johnny can go his way and Blaisedell his," Skinner said. "I can't see why they can't go along and not scratch each other. Blaisedell has never made a move to set himself against Johnny. Not one!"

"I guess Johnny hasn't gone and made any move against Blaisedell, for that," Bacon said. "I guess it just looks like he is going to have to, one of these days."

"Over Morgan," Mosbie said.

"You boys are starting to make me feel real sorrowful over the deputy," Jameson said. "It looks like he is in dommed bad shape."

They all watched a fly circling in flat, eccentric planes over the judge's head. The judge waved it away. "It is the awkward time," he said. "It is where this town don't know yet whether it still needs a daddy to protect it, or not."

"You don't have to kick your daddy in the face when you have got your growth," Bacon said.

Jameson said, "You know what my old dad did to me once? I—"

"Shut up!" Skinner yelled at him.

Mosbie stirred in his chair. "There's some things I wish I knew about Johnny," he said. "I wish I knew how he felt about it when Blaisedell shot Billy. I wouldn't want to think—"

"He don't hold it against Blaisedell," Skinner said. "I can say that for sure."

Mosbie nodded.

Then Bacon spoke. "Man doesn't like to talk about him when he is not here," he said, in an embarrassed voice. "But there's something been bothering me too I'd better speak up about. Maybe somebody can—" He paused, and his wrinkled face turned pink. "Well, that Kate Dollar he is seeing pretty good. There is that talk how she is down on Blaisedell, and why, from Fort James. And Johnny seeing so much of her, you know."

"Set Johnny against the marshal, you think?" Skinner said worriedly. He began to shake his head. "I don't think—"

The judge slapped the palm of his hand down on the table. "If you boys would accept my judgment," he said. "I would say that Johnny Gannon wouldn't do anything any of you wouldn't, nor hold to a reason you wouldn't. And I would say he is more honest with himself than most, too."

Skinner was scowling. "Only—" he said, in a husky voice. "Only, God damn it to hell, if it comes to it, and pray God it don't, Blaisedell is the one I would have to side with. Because—"

"That's where you are wrong," the judge broke in. "Thinking you can put it so you are choosing between two men."

"Well, Judge," Skinner said. "Maybe us poor, simple, stupid common folks has to look at it that way. Us that sees more trees than forest."

"Yes, I suppose so," the judge said. He let his head hang forward; he gripped the neck of his whisky bottle. "But maybe you have to see by now that the deputy here is only doing what the deputy here is going to have to do."

Skinner's red gargoyle's face grew redder still, and deep corrugations showed in his forehead. He took a deep breath. Then he shouted, "Yes,

I can see it! But damned if I want to!" He swung around and stamped out the door.

"He's one for getting upset," Jameson commented. "That one."

"You know what I get to thinking about?" Bacon said. "I get to thinking back on the old days in Texas droving cattle up to the railroad. Didn't own a thing in the world but the clothes I had on and the saddle I sat. So nothing to worry about, and nothing but hard work day in and day out sort of purifies a man. No forests there," he said, smiling faintly at the judge. "It is the forests that wear a man down dead inside, Judge."

"It is the lot of the human race," the judge said. He raised his bottle and shook it. Staring at the bottle he said, "And it is terrible past the standing of it. But I have here the universal solvent. For wine is the color of blood and the texture of tears, and you can drink it to warm your belly and piss it out to get rid of it. And forget the whole damned mess that is too much for any man to face."

"That's not wine," Jameson said. "That's raw whisky."

The judge looked at him with a bleared eye. "I will sleep in a cask of raw whisky," he went on. "Wake me up and pump me out when everyone is dead." His voice shook, and his hand shook, holding the bottle. "What are deputies to me?" he said hoarsely. "Deputies or marshals. They are nothing, and I will not be a hypocrite to sentimentality when I can drink myself above it all. Wake me up when they have killed each other off! Miner and superintendent, vigilante and regulator, deputy and marshal. They are as dead leaves falling and nothing to me. Nothing!" he shouted. He banged the whisky bottle down on the table top, raising it high and crashing it down again, his face twisting and twitching in drunken horror. "Nothing!" he shouted. "Nothing! Nothing!"

They watched him in awe at his grief, as he continued to cry "Nothing!" and bang the bottle. The Mexican's swollen, sleepy face appeared, a square below and to the right of that of Jameson, who whispered, "Listen to the dommed old bastard go!"

56 Morgan Looks at the Cards

I

Sitting in the cane-bottomed rocker in the shade on the hotel veranda, Morgan sat watching Warlock in the morning. There were not many people on the street: a prospector with a beard like a bird's nest sat on the bench before the Assay Office; a white-aproned barkeep swept the boardwalk before the Billiard Parlor; a Cross-Bit wagon was pulled up alongside the Feed and Grain Barn, and Wheeler and a Mexican carried out plump bags which one of Burbage's sons stacked into the wagon-bed. To the southwest the Dinosaurs shimmered in the sun. They seemed very close in the clear air, but improbably jagged and the shadows sharply cut, so that they had a painted look, like a fanciful theater backdrop. The Bucksaws, nearer, were smooth and brown, and he watched a wagon train mounting the circuitous road to the Sister Fan mine.

He stretched hugely, sighed hugely. Inside the dining room behind him he could hear the tinny clink and clatter of dishes and cutlery; it was a pleasant sound. He watched Mrs. Egan bustling down Broadway with her market basket, neat and crisp in starched light-blue gingham, her face hidden in a scoop bonnet. He could tell from the way she carried herself that she was daring any man to make a remark to *her*.

He smiled, strangely moved by the fresh, light color of her dress. He had found himself thus susceptible to colors for the last several days. He had admired the smooth, dark, smoked tan of the burnt-out Glass Slipper yesterday, and the velvet sudden black of the charred timbers in it. Now on the faded front of the Billiard Parlor, where Sam Brown had taken his sign down to have it repainted, there was a rectangle of yellow where the paint had been hidden from the sun; yellow was a fine color. He had begun remembering colors, too; in his mind's eye he could see very vividly the color of the grass in the meadows of North Carolina, and the variety of colors of the trees in autumn—a thousand different shades; he remembered, too, the trees in Louisiana, the sleek, warm, blackish, glistening green of the trunks after it had rained and the sun had come out; and the trees in Wyoming after an ice storm in the sun, when all the world was made of crystal, and all seemed fragile and still; and he remembered the sudden red slashes of earth in west Texas where the dull plains began to turn into desert country.

"Pardon me if I take this other chair here, sir." It was the drummer who had come to town yesterday, and had the room across the hall from his. He sat down. He wore a hard-hat, and a tight, cheap, checked suit. He was smooth-shaven, with heavy, pink dewlaps.

"Fine morning," the drummer said heartily, and offered him a cigar, which he took, smelled, and flung out into the dust of the street. He took one of his own from his breast pocket, and turned and stared the drummer in the eye until he lit it for him.

"I wonder if you could point out Blaisedell for me, if he comes by," the drummer said, not so heartily. "I've never been in Warlock before and we've heard so much of Blaisedell. I swore to Sally—that's my wife —I'd be sure I saw Blaisedell so I could tell her—"

"Blaisedell?"

"Yes, sir, the gunman," the drummer said. He lisped a little. "The fellow that runs things here. That killed all those outlaws in the corral there by the stage depot. I stopped in there yesterday when I got in for a look around."

"Blaisedell doesn't run things here." He stared the drummer in the eye again. "*I* do."

The drummer looked as though he were sucking on the inside of his mouth.

"You can tell your wife Sally you saw Tom Morgan," he said. He felt pleased, watching the fright in the drummer's face, but his stomach contracted almost in a cramp. He flicked his cigar toward the drummer's checked trousers. "Don't go around here saying Clay Blaisedell runs Warlock."

"Yes, sir," the drummer whispered.

The water wagon passed on Broadway, Bacon sitting hunched on the seat, his whip nodding over the team. The rust on the tank shone red with spilled water. The red of rust was a fine color. When the water wagon had passed he saw Gannon coming toward him under the arcade.

"Get out of here," he said to the drummer. "Here comes another one that thinks he runs Warlock."

The drummer rose and fled; Morgan laughed to hear the clatter of his boots diminishing, watching Gannon coming on across Broadway. The sun caught the star on his vest in a momentarily brilliant shard of light.

He came on up on the veranda and sat down in the chair the drummer had vacated.

"Morning, Morgan," he said, and nervously rubbed his bandaged hand upon his leg.

"Is, isn't it?" He crossed his legs and yawned.

Gannon was frowning. "Going to be hot," he said, as though he had just thought it out.

"Good bet." He nodded and looked sideways at Gannon's lean, strained face, his bent nose and hollow cheeks. He touched a finger gently to his own cheek, waiting for Gannon to get his nerve up.

"I've found two of them saw you coming back," Gannon said finally, "the morning after McQuown was killed."

He didn't say anything. He flicked the gray ash from his cigar.

"I heard you when you went by me," Gannon said, staring straight ahead. "Off to the east of me a way. I couldn't say I saw you, though."

"No?"

"I'd like to know why you did it," Gannon said, almost as though he were asking a favor.

"Did what?"

Gannon sighed, grimaced, rubbed the palm of his hand on his leg. The butt of his Colt hung out, lop-eared, past the seat of his chair; if he wanted to draw it he would have to fight the chair like a boa constrictor. "I think I know why," he went on. "But it would sound pretty silly in court."

"Just leave it alone, Deputy," Morgan said gently.

Gannon looked at him. One of his eyes was larger than the other, or, rather, differently shaped, and his nose looked like something that had been chewed out of hard wood with a dull knife. It was, in fact, very like the face of one of those rude *Christos* carved by a Mexican Indio with more passion than talent. It was a face only a mother could love, or Kate.

"Deputy," he said. "You don't hold any cards. You found two men that saw me riding into town, but I know, and you know, that as much as those people down the valley would be pleased if it turned out I had shot McQuown, they have jerked the carpet out from underneath it by all of them swearing up and down it was you that did it. They can't do anything but make damned fools of themselves, and you can't. So just sit back out of the game and rest while the people that have the cards play this one out. It is none of your business."

"It is my business," Gannon said.

"It is not. It's something so far off from you you will only hear it go by. Off to the east a way. You probably won't even hear it."

They sat in silence for a while. He rocked. Finally Gannon said, "You leaving here, Morgan?"

He gazed at the bright yellow patch over the Billiard Parlor. "One of these days," he said. "A few things to tend to first. Like seeing to a thing for Kate."

He waited, but Gannon didn't ask what it was, which was polite of him. So he said, "She thinks you are about to choose Clay out. I promised I'd watch over you like a baby."

Gannon cleared his throat. "Why would you do that?"

Why, for one thing, he thought, because I saw you get that hand punctured by a hammer pin one night; but aloud he said, "You mean why would I do it for her?" He turned and looked Gannon in the eye. "Because she was mine for about six years. All mine, except what I rented out sometimes." He was ashamed of saying it, and then he was angry at himself as he saw Gannon's eyes narrow as though he had caught on to something.

"That's no reason," Gannon said calmly. "Though it might be a reason for you to kill Cletus."

It shook him that Kate should have told her deputy. Or maybe she hadn't, since it was something anybody could pick up at the French Palace, along with a dose. "That wasn't in your territory, Deputy," he said. "Leave that alone too."

Gannon looked puzzled, and Morgan realized he had been speaking of Pat Cletus. He felt a stirring of anxiety, and he thought he had better set Gannon back on his haunches. He stretched and said, "Are you going to make an honest woman of Kate, Deputy?"

Gannon's face turned boiled red.

"Morgan grinned. "Why, fine," he said. "I'll sign over all rights to you, surface and mining. And give the bride away too. Or don't you want me to stay that long?"

Gannon turned away. "No," he said. "I don't want you to stay, since you asked."

"Running me out?"

"No, but if you don't get out I will have to take this I came to ask you about as far as it goes."

"And you don't want to do that."

"I don't want to, no," Gannon said, shaking his head. "And like you say I don't expect I'll get much of anywhere. But I will have to go after it."

"You could leave it alone, Deputy," he said. "Just stand back out of the way awhile. Things will happen and things will come to pass, and none of it concerns you or much of anybody else. I will be going in my own time."

Gannon got to his feet, splinter-thin and a little bent-shouldered. "A couple of days?" Gannon said doggedly.

"In my own good time."

Gannon started away.

"Don't post me out of town, Deputy," Morgan whispered. "That's not for *you* to do."

He regarded what he had just said. He had not even thought of it before he had said it; or maybe he had, and had just decided it.

But it was the answer, wasn't it? he thought excitedly. And maybe he could still keep the cake intact, and let the others think they saw crumbs and icing all over Clay's face. He began to check it through, calculating it as though it were a poker hand whose contents he knew, but which was held by an opponent who did not play by the same rules he did, or even the same game.

II

Later he sat waiting for Clay at a table near the door of the Lucky Dollar. He watched the thin slants of sun that fell in through the louvre doors, destroyed, each time a man entered or departed, in a confusion of shifting, jumbled light and shadow as the doors swung and reswung in decreasing arcs. Then they would stand stationary again, and the barred pattern of light would reform. During the afternoon the light would creep farther in over Taliaferro's oiled wood floor, and finally would die out as the sun went down, and another day gone.

He did not think he would do more today than test the water with his foot, to see how cold it was.

The pattern of light was broken again; he glanced up and nodded to Buck Slavin, who had come in. Slavin nodded back, hostilely. Look out, he thought, with contempt; I will turn you to stone. "Afternoon," Slavin said, and went on down the bar. Look out, I will corrupt you if you even speak to me. He could see the faces of the men along the bar watching him in the glass; he could feel the hate like dust itching beneath his collar. From time to time Taliaferro would appear from his office—to see if he had begun to ride the faro game yet, and Haskins, the half-breed pistolero from the French Palace, watched him from the bar, in profile to him, with his thin mustache and the scar across his brown chin like a shoemaker's seam, his Colt thrust into his belt.

He nodded with exaggerated courtesy to Haskins, poured a little more whisky in his glass, and sipped it as he watched the patterns of light. He heard the rumble of hoofs and wheels in the street as a freighter rolled by, the whip-cracks and shouts. The sun strips showed milky with dust.

Clay came in and his bowels turned coldly upon themselves. He pushed out the chair beside him with a foot and Clay sat down. The bartender came around the end of the bar in a hurry with another glass. Morgan poured whisky into Clay's glass and lifted his own, watching Clay's face, which was grave. "How?" he said.

"How," Clay said, and nodded and drank. Clay grinned a little, as though he thought it was the thing to do, and then glanced around the Lucky Dollar. Morgan saw the faces in the mirror turn away. He listened to the quiet, multiple click of chips. "It is quiet these days," Clay said.

Morgan nodded and said, "Dull with McQuown dead." He supposed Clay knew, although there was no way of telling. Clay was turning his glass in his hands; the bottom made a small scraping sound on the table top.

"Yes," Clay said, and did not look at him.

"Look at scarface over there," he said. "Lew can't make up his mind whether to throw him at me or not."

Clay looked, and Haskins saw him looking. His brown face turned red.

"Before I go after Lew," Morgan said.

"I asked you to leave that alone, Morg."

He sighed. "Well, it is hard when a son of a bitch burns your place down. And hard to see the jacks so pleased because they think one of them did it."

Clay chuckled.

Well, he had backed off that, he thought. He said, "I saw Kate last night. She is gone on that deputy—Kate and her damned puppy-dogs. This one kind of reminds me of Cletus, too."

"I don't see it," Clay said.

"Just the way it sets up, I guess it is."

Clay's face darkened. "I guess I don't know what you mean, Morg. It seems like a lot lately I don't know what you are talking about. What's the matter, Morg?"

I have got a belly ache, he observed to himself, and my feet are freezing off besides. He did not think that he could do it now. "Why, I get to thinking back on things that have happened," he said. "Sitting around without much to do. I guess I talk about things without letting the other fellow in on what I've been thinking."

He leaned back easily. "For instance, I was just remembering way back about that old *Tejano* in Fort James I skinned in a poker game. Won all his clothes, and there he was, stamping around town in his lousy, dirty long-handles with his shell belt and his boots on—he wouldn't put those in the pot. Remember that? I forget his name."

"Hurst," Clay said.

"Hurst. The sheriff got on him about going around that way. 'Indecent!' he yelled. 'Why, shurf, I've been sewed inside these old long-johns for three years now and I'm not even sure I have got any skin underneath. Or I'd had them in the pot too, and then where'd we be?'

"Remember that?" he said, and laughed, and it hurt him to see Clay laughing with him. "Remember that?" he said again. "I was thinking about that. And how people get sewed up into things even lousier and dirtier than those long-handles of Hurst's."

He went on hurriedly, before Clay could speak. "And I was remembering back of that to that time in Grand Fork when those stranglers had me. They had me in a hotel room with a guard while they were trying to catch George Diamond and hang him with me. Kate splashed a can of kerosene around in the back and lit up, and came running up-stairs yelling fire and got everybody milling and running down to see, and then she laid a little derringer of hers on the vigilante watching me. She got me out of that one. Like you did here, you and Jessie Marlow. I have never liked the idea of getting hung, and I owe Kate one, and you and Miss Jessie one."

"What is this talk of owing?" Clay said roughly. He poured himself more whisky. "You can take it the other way too, Morg—that time Hynes and those got the drop on me. But I hadn't thought there was any owing between us."

No? he thought. It would have pleased him once to know that there was no owing between them; it did not please him now, for debts could be canceled, but if there were no debts then nothing could be canceled at all.

"Why, there are things owed," he said slowly. And then he said, "I mean to Kate."

Clay's cheeks turned hectically red. Clay said in an uncertain voice,

"Morg, I used to feel like I knew you. But I don't know you now. What—"

"I meant about the deputy," he said. He could not do it. "She is scared," he said, and despised himself. "She is scared you and the deputy are going to come to it."

"Is that what you have been working around to asking me?"

"I'm not asking you. I'm just telling you what Kate asked me."

"There is going to be no trouble between the deputy and me," Clay said stiffly. "You can tell Kate that."

"I already told her that."

Clay nodded; the color faded from his cheeks. The flat line of his mouth bent a little. "Foolishness," he said.

"Foolishness," Morgan agreed. "My, I have a time saying anything straight out, don't I?"

Clay's face relaxed. He finished the whisky in his glass. Then he said abruptly, "Jessie and me are getting married, Morg. If you are staying maybe you would stand up for me?"

It seemed to him it had been a long time coming, what he knew was coming. But he would not stand up for Clay this time. "When?" he said.

"Why, in about a week, she said. I have to get a preacher down from Bright's City."

"I guess I won't be staying that long."

"Won't you?" Clay said, and he sounded disappointed.

He could not stay and stand up for Clay, and give the proper wedding gift to him and to his bride; not both. "No, I guess I can't wait," he said. "You will be married half a dozen times before you are through —a wonder like you. I will stand up for you at one of the others. Besides, there's an old saying—gain a wife and lose your friend. What a man I used to travel with said. He said he had been married twice and it was the same both times. First wife ran off with his partner, and number two got him worked into a fuss with another one—shot him and had to make tracks himself."

Clay was looking the other way. "I know she is not your kind of woman, Morg. But I'll ask you to like her because I do."

"I admire the lady!" he protested. "It is not every man that gets a crack at a real angel. It's fine, Clay," he said. "She is quite a lady."

"She is a lady. I guess I have never known one like her before."

"Not many like her. She is one to make the most of a man."

"I'm sorry you can't stay to stand for me."

"Not in Warlock," he said. "I'm sorry too, Clay." He wondered what Clay thought he wanted, married to Miss Jessie Marlow—to be some kind of solid citizen, with all the marshaling and killing behind him and his guns locked away in a trunk? He wondered if Clay knew Miss Jessie would not allow it, or, if she would, that the others would not. And what was he, Clay's friend, going to do? I will put you far enough ahead of the game, Clay, so you can quit, he thought. I can do that, and I will do it yet.

"Morg," Clay said, looking at him and frowning. "What got into you just now?"

Morgan picked up his glass with almost frantic hurry. "How!" he said loudly, and grinned like an idiot at his friend. "We had better drink to love and marriage, Clay. I almost forgot."

Grief gnawed behind his eyes and clawed in his thoat as he watched Clay's face turned reserved and sad. Clay nodded in acceptance and grasped his own glass. "How, Morg," he said.

III

When he returned to his room at the hotel it was like walking into a furnace. He threw the window up and opened the door to try to get a breeze to blow the heat out. He had started to strip off his coat when Ben Gough, the clerk, appeared.

"Some miner just brought this by and wanted to know was you here." Gough handed him a small envelope and departed. The envelope smelled of sachet, and was addressed in a thin, spidery script: *Mr. Thomas Morgan.* He tore open the flap and read the note inside.

June 1, 1881

Dear Mr. Morgan,

Will you please meet me as soon as possible in the little corral in back of "The General Peach," to discuss a matter of great importance.

Jessie Marlow

He put his coat back on, and the note in his pocket. He was pleased that she had sent for him—the Angel of Warlock summoning the Black Rattlesnake of Warlock. Probably she would tell him that what she wanted for a wedding present was his departure.

He went outside, across Main Street, and down Broadway. The sun burned his shoulders through his coat. It was the hottest day yet, and it showed no signs of cooling off now in the late afternoon. There were a number of puffy, ragged-edged clouds to the east over the

Bucksaws, some with gray bottoms. When he reached the corner of Medusa Street he saw that one was fastened to the brown slopes by a gray membrane. It was rain, he thought, in amazement. He walked on down past the *carpintería* and turned in the rutted tracks that led to the rear of the General Peach.

There was a small corral there, roofed with red tile. He entered, removing his hat and striking a cobweb aside with it. There was a loud, metallic drone of flies. The June-bride-to-be was sitting on a bale of straw, wearing a black skirt, a white schoolgirl's blouse, and a black neckerchief. She sat primly, with her hands in her lap and her feet close together, her pale, big-eyed, triangular face shining with perspiration.

"It was good of you to come, Mr. Morgan."

"I was pleased to be summoned, Miss Marlow." He moved toward her and propped a boot on the bale upon which she sat; she was a little afraid he would get too close, he saw. "What can I do for you, ma'am?"

"For Clay."

"For Clay," he said, and nodded. "My, it is hot, isn't it? The kind of day where you think what is there to stop it from just getting hotter and hotter? Till we start stewing in our own blood and end up like burnt bacon." He fanned himself with his hat, and saw the ends of her hair moving in the breeze he had created. "Clay has told me you are being married," he said. "I certainly wish you every happiness, Miss Marlow."

"Thank you, Mr. Morgan." She smiled at him, but severely, as though he were to be pardoned for changing the subject since he was observing the amenities. Each time he talked to her she seemed to him a slightly different person; this time she reminded him of his Aunt Eleanor, who had been strict about manners among gentlefolk.

"Mr. Morgan, I am very disturbed by some talk that I have heard."

"What can that be, Miss Marlow?"

"You are suspected of murdering McQuown," she said, staring at him with her great, deep-set eyes. He saw in them how she had steeled herself to this.

"Am I?" he said.

He watched her maiden-aunt pose shatter. "Don't—" she said shakily. "Don't you see how terrible that is for Clay?"

"There is always talk going around Warlock."

"Oh, you must see!" she cried. "Don't you see that it is bad enough that people should think he had something to do with your going down there and—and— Well, and even worse, that—"

"Why, I don't know about that, Miss Marlow. I am inclined to think that whoever killed McQuown did Clay a favor. And you."

"That is a terrible thing to say!"

"Is it? Well, Clay might be terrible dead otherwise."

She opened her mouth as though to cry out again, but she did not. She closed it like a fish with a mouthful to mull on. He nodded to her. "McQuown was coming in here with everything Clay would have had a hard time turning a hand against. I don't mean a bunch of cowboys dressed up to be Regulators, either. I mean Billy Gannon and most of all I mean Curley Burne."

"They were dead," she whispered, but she flinched back as he stared at her and he knew he had been right about Curley Burne.

"Dead pure as driven snow," he said. "Curley Burne, that is, and Billy Gannon not quite so pure but maybe pure enough because of the talk going around Warlock. McQuown was coming in with that and he could have come alone, only he didn't know enough to see it. Clay would have been running yet. But since he wasn't coming alone Clay didn't have to run, and he may be the greatest nonesuch wonder gunman of all time but he wouldn't have lasted the front end of a minute against that crew. The man who shot McQuown did him a favor. And you."

He heard her draw a deep breath. "Then you did kill McQuown," she said, and now she was severe again, as though she had gotten back on track.

He shrugged. Sweat stung in his eyes.

"Well, that is past," she said, in a stilted, girlishly high voice. "It cannot be undone. But I hope I can persuade you—" Her voice ran down and stopped; it was as though she had memorized what she was going to say to him in advance, and now she realized it did not follow properly.

"What do you want, Miss Marlow?"

She didn't answer.

"What do you want of him?" he said. "I think you want to make a stone statue of him."

She looked down at her hands clasped in her lap. "You cannot think me strange if I want everyone to think as highly of him as I do."

It was fair enough, he thought. It was more than that. She had cut the ground right out from beneath him with the first genuine thing she had said. She smiled up at him. "We are on the same side, aren't we, Mr. Morgan?"

"I don't know."

"We are!" Still she smiled, and her eyes looked alight. She was not so plain as he had thought, but she was a curious piece, with her face not so young as the dress she affected and the style of her hair. But her eyes were young. Maybe he could understand why Clay was taken with her.

"What if we are?"

"Mr. Morgan, you must know what people think of you. Whether it is just or not. And don't you see—"

He broke in. "People don't think as highly of him as they should. Because of me."

"Yes," she said firmly, as though at last they had come to terms and understood one another. "And everyone is too ready to criticize him," she went on. "Condemn him, I mean. For men are jealous of him. Too many of them see him as what they should be. I don't mean bad men—I—I mean little men. Like the deputy. Ugly, weak, cowardly little men—they have to see all their own weaknesses when they see him, and they are jealous—and spiteful." She was breathing rapidly, staring down at her clasped hands. Then she said, "Maybe I understand what you meant when you implied he would have been helpless against McQuown, Mr. Morgan. But he is helpless against the deputy, too, because you killed McQuown for *him*, and the deputy is in the right pursuing it."

Her eyes shone more brightly now. There were tears there, and he turned his face away. He had thought he could be contemptuous of her because of the different poses she affected—the faded lady, the maiden aunt, the innocent schoolgirl, the schoolmarm. What she was herself was lost among the poses, and must have been lost years ago. It did not matter to him that there was something piteous in all this, but he was shaken by the sincerity that shone through it all. He had not stopped to think before that she must love Clay.

"He will attack Clay through you," she went on. "He will do it so that Clay will either have to defend you or— Oh, I don't know what!"

He did not speak and after a moment she said, as though she were pleading with him, "I think we are on the same side, Mr. Morgan. I can see it in your face."

What she had seen in his face was the thought that he would rather have someone like Kate scratch his eyes out than Miss Jessie Marlow kiss them. But he could not scorn her concern for Clay. He sighed, removed his foot from the bale, and stood upright to light a cigar. He frowned at the match flame close to his eyes. She must think she was handling him as she would a bad actor among her boarders. "Well," he said finally. "I guess I have a lien to pay off on that buggy ride, don't I? What do you want? Me to pack on out?"

She hesitated a moment. She licked her lips again with a darting movement of her tongue. "Yes," she said, but he had seen from her hesitation that there was more to it and it angered him that she might be one step ahead of him. But he nodded.

"So, since I am going anyway . . ." he said. He drew on the cigar and blew out a gush of smoke. She was working up one of her inadequate little smiles.

He finished it. "He might as well post me out."

"Yes," she said, in a low voice. She took a handkerchief from her sleeve and touched it to her temples. Then she wound it around her hand.

"I'd already thought of that. There is only one thing wrong with it."

"What, Mr. Morgan?"

"Why, I don't expect he'd want to. I don't know if you'd understand why he wouldn't want to, but I am afraid it would take some doing. What am I supposed to do?"

"Oh, I don't know! I—"

"It would have to be something pretty bad," he broke in. He eyed her with an up-and-down movement of his head. She flushed scarlet, but she was watching him closely nevertheless. There was no sound but the buzzing of the flies, and a creaking of buggy wheels in Grant Street.

Finally she said, "Will you try to do something, Mr. Morgan? For my sake?"

"No," he said.

She looked shocked. She flushed again. "I mean for his sake."

"If I can think of something." All of a sudden rain splattered on the tile roof, with a dry, harsh sound like a fire crackling. He glanced up at the roof; a fine mist filtered through the cracks, cool upon his face. Miss Jessie Marlow was still staring at him as though she hadn't noticed the rain.

"Just one thing," he said. "Saying I can think of something and they post me, and I run from him like the yellow dog I am. Afterwards can you let him be?" His voice sounded hoarse. "Can you let him bank faro in a saloon or whatever it is he wants to do? Can *you* let him be? There'll be others that won't, but if you—"

"Why, of course," she said impatiently. "Do you think I would try to force—" She stopped, as though she had decided he had insulted her.

"Did you hear Curley Burne turning in his grave just now?" he said, and she flinched back from him once again as though he had slapped her. He saw the tears return to her eyes. But he said roughly, "You have been telling me a lot of things I ought to see—but you had better see this will be a place he can stop. If he wants to stop I will put it on you to let him. Understand me now!"

Her expression showed that she was not going to quarrel with him, and, more than that, that she thought she had cleverly brought him to the idea of getting himself posted. He had been considering it all day, but it cost nothing to let her think there was no man she couldn't get around.

The rain rattled more sharply on the tiles, and she seemed to become aware of it for the first time. "Why, it's raining!" she cried. She clapped her hands together. Then she got to her feet and put out a hand to him. He took it and she gripped his hand tightly for a moment. "I can promise you that, Mr. Morgan!" she said gaily. "I knew we were on the same side. Thank you, Mr. Morgan. I know you will do your part beautifully!"

He gaped at her. She sounded as though he had promised to play the organ at her wedding and did not know how, but would learn, for her. He laughed out loud and she looked momentarily confused. But then she gathered up her skirts and ran out of the corral and through the pelting rain toward the back steps of the General Peach. She ran as a young girl runs, lightly but awkwardly.

He put on his hat and went out into the rain, and his cigar sizzled and died. The rain beat viciously down on his hat and back from an oyster-colored sky. It made craters in the dust where it fell, and muddy puddles spread in the ruts. He walked back to the Western Star Hotel in the rain.

57. Journals of Henry Holmes Goodpasture

June 3, 1881

IT HAS been most oppressively hot this last week or ten days, as though the sun were burning each day a little closer to the earth. Then this afternoon it rained, a brief and heavy downpour that turned the streets to mud. By tomorrow the mud will be gone, and the dust as fine and dry as ever. Yet we will have a spring: here there is a miniature spring of green leaves and blossoms appearing after any rain. This should cheer us, for all have been tense, or listless.

Six weeks have passed since Whiteside made his promise to us. Buck feels we should set out immediately to put our threats into effect, but I have instead written a strong letter to Whiteside saying that in one more week we will do so. I am sure my further threats are worthless, but it allows me to procrastinate. Hart, more honest than I, readily admits he has no stomach for another journey to Bright's City.

The Sister Fan has had to put on a night crew. The water struck there at the lower levels has become a problem of increasing dimensions. They have a fifty-gallon bucket to bail out the excess and men must be kept working night and day to stay abreast of the flow. Godbold, the superintendent, says it looks as though expensive pumping machinery will have to be brought in. The Medusa strikers are, the doctor says, in despair over this (as they were previously over a rumor that Mexicans were to be brought in to work the idle Medusa), feeling that the Porphyrion and Western Mining Co. will not attempt to settle the strike until it is seen how grave is the water problem at the Sister Fan.

All is quiet in the valley. The Cowboys, now apparently led by Cade and Whitby, have, according to report, descended into Mexico on a rustling and pillaging expedition. This is looked upon as foolhardy at the present time, since the border is supposedly under close surveillance.

It is whispered that a board cross appeared briefly upon McQuown's grave, with the inscription "murdered by Morgan." In a way, I think, people have come to fear Morgan as they once feared McQuown. It is an unreasonable thing, and I suppose it is closely akin to the passions aroused in a lynch mob. Somehow he stands convicted of the murder of McQuown, and other murders as well, by some purblind emotionality for which there seems little basis in fact.

There is talk of bad blood between Gannon and Blaisedell, this stemming, evidently, from the encounter they had when the miner who shot MacDonald took refuge, himself wounded, in the General Peach. No one seems to know what actually passed between them, but I have found from long experience that much smoke can be generated here from no fire at all. The human animal is set apart from other beasts by his infinite capacity for creating fictions.

I must say that I myself have felt it necessary to change my own opinions of the deputy to a degree. I feel he is an honorable, though slow-moving man—a plodder. He has taken on a certain stature here— proof of which lies in the pudding of the speculation and of contention regarding him. He has become what none of the other deputies here has ever been—except possibly, and briefly, for Canning—a man to reckon with.

MacDonald is in Bright's City. I suspect he will soon return, and I suspect that he is plotting reprisal. He is indeed hot-headed enough to seek illegal means of punishing the strikers, who I am sure he feels conspired to take his life by means of a hired assassin. If he is fool enough, however, to attempt to convene his erstwhile Regulators again to this purpose, he will find an angry town solidly aligned against him. MacDonald has no friends in Warlock.

So life in Warlock, with terrors more shadows at play upon the wall than actuality. The atmosphere remains a charged one, yet I wonder if it is not merely something that will go on and on without ever breaking into violence; if it is not, indeed, merely part of the atmosphere of Warlock, with the dust and heat—

I spoke too soon. Another drought is ended. A gunshot; I think from the Lucky Dollar.

June 4, 1881

It is uncertain yet what provoked the shooting last night in the Lucky Dollar. Will Hart, who was present, says that Morgan suddenly accused Taliaferro of cheating, and, in an instant, had swung around and shot a half-breed gunman named Haskins through the head, and swung back evidently with every intention of shooting Taliaferro, who, instead of drawing his own pistol, sought to flee, and, on his hands and knees, was crawling to safety through the legs of the onlookers. Morgan, instead of pursuing him, had immediately to face the lookout, who had brought his shotgun to bear. All this, says Hart, took place in an instant, and Morgan was cursing wildly at Taliaferro for his flight and calling upon the lookout to drop his weapon, which order the lookout had the courage to ignore, or more probably, Hart says, was too paralyzed to comply with. The situation remained in this deadlock while Taliaferro made good his escape, and until Blaisedell, who had previously been present but had absented himself for a stroll along Main Street, burst back in.

Blaisedell immediately commanded Morgan to drop his six-shooter, although, Hart says, Blaisedell did not draw his own. Morgan refused and abused Blaisedell in vile terms. Blaisedell then leaped upon his erstwhile friend and wrested his weapon from him, upon which, Morgan, evidently surprised by Blaisedell's quick action and further infuriated by it, closed with the Marshal and a violent brawl ensued. Evidently Morgan sought to cripple Blaisedell a dozen times by some villainous trick or blow, but Blaisedell at last sent him sprawling senseless to the floor, and then carted him off for deposit in the jail as though he had been any drunken troublemaker.

Last night the town was in part aghast, in part wildly jubilant, and the rumor sprang up immediate and full-blown that Blaisedell had posted Morgan out of town—people here are apt to forget that it is the Citizens' Committee who posts the unworthy, not Blaisedell himself. The judge, however, was promptly summoned to hear Morgan on the murder of Haskins. Morgan claimed he had caught Taliaferro using a stacked deck. This is a strange argument. No doubt it is true, but in these engagements between master gamblers, such as the one that has been in progress for some time between Taliaferro and Morgan, it is clear to all that stacked decks are being used and the whole basis of the game becomes Taliaferro's cunning in arranging a deck against Morgan's cunning at ferreting out the system used. It has been said that Morgan was surpassingly clever at guessing Taliaferro's machinations previous to this, but that for the last two days he has been losing heavily. Morgan also claimed that Haskins had, as Taliaferro's gunman, attempted to shoot him in the back. Will says he could not have known this without eyes in the back of his head, but Morgan's statement in this regard was supported by Fred Wheeler and Ed Secord, who swore that Haskins had indeed drawn his six-shooter as soon as Morgan had accused Taliaferro of cheating, and showed every sign of aiming a shot at Morgan. The judge could do nothing but absolve Morgan for the death of Haskins, and although Morgan had clearly been bent upon Taliaferro's speedy demise, he had been thwarted in this, and was culpable of nothing by our standards of justice, except creating a disturbance, for which he was given a night in jail.

Gannon seems to have arrived in the Lucky Dollar while Morgan and Blaisedell were seeking to maim each other, but was fittingly nonparticipant throughout. I think it can be said of him that he knows his place.

The hearing over, members of the Citizens' Committee met stealthily to discuss the situation, and to remind ourselves that on the occasion of Blaisedell's first encounter with McQuown and Burne, Blaisedell had warned the outlaws in violent terms against starting gunplay in a crowded place, where there was danger to innocent bystanders; the parallel was clear. Still in cowardly secrecy, a general meeting was called at Kennon's livery stable. The secrecy was necessitated by the fact that we were not sure what Blaisedell's attitude toward his friend now was, but we were one and all determined to seize the occasion at its flood and post Morgan out of Warlock, if possible. All were present except for Taliaferro, who was not sought, and the doctor and Miss Jessie, who, it was felt, would make us uncomfortable in our plotting.

It was speedily and unanimously decided that Morgan should be posted. His actions had constituted, we told ourselves, exactly the sort of threat and menace to the public safety with which the white affidavit was meant to deal. The problem lay only in advising Blaisedell of our decision. It might suit him exactly, some felt, while others were afraid it would not suit him at all. Still, there are members of the Citizens' Committee, whose names I shall not mention here, who, in the past weeks and even months, have become restive over Blaisedell's high salary, or wish him gone for other reasons. They now began to speak up, each giving another courage, or so it seemed—I will not say more about them than that Pike Skinner had to be forcibly restrained from striking one of the more outspoken. Their attitude in general was that if Blaisedell refused to honor our instructions to post Morgan out, as he had done in the case of the miner Brunk, then he should resign his post. In the end their view carried, and I am sorry to say that I, in all conscience, felt I had to agree with them. Blaisedell is our instrument. If he will not accept our authority, then he must not accept our money.

The meeting was adjourned, to be reconvened this morning with Blaisedell instructed to attend. He came, much bruised around the face, but he was not told he was to post Morgan out of Warlock. It was he who did the speaking. He said he was resigning his position. He thanked us gravely for the confidence we had previously reposed in him, said that he hoped his fulfillment of his duties had been satisfactory, and left us.

Warlock, since this morning, has been as silent as was the Citizens' Committee when we heard his statement. I think I am, ashamedly, as disappointed as the rest, but I know I think better of Blaisedell than I have ever before. It was clear that he knew exactly what was our intention at the meeting, and, since he did not wish to do it, saw that he must resign. There was no reproach evident in his demeanor. We will reproach ourselves, however, for what was said of him the night before. And I respect him for not wishing to post his friend from Warlock; I think he has acted with honor and with dignity, and I have cause to wonder now if this town, and the Citizens' Committee, has ever been worthy of the former Marshal of Warlock.

58. Gannon Speaks of Love

GANNON lay fully clothed on his bed and contemplated the darkness that enclosed him, the barely visible square of vertical planes that were the walls marred here and there by huddled hanging bunches of his clothing, and the high ceiling that was not visible at all, so that the column of darkness beneath which he lay sprawled seemed topless and infinitely soaring. He had been forced out of the jail tonight not by any danger, but only because there were too many people there end-lessly and repetitiously talking about Morgan and Blaisedell, Blaise-dell and Morgan, and he did not want to hear any more of it.

Yet even now he could hear the excited murmur of voices from one of the rooms down the hall, and he knew that throughout Warlock it was the same, everyone talking it over and over and over, changing and fitting and rearranging it to suit themselves, or rather making it into something they could accept, angrily or puzzledly or sadly. Each time they would come to the conclusion that Blaisedell had better move on, but, having reached that conclusion, they would only start over again. He, the deputy, he thought, must not enter their minds at all; nor could he see in the black blank of his own mind what his part was. He had come, finally, almost to accept what Morgan had said to him—that it was not his business.

He heard the upward creaking of the stairs, and then Birch's high voice: "Now watch your step, ma'am. It is kind of dark here on these steps."

He started up, and groped his way to the table. His hand encountered the glass shade of the lamp; he caught it as it fell. He lit a match and the darkness retreated a little from the sulphur's flame, retreated farther as the bright wedge mounted from the wick. As he replaced the chimney there was a knock. "Deputy!" Birch said.

He opened the door. Kate stood there in the thick shadows; he could smell the violet water she wore. "Here is Miss Dollar to see you," Birch said, in an oily voice.

"Come in," he said, and Kate entered. Birch faded into the darkness, and the steps creaked downward. The voices in the room down the hall were still. Kate closed the door and glanced around; at his cartridge belt hanging like a snakeskin from the peg beside the door, at the clothes hanging on their nails, at the pine table and chair and the cot with its sagging springs. Lamplight glowed in a warm streak upon her cheek. "Sit down, Kate," he said.

She moved toward the chair, but instead of seating herself she put her hands on the back and leaned there. He saw her looking around a second time, with her chin lifted and her face as impassive as an Indian's. "This is where you live," she said finally.

"It isn't much."

She did not speak again for a long time, and he backed up and sat down on the edge of the bed. She turned a little to watch him; one side of her face was rosy from the lamp and the other half in shadow, so that it looked like only half a face. "I'm leaving tomorrow," she said.

"You are?" he said numbly. "Why—why are you, Kate?"

"There is nothing here for me."

He didn't know what she meant, but he nodded. He felt relief and pain in equal portions as he watched her face, which he thought very beautiful with the light giving life to it. He had never known what she was, but he had known she was not for him. He had dreamed of her, but he had not even known how to do that; his dreams of her had just been a continuation of the sweet, vapid day and night dreams embodied once in Myra Burbage, not so much because Myra had been attractive to him as because she was the only girl there was near at hand; knowing then, as he knew now, that there would be no woman for him. He was too ugly, too poor, and there were too few women ever to reach down the list of unmarried men to his name.

"You're going with Morgan?" he asked.

Her face looked suddenly angry, but her voice was not. "No, not Morgan. Or anybody."

He almost asked her about Buck, but he had once and she had acted as though he were stupid. "By yourself?" he asked.

"By myself."

She said that, too, as though it should mean something. But he felt numb. What had been said was only words, but now the realization of the actuality of her leaving came over him, and he began to grasp at the remembrance of those times he had seen her, as though he must hold them preciously to him so that they would not disappear with her. He had, he thought, the key to remember her by.

"When?" he said.

"Tomorrow or— Tomorrow."

He nodded again, as though it were nothing. He could hear the roomers talking down the hall again. He rubbed his bandaged hand upon his thigh and nodded, and felt again, more intensely than he had ever felt it, his ineptness, his inadequacy, his incapacity with the words which should be spoken.

"I guess I didn't expect anything," Kate said harshly. "I guess you are sulking with the rest tonight."

"Sulking?"

"About Blaisedell," she said, and went on before he could speak. "I was the only one that thought it was wonderful to see," she said in a bitter voice. "For I saw Tom Morgan try to do a decent thing. I think it must have been the first decent thing he had ever tried to do, and did it like he was doing a dirty trick. And had it fall apart on him. Because Blaisedell was too—" Her voice caught. "Too—" she said, and shook her head, and did not go on. Then she said, as though she were trying to hit him, "I'm sorry you feel cheated."

"You think if Blaisedell had posted him he would have gone?"

"Of course he would have gone. He was trying to give Blaisedell that—so people would think Blaisedell had scared him out. I think it's funny," she said, but she did not sound as though she did.

They were talking about Blaisedell and Morgan like everyone else, and he knew she did not want to, and he did not want to.

He looked down at his hands in his lap and said, "I'd thought you might be going with Morgan."

"Why?"

"Well, I talked to him. He said you'd been his girl but that you were through with each other. But I thought you might have—"

"*I* told you I'd been his girl," Kate said. Then she said, "Did he tell you more? I told you more, too. I told you what I'd been."

He closed his eyes; the darkness behind his eyes ached.

"I guess I am still," her voice continued. "Though I don't have to work at it any more, since I've got money. That came from men." Again she spoke as though she were hitting him. She said, "I'm damned if I am ashamed of it. It is honest work and kills no one. What are you waiting for, a little country girl virgin?"

Now he tried to shake his head.

"Why, men marry whores," she said. "Even here. But not you. And not me. There is nothing here at all for me, is there?" Her voice began to shake and he looked up at her and tried to speak, but she rushed on. "So I have been a whore by trade," she said. "But I can love, and I can hate by nature. But you can't. You just sit and stare in at yourself and worry everything every way so there is no time nor place for any of that. Is there?"

"Kate," he said in a voice he could hardly recognize. "That is not so. You know well enough I have loved—"

"Don't say that!" she broke in fiercely. Her face looked very red in the lamplight, and her black eyes glittered. "I have never heard you lie before and don't start for me. I know you haven't been to the French Palace," she said, "because I asked." She said it cruelly. "I wanted to know if you were waiting for a little country virgin or not. And I—"

"That's not so, Kate!" he cried in anguish.

Slowly the lines of her face relaxed until it was as gentle and full of pity as that of the little madonna in her room. He had never seen it this way before. "No," she said gently. "No, I guess it isn't. I guess you thought going to a whore wasn't right. And I guess you thought that about me, too."

"Kate—I guess I knew you felt—kindly toward me. I kind of presumed you did. I'm not a fool. But Kate—" he said, and couldn't go on.

"But Kate?" she said.

"Well, this is where I live."

He waited for a long time, but she did not speak. When he looked up he saw the harsh lines around her mouth again. He heard the rustle of her garments as she moved; she clasped her hands before her, staring down at him, her eyes in shadow.

"Another thing," he said. "You have been in the jail and seen those names scratched on the wall there." He took a deep breath. "There was something Carl used to say," he went on. "That there wasn't a man with his name on there that didn't either run or get killed. And Carl used to say who was he to think he was any different? And that he wouldn't run. I think he even knew who was going to kill him."

"I've got money, Deputy," Kate said. "Do you want to come with me? Deputy, this town is going to die and there is no reason for anybody to die with it. I am asking you to take the stage to Bright's City with me tomorrow. Out of here, out of the territory."

"Kate—" he groaned.

"Do you want to, or not?"

"Yes, but Kate—I can't, now."

"Killed or run!" she cried. "Deputy, you can run with me. I have got six thousand dollars in the bank in Denver. We can—" She stopped, and her face twisted in anger and contempt, or grief. "What kind of a fool am I?" she said, more quietly. "To beg *you*. Deputy, you can't give me anything I haven't had a thousand times and better. I can give you what you've never had. But you will lie down and die instead. Do you want to die more?"

"I don't want to die at all. I only have to stay here." He beat his bandaged hand upon his knee. "Anyway till there is a proper sheriff down here, and all that."

"Why?" she cried at him "Why? To show you are a man? I can show you you are more a man than that."

"No." He got to his feet; he rubbed his sweating hands on his jeans. "No, Kate, a man is not just a man that way. I—"

"Because you killed a Mexican once," she broke in. Her tear-shining eyes were fastened to him. "Is that why?"

"No, not that either any more. Kate, I have set out to do a thing." He did not know how to say it any better. "Well, I guess I have been lucky. That's part of it, surely. But I have made something of the deputy in this town, and I can't leave it go back down again. Not till things are—better. I didn't drop it a while back when I was afraid, and, Kate, I can't now because I would rather go off with you"— he groped helplessly for a phrase—"than anything else in the world."

He wet his dry lips. "Maybe to you Warlock is not worth anything. But it is, and I am deputy here and it is something I am proud of. There are things to do here yet that I think I can do. Kate, I can't quit till it is done."

He saw her nod once, her face caught halfway between cruel contempt and pity. He moved toward her and put out a hand to touch her.

"Don't touch me!" she said. "I am tired of dead men!" She stepped to the door and jerked it open. The bottom of her skirt flipped around the door as she disappeared, pulling it half closed behind her.

He took up the lamp and followed her, stopping in the hallway and holding the lamp high to give her a little light as she hurried down the stairs away from him, and, when she was gone, stared steadily at the faces that peered out at him from the other doorways until the faces were drawn back and the doors closed to leave him alone.

59. Morgan Shows His Hand

MORGAN stood at the open window with his tongue mourning after a lost tooth and the night wind blowing cool on his bruised face. The night was a soft, purplish black, like the back of an old fireplace, the stars like jewels embedded in the soot. He stood tensely waiting until he saw the dark figure outlined against the dust of the street, crossing toward the hotel. Then he cursed and flung his aching body down into the chair, and took out a cigar. His hand shook with the match and he felt his face twisting with a kind of rhythmic tic as he listened to the footsteps coming up the stairs, coming along the hall. Knuckles cracked against the panel of his door. "Morg."

He waited until Clay rapped again. Then he said, "Come on in."

Clay entered, taking off his hat and bowing his head as he passed through the doorway. There was a strip of court plaster on his cheek, and his face was knuckle-marked enough. Morgan looked straight into his eyes and said, "You damned fool!"

"What was I supposed to do?" Clay said, closing the door behind him. "Post you out because you were going anyhow?"

The blue, violent stare pierced him, and his own eyes were forced down before it. "Why not?"

"Would you kill two men to serve a trick like that, Morg?"

"Why not?" he said again. His tongue probed and poked at the torn, pulpy socket. "One," he said. "I had to take scarface first and Lew crawled for it." With an effort he looked back to meet the blue gaze. "I told you I couldn't let a man get away with burning me out!"

"I asked you to leave that alone."

"Post me then, damn you!"

Clay moved over to sit on the edge of the bed, with his shoulders slumped and his face sagging in spare, flat planes. He shook his head. "I couldn't anyhow. I am not marshall any more."

"Well, I will back a play I have made. I don't go unless you post me."

Clay shrugged.

"What would it cost you? It might win you something."

"No."

"What does Miss Jessie Marlow say?"

Clay frowned a little. He said in a level voice, "What would you try to do this for, Morg?"

Because I never liked to look a fool, he thought. He had never hated it so much as he did now. "God damn it, Clay! A whole town full of clodhopping idiots aching for you to play the plaster hero for them one time again, and post out the Black Rattlesnake of Warlock. Which is me. And why not? It would have pleased every damned person I know of here except maybe you. Maybe you are yellow, though—a damned hollow, yellow Yankee. I hate to see you show it for these here!"

"They can have it that way if they want it. I have quit."

"You could have posted me and quit after the big pot when I'd run."

"It wasn't a game to cheat and make a fraud of," Clay said. His face looked pasty pale beneath the bruises. He shrugged again, tiredly. "Or maybe it was and it took a thing like this to show me. And maybe if it could be that, it is time and past time to quit."

"Clay, listen. I am sick to death of this town! I am sick of sitting in the Lucky Dollar taking Lew's money away, I am dead sick of watching the gawps from the chair on the veranda. I want to get out of here! It was a good reason for me to get out of here. I am trying to tell you it would have pleased everybody, me included. Now you are a damned has-been and a fool besides." And you have not quit, he added, to himself; now you have not, whatever you think.

"Why, I have pleased myself then," Clay said. He said, quietly, "What are you so mad about, Morg?"

He sat slumped down in his chair with his cold cigar clenched between his teeth. For whom was he doing this, after all? To please himself, was it? At least he wanted a live plaster saint rather than a dead one, and for that he had done what he had done, and for that he would do more. For whom? he wondered. It stuck now to try to say it was for Clay.

"Mad?" he said. "Why, I am mad because I have looked a fool. I am mad because I am used to having my way. I will have my way this time. If you won't post me for that, I will—" He stopped suddenly, and grinned, and said, "I will ask you for it for a favor."

Clay looked at him as though he were crazy.

"For a favor, Clay," he said.

Clay shook his head.

"Then I will see what it takes. Do you think I can't make you do it?"

"Why would you?" Clay said.

"I said I will have my way!" He felt his fingers touch his cheek, and the tic convulsed his face again.

"I have quit," Clay said. "I will post no man again, nor marshal again." He held his hand up before his face and stared at it as though he had never seen it before. "What is all this worth?" he said, in a shaky voice. "What is all this foolish talk? What's my posting you out of Warlock worth to anybody?"

"It is worth something to me," he said, under his breath.

"What are you trying to make of me?" Clay went on. His voice thickened. "You too, Morg! Not a human being at all, but a damned unholy *thing*—and a fraud of a thing in the end. No, I have quit it!"

"Do it for me, Clay," he said. "For a God-damned favor. Post me out and turn me loose. I am sick to death of it here. I am sick of you."

He saw Clay close his eyes; Clay shook his head, almost imperceptibly. He continued to shake it like that for a long time. He said, "Go then. I don't have to post you so you can go. I—"

"You have to post me!"

"As soon as I did you would walk the street against me."

"I've told you I wasn't a stupid boy to play stupid boys' games!"

"I don't know that many of them was stupid boys," Clay said. "But every time now it is that way. If I posted you out for whatever reason you made me—no sooner it was done than you would come against me. No, God, no!" he groaned, and slapped his hand hard against his forehead. "No, no more! What have I done that I was made to shoot pieces off myself forever? No, I have done with it, Morg!"

"Clay—" he started. "Clay, what are you taking on like this for? All I am asking is post me and I will get out of town on the first stage or before it. Good Christ! Do you think I am fool enough to—"

"I will not!" Clay said. His lips were stretched tight over his teeth, and his face looked pitted, as though with some skin disease.

Morgan got up and stood with his back to him. He could not look at that face. He said, "If you had been any kind of marshal here you would have posted me before this. But I guess you couldn't see the hand in front of your nose. That everybody else saw."

"What?" Clay asked.

"You should have posted me for killing McQuown, for one. If you had been any kind of marshal."

Clay said nothing, and he felt a dart of hope. "If you had been any kind of marshal," he said again, "which was supposed to be your trade, but I guess you did not think so much of your trade as you liked to make out. And before that. Those cowboys that stopped the Bright's City stage didn't kill Pat Cletus."

"I don't believe that, Morg," Clay said, almost inaudibly. Then he cleared his throat. "Why?"

Morgan swung around. "Because Kate was bringing him out here to me she had another Cletus to bed her, as big and ugly as the first one. I am tired of watching that parade. Do you think I like her throwing every trick she has rutted with in my face?" His heart beat high and suffocating in his throat as Clay raised his head, and the blue stare was colder than he had ever seen it before. Then, almost in the same instant, it seemed to turn inward upon itself, and Clay only looked gray and old once more.

Do you have to have more? he cried, to himself. For maybe the curse upon him was that now even the truth itself would not be enough. He said calmly, "Why, then, if you will have more I will tell you why Bob Cletus came after you in Fort James."

Clay's head jerked up, and Morgan laughed out loud, proud that he could laugh.

"Are you listening, Clay?" he said. "For I will tell you a bedtime story. Do you know why he came after you? Because he wanted to marry Kate, the son of a bitch. And the bitch—she told him I might make trouble, and he had better see me. So he came to see me. You didn't know you killed Cletus over Kate, did you?"

"Kate?" Clay said; his eyes had a pale, milky look.

"I told him it wasn't me he had to worry about, it was you. You. For you had been rutting Kate and you were jealous by nature and no man to fool with. He was mad because she hadn't told him about you, so I told him if he wanted Kate he had better get you before you got him, and sent word roundabout to you that he was out—"

His breath stopped in his throat as Clay got to his feet. But Clay only went to stand at the window. He leaned one hand upon the sash, staring out.

When Morgan spoke again his voice had gone hoarse. "By God, it was the best trick I ever pulled," he said. "It made you a jackass and him a dead jackass—and Kate—" He stopped to catch his breath again. "Do you know what has always eaten on me? That nobody knew how I had served you all. It was a shame nobody knew. But how I laughed to think of Cletus jerking for that hogleg like it was a fence-post stuck in his belt. And you—"

Clay faced him. "He never did draw," Clay said. "I don't think he ever meant to. You are lying, Morg." There was a little pink in his face and his expression was strangely gentle. "Why, Morg, are you trying to give me that, too? I don't need that any more." Then his eyes narrowed suddenly, and he said, "No, it is not even that, is it? You are telling me something to kill you for, not post you."

"I told you I don't play boys' games!"

"Stop playing this one."

"It is so, God damn you to hell!"

"Why, I expect part of it is," Clay said. "I knew you had been in on it, for I have seen you chewing yourself. I expect you told him something like that to scare him so he would let Kate be. Not thinking he would come to me, though maybe you fixed it so that cowboy told me he'd heard Cletus was after me on account of Nicholson and I had better watch out—just in case Cletus did decide to make trouble. But I don't believe he meant to draw on me; he just wanted to find out about Kate when he called after me. I was just edgy about any friends of Nicholson's, was all, and thought he was out for blood." He stopped, and his throat worked as he shook his head. "It is not so, Morg."

Morgan stared back at him. Strangely it did not shake him that Clay had known, or guessed; he only felt dazed because he could not see what he could do next. He had chewed the end of his cigar to shreds, and with an uncertain movement he took it from his lips. He flung it on the floor. Clay said, "Once I would've wanted pretty bad to think what you just told me was so. But it was more my fault than it was yours. Whatever you did."

"I served you up!" Morgan cried. He could feel the sweat on his face. "Hollow!" he cried. "Hollow as a damned plaster statue."

"It doesn't matter any more," Clay said. "If it hadn't been Bob Cletus dead to teach me a lesson, it would have been another. I learned that day a man could be too fast. I thought I had learned it," he said.

"Damn you, Clay!" he whispered. All at once there was nothing in the world to hold to except this one thing. "Damn you! I will have my way!"

Clay shook his head almost absently. "Do you know what I wish?" he said. "I wish I was some measly deputy in some measly town a thousand miles away. I wish I was not Clay Blaisedell. Morg, you have killed men for my sake—Pat Cletus and McQuown that I know of.

But I can't thank you for it. It is the worst thing you have done to me, because it was *for* me, and I am more of a fraud of a thing than I knew. Morg—we think different ways, I guess." He took up his hat; he turned his face away. When he went out he pulled the door quietly but firmly closed behind him.

"Don't you have the dirty rotten gall to forgive me, damn you to hell!" Morgan whispered, as though Clay were still present. "You didn't take that away too, did you? You didn't take that!" He put his hands to his face; his mouth felt stretched like a knife wound. A burst of laughter caught and froze in his bowels like a cramp. "Well, I am sorry, Miss Jessie Marlow," he said aloud. "But he was iron-mouthed beyond me." You took me to the last chip, Clay, and won my pants and shirt too, and my longjohns are riveted on and too foul to bear. He shook his head in his hands. He would rather Clay had shot him through the liver than say what he had said, as he had said it, meaning what he had meant by it: *We think different ways, I guess.*

He pressed his hands harder to his aching face, suffocating in the sour, dead stench of himself. It was a long time before he remembered that he was lucky by trade, and that no one had ever beaten him.

60. Gannon Sits It Out

THE sun was standing above the Bucksaws in the first pale green light of morning as Gannon came like a sleepwalker along the echoing planks of the boardwalk, along the empty white street. The inside of the jail was like an icehouse, and he sat at the table shivering and massaging his unwashed, beard-stubbled face. He felt sluggish and unrested, and his blood as slow and cold in the morning chill of the adobe as a lizard's blood.

He sat staring out through the doorway at the thin sunlight in the street, waiting for the sounds of Warlock waking and going about its Sunday business, and waiting especially for the sound of the early stage leaving town. Today, like every other day, the sun would traverse its turquoise and copper arch of sky; a particular sun for a particular place, it seemed to him, this sun for this place bounded by the Bucksaws and the Dinosaurs, illuminating indiscriminately the righteous and the unrighteous, the just and the unjust, the wise and the foolish. Shivering in the cold he waited for Warlock to waken, and for Kate Dollar to leave, examining the righteousness that both moved and paralyzed him, the injustice he had performed upon himself because of his love of justice. He called himself a fool and prayed for wisdom, and saw only that he could not change his mind, for nothing was changed. He felt as though he were a monk bound to this barren cell by some vow he had never even formulated to himself. He thought of the end of the vow that Carl had known, and accepted. Maybe the only thing changed now was that that end was so much harder to accept.

The first sound he heard was a horn blowing a military call. It was faint, but clear and precise in the thin air—as out of place and improbable as though a forest with stream, moss, and ferns had showed itself suddenly in the white dust of the street. He did not move, holding his breath, as though he had mistaken the sound of his breathing for that other sound. After a while it came again, a bugle call signifying what, rallying or commanding what, he did not know. The brassy notes hung in the air after the call had ended. He rose and moved to the doorway. A Mexican woman with a black *rebozo* over her head came down Southend Street, and Goodpasture's *mozo* appeared, broom in hand, to speak to her as she passed, and then turned and leaned on the broom and stared east up Main Street.

He went back inside the jail and sat down again. Once he thought he heard the sound of hoofbeats, but it was faint, and, when he listened for it, inaudible, as though it had only been some kind of ghostly reverberation along his nerves. He began to think he had heard the bugle only in a half-dream, too. Immediately the brassy, shivering call came again, close now, a different call this time, and now when he hurried out the door there were many people up and down the street, all staring east.

Back of the Western Star he could see the cloud of tan dust rising, and he could hear the hoofs clearly as the dust rolled nearer. Preceding it, riders wheeled into Main Street on the road from Bright's City. There were ten or twelve of them, in dusty blue and forage caps, one with the fork-tailed pennon on a staff. They came down Main Street at a pounding trot, looking neither right nor left as men hurried out of the street before them, the leader with three yellow Vs on the sleeve of his dark blue shirt, and a dusty-dark, mustachioed face beneath the vicious-looking, flat-vizored cap; the second man holding the pennon staff, and, next to him, the bugler with rows of braid upon his chest. He watched them pass him, and another group appeared, far up the street. The first group trotted to the end of town, wheeled about, and halted. The second turned south down Broadway. A third did not come into Main Street at all, but trotted dustily on past it. Another bugle sounded and more cavalry appeared, this time a much larger body and a mixed one, for there were civilian riders in it. Frozen into his eye for an instant was the image of a huge, uniformed man in a wide, flat hat with one side pinned up, and a white beard blown back against his chest.

Pike Skinner came running across Main Street toward him, shoving his shirttails down into his pants. "What the hell is this, Johnny?"

He could only shake his head. The main body came slowly down Main Street, to halt before the burnt shell of the Glass Slipper. One of the civilians rode on toward him; it was Sheriff Keller. He reined up and dismounted, heavily, and dropped his reins in the dust. Grunting, he mounted the boardwalk, and with a sideways glance at Gannon stamped on into the dimness of the jail. There he slumped down into the chair at the table as Gannon followed him inside. The sheriff wiped his face and the back of his neck with a blue handkerchief and squinted at Pike, who stood in the doorway.

"Glad to've seen you, *hombre*," he said blandly, and made a slight movement with his head.

Pike started to speak, but changed his mind and went out. Down the street someone was yelling in a brass voice that was drowned in another sudden pad of hoofs.

Gannon felt a sudden wild and rising hope that this was to be some kind of ceremony investing a new county. "What's the cavalry down here for, Sheriff?"

The sheriff rubbed his coarse-veined red nose. The plating was worn from his sheriff's star and the brass showed through. "What we forget," he said slowly, staring at Gannon with his flat eyes. "We get to thinking the general runs things. But there is people to run him too."

The hope burst in him more wildly still; but then the sheriff said, "Gent named Willingham. Porphyrion and Western Mining Company, or some such. There is a flock of wagons coming down."

"Wagons?"

"Wagons for miners to ride in."

"Miners?" he said, stupidly.

"Over to Welltown to the railroad," the sheriff said. He sucked on his teeth. "And out," he said, jerking his thumb east. "Out of the territory. Troublemaking miners," he said, nodding, pursing his lips, scowling. "Ignorant, agitating, murdering foreigners, and a criminal conspiracy, what the general's general says. Willingham, that is." He sighed, then he scowled at Gannon. "This Tittle a friend of yours too, son? That was what tore it."

A crutch-tip cracked on the planks. Judge Holloway came in, red-faced and panting. "Oh, it's you, Keller!" the judge said. "Oh, you have come down to Warlock at last, have you?"

"Uh-huh," Keller said. "Sit," he said, vacating the chair grudgingly, and moving his bulk to the other. The judge sat down. His crutch got away from him, and clattered to the floor.

"Will you tell me what damned dirty devilment is going on here, Keller?"

"Run out of Apaches," the sheriff said. His fat face looked tired and disgruntled. In the street Gannon saw a man running, looking back over his shoulder. He started out. "Here!" Keller barked. "Come back here, boy! You are going to have to pay this no mind."

"Pay what no mind?"

"What are you saying about Apaches, Keller?" the judge said.

"Why, they are all cleaned out, so now it is Cousin Jacks to take out after. New flag; it has got Porphyrion and Western wrote on it. Wagons coming. All those striking ones are going to get hauled up to Welltown and a special train is going to haul them back east somewheres and dump them."

"MacDonald," the judge whispered.

"Why, surely, MacDonald. Only he has got his big brother along, name of Willingham. Out from Frisco. Willingham has thrown a scare into old Peach something terrible."

The judge began to hawk as though he would strangle. The sheriff rose and pounded him on the back. "Son," he said to Gannon. "You should have snatched down on that Tittle, what you should have done. You let me down, boy, and I got ordered down here the same as some tight-britches trooper." He pounded the judge on the back once more, and then reseated himself. Gannon leaned back against the wall.

"They can't do it!" the judge cried. "He is crazy!"

"Didn't you people down here in Warlock know that? But he can surely do it. Colonel Whiteside was arguing and stamping around, how he couldn't do it; and Willingham giving it to him he had damned well better. I heard Whiteside telling him Washington'd have his ears for it. But when Peach gets a bee in his bonnet he moves and if you think he can't do it, you just watch him."

Keller took off his hat, ran a hand back over his head, sighed, and said, "Whiteside is a nice old feller for a colonel, and thinks high of Peach too. He says all he wants is for Peach to go out well thought of, which he is near to doing—and this will ruin him for sure. But Peach thinks how Willingham can do him some good in Washington some way, and anyway Willingham is claiming this is armed rebellion against the U.S. down here, and up to Peach to stop it. Why, they are going to round up these jacks like a herd of longhorns and ship them out in cattle cars, and it is a crying shame." He extended a long, spatulate finger. "But judge," he said, "and boy: there is nothing to do about it."

The judge slid the drawer open against his belly and worked his bottle of whisky out of it. He cracked it down on the table before him. He said, "We are overrun with Philistines!"

"Save some of that for me," the sheriff said. "I rid drag all the way down here."

Gannon leaned against the wall and stared at the sheriff's face. "What are you here for, Sheriff?"

The sheriff took the bottle the judge handed him, and drank. His belly began to shake; he was laughing silently. He handed the bottle back and winked. "Why, I am to clean things out down here," he said. "You and me, son. Why, we are to fill up one of those wagons ourself. Road agents, rustlers, murderers, and such trash; we are to round up a bagful. Old Peach heard somewhere that things've got a little out of hand down here."

Gannon turned to watch a squad of cavalry ride slowly by, spaced to fill the street from side to side, carbines held at the ready. "Blaisedell," the sheriff said, and laughed.

Gannon's head swung back. He heard the judge draw in a sharp breath. The sheriff's belly shook again with silent laughter. "Shoot him down like a dog if he don't go peaceable," the sheriff said. "And that's when I unpinned this wore-out old badge here and handed it in. And said I had just *re*tired, being too old for the job."

"Great God!" the judge said.

"MacDonald said how Blaisedell went and interfered with Johnny here in the performance of his duty, which was Tittle," Keller went on. "Only that's not all of it. Peach don't like anything about Blaisedell. Blaisedell's been stealing his thunder. There is a lot of bad things being said about Blaisedell now, too, to give the crazy old horse his due. Some talk he went down and settled McQuown kind of backside-to."

"It is a lie!" the judge said, wearily. "Well, what happened? I see you have your badge back. Did you decide to shoot him down?"

"Worked out so I don't have to," Keller said, grinning. "Whiteside talked him some turkey on that one. Told him how Blaisedell was held innocent up in court, and how Peach would just make him more of a thing down here than he is already if he tried to run him out, and Blaisedell got shot or *I* got shot. What he said to do was, since the Citizens' Committee down here had hired Blaisedell and they wanted a town patent pretty bad, was tell them they could have it if they got rid of Blaisedell. It was slick to see Whiteside getting around him on that, and it worked too. Except—" He looked suddenly depressed. "Except if he don't go, it is back to me again. But I can always resign," he said, brightening. "Pass over that bottle again, will you, Judge?"

The judge handed it to him. "We are a bunch of vile sinners," he said in a blurred voice. "But I am damned if we deserve this. What about Doc Wagner, Keller? Does Peach mean to have him transported too?"

"Yep," the sheriff said. "Now, you just sit down, Judge. There is not a thing in the world you can do. Johnny!" he snapped. "Don't sneak that hand up there to be unpinning that star, or I will load you on my wagon first off and you will wait it out in the hot sun till I catch the rest, which might be a while. Now you just calm yourself. All the arguing and maneuvering to be done's been done already. I have seen Peach take out after Whiteside with that sword of his, fit to take his head off. Don't go trying to interfere with him."

"He can't do that to those poor damned—"

"He can," the sheriff said. "What was you going to do to stop it, son?"

Peter Bacon stuck his head in the door. "Johnny, are you going to stand by and let those blue-leg sons of bitches—" He stopped, staring at the sheriff. "My God, are you here, Keller?" he said, incredulously.

"I'm here," the sheriff said. "And how's things going out there?"

Peter's brown face wrinkled up as though he were going to cry. "Sheriff, they are rounding up those poor fellows from the Medusa like—"

"Going well, huh?" the sheriff said. "Well, drop in some later and see us again, Bacon. Pass me that bottle, Judge."

Peter stared at the sheriff, and turned and looked Gannon up and down. Then he withdrew. Keller tilted the bottle to his lips. Gannon saw the sheriff's hand, lying on the table before him, clench into a fist as there was a burst of shrill shouting down the street.

Gannon started toward the door.

"Don't even look, boy," the sheriff said heavily. "You might turn into a pillar of salt or something."

"Salt's not what I'm worth. Or you."

"I know it, boy. I never said otherwise. But you can't interfere with the cavalry, and the military governor. During maneuvers," he added. "That's what they are calling it; maneuvers."

"And you are supposed to maneuver down to San Pablo?" the judge asked.

"Supposed to. I guess I won't rush things, though."

"You might do well to rush. From what we hear they are all down raiding the Hacienda Puerto range right now."

"Rush," the sheriff said, nodding. Then Keller looked at Gannon again with his sad eyes. "Nothing you can do, boy," he said. "Nor any man. Just stand steady and let it go by. He's put his big foot in it now, and who knows but things might change, maybe, because of this."

"I have thought," the judge said bitterly, "that things were so bad they couldn't get any worse. But they have got worse today like I wouldn't believe if I didn't hear it going on. And maybe there is no bottom to it."

"Bottom to everything," the sheriff said, holding up the bottle and shaking it. Through the door Gannon watched a young lieutenant cantering past on a fine-looking sorrel, followed by a sergeant. He slammed his hand against his leg.

"Hold steady now," the sheriff said.

"Yes, learn your lessons as they come your way," the judge said. "And when you have learned them all they can stick red-hot pokers in your wife and babies and you will only laugh to see it. Because you will know by then that people don't matter a damn. Men are like corn growing. The sun burns them up and the rain washes them out and the winter freezes them, and the cavalry tramps them down, but somehow they keep growing. And none of it matters a damn so long as the whisky holds out."

"This here's gone," the sheriff said. "Go cut some of that corn and stir up some more mash, Judge. Say, did you people get any rain down this way?"

A rumble of bootheels came along the boardwalk. Old man Heck came in the door, his chin whiskers bristling with outrage, and Frenchy Martin and four others, of whom Gannon recognized only one named Daley, a tall, mild, likeable miner. Then he saw the doctor, with a trooper holding his arm. The doctor's face was grayer than ever, but his eyes were bright. There followed two other troopers, a sergeant, and Willard Newman, MacDonald's assistant at the Medusa, who shouldered his way inside past troopers and miners.

"Deputy, these men are to be locked up until the wagons get here."

"Lickspittles, all of you!" the doctor said.

"Now, Doc, that don't do no good," Daley said.

"MacDonald is afraid to look me in the face so he sends his lickspittles!"

Daley thrust himself between the doctor and Newman, as Newman cursed and raised a hand. "You!" the sergeant said, to Newman. "You mistreat the prisoners and I'll drink your blood, Mister!"

"That's the sheriff!" one of the miners said, and Gannon saw Keller's face redden. The doctor moved stiffly inside the cell, and the others followed him.

"I hope you soldiers are proud of your uniforms today!" the judge said, raising his voice above the shuffling of boots.

"You should be in here with me, George Holloway!" the doctor called, standing with the miners in the cell. "This is a thing every man who likes to think himself of a liberal persuasion should know for himself. We belong—"

"I will stay out and drink myself to death instead," the judge said, with his head bent down.

"Lock them up, Johnny," the sheriff said. He held the bottle up, studied it, and then handed it back to the judge.

Newman kicked the door shut.

"I'll not!" Gannon said, through his teeth.

The sergeant turned to look at him; he had a sour, weatherbeaten face and thick graying sideburns. Newman glared at him. "Lock them up, Deputy!"

"By whose orders?"

"General Peach's order, you fool!" Newman cried. "Will you lock these sons of bitches up before I—"

"Not in my jail!" He thrust between the sergeant and Newman, snatched the key ring from its peg, and retreated to stand against the wall where the names were scratched. He put his hand on the butt of his Colt. The sheriff stared at him; the judge averted his face.

The sergeant sighed and said, "Mick!" One of the troopers raised his carbine and started forward. Someone burst in the door behind him.

It was a miner Gannon didn't know; he had gnarled, discolored hands and a stubble of beard on his long, young face. He stopped for a moment, panting; then he thrust one of the troopers aside and leaped forward to hit Newman in the face with a long, awkward sweep of his arm. Newman yelled and fell back the length of the room, while the sheriff came to his feet with surprising swiftness and slammed the barrel of his Colt down above the young miner's ear. The miner crumpled and fell, just as Newman, cursing, regained his balance and pulled the six-shooter from his belt. "Here!" the sergeant bellowed, and there was an outcry from the cell. Gannon jerked his Colt free and stepped toward Newman. The trooper named Mick caught the miner by the collar as he scrambled to his feet, and, with the sheriff's help, thrust him into the cell with the others.

Newman backed up, staring at Gannon's Colt. The sheriff came toward Gannon, pushed the gun barrel down with his fat hand, and took the key ring. The sheriff shook his head at him reprovingly. Newman's nose was bleeding.

"Let's get on, Mr. Newman," the sergeant said, and Newman cursed and replaced his own six-shooter in his belt. He stamped on outside, holding a handkerchief to his nose. Gannon leaned against the wall and watched in silence and despair as the sergeant detailed one of the troopers to guard the cell, and, with the others, followed Newman outside. The one who remained stood before the cell door, scowling uneasily. The sheriff put the key ring on the table, and the judge hung it over the neck of the whisky bottle and brooded down at it.

The miners were whispering together in the cell as Gannon returned his Colt to its scabbard. "That was a foolish thing, Jimmy," he heard the doctor say.

"It was not," the young miner said shakily. He laughed, shakily. "Sheep up in the livery stable, goats in here. I'll not be cheated now."

The doctor said, "I thought you had learned to be careful with those hands."

"Why, I guess there might be a day when having been in Warlock jail will be a big thing, Doc. There is more than one way to grow a goat's beard."

"You young pipsqueak," old man Heck growled. "We are all goats today."

"We are cossacks or peasants," the doctor said, in a strong, clear voice. "How do you like it out there with the cossacks, George Holloway?"

The judge said nothing, and Gannon heard him sigh.

"Have they got Tittle yet, anybody heard?" one of the miners demanded. No one answered him. Another began to sing:

> "Good-by, good-by,
> Good-by to Warlock, good-by.
> Here comes the cavalry, lickety-split,
> Here comes MacDonald to give us a fit,
> Oh, good-by, good-by,
> Good-by, old Warlock, good-by!"

There was laughter. "Hush that up!" the trooper growled. The others immediately began to sing it, and the doctor's voice was loudest among them.

"Looks like a fiesta down by Miss Jessie's boarding house," the sheriff commented, and Gannon joined him in the doorway. There was a huge crowd at the corner of Grant Street, extending out of sight down toward the General Peach.

Then there was a shot. He started out past the sheriff, but Keller grasped his arm tightly. "We'll just stay here and wait it out, boy," the sheriff said. "That is cavalry work down there and nothing to do with us. You and me will just sit it out right here, Johnny Gannon."

61. General Peach

I

THE troopers turned into Grant Street at a trot, eight of them, with a sergeant riding ahead beside the ninth horseman, who was Lafe Dawson. Townsmen watched them from the corner of Main Street as the dust slowly settled in their wake. The troopers carried carbines; they wore dark blue shirts, web cartridge belts, and lighter blue trousers. Beneath their flat caps their faces were bronzed, clean-shaven, and expressionless. A bugle sang off toward the west end of town.

The troopers reined to a halt in a semicircle before the porch of the General Peach boardinghouse. The sergeant dismounted, and, on short calipers of legs, started for the steps. He stopped as Miss Jessie Marlow appeared on the porch. He and Lafe Dawson, who had also dismounted, removed their hats.

"Miss Jessie," Dawson said. "We are sorry to trouble you, but that Tittle is wanted. These fellows have come after him, and—"

"He is not here any more," Miss Jessie said. She stood very straight before the thick shadow of the doorway, with her brown ringlets shining in the sun, her hands clasped before her.

"Well, now, not to be doubting you, ma'am—but these men have orders to look everywhere for him."

The sergeant said politely, "Why, you'll not mind if we look around in there for him, will you, lady?" He had a wizened, dark, Irish face like a dried apple.

"Yes, I mind. There are sick men in here and I will not have your soldiers tramping around disturbing them. You will have to take my word that Tittle is no longer here."

Dawson muttered to himself. The sergeant scratched his head and said, "Well, we can't do that, lady, you see," but he did not move forward.

"Now, see here, Miss Jessie," Dawson said impatiently. "I am sure he isn't here if you say so. Except it's General Peach's orders we are to round up all the strikers from the Medusa, and I *know* there's some of them in there. Now you don't want to interfere with these men trying to do their duty, do you?"

The sergeant signaled with his hand and the troopers dismounted. At the corner of Main the crowd filled the street now, watching silently.

"Will you use force on a woman, Sergeant?" Miss Jessie said.

The sergeant carefully did not look at her as the troopers came forward to join him. Dawson moved toward the steps. Then he stopped, and his hands rose shoulder high as he stared past Miss Jessie. The sergeant and the troopers stared. Blaisedell stood in the shadow just inside the entryway.

"Now, see here, Marshal," Dawson whispered, as though to himself. He dropped his hands slowly to his sides. The sergeant glanced sideways at him. One of the troopers tilted the muzzle of his carbine up; the man beside him struck it down. There was a rustle of whispering from the townsmen at the corner, and titters. Miss Jessie stood gazing down at Dawson and the troopers, her mouth a pinched, severe line.

The sergeant looked at Dawson with one grizzled eyebrow hooked up interrogatively, and a ghost of a smile.

"Well, let's leave this for now, Sergeant," Dawson said, and swung up onto his horse again. The sergeant replaced his cap and waved the troopers back. In silence, they all remounted and rode back up Grant Street the way they had come. The crowd at the corner parted to let them pass through, and, when they had disappeared into Main Street, someone uttered a low, tentative Apache war cry.

Miss Jessie Marlow went back inside the General Peach.

II

The miners stood in silent, stolid groups, in the dining room, in the hall, on the stairs, watching Miss Jessie as she closed the door behind her and put her hand on Blaisedell's arm.

"God bless you and the marshal for that, Miss Jessie!" Ben Tittle said, leaning on the newel post at the bottom of the stairs.

"Looks like they might be back, though," another miner said.

Blaisedell and Miss Jessie stood at right angles to each other in curiously stiff attitudes; she facing him with her great eyes wide as though she had seen a vision, her breast rising and falling rapidly with her breathing and her hand nervously fondling the locket that hung around her neck; Blaisedell facing toward the stairs with his bruised face remote and frowning, his round chin set beneath the broad sweep of his fair mustache.

"I guess they are rounding everybody up," Harris said, in a hushed voice. "I am just as glad I'm not a Medusa man today."

"Ben!" Miss Jessie said suddenly. "I want your head bandaged over like Stacey's, and you are to lie down in Stacey's bed. Stacey will have to go down to one of the houses in Medusa Street; he can walk well enough." She spoke to Stacey. "You help him. Quickly, now!"

Tittle said, "Miss Jessie, I'll not have you and Mr. Blaisedell getting in any mess trying to—"

"Hurry!" she snapped. He turned and hobbled painfully back down the hall, Stacey, with his bandaged head, following him. Blaisedell was watching Miss Jessie. The other miners stirred uneasily.

"That was an Orangeman, that sergeant," O'Brien said from the stairs. "I can smell an Orangeman."

"Are you going to try to stop them from coming in here, Miss Jessie?" Bardaman asked. But he was looking at Blaisedell.

Jones laughed shrilly. "You surely scared that bunch off, Marshal!"

Blaisedell shook his head a little, and frowned more deeply. Miss Jessie was looking from face to face with her eyes blazing and the little muscles tugging at the corners of her mouth.

A bearded miner ran heavy-footed in through the dining room from the rear of the General Peach. "Miss Jessie! They have caught Doc and old Heck and Frenchy and Tim Daley and some others down at

Tim's house. The deputy's got them there in the jail now. Boys, they are scouring the whole town! They have got wagons coming in and all the strikers are going to be transported out!"

There was an immediate uproar. It was a time before the bearded miner could make himself heard again "and the general himself's here, Miss Jessie! They are going to shoot us down if we don't—"

He stopped abruptly and all the others were silent as Miss Jessie raised a hand. "They will not bother you here," she said calmly. She looked up at O'Brien, on the stairs. "Will you go up to a front window where you can see them coming? Let us know when you do. The rest of you are to go back to the hospital room." She stood looking from face to face again until they all started down the hall, shuffling their feet but otherwise silent. Then with a glance at Blaisedell she went into her room, and he followed her.

III

There was a disturbance outside the General Peach, a mutter of voices, a crack of boots on the wooden steps and on the porch. A file of townsmen entered, carrying rifles and shotguns, with six-shooters holstered at their sides or thrust into their belts; their faces were set, their eyes excited—Pike and Paul Skinner, Peter Bacon, Sam Brown, Tim French, Owen Parsons, Hasty, Mosbie, Wheeler, Kennon, Egan, Rolfe, Buchanan, Slator. "Marshal!" Pike Skinner called, and immediately the miners reappeared, crowding silently back down the hallway. The door of Miss Jessie's room opened and Blaisedell came out. Miss Jessie stood in the doorway behind him.

"Marshal," the townsmen said, in a scattered greeting, and one or two removed their hats and said, "Miss Jessie."

"Marshal," Pike Skinner said. "It has come time for vigilantes, looks like." His gargoyle's face was earnest. "Marshal, we don't know what to do but we heard you did and there is a bunch of us here that will back any play you want to make. And more coming. We'll not see this thing happen in Warlock."

"Fight if it comes to that," Mosbie said.

"Ought to be a few of you jacks to make a fight of it, too," Hasty said, nodding toward the miners crowded together in the hallway.

"As well as you people!" one of them cried.

"Well, we didn't all come to make a fight," Peter Bacon said. A chew of tobacco worked in his brown, wrinkled cheek. "But we will make a decent enough stand, and I guess fight if we have to do it."

Blaisedell leaned on the door jamb. His intense blue eyes traversed the faces before him. He smiled a little.

Paul Skinner said, "Marshal, it is time folks in this town stood up to things some. You tell us how we're to do, and we'll do it."

"They won't fire when there's a town full of us against them," Kennon said. "It is a pitiful sight; they are stacking miners in my stable there like cordwood."

Blaisedell still said nothing; Pike Skinner looked at Miss Jessie anxiously.

"We are with you, Marshal," Sam Brown said, cracking the butt of his rifle down on the floor. "You lead us on and we'll chase blue breeches right on back to Bright's. We are with you sink or swim."

"Or stuck in the mud," Bacon said, sadly. "Marshal, the sheriff is down here and got Johnny Gannon hobbled. That couldn't do anything anyway. But we are with you, U.S. Cavalry or not."

"It is his place," Miss Jessie said. Their faces all turned toward her. Blaisedell straightened.

Then they were all silent, watching Blaisedell.

All at once he grinned broadly. "Well, boys," he said. "Maybe we can pull some weight here between us."

There was a concerted sigh. "Why, now then!" Mosbie said.

"You want us in here or outside, Marshal?" Oscar Thompson asked.

"I'll make my place on the porch there, if that's all right with you boys. I don't mean to take it on for myself, but it looks like if I can't handle it without going to shooting maybe we all couldn't." His face turned grave again. "For if it came to shooting there'd be dead men and too many cavalry for us, and nothing gained in the end."

"Except by God we fit the sons of bitches!" one of the miners cried in a high, cracked voice.

"You mean to bluff it, Marshal?" Wheeler said worriedly.

Pike Skinner said, "Don't leave us out of it, Marshal!"

"Marshal," Sam Brown said. He sounded embarrassed. "Well, Marshal, no offense, but—well, that time those jacks tramped you at the jail. I mean, a bluff's a bluff, but—"

Blaisedell looked at him coldly. "You asked me how I wanted to do it," he said. "I am telling you how. I am not going to fire on the U.S. Cavalry, or you either. Do you hear?" He gazed from face to face. "I said I will stand by on the porch here. I'll ask the rest of you to do some climbing and get up on the roof of the barn, and the other places on down the street." He grinned again, in a swift flash of teeth.

"We will have the U.S. Cavalry surrounded and we'll see if they don't bluff."

Tim French laughed out loud. "Why, if we could call old Espirato up from his grave we could hightail Peach out of here at a run!" The others laughed.

"No shooting!" Blaisedell said sharply. "Now maybe you had better move, boys."

"Squads left!" Paul Skinner said, and limped toward the door. The others started after him.

"General!" someone called back. "Send up chuck now and then, and we will hold out for a month." They tramped out, laughing and talking excitedly.

"Let them have their fun," a miner said bitterly. "They don't want any help from us."

"Looks like we are having it from them, though," Bardaman said. "Marshal, you sure you know what you are doing?"

"No," Blaisedell said, in a strange voice. "No man ever is."

"You had better get your six-shooters, Clay," Miss Jessie said. She said it as though she were the general, after all, and turned back inside her room as Blaisedell started for the stairs. Three miners who stood there glanced at him covertly, each in turn, as he mounted the steps past them.

"I hope MacDonald's black soul rots in hell," a miner in the hallway said. "And General Peach with him."

"Amen."

"This might be a fine show here today," the bitter one said. "But we will get shipped further and harder for it."

"Shut up," Bardaman said. "It's a show worth it, isn't it?"

They were silent again as Blaisedell came back down the stairs. He had taken off his coat, and was bareheaded. The sleeves of his fine linen shirt were gartered on his upper arms, pulling the cuffs free of his wrists. He wore two shell belts, two holstered Colts hung low on his thighs. Their gold handles gleamed in the light as he threw the front door open.

"The best show there is," Bardaman whispered, to the miner next to him. Miss Jessie came to stand behind Blaisedell in the doorway and they watched the men appear on the rooftops across the street.

There was a yell from upstairs. Boots thumped in the upstairs hall; O'Brien yelled from the top of the stairwall, "Marshal! Here they come! It is the whole damned army!"

IV

The troopers made their way down Grant Street with difficulty through the crowd that had collected. There were more than thirty of them, and with these were MacDonald, on a white horse, and Dawson and Newman from the Medusa. At the head of the troop were a major and a young captain. A still younger lieutenant rode beside Dawson. The crowd jeered and cheered as they came through. MacDonald toppled in his saddle as someone pulled on his leg, and there was a burst of laughter. MacDonald lashed out with his quirt, blindly, for his hat had slipped forward over his eyes. His left arm was folded into a black sling.

"Mister Mac!" someone shouted. "You have got yourself a passel of new foremen!"

There was more laughter. The lieutenant grinned sheepishly, the captain looked angry; the major was glancing up at the men on the rooftops along Grant Street, and their weapons. MacDonald spurred the white horse toward the porch of the General Peach, where Blaisedell stood, with Miss Jessie Marlow behind him in the doorway.

"This is the United States Cavalry, Marshal!" he cried. As soon as he spoke the crowd fell silent. "You interfere at your own peril! Major Standley has orders—"

Blaisedell's voice boomed out, drowning MacDonald's. "Can't be the U.S. Cavalry. They would not ride down here to do your black-hearted work for you, MacDonald. Own up, now, boys; what quartermaster wagon did you rob for those blue shirts?"

There was another roar of catcalls and laughter. The major raised his hand and the troopers halted. He said, not loudly, "Mr. Blaisedell, we are here under orders to arrest all the strikers from the Medusa mine, and we propose to search this house for a man named Tittle. You won't be fool enough to try to stop us?" He was a plump man with a half-moon of faded blond mustache and eyelashes that looked white in his dark face.

"Why, yes," Blaisedell said, and laid his hands flat against his holsters. "I am fool enough."

"We have orders to shoot if we have to, Marshal!"

"Why, I can shoot too, Major!"

There was a shout of approbation from the crowd. It ceased immediately as Blaisedell raised a hand for quiet. He pointed a finger at the major. "You will be first, Major. Then you, MacDonald. Then you, Captain. Then I will take those two they couldn't find britches to fit," he said, indicating Dawson and Newman. "And then you, young fellow, if you don't mind waiting your turn."

"You won't get that far!" the captain shouted furiously. He rose in his stirrups. "Major—"

The major motioned to him to be silent and said, "You are now in armed rebellion against the United States government. Do you realize that, sir?"

Blaisedell stood with his arms hanging loosely at his sides, his fair hair gleaming in the sun. Behind and to the right of him Miss Jessie stood straight and proud, with her chin held high.

"Major," Blaisedell said. "The United States government was got in armed rebellion before either of us was born. And got for one thing by people wanting to keep soldiers from busting through the houses they lived in, if I remember my history books right."

"*Hear, hear!*" someone cried hysterically. The captain swung his horse and spurred it toward the crowd. There was a rising clamor. A number of whores from the Row had gathered on the far side of Main Street and now the shouting had a higher pitch to it, as they added their voices to the rest.

"—a woman behind you so no man can shoot!" MacDonald was heard to cry.

"And a troop of cavalry behind you, Mister Mac!" Hasty called, from the roof of the Feed and Grain Barn.

The major said, "You are held in some respect, Marshal; but no man can bluff the army. I advise you to stand aside before this has gone too far!"

"Bluff?" Blaisedell said grimly. "Why, I advise *you* not to find out whether it is a bluff or not."

"*Marshal!*" Pike Skinner bellowed, and instantly there was a flat, echoing crack. A trooper's hat flew off. Blaisedell stood wreathed in smoke, one of his Colts in his hand. In the silence, as the smoke blew apart, he said harshly, "Throw it down, sonny." The trooper, who had raised his carbine, pitched it from him as though it were red hot. He raised a hand to feel his bare head. MacDonald's horse was pitching and side-stepping. The captain cursed. The major backed his horse away from the porch. Miss Jessie had disappeared.

The major shouted to make himself heard. He raised a gauntleted hand and the troopers with one movement brought their carbines to the ready. Blaisedell unholstered his other Colt, aimed one at the major, one at MacDonald. Otherwise he did not move, except to glance quickly around as Miss Jessie reappeared. She had a derringer in her hand; another wild shout went up. Some of the troopers lowered their carbines. The major looked frozen with his hand still raised.

"Major, you will go down like Custer!" Pike Skinner shouted. The men on the rooftops had their weapons pointed down on the troopers in the street. Peter Bacon spat tobacco juice onto the cap of a trooper below him.

"You are surrounded, you blue-leg bastards!" Mosbie bellowed enthusiastically. "We will cut hair today, if you fire on those two."

The major swung his horse around and snapped an order. The lieutenant saluted; with eight of the troopers in line behind him he trotted south down Grant Street, and there dismounted with his men, where they could cover the men on the roofs, some of whom now knelt behind the parapets. The major's face was shining with sweat.

There was a new disturbance in the crowd packed into Main Street. "Shame!" a woman's voice cried shrilly. "Shame on the United States Cavalry! Shame, General Peach! Shame—"

"Peach!" someone yelled.

"Here comes the general!"

He appeared at the corner, with another officer behind him. The crowd gave way before him. "Shame!" the shrill voice cried. "Shame! Shame!" General Peach did not appear to notice. He looked huge on his great gray horse; he rode heavily, slumped in the saddle. His white beard lay against his chest, his blouse was unbuttoned, and an unlit cigar jutted from his mouth like the bowsprit of a sailing ship. His great, black, broad-brimmed hat flapped with the motion of the gray's pace. One side of his hat was pinned to the crown with a silver eagle and there were great yellow eagles on the rear corners of his shabrack. He carried a leather-bound stick in his hand. The townspeople in the street thrust aside, and the gray horse came down the alleyway between them at a slow walk. Behind him rode Colonel Whiteside, a frail, worried-looking man with gray mutton-chop whiskers.

"*Shame!*" the voice continued to cry, increasingly hoarse. "Shame, General Peach! Oh, shame! *Shame!*" There were a few catcalls, a gobbling Apache cry. General Peach did not even move his head.

The captain saluted. The major spurred forward to speak to General Peach, but the general ignored him and the gray horse continued steadily forward, with Whiteside close behind. Peter Bacon spat over the parapet again, while Pike Skinner rose to his feet, with his shotgun over his arm. Blaisedell moved only to replace his six-shooters in their scabbards where one of the golden butt-inserts caught the sun like a flame. Miss Jessie stepped slowly to the far side of the porch, the hand holding the derringer at her side.

General Peach reined to a halt close to the steps of the boarding house that bore his name. He spoke in a huge, hollow, reverberating voice. "A long-haired gunman and a pretty woman with a pretty ankle and a pretty little derringer."

Having said it, he sat more erectly in the saddle, blinking sleepily. His eyes looked too small for his broad, squat, fleshy face, his mouth was a pinched dark hole in his beard. He raised his leatherbound stick and scratched behind his ear with its tip. His beard blew and his hat flapped in a gust of wind that ruffled Blaisedell's hair as well.

"All right!" Now there was an edge of anger to the great, blown voice. "You have made your show—" He did not go on, slumping in the saddle again, as though speech had tired him. He sat as though he were waiting for the two on the porch to disappear. There was silence except for the occasional stamp of a hoof or the jingle of harness among the troopers. Blaisedell did not move. Miss Jessie's face looked drawn.

Colonel Whiteside edged his horse forward until he was almost in a line between the general and Blaisedell. "I'm sorry, Miss Marlow!" he said, in his high voice. "We will have to clear the strikers out of your house."

"Have you a warrant, sir?" Miss Jessie said.

"We don't need a warrant, ma'am. We—"

"I say you need a warrant. And I think there can be no warrant for this disgraceful conduct!"

"You stubborn little fool!" MacDonald cried. "This is the military government you are presuming to—"

"Mineowner's government!" a thick Cornish voice shouted, and there was a roar of mocking laughter.

Someone yelled from the rooftops, "Sound the charge, bugler! It is Bull Run all over again." General Peach rose in his stirrups and glanced slowly around him, and up at the roofs.

"We have no government here!" Miss Jessie cried. "Each of us has had to learn to defend his own house!"

"Hear, hear!"

"Shame, General Peach! Oh, *shame* on you!" The clamor began all around. Buck Slavin appeared on the roof of the Feed and Grain Barn. He climbed up on the parapet, waving his arms and shouting for silence.

"When are we going to get a town patent, General?" Slavin shouted.

There were cheers. "When do we get a county of our own without the law a day's ride away?" The cheering and whistling swelled and rose, while Slavin waved his arms again. Colonel Whiteside had swung around in his saddle, but General Peach sat staring stolidly at Blaisedell.

"Mineowners' law!" the man with the Cornish accent bellowed, and MacDonald rose in his stirrups to try to see the offender. There was jeering.

Slavin waved his arms for quiet. "People of Warlock!" he cried. "A motion! A motion! That we call our county Peach County in honor of the general. And Warlock the county seat! All in favor!"

There were groans mingled with cheers. "Medusa County!" someone cried, and the groans drowned the cheers. "Blaisedell County!" and the cheers drowned the groans. General Peach looked around as though he had been waked from sleep. The catcalls and the jeering grew louder and louder, there were rebel yells, Apache war cries. The general waved his gauntlet holding the leather-bound stick high above his head, and there was a sudden hush.

"A county of jackasses run by a murdering gunman and his doxy?" he said, in his huge voice. "Call it Espirato County for all of me!" Then, as there were boos, he shouted, "Standley, clear the damned jackasses out of the street!"

The major spurred his horse toward the crowd with obvious reluctance, the captain more eagerly. The troopers swept into line behind them, and, horses sidling forward, they pushed the townspeople back into Main Street. The Apache cry was taken up now throughout the crowd until the street was filled with turkey gobbling. General Peach sat glowering, chewing on his cigar. Whiteside was whispering to him.

He thrust the colonel aside with a motion of his stick. "Madam!" he roared. "You asked a minute ago if I had a warrant to go through your house. I ask you if you have a warrant to keep such a house!" He stopped, and waited; there was silence again. Then he said, "A disorderly house! A brothel for dirty miners complete with pimp and madam!"

He raised his stick and cut it viciously through the air, so that the gray shied. "Madam, you are a vile disgrace!" he shouted hoarsely. "And your *macquereau* with his pistols has killed more decent men than the typhoid. Filth cohabiting with murderous vile filth and prostituting to filth! And time you were stamped out like filth! You are a notorious pair and a public scandal! I will give you and your—"

There was another flat violent crack, and smoke swirled up before Blaisedell again. The general's raised gauntlet no longer contained the leather-bound stick. The troopers swung their horses around as the major shouted a command; a huge sigh rose from the crowd, an aghast and awed intake of breath that blew out instantly in one great cry of approval and triumph. Colonel Whiteside leaned forward in his stirrups with an arm stretched out toward the general and his mouth wide with some inaudible cry. General Peach snapped his fingers and pointed down, and the colonel dismounted and scampered around the gray to find the stick. The cheering grew louder. The general's face was dark red.

Whiteside handed him back the stick, and then hurried to remount. The clamor slackened and died. General Peach continued in the same voice, as though he had not been interrupted at all. "—thirty seconds to get off that porch. And exactly one hour to get out of this town!"

Then he sat motionless and silent, slumped and sleepily blinking once more. He did not heed the colonel's attempts to whisper to him, waving his stick finally as though to brush away a fly. Blaisedell stood facing him with his boots planted apart and his still smoking Colt slanting down in his hand. Slowly he replaced it in its scabbard, and Miss Jessie retreated a little, one hand still gripping the derringer at her side.

Then, all of a sudden, the general sat erect. Laboriously he swung himself out of the saddle. "Sir!" Whiteside whispered. "Sir!" He scrambled from his saddle and tried to intercept the general, who knocked him aside. General Peach tramped through the dust, grunted as he mounted the boardwalk, slapped the leather-bound stick against a black boot. His bootheel struck the first step resoundingly; he mounted the second step.

"Stop right there!" Blaisedell said.

General Peach stopped. He turned, on the step below where Blaisedell stood, to face his troops. He paused there a moment, in the frozen hush, moving his head from side to side as though he were going to speak. Then, with his back to Blaisedell, ponderously, powerfully, but not even swiftly, he swung his arm backhanded, swung the stick in his hand. It struck Blaisedell's skull with a startling crack. Blaisedell staggered back.

General Peach pivoted with the swing of his arm; grunting, he beat the stick down on the six-shooter in Blaisedell's hand. The six-shooter fell. He slashed the stick with a heavier, duller crack across Blaisedell's face. There was a moan from the crowd as Blaisedell fell back again. Miss Jessie screamed.

General Peach moved after Blaisedell with slow, awkward swings of his arm. His tight blouse split down the back and he grunted hugely with every stroke of the leather-bound stick, which flashed through its arc like a brown snake. Blaisedell crumpled and fell. The general straddled his body and brought the stick down again. Miss Jessie flung herself at him, screaming. He slashed at her and she fell back, clutching at her breast.

Then she raised the derringer in both hands and pointed it, as Colonel Whiteside bounded up the steps toward her crying, "No! No!" The hammer fell with the dry snap of a misfire and the colonel caught her in his arms, and wrested the little pistol away. The general slashed his stick down, and down again, unnoticing, "I!" he shouted suddenly, panting. "*I* am! *I am!*"

Then he desisted. He swung around toward the troopers and roared, "What are you men waiting for? Do I have to cut his onions before you will move?"

Major Standley started and called a command. Half the troopers dismounted, and, in single file, followed the major up on the porch, where Colonel Whiteside held Miss Jessie Marlow and General Peach stood astride Clay Blaisedell, mopping his red face with a blue handkerchief, panting. His vacant, small blue eyes watched the troopers enter, almost sleepily. One of them stumbled over one of the gold-handled six-shooters. The next kicked it off the porch. Colonel Whiteside held Miss Jessie's arms, whispering to her; she was not struggling now.

"See that they find that man Tittle, Whiteside," the general said suddenly. "Willingham wants him in particular."

"Yes, sir," Whiteside said.

Peach nodded solemnly. "Then nothing to do but load 'em up, take 'em out; see to it, Whiteside. Load 'em up, take 'em out," he said, nodding again. "Willingham is a power at the convention, Whiteside. Oh, he is a powerful force at the convention. He will be useful to us, Whiteside."

"Yes, sir," the colonel said.

General Peach took off his great hat and wiped his pink bald head. Then he stepped clear of Blaisedell and walked heavily back down the steps. An orderly helped him mount the gray horse. MacDonald sat staring at the porch with his teeth showing in a kind of paralyzed grimace. Troopers began to come out of the door, herding the boarders before them. None of the miners looked at Miss Jessie, or at Blaisedell. The major came out.

"Where is Tittle, ma'am?" he said.

"I won't tell you!"

"Now, ma'am," the colonel said chidingly. "You would do just as well to tell us. We—"

"What will you do if I do not?" Miss Jessie cried. "Turn me over to your men for rape?"

"Now, ma'am!" the colonel groaned. He released her arms. Instantly she ran down the steps toward the general's horse.

She cried, in a hoarse voice, "An army of jackals led by an old boar with a ring in his nose!"

"Hush!" Whiteside said, catching her again. "Hush now, *please*, ma'am! It is bad enough already. Hush, please!"

"Bloody old boar!" she cried. "Crazy old boar!" She began to sob wildly. General Peach stared down at her in silence, frowning. The men on the roof across the street averted their eyes.

Then there was a gasp as Blaisedell rose. He stood clinging to one of the posts that supported the roof of the porch, his face cruelly striped with red welted lines. Again Miss Jessie broke away from the colonel and ran to him, but now her cry was lost in a shout that went up from the corner, and General Peach awoke from his stupor as though galvanized by an electric shock.

"*Espirato!*" someone was shouting, pushing his way through the crowd. "*Espirato!*" He appeared between two of the troopers' horses; it was Deputy Gannon. He ran toward the general.

"Oh, good God!" the colonel cried, as the general slashed the stick across the gray's rump. The gray leaped forward toward the deputy.

"What's that, man?" Peach roared. "What's that you say?"

"Apaches!" the deputy cried. He grasped the gray's bridle, his narrow, crooked-nosed face bent back to peer up into the general's face. The major appeared and ran down the steps, and troopers hurried out of the door behind him. "It's Apaches!" the deputy cried. "Joe Lacey just rode in to say they have killed a bunch of cowboys in Rattlesnake Canyon! He is at the saloon now!"

His further words were lost in shouting. The gray bucked away from his grasp as the general slashed back with the stick again.

"Whiteside!" Peach shouted. "Whiteside! Espirato, d'you hear? Do you *hear*, Whiteside? By the Almighty we will run him to earth this time, Whiteside! Standley, get your men mounted and ready!" The gray started forward through the townspeople. Men crowded around the deputy, shouting questions. No one looked now to see Miss Jessie Marlow helping Blaisedell back inside the General Peach.

The men descended from the rooftops, and the crowd moved away down Main Street. There were a few backward glances, and those made quickly and almost furtively. When they had all gone only Tom Morgan was left, leaning against the adobe wall of the Feed and Grain Barn, still staring at the porch. There was a fixed, contorted grin upon his face that was part a snarl, like that of a stuffed, savage animal, and part expectant, as though he were waiting for something that would change what had happened there.

62. Journals of Henry Holmes Goodpasture

June 5, 1881

It was a thing I wish I had never seen, a man's downfall and degradation. Poor Blaisedell; should he have pulled that trigger? I have fought the question, pro and con, to exhaustion in my mind. Yet was he not subscribed to it when he made his stand? And was it Miss Jessie's will directing him to that stand? I will not blame her. Poor Blaisedell, we had already seen that incapacity that brought him low today; it was evident too when he was overrun by miners before the jail, that flaw of mercy or humanity, or of a fatal hesitation to be the aggressor at gunplay, or too much awareness of the consequences if he had pulled the trigger, on both occasions—not to himself but to this town.

How would I have him be different? If he had not had this flaw he would have been no more than a hired, calloused killer of men, and we would have turned against him finally for that very heedlessness. Instead, we will turn against him for his failure to be heedless, of consequences or of life, for seeming weakness, for that hesitation that was his ruin; for failure. Now he is pitied, and pity is no more than contempt beribboned and scented.

Pity and shame, a shame for him and for ourselves, who share it. Shame and pain, and pain must savagely turn upon its cause, which is Blaisedell. He should have fired.

Yet how could he have fired upon an old man, an insane old man, but one still to be honored for past deeds and for his position. Ah, but a cunning and treacherous insane old man, who, by the contrivance of turning his back upon Blaisedell, confessed that he knew Blaisedell to be honorable. And must have known that Blaisedell would not fire upon the man who is, after all, the embodiment of law and authority in this place.

Poor devil, he must wish himself dead, honorably dead. That is, perhaps, what should have been. He should have killed General Peach, and been himself instantly, unambiguously, and honorably killed by a volley of carbine fire. We would have crowned him then with laurels for tyrannicide.

Now, too late, I can formulate it: I asked of him only that he not fail. He has failed, yet how can a man be human and not fail? I remember once, before he came, jesting that he would have to be not of flesh and blood to succeed here. He did, until now, succeed, and was human, and is still. I could not grieve for him if he were not. So do most of us grieve; Warlock, for a day, will bleed for those wounds upon his face and spirit, and then, as a man will manage to thrust into oblivion something of which he is mortally ashamed, we will turn away from him.

My first thought, of course, was that Gannon was trying rather ridiculously to create a diversion. It was presently obvious that this was not so. Joe Lacey had indeed arrived in Warlock, with a frightful bullet-furrow across his forehead and a frightful story. It seems that the San Pabloites, including Lacey, Whitby, Cade, Harrison, Mitchell, Hennessey, and others—thirteen in all—were returning empty-handed from Hacienda Puerto, having been driven off by Mexicans, when, yesterday at nightfall, they were ambushed in Rattlesnake Canyon by a band of half-naked Apaches with their bodies horribly daubed with mud. Lacey swears (although this is not given much credence) that he marked Espirato among them, an old man supposedly very tall for an Apache. Any tall Apache immediately becomes Espirato, by which device he was, in the old days, capable of being seen in several places at once. The ambush was carried out with devilish cleverness. The men were riding closely grouped along a narrow and boxlike defile in which the whole group was enclosed at once, when there was a war cry as a signal, whereupon Apaches rose from behind every bush and rock—at least a hundred of them, Lacey says—and began to pour a torrent of hot lead down upon the hapless whites. In a few moments all but Lacey were dead. He saw with his own eyes one brave leap down to cut Whitby's heart from his still living body, and others join to begin the usual disfigurement of the dead.

Lacey himself was in the lead, and miraculously escaped on down the canyon, riding at breakneck speed. He is sure no others escaped their doom.

I was fortunate enough to have entered the Lucky Dollar, where Lacey was steadying his nerves with Taliaferro's whisky, before the rest of the crowd was blocked out by soldiers upon General Peach's entry there. The General, after hearing Lacey's story, announced his intention to depart immediately and with all his troops for the border. Colonel Whiteside interposed that Rattlesnake Canyon is in Mexican Territory, whereupon the General whirled as though he would strike his subordinate. "I will follow Espirato to hell itself, and be damned to the Mexican government!" cried he, to the accompaniment of cheers —for how fickle are men, to whom, a few minutes earlier, Peach had seemed a monster of superhuman powers. Whiteside continued to warn him that if he entered Mexican territory, trouble with that country would result, that he would certainly be court-martialed for it and end his days in disgrace. The General ordered him away contemptuously, and charged Major Standley with the preparation of the cavalry for the ride to the border.

Peach towered over his subordinates like a Titan over pygmies. Hate him as I must, I will admit he was at this moment every inch a general, and an impressive one. He seemed younger. He held himself more erect. His eyes flashed with resolution, and the commands he uttered were clear and terse; he seemed to have recovered himself completely since I had seen him last, in Bright's City.

It was at this time that Willingham entered.* He is a short, rotund man with red whiskers fringing a cold and willful face. He began to seek the General's attention, but Peach rebuffed him and, when Willingham persisted, directed one of his officers to escort the gentleman outside. Peach did this politely enough, but evidently had been holding himself in with some restraint, for when Whiteside again endeavored to make himself heard, Peach bellowed that he would be put under arrest if he uttered another word, and within twenty minutes General Peach and every officer and trooper had departed Warlock for the border.

The position of Willingham, MacDonald, and their henchmen, who

* Director of a number of mining companies, and president of the board of Porphyrion and Western, "Sunny Will" Willingham was a prominent California politician and a former member of Congress.

have taken refuge in the Western Star Hotel, is perilous indeed, for the Medusa strikers have been released from the livery stable where they were confined, and a great number of them are now standing in Main Street outside the hotel, in ominous silence. Their mood does not seem to be one of violence—although as the day progresses and strong waters are imbibed, agitators listened to, and especially when the miners return this evening from the other mines, the mood may rapidly change, and if I were MacDonald and Willingham I would be shaking in my boots. I understand that Morgan has enlisted himself in Willingham's party, and, with a number of foremen, stands guard at the hotel.

One of Blaikie's hands has arrived, early this afternoon, with more news of the ambush in Rattlesnake Canyon. It now seems that Jack Cade and Mitchell have also escaped, and that their assailants were not Apaches at all, but Mexicans! This version of the ambush has immediately been accepted. For one reason, no doubt, because the possibility of Apaches on the loose and murderously inclined is an extremely unpleasant prospect to contemplate, and, for another, because the rumor has long been that McQuown and most of these same San Pablo men once ambushed Hacienda Puerto riders trailing rustled stock in Rattlesnake Canyon in exactly this same manner, masquerading as Apaches; and so it seems very likely that Don Ignacio's vaqueros might have chosen a similar means to vengeance. Horrible though that vengeance seems, there is justice in it, and it is difficult not to wish that men such as Mitchell, and especially Jake Cade, had not been spared.

The Cowboy who brought in this news says he met the cavalry en route, and apprised them of his information—and was summarially brushed aside. It would seem, however, that the marauders will have put many miles between themselves and the border by now, if, indeed, they ever crossed it. And surely General Peach will not cross it himself, in pursuit of what the members of his staff, at least, must come to see are masqueraders.

There is laughter now about his wild, windmill-chasing ride, which, not many hours ago, had a valiant and glorious aspect. But the possibility that he will compound foolishness with idiocy, and lead his force into Mexico, is worrisome. Such an action could easily, in the present state of international relations, lead to reprisals, if not to war. To war in general we are not averse, but we decry it when we are in such an exposed position. Nor is General Peach a military commander in whom it is possible to have much faith.

The crowd of miners before the Western Star seems to have thinned out, and some say that their leaders, who had been let out of jail (the doctor was incarcerated with them!) are now meeting to decide upon a course of action. I fear they may run wild, knowing they have this respite in which to commit whatever arson and destruction they please, before Peach returns and they are rounded up again.

Blaisedell has not been seen. The subject is scrupulously avoided, and gossip is all over General Peach's charge after the nonexistent Apaches. There is a general feeling of the fittingness of the slaughter of the rustlers, and I have heard it said that this ambush took place in exactly the same part of the Canyon as did the previous one, which it avenged. Sheriff Keller I saw in the Lucky Dollar, exceedingly under the influence of strong spirits; with him the judge, equally so. Many Cowboys are coming in from the valley. As usual, the news from Warlock has reached them on the wind, or through the voices of birds. I hope they have not come to gloat over Blaisedell's fall. *They* did not accomplish it. The sight of him dropping mutely beneath General Peach's bludgeon clings to me like an incubus.

63. The Doctor Chooses His Potion

WORD had been sent out that the Medusa strikers were to meet on the vacant ground next to Robinson's wood yard at five o'clock, and a little before that time the doctor set out from Tim Daley's house in company with Fitzsimmons, Daley, Frenchy Martin, and the others, who, as Fitzsimmons had said, had been classified as goats rather than sheep by the fact that they had been incarcerated in the jail rather than in the livery stable with the rank and file. Old man Heck, in a sulk, had refused to attend the meeting.

The afternoon had been spent in argument over policy that had been, by careful indirection, a struggle for power. Old man Heck's supporters had deserted him one by one, until finally even Frenchy Martin and Bull Johnson had been won over. Now the decisions, for better or for worse, lay with the doctor and Fitzsimmons, whom the goats had raised to leadership over themselves, and so over the sheep.

The doctor had been amazed by his own actions this afternoon. They had been entirely foreign to what he had known of himself, Dr. David Wagner. The hatred engendered within the struggle to manipulate words and men just passed, had far outstripped any felt for the Medusa mine, for MacDonald, and for the mineowners. He was not even disgusted with himself to realize that he was as much a subject to this as old man Heck or Bull Johnson. His jealousy, whenever any man had risen to challenge him, had been ruthless, his pleasure, when he had won each separate skirmish, triumphant; he was contemptuous now of those he had beaten.

Fitzsimmons had clung to his coattails throughout, and he had been content to have it so, although he knew, too, that Fitzsimmons was jealous of him, and that he could look forward to a further struggle for power, one day, with Jimmy Fitzsimmons. He did look forward to it, to test again this thing newly discovered in David Wagner against the iron will and cunning, the pure thrust of ambition in a boy more than twenty-five years younger than he.

Fitzsimmons glanced sideways at him and winked, solemnly, and he nodded in reply.

Behind them Daley and Martin were talking in low, excited voices. Several whores peered worriedly from the cribs along the Row, and the dark, wooden faces of Mexican women watched them from the porches of the miners' shacks along Peach Street. Warlock seemed apathetic after an eventful day. Now, the doctor thought, his anger against MacDonald must be regenerated, and yet this done in such a way that he could temper the mood of the strikers at the meeting to the proper course. He began to ponder what he must say to them—different words entirely from those of this afternoon.

"Do you know what, Doc?" Fitzsimmons said, in a low voice. "There is not a miner in this town knows what to do now. They will be so pleased to have us tell them they will wag their tails."

"And do just the opposite," he said, and smiled.

"Not if we tell them what they are going to do is what they *want* to do."

"I think there are more than old Heck who want to burn the Medusa still. Or more than ever."

Fitzsimmons shook his head condescendingly. "They are too scared, Doc. Just so nobody says they are scared. We had just better be damned sure nobody speaks up to say we had better settle quick before the cavalry gets back. That's all we have to watch out for."

"And make sure we show Willingham we think he is in rather a worse position than we are."

"Expect it would be a good idea to get up a torchlight parade tonight?"

"I think it would be very effective, and a good thing for you to turn your energies to. If you are sure you could control it."

"I could control it, all right," Fitzsimmons said stiffly, and glanced at him sideways again.

The little procession passed the wood yard and turned into the vacant property, which had been used for miners' meetings since Lathrop's time. There were a number of miners there already.

The doctor stopped and looked around to meet the eyes that were all fixed upon him. It was as though they knew instinctively that he had been chosen, and deferred without question to the choice. "Doc," Patch said, in grave greeting, and then many of the others took it up. Their tone was different from that of their usual greetings—a pledge of loyalty that had a suspended skepticism in it. They greeted Fitzsimmons by name too, but less deferentially.

"Frenchy," the doctor said, as the rest of the men from Daley's house came up to group around him, "will you see that those planks are set up on the barrels so the speakers will have a place to stand?" Fitzsimmons grinned crookedly as Frenchy went to do it, and the doctor realized why he had spoken so loudly, and to Martin in particular.

"Doc!" Stacey, with his bandaged head, was hurrying toward him. Stacey raised a hand and broke into a trot. "Doc," he panted, as he came up. "You had better come. Miss Jessie needs you at the General Peach."

He felt Fitzsimmons' eyes. "I can't come now," he said curtly. But all at once what had happened at the General Peach, which he had tried to put from his mind as irrelevant, crushed down upon him, and he felt pity for Jessie like a dagger stroke. But not now, he almost groaned; not now. He could not go now.

"It was the marshal sent me," Stacey whispered. Beneath his muslin turban his freckled forehead was creased with worry. "He says she has got the nerves very bad, Doc."

He nodded once. "Get my bag from the Assay Office, will you?" He turned to Fitzsimmons, whose eyebrows rose questioningly in his bland face. "Jimmy, I must go and see about Miss Jessie. You will have to do your best here until I get back."

Fitzsimmons nodded, and then on second thought frowned as though it were a terrible burden and responsibility. "I will do my best, Doc," Fitzsimmons said, massaging the torn knuckles with which he had made sure of his future. "You hurry," he said.

"I will," he replied grimly. He left the lot, ignoring those who called after him; he almost ran down Grant Street to the General Peach. Jessie's door was closed, but he could hear her voice raised shrilly inside her room. Blaisedell opened the door for him.

He stared in shock at Blaisedell's face. It was cross-hatched with great red welts, and his bruised eyes were swollen almost closed. "Thank God you have got here," Blaisedell said, in a low voice. "You had better give her something. She is—"

"David!" Jessie cried, as he entered past Blaisedell. She stood in the center of the room facing him. Her white triangle of a face looked wasted, as though the fire that blazed in her eyes was consuming the flesh around them. Her face contorted into a wild grimace that he realized was meant to be a smile.

Blaisedell closed the door and came up beside him, moving as though he were sore in every fiber. He sounded exhausted. "She wants us to lead the miners up to burn the Medusa mine," he said. "I have been trying to tell her it is—not the right time. I thought if you could give her something to quieten her," he whispered.

"It is the time!" Jessie cried. "It is the time now! David, we will lead them, and we will—"

"Lead the miners, Jessie?" he broke in, and the words seemed a mockery of himself.

"Yes! We will ride up to the Medusa at the head of them, an army of them. How they will cheer and sing! There are barricades there, they say, but that cannot stop us! Oh, Clay!"

"Jessie, Blaisedell is right, I'm afraid. It is not the time."

"It is the time! The cavalry has gone, and—and we have to do *something!*" She had a handkerchief in her hands, which she kept winding around one hand and then the other.

"We don't have to do anything, Jessie," Blaisedell said in a patient voice.

Her sunken, blazing eyes stared at Blaisedell, shifted to stare at the doctor; it was as though she were looking past them both to the Medusa mine, to glory or redemption—he did not know what. She pulled the handkerchief tight between her hands again. "David," she said calmly. "You must help me make him understand."

There was a knock. "That is Stacey with my bag," he said to Blaisedell, who went to open the door. He took Jessie's hands. The handkerchief was wet with perspiration, or with tears. He smiled reassuringly at her and said, "No, Jessie, I'm afraid it really is not the right time. Everything is very confused right now. But maybe tomorrow or the next day you and—"

"Now!" she cried, and her voice was suddenly deep with grief. "Oh, now, *now!*" She swung toward Blaisedell. "Oh, it must be now, before they forget him. Clay, it is for you!"

He took the bag from Blaisedell, and the bottle from it. There was a glass on the bureau and he filled it with water from the pitcher, and stained the water with laudanum. Behind him Jessie said despairingly, "Clay, it is for your sake!"

In the mirror the doctor saw the agony and revulsion written on Blaisedell's cruelly bruised face. Jessie flew to him and pressed her face to his chest, her ringlets flying as she turned her head wildly from side to side, murmuring something to Blaisedell's heart he neither could hear nor wished to hear. Blaisedell stared at him over her brown head as, awkwardly, he patted her back.

The doctor indicated the glass, and Blaisedell said, "Jessie, Doc has got something for you."

Instantly she swung around. Her face darkened with suspicion. "What's that?"

"It is some laudanum to let you rest."

"Rest?" she cried. "Rest! We cannot rest a moment!"

"You had better take it, Jessie," Blaisedell said, in the gentle voice.

The doctor raised the glass with the whisky-colored liquid in it to her, but she lifted a hand as though she would strike it to the floor. "Jessie!" he said sharply.

Her shoulders slumped. She closed her eyes. She began to sob convulsively. She rubbed her knuckles into her closed eyes and swayed, and Blaisedell put an arm around her. The doctor could see the sobs tearing at her frail body. They tore at him as well; with each one he was wrenched with pity for her, and with anger at Clay Blaisedell and the world that had broken her. His hand shook with the glass.

"Drink it, Jessie."

Obediently she drank it down, and he went to turn the coverlet back on the bed. Blaisedell helped her to the bed and she lay down with her hands over her face, her fingers working in her tangled ringlets, her head moving ceaselessly from side to side. The doctor pulled the coverlet up over her as Blaisedell stepped back toward the door.

"I will be going now, Doc," Blaisedell said in his deep voice, and he turned to meet the blue, intense gaze that was almost hidden beneath the swollen lids. Blaisedell said it again, not aloud, but with his lips only, and nodded to him.

"We will do it tomorrow!" Jessie cried suddenly. She raised her head and her eyes swung wildly in search of Blaisedell. "We will lead them to the Medusa tomorrow, Clay. Tomorrow may not be too late!"

"Why, no; tomorrow won't be too late," Blaisedell said, and smiled a little; then he went out, gently closing the door behind him.

The doctor sat down on the bed beside Jessie as she laid her head back again. She closed her eyes, as though she would be glad to rest. As he heard Blaisedell's step upon the stairs he put down the glass and smoothed his hand over her damp, tangled hair.

He glanced up at the mezzotint depicting Cuchulain in his madness, and felt the pain and fury convulse his heart. So Blaisedell would leave, and damned be his soul for ever having come, for having enchanted her, for leaving her forever in the circle of flames and thorns. And the miners and their union? he thought suddenly. There was no choice. He smiled down at her and smoothed his hand over her hair.

"The miners are meeting now, Jessie," he said. "Tomorrow will be time enough."

She nodded and smiled a little, but did not open her eyes. "It would be better today," she said in a small, clear voice. "But he is tired and hurt. I shouldn't have blamed him so. I shouldn't have called him a coward. What a strange thing to say of him!"

"He knew you were disturbed." He looked down at the strong jut of her brows over her sunken, closed eyes, the whitening of her nostrils as she breathed, the determined set to her little chin.

"Oh, I am so glad I thought of it!" she said. "For it will change everything. We will ride, of course, and they will march behind us. We—"

"Tomorrow," he whispered. "Tomorrow, my dear."

He saw her face crumple; she began to sob again, but softly. She said in the small voice, "But you see why I must make him do it, don't you, David? Because what happened here was my fault."

"No, Jessie," he said. "Jessie, you had better try to rest now."

She fell silent, and after a time he thought she must be asleep more from exhaustion than from the effect of the opiate. He left off stroking her hair and gazed at the window, wondering how the miner's meeting was progressing. He felt detached from it now, but there were a few things he would have liked to say. He would have liked to treat with Willingham for them; he thought he would have enjoyed crossing swords with Willingham.

Jessie said sleepily, "He was hurt and sick at heart, and I was so furious— He wanted to leave here tomorrow, he and I. To go somewhere else, and he said he would change his name. It made me so angry that he should think of changing his name! But I should have understood that he was hurt and sick at heart. Oh, dear God, I thought that monster had destroyed him! But it is silly to give in so easily when—"

"Rest," he said. "You must rest."

Again she was silent. He thought of her and Blaisedell leading the miners and wondered if it was any more insane than his trying to lead them himself. He gazed at his world through inward eyes and saw all his ideals and aspirations crumbling gray and ineffectual. He saw himself a fool. Much better, he thought, a torchlight parade than what he would have brought them, if he could have brought them anything; how much finer the flame of the Medusa stope mounting the shafthead frame against the sky, than the gray ashes of reason. He had deluded himself with his ideals of humanity and liberality, but peace came after war, not out of reason. They would have to have fire and blood to make their union. So it had always been, and revolutions were made by men who conquered, or who died, and not by gray thought in gray minds. Peace came with a sword, right with a sword, justice and freedom with swords, and the struggle to them must be led by men with swords rather than by ineffectual men counseling reason and moderation.

He watched the shadows lengthening through the lace curtains. The room was dimmer now, Jessie's pale face shadowed and more peaceful. It was a quiet meeting the miners were having, he thought. He wondered what kind of a showing Fitzsimmons was making, and smiled at these dregs of jealousy in himself. He knew that Fitzsimmons would do well. It was a sad truth that all the masses of men in their causes would be led by ambitious men, by power-hungry, cunningly self-serving men, rather than by the humanists, the idealists; and better led for it, he thought. Fitzsimmons loved neither the miners nor their cause, he loved only himself and the power he might attain through them. Neither did he, David Wagner, love the miners. He loved an ideal, a generality, and hated another. It was more love, and hate, than Fitzsimmons possessed, and yet it had crippled him in the end, because he could see too well how gray and impalpable was a generality, however fine, set against flesh and blood. There was no choice for him between serving an ideal made of straw and serving a single person in unhappiness and pain, whom he loved.

When Jessie spoke again her voice was so blurred he could hardly understand it. "What did Curley Burne matter to him? I cannot understand why Curley Burne mattered to him so, David. He was not good for anything! He was just another rustler. He—" Her voice died, although her lips still moved.

He watched the increasingly slow movement of her lips, and whispered, "Rest." All that is over, he thought; but could not tell her so. There was a knock.

"Doc?" It was Fitzsimmons' voice. He rose quietly, and went to open the door. He put a finger to his lips, and Fitzsimmons glanced past him and nodded. His face was flushed and triumphant. "You and me are to go talk to Willingham!" he whispered excitedly. "We are to work it out somehow. It is up to us!"

"I can't go, Jimmy."

"You can't!" Fitzsimmons avoided his eyes, pouting; but he knew that Fitzsimmons was relieved and pleased.

"My place is here, I'm afraid."

Fitzsimmons made a show of scowling, biting his lip, rubbing a scarred hand over his stubble of beard. "Well—I guess I can't go back and tell them. I guess I will try and go it alone."

"Listen to me. You will have to have something to take back to them. If it looks as though Willingham will give you nothing, tell him they will not go back to work for MacDonald. He will give you that, at least."

Fitzsimmons nodded. "I'll get more than that."

"Good luck, Jimmy." He put out his hand, and took Fitzsimmons' gnarled, scarred hand, shook it once, and released it.

"Thanks, Doc." The other didn't smile. He started away, and then he glanced back, warily, questioningly.

The doctor smiled and said, "No, I won't get in your way. I am a doctor, after all, not a miner. But try to remember that you are serving them, sometimes. Not just yourself, Jimmy."

Fitzsimmons' face flushed more deeply, but his mouth was hard and crookedly set. "Why, it goes together, doesn't it, Doc? Or does sometimes," he said, and grinned and took his leave, his shoulders held very straight, his hands carried before him. No doubt those burned hands would be useful with Willingham, and no doubt Fitzsimmons meant to use them for all they would gain him, and the miners—that went together sometimes. And perhaps, he thought, as he closed the door, it was as much as could be expected in a world of men.

He returned to sit beside Jessie again. As he watched her sleeping face he smiled and felt at rest himself. He thought there was no better vocation he could have asked, had he ever had a choice. Her sleeping face was quite beautiful, but he was worried about her thinness. She was tired, there had been too much strain upon her, but it would be better with Blaisedell gone. He started to touch her hair again, but he was afraid of waking her, so he contented himself with staring at her face as though to memorize it.

He started as there was a shot in Main Street; he frowned as he saw her eyelids move. There were more shots. Her eyes opened.

"What's that?" she whispered.

"Only a cowboy making a little excitement."

Her forehead was wrinkled with worry, her eyes looked troubled. There were more shots, followed by shouting.

"It is just some cowboy," he said soothingly. He took the bottle of laudanum up again and measured ten more drops into her glass, and rose to fill it with water. "Drink this," he said, and she raised her head to drink. The shooting continued, sporadically, and the shouting. Jessie smiled and he saw her relax as Blaisedell's footsteps descended the stairs.

"Clay will stop *that*," she whispered, as she lay back upon the pillow again.

He felt very tense as he listened to Blaisedell's steps in the entryway, and then he too relaxed as they passed Jessie's door and went outside. "I think I will join you, Jessie," he said, smiling down at her. He measured into the glass his usual dosage, in which he had not indulged for some time now, and then added five more drops and poured the water in. He raised the glass ceremoniously. He thought, as he drank the bitter and puckery draught, that it was not too early in the day.

64. Morgan Cashes His Chips

TOM MORGAN sat on the veranda of the Western Star Hotel and watched the sun's slow descent toward the bright peaks of the Dinosaurs. The crowd of miners had drifted away and now there was no one in the street for whom he had to put on a show of being mine-owner-bought, which had made him feel like a fool. Alone now, with the sun going down, he felt at ease.

At the same time he had never felt so excited, nor so pleased with himself. His tongue pried and poked after the tooth he had lost the other night, to Clay, and it seemed to him now that he had played out his life like a kind of bad tooth, merely filling a hole in the jawbone of mankind, to leave, when he had passed on by, a momentary tender spot that not even a blind tongue would remember. But not now; they would remember him.

And now he thought he must have seen the way some time ago. He had told Clay that since he was leaving he might as well be posted out. It was only a step farther, ace over king. He knew what it would do to Clay, clearly he saw that; and yet he knew that it was right, and had to be, for Clay Blaisedell. It would wipe out General Peach, it would do more than that. For after it they could not touch Clay. After it they could make him neither more nor less. Clay would have come the route, and they would have to let him be, for there was no more. And they would remember Tom Morgan.

He felt an urge to crow, like a cock.

But he whispered, "Yes, me too, you poor damned lost son of a bitch!" He glanced to the left where he could see the roof of Miss Jessie Marlow's boardinghouse, where Clay was, and wondered what he was doing now, thinking now, feeling now. He clasped the shot-gun that leaned between his legs and banged the butt gently against the planks. "Clay, I am sorry," he whispered. "But it is the only thing." He counted a few more regrets: that he would not be able to beat Peach's head off with his own leather-bound quirt; Taliaferro. He laughed at himself as he realized that there was another regret, too. He wished that someone might know why he was doing this. He wished that Kate, at least, might know. But there was no way, and he supposed that it was fair enough.

He squinted up at the descending sun. Not so fast there! he thought. A miner walked along the far side of the street, and Morgan made a show of scowling and tipping the shotgun forward. Godbold came out of the hotel and down the steps past him, and walked quickly across Broadway.

He watched, in the late afternoon, the slant of sun under the arcades, the bright, shiny brown of a horse's haunch, the colors of the dresses of two whores looking in the window of Goodpasture's store. Sam Brown had not got his sign back up yet, and the yellow rectangle was fading in the sun. The wind blew up a whirl of dust, which traveled a way and died, and sent a dry weed rolling and rustling along the edge of the boardwalk. The light changed as the sun slid down the western slope of the sky, and the shadow line advanced across the dusty street. Now, where the sun struck, it made darker stronger colors that seemed tinged with red. It was getting late, and it was coming time.

He banged the shotgun butt down again and rose. Dawson leaned in the doorway with a rifle under his arm, and looked as though he were putting a lot into wishing he were someplace else. He went inside past Dawson, and propped the shotgun against the counter. The Medusa people were all in the dining room. Newman sat gazing out the window. Willingham was playing a game of solitaire, his black hard-hat seated squarely on top of his head, a hand pulling at his fringe of red beard. MacDonald, seated across from him, was morosely watching the cards.

"The muckers will be in from the other mines pretty quick now," Morgan called into the dining room. "There will be hell busting the door down then."

MacDonald grimaced, and shifted his black-slinged arm around in front of his body. Willingham turned the cards and said, "Mr. Morgan, you enjoy alarming us." He took a gold watch from his vest pocket and consulted it. "I suppose we can't count on that old idiot getting back here tonight, can we?"

"He's forgotten us," MacDonald said, in a hollow voice. Newman, his shoulders hunched, had turned to watch them. Three foremen sat at another table at the far end of the room. None of them looked as though they had anything to be pleased about.

Willingham said, "I told him I would ruin him. I will feel quite put out if he ruins himself by blundering down into Mexico."

"What you big mining men need is a more reliable army. Chasing off after Apaches!"

"I don't believe there are any Apaches," MacDonald said. "Mr. Willingham, I think we ought to get that coach around and—"

"I will not be driven out of here!" Willingham said. He looked down at his cards again. "Well, Mr. Morgan? I thought our bargain was that you were to maintain the battlements. That is out in front, not here."

"Things are slow out there. I can't pick a fight with anybody."

"Good God!" MacDonald said. "We don't want any fights!"

"I thought I was to pick fights and shoot holes in jacks. Run some of them out of town."

"Good God!"

"Mr. Morgan, kindly remove your dubious frontier humor and yourself. Your post is on the veranda."

"I'm going upstairs and change my shirt, and then remove myself for a walk around town."

"Mr. Morgan—"

"I always take a walk around sundown," he said. "I wouldn't miss it for the Medusa mine." He went on upstairs to his room.

There he stripped off his coat, harness, and shirt, and washed himself in the basin. He sat down on the edge of his bed to check the action of his Banker's Special. A thin edge of the sun came in through the window, throwing a watery red light over the bed. There was a beat like that of great slow wings in his head, and he sat with the revolver in his hand staring at the blank wall opposite him for a long time before he rose and put on a new linen shirt. He found that his fingers were shaking as he tried to insert his gold cuff links into the cuffs. "I'll be damned!" he whispered. "Why, Rattlesnake!" He stood before the distorted mirror in his shirt sleeves, regarding his pale face with the slash of black mustache across it. He brushed his hair until it shone silver. He rubbed his hands hard together, stretching and clenching his fingers until they felt limber, and then he poured a little whisky into a glass, raised it, said, "How," bowed to the setting sun, and drank.

Leaving his coat off, he set the Banker's Special inside the buckle of his belt and swaggered back downstairs. Gough stared at him round-eyed. In the dining room a young miner in clean blue pants and shirt, and with disfigured, scarred hands which he held awkwardly before him, was talking to Willingham, while MacDonald stood glaring at him with his face mottled red and white.

"What goes against what's bred into you?" said Willingham, who was still playing solitaire.

"Stope-burning," the boy said.

"Oh, it's stope-burning, is it?" Willingham said caustically.

"Yes, sir," the boy said. "There's most of them feel that way about it now. They figure when Peach gets back he will load us up and ship us out like he was set to do in the first place, so might as well get shipped for goats as sheep. There is some that get satisfaction from a good fire, and knowing how it'll burn a couple-three years. It just goes against what's bred in, with me. And some others."

"Oh, you are talking for some others, are you?"

"I might be," the boy said.

"Blackguarding young—" MacDonald cried, but he stopped as Willingham waved a hand at him.

"How many do you speak for, my boy?"

Leaning in the doorway, Morgan watched Willingham, who had not looked up at the boy yet. Willingham ran out of plays, and picked up the cards and shuffled them.

The boy rubbed his scarred hands together. "Well, I don't know, Mr. Willingham. I guess that would depend. They'd just about all like to go back to work, sure enough. But you know how people get—they don't much like feeling they've got backed down to nothing. That's how come they've stayed out so long. Mr. MacDonald here wouldn't give an inch."

"Hush, Charlie," Willingham said, as MacDonald started to speak. The boy glanced around at Morgan. He had the shadowy beginnings of a beard, and he looked like a card sharp posing as a country bumpkin.

"Not an inch, eh?" Willingham said, shaking his head.

"I guess they wouldn't ever go back to work for Mr. MacDonald. If you'll pardon me for being frank, Mr. Mac."

"Mr. Willingham!" MacDonald cried, in a strangled voice. Willingham only pushed a hand at him, then began to turn the cards once more. He did not look up even now.

"How many do you speak for?" he said again.

"I guess the more I got from you, the more I could speak for."

"I see," Willingham said. "Well, sit down, my boy." The young miner sat down warily, in MacDonald's chair, and Willingham went on. "Let's see if reasonable men cannot work this out amicably. I will warn you in advance that I do not intend to give much more than an inch, but I have always desired to be fair. Sometimes subordinates become over-eager—I recognize that much."

It looked, Morgan thought, as though it would be a good game, with MacDonald first into the pot. He would have liked to stay to watch it, but the sun was going down. He said loudly, "I guess I had better get moving if I expect to run Blaisedell out of town tonight."

The young miner's head swung toward him. MacDonald's mouth gaped open. Willingham rose out of his chair. "Great God!" one of the foremen said.

"I'll be back to collect that thousand dollars pretty quick," Morgan said, and grinned around the room and seated the Banker's Special more firmly in his belt.

"Mr. Morgan!" Willingham cried, but Morgan went on out, past the wide-eyed clerk. Dawson, at the front door, stared at him; as he passed he jerked Dawson's Colt from its scabbard.

Dawson said, "Whuh—"

"Keep out of the street, Fatty," he said. "There's going to be lead flying." He thrust the other's Colt inside his belt, and went down the steps and started west along the boardwalk.

The sun had swelled and deepened in color. It hung like a red balloon over the sharp-pointed peaks that would soon impale it. It was a sun the equal of which you saw nowhere else, he thought; bigger and brighter than anywhere else, bigger and brighter today. He took his last cigar from his shirt pocket and bit down on it.

He crossed through the dust of Broadway and mounted the board-walk in the next block. He passed the shell of the Glass Slipper. Men stared at his waist, and he turned his head from side to side to gaze back into their faces. Not one would meet his eyes. Once a cowboy chewing on a cud of tobacco looked back at him for a moment, but he slowed his steps and the cowboy turned quickly aside. No one spoke in his wake. Faces peered out at him over the batwing doors of the Lucky Dollar; six or eight horses were tied to the rail there. He heard whispering behind him now, and he saw Goodpasture watching him from his store window. He glanced up toward the French Palace and tipped his hat in salute. Hearing a movement behind him he turned and grinned to see three cowboys hurriedly getting their horses out of the street.

He went on, under the new sign with the one bullet hole through it, and turned into the jail. Gannon glanced up at him from behind the table, and he brought out Dawson's Colt and leveled it. "Hands up," he said.

Stiff-faced, Gannon rose slowly; his hands continued to rise, shoulder high. "What—" he said, and stopped.

Morgan stepped forward and drew Gannon's Colt and jammed it inside his belt. He motioned Gannon toward the open cell door. Gannon didn't move and he thumbed the hammer back. "Get in there!"

"What the hell do you think you are doing?" Gannon said hoarsely.

"Get in there!" He jammed the muzzle into Gannon's belly and Gannon backed into the cell. He slammed the door and locked it, and tossed the key ring toward the back of the jail. He sneered in at Gannon through the bars. "I promised Kate you wouldn't get hurt," he said, and added, "If this comes wrong you had better tell her if I couldn't do it Pat Cletus couldn't've either."

"What are you going to do?"

"Pistol-whip the spots off this town." With Dawson's Colt in his right hand and Gannon's in his left, he stepped outside.

"Morgan!" Gannon called after him. But he raised his hand and drowned his name in a gunblast; the new sign swung wildly, perforated again.

Now the fuse was lit; he vaulted the tie rail, and his boots sank into the soft dust of the street. The sun sat on the peaks, blood-red, like the yolk of a bad egg. He shivered a little in the wind as he turned his back on the sun. He laughed to see the men scampering along the boardwalks as he swaggered out into the street. He had seen towns shot up before. The best he had ever seen at it was Ben Nicholson, but he could beat that. He spat out his cigar, raised Dawson's Colt, and pulled the trigger again. With the blast rocking in his ears he began to howl like a coyote, an Apache, and a rebel all rolled into one.

"Yah-hoo!" he yelled. "I am the worst man in the West! I am the Black Rattlesnake of Warlock! My mother was a timber wolf and my daddy a mountain lion, and I strangled them both the day I was born!

"Yah-hoo!" he yelled. "I will kill anything that moves, so sit still or die, you sons of bitches; or if you move, crawl! I can spit a man through at fifty yards! I have got lightning in both hands, I comb my hair with wildcats and brush my teeth with barbed wire!" He put a bullet through Taliaferro's sign. A man dived inside the pharmacy, and he fired behind him; a puff of dust rose from the adobe.

"Who wants to die?" he shouted, walking slowly forward. "I am spoiling for a fight! Come on, you sons of bitches—I eat dead cowboys!"

His throat was dry and hoarse from shouting. But he grinned idiotically at the white faces that stared at him. His shirt back felt soaked with sweat. He fired into the air again, and he fired at the yellow patch over the Billiard Parlor. "Come on out and fight!" he yelled. "I have killed forty-five men, half with one shot, and I am going to run some score today!

"Any friends of McQuown's here? I will claw them down with Honest Abe! I am the champeen all-time cowboy killer. Any partners of Brunk's? Come on, you muckering chittle-witted muckers and I will dice your livers for you. Any damned Yankees? No, I can hear them scampering now! Anybody! Come on out, you yellow sons of whores, or I will run this whole town out of itself!"

He raised Dawson's six-shooter and pulled the trigger again; the hammer snapped down dry. He tossed it and caught it by the barrel, and with a long sweep of his arm slung it through Goodpasture's window with a smash of glass. He raised his left hand and fired Gannon's.

"Come on, I say! Where are those brave possemen? Where is that bunch of jailhouse bummers!" He saw several of them, standing with some cowboys along the wall near the Glass Slipper. "Step up, boys! Come out of your holes! No? Where is that mighty deputy then? He has locked himself in his own jail. Isn't there a man in this town? Any friends of Blaisedell's then? I will warm up on them. Speak up, boys!"

He fired into the air to liven things again. Left-handed, he shot the panes out of the gunshop window. He flung Gannon's used-up Colt toward the pharmacy. A man dodged out of the way, and then snapped stiffly to a standstill as though he were standing at attention.

He drew the Banker's Special from his belt. He laughed and howled, and fired into the air. He saw a movement in the ruin of the Glass Slipper, and he fired and chipped adobe. The dust of the street darkened as the sun went down behind him. The moon was up over the Bucksaws, pale as a cloud. It was time, he thought.

"Yah-hoo!" he screeched. "Where is Clay Blaisedell? Where is that yellow-bellied, hollowed-out, gold-handled, long-haired marshal of Warlock? Whose skirts is he hiding behind? Come on out, Clay Blaisedell! Out of your hole and let's see the color of your plaster guts!"

He had come up even with the Glass Slipper now, and he saw a movement among the townsmen there; he swung the Banker's Special and howled with laughter to see one of them dive to the boardwalk. He saw Mosbie's dark, scarred face twisted with rage. "Come on, Clay," he whispered. "I am starting to feel like a damned fool!"

He walked on down Main Street, laughing and taunting; he swung toward the Billiard Parlor, and the miners there tumbled back inside. "Yah-hoo!" he screamed, with his voice tearing in his throat. "Every man is afraid of me! Where is Clay Blaisedell! He has posted his last man out of this town! Blaisedell! Come out here and play boys' games with me, you yellow Yankee hound. Blaisedell!"

Come on, Clay; come on! I am sick to death of this game already! He walked on across Broadway, and saw Dawson jump back inside the door of the hotel. He saw Clay at the next corner.

"Morgan!" Mosbie yelled, and he spun and squeezed the trigger, and saw through the smoke Mosbie slam back against the wall in the shadow under the arcade, his Colt flying free of his hand. And in his deafened ears he heard Clay call, "Morg!"

Clay stood in the street now with his black hat pulled down to conceal his face, his wide brown leather belt slanting across his hips, the sleeves of his white shirt fluttering in the wind; with a wild relief and jubilation Morgan knew that his luck still held, and, as he jammed the burning barrel of the Banker's Special back into his belt, he knew, with a sudden pride, that he could beat those hands of Clay's if he wished, and knew he could center-shot that white shirt just beneath the black tie-ends, if he wished. He yelled hoarsely, "I can beat you, Blaisedell! You had better hit it fast!"

He cried out once more, wordlessly, in triumph, as his hand swept up with the Banker's Special, beating Clay's hand. Clay's hat flew off. He heard a cry and it was Kate. "*Tom!*" Instantly he was flung staggering back with white-hot death impaling him. He squeezed the trigger once more, unaimed, and the sound was lost in a totality of deafening sound; he sought frenziedly to grin as he staggered forward toward the motionless figure that faced him wreathed in smoke. The Banker's Special was suddenly too heavy. It slipped from his hand. But still he could raise his hand to his breast, slowly up, slowly across and back, while the world blurred into deeper and deeper shadow.

He fell forward into the dust. It received him gently. One arm felt a little cramped and he managed to move it out from under his body. In his eyes there was only dust, which was soft, and strangely wet beneath him. "Tom!" He heard it dimly. "Tom!" He felt a hand upon his back. It caught his shoulder and tried to turn him, Kate's hand, and he heard Kate sobbing through the swell of a vast singing in his ears. He tried to speak to her, but he choked on blood. The dust pulled him away, and he sank through it gratefully; still he could laugh, but now he could weep as well.

65. The Wake at the Lucky Dollar

I

MORGAN lay face down in the dust of Main Street. Kate Dollar bent over him, pulling weakly at his shoulder, her harsh, dry sobbing loud in the silence, her white face turning to stare at Blaisedell, and then at the men who lined the boardwalk. Buck Slavin ducked under the tie rail and came out to join her.

Blaisedell retrieved his hat. His face was invisible beneath its brim in the fading light. Kate Dollar rose as Slavin bent down and turned

Morgan over. Morgan's face, caked with white dust, was grinning still. His shirt front was muddy and blood welled through the mud.

"Get your hands off him," Blaisedell said, and Slavin straightened hurriedly, wiping his hands on his trouser legs. Blaisedell's face was a mesh of thick, red welts, his eyes were swollen almost closed.

"You weren't worth it," Kate Dollar said, not loudly, as Blaisedell bent down and picked up Morgan's body. He stood for a moment, staring back at her, and then he carried Morgan slowly back up the street toward the Lucky Dollar. He laid him on the boardwalk, ducked under the rail, and, in the silence, picked him up again. He backed through the batwing doors of the Lucky Dollar, gently maneuvering Morgan's sagging, dusty head past the doors.

Inside, grunting a little now with his burden, Blaisedell moved with heavy steps toward the first faro layout. Men scrambled out of his way, and the dealer and the case keeper retreated. He laid Morgan on the layout amid the chips and counters, and the silver. He straightened Morgan's legs and folded his hands upon his muddy chest, and he stood for a long time in the intense and crowded silence staring down at Morgan. Then he glanced slowly around at the men who watched him, his eyes slanting from face to face white-rimmed like those of a frightened stallion: toward Skinner, Hasty, French, and Bacon, who stood nearby; toward the miners at the bar; toward the sheriff and Judge Holloway, who sat at a table with a whisky bottle between them, the sheriff staring at nothing in frozen concentration, the judge leaning forward with his forehead resting in his hands. Blaisedell glanced up at the sweaty-faced lookout sitting stiffly with his hands held rigid six inches above the shotgun laid across his chair arms.

He took a handkerchief from his pocket and gently brushed the dust from Morgan's face; then he covered the face with the handkerchief and said to the lookout in a jarring voice, "Watch him." His bootheels scuffed loudly as he moved toward the bar. The men edged away before him so that by the time he reached it he had a twenty-foot expanse to himself. He put his hands down flat on the bar. "Whisky," he said, staring into the looking-glass opposite him.

One of the barkeepers brought him a bottle and a glass, and retreated as though on wheels. Blaisedell poured a glassful, raised it and said, "How?" He drank and set the glass down with a sharp clatter.

The sound only intensified the silence. Faces peered in the batwing doors, and men close to the doors began silently to edge toward them, and outside. Those beyond Blaisedell remained in rigid attitudes. Skinner, French, Hasty, and Bacon quietly seated themselves at a table near the judge and the sheriff. A chair scraped and Blaisedell looked around; again his white-rimmed, swollen eyes swung from face to face. They fixed themselves finally upon Taliaferro, who stood down at the far end of the bar, and Taliaferro's mole-spotted dark face turned yellow.

With a slow, hunched motion Blaisedell turned toward him. "Taliaferro!" he said.

Taliaferro screamed, raised his hands high above his head, turned, and fled back through his office doorway as Blaisedell's hand slapped to his side. But he did not draw.

Peter Bacon crossed his hands on the table before him, staring down at them; Pike Skinner was gazing fixedly at Morgan lying on the faro layout with the handkerchief over his face. "Oh my sweet God damn!" the sheriff said, almost inaudibly, his lips barely moving with it. "Don't anybody cross him, for God almighty's sake!"

"Oh Lord, deliver us from evil," the judge said suddenly, loudly, in a drunken voice, and the sheriff flinched.

Blaisedell glanced once at the judge, and then turned back to the bar. "How?" he said, as though to himself; he straightened, staring at his dark reflection in the glass. With a slow, deliberate motion he drew his Colt. The explosion jerked the men around him like puppets on strings; one of the miners cried out shrilly, and the bartenders ducked behind the bar. Sound rocked and echoed through the Lucky Dollar, and, in the smoke, the mirror opposite Blaisedell dissolved into a spider web of cracks. A long shard of glass tipped out and fell, and others crashed down in brittle breakage.

The lookout stood gazing straight ahead of him at nothing, with his hands held out before him like a piano player's. The barkeepers raised their heads. The sheriff rose from his chair and, moving like a sleepwalker, slowly and carefully walked toward the batwing doors, and then, in a rush, fought his way through the men there and outside. Blaisedell stood facing the shattered mirror obscured in gunsmoke still. He thrust the gold-handled six-shooter into its scabbard, grasped the whisky bottle by the neck, and swung around.

He moved back to the layout where Morgan lay. He walked around it, putting the bottle down beside Morgan's head, and stood staring at the men beyond with his swollen eyes in his battered, striped face. No one moved. White-faced, they avoided his gaze, and one another's. He turned toward the judge.

"Say something."

The judge drew his arms in closer to his body, hunching his shoulders, his wrists crossed and his hands held flat against his chest; his head sagged lower.

Blaisedell's mustache twisted contemptuously. He turned back to the others. "Say something."

Peter Bacon looked steadily back at him. Hasty was cleaning his fingernails with minute attention. Tim French, with his back to Blaisedell, stared at Bacon, plucking at his lower lip. Pike Skinner, his ugly, great-eared face flushed beet-red, said, "I guess he would've killed somebody. He broke Mosbie's arm for him. He was after trouble. He—"

"What's Mosbie worth?"

"He was out to kill somebody, Marshal," Hasty said. "He—"

"Kill who? You?"

"Might've been me, I guess," Hasty said, uncomfortably.

"What are you worth?"

Hasty said nothing. French turned slightly, carefully, to glance up at Blaisedell.

"Oh Lord, deliver us!" the judge said.

The whites of Blaisedell's eyes flashed again, his teeth showed briefly beneath his mustache. He hooked his thumb in his shell belt. "Was it what you wanted?" he said to French.

French did not reply.

"What you wanted?" he said to Bacon.

"I guess I never much want to see a man killed, Marshal," Bacon said.

"You are talking to your friends here, Marshal," Skinner said.

"I have got no friends!" Blaisedell's breath leaked steadily, noisily through his half-parted lips. "Don't look at me like that!" he said suddenly.

Peter Bacon, to whom he had spoken, leaned back a little in his chair. His wrinkled face was grayish under the dark tan, his washed blue eyes remained fixed on Blaisedell. Then he rose.

"I'll be going," he said, in a shaky voice. "I don't much like seeing this." He started for the door.

"Come back here," Blaisedell said.

"I guess I won't," Bacon said. His face turned toward Blaisedell as Blaisedell drew the gold-handled Colt, but he said, "I'd never be afraid to turn my back on you, Marshal." He went on outside.

"You've got no cause to turn mean against us here, Marshal," Pike Skinner said.

"I've got cause," Blaisedell said. It was almost dark in the Lucky Dollar now, and his face looked phosphorescent in the dim light. "Judge me," he said. "You judged him. Judge me now." He swung toward Judge Holloway. "Judge me," he said, in the jarring voice.

"What will you do?" the judge cried suddenly. "Kill us all for your pain?" He pulled himself upright, trying to fit his crutch beneath his armpit. With a swift movement Blaisedell skipped forward and kicked the crutch loose. The judge fell heavily, crying out. Blaisedell snatched up the crutch and flung it toward the batwing doors. It fell and slid with a clatter.

"I've had too much of you!" Blaisedell said. "Crawl for it. Crawl past him, that was a man and not all talk!"

Pike Skinner got to his feet, and Tim French half rose; Blaisedell swung toward them. The judge crawled, awkwardly, sobbing with fear; he crawled past the faro layout, reached the crutch, and pushed it toward the bar, where he pulled himself up, and, sobbing and panting, swung out through the louvre doors. It was silent again. Blaisedell went back to stand beside Morgan's body. He took off his hat and brushed a hand uncertainly over his pale hair. He pointed a finger at one of the barkeepers.

"Bring me four candles over here." He turned slowly, in the dim room. "Take off your damned hats," he said. His voice cracked. "Sing," he said.

There was no sound. One of the barkeepers scurried forward with four white candles. Blaisedell jammed one in the mouth of the whisky bottle, lit it, and placed it beside Morgan's head. He took the bottle from the judge's table and fixed and lit a second, which he placed on the other side of Morgan's head. He handed the other two candles back to the barkeeper and indicated Morgan's feet.

"Sing!" he said again. Someone cleared his throat. Blaisedell began to sing, in the deep, heavy, jarring voice:

"Rock of ages, cleft for me,
Let me hide myself in thee."

The others began to join in, and the hymn rose. The candle flames soared and shivered at Morgan's head and feet.

"Let the water and the blood
From thy side, a healing flood,
Be of sin the double cure,
Save from wrath, and make me pure."

They sang more loudly as Blaisedell's voice led them. They sang the same verse three times, and then the singing abruptly died as Blaisedell's voice ceased. Blaisedell removed the handkerchief with which he had covered Morgan's face.

"You can come past and pay your respects to the dead," he said, quietly now.

Several of the miners came hesitantly forward, and Blaisedell moved to the other side of the layout, so that they had to pass between him and Morgan. He stared into each face as the man passed. The others began to fall into line. There was a scrape of boots upon the floor. One of the miners crossed himself.

"Have you got a cross on?" Blaisedell said. The man's sweating, bearded face paled. He brought from under his shirt a silver crucifix on a greasy cord, which he slipped over his head. Blaisedell took it from him and fixed it upright between Morgan's hands. The men filed on past the faro layout, under Blaisedell's eyes, and each glanced in his turn at Morgan's grinning dead face, and then passed more quickly outside. The candle flames danced, swayed, flickered. Blaisedell beckoned the lookout down from his stand to join the line, and the men at the tables, and the barkeeps. Some, as they went by, crossed themselves, and some nodded with their hats placed awkwardly against their chests, but all in silence and without protest passed by as Blaisedell had directed, and on outside into the crowd that waited in Main Street.

II

"Where's Gannon?" Pike Skinner said, in a stifled voice, when he joined the others outside in the darkness. "Oh hell, oh, God damn it, oh, Jesus Christ," he said helplessly.

"What's he doing now?" someone whispered. They stood crushed together upon the boardwalk, but at a distance from the louvre doors.

"Breaking bottles, it sounds like."

The sound of breaking glass continued, and then they heard furniture being dragged across the floor. There was a wrenching sound of splintering wood. Presently they noticed that there was more light inside.

"Fire," someone said, in a matter-of-fact voice.

"Fire!" another yelled.

Immediately Blaisedell appeared in the doorway, outlined against the strengthening bluish light. He had the lookout's shotgun in his hands. "Get back!" he said, and, because they did not comply rapidly enough, shouted viciously, "Get on back!" and raised the shotgun and cocked it. They fled before him off the boardwalk into the street, and down the boardwalk right and left. Flames rose in great blue tongues inside the doors. Blaisedell looked huge, black, and two-dimensional standing against them. The fire crackled inside. Soon it coughed and roared, and red and yellow flames were mingled with the blue.

"Fire!" someone shouted. "Fire! It's the Lucky Dollar going!" Others took up the cry. Flames licked out through the louvre doors, and Blaisedell moved aside, and, after a while, walked east along the boardwalk, the men there silently giving way before him, and disappeared into the darkness.

66. Gannon Takes Off His Star

IN THE jail the flame in the hanging lamp was dim behind the smoky shade. Gannon watched the broad, wide-hatted shadow Pike Skinner made as he moved across before the lamp, pacing toward the names scratched on the wall, and back toward the cell where the judge snored in drunken insensibility upon the prisoners' cot. Peter Bacon sat with his shoulders slumped tiredly in the chair beside the alley door, wiping the sweat and ashes from his face with his bandanna. The fire, at least, was out.

Gannon leaned against the wall and watched Pike and wondered that his legs still held him up. He heard the judge snort in his sleep and the clash of springs as he changed position. The whisky bottle clattered to the floor. He had locked himself in the cell and had the key ring in there with him.

"Well, by Christ," Pike said. "Keller's lit out of here like the fiends was after him and the judge's drunk himself to a coma. What's there for you and me, Pete?"

"Go home and sleep," Peter said.

"Sleep!" Pike cried. "Jesus Christ, sleep! Did you see his eyes?"

"I saw them," Peter said.

Pike rubbed a hand over his dirty face. The back of his hand was black with soot. Then Pike turned to face Gannon. "Johnny, he will kill you!"

"Why, I don't know that it will come to that, Pike," he said.

Pike glared at him with his ugly red face wild with grief and anger; Peter was watching him too, the chew of tobacco moving slowly in his jaw. He felt the skin at the back of his neck crawl. They were looking at him as though he were going to kill himself.

"You didn't see his eyes," Pike said. "Leave him be, for Christ's sake, Johnny! Go home and sleep on it. Maybe he will've come to himself by morning."

Gannon shook his head a little. He could look down through himself as through a hollow tube and see that he was a coward and be neither ashamed of it nor proud that he would do what he had to do. He said, "I guess it doesn't matter much whether he comes to himself or not. You can't go around burning a man's place down. The whole town might've gone."

"And a damned good thing," Pike said. He resumed his pacing. "It's what's wrong," he said. "A town of buildings is more important than a man is." The judge groaned and snorted in the cell, in his troubled sleep.

"I hold it poorly on the judge," Peter said, as bitterly as Gannon had ever heard him speak. "I hold a man should face up to a thing he has got to face up to."

"Shit!" Pike Skinner cried. He halted, facing the names scratched upon the wall, his fists clenched at his sides. "Face up to shit!" he said. He swung around. "Johnny, he is still owed something here!"

"I thought maybe I'd tell him I wouldn't come after him till morning. I thought maybe he might go before, then."

"Johnny, who the hell are you to tell him to go, or arrest him either?"

He felt a stir of anger; he said, stiffly, "I am deputy here, Pike."

"He'll kill you!"

"Maybe he has come to himself already," Peter said.

"Is he still down there?"

"He was just now."

Gannon pushed himself away from the wall. He could smell on himself the stench of ashes and sweat, and fear. "I guess I will be going along, then," he said. Neither Pike nor Peter spoke. The judge snored. He picked up his hat from the table and went on outside into the star-filled dark. The cold wind funneled down the street and he could hear the steady creaking of the sign above his head. He shivered in the cold. The moon was down already in the west, the stars very bright. He walked slowly along the boardwalk, with the hollow pound of his footfalls reverberating in the silence.

A light burned in the window above Goodpasture's store. The French Palace was dark. He crossed Southend Street and stepped carefully past the clutter of boards before the Lucky Dollar where a part of the arcade roof had fallen in. He could smell wet ashes now, and smoke, and the stink of char and whisky, and the sweeter, stomach-convulsing odor with them. Further on there were still a few loiterers standing along the railing. Some of them greeted him as he went by. He passed the burnt-out ruin of the Glass Slipper and crossed Broadway. A lamp burned in a second-story window of the hotel. The rocking chairs were dark, low shapes on the veranda. One of them was occupied, and his heart clenched breathless and painful in his chest for a moment, because it was the chair in which Morgan had always sat. But it would be Blaisedell now.

He heard a faint creak as it rocked. He went to the bottom of the veranda steps and halted there, ten feet away from the chairs. He could make out the faint, pale mass of Blaisedell's face beneath his black hat, the smaller shapes of his pale hands on the chair arms.

"I'm sorry, Blaisedell," he said, and waited. The face turned toward him, and he could see the gleam of Blaisedell's eyes. Blaisedell did not speak.

"It is time, Blaisedell," he said, and he hoped that Blaisedell would remember, but still there was no answer. The rocking chair creaked again. He repeated the words.

Then he took a deep breath and said, "Marshal, I will have to come after you if you are still here by morning. I—"

"Not Marshal," Blaisedell said. "Clay Blaisedell." Blaisedell laughed, and he stepped back, against his will, from that laugh. "Are you running me out of town, Deputy?"

He could see Blaisedell's eyes more clearly now, and more of his face; the welts on it looked like tattoo marks. "No, I am just saying I will have to arrest you in the morning. So I am asking you to go before."

"Nobody tells me that," Blaisedell said. "Or asks me. I will come and go as I please."

"Then I will have to come after you in the morning."

"Come shooting if you do."

"Why, I will do that if I have to, Marshal."

"You'll have to."

He stood there staring at Blaisedell, but Blaisedell was not looking at him any longer. "It is a damned shame, Marshal!" he burst out, but Blaisedell said nothing more, and finally he started on, holding himself carefully and tightly as though, if he did not, he would fall apart like something made of wet straw. He moved on east on Main Street without even being aware where he was going. When he looked back he could no longer see Blaisedell in the darkness.

At the corner of Grant Street he saw a light from the General Peach thrown out onto the dust of the street in a long, dim rectangle. He turned away from it and started up toward Kate's house with the key suddenly a very conscious weight and shape in his pocket. He took it out as he mounted the wooden steps. It rattled against the metal of the lock.

When it entered he turned it and thrust the door open. Inside the floor creaked beneath his weight. He closed the door and stood there waiting for his eyes to accustom themselves to the deeper darkness here. His shoulders ached, and dust and ashes itched upon his face and around his neck. He could make out a shape like a deep coffin on the floor between him and the bedroom door, and there was a flicker of light in the doorway beyond it. Kate's disembodied face appeared, filled with shadows, with a candle flame below it. The box before him was one of her trunks.

"Deputy?" she said, in a calm voice, and he answered yes, nodding, but he did not move, shivering still, though it was warmer here. Kate lowered the candle a little and he saw that she wore a loose robe which she held clasped at the waist with her left hand.

Kate watched him without expression as he removed his hat and started toward her. It was a waxen face above the candle flame, with no paint on it, and a cloud of thick black hair framing it. The beauty spot was missing from her cheek. She looked very slim and boyish in the robe, but a dull point of a breast showed through the silk with the pull of her hand at her waist.

As he approached she moved back with a slight inclination of her head, and, hat in hand, he passed into her bedroom. He watched her place the candle on a box beside her bed. The room was barren now, as he had seen it once before, with only a few clothes hanging upon the wire stretched across one corner, the sad-faced Virgin and her other things evidently packed away for her departure. She sat down on the edge of the bed, stiffly, her eyes raised to him. There were blue-black glints in her hair from the candlelight.

His tongue felt thick in his mouth. "I have told Blaisedell he is to get out of town by morning."

"Have you?" Kate said, tonelessly, and he nodded.

"And did he go?" she said.

He shook his head.

Her full, pale lips opened a little and he could hear the sudden whisper of her breathing. He felt sweaty, foul, and exhausted, and there was a slow, crushing movement in his head, like the laboring of a walking beam. "What do you want of me?" Kate whispered. "Are you afraid?" She unclasped her hand and the robe fell open down her white belly. He averted his eyes.

"Why, I can fix that," she continued. "That is what men come to women for, isn't it?"

"I guess I'm not very much afraid," he said.

"Come to brag? What a man you are?"

He flushed and shook his head.

"Someone to be sorry you are dead?" Kate said. He shook his head again, but she went on. "I have seen all those things. When you have seen everything you still have to watch it over and over—" Her voice broke, but immediately she regained control of it. "And over," she said. "The same things happening and coming on. But I have seen one thing new. I have seen Tom Morgan kill himself, and I know he did it for Clay Blaisedell."

"He has to go," he said. "He is on the prod and mean. He burned Taliaferro's place down, and all but burned the town."

"Oh, he will go. You can make him go by letting him kill you. That is brave, isn't it?"

The candlelight gleamed in her black eyes that were like deep ponds. "But not quite brave enough? Did you come to get the rest from me?" She said it as though it were important to her.

"There is no one else but me to do it," he said hoarsely. "And—and everything's come to nothing if I don't. It is up to me; do you think I want to do it?"

"Do what? Die? Or kill him?"

"Why, put it to him, even." He wrenched his hat between his hands, and stared down at the swath of her flesh where the robe hung open.

"Tom would kill himself for Blaisedell, but you would do it for a silly star on your chest," Kate said. "Take it off—I will take a man, I won't take a sharp-pointed tin thing like that against me. Take it off!" she said again, as his fingers fumbled the catch loose. He dropped the star in his pocket.

"Not afraid?" Kate said, mockingly; but her face was not mocking. "Wait!" she said. "Tom to pay for Peach, and you for Tom. But I will have my pay too. What for, Johnny? You are not fool enough to think you can beat him?"

"No, I know I can't. That's it, you see."

Her eyes narrowed. With a blunt movement of her hand she pulled the robe further open. "Then why?"

"If I am killed—"

"Give you the rest of your life in a night?" she said. "All of it?" In her face he saw what seemed to him a half-amused contempt, but triumph in it, and increasing triumph, and then pain showed naked there. "Come here then," she said, in a voice he didn't even recognize.

She pulled at her robe again as he dropped to his knees before her. He stifled a sound that welled in his throat, and flung his arms around her and pressed his face into her flesh. She brushed her hand over his head.

"You smell like a horse barn," she said gently. Her hand pressed his face against her. "Johnny, Johnny," she whispered. "Do you think I'd let him kill you?"

He didn't know what she meant. He felt the heavy swell of her breast against his cheek and stared down in the pale dark between them at the gleam of her thighs. Her breast pressed hard against him as she drew a deep breath; she blew it out, and there was darkness. Both her arms held him against her. She smelled very clean, and he was foul. He ran his hands along her body inside her robe, and he had never felt anything so smooth beneath his hands.

She rocked with him, forward and back, and whispered words in his ear that had no sense and were only disconnected sounds, but that were the sounds he had always wanted to hear without ever knowing it before. He was shivering uncontrollably as her hands rose and pressed flat against his cheeks and pulled his face to hers. Her lips were wonderfully warm in the warm darkness and her sharp-pointed fingers pressed into his back with exquisite pain. He twisted his lips from hers once, panting for breath, and she pulled his face into her throat where he could hear her own swift, shivering breath. Her body arched and strained against him, and he cried her name as they fell back and away through darkness, and her flesh enveloped him.

67. Journals of Henry Holmes Goodpasture

June 5, 1881 (continued)

THE fire in the Lucky Dollar has been quenched, and just in time, for a strong wind has come up. Thank God it did not arise earlier, or this town would have burned as swiftly as dry paper—a burnt offering after a man's reputation, or his sanity. A town to form Morgan's funeral pyre, and Blaisedell's parting salute. Or is it of parting? Those who saw him say he was quite insane. Almost, as I write this, I find I wish he had burned us all out: Warlock gone and ourselves scattered, leaving Blaisedell to brood here alone in his madness.

There will be no sleep this night.

The news of the death of General Peach comes as no shock. Neither have I taken it as a sign of New Hope, as Buck Slavin seems to. It is only a meaningless bit of information. Perhaps it is not even true.

I have had a stream of callers. I suppose they have seen my light and sought a fellow human to talk to. Kennon says he has heard that the strike has been settled. Mosbie's arm is broken, but he is not seriously wounded; I had thought he was dead. Kennon says he will resign from the Citizens' Committee; he does not say why. I feel the same. All reason is gone. Egan says that Morgan had got the drop on Gannon and locked him in the jail, which was why our brave deputy was so little in evidence this evening. He did appear during the fire, and helped organize a bucket brigade, the pumper having broken down. Egan says we will have to have a proper fire department; I stare at him stupidly as he says it.

Buck Slavin has come in again and told me the latest news. It is true, evidently, that General Peach is dead at the border. A Lieutenant Avery was here with a detachment—unobtrusively, for I did not see nor hear of them until now—to dispatch back to Bright's City the wagons that had been brought here to transport the miners to the railroad at Welltown. Peach's body is with the main train, which has hastened back up the valley. Whiteside is now presumably acting governor, and Buck is overjoyed. Avery told him, however, that Whiteside seemed a man in a trance. Evidently he was very close to the General when he fell (as he was always protectively close), and was much shocked by the incident, which was, however, a fortunate one. Avery said it was obvious to all but Peach by the time they reached the border that the massacre had been perpetrated by Mexicans in revenge upon the rustlers, and it had taken place, as well, upon Mexican soil. Peach, however, was determined that it was his old antagonist, Espirato, and seemed prepared to pursue him to South America, if necessary. But before he had passed onto Mexican soil, his horse slipped in a narrow defile at the mouth of Rattlesnake Canyon, he fell and died instantly, and mercifully. Whiteside, accompanying him, was the only man to see it. Afterwards his only concern was to get the cavalry and Peach's body back to Bright's City in order to give him a military funeral before decomposition of the remains begins.

Buck has no doubt that Whiteside will now, according to his promise, rectify all our wrongs and wants, and sees Warlock as a future metropolis of the West. Buck is an optimistic and public-minded man. To his mind Blaisedell is only a small and temporary blight upon the body politic; with all else healthy and aright, he will automatically disappear. Like the rest of us, but perhaps for different reasons, he too is no longer interested in the Citizens' Committee. I am apathetic of his ambitions, I am contemptuous of his optimism. The old, corrupt, and careless god has been replaced in his heaven, and so, he feels, all will be well with the world, which is, after all, the best of all possible ones. It is a touching faith, but I am drawn more to those who wander the night not with excitement for the future but with dread of it.

I can see many of them through my window, unable to sleep now that the fire is out. For what fire is out, and what is newly lighted, and what will burn forever and consume us all? We will fight fire with futile water or with savage fire to the end of this earth itself, and never prevail, and we will drown in our water and burn in our preventive fire. How can men live, and know that in the end they will merely die?

Pike Skinner, who is frantic, says that Gannon has warned Blaisedell that he intends to arrest him at sun-up. Skinner says that Blaisedell will kill him, and I cannot tell whether he feels more horror that Blaisedell should kill the Deputy, or that the Deputy, who is Pike's friend, should be killed. Once I would have stupidly said that the

Deputy would not be such a fool. I have been shown fatuous in my skepticism too many times. Now I neither believe nor disbelieve, and I feel nothing. There is nothing left to feel.

It is four in the morning by my watch. Mine is the only light I can see, the scratching of my pen the only sound. Here astride the dull and rusty razor's edge between midnight and morning, I am sick to the bottom of my heart. Where is Buck Slavin's bright future of faith, hope, and commerce? What is it even worth, after all? For if men have no worth, there is none anywhere. I feel very old and I have seen too many things in my years, which are not so many; no, not even in my years, but in a few months—in this day.

Outside there is only darkness, pitifully lit by the cold and disinterested stars, and there is silence through the town, in which some men sleep and clutch their bedclothes of hope and optimism to them for warmth. But those I love more do not sleep, and see no hope, and suffer for those brave ones who will fall in hopeless effort for us all, whose only gift to us will be that we will grieve for them a little while; those who see, as I have come to see, that life is only event and violence without reason or cause, and that there is no end but the corruption and the mock of courage and of hope.

Is not the history of the world no more than a record of violence and death cut in stone? It is a terrible, lonely, loveless thing to know it, and see—as I realize now the doctor saw before me—that the only justification is in the attempt, not in the achievement, for there is no achievement; to know that each day may dawn fair or fairer than the last, and end as horribly wretched or more. Can those things that drive men to their ends be ever stilled, or will they only thrive and grow and yet more hideously clash one against the other so long as man himself is not stilled? Can I look out at these cold stars in this black sky and believe in my heart of hearts that it was this sky that hung over Bethlehem, and that a star such as these stars glittered there to raise men's hearts to false hopes forever?

This is the sky of Gethsemane, and that of Bethlehem has vanished with its star.

68. Gannon Sees the Gold Handles

I

GANNON came awake with a start and stared at the outline of the window that was emerging gray from the surrounding darkness. He raised himself carefully on one elbow and looked down at Kate's sleeping face, with the soft mass of hair beneath it on the pillow like a heavy shadow, the soft curves of her lashes on her cheeks, and her lips, which looked carved from ivory. He watched the rounding and relaxation of her nostrils as she breathed, and the slow, deep rise and fall of her breast. One arm was thrown across it and her fingers almost touched him.

Slowly, watching her face, he began to slide away from her, stopping when her lips tightened for a moment and then parted as though she would speak. But she did not waken, and he eased himself from her bed, and carried his clothing, shell belt, and boots into the living room to dress. His holstered Colt thumped upon the oilcloth-covered table as he set it down, and he held his breath for a moment, but there was no sound from the bedroom.

He looked in at her one last time before he put on his boots. Her hand had moved over a little farther, to lie where he had lain. He put the key on the table, went outside, and in the dark gray chill set his boots down and worked his feet into them, and softly closed the door.

The town was empty and out of the grayness buildings and houses came slowly at him like thoughts emerging from the gray edges of his mind, to hang there unattached, two-dimensional, and strange in the silence that was broken only by the hollow clump of his boots upon the boardwalk.

Down Grant Street he could just make out the high bulk of the General Peach, lightless and asleep. He turned right down Main Street. A few stars still showed frail shards of light, but almost as he looked up they were gone. He walked past the hotel and the empty rocking chairs upon the veranda, and across Broadway; he felt a strangely intense sense of possession of the vacant town in the early morning. He passed the ruin of the Glass Slipper, the pharmacy and the gunshop with their shattered windows, and skirted again the charred timbers on the boardwalk before the Lucky Dollar. The sickly sweetish stench, and that of whisky, were dissipated now, but inside the wreckage was still smoking. He crossed Southend and halted for a moment beneath the new sign to gaze into the dim interior of the jail, and felt the adobe breathing the night's chill upon him.

He waited there until he heard the judge stir and snore in the cell, and then he went on to Birch's roominghouse, again removing his boots so he would awaken no one as he climbed the stairs to his room. Upstairs there was a dull concert of snoring, which faded when he closed his door. He lit the lamp and held his hands to its small warmth for a moment, and then he stripped off his clothes and washed himself, soaping and scrubbing his white flesh with a rag and icy water from the crockery pitcher; he shaved his face before the triangle of mirror. He laid out clean clothes and dressed himself with care, his best white shirt, his new striped pants—store pants from the legs of which he tried to rub the creases—and dusted off his new, too-tight star boots, and painfully worked his feet into them. After rubbing his star to a shine he fastened it to his vest, and put that on, and donned his canvas jacket against the cold. He rubbed the dust from each crevice between the cartridge-keepers of his shell belt, frowned at the torn hole at the back, and polished the sharp-edged buckle. He buckled on the belt, cinching it a notch tighter than usual against the crawling cold of his stomach, thrust it down as far as it would go, and knotted the scabbard thong around his thigh tightly too.

Then he produced a whisky bottle half full of oil, and a rag, and sat down at the table to clean his Colt, and oil it, and wipe it dry. He did this over and over again with an intense, rapt attention, rubbing patiently at each small fleck of Main Street dust until the old forty-four-caliber shone dully and richly in the lamplight. He oiled the inside of the holster too, and worked the Colt in and out until it slid to his satisfaction. He replaced the cartridges in the cylinder, let the hammer down upon the empty one, seated the Colt in the holster, scrubbed the oil from his hands, and was ready. Now he could hear some of the miners waking and stirring in their rooms.

He rose and blew out the lamp. As he started out he remembered the spare key to the cell door. He took it with him, on its iron ring, to leave at the jail.

Outside it was lighter, harsher gray now, and down Main Street he could see lights burning among the miners' shacks beyond Grant Street. As he walked toward the jail more of them were lit. The dust of the street was cleanly white, and the slight breeze from the northeast was fresh in his nostrils and no longer cold. The gray above the Bucksaws showed a greenish cast now, a yellow green that faded up and out to darken and merge with the gray world, but higher and brighter almost as he watched, so that he began to walk more rapidly. He turned into the jail, where first he hung the key ring on the peg, and then sat down at the table and placed his hat carefully before him to wait these last few moments. He tried to think only of what he might have left undone.

He glanced toward the cell as the judge groaned and moved, made wet smacking sounds with his lips, groaned, and snored again; he could not see him in the darkness there.

Turning again he watched the whitening dust in the street, and leaned on the scarred table top from which the justice of Warlock was dispensed, and waited, and wished only that there were some way he could see Warlock's future before him, and wished, with a sudden, terrible pang, that he could hear how they would speak of him.

But he felt, besides a flat and unfocused anxiety that came over him intermittently like a fever, a kind of peace, a certain freedom. He realized that there was no need for self-examination now, no need to question his decisions, no need to reflect upon his guilt, his inadequacy, nor upon himself at all. There were no decisions to be made any more, for there was only responsibility, and it was a freedom of tremendous scope. And he looked once more at the list of the names of the deputies of Warlock upon the whitewashed wall, at his own name scratched last there, but not last, and felt a pride so huge that his eyes filled, and he knew, too, that the pride was worth it all.

A slow tread of bootheels came along the boardwalk, and Pike Skinner turned in the door. There were heavy smudges beneath his eyes, so that they looked like a raccoon's eyes; the flesh of his face was stretched tight over the bone, and two day's growth of beard made his face look dirty. He wore a sheepskin-lined jacket.

"Pike," he said, and Pike nodded to him, and looked in the cell.

"Chicken old son of a bitch," Pike said, with infinite contempt. Then he glanced at the names on the wall, and nodded again as Gannon slid the table drawer open.

He took out the other deputy's star and handed it to Pike, who tossed it up and caught it once, not speaking. He indicated the key ring on its peg. "I brought the other key along. The judge's got one in there with him."

Pike nodded. He tossed the star again; this time he dropped it, and his face reddened as he bent to pick it up.

"Careful of it," Gannon said.

"Shit!" Pike said, and in the word was a grief for which he was grateful. Pike turned away. "There's people out," he said. "Funny how they hear of a thing."

He looked past the other and saw the first light upon the street. "It's close to time, I guess," he said.

"I guess," Pike said.

Peter came in with Tim French. There was a grunting and scraping within the cell; the judge's hands appeared on the bars, then his face between them, heavy with sleep and liquor. The hot, red-veined eyes stared at him unseeing as he put on his hat and nodded, and nodded to Tim and Peter. Peter glanced down at Pike's hand holding the other star.

"Chilly out," Tim said.

He stepped past them, and outside. Down the boardwalk a way Chick Hasty stood, and with him were Wheeler, old Owen Parsons, and Mosbie, with his right arm in a muslin sling and a jacket thrown over his shoulders. There were men along the boardwalks farther down, too, and he saw the miners collecting at the corner of Grant Street, where the wagons from the Medusa and the other mines would pick them up. The first sliver of the sun showed over the Bucksaws, incredibly bright gold and the peak beneath it flaming.

Chick Hasty looked down at him and nodded. Mosbie leaned back and nodded to him past Hasty, sick-eyed. He could hear the increasing bustle of Warlock awakening. Already, with the half-sun showing, the air was warmer. It would be another hot day. He moved farther out upon the boardwalk to lean against the railing and watch the great gold sun slowly climb from its defilade behind the mountains. All at once it was free, and round, and he walked on down the boardwalk past the men leaning against the railing there, and out into the dust of Main Street.

II

Blaisedell came out of the hotel, and immediately the men began moving back off the boardwalks, into doorways and the ruins of the Glass Slipper and the Lucky Dollar. Blaisedell walked slowly out into the street, and then Blaisedell was facing him, a block away, like some mirror-image of himself seen distant and small, but all in black, and Blaisedell began to walk at the same instant that he did. He could see the slant of Blaisedell's shell belt through the opening of his unbuttoned coat, and the gold-handled Colt thrust into his belt there. Blaisedell walked with a slow, long-legged stride, while his own star boots felt heavy in the dust. The boots hurt his feet and his wrist brushed past the butt of his Colt with almost an electric shock. He watched the dust spurting from beneath Blaisedell's boots.

He could see the angry-looking stripes on Blaisedell's face. He felt Blaisedell's eyes, not so much a force now as a kind of meaningless message in a buzzing like that of a depressed telegrapher's key. The sun was very bright in his face, and the figure approaching him began to dance and separate into a number of black-suited advancing figures, and then congeal again into one huge figure that cast a long, oblique shadow.

Then he saw Kate; she stood against the rail before the Glass Slipper, motionless, as though she had been there a long time. She too was dressed all in mourning black, heavily bustled in a black skirt of many folds, a black sacque with lines of fur down the front, her black hat with the cherries on it, black mesh mitts on her hands that gripped the rail. A veil hid her face. He saw her raise her hands to her breast, and he saw Blaisedell glance toward her, and make a curt motion as though he were shaking his head.

Straight down, straight up, Blaisedell had told him; it burst in his mind so there was room for nothing else. He walked steadily on, trying not to limp in his tight boots, and his eyes fixed themselves on Blaisedell's right hand swinging at his side. He felt the muscles in his own arm tighten and strain at every step. He could feel Blaisedell's eyes upon him and now he felt their thrust and still the confused buzzing inside his mind. But he watched Blaisedell's hand; it would be soon. Now, now, now, he thought, at every jolting step; now, now. He felt himself being crushed beneath a black and corrosive despair. Now, he thought; now, now—

It was as though there had been no movement at all. One instant Blaisedell's hand had been swinging at his side, the next it contained the Colt that had been thrust inside his belt. His own hand slammed down—straight down, straight up—but already he was staring into the black hole of Blaisedell's gun muzzle and saw Blaisedell's mouth shaped into a crooked contemptuous half-smile. He steeled himself against the bullet, halting with his feet braced apart and his body tipping forward as though he could brace himself against the shock. But the shock, the explosion, the tearing pain, did not come. As he brought his own Colt up level, he hesitated, his finger firm against the trigger, and saw Blaisedell's hand turn with a twisting motion. The gold handle gleamed suddenly as the six-shooter was flung forward and down to disappear in the street with a puff of dust.

Blaisedell's hand moved swiftly again, and the mate of the first Colt appeared. Again his finger tensed against the trigger and again he held it back as Blaisedell flung the other down. The slight contemptuous smile still twisted Blaisedell's lips in his battered face. Blaisedell's arms hung at his sides now, and slowly, uncertainly, he let his own hand drop. His eyes caught another splash of dust, in the street below the railing where Kate stood, her right hand extended and open and her face invisible behind the veil. Blaisedell stood staring at him with his swollen eyes looking shut.

The realization burst in him that all he had to do now was walk the remaining thirty feet and arrest Blaisedell. But he did not move. He would not do it, he thought, in sudden rebellion, as though it were his own thought; but now he was feeling intensely the thrust of all the other eyes that watched this, and it was a force much stronger than that of his own gratitude, his own pity, and he knew all he served that was embodied in the vast weight pinned to his vest, and knew, as he made a slight, not quite peremptory motion with his head, that he spoke not for himself nor even a strict and disinterested code, but for all of them.

Blaisedell started forward again, no longer coming toward him but walking along the track of his shadow toward Goodpasture's corner. He walked with the same, slow, long-legged, stiff-backed stride, not even glancing at Gannon, as he passed him, and turned into Southend and disappeared down toward the Acme Corral.

As Gannon turned to face the corner, he saw, past his shoulder, that the sun seemed not to have moved since he had come out into the street. But now he heard the sounds of hoofs and wagon wheels, and saw the wagons turning into Main Street. He watched the miners climbing into them, and the mules stamping and jerking their heads. More wagons appeared; the Medusa miners were going back to work. Miners appeared all along the boardwalks now, glancing back over their shoulders at him and at the corner of Southend as they moved toward the wagons. They made very little noise as they embarked.

Miss Jessie appeared among them, hurrying along the boardwalk with a dark *rebozo* thrown over her shoulders and her brown hair tumbling around her head with her steps. She stopped with one hand braced against one of the arcade posts, and stared at Kate, and then, blankly, at him.

He heard the pad of hoofs. Blaisedell came out of Southend Street on a black horse with a white face, white stockings; the horse pranced and twisted his sleek neck, but Blaisedell's pale, stone profile did not turn. The black swung around the corner, and, hindquarters dancing sideways, white stockings brilliant in the sun, trotted away down Main Street toward the rim.

"Clay!" he heard Miss Jessie call. Blaisedell did not turn, who must have heard. Gannon heard the running tap of heels upon the planks. She stopped and leaned against another post before Goodpasture's store, and then ran out into the street, while the black danced on away. He saw Pike Skinner and Peter Bacon watching from the jail doorway, and more men were crowding out along the boardwalks now, and some into the street.

Miss Jessie ran down Main Street in the dust, holding her skirts up; she would run swiftly for a time, then decrease her pace to a walk, then run again. "Clay!" she cried.

Gannon began to move forward with the others, as Miss Jessie ran on. The black horse dropped down over the edge of the rim, Blaisedell's head and shoulders visible for an instant and his ruined face turning back to glance once toward the town; then abruptly he was gone. "*Clay!*" Miss Jessie screamed, with her voice trailing thinly behind her as she ran. The doctor was hurrying after her.

Gannon walked with the others down Main Street toward the rim, where the doctor had caught up with Miss Jessie. The doctor had an arm around her and was leading her back, her face dusty and white with huge vacantly staring eyes, her mouth open and her breast heaving. He saw the wetness at the corners of her mouth as he passed her and the doctor, and her eyes glared for a moment at him, vacant no longer, but filled with tears and hate. He moved on, and heard the doctor whispering to her as he led her back through the groups of men approaching the rim.

III

From the rim the great, dun sweep of the valley was laid out before them. There were wild flowers on the slopes from the recent rain. The long dead spears of ocotillo were covered with a thin mist of leaves, and from their ends red flaming torches waved and bowed in the breeze. Someone extended an arm to point out Blaisedell, where he guided the black horse among the huge tumbled boulders of the malpais. He was hidden from time to time among the boulders and each time he reappeared it was a smaller figure on a smaller horse, trailing tan clouds of dust that lingered in the air behind him. They watched in silence as he rode on down the stage road toward San Pablo and the Dinosaurs, until they could not be sure they saw him still at all, he was so distant. Yet now and then the tiny black figure on the black horse would stand out clearly against the golden, flower-speckled earth, until, at last, a dust devil rose in a gust of wind. Rising high and leaning across his path, it seemed to envelop him, and, when it had passed and blown itself apart, Blaisedell too was finally lost to sight.

Afterword:

A Letter from Henry Holmes Goodpasture

1819 Pringle St.
San Francisco, Calif.
May 14, 1924

My Dear Gavin: *

It has been a long time now, but I am surprised, as I look into the past in order to answer your letter, how easily it all comes back to me. Perhaps I am able to remember it with such immediacy because you and your brother so often asked me to tell and retell stories of my days in Warlock. That must seem a long time ago to you, who are now in your third year at New Haven, but to me, in my eighty-third upon this planet, it is only yesterday.

I am most pleased that you should recall those old stories, and be interested enough to wish to know, now that you are grown, what happened "After."

To begin with, Warlock did not continue to prosper and grow as her citizens had once hoped, and when I departed for San Francisco in 1882, her decline was well under way. The Porphyrion and Western Mining Company had by then bought up the rest of the mines, and struggled for a number of years to cope with the increasing amounts of water met with at the lower levels; but it was a hopeless task, and Porphyrion, faced too with the fall of the silver market, was finally forced to the wall. By 1890 only the Redgold Mine was still in operation. The hamlet of Redgold then flourished briefly but, after the mine

* Gavin Sands, Goodpasture's grandson.

closed, became in its turn a ghost like Warlock and so many other mining camps.

In answer to your questions, I shall try to be as succinct as it is possible for a garrulous old man to be. Yes, Warlock did become the county seat of Peach County. Its courthouse still stands (or stood the last time I visited Warlock, seventeen years ago), a fine brick structure that was unfortunately gutted by a fire soon after the turn of the century. Curiously, its blackened brick husk seemed to me to have no connection with the adobe husks around it, and even stands near the rim at the southwest corner of the town (where it commands a most striking view of the valley), apart from them. As I say, Warlock was the county seat; but not for long. The county offices were removed to Welltown, I believe in 1891.

Dr. Wagner accompanied Jessie Marlow to Nome, where he died of a heart ailment. Jessie herself operated an establishment there called "The Miners' Rest" for a number of years, and you will find her mentioned in many accounts of the Gold Rush days. I think she married a man named Bogart, or Bogarde, a prospector and saloonkeeper, and himself a figure of minor importance in Nome.

James Fitzsimmons was one of the I.W.W. leaders imprisoned during the Great War. I have heard nothing of him since.

There was never any doubt in Warlock that John Gannon's death was cold-blooded murder. Cade had concealed himself in the alley behind the jail, and the shooting took place in Main Street before my store. I saw the body very shortly after the shooting, and poor Gannon had been clearly shot in the back, nor had his revolver been drawn. I was especially struck by the expression on his face, which was remarkably peaceful; he cannot even have known what struck him down.

Cade took flight, but was apprehended in short order by a posse led by Pike Skinner. His trial was a notorious one, and these stories you have heard stem from his defense, which was based upon the contention that Gannon had not only murdered McQuown but had communicated to the Mexican authorities information which resulted in the massacre of the Cowboys in Rattlesnake Canyon. As far as I could see, Cade mustered no evidence whatever to support this, but his accusations were then, and probably still are, widely believed. I know that Will Hart, an honest and intelligent man, professed to believe Cade's story. I do not.

Although he was tried in Bright's City, Cade was returned to Warlock for execution, and became the first man legally hanged in Peach County. That was a memorable day.

Pike Skinner was Peach County's first sheriff. Judge Holloway presided briefly over the bench in Warlock's new courthouse. Buck Slavin was Warlock's first mayor. I am sure you will remember hearing stories of his career in the U.S. Senate. He was a colorful man, a brilliant politician, and had a matchless eye for the main chance.

Arnold Mosbie, who served as a deputy under Skinner, became one of the last of the famous peace officers. He was Marshal in Harrisonburg.

I have heard that the notorious "Big-nose Kate" Williams, of Denver fame, or ill fame, was Warlock's Kate Dollar. I have also heard that Kate Dollar married a wealthy Colorado rancher. One, both, or neither of these stories may be true.

You will notice that I have kept your questions about Blaisedell to the last. No, I cannot say I wish I had been present to hear you and your "know-it-all" friend argue about him. I have heard in my time too many such arguments, and I think you must have held for him as well as I could have done—perhaps better, for I was always chary of making him out a better man than he may have been. What was he? I think in all honesty I must say I do not know, and if *I* do not know in this late year of Our Lord, then I think that no man can. Certainly your opinionated friend cannot.

Nor do I know what became of him. If anyone ever knew, genuinely, it has been a well-kept secret. Of course there have been many rumors, but never one to which I was able to give any credence. The most common has been that Blaisedell was half-blind when he left Warlock, and soon completely lost his sight. Consequently there were a number of tales, variously embroidered, concerning tall, fair, blind men represented as being Blaisedell.

There was at one time an old prospector living in the Dinosaurs, who claimed that Blaisedell had been murdered there by persons unknown, and for a fee he would lead the gullible to view the lonely grave where he swore he had buried Blaisedell's body. Another story has it that Blaisedell changed his name to Blackburn and was town Marshal in Hyattsville, Oklahoma, where he was killed by a man named Petersen in a gun battle over a local belle. Blaisedell has enjoyed a number of sepultures.

Then there were the writings of Caleb Bane, which I suppose many fools have read as gospel. It was Bane, a fabricator of cheap Western fiction, who had given Blaisedell the gold-handled Colts in Fort James, and Bane (who seems to have felt that Blaisedell, because of that gift, belonged to him) continued to write tales about Blaisedell's imaginary continued career long after the subject himself was lost from sight.

I notice in a recent volume of Western memoirs that Blaisedell is spoken of as more a semi-fictional hero than an actual man. But he was a man: I can attest to that, who have seen him eat and drink, and breathe and bleed. And despite the fictions of Bane and his ilk, there have not been many like him, nor like Morgan, nor McQuown, nor John Gannon.

But sometimes I feel as perhaps you may feel, looking back on the stories of these men I told you about when you were a "young 'un"—that I myself was a fictionalizer with an imagination as active as that of Bane, or that in my own mind (as old men will do!) I had gradually stylized and simplified those happenings, that I had fancifully glorified those people, and sought to give them superhuman stature.

I cry out in pain that it is not so, and at the same time come to doubt myself. But I kept a journal through those years, and although the ink is fading on the yellowing pages, it is all still legible. One of these days, if you are interested beyond merely seeking to bulwark your arguments with a classmate, those pages shall be yours.

Now that your letter has caused me to call to memory all those people and those years, I find myself wishing most intensely that I had left to me Time and the powers to flesh out my journals into a True History of Warlock, in all its ramifications, before the man who was Blaisedell, and the other men and women, and the town in which they lived, are totally obscured. . . .

TITLES IN SERIES